"This collection could be the shot in the arm our imaginations need. It's an important book, and not just for the fiction."
—*Wall Street Journal*

"[A] group of visionaries have banded together to offer stories that are more utopian, which they hope will contribute to a more positive future. . . . The stories still offer plenty of drama, death and destruction, but many have a sort of happy ending."
—*New York Times*

"One can surmise the ingenuity and thoughtfulness in the selections, as well as the felicitous arrangement in how the anthology's stories flow from section to section. . . .There is a great range and diversity to be had for an anthology wanting to embrace a future that the Earth so desperately deserves. . . . This new anthology justly deserves to be ranked alongside the very best collections published within science fiction: Terry Carr's *Universe*, Damon Knight's *Orbit*, or Robert Silverberg's *New Dimensions*."
—*Los Angeles Review of Books*

"...Thought-provoking and fun."   —*Pacific Standard* magazine

HIEROGLYPH

Edited by Kathryn Cramer and David G. Hartwell

HIEROGLYPH

Stories and Visions for a Better Future

EDITED BY ED FINN AND KATHRYN CRAMER

WILLIAM MORROW

An Imprint of HarperCollins*Publishers*

CONTENTS

FOREWORD
Lawrence M. Krauss

SCIENCE FICTION SHARES WITH science a most important driver: a fascination with the possibilities of existence. As a theoretical physicist, my motivation for studying the universe has always been the wonder of what might be possible rather than what is practical. This makes me particularly sympathetic to the challenges facing science fiction writers. After all, perhaps the most significant difference between science and science fiction is that the former explores what is possible in our universe, and the latter what might be possible in any universe.

This is not to minimize the significance of this important distinction. The renowned physicist Richard Feynman once said that "science is imagination in a straitjacket." It is wonderful to let one's imagination roam, but forcing our ideas to conform to the evidence of reality, and being willing to throw out ideas, even beautiful ones, if nature turns out not to use them, is hard even for those of us who spend our lives preparing to do just that.

In my own field of cosmology, for example, we have been forced, kicking and screaming, by the data to give up the comforting notion that the energy of empty space had a commonsense value, namely zero, and have instead had to come to grips with the fact that empty space contains the dominant energy in the universe, producing a kind of cosmic antigravity that will determine our ultimate future.

In this regard it is perhaps appropriate to suggest instead that science fiction is the literature where we keep the beautiful ideas and throw out the data . . . namely, where we are free to conjure new realities that conform to our ideas.

So it is that I am often unimpressed when people claim that science fiction anticipates science. It doesn't. The imagination of the natural world far exceeds that of even the most gifted science fiction writer. The really big advances in science are most often unforeseen, which is one of the things that makes science so fascinating and so much fun to be involved in. These include serendipitous discoveries like the antibiotic capability of penicillin, the weird behavior of the expanding universe I alluded to above, or even the overwhelming social revolution created by the World Wide Web.

When science fiction and science do converge, there is rarely a causal connection, but rather it is generally because creative people can come up with independent but similar solutions to well-known problems. Thus, for example, faced with the possibility that opening someone up to explore inside his or her body might be less desirable than probing metabolic processes from the outside, the writers of *Star Trek* invented the "tricorder," whereas in the real world, scientists came up with ultrasound, CAT scans, and MRI machines. The latter were far more difficult to actually make work than the former of course, so it is not surprising that they arose later.

Of course there are periodically examples of science fiction inspiring real-life designers. The original flip cell phone was inspired by *Star Trek*, and the X-Prize Foundation now has a prize for someone to develop a real-life tricorder. But these are the exception, rather than the rule.

This is what makes the current anthology so intriguing and ambitious. In this collection of stories, science fiction writers, futurists, and technology writers have been challenged to come up with stories on the hairy edge of current reality—exploring possibilities that might actually spur useful collaborations with scientists and engineers to produce new technologies to deal with problems just beyond our current horizon. As Neal Stephenson put it when he founded Project Hieroglyph: the collection should involve a moratorium on "hackers, hyperspace and holocaust." Namely, it should avoid the classic science fiction hooks: a dystopian future or technology so advanced that the world it describes bears little or no relation to our world.

The stories in this anthology range over a locus of possibilities that take up just where current science and technology hang. I suppose one had to expect at least one story about space travel, that area that engenders such disappointment among those who grew up with the agonizing technological coitus interruptus of the Apollo program. Gregory Benford's space-based saga may be mere wishful thinking, but a central facet of it revolves around technology that at least some entrepreneurs are taking seriously—mining asteroids for raw materials that might be used both to relieve scarcities here on Earth and to construct facilities in space. I wouldn't personally invest in this likelihood—I just don't see a business model that actually works—but if you examine my real-life investments, it is not difficult to distinguish my business acumen from Warren Buffett's. And whatever one can say about the remarkable waste of resources associated with human space exploration—which gets in the way of doing good science at NASA—it is hard to argue that our future, if there is to be one, will in the long run expand beyond the confines of our planet.

More grounded, if you will forgive the pun, is Neal Stephenson's piece about building a twenty-kilometer tower on Earth. At first glance it seems to defy reason, but what *are* the actual limits of civil engineering? The Tower of Babel didn't work out well for anyone involved, but like the bulk of the Bible, that story was just a fairy tale, and a pretty boring one at that. What if one seriously contemplates such a project?

Are there any laws of physics that really make this impossible? This idea has spawned a collaboration with engineers at Arizona State University. Time will tell if it leaps from a sparkle in Stephenson's eye to reality. Other stories include subjects at the heart of modern science innovation, from neuroscience and memory storage to 3-D printers. Whatever skepticism one might bring to the likely success of such speculations for productively influencing ongoing scientific or engineering research, the true hallmark of good science fiction is, surprisingly perhaps, not based primarily on the science.

Too often we concentrate on the first word in *science fiction* and not the second. If a science fiction story is not dramatically compelling, it becomes difficult, if not impossible, for readers to suspend disbelief and immerse themselves in the action. In this sense, nothing distinguishes science fiction from the rest of fiction. All these literary works create a make-believe universe that has to be just real enough to make the dramatic tension that arises between the protagonists both convincing and compelling.

Many of the stories in this collection exemplify precisely this development of dramatic tension that turns potentially pale futuristic ideas into compelling pieces of fiction. For example, 3-D printing is a new technology that is already inspiring the public's imagination, from allowing fabrication of intricate mechanical devices in the third world to building human organs cell by cell. Cory Doctorow's beautiful story "The Man Who Sold the Moon," however, pushes these ideas one step further by suggesting that 3-D printers could be put on the moon to create building materials that might one day be used by future colonists. What makes the story truly come alive, however, and allows one to suspend disbelief at the remarkable technological hurdles involved, is the deep friendship between three misfits who meet by accident as drug-addled Burning Man partygoers and who overcome personal demons and disease to build lives together.

Similarly, the emerging attempts to inject neuroscience more fully into the legal system, from the search for some form of lie detection that might actually work to serious efforts to anticipate behavior before it happens, are, for many of us, chilling developments. But perhaps nowhere near as chilling as Elizabeth Bear's "Covenant." Taking the simple idea that eventually we may be able to alter neurophysiology sufficiently to change character, Bear goes inside the mind of a serial killer and inserts that concept in a gripping cat-and-mouse chase where prey and predator can be confused.

Science fiction has also often been a convenient method of projecting social insights in a way that avoids traditional stereotypes that produce emotional baggage that often otherwise distorts reality. Going back all the way to the nineteenth century, Edward Abbott's *Flatland* described a fictitious world of two-dimensional beings, where the highest form of social class, circles, were priests, and the lowest form, lines, were women. Women were dangerous because a line disappears when it is coming toward you and thus could pierce you, so separate entrances were needed for them in every building. In this way Abbott could satirize the Victorian subjugation of women without having to refer to any ongoing political issues.

So too in this collection one finds several stories, notably Madeline Ashby's "By the Time We Get to Arizona" and Karl Schroeder's "Degrees of Freedom," that explore how future advanced technology—in the case of Ashby's piece it is sensor technology and human-machine interfaces, and in Schroeder's it is the increasing sophistication of data analysis and retrieval on the Internet—can nevertheless cast new light on current real-world problems. In Ashby's piece it is the constant fear that many illegal immigrants now feel in the United States about being "outed" and deported in spite of the fact that they may be productive members of our society, and in Schroeder's it is the time invariant struggle of the individual versus the state—the very thing that Rousseau talked about when he said we are all born free and yet will forever be in chains. But that struggle has taken on a new dimension in the virtual world of the Internet. As online interconnections grow, and the data on everything from our shopping preferences to our network of friends becomes accessible, those who can best utilize this information can best manipulate us.

If it is these sorts of dramas that drive good science fiction, rather than merely the science, one might question whether science fiction can play any role at all in pushing forward progress of science and technology. Here, I defer to my friend and colleague Stephen Hawking, who wrote the foreword for my book *The Physics of Star Trek*. As he put it: "Science fiction like *Star Trek* helps inspire the imagination."

I know very few working scientists who did not enjoy science fiction during their formative years. The question then naturally arises: Which came first? Did a love of science fiction inspire a fascination with science, or did a fascination with things scientific engender an interest in a segment of literature with scientific overtones?

Although a natural question, I would argue, in the spirit of Hawking, that it is largely unimportant. There is little doubt that science fiction as a genre legitimizes the activity—especially among impressionable adolescents—associated with imagining both what is possible in the universe and how to find out. It therefore can help promote a fascination with the poetry of reality while providing an outlet for creative imagining about the world. And that creative imagining is at the heart of the process of science. I would be remiss if I didn't note that it also provides another important opportunity for young people to grow. It gives them an excuse to read. I suspect that there are many people today who would have been embarrassed to be caught with a book under their arms, unless that book were a science fiction book. The long connection between science fiction and pulp novels legitimized, for a generation, the possibility that reading, thinking, and enjoyment might actually go hand in hand.

Which brings me back to the beginning of this essay. The beauty of science lies for me not merely in its ability to produce fantastic new technologies that transform and can improve the human condition. It is rather in its ability to open our eyes to the endless wonder of the real universe, which continues to surprise us every time we open a new window upon it, even when that window is a literary one. If we ever stop imagining the myriad possibilities of existence, or stop exploring ways to determine whether reality encompasses them, then the human drama will no longer be worth writing about, either in fiction or nonfiction.

PREFACE: INNOVATION STARVATION
Neal Stephenson

MY LIFE SPAN ENCOMPASSES the era when the United States of America was capable of launching human beings into space. Some of my earliest memories are of sitting on a braided rug before a hulking black-and-white television, watching the early Gemini missions. In the summer of 2011, at the age of fifty-one—not even old—I watched on a flatscreen as the last space shuttle lifted off the pad. I have followed the dwindling of the space program with sadness, even bitterness. Where's my donut-shaped space station? Where's my ticket to Mars? Until recently, though, I have kept my feelings to myself. Space exploration has always had its detractors. To complain about its demise is to expose oneself to attack from those who have no sympathy that an affluent, middle-aged white American has not lived to see his boyhood fantasies fulfilled.

Still, I worry that our inability to match the achievements of the 1960s space program might be symptomatic of a general failure of our society to get big things done. My parents and grandparents witnessed the creation of the automobile, the airplane, nuclear energy, and the computer, to name only a few. Scientists and engineers who came of age during the first half of the twentieth century could look forward to building things that would solve age-old problems, transform the landscape, build the economy, and provide jobs for the burgeoning middle class that was the basis for our stable democracy.

The Deepwater Horizon oil spill of 2010 crystallized my feeling that we have lost our ability to get important things done. The OPEC oil shock was in 1973—almost forty years earlier. It was obvious then that it was crazy for the United States to let itself be held economic hostage to the kinds of countries where oil was being produced. It led to Jimmy Carter's proposal for the development of an enormous synthetic fuels industry on American soil. Whatever one might think of the merits of the Carter presidency or of this particular proposal, it was, at least, a serious effort to come to grips with the problem.

Little has been heard in that vein since. We've been talking about wind farms, tidal power, and solar power for decades. Some progress has been made in those areas, but energy is still all about oil. In my city, Seattle, a thirty-five-year-old plan to run a light rail line across Lake Washington is now being blocked by a citizen initiative. Thwarted or endlessly delayed in its efforts to build things, the city plods ahead with a project to paint bicycle lanes on the pavement of thoroughfares.

In early 2011, I participated in a conference called Future Tense, where I lamented the decline of the manned space program, then pivoted to energy, indicating that the real issue isn't about rockets. It's our far broader inability as a society to execute on the big stuff. I had, through some kind of blind luck, struck a nerve. The audience at Future Tense was more confident than I that science fiction (SF) had relevance—even utility—in addressing the problem. I heard two theories as to why:

1. The Inspiration Theory. SF inspires people to choose science and engineering as careers. This much is undoubtedly true, and somewhat obvious.

2. The Hieroglyph Theory. Good SF supplies a plausible, fully thought-out picture of an alternate reality in which some sort of compelling innovation has taken place. A good SF universe has a coherence and internal logic that makes sense to scientists and engineers. Examples include Isaac Asimov's robots, Robert Heinlein's rocket ships, and William Gibson's cyberspace. As Jim Karkanias of Microsoft Research puts it, such icons serve as hieroglyphs—simple, recognizable symbols on whose significance everyone agrees.

Researchers and engineers have found themselves concentrating on more and more narrowly focused topics as science and technology have become more complex. A large technology company or lab might employ hundreds or thousands of persons, each of whom can address only a thin slice of the overall problem. Communication among them can become a mare's nest of e-mail threads and PowerPoints. The fondness that many such people have for SF reflects, in part, the usefulness of an overarching narrative that supplies them and their colleagues with a shared vision. Coordinating their efforts through a command-and-control management system is a little like trying to run a modern economy out of a politburo. Letting them work toward an agreed-on goal is something more like a free and largely self-coordinated market of ideas.

SPANNING THE AGES

SF has changed over the span of time I am talking about—from the 1950s (the era of the development of nuclear power, jet airplanes, the space race, and the computer) to now. Speaking broadly, the techno-optimism of the Golden Age of SF has given way to fiction written in a generally darker, more skeptical, and ambiguous tone. I myself have tended to write a lot about hackers—trickster archetypes who exploit the arcane capabilities of complex systems devised by faceless others.

Believing we have all the technology we'll ever need, we seek to draw attention to its destructive side effects. This seems foolish now that we find ourselves saddled with technologies like Japan's ramshackle 1960s-vintage reactors at Fukushima when we have the possibility of clean nuclear fusion on the horizon. The imperative to develop new technologies and implement them on a heroic scale no longer seems like the childish preoccupation of a few nerds with slide rules. It's the only way for the human race to escape from its current predicaments. Too bad we've forgotten how to do it.

"You're the ones who've been slacking off!" proclaims Michael Crow, president of Arizona State University (and one of the other speakers at Future Tense). He refers, of course, to SF writers. The scientists and engineers, he seems to be saying, are ready and looking for things to do. Time for the SF writers to start pulling their weight and supplying big visions that make sense. Hence the *Hieroglyph* project, an effort to produce an anthology of new SF that will be in some ways a conscious throwback to the practical techno-optimism of the Golden Age.

SPACEBORNE CIVILIZATIONS

China is frequently cited as a country now executing the big stuff, and there's no doubt they are constructing dams, high-speed rail systems, and rockets at an extraordinary clip. But those are not fundamentally innovative. Their space program, like all other countries' (including our own), is just parroting work that was done fifty years ago by the Soviets and the Americans. A truly innovative program would involve taking risks (and accepting failures) to pioneer some of the alternative space launch technologies that have been advanced by researchers all over the world during the decades dominated by rockets.

Imagine a factory mass-producing small vehicles, about as big and complicated as refrigerators, which roll off the end of an assembly line, are loaded with space-bound cargo and topped off with nonpolluting liquid hydrogen fuel, then are exposed to intense concentrated heat from an array of ground-based lasers or microwave antennas. Heated to temperatures beyond what can be achieved through a chemical reaction, the hydrogen erupts from a nozzle on the base of the device and sends it rocketing into the air. Tracked through its flight by the lasers or microwaves, the vehicle soars into orbit, carrying a larger payload for its size than a chemical rocket could ever manage, but the complexity, expense, and jobs remain grounded. For decades, this has been the vision of such researchers as physicists Jordin Kare and Kevin Parkin. A similar idea, using a pulsed ground-based laser to blast propellant from the backside of a space vehicle, was being talked about by Arthur Kantrowitz, Freeman Dyson, and other eminent physicists in the early 1960s.

If that sounds too complicated, then consider the 2003 proposal of Geoff Landis and Vincent Denis to construct a twenty-kilometer-high tower using simple steel trusses. Conventional rockets launched from its top would be able to carry twice as much payload as comparable ones launched from ground level. There is even abundant research, dating all the way back to Konstantin Tsiolkovsky, the father of astronautics beginning in the late nineteenth century, to show that a simple tether—a long rope, tumbling end over end while orbiting Earth—could be used to scoop payloads out of the upper atmosphere and haul them up into orbit without the need for engines of any kind. Energy would be pumped into the system using an electrodynamic process with no moving parts.

All are promising ideas—just the sort that used to get an earlier generation of scientists and engineers fired up about actually building something.

But to grasp just how far our current mind-set is from being able to attempt innovation on such a scale, consider the fate of the space shuttle's external tanks (ETs). Dwarfing the vehicle itself, the ET was the largest and most prominent feature of the space shuttle as it stood on the pad. It remained attached to the shuttle—or perhaps it makes as much sense to say that the shuttle remained attached to it—long after the two strap-on boosters had fallen away. The ET and the shuttle remained connected all the way out of the atmosphere and into space. Only after the system had attained orbital velocity was the tank jettisoned and allowed to fall into the atmosphere, where it was destroyed on reentry.

At a modest marginal cost, the ETs could have been kept in orbit indefinitely. The mass of the ET at separation, including residual propellants, was about twice that of the largest possible shuttle payload. Not destroying them would have roughly tripled the total mass launched into orbit by the shuttle. ETs could have been connected to build units that would have humbled today's International Space Station. The residual oxygen and hydrogen sloshing around in them could have been combined to generate electricity and produce tons of water, a commodity that is vastly expensive and desirable in space. But in spite of hard work and passionate advocacy by space experts who wished to see the tanks put to use, NASA—for reasons both technical and political—sent each of them to fiery destruction in the atmosphere. Viewed as a parable, it has much to tell us about the difficulties of innovating in other spheres.

EXECUTING THE BIG STUFF

Innovation can't happen without accepting the risk that it might fail. The vast and radical innovations of the mid-twentieth century took place in a world that, in retrospect, looks insanely dangerous and unstable. Possible outcomes that the modern mind identifies as serious risks might not have been taken seriously—supposing they were noticed at all—by people habituated to the Depression, the World Wars, and the Cold War, in times when seat belts, antibiotics, and many vaccines did not exist. Competition between the Western democracies and the communist powers obliged the former to push their scientists and engineers to the limits of what they could imagine and supplied a sort of safety net in the event that their initial efforts did not pay off. A grizzled NASA veteran once told me that the Apollo moon landings were communism's greatest achievement.

In his book *Adapt: Why Success Always Starts with Failure,* Tim Harford outlines Charles Darwin's discovery of a vast array of distinct species in the Galapagos Islands—a state of affairs that contrasts with the picture seen on large continents, where evolutionary experiments tend to get pulled back toward a sort of ecological consensus by interbreeding. "Galapagan isolation" versus the "nervous corporate hierarchy" is the contrast staked out by Harford in assessing the ability of an organization to innovate.

Most people who work in corporations or academia have witnessed something like the following: A number of engineers are sitting together in a room, bouncing ideas off one another. Out of the discussion emerges a new concept that seems promising. Then some laptop-wielding person in the corner, having performed a quick Google search, announces that this "new" idea is, in fact, an old one—or at least vaguely similar—and has already been tried. Either it failed, or it succeeded. If it failed, then no manager who wants to keep his or her job will approve spending money trying to revive it. If it succeeded, then it's patented and entry to the market is presumed to be unattainable, since the first people who thought of it will have "first-mover advantage" and will have created "barriers to entry." The number of seemingly promising ideas that have been crushed in this way must be in the millions.

What if that person in the corner hadn't been able to do a Google search? It might have required weeks of library research to uncover evidence that the idea wasn't entirely new—and after a long and toilsome slog through many books, tracking down many references, some relevant, some not. When the precedent was finally unearthed, it might not have seemed like such a direct precedent after all. There might be reasons why it would be worth taking a second crack at the idea, perhaps hybridizing it with innovations from other fields. Hence the virtues of Galapagan isolation.

The counterpart to Galapagan isolation is the struggle for survival on a large continent, where firmly established ecosystems tend to blur and swamp new adaptations. Jaron Lanier, a computer scientist, composer, visual artist, and author of the book *You Are Not a Gadget: A Manifesto,* has some insights about the unintended consequences of the Internet—the informational equivalent of a large continent—on our ability to take risks. In the pre-Net era, managers were forced to make decisions based on what they knew to be limited information. Today, by contrast, data flows to managers in real time from countless sources that could not even be imagined a couple of generations ago, and powerful computers process, organize, and display the data in ways that are as far beyond the hand-drawn graph-paper plots of my youth as modern video games are to tic-tac-toe. In a world where decision makers are so close to being omniscient, it's easy to see risk as a quaint artifact of a primitive and dangerous past.

The illusion of eliminating uncertainty from corporate decision making is not merely a question of management style or personal preference. In the legal environment that has developed around publicly traded corporations, managers are strongly discouraged from shouldering any risks that they know about—or, in the opinion of some future jury, should have known about—even if they have a hunch that the gamble might pay off in the long run. There is no such thing as "long run" in industries driven by the next quarterly report. The possibility of some innovation making money is just that—a mere possibility that will not have time to materialize before the subpoenas from minority shareholder lawsuits begin to roll in.

Today's belief in ineluctable certainty is the true innovation killer of our age. In this environment, the best an audacious manager can do is to develop small improvements to existing systems—climbing the hill, as it were, toward a local maximum, trimming fat, eking out the occasional tiny innovation—like city planners painting bicycle lanes on the streets as a gesture toward solving our energy problems. Any strategy that involves crossing a valley—accepting short-term losses to reach a higher hill in the distance—will soon be brought to a halt by the demands of a system that celebrates short-term gains and tolerates stagnation, but condemns anything else as failure. In short, a world where big stuff can never get done.

ACKNOWLEDGMENTS

THE EDITORS WISH TO thank the many people who made this book and Project Hieroglyph possible. Many of the people we name here will be named again several times below because of the many roles they served in building and supporting this big idea. First, we'd like to acknowledge Neal Stephenson for founding Project Hieroglyph and President Michael Crow for bringing the Center for Science and the Imagination to life at Arizona State University (ASU).

On behalf of the Center for Science and the Imagination, we thank Kimberly de los Santos for shepherding the idea in its nascent early stages; Safwat Saleem and Joshua Gallagher for establishing Project Hieroglyph's early style; Art Lee, Jim O'Brien, and Karen Liepmann for sage counsel; and Lauren Pedersen, Elizabeth Vegh, and Wesley de la Rosa for their good humor, can-do attitudes, and the many hours they have contributed to making Project Hieroglyph and the center as creative and vibrant as they are today. We wish to specially acknowledge Jennifer Apple, volunteer editor extraordinaire; Chelsea Courtney, business operations specialist and operational wizard; Nina Miller, the tremendously creative designer and architect of the current Project Hieroglyph platform; and Joey Eschrich, a tireless and talented editor, promoter, enthusiast, manager, field marshal, ghostbuster, and majority whip for Project Hieroglyph and the center. For the launch of Project Hieroglyph we thank Jeremy Bornstein, Gary McCoy, Karen Laur, Zoe Glynn, and all those at Subutai Corporation and Brainstem Media for their hard work on the first iterations of the Hieroglyph platform, as well as Jim Karkanias, Stewart Brand, Esther Dyson,

xxiv   Acknowledgments

and the many others who provided key pieces of advice and support during Project Hieroglyph's early days.

As editors we also wish to acknowledge the wit, warmth, and unflagging support of Jennifer Brehl and the entire team at HarperCollins, as well as Michele Mortimer and the charming Liz Darhansoff, of Darhansoff and Verril Literary Agents, who acted as agent for the project, negotiating the complex contract on behalf of ASU.

Ed Finn would like to thank all those at ASU who have made the center's existence not merely possible but a thrilling adventure for their support, their good advice, and their intellectual generosity, especially those who might grant him tenure one day. He'd especially like to thank Michael Crow for letting him just make stuff up and then try it as a job description and Kimberly de los Santos for hiring someone who is, by many objective measures, pretty weird. He is eternally grateful to Anna and Nora for giving him new reasons for optimism every single day.

Kathryn Cramer thanks Neal Stephenson and Ed Finn for the opportunity to work on *Hieroglyph*, Edward Cornell for his support and encouragement, Gregory Benford for conversation and advice, and David Hartwell for suggesting to Neal Stephenson that she might be right for this project.

INTRODUCTION:
A BLUEPRINT FOR BETTER DREAMS
Ed Finn and Kathryn Cramer

WELCOME TO PROJECT HIEROGLYPH, founded by Neal Stephenson and produced by Arizona State University's Center for Science and the Imagination. Our purpose here is to rekindle grand technological ambitions through the power of storytelling. Audacious projects like the Great Pyramids, the Hoover Dam, or a moon landing didn't just happen by accident. Someone had to imagine them and create a narrative that brought that vision to life for others. They are dreams that became real not because they were easy, but because they were hard. The editors firmly believe that if we want to create a better future, we need to start with better dreams. Big dreams—infectious, inclusive, optimistic dreams—are the vital first step to catalyzing real change in the world. As it turns out, sometimes that dreamer is a writer of fiction, often science fiction.

It all started in 2011. Neal Stephenson was on a panel called Future Tense with ASU's president, Michael Crow. Stephenson had recently published "Innovation Starvation," his preface to this volume, and onstage he was talking about how dystopian our visions of the future are, and how we seem to have lost sight of our ability to think and do "big stuff": the Apollo program, national infrastructure projects, and the microchip, for example. Crow responded that maybe it's the science fiction writers who are letting us down by failing to conjure up grand, ambitious futures that will inspire us to get out there and make them real. The two began to discuss how we might get science fiction writers actively involved in shaping the future in a persistent, organized way.

That conversation launched both the Center for Science and the Imagination and Project Hieroglyph, two initiatives with a shared goal: get people thinking creatively and ambitiously about the future. We see this mission as having two interlocking halves. First, we need to share a broader sense of agency about the future. It's not something people in white coats are cooking up in a lab somewhere. Whether we consciously accept it or not, we are all making choices that shape the future we are creating together. Second, we need to become more comfortable with the tools we have for envisioning that future. The university is a particularly good place to see that imagination is the key to moving forward in every discipline, even though the language of professionalism in many of them forbids or discourages unorthodox thinking. So it is our hope that the center, founded and directed by Ed Finn, becomes a vehicle for radical thought experiments, odd conversations, and mind-blowing prototypes and, most important, a venue in which anyone can take intellectual risks.

If the center is the mission control system, Project Hieroglyph is the spacecraft: our first effort to explore the ragged edge of human knowledge and potential. Stephenson assembled a small group of fellow writers interested in taking on the challenge. He also recruited Kathryn Cramer, who has edited *Year's Best Science Fiction* annuals for a decade and who has expertise in hard science fiction. She joined Finn as coeditor and together, we broadened the group to the mix of writers in the current volume. We sought a diverse group with a mix of stylistic, political, and technological viewpoints, including several celebrated science fiction authors who have been writing this kind of technically grounded, optimistic, near-future fiction for years. Project Hieroglyph also leverages an incredible network of people ranging from undergraduates to leading technologists, scientists, and visionaries who are ready to think seriously, and boldly, about the futures we want to realize.

While this network includes scientists and engineers working on very real stuff, our brand of imagination does not reject or edge away from its origins in science fiction. Rather we embrace the power of what science and technology writer Clive Thompson calls the "last great literature of ideas" to open new doors, to ask difficult questions, and to inspire. A good science fiction story can share an iconic vision with millions of people. Isaac Asimov's robots, Robert Heinlein's rocket ships, and William Gibson's cyberspace shaped not just real technologies but the whole cultural frame around them. Such science fiction stories created a kind of indelible symbol, a hieroglyphic imprint that has endured in popular imagination. This variety and range of approaches is crucial to breaking the mold of the status quo future and exploring the full spectrum of possibility for our species in the next few generations.

To explore those possibilities, Project Hieroglyph connects writers with scientists and engineers so they can identify compelling new "moonshot ideas." A moonshot idea is the intersection of a huge problem, a radical solution, and a breakthrough discovery that makes the solution possible now or in the near future. Our challenge to the Hieroglyph community is to develop ideas that could be realized within one professional lifetime and implement technologies that exist today or will exist in the near future. No magic wands, hyperspace drives, or galaxies far, far away—just big ideas about how the world could be very different with a few small adjustments.

The project's home at the center puts the resources of a world-class, ambitiously experimental research university behind our work. While it is not new for science fiction writers to consult scientists—and a number of science fiction writers are themselves scientists—this is the first time that we know of that a university has aggressively recruited its faculty members to further the project of visionary science fiction.

Writers, researchers, and others are talking online, in person, and on the phone, creating a rich feedback loop between science and storytelling. The living, beating heart of Project Hieroglyph is this extended community, and the set of conversations, brainstorms, and debates that shaped the stories in this book.

Science fiction has always been an idea-driven literature that inspires people to become scientists and engineers. And a major part of the job of being a science fiction writer is coming up with ideas good enough, or entertaining enough, to allow for the willing suspension of disbelief, inviting a group of readers in to share the dream. Our key task as editors has been to cultivate stories that would take this further, shepherding ecosystems of interest and innovation around radical ideas. We hope that framing these challenges in an exciting, accessible way will spark some real solutions.

One of the pleasures in this project has been to see several of our science fictions preempted by real research, such as funding for moon printers (NASA and the European Space Agency) and plans for the use of commercial drones (Amazon, among others). Additionally, the collaborations involved in the creation of these stories have launched new avenues of research: for example, Stephenson's Tall Tower raises research questions about wind patterns and electrical activity in the upper atmosphere. In years to come, we aim to continue troubling the boundary between fiction and serious research by seed funding scientific investigations, recruiting more collaborators to the Project Hieroglyph community, and refining our hybrid process for prototyping dreams.

In a traditional anthology, we'd spend a few paragraphs summarizing the general run of stories in the book. Instead we suggest you browse the author notes, commentary, and further reading we have curated for each story on the Project Hieroglyph site (hieroglyph.asu.edu). There you will discover the collaborations, conversations, and technical research authors conducted to create their stories. The problems they tackle range from standbys like interstellar travel to more earthly challenges such as climate change and social justice. (What happens when we treat social injustice not as a symptom of technological innovation, but rather ask how social structures themselves could be radically improved?) In many of these thought experiments, some form of empathy is a key element to the solution of large-scale technological problems. Fiction is a sandbox not just for the future, but for understanding one another. Big problems can be solved only when we work together.

These stories are not the end of our project, but the beginning. This is a sketchbook for the future, with ideas we hope will leap off the page and into real life. This collection of thought experiments, pointed questions, and napkin proofs is backed by research in fields from neuroscience to robotics, from behavioral science to structural engineering. We hope this volume reflects our ambitions. Following the trails blazed here back to the Project Hieroglyph site will lead you to new ideas, technical research, interviews, illustrations, and vibrant discussions. And better dreams.

We hope that Project Hieroglyph will inspire you to join in and help us imagine the way things could be. Think of this book as a blueprint, a manifesto, and an invitation. What are your dreams for the future and how can we get there? We'd like to know.

ATMOSPHÆRA INCOGNITA
Neal Stephenson

IT'S CALLED SOIL," I told him, for the third time.

Carl didn't even like to be told anything *twice*. He drew up short. "To me," he said, "it's all dirt."

"Whatever you call it," I said, "it's got a certain ability to hold things up."

I could tell he was about to interrupt, so I held up a hand to stifle him. Everyone else in the room drew in a sharp breath. But none of them had known Carl since the age of five. "All I'm saying," I said, "is that civil engineers happen to be really, really good at building things on top of *dirt*—" (this was me throwing him a bone) "—and so rather than begin this project—whatever the hell it is—by issuing a *fatwa* against dirt, maybe you should trust the engineers to find some clever way to support *whatever the hell it is you want to build* on top of *whatever kind of soil* happens to cover *whatever the hell site* you want me to buy."

Carl said, "I don't trust dirt to support a tower twenty kilometers high."

That silenced the room. With any other client, someone might have been bold enough to raise their hand and ask if he'd really meant what he said.

Or, assuming he had, whether he was out of his mind.

No hands went up.

"Okay," I said finally, "we'll look for a site where bedrock is near the surface."

"Preferably *is* the surface," Carl said.

"I'm just saying that might be tricky," I pointed out, "combined with your other requirements. What were those, again?"

"Direct access to a Great Lake," he said. "Extra points if it has a steel mill on it."

"What if the steel mill isn't for sale?" someone asked.

"It will be," I said, before Carl could.

WITH ME AND CARL it was one of those relationships where we went for a quarter of a century without having any contact at all and then picked up right where we'd left off at twelve. We'd gone to the same schools and scuffled together on the same playgrounds and even advanced as far as some exploratory kissing, which, for reasons that will shortly become self-evident, hadn't gone very well. Then the coach of the middle-school football team had refused to let me participate, save as manager or cheerleader, and my parents had yanked me out of the place and homeschooled me for a year before sending me to a private academy. This had led to college and grad school and a long dispiriting run of un- and underemployment, since the economy didn't seem interested in comparative religion majors. I'd moved to California with a girlfriend during a window when gay marriage was legal, but broken up with her before we could tie the knot—because something about knowing you *could* really focused one's attentions on what life would be like if you *did*—then met Tess and married her instead. Tess was making decent money as a programmer for a series of tech firms, which left me as one of those stay-at-home spouses with nothing to pass the time except yoga. Eventually, as an alternative to simply going crazy, I had gotten into the real estate business. I was good at all parts of it except dealing with silly homeowners-to-be who couldn't make up their minds about which house they wanted to buy.

Commercial real estate had turned out to be my ticket. Those buyers knew what they wanted and I liked such people.

People like Carl.

I'd followed his career: the cover stories in the business magazines, the photos of him opening the New York Stock Exchange. I hadn't realized that he was Carl, the kid from the playground, until he'd become a billionaire, lost most of it, and become a billionaire a second time: exhibiting a tolerance for risk that fit in perfectly with his behavioral profile during recess.

One year I'd gone home for Christmas. My mom, busy in the kitchen, had dispatched me to the grocery store to buy cranberry relish. I found myself standing next to Carl in the checkout line. He was holding a tub of sour cream and a six-pack of beer. Just me and the eleventh-richest man in America standing there waiting for Old Lady Jones (as we had known her three decades earlier) to finish coupon sorting. Carl and I had strolled across the parking lot to the Applebee's and spent a while catching up. I told him about my marriage. Carl just nodded as if to say, *Yeah, that would be you.* This created an immediate and probably stupid feeling of gratitude and loyalty that saw me through a lot of the crazy stuff that happened later.

Then some internal timer seemed to go off in his head. Maybe he sensed that the sour cream and the beer were both getting warm, or maybe that's just how guys like Carl are hooked up. He turned into a grown-up again. Asked me what I did for a living. Asked me *a lot* of questions about it, then interrupted my answers when they reached the point of diminishing returns. Requested my business card.

A week later I was back in the Bay Area. Finding Carl a hangar to store his collection of restored World War I biplanes. After that it was helping one of his companies move to a new facility in Redwood Shores. Then finding an office building for his microfinancing venture.

And it was always easy between us. Even when he was impatient or downright pissed off about something, it was always Emma and Carl, twelve years old again. Even—no, *especially*—when he came to me with a very twelve-year-old look on his face and said, "I've got a weird one for you."

"YOU WEREN'T KIDDING ABOUT the weird part," I told him, after the engineers and bankers and lawyers and a single lonely astrophysicist had all filed out of the room.

"I was going to keep it secreter, longer," he admitted, "but people can't make good decisions if I don't tell them the plan."

"Is it a plan?" I asked. "I mean, how much of this have you figured out?"

"I've had civil and mechanical engineers on it for a few months," he said, "a small team. What I haven't figured out yet is—"

"Why it makes sense?" I prompted him.

"Ah, I knew there was a reason I hired you."

HOW STEEL IS MADE sounds like the title of one of those earnest educational films that Carl and I had respectively slept through and watched in fourth grade. If you're of a certain age, you can see that film in your mind's eye: the grainy black-and-white footage, the block-letter title cards, the triumphant soundtrack trying to blow out the tiny speakers of your classroom's AV cart. Here I'm using it as a kind of placeholder for the first six months of my tenure in Carl's organization. There was no point in even starting to think about building a twenty-kilometer-high steel tower until we had figured out where the steel was going to come from.

Making no pretenses to narrative coherence, here's that six months broken down into six bullet points:

• There's a reason most of the steel mills were around the Great Lakes. These seemed to have been designed by God to support the production of steel on a massive scale. Iron ore from northern Minnesota came together with coal from Appalachia (or, later, from Wyoming) and poured into mills dotted around the shores of those enormous bodies of water. To you and me, "lake" might mean "fishing and waterskiing," but to industrialists it meant "infinitely wide superhighway for moving heavy things."

• Most of those mills were obsolete.

• The steel industry was, in Carl's unkind phrasing, "the Jurassic Park of the business world." It took a long time to pay off the massive capital investment needed to build a new mill, so owners were resistant to change. Innovation tended to be forced on them by early adopters, elsewhere in the world, who had nothing to lose.

• China was kicking the crap out of us. Most of their mills were new. They produced better product: more consistent, higher quality, easier to work with. They were getting their ore from Australia and their coal domestically. They weren't encumbered by regulations.

• None of the existing U.S. mills were making the stuff we were going to need.

• As a little side project en route to building his tower, Carl was going to have to reboot the American steel Industry.

Our initial idea, which we quite fell in love with, was to plant the tower along the shore of a Great Lake and basically extrude it out the top of a brand-new steel mill. Needless to say, we got a lot of love from Chambers of Commerce in that part of the country until our structural engineers finally achieved mind-meld with some climate scientists and called us in for a little meeting.

The engineers had been getting more and more nervous about wind. It had been clear from early on that the big challenge, from a structural engineering point of view, wasn't supporting the self-weight of the tower. The amount of steel needed to do that was trivial compared to what was needed to prevent its being knocked flat by the upper-altitude winds. Kavanaugh Hughes, our head structures guy, had an effective demo that came to be known as "I am the wind." He would have you stand up in a normal, relaxed attitude, feet shoulder width apart, and then he would get to one side of you and start pushing. First he would get down on his hands and knees and push on your ankle as hard as he could. "Low-level winds," he explained. No one had trouble resisting a force applied that close to the floor. Then he'd rise up to a kneeling position, place his hands on your hip bone, and push. "Note the transfer of weight," he'd say, and he'd keep urging you to articulate what you were feeling until you got the right answer: your "downwind" leg and foot were bearing more weight, your "upwind" leg and foot were more lightly loaded. Your only way to resist the force of Kavanaugh was that differential push-pull between one leg and the other—the "couple," as he called it. "The downwind leg has to be stronger to take that extra force. But since we don't know which direction the wind might blow from, we have to make all of the legs stronger by the same amount. That means more weight, and more steel." Finally, Kavanaugh would stand up, put his hand on your shoulder, and push. It didn't take much force to knock the average person off balance. Short of that, other things were going on: not just the intensifying "couple" between the upwind and downwind feet, but some internal strains in the torso. "My trainer is always nagging me to activate my core," Kavanaugh said, "and what that means to me is a system of internal cross bracing that makes it possible for me to transfer stresses from one part of my body to another—

and eventually down into one of my feet." Then he would push you until you were forced to hop away from him. "The problems are two," he explained. "First, all of that cross bracing requires more steel—and more steel catches more wind, and increases the force!"

"Shit, it's an exponential," Carl said.

"Yes, it is," said Kavanaugh. "Second, the most powerful winds aren't down at ankle height, where it's easy to resist them. They're up near the top—the worst possible place."

"The jet stream," Carl said.

"You got it. Now, I'm not saying we can't build a tower capable of resisting the jet stream. We can do anything we want. But common sense tells us to avoid places where the jet stream is powerful and frequent." He nodded to one of his new climate scientist buddies, who flashed up a map of the world showing where the jet stream wandered most frequently. And it was immediately obvious that the upper Midwest and the industrial Northeast were the worst places in the whole world to construct our tower.

Near the equator and near the poles tended to be better. Carl nixed the poles. So we were left staring at a band of latitude that, roughly speaking, corresponded to the tropics.

"I know what some of you are thinking," Carl said, after studying it for a minute, "but no, I'm not going to build this tower in some third world hellhole only to have it end up being the property of the first junta that comes along."

A few of the people in the room had actually been born and raised in what Carl considered to be third world hellholes.

Carl was oblivious. "Political stability and property rights are nonnegotiable site selection criteria."

"The northernmost capes of Australia look ideal, then," someone pointed out. And for a minute we were all ready to purchase stylish hats and join the Qantas frequent flier program, until someone in the climate science group mentioned that those areas tended to get hit by cyclones.

"Okay," Carl said, "we need a place with boring weather at all altitudes, and political stability."

The answer was the southwestern United States, with California's Central Valley being ground zero. There was quibbling. Left-leaning people denied that the United States was a politically stable entity. Right-leaners took issue with the premise that Americans really had property rights.

And Californians seemed offended by the assertion that their climate was boring. People in every part of the world, it seemed, like to complain about their local weather. We began to search outward from the Central Valley. Could we find a location with better seismic stability? Better access to heavy freight transport? A nice high-altitude plateau, perhaps, so that we could get an extra height boost?

IN DUE TIME WE found promising locations in central California. Southern Nevada. Central Arizona. Southwest Texas. Every time we found a place that would work, my acquisitive instincts kicked in, and I started pestering Carl with text messages and e-mails, wanting to go in for the kill. But it seemed that all he wanted was to string these people along for as long as possible. Hoping to play them off against one another and drive the price down, I reckoned.

Then one day the following text message showed up on my phone:

Buy all 4

To which I replied:

Lol really?

And he answered:

As long as you think they can be resold without serious loss.

And, moments later:

Don't spend it all in one place

Referring, I guess, to the fact that I was about to collect four commissions on four separate purchases—and perhaps as many as three more when he decided to resell the ones he didn't want to use ("losers" in Carl-speak).

I was beginning to suspect that the tower was a ruse and that he was actually making some kind of incredibly complicated play in desert real estate.

The reality became clearer to me when Carl bought all of those properties and then began to visit those towns and show the locals the dog-and-pony show his engineers had been preparing on the subject of why it was such a great thing to have a twenty-kilometer-high tower in one's community. Lots of PowerPoint slides explaining, in the most soothing possible way, why it was impossible for the thing to fall over and crush the town. Even if it got hit by a 747.

I ended up going on many of these dog-and-ponies. I had already done the part I was qualified to do. But my job title kept morphing as the project developed. For Carl was no respecter of titles and credentials. Whomever he trusted, was in his field of vision, and hadn't said anything colossally stupid recently tended to end up being assigned responsibilities. I ended up becoming one of the advocates for this thing, completely trashing my regular business (it was okay, we worked it out in the aftermath), and had to buy a pocketbook to contain all of my loyalty program cards for Hertz, United, Marriott, et al. Then a purse to contain the pocketbook. Then skirts to go with the purse. Which I mention because I'd always been a wallet-in-the-pocket-of-my-jeans kind of girl. Tess watched my sartorial transformations with amusement and alarm, accusing me of traveling to the Intermountain West in drag. It became a little tense between us until one day the lightbulb came on and I explained: "They don't give a shit that I'm gay."

"Really?"

"Really. They actually think it's kind of cool. Most of them."

"I just thought—"

"No. The clothes are about being taken seriously." Tess was mollified, though not fully convinced.

"People are afraid it's going to fall over on them. The explanation of why this is never going to happen needs to come from someone who is not wearing black leather."

I could do the PowerPoint in my sleep. As a matter of fact I often *did* do it in my sleep, tossing and turning in my hotel bed. We'd hired a graphics firm to make a nice animated film showing the transformation of the site. Leveling the ground. Planting trees to make it purty. A new railway line, lollipop-shaped, terminated with a perfectly circular loop nine miles in diameter. Extending inward from that, the spoke lines. Half a dozen of them, one for each of the Primaries—the primary supports that would hold the tower up. A little homily here on the subject of "why six?" In theory you could build a stable tower with only three. But if something happened to one of them—I didn't have to mention a jumbo jet strike, since everyone was clearly picturing it in their heads—the other two wouldn't be able to hold it up. You might be able to make it survivable with four, but it would take some structural legerdemain. Five was a safer bet. Six gave you even more of a safety margin as well as some benefits resulting from symmetry. The greater the number of Primaries, the closer each was to its neighbors, and that simplified, somewhat, the problem of webbing them together structurally. So six it was.

The next step was to construct the foundation strips: six reinforced-concrete tracks, each straddling one of the spoke lines. This part of the presentation went pretty fast; there wasn't much interesting you could say about pavement.

The concept of a rolling factory was harder to explain. Factories they got, but no one had ever seen one crossed with a main battle tank the size of a shopping mall. This was where the computer-graphics renderings really came in handy, showing how the thing was built from the ground up on huge steel treads, how it accepted its inputs (steel! steel! and more steel!) from the railway line that ran right through the middle of it, assembled them into trusses, connected them to the bottom of the Primary, and then pushed them straight up through a hole in the roof. It was all reasonably easy to follow, once you got the gist of it. The one part that was a little hard to convey was that each of these six rolling factories—one for each Primary—was also a structural foundation supporting its share of the tower's whole weight. The factory didn't just have to roll (slowly!) along the runway. It didn't just have to assemble trusses and feed them out its ceiling. It also had to contain hydraulic rams for pushing the tower up, transmitting its share of the weight down through its structure into the big steel tank treads and from there into the foundation strip and finally into Carl's precious bedrock.

Having gotten those preliminaries out of the way, I was able to proceed to the big all-singing all-dancing animation (complete with moving symphonic music) showing the six Struders (as we had come to call the truss-extruding factories) poised at their starting positions at the innermost extremes of the spokes, nearly touching one another. Six trains came chugging up the lollipop handle and went their separate ways around the rim line. A seventh went straight into the center, headed for a central, non-moving Struder designed to extrude the tower's core. Once each of the seven had been supplied by its own train, steel trusses—kinda like radio towers—began to emerge from the holes in their roofs, growing upward like stalks from magic beans. There was a pause as cranes went to work framing in a platform that joined the six Primaries with the core. This was my opportunity to wax poetic as I marveled over the fact that this platform would one day be twenty thousand meters above the ground, for all practical purposes in outer space, where the sky was black and the curvature of the earth visible. Honeymooners would luxuriate in pressurized suites, astronomers would gaze at the universe through glass eyes undimmed by atmospheric pollution. Rockets would launch from it and extreme skydivers would jump off.

And yet 99 percent of the workers who built it would never have to leave the ground.

The reaction to *that* was mixed. Oh, everyone understood why it made sense—you couldn't have a large workforce commuting straight up into the sky every day, breathing from oxygen tanks and swaddled up in space suits. But it did take some of the romance out of it. At some level I think that every blue-collar worker who ever attended one of these presentations was telling himself that he would be one of the tiny minority of employees who would actually get to go up high on the tower, inspecting and trouble-shooting.

The rest of the movie was predictable enough. The trains kept rolling in, the Struders kept extruding, pausing from time to time so that the freshly extruded Primaries and core could be webbed together with stiffening trusses—Kavanaugh's "core muscles." We speeded up the movie, of course, once people got the gist of it. Push, pause, web. Push, pause, web. With each push the factories rolled outward imperceptibly on their tracks, moving about one meter for every fifteen meters of stuff they extruded, keeping the tower's height-to-width ratio fixed. Though, toward the end, they started moving a bit faster, making the base splay out, giving it a bit of an Eiffel Tower feel. Even the people who walked into the room claiming to be worried that it would fall over were convinced by this; it had a wide enough stance that it just *looked* stable. Up and up went the steel as I recited lore that I had picked up from Wikipedia and from meteorology textbooks and long conversations with Ph.D. metallurgists about the different layers of the atmosphere and the varying challenges that the tower would have to contend with: down below, rain and rust. Up higher, icing. Higher yet, wind loading, the possibility of contact with a wandering jet stream (or a wayward jet). Profound cold that would render the metal brittle if we had been dumb enough to use the wrong alloys. Thermal expansion and contraction as the unfiltered sun shone on its higher reaches in the day and then disappeared at night. Each challenge was an opportunity to generate energy with photovoltaics (up high) or convection ducts (down low) or wind turbines (in the middle).

So much for the pitch.

And so much (almost) for my marriage, which barely survived all of the absences, all of those nights in chain hotels far from home, all of those alarming changes in wardrobe and hairstyle.

IF I WERE TO write a book about building the tower, I'd here interpolate a three-year-long chapter entitled "Politics and Lawyers." Halfway through it, I got a text message from Carl:

CALI = LOSER

meaning, "Sell the property in California."
My response was

OK

but my reaction was a little more complicated. I had known all along, of course, that we'd end up selling at least three of the four properties. But I'd spent time in each of those places and had made friends with the locals, and I didn't look forward to breaking them the news that their bid—for by this point, each of these things had mushroomed into a complicated bid package binding together state and local governments, unions, banks, and other worthies—had been rejected.

The answer, simply, was that the tower was going to be visible from the hills above Oakland and Berkeley: a spendy part of the world where lots of rich people were accustomed to looking out the windows of their nice houses and seeing the landscape. And *only* the landscape. They didn't want their views marred by a twenty-kilometer-high "monstrosity" whose "stark, ugly, industrial profile" was going to be "cluttered" with "ungainly industrial encrustations" and "gaudy" with a "Las Vegas–style light show" that would "sully the purity of the skies night and day."

Southwestern Texas got killed six months later by environmentalists being used as sock puppets by an unholy alliance of—well, never mind. Demonstrating in court that their claims were bogus would have been expensive. Bankrolled as well as they were, they could have stretched the process out forever by filing legal challenges. Arizona was the next domino to fall. It had always been a long shot, but we'd held on to it mostly to give us greater bargaining power over the Nevada site, where local politicians had smelled money and begun to let us know, in various ways, that we were going to have to play ball.

So that was how I came to earn four commissions by purchasing four "losers" for Carl, and another four by selling each and every one of them. We made money on two, lost money on another two, and pretty much broke even on the whole deal.

That was how the project ended up where it did: between an Indian reservation and a decommissioned military bombing range, out in the southwestern desert, in an area that had already demonstrated its openness to radical transformations of the landscape, first by bombing the crap out of it, then by building a casino complex, and most recently by its wholehearted acceptance of wind farms.

At about the same time we closed a deal on an aging complex near the Illinois-Indiana border and got to work building a new kind of steel mill. The Great Lakes were still the best place in the world to make steel. This was a far cry from our original scheme to have the mill on-site. But in the intervening years it had become clear that lots of people wanted the kind of steel that a new mill could produce. Hard as it was to believe, the tower had become a minor customer.

Transportation wasn't that big of a deal. Smaller pieces could be shipped southwest on freight trains. Big stuff was barged down the river system to the Gulf, dragged through the Panama Canal, landed at the head of the Gulf of California, and then transported overland using land trains.

The site was twenty minutes' drive from a college town, which gave the employees a place to educate their kids and entertain themselves and gave us a ready supply of fresh young engineering talent.

As well as a cowgirl-themed gay bar. Which became pretty important when Carl told me—as if this should have been obvious from the
beginning—that I was moving there to run the whole thing.

"I'm not qualified to construct a twenty-kilometer-high tower," I
pointed out.

"Since it has never been done before," he said, "no one is."

"The engineering is totally beyond my—"

"We have engineers."

"All the legal ins and outs—"

"Lawyers."

I was dreading the conversation with Tess but she'd seen it coming
long ago. Hell, maybe Carl had even prepped her.

"Let's go," was all she said.

Bless her beautiful heart, I thought. But what I said was "Huh?"

"I've been looking into it. Precleared it with my boss. I'll telecommute."

NEITHER OF US REALLY believed that, of course. Her job lasted for all of
twelve weeks after we moved.

She cashed in some stock options and bought the cowgirl bar for less
than what she had spent on her last car. With what was left over she bought
a pickup truck from a rancher who had sold his land to Carl.

Five years later, the bar had morphed into *the* hangout for all the engineers, gay and otherwise, who had moved to the area.

Another five years after that, Tess was operating the First Bar in Space.

Oh, people argued about it. Space tourism had been gathering steam.
Queasy/giddy tourists drifted around the tiny envelopes of their subor-
bital capsules and sucked premixed cocktails from nippled sacs and this got
billed as the first bar in space. It became like the debate on who had built
the first computer: well, depends on what you consider a computer.

What do you consider a bar? For Tess it had to have a jukebox, a dart-
board, and gravity. You can't get a head on your Guinness in zero gee.

At first it was just a shipping container with portholes plasma-torched
by Tess's eternally grateful clientele of elite ultra-high-altitude steelworkers. This was back in the early days when the Square Kilometer—as we
called the (actually round) platform at the top of the tower—was still only
a couple of thousand meters off the ground. Once we broke through four

thousand meters it became necessary to start running oxygen concentrators full-time, even for the altitude-adjusted regulars. On the day the Top Click (as we called the Square Kilometer by that point) pushed up past the altitude of Mt. Everest, we moved the whole operation into a pressurized Quonset hut and filled it with sea-level atmosphere. Beyond ten thousand meters we just started calling it the First Bar in Space. There was carping on the Internet but the journalists and businesspeople who rode the heli-rail up to the top and sat at the bar taking in the black sky and the curvature of the earth—well, none of them doubted.

I'm leaving a lot out: five years of starting the project, ten years of riding it up. Tess and I had two kids, raised them to teenagerhood, and went through a spell of personal-life hell when she had an affair with a Mohawk ironworker who drifted in from Upstate New York and stormed out a year later when Tess thought better of it. I ran the show for a few years until Carl suddenly announced during a meeting that (a) I had done a fantastic job but (b) I was being replaced effective immediately and (c) he was commencing radiation therapy for prostate cancer forty-five minutes from now. He then gave me the world's most unusual commercial real estate gig: selling off the Top Click. Obvious conflict-of-interest issues were raised by my wife's bar; Carl resolved them by giving us a lease in perpetuity, hand-scrawled on the back of a boarding pass.

Shipping materials to the top of the tower only became more expensive as it went up, so we had framed in the big structures while the Top Click had been on the ground, then stockpiled steel and other goods that could be used to finish it later. All of it got a free—but very slow—ride to twenty thousand meters. Additional structural work proceeded at a leisurely pace during the years that the Top Click was rising up through the Dead Zone—the altitudes from about seven to twelve kilometers. Below seven, humans could breathe (though most needed oxygen bottles), move around without pressure suits, and enjoy a decent enough view. It was cold as hell, but you could wear warm clothes; it was like being at a base camp on a man-made Himalaya. Much above seven, there wasn't enough atmosphere to breathe, but there was enough to supply foul weather in abundance. The view down was often blocked by clouds, the view up not yet enlivened by starlight. Past Everest height—nine kilometers or so—we got up into screaming sub-sub-subzero winds that, at their worse, were close to jet stream intensity. There wasn't much point in trying to keep glass in window frames. Even heavy-looking stuff like shipping containers had to be welded down or it would blow off, fall a few miles, and break something on the ground. There were ways to deal with it, but it basically led to Top Click operations being put in suspended animation until the Struders on the ground pushed it up out the top of the Dead Zone. During that time, we had other things to think about: sheathing the horizontal braces in giant wings, and getting them to work right.

Above the Dead Zone, things got nice in a hurry. The buildings, which had been empty shells for several years, got shelled in by space-suited workers and then pressurized with proper atmosphere so that shirtsleeved workers could get in, lay carpet, and put on doorknobs.

It was during that phase, when the Top Click was about seventeen kilometers above the ground, that we threw a party in the First Bar in Space for the purpose of scattering Carl's ashes. The basic idea being that they would fall for a couple of kilometers, get snatched by the wind, and disperse.

I was the last to arrive, carrying the guest of honor—a Ziploc bag full of Carl—in a messenger bag that looked way too hip for a middle-aged mom in the real estate business. My flight from SFO had been delayed by one monster of a storm front: the kind of thing that had been sweeping west to east across the Great Plains since time immemorial but was rarely seen in our part of the Southwest. But like the proverbial frog in a pan of water, we'd all been getting accustomed to shifts in the climate, and weather events unheard of during the previous century. The airline had found a way to route me around the storm, but as I drove in from the regional airport in Tess's pickup truck, I could see clearly enough that it was determined to catch up with me: an arc of stratocumulus anvil clouds stretching, it seemed, from Baja to Utah, blotting out the late-afternoon sun and flashing here and there with buried lightning.

It was the only thing that could make the tower look small.

One of the engineers, way back at the beginning, had described it as "a gas of metal," which was pretty poetic for an engineer but did convey its gist: the minimum of steel needed to do the job, distributed over the largest volume it could feasibly occupy, but in a specific way meant to solve a host of structural problems. At night, when the lights came on, it looked far more substantial than during the day, when it was a glinting cloud that rose up out of the desert like an inverted tornado. If you let your gaze be drawn up high enough—astonishingly high, far above most clouds—you could see its ladder of wings cruising in the jet stream, like a set of venetian blinds hanging inexplicably in space. Above that, frequently obscured by haze and clouds, was the flare at the very top where it broadened to support the Top Click.

Even though I'd been living with—and on— this thing for going on twenty years, I was still impressed with its scale when I approached it as I was doing now. But having Carl's earthly remains on the passenger seat somehow drew my attention to his ground-level legacy, which now spread out from the base of the tower to a radius of ten or twenty miles. Fanning away to the east-southeast was an expanse of open rangeland, inhabited only by bison, groundhogs, and a few back-to-the-land types: *vaqueros* and the Indians who had always lived in those parts. Part of it was a bombing range. The rest I had acquired, one ranch at a time, using shell companies so that the landowners wouldn't gang up on me. Because one of the questions people had asked was "What if it gets rusty and falls over?" and Carl's answer had been "Then we'll use demolition charges to fell it like a tree down the middle of the Swath," as this territory had come to be known. Which to me had seemed like bending over backward for the NIMBY types, until I'd understood that Carl had always intended to use the tower as a catapult for launching space vehicles, whose trajectories, for the first twenty miles, would pass right down the middle of the Swath, which he therefore needed to keep clear anyway so that failed rockets would have a place to crash.

The new highway from the airport ran along the Swath's northern border for the last few miles, and as I drove in I enjoyed, to the left, a vista of grazing bison and the occasional horse-riding Indian, and to the right, a generic exurban sprawl of strip malls and big-box stores that had sprung up to fill the needs of all the people who had moved here. Behind that line of development I could hear the long blasts of a locomotive whistle: another huge train rolling in from Chicago carrying prefab steel trusses to feed into the Struders.

The ring line encircling the base was discernible as a crescent of five- to ten-story commercial buildings adorned with the logos of the tech firms and contractors that had set up shop here. Mixed in were hotels and apartment buildings housing temporary residents as well as the younger, more urban crowd who wanted to be close to what had developed into a passable nightlife and entertainment district. From their windows they could look out over residential developments spreading away along the state highway connecting to the college town All of this had a temporary feel, since it was understood that when the tower topped out and the Struders ground to a halt, the bottom kilometer would develop into a vertical city, a much cooler place to live—climatically as well as culturally.

For now, though, the tower's lower reaches were a web of bare trusses with steelworkers, and their robots, crawling about. Welding arcs hung in it like bottled fireflies, and cranes pivoted and picked like hollow mantises. In most building sites, a crane had to be capable of hoisting itself higher as the building grew beneath it, but here the cranes had to keep working their way *down* the structure as it pushed up from the Struders. It wasn't rocket science but it did make for some crowd-pleasing erector-set gymnastics, watched by vacationing families and know-it-all retirees from covered viewing platforms spotted around the ring road.

Rocket science was the domain of the innermost core, a ten-meter-diameter chimney running all the way up the tower's central axis. During the first couple of years I had pestered Carl with questions about what specifically was going to go into that empty space—that perfectly round hole at the center of every floor plan.

"You're assuming I have a secret plan," he had said.

"You usually do."

"My secret plan is that I have no secret plan."

"Wow!"

"I am going to sell—you are going to sell—that right-of-way to the highest bidder. On eBay if necessary."

"And what is the highest bidder going to put in it?"

"I have no idea. Since it is twenty kilometers long and pointed straight up, I'm going to make a wild guess that it will be something connected with hurling shit into space."

"But you really don't know what exactly?"

He had thrown up his hands. "Maybe a giant peashooter, maybe a railgun, maybe something that hasn't been invented yet."

"Then why did you pick ten meters for its diameter?"

"It was easier to remember than eleven point one three nine zero two four . . ."

"Okay, okay!"

The secret plan worked. The people who won the bidding war—a coalition of commercial space companies and defense contractors—gave the tower a shot of cash and credibility at a time when both had been a little tight.

Now cutting across the ring road, working against an outflow of traffic—workers coming off the day shift, headed home for the weekend—I passed a security checkpoint and rolled across a flyover that had been thrown across the circular railway line. This ramped down to ground level and became a road paralleling the Northwest Spoke.

Instead of paving the spokes all at once—which would have been a huge up-front expense—we had been building them just in time, a few meters and a few weeks in advance of where and when they would be needed. This made it possible to keep the paving crews employed on a steady full-time basis for years. So directly in front of the astonishing bulk of the Northwest Struder was this fringe of preparatory activity: orange flags marking the locations of soil samples, graded and tamped earth, a gray haze of webbed rebar, plywood forms, freshly poured concrete. The giant linked treads and looming hulk of the Struder rising just behind.

On the top of the Struder, evening-shift workers in safety harnesses were ascending from dressing rooms below to busy themselves on the most recently extruded truss section, inspecting, x-raying, installing sensors and lights and wires. A lot of that work had been done hundreds of miles away when the trusses were being prefabbed, but there didn't seem to be any computer-driven process that couldn't be improved upon by humans crawling around on the actual structure and writing on it with grease pencils. As the tower had risen up from the desert, data pouring in from its millions of strain gauges, thermocouples, cameras, and other sensors had given up oceans of information about how the models had, and hadn't, gotten the predictions right, creating a demand for "tweaking crews" to make adjustments to newly extruded work before it got pushed so high into the sky that it became hard to reach.

There was more than one way to the top. Climbing hand over hand had become a new extreme sport. Helipads were available at various altitudes, and work was under way to build a new regional airport at what would eventually be the twenty-five-hundred-meter level—airplanes would land and take off by flying into and out of apertures in the tower's side, saving them huge amounts of fuel as they avoided the usual ascent and descent.

Surrounding that ten-meter right-of-way in the middle were vertical elevator shafts. But the primary transport scheme was the helirail: a cross between a train, an elevator, and an amusement park ride that corkscrewed up the periphery of the structure, ascending at a steady twenty-degree angle. It was really just a simple ramp, about sixty kilometers long, that had been wrapped around the tower as it was built. Cut a triangle out of paper and roll it around a pencil if you want the general idea. Special trains ran on it with tilted floors so that you always felt you were on the level. Train stations were built around it every two thousand meters altitude. One of those—the second to last—had just been roughed in and was dangling there a few meters off the ground. I was able to clamber up into it via some scaffolding and catch the next up-bound train.

Actually *train* was too grand a word for this conveyance, which was just a single car with none of the luxury appurtenances that would be built into these things later when they were carrying droves of tourists and business moguls. All the regulars knew to empty their bladders first and to bring warm clothes even if it was a warm day at ground level. I shared my car with Joe, an aeronautical engineer who was headed up to fourteen thousand meters to inspect the servomechanisms on a wing; Nicky, an astronomer going to the Top Click to work on the mirror stabilization system for the big telescope a-building there; and Frog, a video producer readying a shoot about the BASE-jumping industry, which was already serving a thousand clients a year. After peppering us with recorded warnings, the car began to hum up the helirail, banking slightly on its gimbals as it picked up speed. A recorded message told us where to look for motion sickness pills and barf bags, then moved on to the more serious matter of what to do if we lost pressurization.

This was a pretty white-collar passenger manifest, but this was Friday afternoon and most of the workers were headed down for the weekend—as we could see when we looked into the windows of the crowded coaches spiraling down the opposite way.

For the hundredth time since leaving the funeral home, I reached out and patted the bundle of ashes in my bag. Carl had had a lot to be proud of and had not been shy about taking credit when earned. But I knew, just from watching his reactions, that he took special pride in having created countless blue-collar jobs. His family back home had been steelworkers, electricians, farmers. Carl had always been more comfortable with them than with the crowd at Sun Valley or TED, and when he had passed, the outpouring of grief from those people had been raw and unaffected.

As we spiraled up, we revolved through all points of the compass every four minutes or so. Views down the brown expanse of the Swath alternated with the panoramic storm front now blotting out the evening sun. The top fringes of the anvils were still afire with bent sunlight but their bases were hidden in indistinct blue-gray murk, cracked open here and there with ice-white lightning.

The car began to hum and keen as it pushed its way up into an eighty-mile-an-hour river of air. Bars of shadow began to flash down over us as we passed upward through a structure that resembled a six-sided ladder, with each rung a giant wing. For this part of the tower was not so much a structure in the conventional sense as a stationary glider. Or perhaps *kite* was the correct word for it.

The idea dated back to the very first months of the design process, when the engineers would work late into the evening tweaking their models and wake up in the morning to find long e-mails from Carl, time-stamped at three A.M. The weight of the tower—what Carl called the Steel Bill—kept growing. Sometimes it would creep up stealthily, others make a sickening upward lurch. The problem was wind. The only way to win that fight—or so the engineers thought at first—was to make the tower beefier, so that the downwind legs could push back. Beefy steel catches more wind, increasing the force that's causing the problem in the first place. Not only that but it demands more steel below to support its weight. This feedback loop produced exponential jumps in the Steel Bill whenever anything got adjusted.

It wasn't long before someone pointed out that, from an aerodynamics standpoint, the tower was a horror show. Basically every strut and every cable was a cylinder—one of the draggiest shapes you can have. If we snapped an airfoil-shaped fairing around each of those cylinders, however, leaving it free to pivot into the wind, the drag went down by an order of magnitude and the Steel Bill dropped like—well, like a wrench dropped from the roof of a Top Click casino. And those fairings would have other benefits too; filled with lightweight insulation, they would reduce the thermal ups and downs caused by sunlight and direct exposure to space. The steel would live at a nice in-between temperature, not expanding and contracting so much, and brittleness would be less of a problem.

Everyone was feeling pretty satisfied with that solution when Carl raised an idea that, I suspect, some of the engineers had been hiding in their subsconscious and been afraid to voice: Why not fly the tower? If we were going to all the trouble to airfoilize everything, why not use the kind of airfoil that not only minimizes drag, but also produces lift?

Wings, in other words. The tower's lateral braces—the horizontal struts that joined its verticals together at regular intervals—would be enclosed in burnished-aluminum wings, actuated by motors that could change their angle of attack, trimming the airfoils to generate greater or lesser amounts of lift. When the jet stream played on the tower's upper reaches like a firehose slamming into a kid's Tinkertoy contraption— when, in other words, the maximum possible crush was being imposed on the downwind legs—the wings on that side would be trimmed so as to lift the whole thing upward and relieve the strain. Performing a kind of aero-dynamic jujitsu, redirecting the very energy that would destroy the tower to actively hold it up. The tower would become half building, half kite.

© 2013, Haylee Bolinger / ASU

People's understandable skepticism about that scheme had accounted for the need to maintain a huge empty swath downwind of it. Many took a dim view of a building that wouldn't stand up without continuous control system feedback.

When we had boarded the helirail, I'd exchanged a bit of small talk with Joe, the engineer sitting across from me. Then he had unrolled a big display, apologizing for hogging so much table space, and spent most of the journey poring over a big three-dimensional technical drawing—the servomechanism he was going to take a look at. My eyes wandered to it, and I noticed he was studying me. When I caught him looking, he glanced away sheepishly. "Penny for your thoughts," he mumbled.

"Oh, I spent years talking to concerned citizens in school gyms and senators in congressional hearings, selling them on this idea."

"Which idea?"

"Exactly," I said. "You've grown so used to it you don't even see it. I'm talking about the idea of flying the tower."

He shrugged. "It was going to require active damping anyway, to control oscillations," he said.

" 'Otherwise, every slot machine on the Top Click will have to come equipped with a barf bag dispenser.' Yeah, I used to make a living telling people that. 'And from there it's a small step to using the same capability to help support the tower on those rare occasions when the jet stream is hitting it.' "

Joe was nodding. "There's no going back," he said. "It snuck up on us."

"What did?"

He was stumped for an answer and smiled helplessly for a moment. Then threw up his hands. "All things cyber. Anything with code in it. Anything connected to the Internet. This stuff creeped into our lives and we got dependent on it. Take it away and the economy crashes—just like the tower. You gotta embrace it."

"Exactly," I said. "My most vociferous opponent was a senator who was being kept alive by a pacemaker with a hundred thousand lines of embedded code."

Joe nodded. "When I was younger, I was frustrated that we weren't building big ambitious stuff anymore. Just writing dumb little apps. When Carl came along with the tower idea, and I understood it was going to have to fly—that it couldn't even stand up without embedded networks—the light went on. We had to stop building things for a generation, just to absorb—to get saturated with—the mentality that everything's networked, smart, active. Which enables us to build things that would have been impossible before, like you couldn't build skyscrapers before steel."

I nodded at the drawing in front of him, which had been looping through a little animation as we talked. "What's new in your world?"

"Oh, doing some performance tweaks. Under certain conditions we get a rumble in the tower at about one-tenth of a hertz—you might have felt it. The servos can't quite respond fast enough to defeat it. We're developing a workaround. More for comfort than for safety. Might force us to replace some of the control units—it's not something you can do by sitting on the ground typing." He nodded toward the luggage rack by the door where he had deposited a bright yellow plastic case, obviously heavy.

"That's okay," I said, "sitting on the ground typing wasn't Carl's style."

As if on cue the car dinged to warn us of impending deceleration. Joe began to collect his things. A minute later the car stopped in the middle of a sort of pod caught in the fretwork of the tower like a spider's egg case in a web. Lights came on, for it was deep dusk at this point. A tubular gangway osculated with the car's hatch, its pneumatic lips inflating to make an airtight seal. Air whooshed as a mild pressure difference was equalized, and my ears popped. The door dilated.

Joe nodded good-bye and lugged his bag case out into the station, which was a windowless bare metal tub. A minute later we were on our way again.

"I just wanted to introduce myself. Nicky Chu." This was the astronomer en route to the Top Click. "Sorry, but I didn't realize who you were until I heard your story."

"Have you spent much time up there, Nicky?"

"Just once, for orientation and safety briefings."

"Well, you're always welcome in the bar. We're having a little private observance tonight, but even so, feel free to stop in."

"I heard," Nicky said, and, perhaps in spite of herself, glanced toward the messenger bag. "I only wish I could have shared one of these rides with the man before . . ."

The pause was awkward. I said what Carl would have said: "Before he was incinerated in a giant kiln? Indeed."

A SENATOR HAD ONCE described the Internet as a series of tubes, which didn't describe the Internet very well but was a pretty apt characterization of the Top Click. "Shirtsleeves environment" had been the magic buzzword. I knew as much because Carl had once banned the phrase from PowerPoint slides—shortly before he had banned PowerPoint altogether, and then attempted to ban all meetings. "The Cape of Good Hope is not a shirtsleeves environment. Neither was the American West. The moon. The people who go to such places have an intrepid spirit that we ought to respect. I hate patronizing them by reassuring them it's all going to be in a shirtsleeves environment!"

This sort of rant had terminated some awkward conversations with casino executives and hoteliers. I had donated a small but significant chunk of my life to getting him to admit that my job would be easier and the Top Click would be more valuable if it had a breathable atmosphere that wouldn't cause simultaneous frostbite and sunburn. Building one big dome on the top was too inflexible, and we had ended up with a mess of cylindrical and hemispherical structures (because those shapes withstood pressurization) joined by tubular skybridges. The Top Click helirail terminal was a hemispherical dome, already awe-inspiring in a Roman Pantheon way even though it was just a shell. Radiating from it were tubes leading to unfinished casinos, hotels, office buildings, and the institute that Carl and some of his billionaire friends had endowed. The observatory was there, and that was where Nicky went after saying good-bye and exchanging contact data with me. I shouldered the bag with Carl in it and hiked down a tube to a lobby where I changed to another tube that took me to the First Bar in Space. Frog, the video producer, walked with me; having slept most of the way through the ride, he was in the mood for a drink. I helped him tow his luggage: a hard-shell case full of video gear and a Day-Glo pink backpack containing the parafoil he intended to use for the return trip.

It was a pretty small party. Carl didn't have a lot of friends. Alexandra, his daughter from a long-dead marriage, had flown in from London with her boyfriend, Roger, who was some sort of whizbang financial geek from a posh family. Tess was there to greet me with a glass of wine and a kiss. Our kids were off at college and at camp. Carl's younger brother Dave, a college volleyball coach, had come in from Ohio. He was already a little tipsy. Maxine, the CEO of Carl's charitable foundation, and her husband, Tom, a filmmaker. We took over one corner of the bar, which was pretty quiet anyway. Marla the bartender and Hiram, one of the regulars, were watching a Canadian hockey game on the big screen. Hiram, a teetotalling Mohawk ironworker, was knocking back an organic smoothie. Frog grabbed a stool at the other end of the bar, ordered a Guinness, whipped out his phone, and launched into a series of "you'll never guess where I'm calling from!" calls.

It was lovely to be home in my bar with my wife. I was just a few sips into that glass of wine, starting to wish that all of these nice guests would go away and leave us alone, when heads began to turn and I noticed that we had been joined by a woman in a space suit.

Not totally. Nicky Chu had had the good manners to remove the helmet and tuck it under her arm. She said, "Sorry, but I think we all need to get under cover. Or *over* cover is more like it."

"Over cover?" I asked.

Roger broke the long silence that followed. I don't know, maybe it was that British penchant for wordplay. "What's coming up from beneath?" he asked. "And how's it going to get through the floor?"

"High-energy gamma ray bursts," Nicky said, "and some antimatter."

"Antimatter?" several people said at once.

"I'll explain while you're donning," she said, and started backing toward the exit. "I'm afraid you're going to have to put down your drinks."

Donning, as most of us knew, meant putting on space suits. It was to living on the Top Click what the life vest drill was to an ocean cruise. Thanks to the space tourism industry, it had become pretty idiot proof. Even so, it did take a few minutes. They were stored in a vestibule, which for very sound reasons was a sealable windowless capsule. Nicky insisted we drag them out into an adjacent sky lobby—a future restaurant—with big west-facing windows. She wanted us to get a load of the storm.

And this bore no resemblance to watching a storm approach on the ground. We've all done that. From a distance you can look up into the structure of the high clouds, but as it gets closer all is swallowed in murk. Lightning bolts, hail, torrents of rain, and wind gusts jump out at you from nowhere.

Here, we were miles above the uppermost peaks of the anvil clouds, enjoying an unobstructed view of outer space. The Milky Way shot up like an angled fountain above the storm front, which from this height looked like a layer of ground-hugging dry ice fog in a disco. Sometimes it would glow briefly.

Nicky's warning had put me in mind of nuclear war and so I had to wait for my logical mind to catch up and tell me that those flashes were nothing more than lightning bolts, seen from above.

Nicky had turned toward me—but she wasn't looking at me. She was staring unfocused. "They're easiest to see in your peripheral vision," she remarked. "They'll be very high up—in space."

"What are you talking about?" Dave demanded. He wasn't handling this especially well. Fortunately Hiram interceded. "Sprites," he explained. "We see 'em all the time."

From anyone else this would have provoked a sarcastic rejoinder from Dave. Coming from a crag-faced, 250-pound Mohawk, it took on more gravity.

"Oh!" Tess exclaimed.

I heard the smile in Nicky's voice. "Big one there!"

"Where?" people were asking.

"It's already faded," Nicky said. But then I saw a disk of red light high up, which expanded while darkening in its center, becoming a scarlet halo before it winked out.

I turned back to Nicky to ask a question, which never made it out of my mouth as something huge registered in my peripheral vision: a cloud of red light, jellyfish-like, trailing hundreds of streaming filaments. By the time I had snapped my head around to focus on it, this had shrunk to a tiny blob that went dark.

Within a minute, everyone had witnessed at least one of these sprites and so all questions as to Nicky's credibility had gone away. For the most part they all faded in the blink of an eye. But sometimes, ghostly orbs of blue light would scamper up the red tendrils for a few moments afterward, prompting gasps of delight. These I heard over the wireless voice com system built into my suit—by this point I had my helmet on.

Nicky was watching their reactions uneasily, clearly wishing they would take this a little more seriously. "A couple of decades ago," she said, "some of our orbiting gamma ray observatories began picking up incredibly powerful bursts. Long story short, it became obvious that these were coming not down from deep space but up from *below*—from the earth. So powerful that they maxed out the sensors, so we couldn't even tell how massive they actually were. Turned out they were coming from thunderclouds. The conditions in those storm towers down there are impossibly strange. Free electrons get accelerated upward and get kicked up into a

hyperenergetic state, massively relativistic, and at some point they bang
into atoms in the tops of the storm towers with such energy that they produce gamma rays which in turn produce positrons—antimatter. The positrons have opposite charges, so they get accelerated downward. The cycle
repeats, up and down, and at some point you get a burst of gamma rays
that is seriously dangerous—you could get a lifetime's worth of hard radiation exposure in a flash." She paused for a moment, then stared directly at
me with a crazy half smile. "The earth," she said, "is an alien world."

The story was jogging memories. This was one of those "gotchas" that
had come along halfway through the project and precipitated a crisis for
a few weeks. The hard part, actually, had been getting Carl and the other
top decision makers to believe that it was for real. The engineering solution hadn't been that complicated—shield the floors of the buildings with
radiation-stopping materials, and, during thunderstorms, evacuate any
parts of the structure that hadn't been shielded yet—

"Thank you," I said, "you're a sharp one."

Nicky nodded.

"What is your idea? Why are we donning?" I asked her.

"There's a place over in the depot where some plate steel has been
stacked up—I reckon if we huddle on top of that, it should stop most of the
gamma rays coming up from the storm."

Roger had been listening intently to all this. In a weird burst of insight,
I understood why: Alexandra was pregnant. She wasn't showing yet. So
there was no real evidence to support my intuition. But she had declined
the offer of a drink, which was unusual for her, and there'd been something in the way she and Roger looked at each other . . . Carl's grandchild
was up here, taking shape in her womb. We had to get her over cover.

The depot that Nicky had spoken of was the old construction materials dump, near the middle of the Top Click. It was all out in the open,
which was why we'd had to don in order to get there. In a few minutes'
time we were all able to put on our helmets and let our suits run through
their self-check routines. We stepped out into an airlock and experienced
the weird sensation of feeling the suits stiffen around us as the outside
pressure dropped. They were awkward to move in, and none of us was
really trained in their use—they were for survival purposes only. For that
reason a number of electrically powered scooters were parked in their
charging docks right outside the exit. We merely had to waddle over to

them, climb aboard, and then steer them away. In an ungainly queue we followed Nicky in a circuitous path among buildings-in-progress. Shortly we arrived at the depot and followed her to a place where corrugated steel floor panels had been stacked up in neat rectangular blocks almost as tall as our heads. Hiram, who of all of us was most adept at moving around in a suit, clambered up onto the top of a stack and then reached down to pull the rest of us after him.

The view here wasn't as good, but none of us doubted Nicky's judgment as to the gamma rays, so we didn't mind. Soon the most intense part of the storm was passing beneath us. We could tell as much from the fact that the red sprites were directly overhead. Most of us ended up lying on our backs so that we could gaze straight up and watch the light show.

We had taken all of these precautions for one reason: to avoid exposure to gamma radiation. The storm was nowhere near us. Far below, winds were buffeting the lower structure, but we didn't even feel it. Our view down blocked by tons of steel, our only clue that a storm was in progress was the sprites blooming tens of thousands of meters overhead.

All of which made the superbolt just that much more surprising.

Of course, we didn't know it was something called an "upward superbolt" until much later. At the time, I just assumed that I was dead for some reason, and that the transition to heaven, or hell, was a much more jarring event than what tended to be described by survivors of near-death experiences. My next hypothesis was that I was still alive, but not for long—I remember reaching up to touch my helmet, fearing that it had popped off. Nope, it was still there. Then, for a minute or two, I was convinced that terrorists had set off a small nuclear device somewhere on the Top Click. Buildings were damaged, debris—glowing hot—was cascading to the deck. Finally my ears recovered to the point where I could hear Nicky saying "lightning," and despite all of this chaos some part of my brain was registering the schoolgirlish objection that lightning was a cloud-ground interaction, and we were not between the clouds and the ground, so how could that be? Now, of course, I know more than I want to about upward superbolts: another fascinating middle-atmospheric phenomenon that Nicky hadn't gotten around to lecturing us about.

Shock and awe only last for so long and then you begin to take stock of reality.

The First Bar in Space was mostly gone. The superbolt had melted a hole through its floor and roof and it had explosively decompressed, vomiting its contents—barstools, dartboards, Carl's ashes—into space. So Nicky's precaution about the gamma rays had not only saved us from a stiff dose of radiation but, by dumb luck, kept us from being blown to bits and sprayed across the desert.

Several other buildings were no longer shirtsleeves environments. Some looked undamaged. Safety doors ought to have slammed down in the tube network, preventing depressurization of the whole Top Click. When the storm had passed and the danger of gamma rays was over, we'd move into one of the undamaged structures and wait for rescue.

In the meantime, we were in for a wild ride, because the tower had begun swaying and shuddering beneath us.

Panic would have been too obvious. I confess I was headed in that general direction, though, until Hiram's voice came through: "I don't care how big the lightning was," he said. "I rode that steel up and there is just no way it could have taken that much damage." He rolled off the stack of plates and let himself down to the deck. "I'm going to go have a look."

What the heck. My kid-having days were over. I had responsibilities. First and foremost to Carl's grandkid-in-the-making.

"Emma, what the *heck*?!" Tess called.

"The storm is over, baby," I said, and followed Hiram, who let me down easy to the deck.

Some touristy impulse led us straight to the wreckage of the First Bar in Space. We dropped to our knees and approached the hole in the deck on all fours.

Staring down through the hole, we could see, a couple of kilometers below us, something like a venetian blind that had been attacked with a blowtorch. Several of those burnished-aluminum airfoils had been blasted by the superbolt. A huge strip of aluminum had peeled away from one of them and gotten wrapped around the one below it.

"Well, there's your problem," Hiram pronounced. "No wonder the tower ain't flying right." As if on cue, the structure lurched beneath us, eliciting squeals of horror from our friends back in the depot.

"Is it dangerous?" I asked him. Because one of the advantages of being a middle-aged chick in this world was the freedom to ask questions that a young male would be too insecure to voice.

"To people below? If some of that crap falls off? Sure!" he said. "To us?

Nah. Structure's fine. Just ain't flying right. Only real risk is barfing in our helmets."

I wasn't about to second-guess Hiram, who had ridden the tower up from day one and had a strong intuitive feel for what made it stand up. But uneasy memories were stirring of briefings, years ago, about top-down failure cascades. The classic example being the Twin Towers, which had collapsed in toto despite the fact that all the initial damage had been confined to their upper floors. Debris from a high-level event could damage structural elements far below, with incalculable results. The thin, almost nonexistent atmosphere up here would allow debris to fall at supersonic velocity. Energy, and damage, would increase as the velocity *squared* . . .

Where was the problem, I wondered, that was preventing the tower from "flying right"? Had the superbolt fried the electronics? Jammed a mechanism? Bent a control surface?

Which caused me to remember one other detail from earlier in the evening . . .

"Crap," I said. "There's a guy down there. Working on the system. Joe. An engineer. I hope he's okay."

"I wonder if there's any way to reach him?" Tess asked. Reminding me that all of us up here were linked in a single conversation by a wireless mesh network.

"First things first," I said. "The absolute top priority is patrolling the edge of the Top Click to make sure no debris falls off the edge. Spread out and do that. If you see anything, report it to Hiram. Hiram, you'll have to jury-rig something . . ."

"I'll get a welding cart. Should be great for tacking things down."

"Everyone should be spreading out now," I insisted. "Storm's over, folks. I see clear air below, headed our way. Look for anything that might go over the edge, or get jostled loose by all this shaking. And while you're at it, look for buildings that are still pressurized, where we can take shelter before our suits run out of air."

"GOOD NEWS, BAD NEWS," Dave announced a minute later. "I found a little dome—a construction shack—that still has pressure. But this thing next to it got zapped real hard—it's about to shed a roof truss over the edge."

"I know the place. On my way," Hiram announced.

It didn't rain up here, so "roof" meant a piece of steel to rduce ing the flux of cosmic rays. The point being, a roof was a heavy object, and not something we wanted to drop off the top of the tower.

Toddling around in my suit, I caught sight of Hiram trundling a welding cart as fast as he could manage it. These carts weren't like terrestrial welders. They had built-in engines to generate power, fueled by liquid propane—but since there was little air up here, they also carried their own supply of liquid oxygen. It made an unwieldy package even for a big man like Hiram, but presently Dave waddled over to lend a hand.

Inside, our little refuge was like any other construction site office, decorated with freebie catalogs from tool companies and beer posters featuring sexy babes. Once we got through the airlock and pulled off our helmets, we were able to sit down and take stock. Outside, Hiram was tack-welding the wayward truss into place, assisted by Dave and a contractor who had joined up with our little band. He'd been working late on the top floor of a casino when the lights had gone out and a six-foot-long arc had jumped out of a nearby faucet and connected with an electrical outlet, passing close enough to his head to singe his hair. Once we'd heard his story, we understood why we couldn't get Internet. But we could make cell-phone calls, connecting, albeit patchily, with towers on the ground.

Tess and Marla the bartender, who knew their way around the Top Click as well as anyone, swapped in new oxygen supplies and went out to reconnoiter for injured stragglers. I was able to get through on the phone to Joe's boss and hear the troubling, but hardly surprising, news that he hadn't checked in.

Which was how Roger, Frog, and I ended up abseiling three kilometers straight down the tower's central shaft on a rescue mission.

Why us three? Well, Frog was the veteran BASE jumper, a little past his prime and above his station, but—bottom line—the only way to prevent him from coming would have been to hit him on the head with a wrench and ziptie him to a girder. Roger, true to his pedigree, had mountaineering experience.

And I knew as much about the tower's weird little ins and outs as anyone.

The central shaft, which would one day be filled with some as-yet-unbuilt space launch tech, was empty. Ever-pragmatic construction workers had strung long cables down it, like mountaineers' ropes. They used mechanical descenders to glide down when they wanted to get lower but didn't have time to mess about with helirails. There were also elevators, but these had all shut themselves off when the superbolt had fritzed their electronics, and there seemed no way to reboot them without getting through to a customer service rep in Pakistan. Roger, the biggest member of our group, slung an extra space suit on his back (these folded up, sort of, into backpackable units, bulky but manageable). This was just in case Joe was in need of one. Hiram showed us how to harness the descenders to the outside of our suits. Each of us connected to a different cable—there were plenty of them—and then we backed off the rim of the shaft and let ourselves drop.

So this was a tubular vacancy, ten meters across and (currently) seventeen thousand meters long. Walking to the edge of it and looking straight down had become a popular tourist activity on the Top Click. To put this in perspective, it had the same relative dimensions as a forty-foot-long soda straw. As a rule, it was perfectly straight, as if it had been laser-drilled through a cube of granite. Quite a trick given that it was held in place by a wind-buffeted gas of metal.

Tonight, though, it was sashaying. You couldn't see the bottom from the top. It was like staring down the gullet of an undulating snake. Because, in Hiram's phrasing, the tower wasn't flying right. Its accustomed straightness was a process, not a state; it was made straight from one moment to the next by a feedback loop that had been severed.

As alarming as it looked, the undulation wasn't as huge as it appeared from above, and once we had adjusted the tension in our descenders, we were able to plunge more or less straight down. In a forty-foot soda straw, even a little bend looks enormous.

The self-weight of the cables became a problem after a while and so they terminated every hundred meters, forcing us to stop and transfer to new ones. It took us thirty transfers, and as many minutes, to get down to the altitude where Joe had detrained some hours ago.

This brought us into the Neck, the skinniest part of the tower, but in some ways the most complicated. The Top Click was destined to be the domain of gamblers and scientists. The bottom kilometers would be a city with an airport on its roof. The central core, a somewhat mysterious ballistics project. But the Neck was the domain of engineers: mechanical, control-system, and aeronautical. That's because it was here that the wind stress was at its peak, and here that it had to be addressed with what were called "active measures." The most conspicuous of these were the airfoils, large enough for people to walk around inside of them. At one level there was also an array of turbofan engines, the same as you see on airliners, which had been put there as a last-ditch measure in the event of a full-on jet stream hit. If that ever happened we would just fuel them up, turn them on, and run them full blast, thrusting back against the force of the wind, until the jet stream wandered away, a few hours or days later.

All of this gear for playing games with enormous forces had made the Neck beefier by far than the rest of the tower, and so as we descended silently into it, our view of the stars and of the curving horizon was interrupted, then cluttered, and finally all but blotted out by a mare's nest of engineering works, most of it wrapped in streamlined airfoils to make it less draggy.

At our target altitude, six horizontal braces radiated from the core to the six primary legs of the tower. These were trusses, webs of smaller members triangulated into rigid systems, looking a bit like radio towers laid on their sides. Plastic tubes had been built around them, forming airtight corridors. Those in turn had been encased in aerodynamic sheaths. Six of those converged like spokes on the place where we stopped our descent and unhooked ourselves from the descenders. Moving deliberately, clipped to safety rails, leapfrogging from one handhold to the next— for the wind was fearsome—we made our way to the airlock that afforded entry to the southeastern strut/truss/tube/airfoil. Based on information from Joe's boss, I believed we would find him at the end of it. So I was dismayed when the airlock's control panel gave us the news that the tube was depressurized. This thing was supposed to be full of a proper atmosphere so that engineers could move along it without having to leave that all-important shirtsleeves environment. But apparently the superbolt had caused it to spring a leak. This was okay for me, Roger, and Frog, but I didn't know what it might portend for Joe.

In any case, opening the door was easy since we didn't have to cycle the airlock. We were confronted by a view down a straight tube a thousand meters long, illuminated dimly by blue LEDs. The steel truss had been equipped with plastic catwalk grating. We started walking. This would have been a lot easier in an atmosphere. As it was, I wished we'd had some of those electric scooters, like on the Top Click. The designers of those suits had made the best of a tough design challenge, but at the end of the day they were made for passive survivors awaiting rescue by people in *real* space suits. Hiking down a catwalk wasn't in the design spec. It was like wading through wet cement and feeling it start to harden whenever you planted a foot. I wanted to break the mood with a joke about what great cardio this was, but I was too out of breath, and judging from the sound effects in my headphones, Roger and Frog weren't doing much better.

I was about ready to start whining about how hard it all was when we got to the end of the tube—meaning we had reached the southeastern Primary—and walked through another dead airlock into the pod where Joe had been working.

The pod was spherical. A floor and a ceiling had been stretched across it to turn it into a round room about the size of a two car garage. The dome-shaped spaces above and below were packed respectively with electronics and with survival gear. The first thing I noticed when I walked in was an open floor hatch, which gave me hope that Joe had had time to yank it open and grab a suit.

But Joe wasn't in here.

My eye was drawn to a scarlet flash on the other side of the darkened room. I realized I was looking straight out through a hole that had been blasted in the spherical shell. The red flash had been one of those sprites, off in the distance, high above the top of the thunderstorm as it migrated eastward.

Frog bent down and picked up an overturned swivel chair. Its plastic upholstery was patchy where it had melted and congealed.

On the workspace where Joe had been seated, and on the jagged twists of metal around the rupture, was a mess that I couldn't identify at first—because I didn't want to. And when I did, I almost threw up in my suit. Joe hadn't opened the floor hatch, I realized. It had been blown open when this whole pod had explosively decompressed. The atmosphere had blasted out the hole, taking Joe with it. Later forensic analysis suggested he'd been killed instantly by the superbolt, so at least he'd been spared the experience of being spat out, fully conscious, into free fall. But none of that changed the fact that, through no fault of his own, he'd been sitting in the wrong place at the wrong time. He had become the third accidental fatality on the tower construction project. Number one had been early—a forklift mishap, moving some steel around. Number two had been only a couple of months ago: a taut cable had been snapped by a wayward crane; the broken end recoiled under tension and struck a worker hard enough to break his neck. Joe was number three, killed instantly by an upward superbolt: a species of upper-atmosphere monster of which we had known only traces and rumors when the tower had been designed.

What we did next got described all wrong in the news reports. Oh, they weren't factually incorrect, but they got the emotional tenor wrong. Yes, seeing that the southeastern control node had been blitzed off the network, we concluded that its responsibilities would have to be shunted to other nodes on the same level that still had luxuries such as power and atmosphere. Lacking communication with the ground, we had to make do with a few erratic cell-phone conversations. Roger, Frog, and I spread out to the south, northeast, and north control nodes on the same level—lots more cardio—and finally took those cursed suits off and, following instructions from the ground, repatched cables and typed in arcane computer commands until control had been transferred. The tower stopped swaying and, as the control loops recalibrated to its new aerodynamics, stopped vibrating as well. All of that was true. But the news feeds described it as an Apollo 13 type of crisis, which it never was. They made it sound like we were doing really cool, difficult work under pressure, when in reality most of it was sitting in shirtsleeves (sorry, Carl!) and typing. And they totally failed to understand the context and the tone that had been set by the death of Joe.

The one thing they got right was what happened in the wee hours that followed: Hiram and Frog going out on the damaged airfoil to corral loose pieces of metal that were banging around in the wind and that could have inflicted catastrophic damage had they come loose. That was really dangerous work, performed at great personal risk without proper safety lines and, because it took longer than expected, with dwindling air supplies and cold-numbed digits. Frog, true to BASE-jumper tradition, went out the farthest, and took the biggest risks—maybe because he had a parasail strapped to his back. And, though he later denied it, I think he had a plan. Only after all of the loose debris had been securely lashed and tack-welded down did he "fall off" in an "unexpected wind gust" and free-dive for a few thousand meters before deploying his parasail and enjoying a long ride down to terra firma. You've seen the YouTube of him touching down in the desert at dawn, popping off his helmet, gathering up his chute, and striding toward the camera to make the grim announcement that a man had died up on the tower last night. Standing there in his space suit, unshaven, exhilarated by his "fall" but sobered by the grisly scene he'd witnessed in the pod, he looked like nothing other than an astronaut.

And an astronaut he was, on that morning. One without a rocket. Exploring, and embracing the dangers, not of outer space but of the atmosphæra incognita that, hidden from earthlings' view by thunderheads, stretches like an electrified shoal between us and the deep ocean of the cosmos.

STORY NOTES—Neal Stephenson

The Tall Tower idea is based on papers written by Geoffrey A. Landis ("Compression Structures for Earth Launch," 1998) and Landis and Vincent Denis ("High Altitude Launch for a Practical SSTO," 2003). In addition, the author is grateful to Keith D. Hjelmstad of Arizona State University for many illuminating discussions of the structural ramifications; Ed Finn and Michael Crow, also of ASU, for fostering Project Hieroglyph and the Center for Science and the Imagination; and Daniel MacDonald, Jenny Hu, and Kevin Finke for their participation in further analysis of the tower idea. The idea of using engines to push back against jet stream events should be credited to Jeff Bezos. Finally, Gregory Benford's enthusiasm for the idea and the story are noted with warm appreciation.

STRUCTURAL DESIGN OF THE TALL TOWER—Keith D. Hjelmstad

Read a technical paper about the structural design of the Tall Tower by Keith D. Hjelmstad of Arizona State University at hieroglyph.asu.edu/tall-tower.

GIRL IN WAVE : WAVE IN GIRL
Kathleen Ann Goonan

When humanity is primarily illiterate, it needs leaders to understand and get the information and deal with it. When we are at the point where the majority of humans them-selves are literate, able to get the information, we're in an entirely new relationship to Universe. We are at the point where the integrity of the individual counts and not what the political leadership or the religious leadership says to do.

—Buckminster Fuller, *Only Integrity Is Going to Count*

MY MANY-GREAT-GRANDMOTHER MELODY IS beautiful. Her eyes are huge, dark, and laughing in her smooth, light brown face, and she is muscular, even a bit wiry, but most fivers (five quarters, 125 years old) are.

She sits cross-legged next to me on the Jump Rock, a coral arc rising like the back of a dolphin in Waimea Bay. Her wings, nearly invisible, overlap smoothly across her back.

Mammoth winter waves rise from the sea and break in perfect translucent curls. No one is jumping off Jump Rock today; those waves crash against and spray up the sides of the rock and swirl around the bottom. The tow skis are busy pulling surfers out to where the curl begins, and thirty or so surfers sit on their boards bobbing up and down. Acres of white foam, with an undertow deep and powerful enough to drag strong men to their death, suck at the beach.

"It was like that, Alia," says Melody. "The change. Like a wave, and we are still on it. We—the entire human world—could have been smashed, like that foam, from a lot of convergent factors."

"Yeah, that's what everybody says. The dark ages." Melody mentions the change a lot, but not much about how it happened. Maybe getting her to talk about it will soften her up. This is one way to go about it, but maybe there is no good way. I've never been able to manipulate her. She has an unfair advantage, being older, smarter, and a Mentor. I'm just hoping she'll understand me, understand why I want to see her, and help me.

I want gills. They're not like fish gills, but that's what everyone calls them.

"You make it sound like a war."

"It was a war. It was even called a war. Back then that kind of language seemed the only way to mobilize people. In the early twenty-first century, we were feeling like a pretty successful species, but we were sowing the seeds of our own destruction. Mass starvation, the breakdown of civilization, the loss of information was a hairsbreadth away, for those who spoke the language of chaos theory and statistics. The history of humanity was the history of war. Most people viewed the idea of world peace with tremendous suspicion. They believed it could only exist in a world where extreme submission was the byword, or if some essential bit of humanity was crushed to dust. Rarely was it seen to be a state of balance in which the highest capability of humans—to be freely creative—would be possible for a huge percentage of people, and if they saw it that way, they saw it as a danger. War defined humanity. We used wealth to amass munitions and armies. It seemed necessary, because nature really is, as Darwin said, 'red in tooth and claw.' War was our peculiar sickness. It always seemed inevitable, something we had to return to despite our horror and reluctance."

"It's hard to believe."

"There's been a fundamental change in how we communicate, and how we see ourselves. Back then, everyone could easily relate to the idea of being at war. 'The War on Poverty.' 'The War on Cancer.' 'The War on Illiteracy.'"

"What's cancer?"

"Right. What's polio, what's tuberculosis, what's smallpox. If you want to be a physician—"

"I want to be a world-champion surfer."

"You can be both. If you want to be a physician—that was one career you modeled, remember?—you need to study the history of disease, and in the early twenty-first century illiteracy was classified as a public health problem. That freed us to bring a lot of different resources to bear on solving the problem."

Now, she'd roped me in and I had to go along. "What caused it?"

"Lots of things . . . but maybe we were just going through adolescence, as a species. Maybe our stubborn adherence to warehousing children in schools or, in poorer countries, sending them to work, or outright selling them, might not have crashed civilization, but willful ignorance about how humans learn, based on scientific evidence, wasted billions of lives and their potential. World economies were in a tailspin. People were mostly very rich or very poor; very healthy or slated to die young. It just wasn't working. There was an illusion, among the well-to-do, that it was working, but it wasn't."

She caresses the gill pattern I have tattooed, like an ancient Polynesian hieroglyph, on my right cheek, a scream for independence, for control over my own body.

"Your mother says eighteen."

"Why do I have to wait? You need to help me—Mom will listen to you. Look, out there—JJ has gills—see, she's the purple one—wow! Pounded!" I scan the vast undertow and see her pop up, so tiny in that big sea of white foam, about a hundred yards away. "See how much fun it is?"

"I see."

"I'm fourteen, and she's only thirteen. I'm already way behind. Look, what happened to you—you were twelve, thirteen, right? When you got changed? It was radical, eh? Scary as gills. And look at you!"

"So you called me here to advocate for you." Her smile is teasing, and I'm pretty sure that I have no hope. Still, I push.

"I know I could be a champion! I came in second in the Girls' Division, Natural, last year, but to go big you really need gills."

"Gills won't protect you from getting smashed on the reef. Your mother feels they'll let you think you can take dangerous chances. And there's another one of your career models— physical Tell me. What are you thinking right now, as you look out over the ocean?"

I realize: I'm hypnotized by the way the waves rise up, rush shoreward, curl, and break.

They are mathematically alluring. I study the sea, with its patches of azure, deep blue, shadowy reefs, and swirling foam, for at least five minutes. I always spend a lot of time up here, studying how the waves break in different situations. I can tell if tons of sand have shifted. I know the storm waves. I know when not to go out.

Now, as if the wind has changed, I'm seeing it through new eyes. "With gills, I could get inside the waves. Study them from the inside. Instead of only using the gills to give me an edge."

Melody just smiles. The wind lifts her long white hair in fascinating tendrils, and I want to know, too, about the chaotic yet graceful mechanics of what is happening now, now, now. I want to be able to describe it in a way that is replicable, without words. I have given you a video of what is happening—you can see it in your head, no?—but I want to be able to replicate it in other mediums. I want to study it, and give voice to what I see. Maybe my voice will be a new voice, or maybe my discoveries will have been made before, but I want to be a part of that music.

I realize, suddenly, that I've just learned to think this way—just learned that it is *possible* to think this way—because of Melody's question. I see the potential of entering the phenomena I'm curious about in new ways, seeing them from different angles.

It is a form of love. I gaze at wingsurfers as they dip and fly, tumbling through the air, banzai-style, with this love, and frown.

She is trying to get me off course. She is going to try to make me think I don't need gills to do this. This won't work, of course. It seems obvious that immersion, tumbling in a suit designed to gather information about flow, force, turbulence, is the best way to study waves.

"You have wings. I thought you would understand."

She laughs. "They're fun, but they're mainly dangerous toys. You put yourself at risk." She smiles. "You want to be out there anyway, eh? Even without gills." She pats my knee. "I know."

"If I could stay inside the waves. I could know them. I could learn them. From the inside out."

Even though she sits so solidly, and reaches out from time to time, to touch my knee, she is attending virtually to the twenty or so students, of all ages, whom she mentors around the world and even in space, via holographic avatars and many other not-so-elementary interfaces, depending on the learning style of the mentee. Some, she tells me, require more attention than others—a bit more intensive linking with resources, an encouraging nod, questions that will help them think in a more focused way about the intent of their research, or the process in which they are engaged.

"You *are* inside a wave," she says gently. "In the curl, riding just ahead of the break, at enormous speed. Because you are on the inside, it's hard for you to see. The world has always been this way for you."

"What way?"

"At peace. Most everyone able to be literate in many ways, reading . . ."

I snort. "There's no way *anyone* couldn't learn how to read. No matter how lazy they are. It's like breathing."

"I couldn't read. I couldn't do math. And I was not lazy."

"What?" I stare at her, astonished. "You helped develop *Zebra!*" That's the mudra-language everyone uses now.

She throws her head back and laughs until tears come to her eyes, then looks at me with a grin. "You know that I *changed,* but you have no idea how or why. It wasn't at all what you think. You need a history lesson a lot more than you need gills! Let me show you how different it was. Okay?"

I look with longing at the perfect shorebreak, just this side of deadly, glance at my short board, and feel tricked. But intrigued.

"So what happened? What was it like? Was it fun? As much fun as surfing?"

"Not at all," she says soberly. "I guess it was just as thrilling, because it was scary. We—*I*—didn't know what would happen. But once the incalculable power of creativity was released, and evenly distributed, it was like an atomic reaction: we could not put the genie back into the bottle."

She is silent for a moment, hands moving this way and that, choosing, plucking, and assembling from her Immanent Library the stories she wants for the lesson I know is coming.

I am actually excited. And honored, really. Melody's stories always change me, somehow—I feel stronger afterward. They are precious; I don't get them often. I can barely remember the last time she visited me in person.

"You always seem to know exactly what I need. Like medicine."

She holds my gaze with hers. "I'm a Mentor. It's my job. I listen to my students, I see gaps, I figure out, from an array of possibilities, how best to show them information that might be useful in that particular time on their journey. Learning is all about timing, and understanding what media will most entice any particular person: which stories—and stories can be in words, numbers, Zebra, pictures, music—might draw them into the neuroplastic state of learning, of changing their brain in focused ways. You are right about medicine, in a way, but it seems more like food to me. This is your first grok, right?"

"A *grok*?" I've been biologically ready for a year, but a grok is a serious thing, and I hadn't been sure when I should try it. It's kind of like gauging whether to go over or under a wave, judging break.

I look at the waves and think, *Now.*

When I look back, I see that Melody has assembled spheres, which glow in the air like juggling balls, unaffected by the wind. She tosses me a golden sphere, a green sphere, and one that looks like Jupiter, pulsing with many dark swirling colors. I catch them—they feel like nothing but a slight tingle—and press them to my chest, where they melt into the interface on my skin. I smile and nestle into a smooth curve of volcanic rock as wind and sun wash my bare skin. I close my eyes and grok.

A VIOLENT WRENCH. IT is dark. I seem to be looking at the pages of a book, but the letters dance and mock me, writhing like animated dream-creatures, and I feel bound up, like a prisoner.

When grokking, you can maintain awareness that you are separate from the grok. I know that I can end it whenever I choose, that I cannot be trapped in a bad nightmare. That is what I know, but I need to test it. I need to know I can get out.

I open my eyes and see luminous blue sky, a few white wisps of cumulus, the old clock tower across the bay, and a kind of sideways view of Melody, her eyelids at half-mast, gesturing in graceful Zebra to one of her students. She has implants that record and transmit that three-dimensional language, and, again, I feel a powerful urge to think of ways to describe it mathematically.

She stops gesturing and glances at me. "Pretty hard to believe, right?"

"I was looking right at the screen—through your eyes—and I could only kind of . . . catch the tail end of things, or . . . I don't know. It was kind of weird."

"It was called dyslexia. I had dyslexia, dysgraphia, and dyscalculia. Couldn't read, write, or do any kind of math, even though I knocked myself out trying. But—keep going. Call me if you need me, but I think you can handle it. I've waited a long time to show you. Okay?"

"Sure."

She smiles at someone who I can't see and returns to gesturing.

I am confused. Back then she couldn't even read or write, but she learned how to do all this?

It's weird to be back over a hundred years ago—immersed in it, although I can leave at any moment. I would definitely like to avoid feeling Melody's emotions—they seem too personal—but that's what I'm in for. I guess it's like reading words, where you feel what the characters feel, but a lot more powerful. She thinks I'm strong enough, though. Maybe it will get me my gills, but I suspect the issue has been reframed, and that she even thinks it will change my mind.

If I can drop down the face of a four-ton wave, I can stand this. And that's about what it takes. I close my eyes again.

I grok.

I am Melody Smith. It is 2121, and I am thirteen years old.

I WAS BORN IN the days when *terror* was a byword, a fear to which everyone in the world relinquished rights, and, in the case of many, blood and life.

I think it surprised everyone when infinitely plastic OPEN ROAD was introduced to the world in one bright flash (so it seems now, despite the years of violence, marches, demonstrations) by a globe-spanning group of people.

No one person pushed a button. It emerged, evolved, changed as connectivity increased, with bottom-up feedback. All kinds of people—neurologists, biologists, cognitive scientists, artists, computer scientists, musicians, and visionaries—had been working on aspects of it, first separately, and then connectedly, for years.

It was an offshoot of research on how the brain works, what consciousness is, what makes a brain healthy, how human children link to and explore the environment, explorations that lay down specific neuronal pathways. Research on what makes people mentally ill, criminal, violent, and otherwise challenged, and how to change that.

It was a time of chaos and glorious growth, a watershed as important as the printing press. How much more dangerous than the atomic bomb the release of universal literacy seemed to the settled, privileged way of doing things. You would have thought that it would be the end of the world, and, indeed, it was a war of power and money that permeated the entire structure of society.

It was the removal of mind-blindness. Literacy enhanced empathy, because it makes people able to experience what being someone else might feel like and stretches the range of emotions.

I was there.

I AM THERE.

On the morning of the day that everything changed, I wake in my bedroom, my oasis, in early-morning dark, ready to brave the daily nightmare.

No, that's not right. I'm never ready.

The night before had been very unpleasant. I lie there in the darkness and decide not to bother with going to school today.

I hate to leave my room. I hate even to go into the living room. My two older brothers are always there, sprawled in front of the television—an old-fashioned screen-viewing device, where car crashes and murders pop out into the room in front of it—ready to say something nasty.

When I was six, my parents gave me my room, and paints, all the paints I could want, a big shelf with gallons and quarts and pints of bright hardware-store paints and stiff hardware-store brushes, spray paints, an industrial-strength fan to vent the fumes, a laundry sink, and boxes of rags. It was an act of desperation for them. They gave me all that because it kept me happy. I had my own world.

I repaint my room all the time. My bed is painted. My dresser is painted. My walls are painted. Layers of other years, other parts of me, peek through; it's an archaeology of me. I paint patterns I see in my head, zigzags and dots, like that. I lie in bed, see a picture or colors in my head, jump up, and get started. Or I'm in school, and think of what I'm going to paint when I get home—what colors and brushes to use, how I'll blend this or that.

Sometimes I just get a rage on and start splashing paint around.

When I try to paint people, they come out funny, their arms too long, their faces crazy, but that's okay, I tell myself, and I tell myself that all the time. Sometimes I wrap my arms around my knees and put my head down and say it's okay, it's okay, it's okay.

Last night I was screaming "It's okay! It's okay!" out loud and Dad ran into the room and said, "Melody, what's going on?" And I saw that I had thrown the can at the wall and made a big yellow cartwheel of paint across the floor that he had run through, leaving yellow sockprints. He grabbed me and held me tight, and I stopped screaming and trembling. "Look!" He pried open a red can of paint and mixed to orange and made more foot-prints on the floor until we were both laughing.

Then Mom opened the door and yelled, "I'm working two jobs for this?"

My father's face moved from laughing to fixed, like a statue, like he was a different person, in a blink. He said, "Come on out and do your homework now, you have to let that dry," and I felt trapped. We opened the windows, left our painty socks on the floor, and closed the door on my kingdom.

I sat at the dining room table with my tablet and pulled up my assign-ments. I looked at the wall of my mother's books, all neatly arranged and never pilfered, never leaning into the gaps as they used to be: she had no time to read anymore. I closed my eyes and remembered myself nestled next to her, an open book spanning our laps, and she was trying to make me say the words on the page when one of her tears fell and shimmered, a delicate hemisphere magnifying one spoke of a wheel in a picture of a train.

"Melody?" I opened my eyes. The homework words leaped around on the screen; I had an instant headache, a dark hole in the center of my chest, and a stomachache.

"Honey," said my father, who had pulled up a chair next to me. "What's wrong?" He knew what was wrong. We both did.

"I can't read with all that noise." I pointed to the TV.

"Turn it off," said Dad. Alex flipped me the bird behind Dad's back. He and Jake slunk back to their rooms. "Okay, try again."

Mom's shadow fell across the tablet. "Go on," she said. "Sound it out."

"Wh . . . wh . . . when!"

"Good guess," Dad told me. He pushed the screen and it said, *"Where."*

"Why do you coddle her?" snapped Mom, and walked away.

He went to the next screen, which had three words on it. "Which one is 'what'?" asked the voice.

I had no idea, but pointed to one of the words.

"Think about it," said Dad.

Those words were always like a slap in the face. I burst into tears, ran back into my room, slammed the door, and dove into bed. Outside the door, I heard Mom and Dad fighting: his quiet words; her screams. I put pillows over my head and cried myself to sleep. Again.

SO I OPEN MY eyes the next morning, when everything was about to change, remembering all that, and like a robot getting shorted out, my arms heavy and my eyes aching, I finally get dressed.

When I emerge from my room, Alex is in the kitchen getting his breakfast soda. He and Jake, eighteen and nineteen, are unemployed lay-abouts who do nothing but play video games and eat potato chips. They do not help our parents around the house, and our parents seem power-less against their combined indolence, against the dronelike lifelessness of their pale faces drifting from computer to television to refrigerator. They somehow suck money from the Internet, and Jake won a ragged-out old car while online gambling, but they kept that secret from Mom and Dad and made me keep it secret too.

On my way to the bus stop, I glance down the block at the house Mom and Dad used to own, a pretty bungalow with trees in the yard and tulips, in spring, that Mom planted. They lost it in the crash. Growing up in that house gave my brothers a sense of entitlement I don't have. I'd been a baby when it happened. Dad had been an artist then, but after that took what jobs he could get. Right now he's managing a fast-food restaurant. He's a nice man; he never yells, but he never seems to be able to keep a job for long. Mom works in an office.

A thin, pasty boy on the bus makes quiet, nasty-sounding remarks behind me. I don't know what they mean but I know they're nasty and there is no other seat. He always seems to sit behind me. I endure him every day, my stomach in a knot.

When we pass the Supreme Court, I focus on the sign wavers to keep my mind off other things. Today, I hear, muffled through the window, "NO TRANSGENIC HUMANS! STOP PLAYING GOD!" "Transgenic," I whisper to myself to cement it in my mind. I like new words, and I can remember them if I repeat them to myself. I open my tablet and say it, but close it instantly when the guy behind me bats me on the back of my head with his open palm and says, "Try 'idiot,' bitch."

I imagine swirling around like a tornado, using the superpowers my brothers are always trading in their games, and ripping his head off. I know there is more to me than anger and sadness. I know that if I could read, I could go anywhere and do anything.

I ask the kid next to me, "What do the signs say?"

"'BAN BIONAN. NO TO NANO-NORMALIZATION.' That other group's signs say 'HELP OUR KIDS LEARN. FREE HUMAN POTENTIAL.'"

"Thanks." Both groups are now chanting "SAVE! OUR! CHILDREN!," which about sums up all these protests: everybody likes kids.

I stick in my earpod. "Oona," I say, holding my hand over my tablet to block out the noise on the bus, "tell me about nano-normalization."

"Sure, honey," Oona begins, in my aunt's voice, who reads about fifty pages of stuff out loud to train the device and whips me to a website. Oona reads, "Humans are born to learn. We have taken over the world because we are curious and we explore. We take things apart and build new things. We invent . . ."

"Okay. So?"

I think I hear Oona sigh. "So all the little things you do from the time you're born train your neurons. They grow really, really fast and develop dedicated neural pathways for all of your senses. Your brain is self-organizing when you're an infant, and you start to see the edges of things, you start to hear subtle differences between the sounds of your native language, you start linking things together, but then—"

"Then things go wrong," I say. "Like with me, right? Go ahead, you can tell me. You won't hurt my feelings."

"The neurons are pruned."

Pruned. An ugly word. "Yeah! Like I said!"

"Melody, it happens to everyone when they're infants. Calm down. I'm going to shut down—"

"No! I won't smash you. I promise!" Social Services had given me Magic Man, Oona's predecessor, and I'd had anger issues with him. Aunt

Oona bought this one for me, but the main program remembers being Magic Man.

Oona starts talking again. "It says that there is an international coalition of neuroscientists, educators, and governments—all kinds of vectors are involved, actually—working on improving education for people like you and for everyone, but that business interests keep them from moving forward. This Supreme Court case is about whether or not new medical strategies can be used in education. Next week, they will consider whether the patents on a learning neurobiologic called OPEN are legal. But some kind of business bots are stopping me from further exploration."

"How can they?"

"Education is all about business, not people. Not teachers, and not children. Testing companies rake in billions every year administrating the mandatory testing program . . ."

Oona stutters and the screen freezes. Alex is good for one thing: adept with computers, he told me that was what happened when business, or government, which controls the Internet, television, everywhere we get information, does not want you to know something. But what you want to know is usually there, somewhere. My fingers do the little dance that he taught me to reach the more radical sites and Oona is back. She shows me a video of a woman talking.

"Everything is upside down. All scientific evidence points to a model of the most efficient human learning as being completely individual. Humans, from infants to the elderly, learn in their own style, in their own time, driven by curiosity. February tenth is not the day that every third-grader in the country is ready to learn their four times table, and but that's how it's been taught for a hundred years. Without teachers' unions, it was easy to replace teachers with teacher-technicians. They only know scripts; they don't know anything about *how* children learn. They have a few layers of how to keep everyone on the same page; that's all. If that doesn't work, then they fail the children, hold them back to go through the same fruitless exercises. So one key move is to take education out of the hands of business and put it into the hands of kids and of educators, in that order. We call the people who will help coordinate the learning process Mentors. Mentors will have to know a lot about neuroscience, about learning styles, about their subject matter, and they will take their cues from the children, instead of the other way around. The child will show them what . . ."

We pull into the school parking lot. Just as we step into the milling crowd the pasty kid whispers in my ear once more. In my mind, I turn and knee him in the crotch, leaving him groaning, but really, I slide through the crowd fast as a pixel trace and enter the long, low building: East Side High.

Jarring sounds: slamming locker doors, kids shouting. Every room is full of different people at different times of the day. A gray window of dread falls between me and everything around me. I don't know what's worse—spending every day with the same unpleasant kids or being constantly among strangers. No one stops the kids from being mean. It's too much work. I'm in the principal's office a lot, because of my anger issues, but it's restful. Mr. Beadley is a kind, quiet man who lets me listen to music and chill.

"The model of a public school has not changed in over a hundred years." Right. I believe it. Mine was built in the 1960s and is rectangular, full of rectangular rooms. I am really interested in learning Thai, because I have a cousin who speaks Thai and English and I'm jealous, but they told me that I could only learn Spanish or Latin. I am in remedial math and reading, which is why Alex always calls me Loser and says I should just give up and flip burgers, but I don't want to. It's like there's a beautiful picture in my head of me reading a book and using all those weird symbols I sometimes glimpse in my math program. I'm up on a high mountain peak, where the wind blows hard and the air is clear and I can see forever, but I can't even find the beginning of the trail that leads to the top. I work hard. I just don't get it, despite my meds. I love my special teachers, but all day I'm yanked from class to class, from world to world, expected to keep track of multiple fragments of tenth-hand information. I have a great memory, and I know I have good questions, but when I ask them, the teachers say we all have to get through the day's lessons and don't have much time, and I suspect that they don't even know the answer or how to find it or how to even think about it. Being in school is like being on a conveyor belt in a cafeteria. I'm whisked past smells that might be tantalizing as new-baked bread or as sour as overcooked cabbage, but, whether it's good or bad, there's never enough time for me to put food on my plate and eat it. Maybe I can, they tell me, sometime in the future, if I play my cards right, the cards that everyone assures me exist but that I have never seen. What cards?

My first class is Math for Idiots. I sit at the back of the room, so I can paint on my tablet, but the teacher looks at me from the front of the room, where she's monitoring everyone, and the math program breaks through my fix and takes over. "Melody, here are six groups of two ducks. Write a multiplication problem that will tell you how many ducks there are." The ducks are swimming in a pond, but they may as well be flying over Antarctica. I try to touch one with my finger and stop it from moving, but my finger hits the empty screen. I try to return to my art program. "Melody," says a male voice behind me and I look up. It is Mr. Beadley. "Come to my office, please."

I am very surprised to see my parents there, my mother in an impeccable suit and my dad in his manager's uniform. I can't believe that they both took time off work. Something must be terribly wrong.

We sit around a big round table like grown-ups and Mr. Beadley says, "This is a very sensitive issue, and I apologize if I am out of bounds, but I have been looking over some data and I believe that Melody is the perfect candidate for the OPEN ROAD project at NIH. I would like to recommend her as a participant."

"You mean she could be an experiment. Like a lab rat," says my mother. She looks tired, as usual; her dark brown hair curves perfectly around her chin and her mouth is a thin line.

"She would be part of an experiment, yes, but let me give you my thoughts. I am probably the only person who has observed her steadily over the years. I have all her records here; I've printed them out for you." He kindly gives us all a copy. I catch a few words in mine before they dance away, but I know what the evidence shows: I'm a mess. This is, basically, my picture: I am in seventh grade and cannot read, have no symbolic numeracy skills, and can't write worth beans. I can talk, though. That's something, isn't it? A program changes my spoken words to writing. What more do they want?

"She is gifted in several areas, as you can see," says the ever-kind Mr. Beadley.

My mother presses her lips together more tightly, which means, *none that matter*. She bows her head and flips the pages.

My father says, "We know she has challenges. What kind of experiment are you talking about?"

THE NEXT MORNING DAD and I are in a beautiful glass building in a room looking out over the National Institutes of Health campus. Dr. Campbell, a research scientist with long red hair, explains to us that I probably have an unusual brain that keeps me from being able to focus. I can't correctly process what I see and hear, or organize and use that information. She says they might have a cure. They might be able to tweak with my brain, make it like the brains of everyone around me.

Might. Still, my heart beats faster.

"We are actually in the last stages of our research, and we are getting ready to put this through the FDA approval process. This process has been approved and used in Europe and other countries for the last six months. It's called OPEN. Operational, Procedural, and Educational Neuroplasticity. Perhaps you've heard of it?"

"I don't know," says Dad. "Maybe on the news?"

I ask, "What is it?"

"I will show you some pictures. Here is a picture of a normal brain in a functional MRI machine. A ten-year-old boy whose brain is normal—that is, pretty much the same as 90 percent of all brains—is reading silently. In this one, the boy is reading out loud. See how these regions light up?" She defined the different areas—Wernicke's, Broca's, the motor cortex, and others—and explained what they did.

"This is an image of a dyslexic boy trying to perform the same task. And here are images of that same dyslexic boy who was given an earlier generation of the therapies we propose to administer to you, if you qualify, and if you wish."

It gives me a simple picture: parts of my brain are not connecting to other parts the way most people's brains do.

And shows me that there is a way to fix it.

My father says, "There are many, many creative people who are dyslexic. Steven Spielberg . . ."

You, I suddenly think, surprised by the word as it pops into my mind and then understanding its truth as if I had snapped a puzzle piece into place. *You, and me. Maybe Alex.*

"*Dyslexia* is a blanket word that describes a very broad spectrum of disabilities. Melody's tests show that she has all the symptoms of dyslexia and dyscalculia, which we can confirm or discard as a diagnosis with fMRI studies. We are now able to break these challenges down into more finely defined pictures. Reading takes place in different parts of the brain; if these locations do not connect, it is difficult to read. When pathways between these areas are naturally lacking, they can be developed through genetic and bionan interventions, combined with hands-on exercises. Together the eyes, the hands, and the brain build pathways. We predict that by using OPEN, many people who now have trouble reading can master the processing skills from which reading springs. There is nothing wrong with these people—they are just different. If most brains were like this boy's brain, we would all be communicating in different ways, and I would be the odd person out."

She looks at my father. "I know it may be difficult to come to terms with this, but the way your daughter processes information will make it hard for her to do what she wants to do. She may indeed develop creative responses and strategies, but why deny her the opportunity to communicate with the rest of society? You can find hundreds of fascinating and successful people who were and are, supposedly, dyslexic, but you will not hear about the billions of other dyslexics who were not able to overcome their problems despite all their truly remarkable creative ways of dealing with it."

My father says, "Neurodiverse individuals make important contributions to humanity. Think of Darwin. Leonardo da Vinci. Einstein. Winston—"

I'm looking at the pictures of the brains. You can see the difference. My brain is "before."

I interrupt. "I want my brain to connect."

Dad becomes agitated, urgent. "You're a creative person, Melody. Maybe a genius! You've won art awards—you can maybe get scholarships. You don't have to be the same as everyone! You can be unique!"

"I will always be unique," I shout, though I have no idea why I believe this. "The only thing I'll lose is being so miserable!" He looks very sad at that. I lean over and hug him. "It's okay, Dad, it's okay. I love being able to paint. I always will. I want to know how to read, too."

His arms tighten around me. He pats my back. I hear him swallow hard. "Do it, then."

Dr. Campbell nods. "Good. It is up to your parents to agree to this, and I want all of you to know everything there is to know. I'm sorry your mother couldn't come."

"She had to work. She already took one day off."

"I will get in touch with her and discuss any questions she might have."

"She already said yes," says Dad.

"Still, I need to engage with her. This is a family endeavor."

I ENJOY BEING IN the Connectome MRI, which maps my brain and the changes as I perform tasks on a very fine level. I am safe: no one can bully me. I can relax completely and respond to questions knowing that I will not be judged harshly for wrong answers: I'm giving information that will help heal me. Yes, my father keeps telling me that there is nothing wrong, and that I don't need healing, so I change that word to *enhance* and somehow it makes him happy.

I love the deep, harsh sounds the machine makes; the odd rhythms; the silences. They're like music for me. I do some research on how the machine works and why it makes these sounds, using videos, and realize: soon, when I can read, I will be able to take in information a lot faster than I can when I'm listening to someone talk. I'm thrilled!

After the fMRI—which, I learn, is by now almost primitive—I move through many more advanced ways of looking at my brain. The data, rendered in pictures, in sounds, in graphs, astound me: I'm looking at myself. The tests finely target my learning challenges and their causes.

I return to school while an international team, a keen and fascinating group of people, the members of which I meet online, readies my therapies. Soon, they say, studies like the one that I am in will make this process swift. One man envisions international kiosks in which people will be evaluated and receive therapies in a matter of minutes.

After a month, they call us back with the assembled information. We meet with Dr. Campbell and some of the team in person: a neurogeneticist, a nanobiologist, and two educators, all from OPEN ROAD. It's fascinating to see how information moves through my brain, and the model of how the pathways will grow and strengthen.

With excitement and pride, the team shows me around the Neuroplasticity Lab, equipped with all kinds of specially developed hands-on equipment that seems oddly simple—large sandpaper letters glued on boards, for instance—but intelligent. When I traced the *W,* for instance, it says, "Wah. As in white, water, willow . . ." I remember my mother doing those things long ago, and, as then, the associations fly out of my head as soon as I stop hearing them. In a cabinet hang chains of small, grouped colored beads to show what multiplication is. The five-bead chain, for instance, has five groups of five beads each, and when you fold it up it makes a square of twenty-five beads. That is weird, I never knew what the word *squared* meant before. Just being able to make a square with my hands makes me understand it. There are also little arrows with numbers on them that speak their names when touched—5, 10, 15, 20, and 25—but I can't read them.

The educators have developed a personalized program for a computer that is kind of like a brain prosthetic/stimulator, which they give me. It is a portable analog of the physical lab and projects 3-D images I can move with special gloves. They watch me put it through its paces. I count the five-square bead chain and when I say "five," the number 5 manifests next to the fifth bead. I forget what it looks like as soon as the projections vanish, but it's cool.

I pick up objects—a sphere, a cube, a dodecahedron—and take them apart in various ways, reassemble them, play with them in any way I choose, and as I do so, verbal and the corresponding written information— usually equations—appear in the air. I can move those numbers around, too, and fly through different kinds of mathematics that explain, in their various ways, what I am doing and seeing.

They confer off to one side, heads bowed, come back with smiles and say that they will tweak and continue to tweak. They are as exuberant as kids let loose on a playground. I can almost see them jumping up and down and clapping their hands.

ON THE MORNING I am to get the shot containing the nanobots and genetic information that will bestow upon me a finely calibrated neuroplasticity for a limited time, I wake up sweating. Do I really want to go through with this? Will I really still be myself? Will I die? They told me that developing leukemia from genetic therapies is a thing of the past, but they are not superheroes, just humans. Will it go wrong and make me worse?

Perhaps the bravest and at the same time the most stupid thing I ever did was get into the car with my dad. On the way to NIH, we listen to a pep talk from a boy in Brussels and a girl in Amsterdam and another girl in Libya who have taken the shot. They are all ecstatic. I asked for negative reports too, so I listen to one girl from Rio who says it did nothing, and to parents who blamed their boy's subsequent tic on it. My father, who is driving, holds my hand the entire time. He tells me repeatedly that I can change my mind.

We enter a cubicle and Dr. Campbell swipes my arm with alcohol, talking all the time in a low, soothing voice. "Someday soon this will be something you can drink. We're working on developing a reset, or, really, a going-forward process that would restore one's previous mental environment if the client prefers it. Some people who are blind and gain vision, or who are deaf and gain hearing capability, have a difficult time learning how to process that new information and are unhappy. We want to make everything as smooth as possible for you."

"Science," murmurs my father, as the needle goes in.

The injection is very, very expensive—so expensive that few people in the world can afford it, so radical that use of the individually tailored cocktail is illegal in much of the world, and so controversial that I have been afforded—quite annoyingly to my brothers in particular, whose shady activities, I discovered later, ceased abruptly—round-the-clock security.

"Now," says Dr. Campbell, "I'd like you to meet Glinda. She had the shot a few weeks ago. She'll be your Mentor." She ushers me into the lab.

Maybe it's my imagination, but everything seems brighter, more sharply defined. "I feel a bit nauseated," I say, and Dr. Campbell gets me a ginger ale and some crackers. I am opening the package when an African American girl about my size bounces into view.

"Hi! I'm Glinda!"

She sticks out her hand and I shake it. "Nice to meet you. I'm Melody."

"Okay!" Her eyes are merry and she has a big smile on her face. "I had my shot about a month ago and I'm going to be your guide here. Yeah, I felt kind of woozy for an hour or so. Want to lie down?"

I finish my crackers. "No, I'm fine. So what's this over here?"

"You left-handed?"

I nod.

"Okay, get on your gloves and let's get started." She notices me staring at her long dreads.

"Cool beads."

"Step back," she says, and gives her head a shake. Her dreads swirl; the beads clack together in a kind of music. "Hair as a weapon. Once people get a smack of beads in their face, they don't bother me. Okay. All these exercises look simple, but you know they're tough. And even with all the fancy help, English is a joke. It doesn't make any sense. Well, it makes sense sometimes, and that tricks you into thinking it makes sense all the time. You just have to learn a whole lot of rules and, sometimes, just the way a bunch of words look. It's a lot easier in phonetic languages, like Italian. You're not stupid—English is. What do you do?"

I know immediately what she means. "I paint."

"I play the saxophone. Now I can actually read music! I learned how to play by ear, and I'm an ace at memorizing—y'know?—but wow! Now I can play what I see on the page. When I see a score, I hear it in my head. It's like magic."

The first thing I have to do, she tells me, is connect each letter to a sound and to a motion. "Making the motion with your hand, or your finger, wires it into the brain." She laughs. "Not that there are wires in your brain."

"It seems more like a light show."

We even sleep in the lab—there are cozy little bedrooms there—so we won't miss a second of our enhanced developmental time. Grad students drift around, taking notes and making videos, and everything I do is recorded, somehow, by a light cap that I wear with sensors in it. I forget about it after the first day. Being able to concentrate is such a change that all distractions vanish. I'm climbing a trail up a steep, windy ridge, the trailhead far below me.

I dream the things I'm learning—sounds, pictures—and sometimes I wake at night, remember where I am, dash out, and start where I'd left off. I'm beginning to be able to sort out letters, because they stay solid, but also because I'm doing a lot of tracing work with my fingers and just simple writing of sounds on paper. "Ssss," I say, as I write a sinuous s over a dotted line. There is a set of letters in a partitioned box, and when I pick one up it says its sound, "mmm," and I begin playing with them—there is no other word for I'm doing; it is not work; and soon I'm putting together words that sing at me—"ffaassst!" It's crazy. I'm doing preschool things, and I'm thirteen. But it's the most fun I've ever had.

I'm laughing and crying the day when, after a solid two weeks of work, the lights come on. "Cat! Sun! We went to the park!"

Glinda is sitting cross-legged on the floor, holding up cards, and she tosses them into the air. We jump up and down, hugging, crying, and screaming.

The days go by. We play spades, gin rummy, Scrabble, all kinds of games I couldn't play before. We're like a big family, the whole lot of us, a dozen kids of all ages who have had the shot. I feel as if I've been asleep my whole life and now I'm awake. There's a whole new world around me—a world I can participate in, and change. I run around reading everything I see out loud, and then the words are in my head, silent, giving me pictures, feelings, information. Thanks to the bots in my brain, which transmit information to a screen, I can see that solving a puzzle releases a cascade of pleasure-giving chemicals. I can hear the names of the chemicals, even see a statistical rendering of how many neurons are changed. The amazing thing is that it was just tiny little bleeps of stuff that woke me.

Over the next few weeks, the lab—it is a cold word for the warm, inviting world we have, with its cushions, its books, its bright colors, and the incredibly gifted helpful people, adults and children, in our learning environment—fills with other children who had had their shot, and it is a great thrill to find that I can actually help *them*. Mom and Dad visit every few days. Both seem satisfied in their own ways about what's going on— even Dad, when he sees how happy I am. A great weight lifts from me: I hadn't known that my inability to please them had been so much a part of my life.

Too soon, it's time to go back to the real world, to integrate back into my school.

I am supposed to be subject A4957, a closely guarded secret, a bit of data, like Glinda and the other kids in the lab. Like the other kids in the world. No interviews allowed.

But someone had leaked the news.

I'D BEEN COMPLETELY SHELTERED at NIH, but Dr. Campbell warns me about it and says that it is perfectly all right to say "no comment." A dark limo takes me out the back entrance, but I get a glimpse of picketers at the front gate of NIH. To the delight of my brothers, they've been staying at a hotel for the last week. Unfortunately, they hadn't been shy about giving interviews; Mom and Dad couldn't be with them all the time.

"This is crazy," says Alex, looking out the hotel window. "There are people who are afraid of you learning how to read!"

"They're afraid that it might be forced on them and their children," says Dad.

"But if it works, what's so bad about it?"

"What if it works today and not tomorrow? What if it has some kind of terrible side effect that they don't know about? What might happen when people denied education because of their gender, their religion, their race, or their social strata learn about the world, about science, about history, about how other people live? What will happen to the way things are if the thinking of a lot of people changes?"

"Doesn't everybody already know?" I ask. "We have television. We have the Internet."

"As you know," says Alex, "both are edited."

"And not equally distributed," says Jake. "I heard that somewhere."

I peek out the window. We're on the fourth floor, and when the crowd glimpses me, signs pump up and down in the air. "Dad, I can read the signs now! I can read the signs!" I dance around the room. "And I can read *complicated* words!" I'd raced through lists of words and their definitions and usages, thrilled at the depth and complexity of my language skills. I already knew a lot more words than most kids my age, because I worked so hard at memorizing them for so many years.

"Like what?" asks Jake.

"Like . . ." I look out the window and a woman with long black hair scowls and waves her sign. " 'Harbinger of Doom,' for instance."

"Yeah? What's a harbinger?"

"Like an avatar," I said, smugly. "Like a signal of the future."

"Yeah, right." But he looks impressed despite himself.

I'd been looking forward to seeing my room again, and everyone was feeling pent-up. But it didn't look like we could leave yet; the house was too insecure. Mom asked me if I wanted to go back to school and I was able to edit "Hell" out of my "Yeah!" response. But yeah. Hell yeah.

THE NEXT DAY, PAPARAZZI follow the black Suburban that takes me to school. I feel like I'm in an unpleasant movie. They treat me like a bomb: streets are cleared for a two-block radius. My bodyguards open a path for me to get into the building. It's really annoying. I can hardly concentrate and show off like I'd planned, though I whiz through a few segments of math and get out of the Math for Idiots screen. I hear that the principal got a few death threats, but he refuses to send me home.

It's all pretty unsettling, so around lunchtime I tell my bodyguards that I want to give an interview. Maybe that will make them go away.

I choose the place in the front of the school where I'd pretend-kneed bully-kid in the crotch.

"How do you feel about being an experiment?"

"Like a rat," yells someone in the crowd.

"Great," I say into the microphones. "I hope that it helps other kids like me."

"How do you feel about being the first?" That's a hard one. Should I throw the other kids I know about to the wolves? Finally I say, "I think everyone knows I'm not, and I wish you would leave me alone to get on with my life."

"Read this." That woman with the long black hair thrusts a piece of paper with writing on it into my hand. It's crystal clear: "I am the harbinger of deadly change." Must be their script. I hold it up for the videos, feeling an instant's thrill of knowing I hold a trump card. I crumple it up and toss it to the ground.

"I *am* a harbinger. I am a harbinger of free literacy for millions of people, all around the world. It is a radical change. It is as radical a change as the polio vaccine, as the smallpox vaccine, only this liberates people from the disease of illiteracy. Thank you. That's all."

Next day, the picket signs read ILLITERACY IS NOT A DISEASE. What makes the news is the one that says ILLITERACY IS NOT A DISESE.

WITHIN THE GROK, I move back into myself: Alia. Melody's narrative shifts to a stream of images, narrative, songs, music, poems, that move through my mind in a particular cadence. As soon as I discern a pattern, that pattern shifts, and I feel like a living fractal, a meta-human, a big music flashing with color, intensity, emotion that clamps shut my chest or makes me join with others, briefly, in strange new song.

LONG WALK. FLIES. DAB of goo in eye, don't rub it! Zahra screams for food. Sea of long white tents. Soldiers with candy. Missionaries; lentil soup. Mind your manners, now. Water warm and muddy. Drone of distant trucks.

A mob of kids runs past. *Candycandycandy!*

Back doors of trucks burst open. Out come people, tables, boxes, chairs. A Sheng-man shouting, "English line! Cold Nehi! Take your shot!" I push up front; a fast bright sting, cold! Orange Nehi pop.

Beneath a tree we get rough lines and circles stuck to cardboard. I try to peel them off. Big hands lead mine: **ssss ssss** for **sss**nake! **sss**un! **sss**assy, **sss**oon, and **sss**illy! We all laugh. She tries to take my card back: No! No! No! It's mine! She trades for **aaaa**, like **aa**pple, c**aaa**t, and h**aaa**ppy. Then **tah! tah! tah!** Like **t**ick and **t**ime and **t**ummy!

Soldiers drive up. Shouting. Then they leave. We sing fast songs of words. I feel a loud excitement in my head.

SILHOUETTES OF BOBBING HEADS in a tunnel. Burst of light ahead: emerge to soldiers clubbing people down; young men rise and rush them shouting LET! US! READ! LET! US! READ!

AN INTERVIEW AROUND A lighted table, earnest talking faces, all else in dramatic shadow.

"Research has yielded conclusively that normal brains are not damaged, as many claimed they would be, by use of OPEN. It accelerates the process of learning to read for everyone."

"But people want this for their babies."

"It is not presently recommended for use until the age of four, but it won't hurt them. It doesn't accelerate normal developmental milestones. When natural stages of plasticity occur, the responses of the babies are optimized."

The interviewer leans forward. "So there is a potential for them being smarter than children who don't use it."

"Possibly."

"Which may lead to a two-tiered society."

"If it is limited, of course. That is why many groups are working to prevent that from happening."

"But it's expensive."

The woman shakes her head. "It was at first, but the fancy labs and computers we once used are rapidly becoming obsolete as the number of Mentors increases. They know how to create learning tools from the environment—so cheap and simple it's laughable. And tragic. Beans for counting. Sitting next to someone and helping them sound out words. Most people who have had the shot, or the serum, are thrilled to be able to pay it forward by taking time to mentor."

The interviewer turns to a man in a tweed suit. "Dr. Eltor, the education system is in great flux, is it not?"

"Indeed. It's almost as if we have been stultifying as many children as possible, based on ancient models that probably worked well in smaller, more intimate populations, or models that worked well for homogenization of immigrant populations slated for factory work in the early twentieth century. That a good portion of children were able to succeed in old-style schools was used as proof that it was the best way for children to learn, for it was assumed that a certain percentage of children were unable to master what we wished them to learn. But without that framework, and with new information from the field of neurology about how learning really occurs, and with new, universally available computerized learning tools, children are learning more, and faster, so much faster that it seems that they are all geniuses compared with children just five years ago.

"It is causing social upheaval in many sectors. Everything is affected. Business and trade, political structure, science, the arts, religion—everything. Universal literacy might seem like a simple change, but even American slaveowners knew the power of reading would not lead to simple results."

The interviewer remarks, "It is anything but simple. I'm going to turn to our legal expert. Can you help us understand yesterday's UN mandate that calls for governments to support free distribution of OPEN to all children in the world?"

"It is indeed . . ."

LEARNING TO READ: *An Anthology.* Read by people of many ethnicities—girls, boys, women, men—translated into English by the grok:

> *How language*
> *Feels in my hand:*
> *Sharp*

Sinuous
Like cutting into rainbows
With my brain.

Pathways arise
I follow them
As if up a rope,
Pulling myself up
Hand over hand.

A rough tongue licks my brain
Vision ripples; re-forms. Once
Small, I ride the wave,
Made huge
By just
A word.

I am made Other
I am made Past
I am made Future
I am the stranger
Walking past me in the street;
I am the cat
Asleep at my feet.

Word-lightning zigzags;
Inner.
No other hears
When I hear
Each thought
So private
Yet utterly public.

I read my great-grandmother's letters.
She is dead
Yet her voice speaks to me
As if she were alive. She rings in my mind;

She sits next to me
On this summer afternoon in Cairo.

Words leap through mind like wild gazelles, their flight
A bright path etched on air.
Meaning strikes like sunlight: story feeds me.

When my mother went to the protest in Kabul,
She wore her brave blue burqa.
She did not come back.

My video flies to YouTube:
The million-colored scarves
Of women chanting in the street
Light spills across them
They are like ridge beyond ridge
Of mountains, transparent
In the sunrise

They are thoughts! They are thoughts! They are thoughts!

Reading my first novel:
I do not finish so much as
Let it fall
And move amazed
Through a changed day
Where all seems hushed and new

I was like a red horse
With a sun in my heart
Running through the woods
Of northern Michigan
And I could write it down for other kids
To be that horse
To be that day.

Reading was like a stranger
Who came to town and stayed.
Some said she was dangerous,
But that seemed so unlikely.
She pitched in where she was needed.
Helped with the kids and cooking, built web pages, organized yard sales,
Set up carpools, organized like-minded people
Soon we could not live without her
After a year she started her own business.
Now she owns the town.

Learning speech sounds: letters
Stand out, flamed with color
A fleeting stage, they tell me.
They flip and mirror: my brain follows
And soon they settle; normal.

But now I know their ancient selves
Stretch far back in time.
Once things, before they changed to sounds
And then sounds changed to lines
Stood on their own feet, walked through time,
Omnipotent
Taking on local color
In neighborhoods of minds.

WAVES OF PEOPLE MARCH down Wilson Boulevard, their chant "O-P-E-N" a roar. Their signs read RADICAL LITERACY FOR ALL.

Camera pans to coming clash: BAN BRAIN MEDDLING. KEEP OUR CHILDREN FREE.

A MURMURING UNDERTONE THROUGHOUT the flashes, like words a running brook makes when you listen without thinking: What does it mean what does it mean to be what does it mean to be human?

DO WE WANT TO be human, or not?

I DISCOVER A SEARCH function and follow the bright ping of Melody.

Melody's twenty-year-old voice, low in my head; her bright face above a podium: "All the *with* words. Com-munication. Com-plete. Com-munity. We kids glimpse this vision"—a short, lilting laugh—"I know, I'm an adult now, but when I chose this path I was a child and became part of a network that is actually growing younger, as more children—nearly a billion, now—are reading fluently, with understanding, by age seven, because more of us are reading than ever in history. We are also producing our own literatures—trading them, learning about other cultures and also learning how universal some problems are. Just as there is a natural 'sensitive period' for laying down language skills, which OPEN replicates, we are finding that there may be a 'sensitive period' for incorporating and practicing one's ethical and moral framework. When loyalty is freely chosen, based on conscious decisions, we find it is fluid and dynamic. When loyalty is fear induced, as in many repressive regimes, it is deeply damaging. We are learning the kinds of strengths and skills we may need to determine the difference between the two for ourselves, so that we can make positive decisions about our own commitments as we mature. I may find out I am wrong when I am older, but in my personal experience I have found that most very young children are idealistic. They can tell the good from the bad, and, mostly, want to emulate the good, to be good people. But when we are children, we are powerless, and, being plastic, we emulate the behavior of those around us and mirror their emotions. Thus, even in families where you might expect a happy result, unhappiness and resulting unpleasant behaviors are a part of life. Perhaps the gray areas of human behavior—lying, cheating, stealing—and most definitely the black areas of psychopathology—may be deviations from the norm that are actually sicknesses, illnesses that can be healed by the proper application of OPEN and optimal experience of empathic states, so that it will become almost physically impossible to hurt others and look on without feeling remorse, pity, sorrow. However naive it may be, most children believe that a perfect world is possible—that their parents will once again love each other and remarry, for instance. Unlike earlier children, we have a new power. With the invisible power of literacy we can put ourselves in the place of others. We can't help it. We feel deeply the power of anger. The anguish of injustice. We can rejoice in our own individuality and in the group with which we identify without needing to do away with others. We are far too addicted to the joy of learning and life to have time to contemplate the destruction of others.

"The religious instinct, at its best, builds vast cathedrals and motivates people to be empathic, to help others, to share, to do no harm. At its worst, it is a means of creating sharply defined classes of people—those in power, who can bully with impunity, and those without power, without human rights, who must submit or be hurt, ostracized, or even killed. This is the history of all religions through all time. In an initiate, pathways of thought are established in the mind that, in some cases, claim to obviate the need for deep thought regarding morally complex issues. We have seen both escape from cults through the use of OPEN and the paradoxical establishment of new cults. It takes strength and help to leave a cult, where all of one's important relationships exist, and seek a more healthy life. No one can predict what effect OPEN will have on religion, though it is interesting to try.

"These issues are, of course, far more complex than any one person can fathom. Systems and philosophies from religions to economic treatises to legal and governmental frameworks and science have proposed cures for the ills that so visibly plague humanity. Some even claim that human nature is itself to blame and that we cannot change what is worst in us without losing what is best in us.

"I think that is an empty, morally bankrupt approach. When we look around and become aware of human suffering, all of us must think of how best we can improve matters. Perhaps new ways to manage resources will bring an end to war. I don't know.

"But I do know that universal literacy, however radically it comes about, will be part of the solution." Applause. A woman approaches from the right side of the stage, smiling.

IT IS SUDDENLY A new world.

MY BROTHERS GET THE shot and grow up, to my great surprise, to be great guys.

A STUTTERING RUSH OF sound, pictures, words, sharp and colorful feelings, then Melody's voice and pictures cease.

I am Alia again, and the tang of salt water, the rush of wind, and the roar of surf bring me back to my surroundings.

I open my eyes. The blue sky and the sparsely populated landscape (I'd been spun across the globe, into classrooms, threaded through history with tremendous speed), and the random cries of the children on the beach below take me by surprise, as when you stop moving suddenly and the world surges forward.

"Do you still paint?"

Melody seems surprised. It takes her a moment to answer, and her voice is slow and thoughtful. "I stopped painting for some years. I was too busy, too happy. I think my painting came from anger. I've painted now and then over the years, in spurts. But it's not the same, and I think that my father was always sad about that. He thought I'd lost my genius. I certainly lost my anger, and that was what propelled my painting, back then. I had no other way to express myself. Dead ends inspire creativity. I've found new challenges, though, that give me the same deep satisfaction as painting once did."

She touches her fingers to her thumbs in a certain combination, and her body glows with complex bioluminescent patterns. "I still love to explore color, pattern, and form. To create these, I studied bioluminescence for two years."

My eyes widen. "Can you give me some?"

She laughs. "See? Design your own! Figure out how to do it!"

I gaze back out at the sea and breathe in sharply at the wonder it now, quite suddenly, contains—a new wonder that wells from all that I see and hear—coordinated, strident, almost as if it is shouting at me, a complex combination of forces and properties, chemistries and habitats, no longer a toy but an astonishing field of information and relationships, some, probably, unknown. Some that I might discover.

LIFE BURSTS OPEN.

I SAY TO MELODY, "This is your art. Opening minds."

Still sitting cross-legged, hands clasped in her lap, Melody lowers her head and nods fiercely, so that her whole body rocks. When she looks up again, her face glows with quiet satisfaction. "I think that's true. I never realized that." She leans over and gives me a long, strong hug, whispers in my ear, "Thank you, Alia."

She stands, spreads her wings, leaps, and dances with the wind, furling, diving, spinning, and gliding, until she is another pixel of blue in the distance, indistinguishable from sky and sea. A dot of infinity.

Leaving nothing resolved, I think, with slight vexation, watching my friend take yet another pounding in the surf below.

Except: everything has changed.

I pick up my board and carefully make my way down to the swirling surf.

STORY NOTES—Kathleen Ann Goonan

I was intrigued by the *Hieroglyph* project when I was asked to participate by editors Kathryn Cramer and Edward Finn and began thinking about what might lead to meaningful change in our future.

I have read widely in the field of neuroscience for many years and had just finished a story about a girl with a particular form of synesthesia (*Arc Magazine,* 2014), and another about the possible effects of a neuroplasticity drug on PTSD victims (*TRSF,* 2013). My novel *This Shared Dream* (Tor, 2011) draws heavily on the fast-changing field of memory research and on the much more slowly implemented field of education research.

Therefore, I asked Joey Eschrich, senior coordinator for the Center for Science and the Imagination at ASU, and my bridge to ASU researchers, to introduce me to someone working in neuroscience. Stephen L. Macknik, Ph.D., is director of the Laboratory of Behavioral Neurophysiology at the Barrow Neurological Institute in Phoenix, Arizona, and Susana Martinez-Conde, Ph.D., is director of the Laboratory of Visual Neuroscience at BNI. We had several e-mail exchanges, and I read their book, *Sleights of Mind: What the Neuroscience of Mind Reveals About Our Everyday Deceptions* (Henry

Holt & Co., 2010). It is a fascinating book but did not particularly yield a focus for my story.

Through Joey, I was eventually able to Skype with Ruth Wylie, Ph.D., at ASU's Chi Learning and Cognition Lab in the Learning Sciences Institute. The lab engages in the kind of hands-on research and development that interests me. Fellows investigate how children learn and how they interact with various materials, and develop and test teaching/learning strategies. In our Skype chat, we talked about Dr. Wylie's particular research, which engages in developing strategies to expand computer-enhanced and computer-tracked learning.

By the time I spoke with Dr. Wylie, I had decided to focus on the process of learning to read, and how future education based on what we are discovering about how we learn might facilitate universal literacy.

Our present U.S. educational system is not science based; instead, it has become business based as the dehumanizing loop of frequent, expensive standardized testing, and targeted materials developed and sold to enable school systems to focus on testing success, have become government mandated. Though this method of teaching and evaluation might not be detrimental to students who are able to learn in this manner, many normal students might fall outside the effective parameters of this method of teaching. Additionally, all bodies are slightly different. Some of us have brains that process information in ways that do not meet the norm, such as children who fall under the broad definitions of dyslexia and dyscalculia, and who are therefore unnecessarily challenged and frustrated by our public schools.

Despite fits of reform enthusiasm, the teaching methods used in our public schools, even in this age of science, are not based on scientific information about how children learn. They are, instead, still based on models developed to homogenize large groups of multiethnic immigrants—to teach immigrant children to be good factory workers by learning English, obeying bell-regulated time signals, and receiving information in boring formats without questioning it rather than participating in shaping their own learning process.

My interest in neuroplasticity springs from my long experience as a Montessori teacher. When young children learn, they go through finely delineated periods of neuroplasticity, several of which, as an example, make learning to speak one's native language effortless and accent-free.

I began Association Montessori Internationale training, in 1975, as a skeptic. I planned to be a writer, but I realized, after finishing my degree in English, that I would not be able to support myself as a writer for some time. Having my own preschool seemed a good way to spend time with young children (not everyone's idea of fun, but it is for me), have my own business, and write in my "spare time." Spare time did not materialize, of course, because within a year of opening my school I had a hundred students, an elementary school, two locations, and many employees. But for fourteen years, I closely observed how well a science-based approach to learning works, and this fostered a great curiosity about neuroscience and the ways in which learning occurs. I learned a lot about early childhood development, observing firsthand how effortlessly most of the four-year-olds I taught could read, write, add, subtract, and multiply. In fact, I had to discourage parents from having their children labeled as gifted. They were, for the most part, normal children in a very good science-based learning environment, doing what normal children are able to do.

The underlying tenets of this approach to early childhood learning, developed in the early twentieth century, have been borne out by science. This is not surprising, for Maria Montessori was a scientist. The first woman to graduate from the University of Rome with a medical degree, in 1896, she became an instant worldwide celebrity when she spoke at the first International Congress for Women's Rights in Berlin that same year. During the next few years, she established herself as an advocate of children with learning difficulties. Being a scientist, she took nothing for granted and developed her educational philosophy and materials using the tool of dispassionate observation. The challenged children in the first learning environment she established, for the City of Rome, passed the city's tests in normal range, which made Dr. Montessori wonder why normal children were not learning at a higher level.

One reason I wanted to teach preschoolers instead of high schoolers, as I could easily have done with my English degree, was that, despite being in one of the best school systems in the country from the time I was in seventh grade, I found it stultifying. I knew there had to be a better way. And there is. In fact, there are many different ways. All of them depend on becoming literate, and the best and most effortless age to become literate is in early childhood, when children are naturally learning language, numeracy, and spatial skills; when children's growing motor skills can be engaged in learning through their exploration of an environment that holds finely targeted learning materials. However, early childhood education, or for that matter, public education in general, is not held in very high esteem in the United States. Perhaps that is the reason it consistently ranks average in international measurements of student mastery of science, math, and reading.

Finland, and various Asian countries and locales, including South Korea and Taiwan, consistently rank very high in tests administered annually by the Program for International Student Assessment. In 1963, Finland made a decision to make education its number one economic priority, and the highly effective educational system that emerged is the result. To find out more about it, I read *Finnish Lessons: What Can the World Learn from Educational Change in Finland* by Pasi Sahlberg (Teachers College Press, 2013). I also investigated educational methods used in the Asian schools that top the list and learned that Finnish and Asian methods differ greatly. However, they both work. It seems that wherever good education is a cultural priority, as it is in all the top-rated countries, teaching is a highly respected profession. I also read a number of books that offer alternatives to the way education is usually handled in the United States, such as *Who Owns the Learning? Preparing Students for Success in the Digital Age* by Alan November (Solution Tree Press, 2012) and *World Class Learners: Educating Creative and Entrepreneurial Students* by Yong Zhao (Corwin Press, 2012).

When I finally decided to focus on writing science fictionally about helping dyslexics learn to read, I found one of the best books I have ever come across about the neuroscience of reading, *Reading in the Brain: The New Science of How We Read* by Stanislas Dehaene (Penguin Group, 2009). I also read books about dyslexia, such as *Living "Lexi": A Walk in the Life of a Dyslexic* by Shelly Trammell, and other first-person accounts of dyslexia. I also read quite a lot of research about some of the causes of dyslexia.

The process I went through in researching the facets of this story, and of writing it, is similar to my process when writing any fiction. I thank ASU for putting me in touch with some of the top researchers in the field. I hope that the result is interesting enough to spur individual interest in the importance and possibility of literacy for everyone in the world.

RESPONSE TO "GIRL IN WAVE : WAVE IN GIRL"—Erin Walker

Erin Walker, a researcher in the field of personalized learning technology at Arizona State University, responds to "Girl in Wave : Wave in Girl" at hieroglyph.asu.edu/grokking.

FORUM DISCUSSION—Mad Scientist Island

Kathleen Ann Goonan, Bruce Sterling, and other Hieroglyph community members consider the prospect of a radically deregulated "Mad Scientist Island" at hieroglyph.asu.edu/grokking.

BY THE TIME WE GET TO ARIZONA
Madeline Ashby

THE BUZZ IN ULICEZ'S molars intensified as he drew nearer to the border. They'd said it would help him find his way; so long as he kept north it would keep humming along, a tiny siren song buried deep in his mouth to lead him ever onward. Really there was no need for the chip to vibrate, but the folks from Mariposa said it had to do *something* more than just tell the drones where you were all the time. It had to *add value*, they said. It had to be *user friendly*, so Ulicez and all the others wouldn't have sat in the dentist's chair for nothing.

They could have put the chip under the skin, but then Ulicez might have been tempted to pick it out and sell it. So now it sat there in one of his teeth. He didn't know which one. They'd put him under for the surgery, and there were a couple way in the back, on the right side, that really fucking hurt. But they both felt just like bone when he ran his tongue over them. And neither one ached any more than the other when he sipped from his canteen.

"Why are you walking?" his mother had asked. "They said they would send a truck for you. You know, a truck? With air-conditioning? Like they did for Elena?"

Elena was waiting for him in Mariposa. Apparently they processed women differently. Something about establishing baseline reactions. Hormones. That was the official explanation: they needed more than the three-month probationary period with women, because the pheromone detectors positioned all through town could be totally thrown by menstrual cycles. But maybe they just wanted to see what the reunion would be like. If it would be romantic enough. Real enough. That was what Elena suspected. So she'd stepped up into the truck. She was smiling at him when the locks clicked down behind her. The black trucks that rumbled down from Mariposa had no drivers. Their doors locked automatically. They could take you anywhere, and you couldn't do a thing about it. To him, getting inside one of those things sounded like a pretty stupid idea. And technically, they hadn't said he *couldn't* walk in.

He started just before dawn, when the sky was a bad bruise. He stopped in the living room, where his mother slept in the good chair. She was still half asleep when she stood up and kissed him good-bye.

"There's extra ammo in the blue tin," he said, before he left. "I left the latch open, so you can get it open quick."

She rubbed the swollen joints in her hands and smiled at him. "Things aren't like that, anymore," she said. "It's better, now."

He didn't know if she was talking about the war, or her arthritis. Either way, he waited until she'd turned all the locks in the door before starting down the hallway and out of the building.

It was not far to Mariposa; the desert was all solar farmland, now, and much smaller than it used to be. That was what the border looked like, now: a river of black photovoltaic cells open like flowers to the sun. Corporate surveillance flutterbys zoomed over and around them, automatically alerting the Border Patrol when they spotted a human darting northward whose gait, temperature, expression, and other secret factors did not fit the proprietary algorithmic definition of "employee." Where the river stopped, Mariposa and the other border towns began. Mariposa was the latest.

Mariposa sat in the space once occupied solely by tarantulas and the rocks they hid under. It sat half on one side, half on the other. They'd dropped it just west of the Nogales-Hermosillo highway like a flat-pack explosive device. It was still in the process of unfolding itself, Tab A into Slot B, still growing into a "planned prototyping community" or "cultural moat" or "probationary testing ground" or whatever it was meant to be. Ulicez had looked up pictures of it and it still looked raw and new, more like a movie set than an actual town. Given that everyone going there was auditioning for something, he supposed that made sense.

On the way out of Nogales, El Tejón joined him. Ulicez had no idea what the old man's real name was. He'd been called Tejón forever, likely because the whiskers on his chin were streaked with white like a badger's. But now he melted out of the alley like a tomcat and kept pace with Ulicez without any appearance of effort or exertion. It was as though he'd been waiting for Ulicez to pass by, even though Ulicez had told only his mother that he planned to walk. Then again, it was somehow fitting that the old man be the one to take Ulicez across. They had crossed the same distance together so many times before, although by another route.

"Mariposa?" the old man asked.

Ulicez nodded.

"Teeth hurt?"

He nodded again.

Tejón sucked his teeth and spat. Such was the extent of his commentary on that particular subject. As they headed for the highway, the ads began to diminish, the surfaces rendered inert by their shared demographics and direction. The last bus stop woke up as they shuffled by. It noticed the logo on Ulicez's backpack and gave him the old bit about working at Walmart, where it surely must have come from. It told him how you could train at the nearest location and go anywhere with that training, because the system was the same everywhere, world without end, amen. *Siempre más trabajo. Siempre.*

"Jesus," Tejón said. "That ad hasn't changed in, what, ten years?"

"It was around when I was little." Ulicez whistled the jingle and the old man laughed. They each waved good-bye to the ad (it was bad luck to be rude to the ads) and kept walking. At the highway interchange, Ulicez went ahead to help Tejón over the guardrail, but the old man threw his leg over without any trouble. They stood together on the rise by the crossroads, the old city at their backs and the new one burning white like a star in a field of glittering black. Above them, the real stars were winking out. Beyond the mountains, the night sky crinkled away from the horizon like burning paper.

"Have you been back here, since?"

"For school. Once. Field trip."

Tejón laughed. It came out all at once in a sharp bark. "Field trip. *Puta madre.*" He shook his head and spat again. "Did they tell you how many people used to die here, on your field trip?"

Ulicez said nothing. Of course they hadn't mentioned it. They were there to look at the solar farms, after all, not to relive ancient history. The corporate outreach lady stood in front of his class with her transparent tablet shimmering in her hand and never breathed a word about the war. The guns. The heads.

"They don't know, do they? About before?"

Ulicez shook his head.

"Well, they'll never hear it from me," Tejón said.

TEJÓN SAID NOTHING AS Ulicez approached Mariposa. There was a clear demarcation between the farms and the town; the farms grew in gleaming black rows behind neatly cut curbs, and beyond the curbs were *maquilas,* and beyond the *maquilas* stood Mariposa, the city of transformation. The hum in Ulicez's teeth stopped and he turned to mention it to Tejón, but the old man was already gone.

Then the *maquilas* began to trill the end of the night shift. Squinting, he thought he saw Tejón drifting into the crowds of exhausted factory workers hustling toward the buses that would take them home. Or maybe it was just another old man with salt in his beard. For a split second, Ulicez wished he could access the logs from all the drones they had passed under during their walk. It would help him confirm that Tejón had really been there. It was like that in the night, way back when. One minute the old man would be at his side, or his father's, hefting a shovel or pickaxe or flashlight, and the next he would be gone, having disappeared down a bend in the tunnel like the badger he was.

Now Ulicez faced the white stucco wall and the tiled arch that bridged its welcoming gap alone. He peered up at the lantern they'd hung from its center. It flickered, golden, with artificial candlelight. Slender palms, bereft of any dust, grazed the edge of the wall. He stepped through the arch.

Nothing happened.

He looked to his left, then to his right. No guards. No helpful theme park types, no strategically placed neighbors circling him like sharks. This early, no one was out. He saw another brown guy delivering mail. The mailman lifted his eyebrows at him, gave him a silent nod, but said nothing. And maybe that was that. The mailman's eyes had clocked him. Maybe that was enough.

He pushed forward into town, past the rows of bone-white stucco homes with pretty new red roofs. Why did everybody do that Spanish Revival thing out this way, Ulicez wondered, when it just made the houses look like shopping malls? Here everything was raw: the pavement black and even and soft as the soles of new shoes, the skinny little lemon trees leaning perilously over fresh sod lawns, the botflies so clean and quiet he didn't notice them until they flitted away. Here they didn't drain your blood, or chew your tissue; botflies harvested only data.

Mariposa extended fifteen miles from the border on either side, subdivided into a compass rose of quadrants with their own set of homes, businesses, schools, and service centers. In the center was a brick-paved plaza. And in the center of that stood a labyrinth of cacti and other succulents. They grew exactly where the old border crossing station used to be. He knew the spot all too well. Blindfolded, he could have pinpointed it on a map. They must have planted the maze on sod; obviously, they had not dug very deeply. Ulicez had seen aerial views of it: a twisted, thorny spiral buried deep in the new city's heart. Try as he might, he could never plot the way out. The thorns meshed together too tightly.

Now he stood before it, fingers curled tightly around the scorching wrought iron that made up its fence, and peered inside. He lifted one hand and poked his index finger between the thorns. Beside him, one of the dusty pink prickly pear flowers in the garden unfurled. "Are you lost?" it asked.

"Not really," Ulicez said. "Actually, I'm going home to my wife."

"You should take one of my flowers, then," the cactus said. Ulicez could not spot the speaker doubtless hidden somewhere in its folds, but that didn't matter. "It'll score you some points at home."

It wasn't until he was walking away that Ulicez realized the cactus had made a joke.

THE HOUSE LOOKED LIKE all the others on its street: eggshell white with an unscuffed wood door in muted turquoise and a dusty red tile roof, with a stubby little palm tree out front and some pink gravel in the yard. It was like that book about the kids who go to different worlds, and on the final one all the kids come out and bounce their balls in unison. Ulicez couldn't remember the title, or even what the story was about. All he remembered was that image: all the kids outside, bouncing their balls in rhythm with one another, like the whole street was really just made up of two mirrors reflecting one very lonely child. It had given him nightmares. Now he lived there.

Elena opened the door before he could even knock on it.

He'd been hers since he saw her step off a bus and into the driveway of his school, holding a melting bottle of frozen water to her bare neck. The sight of her rooted him to the spot, as though he'd accidentally shocked himself on the old metal plate surrounding the streetlight across from his building. She had looked up and smiled, and for the first time in his life, he had not looked away. He had looked right back. She walked over to him, held out the bottle of water, and asked him if he was thirsty. And that was that.

Now she stepped through the door, wrapped her arms around his neck, and gave him a kiss worthy of a telenovela. Lots of sucking, lots of licking. She cheated a little to her right as she did, and he couldn't figure out why she was turning him in that direction until she kissed his right ear and whispered: "There's a camera in the planter just over there."

She pulled away and gave him a big smile. "You walked?"

He plastered on his own smile. "Why does everybody keep asking me that?" He looked her up and down and squeezed her wrists. "You look great."

In truth, Elena looked WASP-ish in her little white sundress and her tiny gold sandals and her baby-pink fingernail polish. She'd washed her hair and ironed it flat. If she'd been wearing black, he'd have thought her on her way to a funeral. Instead, he noticed the way she'd done her makeup. It was streaky with inexperience: the stuff under her eyes was paler than it had any business being, somehow highlighting the shadows there instead of hiding them. She didn't meet his gaze.

"Is there something wrong?" he asked.

Her smile's wattage increased substantially. Her voice climbed an octave. "No, nothing. Come inside."

He followed her. The house was pure MUJI: bland, brand-free, everything all eggshell and fake white pine, all the way down to the pearly tile floor in the foyer and the not-quite-Mason-jar pendant lamp above it. It seemed bigger inside, airy. The kind of house white people had on network television.

"Let's have a shower," Elena said.

Maybe constant surveillance and performing a good marriage would have fringe benefits beyond citizenship. "Twist my arm."

The mirror smiled at them as they entered the bathroom. "CUSTOM-IZE PROFILE DATA?" it asked, when Ulicez stood in front of it. He said no, thank you, and started stripping. It blanked once his nipples were reflected in its surface.

"They shy away from nudity," Elena said. "Automatic. Antilitigation factory default."

Not for the first time, Ulicez realized that Elena was the brains of their particular operation. He touched her elbow and turned her around and kissed her for real, this time, just something simple and closed mouthed with a long hug at the end, like normal people who hadn't seen each other in a long time. A sigh shuddered out of her. Something really was wrong.

"You missed me that bad, huh?" he asked.

Something coughed up out of her: a laugh, a sob, he couldn't tell. She hugged him tighter. "Yeah."

She pulled away and they stripped off the rest of their clothes. Even the shower mechanism was absurdly minimalist: you had to wave your hand to start it, and then do some complicated gesture-fu to make it warmer or colder. They'd obviously been going for *Minority Report* and wound up with *Close Encounters* instead. Finally the water reached a reasonable temperature and Elena stepped in. They'd got their hair wet when her eyes finally met his.

"I'm late."

It was as though the water temperature had dipped suddenly and steeply. Out of habit, he remained perfectly still. They used to do that, in the tunnel, when they heard someone walking above. Now he did it every time he felt the slightest shift in adrenaline.

"Aren't you going to say something?"

His voice had disappeared along with his motion. He worked his mouth a little to get it back. "You sure?"

"My app is."

"But you have an IUD."

"I know." She swallowed. "I checked. The strings are still in. But the test still came back positive. It's in a drawer over there, if you want to see."

"I'm not going to go look at your old pee stick. Gross." He frowned. "What, did you think I wouldn't believe you?"

She looked away. That was that. Two weeks in this little Uncle Sam theme park town, and they were already distrusting each other. He leaned back against one wall of the shower. So far Elena didn't look any different. Her mascara was running, and when she paused to wipe the water from her face it smeared away from her eyes, making her seem instantly younger.

"I'm sorry," she said. "I didn't . . . I wasn't . . . I know we can't stay, if we keep it . . ."

"That's just a rumor. We don't know that for sure."

She gave him the look that meant he was being stupidly hopeful and hopelessly naive. "Remember what happened to Maria and Guillermo?"

Christ. She was right. Guillermo should have been a perfect candidate. He was supposed to be teaching magical realism to bored freshmen by now, putting his double Ph.D.s to use. His wife had a degree in early childhood education. They had a good relationship: the kind where everybody picked up their socks and the coffee was always fresh and the dishes got stacked at night. Exemplary. And they were doing well in Mariposa, or so they'd said: the kids at the daycare loved Maria, and Guillermo stayed out with his students, but not too late.

Then they'd gotten pregnant and come back to Nogales.

"Anchor babies," Elena spat. "Fucking anchor babies. That's what they're worried about."

"That's not it. It's just the cost—"

"It's the same fucking thing, Ulicez. The exact same fucking thing."

He checked the dial. Their time was running out in more ways than one. "Come on. The water's about to get cold."

He helped her out and reached blindly. "Where do we keep the towels?"

"Oh. Sorry. Shit. I was going to set some out, and then . . ." Her breath hitched. She was still digging in the closet. She leaned inside it with her back to him. "Oh, shit, Ulicez. I'm sorry. I'm really sorry. I thought we'd be okay. I mean, it's .6 percent. Six-tenths. *Six* fucking *tenths.*"

Despite himself, he smiled. He reached past her, into the closet, and grabbed a towel. He hung it across her shoulders. "Well, at least we've got one thing going for us."

"What's that?"

"You're getting better at swearing in English."

THE NEXT DAY WAS orientation. Ulicez had to set up a separate appointment, because he'd come in earlier than the others on the bus, and he'd missed a last-minute time change that only the guys on the bus heard. That suited him just fine. He had enough to worry about and didn't want to have to sit through a lecture on folding chairs with his fellow competitors.

The guy at the Newcomer Processing Center said his name was Paul. He seemed like a grad student: sandals, tawny curls in a ponytail, finally developing a real tan, occasionally pausing to check that the tattoo inside his left wrist was just as edgy as he remembered. The NPC was a big, airy building with exposed pipes and finished white oak beams against deeply saturated pastels: creamy mint, shrimpy pink. Ulicez guessed he was supposed to feel like he was in an artist's converted loft space, and not an immigration office. Paul called up some forms and toggled them over to a glass panel on his desk. Together, the two of them looked at Ulicez's file. It was all there: his height and weight and color stats, his birthdate, every address, every job. Every job they knew about, anyway. He had never been paid for the other work. That was really his dad's job, anyway. Sometimes his dad needed help. That was all.

"Are my eyes really brown?" he asked. Paul cocked his head, as though he hadn't quite heard him right. He didn't get the joke. So much for shibboleths. "Is everything in order?" Ulicez asked.

Paul nodded. "Yeah, everything looks good. This is your new job." He tapped one form, and the position appeared: *junior laser technologist.* His new responsibilities unfolded into a point-form list. He'd be working for a carbon capture company called GreenLock, using small autonomous lasers to inspect the integrity of the intake pipes, and maybe doing some repairs if the rods or mirrors inside them misaligned. He'd also have to make sure their power sources were all up to par, and that he knew the exact position of each and every one of them at all times, so none of them went around blinding the neighbor's cat by mistake. There was his signature at the bottom of the list.

"Wow," Paul said. "That all sounds really technical."

No shit, Ulicez thought. He opened up some footage of his work in the repair simulator, adjusting a YLF rod. "It's easy, after a while. You just have to have good hands."

Paul smiled. "You must be a real hit with the ladies."

Ulicez wiggled his fingers. "If my wife's testimony counted for anything, I'd already be a citizen by now."

Paul's face took on a concerned aspect. "How is your wife, by the way?"

Ulicez went perfectly still. "Excuse me?"

"Well, the house is saying that she hasn't been feeling too well. The, uh . . ." Paul winced. "The *toilet* has been logging some extra activity . . ."

Morning sickness. Of course. Given how tightly they watched the water out here, the water meter would have probably noticed the difference in their usage from the other users on the line, and the toilet would have accounted for it.

"She gets nervous diarrhea," Ulicez lied. He watched Paul turn a gringo shade of green. When lying, it was best to go for something that made the person hearing it not want to hear anything more. Something embarrassing. His father had taught him that much. "I think, you know, with this whole thing, this whole setup, she's just on edge."

"Right . . ."

"She'll be fine now that I'm here."

"Great." Paul tried to adjust his posture. Something tugged at the edge of Ulicez's awareness. Something he had missed. But now Paul was talking again. "You know how this works, right?" .

"Yeah. It works like Murder, right? Like the game?"

Paul sighed heavily before starting what was obviously a memorized routine. "Your likelihood of obtaining a visa increases or decreases based on your social capital at the end of your six-week trial period. That capital is determined by the people who live in Mariposa. Every day, a new set of

Mariposans is granted a certain number of upvotes and downvotes. If they tell anybody they're a voter, they lose their votes. Even if they're lying. The people who *do* play by the rules get more upvotes than downvotes to play with, but they can always choose to abstain, and not vote at all. If they do, the algorithm sorts them right back to the bottom of the deck."

"So people who vote frequently, they're sorted to the top?"

Paul smiled. "Yeah. It's an incentive."

Ulicez nodded. It was always possible that the closet racists voted constantly, of course. But he chose not to bring that up. Instead, he asked: "When does the voting happen?"

"At the end of the day. Around eight."

"So after the voters have probably talked to their spouses?"

Paul squirmed in his chair. "Yeah. We started doing it at five thirty, and then at noon, but fewer people voted when they were on their way home, or at lunch, or something. We're going to try it in the morning next." He smiled sheepishly. "After they've had their coffee, of course."

It wasn't like Ulicez didn't know all these things going in. It was on the waiver he signed when he began the application process. Everybody back home said it would work out for him—that he was a good boy, a nice boy; that years of being a nerdy kid who found Lego cooler than guns would finally count for something in a place like Mariposa. Still, it was different hearing somebody lay it out like this. Back home, with Elena asleep on his shoulder or his mother's stories on the display, it hadn't seemed entirely real. But here he was, his nervous sweat wicked away by aggressively conditioned air.

"How do the voters know they've been chosen? Do they just get a ping?"

"No. We tell them in person, the day before." His eyes widened. "I mean, not *we*, not *me*, but someone on the, you know, team." He didn't say *task force*. He didn't say *agency*. He didn't say *officer*. But the words hung there all the same.

"Okay." Ulicez looked at the documents on the desk. "I guess I should get going to my next stop, huh?"

Paul checked the time display. "Oh, yeah, jeez. Sorry." He offered his hand and Ulicez shook it.

"Can you tell me where your restroom is?" Ulicez asked. "Best not to be fidgeting on my first day on the job."

Paul tittered. Until this moment, Ulicez had not known that men could even make that particular sound. "Last door on the left," Paul said.

It wasn't until he was zipping up that Ulicez understood what he'd missed. The toilet had only logged usage, not content. It was not detecting the change in her hormones. The only hormone detectors in the town were ambient, meant to find explosions of cortisol that might indicate dishonesty.

They didn't know she was pregnant. And they wouldn't know for a good while, at least. They had time.

"WE DON'T HAVE ANY time. Arizona cuts off at twelve weeks."

"Seriously?" In Mexico, the procedure was allowed until twenty. They'd have a full five months, two months longer than the probationary period in Mariposa. Ulicez chewed halfheartedly at the remainder of his *elotes*. The lime here tasted all wrong. Too acidic. Not sweet. And the cheese was too salty. He had no room to complain, though. Elena couldn't even keep hers down.

"Do you have any idea how far along you are?"

"For the millionth time, *no*." She sighed. "I'm sorry. But it doesn't matter, now, does it? We're stuck. If I go to a doctor, they'll know, and we'll get kicked out. If I don't go to a doctor, we'll be accused of lying when they figure it out, and *then* we'll get kicked out." She smoothed her hair back. "Fuck. I'll have to keep buying tampons just to grief the data."

"We don't know if it goes that far—"

"Of *course* it goes that far, Ulicez. Of *course* it does. You think they'd let a whole data-mining infrastructure that's worked well enough for decades just sit there, going to waste? Why do you think they issued us special discount cards at Target? Because *Target is the best at this game.* Target probably already knows I'm knocked up."

Her voice caught. By the time Ulicez stood up to rub her shoulders, she had swiped the tears away with the heel of her hand.

"I hate these fucking hormones," she said.

"I know." He kept squeezing. "You should try to eat something. Even if it's just ice cream."

She sniffed. "That might be nice."

"I'll go get some." He paused at the freezer. "Should I even bother with a bowl?"

"Shut up."

Ulicez kept scooping. He wished they had condensed milk to go on top. If they had, he could simmer the can in a pot of water and caramelize its contents.

Elena would probably like that. His own mother had mentioned enjoying it when she was carrying him. Jesus, what were they going to tell his mother?

"If they would just stock some damn misoprostol in this godforsaken country, I could take care of this whole thing by myself."

There was no condensed milk. Ulicez picked up the bowl of ice cream and set it down in front of his wife. Even the dishware was bland here. He'd seen more interesting designs at his last trip to Denny's. "Misoprostol?"

"Cytotec. It's for ulcers. And abortions. Well. Misoprostol and some other thing. That's what RU-486 is."

"And they don't sell it here?"

"Nope. Not without a prescription." She laughed. "But they do in Mexico! My sister even asked me if I wanted to take some with me. You know. Just in case. Shit."

"Eat your ice cream."

She dug in. "Thank you."

Ulicez took a pull of his beer. He watched the smaller kitchen screen embedded in the refrigerator. Madrigal wasn't going to get anywhere in this game if he kept flailing around the pitch like that with his elbows sticking out and his knees going nowhere. The man ran like a child. It was only because he was big that they'd let him into the league; he was a bruiser and he had a chilling effect on a passing game. He was a solid wall of muscle and bone that just plunked itself down on the pitch, looming down over the triangle formations of smaller, nimbler players.

A wall.

Of course.

"To save us some time," he said, "let me ask you one question."

Her spoon clinked in the bowl. "Sure."

"Would you be comfortable buying it online? This miso thing."

"It would have to go through customs." She snorted. "Whatever that means, out here."

"Right then." He nodded to himself, then to her. "There's a way around this. Or a way through it, anyway. But it'll involve me getting some things from work."

FIRST, THEY WERE GOING to need a spider bot.

Well, that wasn't quite true. First, they were going to need a way into the labyrinth. And a couple of shovels. And then they were going to need a spider bot. And then, after that . . .

After that they would need the Badger himself.

"Are you sure he'll even remember the code?" Elena asked him, in the shower.

"He's the one who taught it to me, so he had fucking better," Ulicez said. "Where did you say that postcard was?"

On the postcard, he expressed a longing for his mother's plum jam, the likes of which he had not found in the land of the free and the home of the brave. He then mentioned an event that took place in April 1986: Chernobyl. It was surprisingly easy to tie plum jam and nuclear disaster together—all he had to do was make a joke about his mother's inability to properly latch a pressure cooker, and done was done.

"When should we say we'd like to see him again?" Ulicez asked, carefully.

"As soon as possible," Elena said. "Tell him we wish we could spend the weekend with him. You know. Like we used to."

At the mailbox, she turned to him and whispered: "Plum jam? *That's* the secret code word?"

He nodded. "Sure is."

"*Plum jam* means *abortion pills*. You're sure."

"I'm sure."

"Why?"

"Well, because I remember, and because—"

"No, no. Why plum jam?"

He winced. "If this all works out the way we want, the meaning should become pretty clear."

The next day he asked to take a look at the autonomous pipeline inspectors, "just to be sure he was familiar with them."

His boss thought that was a great idea. His boss was a Ph.D. who insisted on being called by his first name, Terry. Terry was a short, skinny man whose blond hair was turning white and whose salmon-colored polo shirts tended to highlight the rosacea around his nose. But he seemed genuinely happy to be in Mariposa: he kept a golf bag in his office, and he insisted that there would be a team-building event out on the links some Friday or other.

Each spider bot was kept in an opaque plastic terrarium about the size of a shoebox. The boxes rustled as he strode past. Pressure sensors in their claws must have sensed his movement. He willed himself to ignore the inherent creepiness of their blind skittering. He needed one of them. *They needed one.*

Way at the end of the steel racks was a box of various bots in states of disrepair. The sticker said they were older models; the parts didn't exist to fix them any longer. "They're spares," his boss said, when he carried the box out of the room with him. "We just use them for the parts that still work, when the printer gets buggy."

"Could I make one on my own, at home?" Ulicez asked. "I wouldn't be using company time. I just want to get to know them better if I'm going to be fixing them, and it's probably better if I just tinker alone on my own—"

"—in a low-stakes environment. I hear you." Terry beamed. "No problem. Just run them through the scanner and sign out for the manifest it spits out."

"Thank you. I really appreciate it."

"And I, for one, appreciate you taking the initiative! We need more of that kind of thinking around here."

And then Terry winked at him.

Ulicez had the strangest feeling that he had just scored some points. Maybe the game wasn't so random after all.

"**WHEN DID YOU START** working on this?"

Ulicez shone his flashlight down the tunnel. It was still as he remembered it: a surprisingly cool, clean space seven feet high and five feet across. Cheap, unfinished Home Depot wainscoting secured the earthen walls. Orange and black extension cords extended all the way down the ceiling; back in the day they'd had it hooked to generators in basements on the other side of the border and lit the thing with utility lamps purchased one hopeful Saturday on clearance at the last auto shop in town. Now both those buildings that supplied electricity were gone, and Ulicez and Elena had to make do with the flashlights.

"I was a kid," he answered. "The work had already started before I was born, I think. I mean, they built a lot of these tunnels back then. This is just one they never found."

"Did you ever move anybody?"

Ulicez shook his head. "My dad didn't like me to do any of the real work. He just needed help with the engineering. You know, telling guys where and how to dig, how to shore it up, stuff like that."

"It looks pretty solid."

"It is. But you can't be too careful." Ulicez put down his backpack and withdrew a shoebox from it. Carefully upending it on the ground, he waited until the spider bot had crawled out. Lights on each of its eight legs twinkled to life, and he watched as it skittered on ahead of them, forming tight spirals from the floor to the right wall to the ceiling, down the left wall and back again, over and over.

"I hate those things," Elena said. "They're creepy."

"They save lives. They work in pipelines all over the world."

"And they do tunnels, too?"

Ulicez smiled. "Yes. They do tunnels, too."

They followed the spider along the tunnel, pausing when it paused, waiting as it fired light from its joints at various sections of wall. Occasionally its green glow would shift into yellow, but it never turned red. That was good; Ulicez hadn't supervised the entire tunnel build, but he had confidence in the guys who did the job. The cartel had paid them good money, after all. And there were certain consequences for not doing the job right.

"I wish I could have spent more time with him," Elena said. "Your father, I mean."

"Me too." Ulicez watched the spider appear to work something out before scrabbling on ahead. "He liked you. He liked us, together."

"Really?"

He nodded. "Mom said so, anyway. After."

Elena took his hand. "I'm sorry. For everything."

Ulicez pulled up short. He let his flashlight dangle from his hand. It was easier to say the words in the shadows. "Stop. It's like you said. Point six percent. You couldn't see that coming. Nobody could. I sure as hell didn't."

"But—"

"Stop. Really. It's done. We're taking care of it. Together." He pointed down the tunnel with his flashlight. "El Tejón is down there, waiting. It's all going to be fine." He tilted his head. "Isn't it?"

"There's going to be a lot of blood. It'll hurt."

"But I'll be there. And we can go to a doctor. We can say it's a miscarriage."

Elena looked like she wanted to say something more, but instead she just launched herself at him and wrapped both her arms around him like she expected him to blow away somehow. He set his chin on her head after a minute.

"Are you having second thoughts?" he asked.

She nodded.

"We have to get the drugs, Elena. Having some choice is better than having no choice at all. That's why we're here. Or there. In Mariposa, I mean. That's why we came."

She sniffed. "I know." She hugged him even harder, which he hadn't known was possible. The woman was a lot stronger than she looked. "It's just that you're being so nice. And so brave. And I'd like a little more of that in the world, you know?"

She pulled away and wiped her eyes. She smiled. "Fucking hormones. Sorry."

He reached out and held her hand. "Let's just get the stuff. If you decide this isn't what you want, then—"

"No, it *is* what I want, I just—"

"Let's just keep it a decision, okay? You can't say it's a real decision if there aren't any other options."

She appeared to gather herself. "Okay."

They were still holding hands when El Tejón appeared at the end of the tunnel. He was in some sort of gentleman adventurer costume, down to the pith helmet and elegant riding boots.

"Why are you dressed as the Most Interesting Man in the World?" Ulicez asked.

"It was the only way they'd let me inspect the rapid transit system," the old man said. He waved a fake badge at them. "Had to get underground somehow."

Ulicez whistled. "Wow."

Tejón brought Elena in for a hug and a kiss. Then he brought out a couple of boxes. "The directions are on the tape," he said. "And this one is some Valium. For the pain."

She beamed. "You think of everything!"

"Make sure to drink lots of water first. Maybe take this with a little food."

"I will."

"And you'll have to go to the hospital. Are you ready for that?"

Elena's lips pursed. "Yes," she said after a long moment. "I think so."

Tejón sighed heavily. "The sooner you use these, the better. The longer you wait, the less they work. Okay?"

"Okay."

"Okay." Tejón looked at Ulicez. "You take care of this one. She's going to need you."

"I know." Something occurred to him. "Have you spoken to my mother?"

Tejón shook his head. "There's no reason for her to know, I don't think."

"Agreed."

Tejón tried to smile. "I wish things could be different for you two. But they *will* be different, soon enough. Very different. You'll be Americans!"

"We're already Americans," Elena said. "This whole continent is America."

Tejón's laugh echoed down the tunnel. He gave them each hugs and kisses. Then he shooed them on their way. When Ulicez turned around, the old man was gone. He really was a badger.

"Should it be glowing red like that?" Elena tugged on his sleeve. "The spider? Isn't red bad?"

Ulicez aimed his flashlight down the tunnel. A cloud of dust was wafting their way. "Yes," he said. "Red is bad. Very bad." He pointed the flashlight at the ceiling. A fine crack had worked its way along under the cable. He thought he heard trucks. He watched root hairs trembling in the light. Then he was digging in his backpack.

"What's happening?"

"There's been a cave-in up ahead," he said. "We have to dig. Come on."

"But we're not on the other side yet! Are we?"

Ulicez checked the map. Shit. "No. We're not. We're . . . we're in the solar farm. We're on the American side, still." He withdrew one shovel, then another. He held it out to Elena.

She refused to take it. "Ulicez. Think. They're going to find two Mexicans digging their way out of a tunnel. They'll see it. The solar people. *They'll see us trying to get back into America.*"

Ulicez looked back at the cloud of dirt. *Fuck.* As if on cue, the spider bounded back to him. It was covered in grit. One of its leg joints had a pebble stuck in it. Its antennae were broken. Whatever had happened up ahead, it was still happening.

"Elena," he said. "We have to dig our way out. Now. Before we're buried alive."

"And saying we make it out, what do we tell the people up there?" She pointed at the ceiling.

Ulicez started digging. "I'll think of something."

"I have a feeling I won't like it."

"Oh, I'm almost certain that you won't."

"GET NAKED. NOW."

"What?"

"I have an idea."

Elena gave him a look that said this had better be good. But she kicked off her shoes and started stripping anyway. White and green light strobed across her increasing expanse of skin. Ulicez unbuckled his pants and shucked them down.

Then he tackled his wife.

"What the fuck? You asshole, my bra isn't even—"

"STOP! SHOW US YOUR HANDS!"

Ulicez grinned. He knelt down on the ground and held up his hands. Beneath him, Elena shot him a look that was pure death. Grudgingly, she got up on her knees and held her hands up. Behind them, keys jingled and flashlights bobbed. Ulicez had one moment to take a look around at the massive black lotuses open to the night around them, and how the stars were reflected in their gleaming surfaces, before his hands were forced down and back and enclosed in bread-tie cuffs. A very distant point was surprised and pleased at how well he was taking it. This was everything he'd ever feared, everything he'd worked his whole life to avoid: getting caught on the wrong side of the border, getting arrested. Flashlights and weapons and the desert cruel and quiet all around them.

"What the . . ." The voice was panting, winded. Whoever they were, they'd run.

"Ma'am, are you doing okay?" another voice asked. A woman. Stern.

"What?" Elena almost brought her hands down, then appeared to think better of it. "I mean, yes. No. I'm okay."

"Was this man attacking you?"

Of course. He almost laughed. Then something wiser in him reminded him that he was in front of people holding Tasers, and he reined himself in. The border botflies had motion-activated computer vision programmed to recognize all sorts of motion: running, walking, jumping. It made sense that fucking would be on the list. It was pretty distinctive, after all. And to the cameras, what Ulicez had done probably looked a lot like an attempted rape.

"What? No! This man is my husband."

"Marital rape is a serious problem, ma'am, you don't need to be afraid of telling—"

"*He wasn't trying to rape me, you fucking idiots!*" Elena brought her hands down and turned around. "He was trying to *fuck* me. We live over there." She pointed vaguely north, at the bright lights of Mariposa. "We . . ." She was panting, now. The adrenaline was clearly washing out of her, leaving her at a loss for words. "We were just . . ."

"We just wanted to get away from the cameras," Ulicez said. His voice sounded remarkably steady in his ears. "From the observation. We're on probation, in Mariposa, and there's this points system, and it's basically to see if you love your wife enough, and . . ." He licked his lips. "It kinda . . . puts a damper on things? You know?"

"So we thought we'd go outside," Elena said.

"Don't y'all have, like, a *yard* or something?" This was a kid. A rookie.

"There are cameras in the yard!" Elena was gesticulating, now, playing into the whole fiery-Latina-woman bullshit. "Seriously, they watch us all the time."

"Is that even legal?" the woman asked. "Arizona has a Peeping Tom law, I know 'cause my ex—"

"Shut up about your ex, already." There was warmth at Ulicez's back. "If I let you go, son, are you gonna run?"

"No, sir. I just want to go home."

"All right, then. Shut your barn door and turn around."

Ulicez did up his fly and stood up, slowly. They were rent-a-cops. Not border security, not BORSTAR, not a militia, just corporate night-shifters with orange cheese-worm dust on their shirts and dark rings under their eyes. Above them, botflies glowed green and hovered, perfectly still. Ulicez resisted the temptation to address them directly.

"We're sorry," he said.

"Really sorry," Elena added.

"Yeah. We just . . ." He heaved a very heavy sigh. "That place will drive you crazy, you know? Just knowing how much rides on it, on how you look and how you act and everything, and . . ."

"We haven't had sex in weeks," Elena said. "Really."

"You married?" the man asked.

"Yes," they answered in unison.

As one, all three rent-a-cops laughed. "Well shit, son, welcome to the new normal," the man said. "Get your lady her sweater. Y'all want a ride back to town? We'll help you straighten everything out."

Ulicez almost choked, but Elena stepped forward. "That would be so great. Thank you." She jerked her head at him. "Did I mention this was *his* idea?"

The woman rolled her eyes. She flipped her long gray braid to the other side of her head and helped Elena put her shirt back on. "My ex, he was like that," she said. "One time he wanted to go under the bleachers at the high school. Naturally, after that, I found out he was running around with some freshman at the community college, and I had to end it."

"Obviously," Elena said.

"Would you shut up about that asshole?" the man said. "Honestly, Joanne, it's bad enough when you talk our ears off about it—"

"And it just means you're really not over it, yet," the kid said. He jingled some keys. "Can I drive?"

"No, you cannot drive, I keep telling you, not at night. You let me drive, and you let me do the talking when we get up to . . ." He held up a key fob and in the distance, a massive truck started. "What's it called, again?"

"Mariposa," Ulicez said. "We live in Mariposa."

STORY NOTES—Madeline Ashby

International borders are a work of fiction. They are a consensual hallucination that we all engage in to perpetuate the status quo. In that regard, they are much like currency in that they have value, but the value itself is a fragile social construct vulnerable to the whims of history,

Trust me. I'm an immigrant.

In January 2006, I was denied entry to Canada. I entered the next month, after spending an hour pleading my case with border security. Finally, I immigrated to Canada. Two years later, a friend of mine was arrested at the U.S. border, and then convicted of assaulting a federal officer when he was the one who took the beating. I decided to write a design thesis on the future of border security, and what I imagined was nightmarish: a world of invisible, invasive surveillance, the kind the NSA dreams about.[1] This story is an effort to imagine another future.

I kept some of the surveillance, but not all of it. Instead, I focused on the border space as a kind of third space, wherein social norms and other mores can be temporarily left behind like so much cultural baggage. I was drawn to stories like the 1967 TV series *The Prisoner,* where a man wakes up in a village full of people whose names have become numbers. And I was thinking of novels like China Miéville's *The City & the City,* where the border isn't so much a line as it is a ritual. I was also forced to reconsider some of the materials I had read during my stint in the Border Town Design Studio, which exhibited at the Detroit Design Festival in 2011. Among these was a paper by Adham Selim called "Emergent Border Cities,"[2] which suggested a design intervention in the border space that would act like a cultural moat as well as a border town. The community would enforce the border. The border would become the community. I was fascinated by the idea and ran with it after talking with Darren Petrucci at Arizona State University about things like corporate sponsorship and branded communities. It was then that I lit on the idea of terraforming the desert around Nogales as solar farmland. To me, corporate security acting in the interests of protecting a technology investment would do a better job than a bunch of police academy washouts whose hiring requirements don't even include a college degree.

To understand the need to blacken the desert with photovoltaic cells, you have to understand the punitive nature of the Sonora Desert. Thanks to Operation Gatekeeper[3] the majority of illegal immigrants have to hike or ride through it to avoid border checkpoints. To borrow a phrase from David Lean, the Sonora is God's anvil. In the summer, average temperatures hit 120°F. Every day, No More Deaths picks up the migrants that U.S.

Customs and Border Protection dumps back in Mexico and gives them water and food, bandages their blistered feet, and treats their tarantula bites. But in reality, people die in the borderland all the time. Between 1998 and 2009, they numbered over four thousand.[4] Most of those men, women, and children died of exposure. I realized the solar energy that was killing them could be fueling both countries instead.

At the same time, news was coming out of the American Southwest that looked like it belonged in the pages of a Margaret Atwood novel. Texas women were crossing the border to obtain Cytotec, because new laws were (and still are) eliminating abortion clinics and making preprocedural sonograms mandatory.[5] It was a bad year for Texas women. It was a bad year for women, period. What was life like for the immigrant women of Texas? I wondered. What would it be like to sacrifice so much for a dream of freedom, only to have that freedom taken away? It was in that spirit that I named this story after the Public Enemy song "By the Time I Get to Arizona," written about Governor Evan Mecham's racist policies[6] in that state. Arizona's current stop-and-frisk policies, and its measurement of the "border" as "anywhere 200 miles north of the fence,"[7] haven't evolved much since 1991.

You might think my research and personal experience would have made the story easier to write. It didn't. I struggled with it at each step. Writing it uncovered a well of bad memories inside me, and every time I stared at the blank white page I felt I was really looking down a deep dark hole. The same history that compelled me to write about the border also frustrated my attempts to pin it down with words. When I was in the process of immigrating, so much of my anxiety was wordless. It's only now that I understand how the invasiveness of it damaged my sense of dignity. And I'm one of the lucky ones.

In the end, I had to decide on an ending that was just as absurd as the border itself. Sometimes absurdity is the only thing that can combat absurdity. So what was a story about how surveillance causes us to perform citizenship as an identity became a story about how, for the people in the audience watching that performance, the ubiquitous surveillance is nothing but an unfortunate nuisance. Tragic when it happens to me, funny when it happens to you. What's really funny, of course, is that American citizens are surveilled just as closely as the people outside its borders, and the ones trying to get in. The whole country is one big border town, to read the Snowden documents. We are all performing our citizenship. We are all living in the Village.

Notes

1. http://madelineashby.com/?p=1068
2. http://adhamselim.blogspot.ca/2011/05/emergent-border-cities.html
3. http://en.wikipedia.org/wiki/Operation_Gatekeeper
4. http://online.wsj.com/news/articles/SB10001424127887323741004578417
   113103350812
5. http://austinist.com/2012/08/14/texas_women_are_crossing_the_
   border.php
6. http://en.wikipedia.org/wiki/Apocalypse_91 . . . _The_Enemy_
   Strikes_Black
7. http://www.nytimes.com/2010/04/24/us/politics/24immig.html?_r=0

EMERGENT BORDER CITIES—Adham Selim

Architect Adham Selim theorizes the emergent border city at hieroglyph.asu.edu/mariposa.

Work-in-Progress Update: April 2013

Read a work-in-progress update from Madeline Ashby in April 2013 at hieroglyph.asu.edu/mariposa to see how a conversation with Arizona State University architecture and urban design professor Darren Petrucci influenced her thinking.

THE MAN WHO SOLD THE MOON
Cory Doctorow

HERE'S A THING I didn't know: there are some cancers that can only be diagnosed after a week's worth of lab work. I didn't know that. Then I went to the doctor to ask her about my pesky achy knee that had flared up and didn't go away like it always had, just getting steadily worse. I'd figured it was something torn in there, or maybe I was getting the arthritis my grandparents had suffered from. But she was one of those doctors who hadn't gotten the memo from the American health-care system that says that you should only listen to a patient for three minutes, tops, before writing him a referral and/or a prescription and firing him out the door just as the next patient was being fired in. She listened to me, she took my history, she wrote down the names of the anti-inflammatories I'd tried, everything from steroids to a climbing buddy's heavy-duty prescription NSAIDs, and gave my knee a few cautious prods.

"You're insured, right?"

"Yeah," I said. "Good thing, too. I read that knee replacement's going for seventy-five thousand dollars. That's a little out of my price range."

"I don't think you need a knee replacement, Greg. I just want to send you for some tests."

"A scan?"

"No." She looked me straight in the eyes. "A biopsy."

I'm a forty-year-old, middle-class Angeleno. My social mortality curve was a perfectly formed standard distribution—a few sparse and rare deaths before I was ten, slightly more through my teens, and then more in my twenties. By the time I was thirty-five, I had an actual funeral suit I kept in a dry-cleaning bag in the closet. It hadn't started as a funeral suit, but once I'd worn it to three funerals in a row, I couldn't wear it anywhere else without feeling an unnamable and free-floating sorrow. I was forty. My curve was ramping up, and now every big gathering of friends had at least one knot of somber people standing together and remembering someone who went too early. Someone in my little circle of forty-year-olds was bound to get a letter from the big C. There wasn't any reason for it to be me. But there wasn't any reason for it not to be either.

Bone cancer can take a week to diagnose. A week! During that week, I spent a lot of time trying to visualize the slow-moving medical processes: acid dissolving the trace of bone, the slow catalysis of some obscure reagent, some process by which a stain darkened to yellow and then orange and then, days later, to red. Or not. That was the thing. Maybe it wasn't cancer. That's why I was getting the test, instead of treatment. Because no one knew. Not until those stubborn molecules in some lab did their thing, not until some medical robot removed a test tube from a stainless steel rack and drew out its contents and took their picture or identified their chemical composition and alerted some lab tech that Dr. Robot had reached his conclusion and would the stupid human please sanity-check the results and call the other stupid human and tell him whether he's won the cancer lottery (grand prize: cancer)?

That was a long week. The word *cancer* was like the tick of a metronome. Eyes open. Cancer. Need a pee. Cancer. Turn on the coffee machine. Cancer. Grind the beans. Cancer. Cancer. Cancer.

On day seven, I got out of the house and went to Minus, which is our local hackerspace. Technically, its name is "Untitled-1," because no one could think of a better name ten years ago, when it had been located in a dirt-cheap former car-parts warehouse in Echo Park. When Echo Park gentrified, Untitled-1 moved downtown, to a former furniture store near Skid Row, which promptly began its own gentrification swing. Now we were in the top two floors of what had once been a downscale dentist's office on Ventura near Tarzana. The dentist had reinforced the floors for the big chairs and brought in 60 amp service for the X-ray machines, which made it perfect for our machine shop and the pew-pew room full of lasers. We even kept the fume hoods.

I have a personal tub at Minus, filled with half-finished projects: various parts for a 3D-printed chess-playing automata; a cup and saucer I was painstakingly covering with electroconductive paint and components; a stripped-down location sensor I'd been playing with for the Minus's space program.

Minus's space program was your standard hackerspace extraterrestrial project: sending balloons into the upper stratosphere, photographing the earth's curvature, making air-quality and climate observations; sometimes lofting an ironic action figure in 3D-printed astronaut drag. Hacker Dojo, north of San Jose, had come up with a little powered guidance system, but they'd been whipped by navigation. Adding a stock GPS with its associated batteries made the thing too heavy, so they'd tried to fake it with dead-reckoning and it had been largely unsuccessful. I'd thought I might be able to make everything a lot lighter, including the battery, by borrowing some techniques I'd seen on a performance bike-racing site.

I put the GPS on a workbench with my computer and opened up my file of notes and stared at them with glazed eyes. Cancer. Cancer. Cancer.

Forget it. I put it all away again and headed up to the roof to clear my head and to get some company. The roof at Minus was not like most roofs. Rather than being an empty gravel expanse dotted with exhaust fans, our roof was one of the busiest parts of the space. Depending on the day and time, you could find any or all of the above on Minus's roof: stargazing, smoking, BASE jumping, solar experiments, drone dogfighting, automated graffiti robots, sensor-driven high-intensity gardening, pigeon-breeding, sneaky sex, parkour, psychedelic wandering, Wi-Fi sniffing, mobile-phone tampering, HAM radio broadcasts, and, of course, people who were stuck and frustrated and needed a break from their workbenches.

I threaded my way through the experiments and discussions and build-projects, slipped past the pigeon coops, and fetched up watching a guy who was trying, unsuccessfully, to learn how to do a run up a wall and do a complete flip. He was being taught by a young woman, sixteen or seventeen, evidently his daughter ("Daaad!"), and her patience was wearing thin as he collapsed to the gym mats they'd spread out. I stared spacily at them until they both stopped arguing with each other and glared at me, a guy in his forties and a kind of miniature, female version of him, both sweaty in their sweats. "Do you mind?" she asked.

"Sorry," I mumbled, and moved off. I didn't add, *I don't mean to be rude, just worried about cancer.*

I got three steps away when my phone buzzed. I nearly fumbled it when I yanked it out of my tight jeans pocket, hands shaking. I answered it and clapped it to my ear.

"Mr. Harrison?"

"Yes."

"Please hold for Doctor Ficsor." A click.

A click. "Greg?"

"That's me," I said. I'd signed the waiver that let us skip the pointless date-of-birth/mother's maiden name "security" protocol.

"Is this a good time to talk?"

"Yes," I said. One syllable, clipped and tight in my ears. I may have shouted it.

"Well, I'd like you to come in for some confirming tests, but we've done two analyses and they are both negative for elevated alkaline phosphatase and lactate dehydrogenase."

I'd obsessively read a hundred web pages describing the blood tests. I knew what this meant. But I had to be sure. "It's not cancer, right?"

"These are negative indicators for cancer," the doctor said.

The tension that whoofed out of me like a gutpunch left behind a kind of howling vacuum of relief, but not joy. The joy might come later. At the moment, it was more like the head-bees feeling of three more cups of espresso than was sensible. "Doctor," I said, "can I try a hypothetical with you?"

"I'll do my best."

"Let's say you were worried that you, personally, had bone cancer. If you got the same lab results as me, would you consider yourself to be at risk for bone cancer?"

"You're very good at that," she said. I liked her, but she had the speech habits of someone who went to a liability insurance seminar twice a year. "Okay, in that hypothetical, I'd say that I would consider myself to be provisionally not at risk of bone cancer, though I would want to confirm it with another round of tests, just to be very, very sure."

"I see," I said. "I'm away from my computer right now. Can I call your secretary later to set that up?"

"Sure," she said. "Greg?"

"Yes."

"Congratulations," she said. "Sleep easy, okay?"

"I will try," I said. "I could use it."

"I figured," she said. "I like giving people good news."

I thought her insurance adjuster would not approve of that wording, but I was glad she'd said it. I squeezed the phone back into my pocket and looked at the blue, blue sky, cloudless save for the scummy film of L.A. haze that hovered around the horizon. It was the same sky I'd been standing under five minutes ago. It was the same roof. The same building. The same assemblage of attention-snagging interesting weirdos doing what they did. But I was not the same.

I was seized by a sudden, perverse urge to go and take some risks: speed down the highway, BASE jump from Minus's roof, try out some really inadvisable parkour moves. Some part of me that sought out patterns in the nonsense of daily randomness was sure that I was on a lucky streak and wanted me to push it. I told that part to shut up and pushed it down best as I could. But I was filled with an inescapable buoyancy, like I might float right off the roof. I knew that if I'd had a hard time concentrating before, I was in for an even harder time getting down to business now. It was a small price to pay.

"Hey," someone said behind me. "Hey, dude?"

It occurred to me that I was the dude in question, and that this person had been calling out to me for some time, with a kind of mellow intensity—not angry, but insistent nonetheless. I turned around and found myself staring down at a surfer-looking guy half my age, sun-bleached ponytail and wraparound shades, ragged shorts and a grease-stained long-sleeved jersey and bare feet, crouched down like a Thai fisherman on his haunches, calf muscles springing out like wires, fingertips resting lightly on a gadget.

Minus was full of gadgets, half built, sanded to fit, painted to cover, with lots of exposed wiring, bare boards, blobs of hot glue and adhesive polymer clinging on for dear life against the forces of shear and torque and entropy. But even by those standards, surfer-guy's gadget was pretty spectacular. It was the lens—big and round and polished, with the look of a precision-engineered artifact out of a real manufacturer's shop—not something hacked together in a hacklab.

"Hey," I said.

"Dude," he said. "Shadow."

I was casting a shadow over the lens. I stepped smartly to one side and the pitiless L.A. sun pierced it, focused by it down to a pinprick of white on a kind of bed beneath the lens. The surfer guy gave me an absentminded thumbs-up and started to squint at his laptop's screen.

"What's the story with this thing?" I said.

"Oh," he said, "Solar sintering 3D printing with the sun." The bed started to jerk and move with the characteristic stepper-motor dance of a 3D printer. The beam of light sizzled on the bed like the tip of a soldering iron, sending up a wisp of smoke like a shimmer in the sun's glare. There was a sweet smell from it, and I instinctively turned upwind of it, not wanting to be sucking down whatever aromatic volatiles were boiling off the print medium.

"That is way, way cool," I said. "Does it work?"

He smiled. "Oh yeah, it works. This is the part I'm interested in." He typed some more commands and the entire thing lifted up on recessed wheels and inched forward with the slow grace of a tortoise.

"It walks?"

"Yeah. The idea is, you leave it in the desert and come back in a couple of months and it's converted the sand that blows over its in-hopper into prefab panels you can snap together to make a shelter."

"Ah," I said. "What about sand on the solar panel?" I was thinking of the Mars rovers, which had had a tendency to go offline when too much Martian dust blew over their photovoltaics.

"Working on that. I can make the lens and photovoltaic turn sideways and shake themselves." He pointed at a couple of little motors. "But that's a lot of moving parts. Want it to run unattended for months at a time."

"Huh," I said. "This wouldn't happen to be a Burning Man thing, would it?"

He smiled ruefully. "That obvious?"

Honestly, it was. Half of Minus were burners, and they all had a bit of his look of delightful otherworldly weirdness. "Just a lucky guess," I said, because no one wants to be reminded that they're of a certain type—especially if that type is nonconformist.

He straightened up and extended his hand. He was missing the tip of his index finger, and the rest of his fingernails were black with grease. I shook, and his grip was warm, firm and dry, and rough with callus. You could have put it in a museum and labeled it "Hardware hacker hand (typical)."

"I'm Pug," he said.

"Greg."

"So the plan is, bring it out to the desert for Fourth of Juplaya, let it run all summer, come back for Burning Man, and snap the pieces together."

"What's Fourth of Jup-whatever?"

"Fourth of Juplaya. It's a July Fourth party in Black Rock. A lot like Burning Man used to be like, when 'Safety Third' was the guiding light and not just a joke. Much smaller and rougher, less locked down. More guns. More weird. Intense."

His gadget grunted and jammed. He looked down at it and nudged one of the stepper motors with his thumb, and it grunted again. "'Scuse me," he said, and hunkered down next to it. I watched him tinker for a while, then walked away, forgotten in his creative fog.

I went back down into Minus, put away my stuff, and chatted with some people I sort of knew about inconsequentialities, in a cloud of unreality. It was the hangover from my week of anxiety and its sudden release, and I couldn't tell you for the life of me what we talked about. After an hour or two of this, I suddenly realized that I was profoundly beat, I mean beat down and smashed flat. I said good-bye—or maybe I didn't, I wouldn't swear to it—and went out to look for my car. I was wandering around the parking lot, mashing the alarm button on my key chain, when I ran into Pug. He was (barely) carrying a huge box, shuffling and peering over the top. I was so tired, but it would have been rude not to help.

"Need a hand?"

"Dude," he said, which I took for an affirmative. I grabbed a corner and walked backward. The box was heavy, but it was mostly just huge, and when we reached his beat-up minivan, he kicked the tailgate release and then laid it down like a bomb-disposal specialist putting a touchy IED to sleep. He smacked his hands on his jeans and said, "Thanks, man. That lens, you wouldn't believe what it's worth." Now that I could see over the top of the box, I realized it was mostly padding, layers of lint-free cloth and bubblewrap with the lens in the center of it all, the gadget beneath it. "Minus is pretty safe, you know, but I don't want to tempt fate. I trust 99.9 percent of 'em not to rip it off or use it for a frisbee, but even a one-in-a-thousand risk is too steep for me." He pulled some elasticated webbing over it and anchored it down with cleats bolted inside the oily trunk.

"Fair enough," I said.

"Greg, buddy, can I ask you a personal question?"

"I suppose."

"Are you okay? I mean, you kind of look like you've been hit upside the head with a brick. Are you planning on driving somewhere?"

"Uh," I said. "Truly? I'm not really okay. Should be, though." And I spilled it all out—the work, the diagnosis.

"Well, hell, no wonder. Congratulations, man, you're going to live! But not if you crash your car on the way home. How about if I give you a ride?"

"It's okay, really—"

He held up a hand. "Greg, I don't know you and you don't know me, but you've got no more business driving now than you would if you'd just slammed a couple tequila shots. So I can give you a ride or call you a cab, but if you try and get into your car, I will argue with you until I bore you into submission. So what is it? Ride? Taxi?"

He was absolutely, totally right. I hated that. I put my keys back into my pocket. "You win," I said. "I'll take that ride."

"Great," he said, and gave me a Buddha smile of pure SoCal serenity. "Where do you live?"

"Irvine," I said.

He groaned. "Seriously?" Irvine was a good three-hour drive in traffic.

"Not seriously," I said. "Just Burbank. Wanted to teach you a lesson about being too free with your generosity."

"Lesson learned. I'll never be generous again." But he was smiling.

I slid into the passenger seat. The car smelled like sweat and machines. The floor mats were indistinct gray and crunchy with maker detritus: dead batteries, coffee cups, multidriver bits, USB cables, and cigarette-lighter-charger adapters. I put my head back on the headrest and looked out the grimy windows through slitted eyes as he got into the driver's side and started the engine, then killed the podcast that started blasting from the speakers.

"Burbank, right?"

"Yeah," I said. There were invisible weights on my chest, wrists, and ankles. I was very glad I wasn't behind the wheel. We swung out onto Ventura Boulevard and inched through the traffic toward the freeway.

"Are you going to be all right on your own?"

"Tonight? Yeah, sure. Seriously, that's really nice of you, but it's just, whatever, aftermath. I mean, it's not like I'm dying. It's the *opposite* of that, right?"

"Fair enough. You just seem like you're in rough shape."

I closed my eyes and then I felt us accelerate as we hit the freeway and weaved over to the HOV lanes. He put down the hammer and the engine skipped into higher gear.

"You're not a burner, are you?"

I suppressed a groan. Burners are the Jehovah's Witnesses of the counterculture. "Nope," I said. Then I said what I always said. "Just seemed like a lot of work."

He snorted. "You think Burning Man sounds like a lot of work, you should try Fourth of Juplaya. No rules, no rangers. A lot of guns. A lot of serious blowing shit up. Casual sex. No coffee shop. No sparkleponies. Fistfuls of drugs. High winds. Burning sun. Non-freaking-stop. It's like pure distilled essence of playa."

I remembered that feeling, like I wanted to BASE jump off the roof. "I have to admit, that sounds totally amazeballs," I said. "And demented."

"Both, yup. You going to come?"

I opened my eyes wide. "What?"

"Well, I need some help with the printer. I looked you up on the Minus database. You do robotics, right?"

"A little," I said.

"And you've built a couple RepRaps, it says?"

"Two working ones," I said. Building your own 3D printer that was capable of printing out nearly all the parts to build a copy of itself was a notoriously tricky rite of passage for hackerspace enthusiasts. "About four that never worked, too."

"You're hired," he said. "First assistant engineer. You can have half my van, I'll bring the cooler and the BBQ and pork shoulder on dry ice, a keg of beer, and some spare goggles."

"That's very nice of you," I said.

"Yeah," he said. "It is. Listen, Greg, I'm a good guy, ask around. I don't normally invite people out to the Fourth, it's a private thing. But I really do need some help, and I think you do, too. A week with a near-death experience demands a fitting commemoration. If you let big stuff like this pass by without marking it, it just, you know, builds up. Like arterial plaque. Gotta shake it off."

You see, this is the thing about burners. It's like a religion for them. Gotta get everyone saved.

"I'll think about it," I said.

"Greg, don't be offended?"

"Okay."

"Right, Just that, you're the kind of guy, I bet, spends a lot of time 'thinking about it.'"

I swallowed the snappish reply and said nothing.

"And now you're stewing. Dude, you are so *buttoned down*. Tell you what, keep swallowing your emotions and you will end up dying of something fast and nasty. You can do whatever you want, but what I'm offering you is something that tons of people would kill for. Four days of forgetting who you are, being whoever you want to be. Stars, dust, screwing, dope, explosions, and gunfire. You're not going to get a lot of offers like that, is what I'm saying."

"And I said I'd think about it."

He blatted out a raspberry and said, "Yeah, fine, that's cool." He drove on in silence. The 101 degenerated into a sclerotic blockage. He tapped at the old phone velcroed to the dashboard and got a traffic overlay that showed red for ten miles.

"Dude, I do *not* want to sit in this car for the next forty-five minutes listening to you not say anything. How about a truce? I won't mention the Fourth, you pretend you don't think I'm a crazy hippie, and we'll start over, 'kay?"

The thing that surprised me most was how emotionally mature the offer was. I never knew how to climb down from stupid fights, which is why I was forty and single. "Deal," I said.

Just like that, he dropped it. We ended up talking about a related subject—selective solar laser-sintering—and some of the funky things he was having to cope with in the project. "Plenty of people have done it with sand, but I want to melt gypsum. In theory, I only have to attain about 85 percent of the heat to fuse it, but there's a lot of impurities in it that I can't account for or predict."

"What if you sift it or something first?"

"Well, if I want it to run unattended, I figure I don't want to have to include a centrifuge. Playa dust is nanofine, and it gets into everything. I mean, I've seen art cars with sealed bearings that are supposed to perform in *space* go gunky and funky after a couple of years."

I chewed on the problem. "You could maybe try a settling tray, something that uses wind for agitation through graduated screens, but you'd need to unclog it somehow." More thinking. "Of course, you *could* just melt the crap out of it when you're not sure, just blaze it into submission."

But he was already shaking his head. "Doesn't work—too hot and I can't get the set time right, goes all runny."

"What about a sensor?" I said. "Try to characterize how runny it is, adjust the next pass accordingly?"

"Thought of that," he said. "Too many ways it could go wrong is what I'm thinking. Remember, this thing has to run where no one can tend it. I want to drop it in July and move into the house it builds me by September. It has to fail very, very safe."

I took his point, but I wasn't sure I agreed. Optical sensors were pretty solved, as was the software to interpret what they saw. I was about to get my laptop out and find a video I remembered seeing when he slammed on the brakes and made an explosive noise. I felt the brakes' ABS shudder as the minivan fishtailed a little and heard a horn blare from behind us. I had one tiny instant with which to contemplate the looming bumper of the gardener's pickup truck ahead of us before we rear-ended him. I was slammed back into my seat by the airbag a second before the subcompact behind us crashed into us, its low nose sliding under the rear bumper and raising the back end off the ground as it plowed beneath us, wedging tight just before its windshield would have passed through our rear bumper, thus saving the driver from a radical facial rearrangement and possible decapitation.

Sound took on a kind of underwater quality as it filtered through the airbag, but as I punched my way clear of it, everything came back. Beside me, Pug was making aggrieved noises and trying to turn around. He was caught in the remains of his own airbag, and his left arm looked like it might be broken—unbroken arms don't hang with that kind of limp and sickening slackness. "Christ, the lens—"

I looked back instinctively, saw that the rear end was intact, albeit several feet higher than it should have been, and said, "It's fine, Pug. Car behind us slid _under_ us. Hold still, though. Your arm's messed up."

He looked down and saw it and his face went slack. "That is not good," he said. His pupils were enormous, his face so pale it was almost green.

"You're in shock," I said.

"Yes," he said, distantly.

I did a quick personal inventory, moving all my limbs and experimentally swiveling my head this way and that. Concluding that I was in one piece, I did a fast assessment of the car and its environs. Traffic in the adjacent lane had stopped, too—looking over my shoulder, I could see a little fender bender a couple car lengths back that had doubtless been caused by our own wreck. The guy ahead of us had gotten out of his pickup and was headed our way slowly, which suggested that he was unharmed and also not getting ready to shoot us for rear-ending him, so I turned my attention back to Pug. "Stay put," I said, and pushed his airbag aside and unbuckled his seat belt, carefully feeding it back into its spool without allowing it to jostle his arm. That done, I gave him a quick once-over, lightly running my hands over his legs, chest, and head. He didn't object—or shout in pain—and I finished up without blood on my hands, so that was good.

"I think it's just your arm," I said. His eyes locked on my face for a moment, then his gaze wandered off.

"The lens," he said, blearily.

"It's okay," I said.

"The lens," he said, again, and tried once more to twist around in his seat. This time, he noticed his limp arm and gave out a mild, "Ow." He tried again. "Ow."

"Pug," I said, taking his chin and turning his face to mine. His skin was clammy and cold. "Dude. You are in shock and have a broken arm. You need to stay still until the ambulance gets here. You might have a spinal injury or a concussion. I need you to stay still."

"But the lens," he said. "Can't afford another one."

"If I go check on the lens, will you stay still?" It felt like I was bargaining with a difficult drunk for his car keys.

"Yes," he said.

"Stay there."

The pickup truck's owner helped me out of the car. "You okay?" he asked. He had a Russian accent and rough gardener's hands and a farmer's tan.

"Yeah," I said. "You?"

"I guess so. My truck's pretty messed up, though."

Pug's minivan had merged catastrophically with the rear end of the pickup, deforming it around the van's crumple-zone. I was keenly aware that this was probably his livelihood.

"My friend's got a broken arm," I said. "Shock, too. I'm sure you guys'll be able to exchange insurance once the paramedics get here. Did you call them?"

"My buddy's on it," he said, pointing back at the truck. There was someone in the passenger seat with a phone clamped to his head, beneath the brim of a cowboy hat.

"The lens," Pug said.

I leaned down and opened the door. "Chill out, I'm on it." I shrugged at the guy from the truck and went around back. The entire rear end was lifted clean off the road, the rear wheels still spinning lazily. To a first approximation, we were unscathed. The same couldn't be said for the low-slung hybrid that had rear-ended us, which had been considerably flattened by its harrowing scrape beneath us, to the extent that one of its tires had blown. The driver had climbed out of the car and was leaning unsteadily on it. She gave me a little half wave and a little half smile, which I returned. I popped the hatch and checked that the box was in one piece. It wasn't even dented. "The lens is fine," I called. Pug gave no sign of having heard.

I started to get a little anxious feeling. I jogged around the back of the subcompact and then ran up the driver's side and yanked open Pug's door. He was unconscious, and that gray sheen had gone even whiter. His breath was coming in little shallow pants and his head lolled back in the seat. Panic crept up my throat and I swallowed it down. I looked up quickly and shouted at the pickup driver. "You called an ambulance, right?" The guy must've heard something in my voice because an instant later he was next to me.

"Shock," he said.

"It's been years since I did first aid."

"Recovery position," he said. "Loosen his clothes, give him a blanket."

"What about his arm?" I pointed.

He winced. "We're going to have to be careful," he said. "Shit," he added. The traffic beyond the car was at a near standstill. Even the motor-cycles were having trouble lane-splitting between the close-crammed cars.

"The ambulance?"

He shrugged. "On its way, I guess." He put his ear close to Pug's mouth, listened to his breathing, put a couple fingers to his throat and felt around. "I think we'd better lay him out."

The lady driving the subcompact had a blanket in her trunk, which we spread out on the weedy ground alongside the median, which glittered with old broken glass. She—young, Latina, wearing workout clothes—held Pug's arm while the gardener guy and I got him at both ends and stretched him out. The other guy from the pickup truck found some flares in a toolkit under the truck's seat and set them on the road behind us. We worked with a minimum of talk, and for me, the sounds of the highway and my weird postanxiety haze both faded away into barely discernible background noise. We turned Pug on his side, and I rolled up my jacket to support his arm. He groaned. The gardener guy checked his pulse again, then rolled up his own jacket and used it to prop up Pug's feet.

"Good work," he said.

I nodded.

"Craziest thing," the gardener said.

"Uh-huh," I said. I fussed awkwardly with Pug's hair. His ponytail had come loose and it was hanging in his face. It felt wiry and dry, like he spent a lot of time in the sun.

"Did you see it?"

"What?"

He shook his head. "Craziest thing. It crashed right in front of us." He spoke in rapid Russian—maybe it was Bulgarian?—to his friend, who crunched over to us. The guy held something out for me to see. I looked at it, trying to make sense of what I was seeing. It was a tangle of wrecked plastic and metal and a second later, I had it worked out—it was a little UAV, some kind of copter. Four rotors—no, six. A couple of cameras. I'd built a few like it, and I'd even lost control of a few in my day. I could easily see how someone like me, trying out a little drone built from a kit or bought fully assembled, could simply lose track of the battery or just fly too close to a rising updraft from the blacktop and *crash*. It was technically illegal to fly one except over your own private property, but that was nearly impossible to enforce. They were all over the place.

"Craziest thing," I agreed. I could hear the sirens.

THE EMTS LIKED OUR work and told us so, and let me ride with them in the ambulance, though that might have been on the assumption that I could help with whatever insurance paperwork needed filling out. They looked disappointed when I told them that I'd only met Pug that day and I didn't even know his last name and was pretty sure that "Pug" wasn't his first name. It wasn't. They got the whole thing off his driver's license: Scott Zrubek. "Zrubek" was a cool name. If I'd been called "Zrubek," I'd have used "Zee" as my nickname, or maybe "Zed."

By the time they'd x-rayed Pug and put his arm in a sling and an air cast, he was awake and rational again and I meant to ask him why he wasn't going by Oz, but we never got around to it. As it turned out, I ended up giving *him* a lift home in a cab, then getting it to take me home, too. It was two in the morning by then, and maybe the lateness of the hour explains how I ended up promising Pug that I'd be his arm and hand on the playa-dust printer and that I'd come with him to Fourth of Juplaya in order to oversee the installation of the device. I also agreed to help him think of a name for it.

THAT IS HOW I came to be riding in a big white rental van on the Thursday before July Fourth weekend, departing L.A. at zero-dark-hundred with Pug in the driver's seat and classic G-funk playing loud enough to make me wince in the passenger seat as we headed for Nevada.

Pug had a cooler between us, full of energy beverages and electrolyte drink, jerky, and seed bars. We stopped in Mono Lake and bought bags of oranges from old guys on the side of the road wearing cowboy hats, and later on we stopped at a farm stall and bought fresh grapefruit juice that stung with tartness and was so cold that the little bits of pulp were little frost-bombs that melted on our tongues.

Behind us, in the van's cargo area, was everything we needed for a long weekend of hard-core radical self-reliance—water cans to fill in Reno, solar showers, tents, tarps, rebar stakes, booze, bikes, sunscreen, first-aid kits, a shotgun, an air cannon, a flamethrower, various explosives, crates of fireworks, and more booze. All stored and locked away in accordance with the laws of both Nevada and California, as verified through careful reference to a printout sheathed in a plastic paper-saver that got velcroed to the inside of the van's back door when we were done.

In the center of all this gear, swaddled in bubblewrap and secured in place with multiple tie-downs, was the gadget, which we had given a capital letter to in our e-mails and messages: the Gadget. I'd talked Pug out of some of his aversion to moving parts, because the Gadget was going to end up drowning in its own output if we didn't. The key was the realization that it didn't matter *where* the Gadget went, so long as it went *somewhere,* which is how we ended up in Strandbeest territory.

The Strandbeest is an ingenious wind-powered walker that looks like a blind, mechanical millipede. Its creator, a Dutch artist called Theo Jansen, designed it to survive harsh elements and to be randomly propelled by wind. Ours had a broad back where the Gadget's business end perched, and as the yurt panels were completed, they'd slide off to land at its feet, gradually hemming it with rising piles of interlocking, precision-printed pieces. To keep it from going too far afield, I'd tether it to a piece of rebar driven deep into the playa, giving it a wide circle through which the harsh winds of the Black Rock Desert could blow it.

Once I was done, Pug had to admit I'd been right. It wasn't just a better design, it was a *cooler* one, and the Gadget had taken on the aspect of a centaur, with the printer serving as rising torso and head. We'd even equipped it with a set of purely ornamental goggles and a filter mask, just to make it fit in with its neighbors on the Playa. They were a very accepting lot, but you never knew when antirobot prejudice would show its ugly head, and so anything we could do to anthropomorphize the Gadget would only help our cause.

Pug's busted arm was healed enough to drive to the Nevada line, but by the time we stopped for gas, he was rubbing at his shoulder and wincing, and I took over the driving, and he popped some painkillers and within moments he was fast asleep. I tried not to envy him. He'd been a bundle of nerves in the run-up to the Fourth, despite several successful trial runs in his backyard and a great demo on the roof of Minus. He kept muttering about how nothing ever worked properly in the desert, predicting dire all-nighters filled with cursing and scrounging for tools and missing the ability to grab tech support online. It was a side of him I hadn't seen up to that point—he was normally so composed—but it gave me a chance to be the grown-up for a change. It helped once I realized that he was mostly worried about looking like an idiot in front of his once-a-year friends, the edgiest and weirdest people in his set. It also hadn't escaped my notice that he, like me, was a single guy who spent an awful lot of time wondering what this said about him. In other words: he didn't want to look like a dork in front of the eligible women who showed up.

"I'm guessing two more hours to Reno, then we'll get some last-minute supplies and head out. Unless you want to play the slots and catch a Liza Minnelli impersonator."

"No, I want to get out there and get set up."

"Good." Suddenly he gorilla-beat his chest with his good fist and let out a rebel yell. "Man, I just can't *wait*."

I smiled. This was the voluble Pug I knew.

He pointed a finger at me. "Oh, I see you smiling. You think you know what's going to happen. You think you're going to go drink some beers, eat some pills, blow stuff up, maybe get lucky. What you don't know is how *life-changing* this can all be. You get out of your head, literally. It's like—" He waved his hands, smacked the dashboard a couple times, cracked and swigged an energy beverage.

"Okay, this is the thing. We spend all our time doing, you know, stuff. Maintenance. Ninety-eight percent of the day, all you're doing is thinking about what you're going to be doing to go on doing what you're doing. Worrying about whether you've got enough socked away to see you through your old age without ending up eating cat food. Worrying about whether you're getting enough fiber or eating too many carbs. It's being alive, but it's hardly living.

"You ever been in a bad quake? No? Here's the weird secret of a big quake: it's actually pretty great, afterward. I mean, assuming you're not caught in the rubble, of course. After a big one, there's this moment, a kind of silence. Like you were living with this huge old refrigerator compressor humming so loud in the back of your mind that you've never been able to think properly, not once since about the time you turned, you know, eleven or twelve, maybe younger. Never been *present* and *in the moment*. And then that humming refrigerator just *stops* and there's a ringing, amazing, all-powerful *silence* and for the first time you can hear yourself think. There's that moment, after the earth stops shaking, when you realize that there's you and there's everyone else and the point of it all is for all of you to figure out how to get along together as best as you can.

"They say that after a big one, people start looting, raping, eating each other, whatever. But you know what I saw the last time it hit, back in 2019? People figuring it out. Firing up their barbecues and cooking dinner for the neighborhood with everything in the freezer, before it spoils anyway. Kids being looked after by everyone, everyone going around and saying, 'What can I do for you? Do you have a bed? Water? Food? You okay? Need someone to talk to? Need a ride?' In the movies, they always show everyone running around looting as soon as the lights go out, but I can't say as I've ever seen that. I mean, that's not what I'd do, would you?"

I shook my head.

"'Course not. No one we know would. Because we're on the same side. The human race's side. But when the fridge is humming away, you can lose track of that, start to feel like it's zero sum, a race to see who can squirrel away the most nuts before the winter comes. When a big shaker hits, though, you remember that you aren't the kind of squirrel who could live in your tree with all your nuts while all the other squirrels starved and froze out there.

"The Playa is like a disaster without the disaster—it's a chance to switch off the fridge and hear the silence. A chance to see that people are, you know, basically awesome. Mostly. It's the one place where you actually confront reality, instead of all the noise and illusion."

"So you're basically saying that it's like Buddhism with recreational drugs and explosions?"

"Basically."

We rode awhile longer. The signs for Reno were coming more often now, and the traffic was getting thicker, requiring more attention.

"If only," he said. "If only there was some way to feel that way all the time."

"You couldn't," I said, without thinking. "Regression to the mean. The extraordinary always ends up feeling ordinary. Do it for long enough and it'd just be noise."

"You may be right. But I hope you're not. Somewhere out there, there's a thing so amazing that you can devote your life to it and never forget how special it is."

WE CRAWLED THE LAST thirty miles, driving through Indian country, over cattle gratings and washed-out gullies. "The local cops are fine, they're practically burners themselves. Everyone around here grew up with Burning Man, and it's been the only real source of income since the gypsum mine closed. But the feds and the cops from over the state line, they're bad news. Lot of jack Mormons over in Pershing County, don't like this at all. And since the whole route to the Playa, apart from the last quarter mile, is in Washoe County, and since no one is supposed to buy or sell anything once you get to the Playa, all the money stays in Washoe County, and Pershing gets none of it. All they get are freaks who offend them to their very souls. So basically, you want to drive slow and keep your nose clean around here, because you never know who's waiting behind a bush to hand you a giant ticket and search your car down to the floor mats."

I slowed down even more. We stopped for Indian tacos—fried flatbread smothered in ground beef and fried veggies—that sat in my stomach in an undigestable, salty lump. Pug grew progressively more manic as we approached the turnoff for Black Rock Desert and was practically drumming on the dashboard by the time we hit the dusty, rutted side road. He played with the stereo, put on some loud electronic dance music that made me feel old and out of it, and fished around under the seat for a dust mask and a pair of goggles.

I'd seen lots of photos of Burning Man, the tents and shade structures and RVs and "mutant vehicles" stretching off in all directions, and even though I knew the Fourth was a much smaller event, I'd still been picturing that in my mind's eye. But instead, what we saw was a seemingly endless and empty desert, edges shrouded in blowing dust clouds with the hints of mountains peeking through, and no sign at all of human habitation.

"Now where?" I said.

He got out his phone and fired up a GPS app, clicked on one of his waypoints, waiting a moment, and pointed into the heart of the dust. "That way."

We rumbled into the dust cloud and were soon in a near-total whiteout. I slowed the car to walking pace, and then slower than walking pace. "Pug, we should just stop for a while," I said. "There's no roads. Cars could come from any direction."

"All the more reason to get to the campsite," he said. "We're sitting ducks out here for anyone else arriving."

"That's not really logic," I said. "If we're moving and they're moving, we've got a much better chance of getting into a fender bender than if we're staying still."

The air in the van tasted dusty and alkali. I put it in park and put on the mask, noticed my eyes were starting to sting, added goggles—big, bug-eyed Soviet-era MiG goggles.

"Drive," he said. "We're almost there."

I was starting to catch some of his enthusiasm. I put it back into drive and rode the brakes as we inched through the dust. He peered at his GPS, calling out, "Left," then "straight," then "right" and back again. A few times

I was sure I saw a car bumper or a human looming out of the dust before us and slammed on the brakes, only to discover that it had been a trick of the light and my brain's overactive, nerve-racked pattern-matching systems.

When I finally *did* run something over, I was stretched out so tight that I actually let out a scream. In my defense, the thing we hit was a tent peg made out of rebar—the next five days gave the chance to become endlessly acquainted with rebar tent pegs, which didn't scar the playa and were cheap and rugged—pushing it through the front driver's-side tire, which exploded with a noise like a gunshot. I turned off the engine and tried to control my breathing.

Pug gave me a moment, then said, "We're here!"

"Sorry about the tire."

"Pfft. We're going to wreck stuff that's a lot harder to fix than a flat tire. You think we can get to the spare without unpacking?"

"No way."

"Then we'll have to unpack. Come on, buddy."

The instant he opened the door, a haze of white dust followed him, motes sparkling in the air. I shrugged and opened my door and stepped out into the dust.

THERE WERE PEOPLE IN the dust, but they were ciphers—masked, goggled, indistinct. I had a job to do—clearing out the van's cargo and getting it moved to our site, which was weirdly precise—a set of four corners defined as GPS coordinates that ran to the tenth of a second—and at the same time, such a farcically huge tract of land that it really amounted to "oh, anywhere over there's fine."

The shadowy figures came out of the dust and formed a bucket brigade, into which I vanished. I love a good bucket brigade, but they're surprisingly hard to find. A good bucket brigade is where you accept your load, rotate 180 degrees and walk until you reach the next person, load that person, do another volte-face, and walk until someone loads you. A good bucket brigade isn't just passing things from person to person. It's a dynamic system in which autonomous units bunch and debunch as is optimal given the load and the speed and energy levels of each participant. A good bucket brigade is a thing of beauty, something whose smooth coordination arises from a bunch of disjointed parts who don't need to know anything about the system's whole state in order to help optimize it. In a good bucket brigade, the mere act of walking at the speed you feel comfortable with and carrying no more than you can safely lift and working at your own pace produces a perfectly balanced system in which the people faster than you can work faster, and the people slower than you can work slower. It is the opposite of an assembly line, where one person's slowness is the whole line's problem. A good bucket brigade allows everyone to contribute at their own pace, and the more contributors you get, the better it works.

I love bucket brigades. It's like proof that we can be more together than we are on our own, and without having to take orders from a leader. It wasn't until the van was empty and I pulled a lounger off our pile of gear and set it up and sank down into it that I realized that an hour had slipped by and I was both weary and energized. Pug handed me a flask and I sniffed at it, got a noseful of dust and whiskey fumes, and then sipped at it. It was Kentucky bourbon, and it cut through the dust in my mouth and throat like oven cleaner.

Pug sprawled in the dust beside me, his blond hair splayed around his head like a halo. "Now the work begins," he said. "How you holding up?"

"Ready and willing, Cap'n," I said, speaking with my eyes closed and my head flung back.

"Look at you two," an amused female voice said. Fingers plucked the flask out of my hands. I opened my eyes. Standing over us was a tall, broad-shouldered woman whose blue Mohawk was braided in a long rope that hung over her shoulder. "You just got here and you're already pooped. You're an embarrassment to the uniform."

"Hi, Blight," Pug said, not stirring. "Blight, this is Greg. He's never been to the Playa before."

"A virgin!" she said. "My stars and garters." She drank more whiskey. She was wearing overalls with the sleeves ripped off, showing her long, thick, muscled arms, which had been painted with stripes of zinc, like a barber pole. It was hard to guess her age—the haircut suggested midtwenties, but the way she held herself and talked made me think she might be more my age. I tried not to consider the possibilities of a romantic entanglement. As much of a hormone-fest as the Playa was supposed to be, it wasn't summer camp. "We'll be gentle," she said.

"Don't worry about me," I said. "I'm just gathering my strength before leaping into action. Can I have the whiskey back, please?"

She drank another mouthful and passed it back. "Here you go. That's good stuff, by the way."

"Fighting Cock," Pug said. "I bought it for the name, stayed for the booze." He got to his feet and he and Blight shared a long hug. His feet left the ground briefly.

"Missed you, Pug."

"Missed you, too. You should come visit, sometime."

They chatted a little like old friends, and I gathered that she lived in Salt Lake City and ran a goth/alternative dance club that sounded familiar. There wasn't much by way of freak culture out in SLC, so whatever there was quickly became legendary. I'd worked with a guy from Provo, a gay guy who'd never fit in with his Mormon family, who'd spent a few years in SLC before coming to L.A. I was pretty sure he'd talked about it. A kind of way station for Utah's underground bohemian railway.

Then Pug held out his hand to me and pulled me to my feet and announced we'd be setting up camp. This involved erecting a giant shade structure, stringing up hammocks, laying out the heavy black rubber solar-shower bladders on the van's roof to absorb the day's heat, setting out the grill and the bags of lump charcoal, and hammering hundreds of lengths of bent-over rebar into the unyielding desert floor. Conveniently, Pug's injured arm wasn't up to the task, leaving me to do most of the work, though some of the others pitched in at the beginning, until some more campers arrived and needed help unloading.

Finally, it was time to set up the Gadget.

I'd been worried about it, especially as we'd bashed over some of the deeper ruts after the turnoff onto Route 34, but Pug had been awfully generous with the bubblewrap. I ended up having to scrounge a heavy ammo box full of shotgun shells to hold down the layer after layer of plastic and keep it from blowing away. I drew a little crowd as I worked—*now* they weren't too busy!—and Blight stepped in and helped toward the end, bundling up armloads of plastic sheeting and putting it under the ammo box. Finally, the many-legged Gadget was fully revealed. There was a long considering silence that broke when a breeze blew over it and it began, very slowly, to walk, as each of the legs' sails caught the wind. It clittered along on its delicate feet, and then, as the wind gusted harder, lurched forward suddenly, scattering the onlookers. I grabbed the leash I'd clipped to its rear and held on as best as I could, nearly falling on my face before I reoriented my body to lean away from it. It was like playing one-sided tug-of-war. I whooped and then there were more hands on the leash with mine, including Blight's, and we steadied it.

"Guess I should have driven a spike for the tether before I started," I said.

"Where are you going to spike it?" Blight asked.

I shrugged as best as I could while still holding the strong nylon cable. "I don't know—close enough to the shade structure that we can keep tools and gear there while we're working on it, but far enough away that it can really get around without bashing into anything."

"Stay there," she said, and let go, jogging off toward the back forty of our generous plot. She came back and grabbed our sledgehammer and one of the longest pieces of rebar, and I heard the ringing of a mallet on steel—sure, rhythmic strokes. She'd done this a lot more than me. She jogged back a moment later, her goggles pushed up on her forehead, revealing dark brown eyes, wide set, with thick eyebrows and fine crow's-feet. The part of me that wasn't thinking about the Gadget was thinking about how pretty she was and wondering if she was single, and wondering if she was with Pug, and wondering if she was into guys at all, anyway.

"Let's get it tied off," she said. We played out the rope and let it drag us toward the rebar she'd driven nearly all the way into the hardpack, the bent double tips both buried deep, forming a staple. I threaded the rope's end through and tied a sailor's knot I'd learned in the one week I'd attended Scouts when I was nine, the only knot I knew. It had never come loose. If it came loose this time, there was a chance the Gadget would sail all the way to Reno over the coming months, leaving behind a trail of interlocking panels that could be formed into a yurt.

The sun was starting to set, and though I really wanted to go through my maintenance checklist for the Gadget, there was dance music playing (dubstep—I'd been warned by Pug in advance and had steeled myself to learning to love the *wub-wub-wub*), there were people milling about, there was the smell of barbecue. The sun was a huge, bloody red ball on the horizon and the heat of the day was giving way to a perfectly cool night. Laser light played through the air. Drones flew overhead, strobing with persistence-of-vision LED light shows and doing aerobatics that pushed their collision-avoidance routines to the limit (every time one buzzed me, I flinched, as I had been doing since the accident).

Blight dusted her hands off on her thighs. "Now what?"

I looked around "Dinner?"

"Yeah," she said, and linked arms with me and led me back to camp.

SOMETIME AROUND MIDNIGHT, I had the idea that I should be getting to bed and getting a good night's sleep so I could get the Gadget up and running the next morning. Then Pug and I split a tab of E and passed a thermosful of mushroom tea back and forth—a "hippie flip," something I hadn't tried in more than a decade—and an hour later I was dancing my ass off and the world was an amazing place.

I ended up in a wonderful cuddle puddle around 2 A.M., every nerve alive to the breathing chests and the tingling skin of the people around me. Someone kissed me on the forehead and I spun back to my childhood, and the sensation of having all the time in the world and no worries about anything flooded into me. In a flash, I realized that this is what a utopian, postscarcity world would be like. A place where there was no priority higher than pleasing the people around you and amusing yourself. I thought of all those futures I'd read about and seen, places where everything was built atop sterile metal and polymer. I'd never been able to picture myself in those futures.

But this "future"—a dusty, meaty world where human skin and sweat and hair were all around, but so were lasers and UAVs and freaking *windwalking robots*? That was a future I could live in. A future devoted to pleasing one another.

"Welcome to the future," I said into the hollow of someone's throat. That person chuckled. The lasers lanced through the dust overhead, clean multicolored beams sweeping the sky. The drones buzzed and dipped. The moon shone down upon us, as big as a pumpkin and as pale as ancient bone.

I stared at the moon. It stared back. It had always stared back, but I'd always been moving too quickly to notice.

I AWOKE THE NEXT day in my own airbed in the back of the van. It was oven hot inside and I felt like a stick of beef jerky. I stumbled out shirtless and in jeans and made it to the shade structure, where I found my water pack and uncapped the hose. I sucked it dry and then refilled it from a huge water barrel we'd set up on a set of sawhorses, drank some more. I went back into the van and scrounged my shades and goggles, found a T-shirt, and reemerged, made use of the chem toilet we'd set up behind a modesty screen hammered into the playa with rebar and nylon rope, and then collapsed into a hammock under the shade structure.

Some brief groggy eternity later, someone put a collection of pills and tablets into my left hand and a coffee mug into my right.

"No more pills, thank you."

"These are supplements," he said. "I figure half of them are harmless BS, but the other half really seem to help with the old seratonin levels. Don't know which half is which, but there're a couple neuroscientists who come out most years who could argue about it for your amusement if you're interested. Take 'em."

Pug thrust a paper plate of scrambled eggs, sausages, and slices of watermelon into my hands. Before I knew it, I'd gobbled it all down to the watermelon rind and licked the stray crispy bits of sausage meat. I brushed my teeth and joined Pug out by the Gadget. It had gone walking in the night, leaving a beautiful confusion of footprints in the dust. The wind was still for the moment, though with every gust it creaked a little. I steadied Pug as he climbed it and began to tinker with it.

We'd put a lot of energy into a self-calibration phase. In theory, the Gadget should be able to tell, by means of its array of optical sensors, whether its test prints were correct or not, and then relevel its build plate and recenter its optics. The unfolded solar collectors also acted as dust collectors, and they periodically upended themselves into the feedstock hopper. This mechanism had three fail-safes—first, it could run off the battery, but once the batteries were charged, power was automatically diverted to a pair of servos that would self-trip if the battery ran too low. They each had enough storage to flip, shake, and restore the panels—working with a set of worm-gears we'd let software design and had printed off in a ceramic-polymer mix developed for artificial teeth and guaranteed not to chip or grind away for years.

There was a part of me that had been convinced that the Gadget just couldn't possibly work. Too many moving parts, not enough testing. It was just too weird. But as Pug unfurled the flexible photovoltaics and clipped them to the carbon-fiber struts and carefully positioned the big lens and pressed the big, rubberized ON button, it made the familiar powering-up noises and began to calibrate itself.

Perfectly.

Dust had sifted into the feedstock hopper overnight and had blown over the build plate. The sun hit the lens, and smoke began to rise from the dust. The motors clicked minutely and the head zipped this way and that with pure, robotic grace. Moving with the unhurried precision of a master, it described a grid and melted it, building it up at each junction, adding an extra two-micron Z-height each time, so that a tiny cityscape emerged. The sensors fed back to an old phone I'd brought along—we had a box of them, anticipating a lot more failure from these nonpurpose-built gadgets than our own—and it expressed a confidence rating about the overall accuracy of the build. The basic building blocks the Gadget was designed to print were five-millimeter-thick panels that snap-fit without any additional fixtures, relying on a clever combination of gravity and friction to stay locked once they were put together. The tolerances were fine, and the Gadget was confident it could meet them.

Here's a thing about 3D printing: it is exciting; then very, very boring; then it is exciting again. It's borderline magic; when the print-head starts to jerk and shunt to and fro, up and down, and the melting smell rises up off the build platform, and you can peer through that huge, crystal-clear lens and see a precise form emerging. It's amazing to watch a process by which an idea becomes a thing, untouched by human hands.

But it's also s-l-o-w. From the moment at which a recognizable object begins to take shape to the moment where it seems about ready to slide off, there is a long and dull interregnum in which minute changes gradually bring the shape to fruition. It's like watching soil erosion (albeit in reverse). This is the kind of process that begs for time-lapse. And if you *do* go away and come back later to check in on things, and find your object in a near-complete state, you inevitably find that, in fact, there are innumerable, mysterious passes to be made by the print-head before the object is truly *done*-done, and once again, you wish that life had a fast-forward button.

But then, you hold the object, produced out of nothing and computers and light and dust, a clearly manufactured *thing* with the polygonal character of everything that comes out of a 3D-modeling program, and once again—*magic*.

This is the cycle that the spectators at the inauguration of the Gadget went through, singly and in bunches, on that day. The Gadget performed exactly as intended—itself the most miraculous thing of the day!—business end floating on a stabilization bed as its legs clawed their way across the desert, and produced a single, interlocking shingle made of precision-formed gypsum and silicon traces, a five-millimeter, honeycombed double-walled tile with snap-fit edges all around.

"That's what it does, huh?" Blight had been by to see it several times that day, alternating between the fabulous dullness of watching 3D paint dry and the excitement of the firing range, from which emanated a continuous *pop-pop-pop* of gleeful shooting. Someone had brought along a junker car on a trailer, covered in improvised armor, rigged for remote control. The junker had been lumbering around on the desert while the marksmen blasted away at its slowly disintegrating armor, raising loud cheers every time a hunk of its plating fell away, exposing the vulnerable, rusted chassis beneath.

"Well, yeah. One after another, all day long, so long as the sun is shining. We weren't sure about the rate, but I'm thinking something like five per day in the summer sun, depending on the dust storms. It'll take a couple hundred to build a decent-sized yurt on Labor Day, and we should easily get that many by then." I showed her how the tiles interlocked, and how, once locked, they stayed locked.

"It's more of an igloo than a yurt," she said.

"Technicality," I said. "It's neither of those things. It's a 3D-printed, human-assembled temporary prefabricated experimental structure."

"An igloo," she said.

"Touché."

"Time for some food," Pug said. It could have been anywhere between three and seven P.M. None of the burner phones we were using to program and monitor the Gadget had network signal, so none of them had auto-set their clocks. I wasn't wearing a watch. I woke when the baking heat inside the van woke me, and ate when my stomach rumbled, and worked the rest of the time, and danced and drank and drugged whenever the opportunity presented itself.

My stomach agreed. Blight put a sweaty, tattoo-wreathed arm around each of our shoulders and steered us to the plume of fragrant BBQ smoke.

I AM PROUD TO say I administered the killing shot to the target car. It was a lucky shot. I'd been aiming for center mass, somewhere around the bullet-pocked midsection, staring through the scope of the impossibly long rifle that a guy in cracked leathers had checked me out on. He was some kind of physicist, high energy at JPL, but he'd been coming out since he was a freshman and he was a saucer implied neuronaut down to his tattooed toes. He also liked big hardware, guns that were some kind of surrogate supercollider, like the rifle over which I'd been given command. It was a sniper's tool, with its own tripod, and he told me that he had to keep it locked up in a gun club over the Nevada state line because it was radioactively illegal in sweet gentle California.

I peered down the scope, exhaled, and squeezed the trigger. Just as I did, the driver jigged the toy wheel she was using to control it, and the car swung around and put the middle of its grille right in my crosshairs. The bullet pierced the engine block with a fountain of black smoke and oil, the mighty crash of the engine seizing, and a juddering, shuddering, slewing cacophony as the car skidded and revved and then stopped, flames now engulfing the hood and spreading quickly into the front seat.

I had a moment's sick fear, like I'd done something terrible, destroying their toy. The silence after my shot rang out couldn't have lasted for more than a second, but then it broke, with a wild whoop!, and a cheer that whipped up and down the firing line.

The car's owner had filled it with assorted pyro—mortars and Roman candles—that were touched off by the fire and exploded out in every direction, streaking up and out and even down, smashing into the playa and then skipping away like flat stones. People pounded me on the back as the car self-destructed and sent up an oily black plume of smoke. I felt an untethered emotion, like I'd left behind civilization for good. I'd killed a car!

That's when my Fourth of Juplaya truly began. A wild debauch, loud and stoned and dangerous. I slept in hammocks, in piles of warm bodies, in other people's cars. I danced in ways I'd never danced before, ate spectacular meals of roasted meat and desserts of runny, melted chocolate on fat pancakes. I helped other people fix their art cars, piloted a drone, got a naked (and curiously asexual) massage from a stranger, and gave one in return. I sang along to songs whose words I didn't know, rode on the hood of a car while it did slow donuts in the middle of the open desert, and choked on dust storms that stung my skin and my eyes and left me huddled down in total whiteout while it blew.

It was glorious.

"How's your windwalker?" Blight said, as I passed her back her water bottle, having refilled it from our dwindling supply.

"Dunno," I said. "What day is it?"

"Monday," she said.

"I don't think I've looked in on it today. Want to come?"

She did.

In the days since we'd staked out the Gadget, more tents and trucks and cars and shade structures and exotic vehicles had gone up all around it, so that its paddock was now in the midst of a low-slung tent city. We'd strung up a perimeter of waist-high safety-orange tape to keep people from blundering into it at night, and I saw that it had been snapped in a few places and made a mental note to get the spool of tape off the post where we kept it and replace it.

The wind had been blowing hard earlier that day, but it had died down to a breathless late afternoon. The Gadget was standing and creaking softly at the end of its tether, and all around it was a litter of printed panels. Three of its legs were askew, resting atop stray tiles. We gathered them up and stacked them neatly and counted—there were forty all told, which was more than I'd dared hope for.

"We're going to be able to put together two or three yurts at this rate."

"Igloos."

"Yours can be an igloo," I said.

"That's very big of you, fella."

"Monday, you said?"

She stretched like a cat. She was streaked with dust and dirt and had a musky, unwashed animal smell that I'd gotten used to smelling on myself. "Yeah," she said. "Packing up tonight, pulling out tomorrow at first light."

I gulped. Time had become elastic out there on the desert, that school's-out Junetime feeling that the days are endless and unrolling before you and there are infinite moments to fill and no reason at all in the whole world to worry. Now it evaporated as quickly as sweat in the desert. I swallowed again.

"You're going to get up at first light?" I said.

"No," she said, and pressed a couple of gel caps into my palm. "I was going to stay up all night. Luckily, I'm not driving."

At some point we worked out that Pug and I had three filled solar showers warm on the van's roof and then it was only natural that we strung them up and pulled the plug on them, sluicing the hot, stale, won-derful water over our bodies, and we took turns soaping each other up, and the molly and whatever else had been in her pills made every nerve ending on my body thrum. Our gray water ended up in a kiddie pool at our feet, brown and mucky, and when we stepped out of it the dust immedi-ately caked on our feet and ankles and calves, gumming between our toes as we made a mad, giggling dash for the van, threw our bodies into it and slammed the door behind us.

We rolled around on the air mattresses in the thick, superheated air of the van, tickling and kissing and sometimes more, the madness of the pills and that last-night-of-summer-camp feeling thrumming in our veins.

"You're thinking about something," she said, lying crosswise so that our stomachs were pressed together and our bodies formed a wriggling plus sign.

"Is that wrong?"

"This is one of those live-in-the-moment moments, Greg."

I ran my hands over the small of her back, the swell of her butt, and she shivered and the shiver spread to me. The dope made me want to knead her flesh like dough, my hands twitching with the desire to clench.

"It's nothing, just—" I didn't want to talk about it. I wanted to fool around. She did too. We did.

"Just what?" she said, some long time later. At one point, Pug had opened—and then swiftly shut—the rear van doors.

"You and Pug aren't . . . ?"

"Nope," she said. "Are you?"

"Nope," I said.

"Just what, then?"

I rewound the conversation. I'd already peaked and was sliding into something mellow and grand.

"Just, well, default reality. It's all so—"

"Yeah," she said. *Default reality* was cutesy burner-speak for the real world, but I had to admit it fit. That made what we were in *special reality* or maybe *default unreality.*

"I know that we're only here to have fun, but somehow it feels like it's been . . ." *Important* was the word on the tip of my tongue, but what an embarrassing admission. "More." Lame-o!

She didn't say anything for so long that I started to get dope paranoia, a fear that I'd said or done something wildly inappropriate but been too high to notice.

"I know what you mean," she said.

We lay together and listened to the thump of music out in the desert night. She stroked my arm lazily with fingertips that were as rough as sandpaper, rasping over my dry, scaly skin. I could distinctly feel each nerve impulse move up my arm to my spine and into my brain. For a while, I forgot my curious existential sorrow and was truly, totally in the moment, just feeling and hearing and smelling, and not thinking. It was the refrigerator hum that Pug had told me about, and it had finally stopped. For that moment, I was only thinking, and not thinking about thinking, or thinking about thinking about thinking. Every time my thoughts strayed toward a realization that they were only thinking and not meta-cognizing, they easily and effortlessly drifted back to thinking again.

It was the weirdest moment of my life and one of the best. The fact that I was naked and hot and sweaty with a beautiful woman and stoned off my ass helped. I had found the exact perfect mixture of sex, drugs, and rock and roll to put me into the place that my mind had sought since the day I emerged from the womb.

It ended, gradually, thoughts about thoughts seeping in and then flowing as naturally as they ever had. "Wow," I said.

"You too?" she said.

"Totally."

"That's what I come here for," she said. "If I'm lucky, I get a few minutes like that here every year. Last time was three years ago, though. I went home and quit my job and spent three hours a day learning to dance while I spent the rest of my time teaching small-engine repair at a halfway house for rehabilitated juvenile offenders."

"Really?" I said.

"Totally."

"What job did you quit?"

"I was CTO for a company that made efficient cooling systems for data centers. It had some really interesting, nerdy thermodynamic problems to chew through, but at the end of the day, I was just trying to figure out how to game entropy, and that's a game of incremental improvements. I wanted to do stuff that was big and cool and weird and that I could point to and say, 'I did that.' Some of my students were knuckleheads, a few were psychos,

but most of them were just broken kids that I helped to put together, even
a little. And a few of them were amazing, learned everything I taught them
and then some, taught me things I'd never suspected, went on to do amazing things. It turns out that teaching is one of those things like raising a
kid or working out—sometimes amazing often difficult and painful, but,
in hindsight, amazing."

"Have you got a kid?"

She laughed. "Maya. She's thirteen. Spending the week with her dad
in Arizona."

"I had no idea," I said. "You don't talk about her much."

"I talk about her all the time," she said. "But not on the Playa. That's
a kind of vacation from my other life. She keeps asking me to come out.
I guess I'll have to bring her some year, but not to the Fourth. Too crazy.
And it's my Blight time."

"Your name's not Blight, is it?"

"Nope," she said. I grinned and smacked her butt, playfully. She
pinched my thigh, hard enough to make me yelp.

"What do you do?" she said.

I hated that question. "Not much," I said. "Got in with a start-up in
the nineties, made enough to pay cash for my house and then some. I do a
little contract coding and the rest of the time, I just do whatever I feel like.
Spend a lot of time at the hackerspace. You know Minus?"

"Yeah. Are you seriously rich?"

"No," I said. "I'm just, I don't know what you'd call it—I'm rich enough.
Enough that I don't have to worry about money for the rest of my life, so
long as I don't want much, and I don't. I'm a pretty simple guy."

"I can tell," she said. "Took one look at you and said, that is one simple
son of a bitch."

"Yeah," I said. "Somehow, I thought this life would be a lot more interesting than it turned out to be."

"Obviously."

"Obviously."

"So volunteer. Do something meaningful with your life. Take in a foster kid. Walk dogs for cancer patients."

"Yeah," I said.

She kissed my shin, then bent back my little toe and gave it a twist.
"Just do something, Greg. I mean, you may not get total satori out of it, but

sitting around on your butt, doing nothing, of *course* that's shit. Be smart."

"Yeah," I said.

"Oh, hell," she said. She got up on her knees and then toppled forward onto me. "Do what you want, you're an adult."

"I am of adult age," I said. "As to my adulthood—"

"You and all the rest of us."

We lay there some more. The noise outside was more frenetic than ever, a pounding, throbbing relentless mash of beats and screams and gunshots and explosions.

"Let's go see it," she said, and we staggered out into the night.

THE SUN WAS RISING when she said, "I don't think happiness is something you're supposed to have, it's something you're supposed to want."

"Whoa," I said, from the patch of ground where I was spread-eagled, dusty, and chilled as the sky turned from bruisey purple to gaudy pink.

She pinched me from where she lay, head to head above me. I was getting used to her pinches, starting to understand their nuances. That was a friendly one. In my judgment, anyway.

"Don't be smart. Look, whatever else happiness is, it's also some kind of chemical reaction. Your body making and experiencing a cocktail of hormones and other molecules in response to stimulus. Brain reward. A thing that feels good when you do it. We've had millions of years of evolution that gave a reproductive edge to people who experienced pleasure when something pro-survival happened. Those individuals did more of whatever made them happy, and if what they were doing more of gave them more and hardier offspring, then they passed this on."

"Yes," I said. "Sure. At some level, that's true of all our emotions, I guess."

"I don't know about that," she said. "I'm just talking about happiness. The thing is, doing stuff is pro-survival—seeking food, seeking mates, protecting children, thinking up better ways to hide from predators . . . Sitting still and doing nothing is almost never pro-survival, because the rest of the world is running around, coming up with strategies to outbreed you, to outcompete you for food and territory . . . If you stay still, they'll race past you."

"Or race backward," I said.

"Yeah, there's always the chance that if you do something, it'll be the wrong thing. But there's zero chance that doing nothing will be the right thing. Stop interrupting me, anyways." She pinched me again. This one was less affectionate. I didn't mind. The sun was rising. "So if being happy is what you seek, and you attain it, you stop seeking. So the reward has to return to the mean. Happiness must fade. Otherwise, you'd just lie around, blissed out and childless, until a tiger ate you."

"Have you hacked my webcam or something?"

"Not everything is about you," she said.

"Fine," I said. "I accept your hypothesis for now. So happiness isn't a state of being, instead it's a sometimes-glimpsed mirage on the horizon, drawing us forward."

"You're such a fucking poet. It's a carrot dangling from a stick, and we're the jackasses plodding after it. We'll never get it though."

"I don't know," I said. "I think I just came pretty close."

And that earned me another kiss, and a pinch, too. But it was a friendly one.

BLIGHT AND HER CAMPMATES pulled up stakes shortly thereafter. I helped them load their guns and their ordnance and their coolers and bales of costumes and kegs and gray water and duffel bags and trash bags and flaccid sun showers and collapsed shade structures, lashing about half of it to the outside of their vehicles under crackling blue tarps. Her crew had a storage locker in Reno where they'd leave most of the haul, only taking personal gear all the way home.

Working my muscles felt good after a long, wakeful night of dancing and screwing and lying around, and when we fell into a bucket-brigade rhythm, I tumbled directly into the zone of blessed, tired physical exertion, a kind of weary, all-consuming dance of moving, lifting, passing, turning, moving . . . And before I knew it, the dawn was advanced enough to have me sweating big rings around my pits and the cars were loaded, and Blight was in my arms, giving me a long hug that continued until our bodies melted together.

She gave me a soft, dry kiss and said, "Go chase some happiness."

"You too," I said. "See you at the Burn."

She pinched me again, a friendly one. We'd see each other come Labor

Day weekend, assuming we could locate each other in the sixty-thousand-person crush of Burning Man. After my intimate, two-hundred-person Fourth of Juplaya, I could hardly conceive of such a thing, though with any luck, I'd be spending it in the world's first 3D-printed yurt. Or igloo.

PUG GOT US EARLY admission to the Burn. From the turnoff, it seemed nearly as empty as it had when we'd been there in July, but by the time we reached the main gate, it was obvious that this was a very different sort of thing from the Fourth.

Once we'd submitted to a search—a search!—of the van and the trailer and been sternly warned—by a huge, hairy dude wearing the bottom half of a furry monkey costume, a negligee, and a ranger's hat—to stay under 5 mph to keep the dust plumes down, we were crawling forward. No GPS this time. During the months that we'd spent in L.A. wondering whether the Gadget was hung up, crashed, stuck, blown away, or stolen, so many vehicles had passed this way that they'd worn an unmistakable road into the Playa, hedged with orange-tipped surveyors' stakes and porta-sans.

The sun was straight overhead, the air-conditioning wheezing as we crept along, and even though the sprawling, circular shape of Black Rock City was only 10 percent full, we could already make it out against the empty desert-scape. In the middle of it all stood the Man, a huge, angular neopagan idol, destined for immolation in a week's time.

Pug had been emailing back and forth with the Borg—the Burning Man Organization, a weird cult of freak bureaucrats who got off on running this circus—all summer, and he was assured that our little paddock had been left undisturbed. If all went according to plan, we'd drop off the van, unpack it and set up camp, then haul bike-trailers over to the paddock and find out how the Gadget had fared over the summer. I was 90 percent convinced that it had blown over and died the minute we left the desert and had been lying uselessly ever since. We'd brought along some conveniences that could convert the back of the van into a bedroom if it came to that, but we were absolutely committed to sleeping in the yurt. Igloo.

We set off as quickly as we could, in goggles and painter's masks against the light, blowing dust. Most of the campsites were empty and we were able to slice a cord across Black Rock City's silver-dollar, straight out to walk-in camp, where there were only a few tents pitched. Pug assured me that it would be carpeted in tents within a couple of days.

Just past walk-in camp, we came upon the Gadget.

It had changed color. The relentless sun and alkali dust had turned the ceramic/polymer legs, sails, and base into the weathered no-color of driftwood. As we came upon it, the solar panels flickered in the sun and then did their dust-shedding routine, spinning like a drum-major's batons and snapping to with an audible crack, and their dust sifted down into the feedstock hoppers, and then over them. They were full. Seeing that, I felt a moment's heartsickness—if they were covered with dust, there'd be no power. The Gadget must not have been printing.

But that only lasted a moment—just long enough to take in what I should have seen immediately. The Gadget's paddock was *mounded* with tiles.

"It's like a bar chart of the prevailing winds," Pug said. I instantly grasped what he meant—the mounds were uneven, and the hills represented the places where the wind had blown the Gadget most frequently. I snapped several photos before we swarmed over the Gadget to run its diagnostics.

According to its logs, it had printed 413 tiles—enough for two yurts, and nearly double what we'd anticipated. The data would be a delicious puzzle to sort through after the Burn. Had the days been longer? The printer more efficient?

We started to load the trailers. It was going to take several trips to transport all the tiles, and then we'd have to walk the Gadget itself over, set up a new paddock for it on our site, and *then* we'd have to start assembling the yurt. Yurts! It was going to be punishing, physical, backbreaking work, but a crackle of elation shot through us at the thought of it. *It had worked!*

"MASTER, THE CREATURE LIVES!" I bellowed, in my best Igor, and Pug shook his head and let fly with a perfect mad-scientist cackle.

We led the Gadget back by means of a pair of guide ropes, pulling for all we were worth on them, tacking into the wind and zigzagging across the Playa, stumbling over campsites and nearly impaling ourselves on rebar tent pegs. People stopped what they were doing to watch, as though we were proud hunters returning with a kill, and they waved at us and squinted behind their goggles, trying to make sense of this strange centaur with its glinting single eye high above its back.

We staked it into the ground on our site on a much shorter tether and dusted it off with stiff paintbrushes, working the dust out of the cracks and joints, mostly on general principle and in order to spruce it up for public viewing. It had been running with amazing efficiency despite the dust all summer, after all.

"Ready to get puzzling?" Pug said.

"Aye, Cap'n," I said.

We hadn't been sure how many tiles we'd get out of the Gadget over the course of the summer. They came in three interlocking sizes, in the Golden Ratio, each snapping together in four different ways. Figuring out the optimal shape for any given number of panels was one of those gnarly, NP-complete computer science problems that would take more computational cycles than remained in the universe's lifetime to solve definitively. We'd come up with a bunch of variations on the basic design (it did look more like an igloo than a yurt, although truth be told it looked not very much like either) in a little sim, but were always being surprised by new ways of expanding the volume using surprisingly small numbers of tiles.

We sorted the printouts by size in mounds and counted them, plugging the numbers into the sim and stepping through different possibilities for shelter design. There was a scaling problem—at a certain height/diameter ratio, you had to start exponentially increasing the number of tiles in order to attain linear gains in volume—but how big was big enough? After a good-natured argument that involved a lot of squinting into phone screens against the intense glare of the high sun, we picked out two designs and set to work building them.

Pug's arm was pretty much back to normal, but he still worked slower than me and blamed it on his arm rather than admitting that he'd picked a less-efficient design. I was half done, and he was much less than half done, when Blight wandered into camp.

"Holy shit," she said. "You did it!"

I threw my arms around her as she leaped over the knee-high wall of my structure, kicking it slightly askew. She was wearing her familiar sleeveless overalls, but she'd chopped her hair to a short electric-blue fuzz that nuzzled against my cheek. A moment later, another pair of arms wrapped around us and I smelled Pug's work sweat and felt his strong embrace. We shared a long, three-sided hug and then disentangled ourselves and Pug and I let fly with a superheated sitrep on the Gadget's astounding debut performance.

She inspected the stacks of tiles and the walls we'd built thus far. "You guys, this is *insane*. I didn't want to say anything you know, but I never bought this. I thought your gizmo"—Pug and I both broke in and said *Gadget,* in unison and she gave us each the finger, using both hands—"would blow over on its side in a windstorm, break something important, and end up buried in its own dune."

"Yeah," I said. "I had nightmares about that, too."

"Not me," said Pug. "I knew from day one that this would work. It's all so fault tolerant, it all fails so gracefully."

"You're telling me that you never once pictured yourself finding a pile of half-buried, smashed parts?"

He gave me that serene look of his. "I had faith," he said. "It's a gadget. It does what it does. Mechanism A acts on mechanism B acts on mechanism C. If you understand what A, B, and C do, you know what the Gadget does."

Blight and I both spoke at the same time in our rush to explain what was wrong with this, but he held his hands up and silenced us.

"Talk all you want about chaos and sensitivity to initial conditions, but here's the thing: I thought the Gadget would work, and here we are, with a working Gadget. Existence proofs always trump theory. That's engineering."

"Fine," I said. "I can't really argue with that."

He patted me on the head. "It's okay, dude. From the day I met you, I've known that you are a glass-half-empty-and-maybe-poisonous guy. The Playa will beat that out of you."

"I'll help," Blight said, and pinched my nipple. I'd forgotten about her pinches. I found that I'd missed them.

"I hate you both," I said. Pug patted me on the head again and Blight kissed me on the cheek.

"Let me finish unpacking and I'll come back and help you with your Playa-Tetris, okay?"

Looking back on it now, I think the biggest surprise was just how *hard* it was to figure out how to get the structure just right. If you fitted a tile the wrong way in row three, it wasn't immediately apparent until row five or six, and you'd have to take them all down and start over again. Pug said it reminded him of knitting, something he'd tried for a couple years.

"It's just that it's your first time," Blight said, as she clicked a tile into place. "The first time you put together a wall of Lego you screwed it up, too. You've been living with this idea for so long, you forgot that you've never actually dealt with its reality."

We clicked and unclicked, and a pile of broken tiles grew to one side of the site. As we got near the end, it became clear that this was going to be a close thing—what had started as a surplus of tiles had been turned into a near shortage thanks to our breaking. Some of that had been our fault—the tiles wanted to be finessed into place, not forced, and it was hard to keep a gentle approach as the day lengthened and the frustration mounted—but some was pure material defect, places where too many impurities had ganged up along a single seam, waiting to fracture at the slightest pressure, creating a razor-sharp, honeycombed gypsum blade that always seemed to find exposed wrists above the glove line. A few times, chips splintered off and flew into my face. The goggles deflected most of these, but one drew blood from the precise tip of my nose.

In the end, we were three—three!—tiles short of finishing; two from mine, one from Pug's. The sun had set, and we'd been working by head-lamp and the van's headlights. The gaps stared at us.

"Well, *shit,*" Pug said, with feeling.

I picked through our pile of postmodern potsherds, looking for any salvageable pieces. There weren't. I knew there weren't, but I looked anyway. I'd become a sort of puzzle-assembling machine and I couldn't stop now that I was so close to the end. It was the punch line to a terrible joke.

"What are you two so freaked out about?" Blight said. "Just throw a tarp over it."

We both looked at each other. "Blight—" Pug began, then stopped.

"We don't want to cover these with *tarps,*" I said. "We want to show them off! We want everyone to see our totally awesome project! We want them to see how we made bricks out of dust and sunshine!"

"Um, yeah," Blight said. "I get that. But you can use the tarps for tonight, and print out your missing pieces tomorrow, right?"

We both stared at each other, dumbfounded.

"Uh," I said.

Pug facepalmed, hard enough that I heard his glove smacking into his nose. When he took his hand away, his goggles were askew, half pushed up his forehead.

"I'll get the tarps," I said.

THEY CAME. FIRST IN trickles, then in droves. Word got around the Playa: these guys have 3D printed their own yurt. Or igloo

Many just cruised by, felt the smooth finish of the structures, explored the tight seams with their fingernails, picked up a shard of cracked tile to take away as a souvenir. They danced with the Gadget as it blew back and forth across its little tethered paddock, and if they were lucky enough to see it dropping a finished tile to the desert, they picked it up and marveled at it.

It wasn't an unequivocal success, though. One old-timer came by, a wizened and wrinkled burner with a wild beard and a tan the color of old leather—he was perfectly naked and so unself-conscious about it that I ceased to notice it about eight seconds into our conversation—and said, "Can I ask you something?"

"Sure," I said.

"Well, I was just wondering how you turn these bricks of yours back into dust when you're done with them?"

"What do you mean?"

"Leave no trace," he said. His eyes glittered behind his goggles. "Leave no trace" was rule number eight of the ten hallowed inviolable holy rules of Burning Man. I suppose I must have read them at some point, but mostly I came into contact with them by means of Burnier-Than-Thou dialogues with old-timers—or anxious, status-conscious noobs—who wanted to point out all the ways in which my Burn was the wrong sort of Burn.

"Not following you," I said, though I could see where this was going.

"What are you going to do with all this stuff when you're done with it? How are you going to turn your ceramics back into dust?"

"I don't think we can," I said.

"Ah," he said, with the air of someone who was winning the argument. "Didn't think so. You going to leave this here?"

"No," I said. "We'll take it down and truck it out. Leave no trace, right?"

"But you're taking away some of the desert with you. Do that enough, where will we be?"

Yep. Just about where I figured this was going. "How much playa dust do you take home in your"—I was about to say *clothes*—"car?"

"Not one bit more than I can help bringing. It's not our desert to take away with us. You've got sixty thousand people here. They start doing what you're doing, next thing you know, the whole place starts to vanish."

I opened my mouth. Shut it. Opened it again.

"Have you got any idea of the overall volume of gypsum dust in the Black Rock Desert? I mean, relative to the amount of dust that goes into one of these?" I patted the side of the structure—we d started calling them *yurtgloos.*

"I knew you'd say that," he said, eyes glittering and beard swinging. "They said that about the ocean. Now we've got the Great Pacific Garbage Patch. They said it about space, and now Low Earth Orbit is one stray screwdriver handle away from a cascade that wipes out every communications satellite and turns the Lagrange points into free-fire zones. Anywhere you go in history, there's someone dumping something or taking something away and claiming that the demand'll never outstrip the supply. That's probably what the first goat-herder said when he turned his flock out on the Sahara plains. 'No way these critters could ever eat this huge plot down to nothing.' Now it's the Sahara!"

I had to admit he had a point.

"Look," I said. "This is the first time anyone's tried this. Burners have been changing the desert for years. They excavate tons of the surface every year to get rid of the Burn platform and the scars from the big fires. Maybe we'll have to cap how many robots run every year, but you know, it's kind of a renewable resource. Dust blows in all the time, over the hills and down the road. It goes down for yards and yards. They mined around here for a century and didn't make a dent in it. The only thing that doesn't change the world is a corpse. People who are alive change the planet. That's part of the deal. How about if we try this thing for a while and *see* whether it's a problem, instead of declaring it a disaster before it's gotten started?"

He gave me a withering look. "Oh yeah, I've heard that one before. 'Give it time, see how it goes!' That's what they said in Fukushima. That's what they said when they green-lit thalidomide. That's what they said at Kristallnacht."

"I don't think they said that about Kristallnacht," I said, and turned on my heel. Decades on the Internet had taught me that Godwin's law was ironclad: as soon as the comparisons to Nazis or Hitler came out, the discussion was over. He shouted something at my back, but I couldn't hear it over the *wub-wub* of an art car that turned the corner at that moment, a huge party bus/pirate ship with three decks of throbbing dancers and a PA system that could shatter glass.

But that conversation stayed with me. He was a pushy, self-righteous prig, but that didn't mean he was wrong. Necessarily.

IF YOU'RE A BURNER, you know what happened next. We kickstarted an entire flock of Gadgets by Christmas; built them through the spring, and trucked them out in a pair of sixteen-wheelers for the next Fourth, along with a crew of wranglers who'd helped us build them. It was the biggest Fourth of Juplaya ever and there were plenty of old-timers who still say we ruined it. It's true that there was a lot less shooting and a lot more lens-polishing that year.

The best part was the variation. Our three basic tiles could be combined to make an infinite variety of yurtgloos, but to be honest, you'd be hard-pressed to tell one from another. On our wiki, a group of topology geeks went bananas designing a whole range of shapes that interlocked within our three, making it possible to build crazy stuff—turrets, staircases, trusses. Someone showed how the polyominoes could be interlocked to make a play-ground slide and sure enough, come the summer, there was a huge one, with a ladder and a scaffolding of support, and damned if it wasn't an *amazing* ride, once it was ground down to a slippery sheen with a disc-polisher.

The next year, there were whole swaths of Black Rock City that were built out of dust-bricks, as they were called by that time. The backlash was predictable, but it still smarted. We were called unimaginative suburban-ites in tract-house gated communities, an environmental catastrophe—that old naked guy turned out to be a prophet as well as a crank—and a blight on the landscape.

Blight especially loved this last. She brought Maya, her daughter, to the Playa that year, and the two of them built the most amazing, most ambitious yurtgloo you'd ever seen, a three-story, curvy, bulbous thing whose surfaces were finely etched with poems and doodles that she'd fed to the paramaterizer in the 3D-modeling software onboard her Gadgets. The edges of the glyphs were so sharp at first that you could literally cut yourself on them, and before the wind and dust wore them down, they cast amazing shadows down into the gullies of the carve-outs when the sun was rising and setting, turning the wall into a madman's diary of scrib-bles and words.

Maya was indifferent to the haters. She was fifteen and was a trouble-seeking missile with a gift for putting creepers in their place that I was in absolute awe of. I watched her fend off the advances of fratty jocks, weird old dudes like me, and saucer-eyed spacemen dancing to the distant, omnipresent thunder of EDM.

"You raised her right, huh?" I said to Blight.

Blight shrugged. "Look, it sucks to be a fifteen-year-old girl. All that attention, it just gets in the way of figuring out who you are. I'm glad she's good at this, but I wish she didn't have to do it. I wish she could just have a Burn like the rest of us."

I put my arm around her shoulders. "Yeah," I said. "Yeah, that sucks."

"It does. Plus, I don't want to get high because I feel like I've got to keep an eye on her all the time and—" She threw her hands up in the air and looked angrily at the white-hot sky.

"You're feeling guilty for bringing her, aren't you?"

"No, Dr. Freud. I'm feeling guilty for regretting that I brought her."

"Are you sure you're not feeling guilty for regretting that you feel guilty that you brought her?"

She pinched me. "Be serious."

I wiped the smile off my face. "Blight, I love you." I'd said it the first time on a visit to her place just after the last Burn, and she'd been literally speechless for a good ten minutes. Ever since, it had become my go-to trick for winning arguments.

She pinched me hard in the arm. I rubbed the sore spot—every time I came back from a visit to see her, I had bruises the size of grapefruits and the color of the last moment of sunset on both shoulders.

Maya ran past, pulling a giant stunt kite behind her. She'd spent the whole Burn teaching herself new tricks with it and she could do stuff with it that I never would have believed. We cheered her on as she got it into the sky.

"She's an amazing kid," I said. "Makes me wish I'd had one. I would have, if I'd known she'd turn out like that."

Maya's dad was a city manager for a small town in Arizona that was entirely dependent on imported water. He came out twice a year for visits and Maya spent three weeks every summer and alternate Christmases and Easters with him, always returning with a litany of complaints about the sheer tedium of golf courses and edge-city megamalls. I'd never met him but he sounded like a good guy, if a little on the boring side.

"Never too late," Blight said. "Go find yourself some nubile twenty-five-year-old and get her gravid with your child."

"What would I want with one of those flashy new models? I've got an American classic here." I gave her another squeeze, and she gave me another pinch.

"Nothing smoother than an automotive comparison, fella."

"It was meant as a compliment."

"I know," she said. "Fine. Well, then, you could always come down and spend some time when Maya is around, instead of planning your visits around her trips to see her dad. There's plenty of parenting to go around on that one, and I could use a break from time to time."

I suddenly felt very serious. Something about being on the Playa made it seem like anything was possible. I had to literally bite my tongue to stop myself from proposing marriage. Instead, I said, "That sounds like a very good plan. I shall take you up on it, I think."

She drew her fingers back to pinch me, but instead, she dragged me to her and gave me a long, wet, deep kiss.

"Ew," shouted Maya as she buzzed us, now riding a lowrider playa bike covered in fun fur and duct tape. She circled us twice, throwing up a fantail of dust, then screeched to a hockey stop that buried our feet in a small dune that rode ahead of her front wheel like a bow wave.

"You've gone native, kiddo," I said.

She gave me a hilarious little-girl look and said, "Are you my new daddy? Mommy says you're her favorite of all my uncles, and there's *so many* of them."

Blight pounced on her and bore her to the ground, where they rolled like a pair of fighting kittens, all tickles and squeals and outflung legs and arms. It ended with Maya pinned under Blight's forearms and knees.

"I brought you into this world," she said, panting. "I can take you out of it, too."

Maya closed her eyes and then opened them again, wide as saucers. "I'm sorry, Mom," she said. "I guess I took it too far. I love you, Mom."

Blight relaxed a single millibar and Maya squirmed with the loose-jointed fluidity of wasted youth and bounced to her toes, leaped on her bike and shouted, "Suck-errrr!," as she pedaled away a good ten yards, then did a BMX-style front-wheel stand and spun back around to face us. "Bye-ee!"

"Be back for dinner!" Blight shouted.

" 'Kay, Mom!"

The two stared at each other through the blowing dust.

"He's pretty good," Maya shouted again. "You can keep him."

Blight took a step toward her. Maya grinned fearlessly. "Love you, Mom! Don't worry, I won't get into any trouble."

She jammed down on the pedals and powered off toward open playa.

"You appear to have given birth to the Tasmanian Devil," I said.

"Shut up, amateur," she said. "This is what they're supposed to be like at fifteen. I'd be worried otherwise."

BY THE TIME THEY sent Pug home to die, Blight was practically living with me—after getting laid off and going freelance, there was no reason not to. I gave her the whole garage to use as workspace—parked my car in the driveway and ran an extension cord out to it to charge it overnight—but half the time she worked at Minus. Its latest incarnation was *amazing,* a former L.A. Department of Water and Power substation that was in bankruptcy limbo. After privatization and failure, the trustees had inventoried its assets and found that it was sitting on all these mothballed substations and offered them out on cheap short-term leases. Minus was practically a *cathedral* in those days, with thirty-foot ceilings, catwalks, even two behemoth dynamos that had been saved from the scrappers out of pure nostalgia. They gave the place a theatrical, steampunk air—until someone decided to paint them safety orange with hot-pink highlights, which looked pretty damned cool and pop art, but spoiled the theater of the thing somewhat.

Pug was no idiot—not like me. So when he found a lump and asked the doctor to look into it and spent a week fretting about it, he'd told me and Blight and a bunch of his other friends and did a week of staying on people's couches and tinkering with the Gadget and going to yoga class and cooking elaborate meals with weird themes—like the all-coconut dinner that included coconut chicken over coconut rice with coconut flan for dessert. And he arranged for me to drive him to the doctor's office for his follow-up visit.

We joked nervously all the way to the waiting room, then fell silent. We declined to be paged by the receptionist and sat down instead, looking from the big, weird, soothing animation on the fifty-inch TV to the health

pamphlets that invited us to breathe on them or lick them for instant analysis and follow-up recommendations. Some of them seemed to have been
licked already.

"Scott Zrubek?" said the receptionist from the door, looking from her
screen to Pug's face.

"That's my slave name," he said to me as he got up and crossed to her.
"Forget you ever heard it."

Twenty minutes later, he was back with a big white smile that went all
the way to the corners of his eyes. I stood up and made a question of my
raised eyebrows. He high-fived me and we went out to the car. The nurse
who'd brought him back watched us go from the window, a worried look
on her face, and that should have tipped me off.

"All okay, then," I said. "So now where?"

"Let's get some lunch," he said. "There's a chicken shack up on the left;
they serve the best chili fries."

It was one of those drive-in places where the servers clipped trays to
the windows and served your food on them, a retro-revival thing that
made me glad I had vinyl seats.

"What a relief," I said, slurping on my shake. They had tiger-tail ice
cream—a mix of orange and black licorice flavor—and Pug had convinced
me to try it in a shake. He'd been right—it was amazing.

"Uh-huh," he said. "About that."

"About what?"

"Doc says it's in my liver and pancreas. I can do chemo and radio-
therapy, but that'll just tack a couple months on, and they won't be good
months. Doc says it's the kind of cancer where, when a doctor gets it, they
refuse treatment."

I pulled the car over to the side of the road. I couldn't bring myself to
turn my head.

"Pug," I said. "I'm so sorry—"

He put his hand on mine and I shut up. I could hear his breathing, a
little fast, a little shallow. My friend was keeping it together so much better
than I was, but he was the one with the death sentence.

"Remember what you told me about the curve?" he said. "Back when
you thought you had cancer? The older you get, the more friends will die.
It's just statistics. No reason I shouldn't be the next statistic."

"But you're only thirty—"

"Thirty-three," he said. "A little lower on the curve, but not unheard of." He breathed awhile longer. "Not a bad run."

"Pug," I said, but he squeezed my hand.

"If the next sentence to come out of your mouth includes the words 'spontaneous remission,' I'm going upside your head with a roll of quarters. That's the province of the Smurfs' Family Christmas, not the real world. And don't talk to me about having a positive attitude. The reason all those who've died of cancer croaked is because they had cancer, not because they were too gloomy."

"How about Laura?" I said. They'd been dating on and off for a couple months. She seemed nice. Did some kind of investment analysis for an ethical fund.

"Oh," he said. "Yeah. Don't suppose that was going to be serious. Huh. What do you think—tell her I'm dying, then break up; break up and then tell her I'm dying; or just break up?"

"What about telling her you're"—I swallowed—"dying, then giving her the choice?"

"What choice? Getting married? Dude, it's not like I've got a life-insurance policy. She's a nice person. Doesn't need to be widowed at thirty-two." He took his hand back. "Could you drive?"

When we got onto the 10, he chuckled. "Got some good birthdays in at least. Twenty-seven, that's a cube. Twenty-nine, prime. Thirty-one, prime. Thirty-two, a power of two. Thirty-three, a palindrome. It's pretty much all downhill from here."

"Thirty-six is a square," I said.

"Square," he said. "Come on, a *square*? Don't kid yourself, the good ones are all in that twenty-seven to thirty-three range. I got a square at twenty-five. How many squares does a man need?"

"Damn, you're weird," I said.

"Too weird to live, too beautiful to die." He thumped his chest. "Well, apparently not." He sighed. "Shit. Well, that happened."

"Look, if there's anything you need, let me know," I said. "I'm here for you."

"You're a prince. But you know what, this isn't the worst way to go, to tell the truth. I get a couple months to say good-bye, put things in order, but I don't have to lie around groaning and turning into a walking skeleton for six months while my body eats itself. It's the best of both worlds."

My mouth was suddenly too dry to talk. I dry-swallowed a few times, squeezed my eyes shut hard, put the car in gear, and swung into traffic. We didn't speak the rest of the way to Pug's. When we pulled up out front, I blurted, "You can come and stay with me, if you want. I mean, being alone—"

"Thanks," he said. He'd gone a little gray. "Not today, all right?"

Blight wasn't home when I got back, but Maya was. I'd forgotten she was coming to stay. She'd graduated the year before and had decided to do a year on the road with her Net-friends, which was all the rage with her generation, the second consecutive cadre of no-job/no-hope kids to graduate from America's flagging high schools. They'd borrowed a bunch of tricks from their predecessors, most notably a total refusal to incur any student debt and a taste for free online courses in every subject from astronomy to science fiction literature—and especially things like agriculture and cookery, which was a critical part of their forager lifestyle.

Maya had cycled to my place from the Greyhound depot, using some kind of social bike-share that I hadn't ever heard of. On the way, she'd stopped and harvested berries, tubers, herbs, and some soft-but-serviceable citrus fruit. "The world'll feed you, if you let it," she said, carefully spitting grapefruit seeds into her hand. She'd scatter them later, on the next leg of the bike journey. "Especially in L.A. All that subsidized pork-barrel water from the Colorado River's good for something."

"Sounds like you're having a hell of a time," I said.

"Better than you," she said. "You look like chiseled shit." She grabbed my shoulders and peered into my eyes, searched my face. It struck me how much like her mom she looked, despite the careful checkerboard of colored zinc paste that covered her features in dazzle-patterns that fooled facial-recognition algorithms and fended off the brutal, glaring sun.

"Thanks," I said, squirming away, digging a glass bottle of cold-brewed coffee out of the fridge.

"Seriously," she said, pacing me around the little kitchen. "What's going on? Everything okay with Mom?"

"Your mother's fine," I said. "I'm fine."

"So why do you look like you just found out you're going to have to bury euthanized dogs for community service?"

"Is that real?"

"The dogs? Yeah. You get it a lot in the Midwest. Lot of feral dogs around Ohio and Indiana. They round 'em up, gas 'em, and stack 'em. It's pretty much the number one vagrancy penalty. Makes an impression."

"Jesus."

"Stop changing the subject. What's going on, Greg?"

I poured myself some coffee, added ice, and then dribbled in a couple of teaspoons' worth of half-and-half, watching the gorgeous fluid dynamics of the heavy cream roiling in the dark brown liquid.

"Come on, Greg," she said, taking the glass from me and draining half of it in one go. Her eyes widened a little. "That's *good*."

"It's not my story to tell," I said.

"Whose story is it?"

I turned back to the fridge to get out the cold-brew bottle again. "Dude, this is weak. Come on, shared pain is lessened, shared joy is increased. Don't be such a *guy*. Talk."

"You remember Pug?"

She rolled her eyes with teenage eloquence. "Yes, I remember Pug."

I heaved in a breath, heaved it out again. Tried to find the words. Didn't need to, as it turned out.

She blinked a couple times. "How long has he got?"

"Couple months," I said. "Longer, if he takes treatment. But not much longer. And he's not going to take it anyway."

"Good," she said. "That's a bad trade anyway." She sat down in one of my vintage vinyl starburst-upholstered kitchen chairs—a trophy of diligent L.A. yard-saling, with a matching chrome-rimmed table. She looked down into her coffee, which had gone a thick, uniform pale brown color. "I'm sorry to hear it, though."

"Yeah," I said. "Yeah. Me too." I sat with her.

"What's he going to do now?"

I shrugged. "I guess he's got to figure that out."

"He should do something *big*," she said, under her breath, still staring into the drink. "Something *huge*. Think about it—it doesn't matter if he fucks it up. Doesn't matter if he goes broke or whatever. It's his last chance, you know?"

"I guess," I said. "I think it's really up to him, though. They're his last months."

"Bullshit," she said. "They're our last months with *him*. He's going to turn into ashes and vanish. We're going to be left on this ball of dirt

for however many years we've got left. He's got a duty to try and make
something of it with whatever time he's got left. Some thing for me to try
on. Come on, Greg, think about it. What do you do here, anyway? Try
to live as lightly as possible, right? Just keep your head down, try not to
outspend that little precious lump of dead money you lucked into so that
you can truck on into the grave. You and Mom and Pug, you all 'know'
that humans aren't really needed on Earth anymore, that robots can do all
the work and that artificial life forms called corporations can harvest all
the profit, so you're just hiding under the floorboards and hoping that it
doesn't all cave in before you croak."

"Maya—"

"And don't you *dare* give me any bullshit about generational politics
and demographics and youthful rage and all that crap. Things are true or
they aren't, no matter how old the person saying them happens to be." She
drained her drink. "And you know it."

I set down my glass and held my hands over my head. "I surrender.
You're right. I got nothing better to do, and certainly Pug doesn't. So, tell
me, wise one, what should we be doing?"

Her veneer of outraged confidence cracked a tiny bit. "Fucked if I
know. Solve world hunger. Invent a perpetual motion machine. Colonize
the moon."

WE WROTE THEM ON the whiteboard wall at Pug's place. He'd painted
the wall with dry-erase paint when he first moved into the little house in
Culver City, putting it where the TV would have gone a few decades before, and since then it had been covered with so much dry-erase ink and
wiped clean so many times that there were bald patches where the underlying paint was showing through, stained by the markers that had strayed
too close to no-man's-land. We avoided those patches and wrote:

SOLVE WORLD HUNGER
PERPETUAL MOTION MACHINE
MOON COLONY

The first one to go was the perpetual motion machine.

"It's just stupid," Pug said. "I'm an engineer, not a metaphysician. If I'm going to do something with the rest of my life, it has to be at least possible, even if it's implausible."

"When you have eliminated the impossible, whatever remains, however implausible, must be—"

"How have you chosen your projects before?" Maya said. She and Blight sat in beanbag chairs on opposite sides of the room, pointedly watching the wall and not each other.

"They chose me," Pug said. She made a wet, rude noise. "Seriously. It never came up. Any time I was *really* working my nuts off on something, sweating over it, that was the exact moment that some other project demanded that I drop everything, right now, and take care of it. I figure it was the self-destructive part of my brain desperately trying to keep me from finishing anything, hoping to land a Hail Mary distraction pass."

"More like your own self-doubt," Maya said. "Trying to keep you from screwing something up by ensuring that you never finished it."

He stuck his tongue out at her. "Give me strength to withstand the wisdom of teenagers," he said.

"Doesn't matter how old the speaker is, it's the words that matter." She made a gurulike namaste with her hands and then brought them up to her forehead like a yoga instructor reaching for her third eye. Then she stuck her tongue out, too.

"All right, shut up, Yoda. The point is that I eventually figured out how to make that all work for me. I just wrote down the ideas as they came up and stuck them in the 'do-after' file, which means that I always had a huge, huge do-after file waiting for me the second I finished whatever I was on at the time."

"So fine, what's the next on your do-after file."

He shook his head. "Nothing worth my time. Not if it's going to be the last splash. Nothing that's a legacy."

Blight said, "You're just overthinking it, dude. Whatever it is, whip it out. There's no reason to be embarrassed. It'd be much worse to do nothing because nothing was worthy of your final act than to do something that wasn't as enormous as it could have been."

"Believe me, you don't want to know," Pug said. "Seriously."

"Okay, back to our list." She closed her eyes and gave a theatrical shudder. "Look, it's clear that the methods you use to choose a project when you have all the time in the world are going to be different from the method you use when there's almost no time left. So let's get back to this." She drew a line through PERPETUAL MOTION. "I buy your rea sons for this one. That leaves MOON COLONY and WORLD HUNGER." She poised her pen over MOON COLONY. "I think we can strike this one. You're not going to get to the moon in a couple of months. And besides, world hunger—"

"Fuck world hunger," Pug said, with feeling.

"Very nice," she said. "Come on, Pug, no one needs to be reminded of what a totally with-it, cynical dude you are. We've all known all along what it had to be. World hunger—"

"Fuck. World. Hunger," Pug repeated.

Blight gave him a narrow-eyed stare. I recognized the signs of an impending eruption.

"Pug," I said, "perhaps you could unpack that statement a little?"

"Come on," he said. "Unpack it? Why? You know what it means. Fuck world hunger because the problem with world hunger isn't too many people, or the wrong kind of agriculture, or, for fuck's sake, the idea that *we're not doing enough* to feed the poor. The problem with world hunger is that rich, powerful governments are more than happy to send guns and money to dictators and despots who'll use food to control their popula-tions and line their pockets. There is no 'world hunger' problem. There's a corruption problem. There's a greed problem. There's a gullibility prob-lem. Every racist fuck who's ever repeated half-baked neo-Malthusian horseshit about overpopulation, meaning, of course, that the 'wrong' kind of people are having babies, i.e., poor people who have nothing to lose and don't have to worry about diluting their fortunes and squandering their pensions on too many kids—"

"So there's a corruption problem," I said. "Point taken. How about if we make a solution for the corruption problem, then? Maybe we could build some kind of visualizer that shows you if your Congresscritter is tak-ing campaign contributions from companies and then voting for laws that benefit them?"

"What, you mean like every single one of them?" Maya pushed off the wall she'd been leaning against and took a couple steps toward me. "Get serious, Greg. The average elected official spends at least half of their time in office fund-raising for their next election campaign. They've been try-ing to fix campaign financing for *decades* and somehow, the people who

depend on corrupt campaign contributions don't want to pass a law limit-
ing corrupt campaign contributions. Knowing that your senator is on the
take only helps if the guy running against him isn't also on the take.

Come on, dude," she said. "The guy is *dying*, you want him to spend
his last days making infographics? Why not listicles, too?" She framed a
headline with her hands. "Revealed: the ten most corrupt senators! Except
that you don't need a data analysis to find the ten most corrupt—they'll
just be the ten longest-serving politicians."

"Okay," I said. "Okay, Maya, point taken. So what would you do to
fight corruption?"

She got right up in my face, close enough that I could see the fine
dark hairs on her upper lip—she and her cohort had rejected the hair
removal mania of the previous decade, putting umpteen Brazilian wax-
ers and threaders and laser hair zappers on the breadline—and smell the
smoothie on her breath. "Greg, what are you talking about? Ending corruption? Like there's a version of this society that isn't corrupt? Corruption isn't the exception, it's the norm. It's baked in. The whole idea of
using markets to figure out who gets what is predicated on corruption—
it's a way to paper over the fact that some people get a lot, most of us get
not much, and so we invent a deus ex machina called market forces that
hands out money based on merit. How do we know that the market is
giving it to deserving people? Well, look at all the money they have! It's
just circular reasoning."

"So, what then? Anarchist collectivism? Communism?"

She looked around at all of us. "Duh. Look at you three. You've organized your whole lives around this weird-ass gift-economy thing where
you take care of yourself and you take care of everyone else."

"Burning Man isn't real life," Blight said. "God, I knew I should have
waited until you were over eighteen before I took you to the Playa." Her
tone was light, but given their earlier fury at each other, I braced for an
explosion.

But Maya kept her cool. "It's a bitch when someone reminds you of
all the contradictions in your life, I know. Your discomfort doesn't make
what I'm saying any less true, though. Come on, you all know this is true.
Late-stage capitalism isn't reformable. It's an idea whose time has passed."

We all stared at one another, a triangle of adulthood with solitary, furious adolescence in the center.

"You're right, Maya. She's right. That's why the only logical choice is the moon colony."

"You're going to secede from Earth?" Blight said. "Start a colony of anarcho-syndicalist moon-men?"

"Not at all. What I want is, you know, a gift economy dangling like a carrot, hanging in the sky over all our heads. A better way of living, up there, in sight, forever. On the moon. If civilization collapses and some chudded-out mutant discovers a telescope and points it at the moon, she'll see the evidence of what the human race could be."

"What the hell are you talking about?" I said.

He stood up, groaning a little, the way he'd started to do, and half shuffled to his bookcase and picked up a 3D-printed miniature of the Gadget, run up on one of Minus's SLS powder printers. It even had a tiny, optically correct lens that his favorite lab in Germany had supplied; the whole thing had been a premium for a massively successful kickstarter a couple of years before. He handed it to me and its many legs flexed and rattled as it settled on my palm.

"I want to put Gadgets on the Moon. Mod 'em to print moondust, turn 'em loose. Years will pass. Decades, maybe. But when our kids get to the moon, or maybe Maya's kids, or maybe their kids, they'll find a gift from their ancestors. Something for nothing. A free goddamned lunch, from the first days of a better nation."

One part of me was almost in tears at the thought, because it was a beautiful one. But there was another part of me that was violently angry at the idea. Like he was making fun of the world of the living from his cozy vantage point on the rim of the valley of death. The two of us had a way of bickering like an old married couple, but since his diagnosis, every time I felt like I was about to lay into him, I stopped. What if, what if. What if this was the last thing I said to him? What if he went to his deathbed with my bad-tempered words still ringing in the air between us? I ended up with some kind of bubbling, subcutaneous resentment stew on the boil at all times.

I just looked thoughtfully at the clever little Gadget in my palm. We'd talked about making it functional—a $7 Gorseberry Pi should have had the processing power, and there were plenty of teeny-tiny stepper motors out there, but no one could figure out a way of doing the assembly at scale, so we'd gone with a nonfunctional model.

"Can you print with moondust?"

Pug shrugged his shoulders. "Probably. I know I've read some stuff about it along the way. NASA runs some kind of 'what the fuck do we do with all this moondust?' challenge every year or two—you can order synthetic dust to play around with."

"Pug, I don't think we're going to get a printer on the moon in a couple of months."

"No," he said. "No, I expect I'll be ashes long before you're ready to launch. It's gonna take a lot of doing. We don't know shit about engineering for low-gravity environments, even less about vacuum. And you're going to have to raise the money to get the thing onto the moon, and that's gonna be a lot of mass. Don't forget to give it a giant antenna, because the only way you're going to be able to talk to it is by bouncing shortwave off the moon. Better hope you get a lot of support from people around the equator; that'll be your best way to keep it in range the whole time."

"This isn't a new idea, is it?"

"Honestly? No. Hell no. I've had this as a tickle in the back of my brain for years. The first time we put a Gadget out in the dust for the summer, I was 99 percent certain that we were going to come back and find the thing in pieces. But it worked. And it keeps on getting better. That got me thinking: Where's there a lot of dust and not a lot of people? I'd love to stick some of these on Mars, send 'em on ahead, so in a century or two, our great-greats can touch down and build Bradburytown pretty much overnight. Even better, make a self-assembling RepRap version, one that can print out copies of itself, and see how fast you can turn any asteroid, dustball, or lump of interstellar rock and ice into a Hall of Martian Kings, some assembly required."

None of us said anything for a while.

"When you put it that way, Pug . . ." Blight said.

Pug looked at her and there were bright tears standing in his eyes. Hers, too.

"Oh, Pug," she said.

He covered his face with his hands and sobbed. I was the first one to reach him. I put an arm around his shoulders and he leaned into me, and I felt the weird lump where his dislocation hadn't set properly. He cried for a long time. Long enough for Blight, and then Maya, to come and put their arms around us. Long enough for me to start crying.

When he straightened up, he took the little Gadget out of my hand.

"It's a big universe," he said. "It doesn't give a shit about us. As far as we can tell, there's only us out here. If our grandchildren—*your* grandchildren, I mean—are going to meet friendly aliens, they're just going to be us."

PUG LIVED LONGER THAN they'd predicted. The doctors said that it was his sense of purpose that kept him alive, which sounded like bullshit to me. Like the stuff he'd railed against when he'd bitten my head off about "positive attitudes." If having a sense of purpose will keep you alive, then everyone who died of cancer must not have had enough of a sense of purpose.

As Pug would have said, *Screw that with an auger.*

It was a funny thing about his idea: you told people about it and they just *got it*. Maybe it was all the Gadgets out on the playa percolating through the zeitgeist, or maybe it was the age-old sorcerer's apprentice dream of machines that make copies of themselves, or maybe it was the collapse of the Chinese and Indian Mars missions and the bankruptcy of the American company that had been working on the private mission. Maybe it was Pug, or just one of those things.

But they got it.

Which isn't to say that they liked it. Hell no. The day we broke our kickstarter goal for a private fifty-kilo lift to the moon—one-fifth the weight of a standard-issue Gadget, but that was an engineering opportunity, wasn't it?—the United Nations Committee on the Peaceful Uses of Outer Space called a special meeting in Geneva to talk about prohibitions on "environmental degradation of humanity's moon." Like we were going to mess up their nice craters.

The Green Moon Coalition was a weird chimera. On the one hand, you had a kind of axis of paranoid authoritarianism, China and Russia and North Korea and what was left of Greece and Cyprus, all the basket-case countries, and they were convinced that we were a stalking horse for the American spookocracy, striking in the hour of weakness to establish, I don't know, maybe a weapons platform? Maybe a listening post? Maybe a killer earthquake machine? They weren't very coherent on this score.

Say what you will about those weird, paranoid creeps: they sure understood how to play UN procedure. No one could game the UN better except for the USA. If only we'd actually been a front for Big Snoop, maybe they would have had our back.

But that was only to be expected. What I didn't expect was the other half of Green Moon: the environmental movement. I sincerely, seriously doubt that anyone in the politburo or Damascus or the Kremlin or Crete gave the tiniest, inciest shit about the moon's "environment." They just hated and feared us because our government hated and feared them.

But there were people—a *lot* of people—who thought that the moon had a right to stay "pristine." The first time I encountered this idea—it was on a voice chat with a reporter who had caught a whiff of our online chatter about the project—I couldn't even speak coherently about it.

"Sorry, could you say that again?"

"Doesn't the moon have a right to be left alone, in a pristine state?"

"There's a saying, 'That's not right. It's not even wrong.' The moon doesn't have rights. It's a rock and some dust, and maybe if we're very lucky, there's some ice. And the moon doesn't do 'pristine.' It's been hammered by asteroids for two billion years. Got a surface like a tin can that's been dragged behind a truck for a thousand miles. There's no one there. There's nothing there."

"Except for craters and dust, right?"

"Yes, except for those."

The call developed the kind of silence I recognized as victorious. The reporter clearly felt that she'd scored a point. I mentally rewound it.

"Wait, what? Come on. You're seriously saying that you think that craters and dust need to be preserved? For what?"

"Why shouldn't they?"

"Because they're inanimate matter."

"But it's not your inanimate matter to disturb."

"Look, every time a meteor hits the moon, it disturbs more dust than I'm planning on messing up by, like, a millionfold. Should we be diverting meteors? At what point do we draw a line on nature and say, all right, now it's time for things to stop. This is it. Nature is finished. Any more changes to this would be unnatural."

"Of course not. But are you saying you don't see the difference between a meteor and a machine?"

There was no hesitation. "Human beings have just about terminally screwed up the earth and now you want to get started on the moon. Wouldn't it be better to figure out how we all want to use the moon before we go there?"

I don't remember how I got out of the call. It wasn't the last time I had that discussion, in any event. Not by a very, very long chalk. They all ended up in the same place.

I don't know if the mustache-and-epaulet club were useful idiots for the deep greens or vice versa, but it was quite a combo.

The one thing we had going for us was the bankruptcy of Mars Shot, the private Mars expedition. They'd invested a *ton* in the first two stages of the project: a reusable lifting vehicle and a space station for it to rendezvous with. The lifter had been profitable from day one, with a roaring trade in comsat launches. But Mars Shot pumped every dime of profit into SkyHaven, which was meant to be a shipyard for the *Burroughs,* a one-way, twenty-person Mars rocket with enough technology in its cargo pods to establish a toehold on our neighboring planet. And SkyHaven just turned out to be too goddamned expensive.

I can't fault them. They'd seen Mir and SkyLab and decided that they were dead ends, variations on a short-lived theme. Rather than focusing on strength, they opted for metastability: nested, pressurized spheres made of carbon-fiber plastic that could be easily patched and resealed when—not if—it ripped. Free-floating, continuously replenished gummed strips floated in the void between the hulls, distributed by convection currents made by leaking heat from within the structure. They'd be sucked into any breach and seal it. Once an outer hull reached a critical degree of patchiness, a new hull would be inflated within the inner hull, which would be expanded to accommodate it, the inside wall becoming the outside and the outside becoming recyclable junk that could be sliced, gummed, and used for the next generation of patchwork. It was resilient, not stable, and focused on failing well, even at the expense of out-and-out success.

This sounded really good on paper, and even better on video. They had a charismatic engineering lead, Marina Kotov, who'd been laid off from JPL during its final wind-down, and she could talk about it with near-religious zeal. Many were the engineers who went into one of her seminars ready to laugh at the "space condom" and bounded out converts to "fail well, fail cheap, fail fast," which was her battle cry.

For all I know, she was totally right. There were a lot of shakedown problems with the fabric, and one of their suppliers went bust halfway through, leaving them with a partial balloon and nothing they could do about it. Unfortunately for them, the process for making the fabric was patented to hell and back, and the patents were controlled by a speculator who'd cut an exclusive deal with a single company that was a lot better at bidding on patent licenses than it was at making stuff. There was a multi-month scramble while the bankruptcy trustees were placated and a new licensor found, and by then, SkyHaven was in deep shit.

Mars Shot had attracted a load of investment capital and even more in convertible bonds that they'd issued like raffle tickets. Building a profitable, efficient orbit-lifter wasn't cheap—they blew billions on it, sure that they'd be able to make it pay once SkyHaven was done and the Mars Shot was launched. I've seen convincing analysis that suggests that they would never have gotten there—not if they'd had to repay their lenders and make a 10x or 20x exit for their investors.

Bankruptcy solved that. I mean, sure, it wiped out thousands of old people's pensions and destroyed a bunch of the frail humans who'd been clinging to financial stability in a world that only needed banks and robots—people like me. That sucked. It killed people, as surely as Pug's cancer had killed him.

The infrastructure that Mars Shot owned was broken up and sold for parts, each of the lifter vehicles going to different consortia. We thought about kickstarting our own fund to buy one, but figured it would be better to simply buy services from one of the suckers who was lining up to go broke in space. Blight had been a small child during the dot-com crash of the 1990s, but she'd done an AP history presentation on it once, about how it had been the last useful bubble, because it took a bunch of capital that was just being used to generate more capital and turned it into cheap dark fiber bundles and hordes of skilled nerds to fill it with stuff. All the bubbles since had just moved money from the world of the useful into the pockets of the hyperrich, to be flushed back into the financial casino where it would do nothing except go around and around again, being reengineered by high-speed-trading ex-physicists who should know better.

The dot-com legacy was cheap fiber. Once all the debt had been magically wiped off the books and the investors had abandoned the idea of 10–20x payouts, fiber could be profitable.

Mars Shot's legacy was cheap lift. All it took was a massive subsidy from an overly optimistic market and a bunch of hedgies with an irrational belief in their own financial infallibility and bam, there it was, ten glorious cents on the dollar, and all the lift you could want, at a nice, sustainable price.

IT'S A GOOD THING there was more than one consortium running lifters to orbit, because our Indonesian launch partner totally chickened out on us a month before launch. They had deep trade ties to Russia and China, and after one of those closed-door plurilateral trade meetings, everyone emerged from the smoke-filled room convinced that nothing destined for the moon should be lifted by any civilized country.

It left me wishing for the millionth time that we really were a front for Uncle Sam. There was a juicy Colombian lift that went up every month like clockwork, and Colombia was the kind of country so deep in America's pocket that they'd do pretty much anything that was required of them. OrbitaColombia SA was lifting all kinds of weird crap that had no business being in space, including a ton of radioisotopes that someone from GE's nuclear division blew the whistle on much later. Still gives me nightmares, the thought of all those offensive nukes going into orbit, the ghost of Ronald Reagan over our heads for the half-life of plutonium.

In the end, we found our home in Brazil. Brazil had a strong environmental movement, but it was the sort of environmental movement that cared about living things, not rocks. My kind of movement, in other words.

We knew Pug's death was coming all along, and we had plenty of warning as he got sicker and the pain got worse. He got a morphine pump, which helped, and then some of his chemist friends helped him out with a supply of high-quality ketamine, which really, really helped. It wasn't like he was going to get addicted or OD. At least, not accidentally.

The last three weeks, he was too sick to get out of bed at all. We moved his bed into the living room and kept the blinds drawn and the lights down. We worked in whispers. Most of the time, he slept. He didn't get thin the way that people with cancer can get at the end, mostly because of his decision to bow out early, without chemo and radiation therapy. He kept his hair, and it was only in the last week when I was changing his bedpan that I noticed his legs had gotten scarily thin and pale, a stark contrast to the day we'd met and the muscular, tanned legs bulging with veins as he crouched by the proto-Gadget.

But he kept us company, and when he was awake, he kibbitzed in a sleepy voice. Sometimes he was too stoned and ended up making no sense, just tapering off into mumble-mumble, but he had surprisingly lucid moments, when his eyes would glitter and he'd raise his trembling arm and point at something on the whiteboard or someone's screen and bust out a change or objection that was spot-on. It was spooky, like he was bringing us insights from the edge of death, and we all started jumping a little when he'd do it. In this way, little by little, the project's road map took shape: the order of lifter consortia to try, the approaches to try with each, the way to pitch the kickstarter, and even the storyboard for the video and engineering suggestions for sifting regolith.

Pug slept on his hospital bed in the living room. In theory, we all took turns sleeping on the sofa next to him, but in practice, I was the only one who could sleep through the groans he'd make in his sleep but still wake up when he rasped hoarsely for his bedpan. It was just after two, one night, when he woke me up by croaking my name, "Greg, hey, Greg."

I woke and found that he'd adjusted the bed to sit up straight, and he was more animated than he'd been in weeks, his eyes bright and alert.

"What is it, Pug?"

He pointed at a crack in the drapes, a sliver of light coming through them. "Full moon tonight," he said.

I looked at the blue-white triangle of light. "Looks like it," I said.

"Open the curtains?"

I got up and padded to the window and pulled the curtains back. A little dust rained down from the rods and made me sneeze. Out the window, framed perfectly by it like an HD shot in a documentary, was the moon, so big and bright it looked like a painted set lit up with a spotlight. We both stared at it for a moment. "It's the moon illusion," he said. "Makes it seem especially big because we don't have anything to compare it to. Once it dips a little lower on the horizon and the roofs and tree branches are in the same plane, it'll seem small again. That's the Sturgeon moon. August's moon. My favorite moon, the moon you sometimes get at the Burn." It was almost time for the Burn, and my email had been filled with a rising babble of messages about photovoltaics and generators, costumes and conductive body paint, bikes and trailers, coffee and dry ice, water and barbecues and charcoal and sleeping bags. Normally, all this stuff would be a steadily rising chorus whose crescendo came when we packed the latest Gadgets into the van, wedged tight amid groceries and clothes and tents, and closed the doors and turned the key in the ignition.

This year, it was just an annoying mosquito whine of people whose lives had diverged from our own in the most profound way imaginable. They were all off for a week of dust and hedonism; we were crammed together in this dark, dying room, planning a trip to the moon.

"Outside," he said, and coughed weakly. He reached for his water bottle and I helped him get the flexible hose into his mouth. "Outside," he said again, stronger.

I eyed his hospital bed and looked at the living room door. "Won't fit," I said. "Don't think you can walk it, buddy."

He rolled his eyes at the wall, and I stared at it for a moment before I figured out what he was trying to tell me. Behind the low bookcase, the garbage can, and the overstuffed chair, that wall was actually a set of ancient, ever-closed vertical blinds. I dragged the furniture away and found the blinds' pull chain and cranked them back to reveal a set of double sliding doors, a piece of two-by-four wedged in the track to keep them from being forced open. I looked back at Pug and he nodded gravely at me and made a minute shooing gesture. I lifted out the lumber, reaching through a thick pad of old cobwebs and dust bunnies. I wiped my hand on the rug and then leaned the wood against the wall. I pulled the door, which stuck at first, then gave way with a crunchy, squeaky sound. I looked from the hospital bed to the newly revealed door.

"All right, buddy, let's get this show on the road. Moon don't wait for no one."

He gave me a thumbs-up and I circled the bed, unlocking each of the wheels.

It was a good bed, a lease from a company that specialized in helping people to die at home. If that sounds like a ghoulish idea for a start-up, then I'm guessing you've never helped a friend who was dying in a hospital.

But it was still a hell of a struggle getting the bed out the door. It *just* fit, without even a finger's width on either side. And then there was the matter of the IV stand, which I had to swing around so it was over the head of the bed, right in my face as I pushed, until he got wedged and I had to go out the front door and around the house to pull from the other side, after freeing the wheels from the rubble and weeds in the backyard.

But once we were out, it was smooth rolling, and I took him right into the middle of the yard. It was one of those perfect L.A. nights, the cool dividend for a day's stifling heat, and the moon loomed overhead so large I wanted to reach out and touch it. Pug and I were beside each other, admiring the moon.

"Help me lower the back," he said, and I cranked the manual release that gently lay the bed out flat, so he could lie on his back and stare up at the sky. I lay down in the weeds beside him, but there were pointy rocks in there, so I went inside and got a couple of sofa cushions and improvised a bed. On my way out the door, I dug out a pair of binoculars from Pug's Burning Man box, spilling fine white dust as I pulled them free of the junk inside.

I held the binocs up to my eyes and focused them on the moon. The craters and peaks came into sharp focus, bright with the contrast of the full moon. Pug dangled his hand down toward me and wriggled his fingers impatiently, so I got to my feet and helped him get the binoculars up to his face. He twiddled the knobs with his shaking fingers, then stopped. He was absolutely still for a long time. So long that I thought he might have fallen asleep. But then he gently lowered the binocs to his chest.

"It's beautiful," he said. "There'll be people there, someday."

"Hell yeah," I said. "Of course."

"Maybe not for a long time. Maybe a future civilization. Whatever happens, the moon'll be in the sky, and everyone will know that there's stuff waiting for them to come and get it."

I took the binocs out of his loose fingers and lay back down on my back, looking at the moon again. I'd seen the Apollo footage so often it had become unreal, just another visual from the library of failed space dreams of generation ships and jetpacks and faster-than-light travel. Despite all my work over the past weeks and months, the moon as a place was . . . *fictional*, like Narnia or Middle Earth. It was an idea for a theme camp, not a place where humans might venture, let alone *live there*.

Seen through the binocs that night, all those pits, each older than the oldest living thing on Earth, I came to understand the moon as a place. In that moment, I found myself sympathizing with the Green Moonies, and their talk of the moon's pristineness. There was something wonderful about knowing that the first upright hominids had gazed upon the same moon that we were seeing, and that it had hardly changed.

"It's beautiful," I said. I was getting drowsy.

"Jewel," he said, barely a whisper. "Pearl. Ours. Gotta get there. Gotta beat the ones who think companies are people. The moon's for people, not corporations. It's a free lunch. Yours, if you want it."

"Amen," I said. It was like being on a campout, lying with your friends, staring at the stars, talking until sleep overcame you.

I drifted between wakefulness and sleep for a long, weird time, right on the edge, as the moon tracked across the sky. When I woke, the birds were singing and the sun was on our faces. Pug was lying in a stoned daze, the button for his drip in his loose grasp. He only did that when the pain was bad. I brought his bed inside as gently as I could, but he never gave any sign he noticed, not even when the wheels bumped over the sliding door's track. I put things back as well as I could and had a shower and put breakfast on and didn't speak of the moon in the night sky to Blight or Maya when they arrived later that morning.

PUG DIED THAT NIGHT. He did it on purpose, asking for ketamine in a serious voice, looking at each of us in turn as I put the pills in his hand. "More," he said. Then again. He looked in my eyes and I looked in his. I put more tablets in his hand, helped him find the hose end for his water as he swallowed them. He reached back for the morphine switch and I put it in his hand. I took his other hand. Blight and Maya moved to either side of me and rested their hands on the bed rail, then on Pug, on his frail arm, his withered leg. He smiled a little at us, stoned and sleepy, closed his eyes, opened them a little, and nodded off. We stood there, listening to him breathe, listening to the breath slowing. Slowing.

Slowing.

I couldn't put my finger on the instant that he went from living to dead.

But there was a moment when the muscles of his face went slack, and in the space of seconds, his familiar features rearranged themselves into the face of a corpse. So much of what I thought of as the shape of Pug's face was the effect of the tensions of the underlying muscles, and as his cheeks hollowed and slid back, the skin on his nose stretched, making it more bladelike, all cartilage, with the nostrils flattened to lizardlike slits. His lips, too, stretched back in a toneless, thin-lipped smile that was half a grimace. His heart may have squeezed out one or two more beats after that; maybe electrical impulses were still arcing randomly from nerve to nerve, neuron to neuron, but that was the moment at which he was more dead than alive, and a few moments after that, he was altogether and unmistakably dead.

We sat there in tableau for a moment that stretched and stretched. I was now in a room with a body, not my friend. I let go of his hand and sat back, and that was the cue for all of us to back away.

There should be words for those moments, but there aren't. In the same way that every human who ever lived has gazed upon the moon and looked for the words to say about it, so have we all looked upon the bodies of the ones we've loved and groped for sentiment. I wished I believed in last rites, or pennies on the eyelids, or just, well, anything that we could all acknowledge as the proper way to seal off the moment and return to the world of the living. Blight slipped her hand in mine and Maya put her elbow through my other arm and together we went out into the night. The moon was not quite full anymore, a sliver out of its huge face, and tonight there were clouds scudding across the sky that veiled and unveiled it.

We stood there, the three of us, in the breeze and the rattle of the tree branches and the distant hum of L.A. traffic and the far-off clatter of a police helicopter, with the cooling body of our friend on the other side of the wall behind us. We stood there and stared up at the moon.

ADAPTING THE GADGET TO work in a lunar environment was a substantial engineering challenge. Pug had sketched out a map for us—gathering regolith, sorting it, feeding it onto the bed, aligning the lens. Then there was propulsion, which was even more important for the moon than it was on Earth. We'd drop a Gadget on the Playa in July and gather up its tiles a couple of months later, over Labor Day. But the moonprinter might be up there for *centuries,* sintering tetroid tiles and pooping them out while the humans below squabbled and fretted and cast their gaze into the stars. If we didn't figure out how to keep the Gadget moving, it would eventually end up standing atop a bed of printed tiles, out of dust and out of reach of more dust, and that would be that.

This wasn't one Pug had a solution for. Neither did I, or Blight, or Maya. But it wasn't just us. There was a sprawling wiki and mailing list for the project, and at one point, we had three separate factions vying to go to the moon first. One was our project, one was nearly identical in goals except that its organizers were totally committed to a certain methodology for sealing the bearings that our side had voted down.

The third faction—they were *weird*. /b/ was a clutch of totally bizarro trolls, a community that had cut its teeth drawing up detailed plans for invading Sealand—the offshore drilling platform that had been converted to an ill-starred sovereign data haven—moved on to gaming *Time* magazine polls, splintered into the Anonymous movement with all its many facets and runs and ops, fighting everyone from the Church of Scientology to the Egyptian government to the NSA and that had proven its ability to continuously alter itself to challenge all that was sane and complacent with the world, no matter what it took.

These people organized themselves under the banner of the Committee to Protect Luna (SRSLY), and they set out to build a machine that would hunt down *our* machine, and all the tiles it dropped, and smash it into the smallest pieces imaginable. They had some pretty talented engineers working with them, and the designs they came up with solved some of the issues we'd been wrestling with, like a flywheel design that would also act as a propulsive motor, its energy channeled in one direction so that the Gadget would gently inch its way along the lunar surface. They produced innumerable videos and technical diagrams showing how their machine would work, hunting ours down by means of EMF sensors and an onboard vision system. For armament, it had its own sinterer, a clever array of lenses that it could focus with software-controlled servos to create a bug-under-a-magnifying-glass effect, allowing it to slowly but surely burn microscopic holes through our robot.

The thing was, the technical designs were absolutely sound. And though 90 percent of the rhetoric on their message boards had the deranged tinge of stoned giggles, the remaining 10 percent was deadly serious, able to parrot and even refine the Green Moon party line with stony earnestness. There were a lot of people in our camp who were convinced that they were serious—especially after they kickstarted the full load for a killer bot in thirty-six hours.

I thought it was trolling, just plain trolling. *DON'T FEED THE TROLLS!* I shouted online. No one listened to me (not enough people, anyway), and there was an exhausting ramble about countermeasures and armor and even, God help us all, a lawsuit, because yeah, totally, that would work. The wrangle lasted so long that we missed our launch window. The leaders of the paranoiac faction said that they'd done us all a favor by making us forfeit the deposit we'd put down, because now we'd have time to get things *really* right before launch time.

Another group said that the important thing wasn't countermeasures, it was *delay*—if we waited until the /b/tards landed their killer bot on the moon, we could just land ours far enough away that it would take five hundred years for the two to meet, assuming top speed and flat terrain all the way. That spun out into a brutal discussion of game theory and strategy, and I made the awful mistake of getting involved directly, saying, "Look, knuckleheads, if your strategy is to outwait them, and their goal is to stop us from doing anything, then their optimal strategy is to *do nothing*. So long as they haven't launched, we can't launch."

The ensuing discussion ate my life for a month and spilled over into the real world, when, at an L.A. burners' event, a group of people who staunchly disagreed with me made a point of finding me wherever I was to make sure I understood what a dunderhead I was.

I should have known better. Because, inevitably, the /b/tard who was in charge of the money fucked off with it. I never found out what he or she did with it. As far as I know, no one ever did.

After that, I kept my mouth shut. Or rather, I only opened it to do things that would help the project go forward. I stopped knocking heads together. I let Maya do that. I don't believe in generalizations about demographics, but man, could that girl *argue*. Forget all that horseshit about "digital natives," which never meant anything anyway. Using a computer isn't hard. But growing up in a world where how you argue about something changes what happens to it, that was a *skill*, and Maya had it in ways I never got.

"WHAT'S WRONG WITH CALLING it the Gadget?"

Blight looked up from her weeding and armed sweat off her forehead, leaving behind a faint streak of brown soil. She and I traded off the weeding and this was her day, which meant that I got to spend my time indoors with all the imaginary network people and their arguments.

"Leave it, Greg," she said, in that tone that I'd come to recognize as perfectly nonnegotiable. We'd been living together for two years at that point, ever since I sank a critical mass of my nest egg into buying another launch window and had had to remortgage my house. The vegetable garden wasn't just a hobby—it was a way of life and it helped make ends meet.

"Come on," I said. Come *on*. We've always called it 'the Gadget.' That's what *Pug* called it—"

She rocked back on her heels and rose to her feet with a kind of yogic grace. Her eyes were at half-mast, with that cool fury that I'd come to know and dread.

"Pug? Come on, Greg, I thought we agreed: no playing the cult of personality card. He's dead. For years now. He wasn't Chairman Mao. He wasn't even Hari Seldon. He was just a dude who liked to party and was a pretty good engineer and was an altogether sweet guy. 'That's what Pug called it' is pure bullshit. 'The Gadget' is a dumb name. It's a way of announcing to the world that this thing hasn't been thought through. That it's a lark. That it's not serious—"

"Maybe that's good," I said. "A good thing, you know? Because that way, no one takes us seriously and we get to sneak around and act with impunity until it's too late and—"

I fell silent under her stony glare. I tried to keep going, but I couldn't. Blight had the opposite of a reality distortion field. A reality *assertion* field.

"Fine," I said. "We won't call it the Gadget. But I wish you'd told me before you went public with it."

She pulled off her gardening gloves and stuffed them into her pockets, then held out her hands to me. I took them.

"Greg," she said, looking into my eyes. "I have opinions. Lots of them. And I'm not going to run them past you before I 'go public' with them. Are we clear on that score?"

Again, I was stymied by her reality assertion field. All my stupid rationalizations about not meaning it that way refused to make their way out of my mouth, as some latent sense of self-preservation came to the fore.

"Yes, Blight," I said. She squeezed my fingers and dropped her stern demeanor like the mask it was.

"Very good. Now, what shall we call it?"

Everyone who had come to know it through Burning Man called it the Gadget. Everyone else called it the moonprinter. "Not moonprinter."

"Why not? It seems to have currency. You going to tell everyone the name they chose is wrong?"

"Yes," I said.

"Okay, go," she said.

"Well, first of all, it's not a printer. Calling it a 3D printer is like calling a car a horseless carriage. Like calling videoconferencing 'the picturephone.' So long as we call it an anything printer, we'll be constrained by printerish thinking."

"All right," she said. "Pretty good point. What else?"

"It's not printing the moon! It's using moondust to print structural materials for prefab habitats. The way you 'print' a moon is by smashing a comet into a planet so that a moon-sized hunk of rock breaks off and goes into orbit around it."

"So what do you think we should call it?"

I shrugged. "I like 'the Gadget.'"

I ducked as she yanked out one of her dirty, balled-up gloves and threw it at my head. She caught me with the other glove and then followed it up with a muscular, rib-constricting hug. "I love you, you know."

"I love you, too." And I did. Despite the fact that I had raided my nest egg, entered the precariat, and might end up someday eating dog food, I was as happy as a pig in shit. Speaking of which.

"Dammit, I forgot to feed Messy."

She gave my butt a playful squeeze. "Go on then."

Messy was our pig, a kunekune, small enough to be happy on half an acre of pasture grass, next to the chicken run with its own half acre. The chickens ate bugs and weeds, and we planted more pasture grass in their poop, which Messy ate, leaving behind enough poop to grow berries and salad greens, which we could eat. We got eggs and, eventually, bacon and pork chops, as well as chickens. No external fertilizer, no phosphates, and we got more calories out for less energy and water inputs than even the most efficient factory farm.

It was incredibly labor-intensive, which was why I liked it. It was nice to think that the key to feeding nine billion people was to measure return on investment by maximizing calories and minimizing misery, instead of minimizing capital investment and maximizing retained earnings to shareholders.

Messy's dinner was only an hour late, and she had plenty of forage on her half acre, but she was still pissed at me and refused to come and eat from my hand until I'd cooed at her and made apologetic noises, and then she came over and nuzzled me and nipped at my fingers. I'd had a couple dogs, growing up, but the most smartest and most affectionate among them wasn't a patch on a pig for smarts and warmth. I wasn't sure how we'd bring ourselves to eat her. Though, hell, we managed it with the chickens, which were smarter and had more personality than I'd ever imagined. That was the other thing about permaculture: it made you think hard about where your food came from. It had been months since I'd been able to look at a jar of gas-station pepperoni sticks without imagining the animals they had once been.

Messy grunted amiably at me and snuffled at my heels, which was her way of asking to be let out of her pasture. I opened the gate and walked around to the small part of the house's yard that we kept for human leisure. I unfolded a chair and sat in it and picked up her ball and threw it and watched her trot off excitedly to fetch it. She could do this for hours, but only if I varied where I threw it and gave her some tricky challenges.

Maya called them the "brickshitters," which was hilarious except that it was a gift for the Green Moon crowd, who already accused us of shitting all over the moon. Blight wanted "homesteaders," which, again, had all kinds of awful baggage about expropriation of supposedly empty lands from the people who were already there. She kept arguing that there were no indigenous people on the moon, but that didn't matter. The Green Moon people were determined to paint us as rapacious land grabbers, and this was playing right into their hands. It always amazed me how two people as smart as Blight and Maya could be so dumb about this.

Not that I had better ideas. "The Gadget" really was a terrible name.

I threw the ball and thought some more.

WE ENDED UP CALLING it "Freelunch." It wasn't my coinage, but as soon as I saw it, I knew it was right. Just what Pug would have wanted. A beacon overhead, promising us a better life if only we'd stop stepping on one another to get at it.

The name stuck. Some people argued about it, but it was clear to anyone who did lexicographic analysis of the message boards, chats, tweets, and forums that it was gaining with that Internet-characteristic, winner-take-all, hockey-stick-shaped growth line. Oh, sure, the localization projects argued about whether *free* meant "libre" or "gratis" and split down the middle. In Brazil, they used "livre" (Portugal's thirty-years-and-counting technocratic "interim" managers translated it as "grátis").

More than eight thousand of us went to Macapá for launch day, landing in Guyana and taking the new high-speed rail from Georgetown. There had been dozens of Freelunch prototypes built and tested around the world, with teams competing for funding, engineer time, lab space. A co-op in Asheville, blessed by NASA, had taken over the production of ersatz regolith, a blend whose composition was (naturally) hotly debated.

The Brazilian contingent went all out for us. I stayed up every night dancing and gorging, then slept in a different family's living room until someone came to take me to the beach or a makerspace or a school. One time, Maya and Blight and I were all quartered in a favela that hung off the side of an abandoned office tower on impossibly thin, impossibly strong cables. The rooms were made of waxed cardboard and they swayed with the wind and terrified me. I was convinced I'd end up stepping right through the floor and ended up on tiptoes every time I moved. I tried not to move.

Celesc Lifter SA had a little VIP box from which customers could watch launches. It held eight people. The seats were awarded by lottery and I didn't get one. So I watched the lift with everyone else (minus eight), from another favela, one of the old, established ones with official recognition. Every roof was packed with viewers, and hawkers meandered the steep alleys with bulbs of beer and skewers of meat and paper cones of seafood. It was Celesc's ninety-third lift, and it had a 78 percent success rate, with only two serious failures in that time. No fatalities, but the cargo had been jettisoned over the Pacific and broke up on impact.

Those were good odds, but we were still all holding our breath through the countdown, through the first flames and the rumble conveyed by a thousand speakers, an out-of-phase chorus of Net-lagged audio. We held it through the human-piloted takeoff of the jumbo jet that acted as a first stage for the lifter and gasped when the jet's video stream showed the lifter emerging from its back and rising smoothly into the sky. The jet dropped precipitously as the lifter's rockets fired and caught it and goosed it up, through the thin atmosphere at the edge of space in three hundred seconds.

I watched the next part from the lifter, though others swore it was better from Al Jazeera's LEO platform, framed against the earth, the day/night terminator arcing across the ocean below. But I liked the view from the lifter's nose, because you could see the moon growing larger, until it dominated the sky.

Decades before, the *Curiosity* crew had endured their legendary "seven minutes of terror" when its chute, rockets, and exterior casings had to be coordinated with split-second timing to land the spunky little bot on our nearest neighbor without smashing it to flinders. Landing the first Freelunch on the moon was a lot simpler, thankfully. We had a lot of things going for us: the moon was close enough for us to get telemetry and send new instructions right up to the last second, it exerted substantially less gravity than Mars, and we had the advantage of everything NASA had learned and published from its own landing missions. And let us not forget that Earth sports a sizable population of multigenerational lunar lander pilots who've trained on simulators since the text-based version first appeared on the PDP-8 in 1969.

Actually, the last part kind of sucked. A lot of people believed they were qualified to intervene in the plan, and most of them were not. The signal:noise ratio for the landing was among the worst in the whole project, but in the end the winning strategy was the one that had been bandied about since the ESA's scrapped lunar lander competition, minus the observational phase: a short series of elliptical orbits leading to a transfer orbit and a quick burn that set it falling toward the surface. The vision systems that evaluated the landing site were able to autonomously deploy air jets to nudge the descent into the clearest, smoothest patch available.

Celesc's lifter released the Freelunch right on time, burning a little to kick itself back down into a lower orbit to prepare for descent. As their vectors diverged, the Freelunch seemed to arc away, even though it was actually continuing on the exact curve that the lifter had boosted it to. It dwindled away from the lens of AJ's satellite, lost against the looming moon, winking in and out of existence as a black speck that the noise-correction algorithms kept erasing and then changing their mind about.

One by one, all the screens around me converged on the same feed: a split screen of shaky, high-magnification real-time video on one side, a radar-fed line-art version on the other. The Freelunch wound around and around the moon in four ever-tightening orbits, like a tetherball winding around a post. A tiny flare marked its shift to transfer orbit, and then it was sailing down in a spiral.

"Coming in for a landing," Blight said, and I nodded, suddenly snapped back to the warm Brazilian night, the smell of food and the taste of beer in my mouth.

It spiraled closer and closer, and then it kicked violently away, and we all gasped. "Something on the surface," Blight said.

"Yeah," I said, squinting and pinch-zooming at the view from its lower cameras. We'd paid for satellite relay for the landing sequence, which meant we were getting pretty hi-res footage. But the moon's surface defies the human eye: tiny pebbles cast long, sharp shadows that look like deep cracks or possibly high shelves. I could see ten things on the landing site that could have been bad news for the Freelunch—or that could have been nothing.

No time. Freelunch was now in a wobbly, erratic orbit that made the view from its cameras swing around nauseously, a roil of Earth in the sky, mountains, craters, the ground, the black sky, the filtered gray/white mass of the sun. From around us came a low "Wooooah!" from eight thousand throats at once.

Maya switched us to the magnified AJ sat feed and the CGI radar view. Something was wrong—Freelunch was supposed to circle two or three times and land. Instead, it was tumbling a little, not quite flipping over on its head, but rolling more than the gyros could correct.

"Fuck no," I whispered. "Please. Not now. Please." No idea who I was talking to. Pug? Landing was the riskiest part of the whole mission. That's why we were all here, watching.

Down and down it fell, and we could all see that its stabilizers were badly out of phase. Instead of damping its tumble, the stabilizer on one side was actually accelerating it, while the other three worked against it.

"Tilt-a-whirl," Maya said. We all glared at her. In a few of the sims that we'd run of the landing, the Freelunch had done just this, as the stabilizers got into a terminal argument about who was right. One faction—Iowa City–led, but with supporters around the world—had dubbed it the Tilt-a-whirl and had all kinds of math to show why it was more likely than we'd estimated. They wanted us to delay the whole mission while they refactored and retested the landing sequence. They'd been outvoted but had never stopped arguing for their position.

"Shut up," Blight said, in a tight little voice. The tumble was getting worse, the ground looming.

"Fuck off," Maya said absently. "It's the Tilt-a-whirl, and that means that we should see the counterfire any . . . second . . . now!"

If we hadn't been watching closely, we'd have missed it. The Freelunch had a set of emergency air puffers for blowing the solar collectors clear if the mechanical rotation mechanism jammed or lacked power. The Tilt-a-whirlers had successfully argued for an emergency command structure that would detect tumble and deploy the air jets in one hard blast in order to cancel out the malfing stabilizer. They emptied themselves in less than a second, a white, smudgy line at right angles to the swing of the Freelunch, and the roll smoothed out in three short and shortening oscillations. An instant later, the Freelunch was skidding into the lunar surface, kicking up a beautiful rooster-tail plume of regolith that floated above the surface like playa dust. We watched as the moondust sifted down in one-sixth gee, a TV tuned to a dead channel, shifting snow out of which slowly emerged the sharp angles of the Freelunch.

I registered every noise from the crowds on the roofs and in the stairways, every moan and whimper, all of them saying, essentially, "Please, please, please, please let it work."

The Freelunch popped its protective covers. For an instant they stayed in place, visible only as a set of slightly off-kilter corners set inside the main boxy body of the lander. Then they slid away, dropping to the surface with that unmistakable moon-gee grace. The simultaneous intake of breath was like a city-sized white-noise generator.

"Power-on/self-test," Maya said. I nodded. It was going through its boot-up routines, checking its subsystems, validating its checksums. The whole procedure took less than a minute.

Ten minutes later, nothing had happened.

"Fuck," I said.

"Patience," Blight said. Her voice had all the tension of a guitar string just before it snaps.

"Fuck patience," I said.

"Patience," Maya said.

We took one another's hands. We watched.

An hour later, we went inside.

THE FREELUNCH HAD NOTHING to say to us. As Earth spun below the moon, our army of HAM operators, volunteers spread out across the equator, all tried valiantly to bounce their signals to it, to hear its distress messages. It maintained radio silence.

After forty-eight hours, most of us slunk away from Brazil. We caught a slow freighter up the Pacific Coast to the Port of Los Angeles, a journey of three weeks where we ate fish, squinted at our transflective displays in the sun, and argued.

Everyone had a theory about what had happened to the Freelunch. Some argued that a key component—a sensor, a power supply, a logic board—had been dislodged during the Tilt-a-whirl (or the takeoff, or the landing). The high-mag shots from the Al Jazeera sat were examined in minute detail, and things that were either noise or compression artifacts or ironclad evidence of critical damage were circled in red and magnified to individual pixels, debated and shooped and tweaked and enhanced.

A thousand telescopic photos of the Freelunch were posted, and the supposed damage was present, or wasn't, depending on the photo. It was sabotage. Human error. Substandard parts. Proof that space was too big a place for puny individual humans, only suited to huge, implacable nation-states.

THERE AIN'T NO SUCH THING AS A FREELUNCH, the /b/tards trumpeted, and took responsibility for all of it. An evangelical in Mexico claimed he'd killed it with the power of prayer, to punish us for our hubris.

I harbored a secret hope: that the Freelunch would wake up someday, having hit the magic combination of rebooting, reloading, and reformatting to make it all work. But as the Freelunch sat there, settled amid the dust of another world—well, moon—inert and idle, I confronted the reality that thousands of people had just spent years working together to litter another planet. Or moon.

Whatever.

THAT WASN'T A GOOD year. I had another cancer scare because life sucks, and the doc wanted a bunch of out-of-policy tests that cost me pretty much everything left in my account.

I made a (very) little money doing some writing about the Freelunch project, postmortems and tit-for-tats for a few sites. But after two months of rehashing the same ground, and dealing with all the stress of the health stuff, I switched off from all Freelunch-related activity altogether. Blight had already done it.

A month later, Blight and I split up. That was scary. It wasn't over any specific thing, just a series of bickery little stupid fights that turned into blow outs and ended up with me packing a bag and heading for a motel. The first night, I woke up at 3 A.M. to vomit up my whole dinner and then some.

Two weeks later, I moved back in. Blight and I didn't speak of that horrible time much afterward, but when we held hands or cuddled at night, there was a fierceness to it that hadn't been in our lives for years and years. So maybe we needed it.

Money, money, money. We just didn't have any. Sold the house. Moved into a rental place, where they wouldn't let us keep chickens or pigs. Grocery bills. Moved into another place, this one all the way out in Fresno, and got a new pig and half a dozen new chickens, but now we were a three hours' drive from Minus and our friends.

Blight got work at a seniors' home, which paid a little better than minimum wage. I couldn't find anything. Not even gardening work. I found myself sitting very still, as though I was worried that if I started moving, I'd consume some of the savings.

She was working at a place called Shadow Hills, part of a franchise of old folks' homes that catered to people who'd kept their nest eggs intact into their long senescences. It was like a stationary cruise ship—twenty-five stories of "staterooms" with a little living room and bedroom and kitchenette, three dining rooms with rotating menus, activities, weekly crafts bazaars, classes, gyms and a pool, a screening room. The major difference between Shadow Hills and a cruise ship—apart from Fresno being landlocked—was the hospital and palliative care ward that occupied the tenth and eleventh floors. That way, once your partner started to die, you could stay in the stateroom and visit her in the ward every day, rather than both of you being alone for those last days. It was humane and sensible, but it made me sad.

Blight was giving programming classes to septuagenarians whose high schools had offered between zero and one "computer science" classes in the early 1980s, oldies who had managed to make it down the long road of life without learning how to teach a computer how to do something new. They were enthusiastic and patient, and they called out to Blight every time she crossed the lobby to meet me and shouted impertinent commentary about my suitability as a spouse for their beloved maestra and guru.

She made a point of giving me a big kiss and a full-body hug before leading me out into the gardens for our picnic, and the catcalls rose to a crescendo.

"I wish you wouldn't do that," I said.

"Prude," she said, and ostentatiously slapped my ass. The oldies volubly took notice. "What's for lunch?"

"Coconut soup, eggplant curry, and grilled pumpkin."

"Hang on, I'll go get my backup PB and J."

I'd been working my way through an online cooking course one recipe at a time, treating it like a series of chemistry experiments. Mostly, they'd been successful, but Blight made a big show out of pretending that it was inedible and she demanded coaxing and pushing to get her to try my creations. So as she turned on her heel to head back into work, I squeezed her hand and dragged her out to the garden.

She helped me lay out the blanket and set out the individual sections of the insulated tiffin pail. I was satisfied to see that the food was still hot enough to steam. I'd been experimenting with slightly overheating food before decanting it for transport, trying to find exactly the right starting point for optimal temperature at the point of consumption. It was complicated by the fact that the cooldown process wasn't linear, and also depended on the volume and density of the food. The fact that this problem was consuming so many of my cycles was a pretty good indicator of my degraded mental state. Further evidence: I carefully noted the temperature of each tiffin before I let Blight tuck in, and associated the correct temperature with the appropriate record on my phone, which already listed the food weight and type details, entered before I left home.

Blight pulled out all the stops, making me scoop up spoonfuls of food and make airplane noises and feed her before she'd try it, but then she ate enthusiastically. It was one of my better experiments. At one point, I caught her sliding my sticky rice pudding with mango coulis across to her side of the blanket and I smacked her hand and took it back. She still managed to sneak a spoonful when I wasn't looking.

I liked our lunches together. They were practically the only thing I liked.

"How long do you figure it'll be before you lose your marbles altogether?" she asked, sipping some of the iced tea I'd poured into heavy-bottomed glasses I'd yard-saled and which I transported rolled in soft, thick dish towels.

"Who'd notice?"

I started to pack up the lunch, stacking the tiffin sections and slipping the self-tensioning bands over them. Blight gently took them out of my hands and set them to one side.

"Greg," she said. "Greg, seriously. This isn't good. You need to change something. It's like living with a ghost. Or a robot."

A bolt of anger skewered me from the top of my head to my asshole, so sharp and irrational that I actually gasped aloud. I must be getting mature in my old age, because the sheer force of the reaction pulled me up short and made me pause before replying.

"I've tried to find work," I said. "There's nothing out there for me."

"No," she said, still holding my arm, refusing to surrender the physical contact. "No, there's no *jobs*. We both know that there's plenty of *work*."

"I'll think about it," I said, meaning, *I won't think about it at all.*

Still, she held on to my arm. She made me look into her eyes. "Greg, I'm not kidding. This isn't good for you. It's not good for *us*. This isn't what I want to do for the rest of my life."

I nearly deliberately misunderstood her, asked her why she wasn't looking for work somewhere else. But I knew that the "this" she meant was living with me, in my decayed state.

"I'll think about it," I repeated, and shrugged off her hand. I packed up the lunch, put it on the back of my bike, and rode home. I managed to stop myself from crying until I had the door closed behind me.

THAT NIGHT WE HAD sex. It was the first time in months, so long that I'd lost track of how long it had been. It started with a wordless reaching out in the night, our habitual spooned-together cuddle going a little further, bit by bit, our breath quickening, our hands and then our mouths exploring each other's bodies. We both came in near silence and held each other tighter and longer than normal. I realized that there'd been a longer gap since our last clinging, full-body hug than the gap since our last sex. I found that I'd missed the cuddling even more than the sex.

I CIRCLED THE FREEBRUNCH—AS the Freelunch's successor had been inevitably named—nervously. For days, I poked at the forums, downloaded the prototypes, and watched the videos, spending a few minutes at a time before clicking away. One faction had a pretty credible account of how the landing had been blown so badly, and pretty much everyone accepted that something about the bad landing was responsible for the systems failure. They pointed to a glitch in the vision system, a collision between two inference engines that made it misinterpret certain common lunar shadows as bad terrain. It literally jumped at shadows. And the Tilt-a-whirl faction was totally vindicated and managed to force a complete redesign of the stabilization software and the entry plan.

The more I looked over Freebrunch, the more exciting it got. Freelunch had transmitted telemetry right up to the final moments of its landing, definitively settling another argument: "How much should we worry about landing telemetry if it only has to land *once*?" The live-fire exercise taught us stuff that no amount of vomit-comet trial runs could have surfaced. It turned out, for example, that the outer skin of the Freelunch had been totally overengineered and suffered only a fraction of the heating that the models had predicted. That meant we could reduce the weight by a good 18 percent. The cost of lifting mass was something like 98 percent of the overall launch cost, so an 18 percent reduction in mass was something like a 17.99 percent reduction in the cost of building Freelunch and sending it to the surface of the moon.

Blight knew I was hooked before I did. The third time I gave her a cold sandwich and some carrot sticks for lunch, she started making jokes about being a moon widow and let me know that she'd be packing her own lunch four days a week, but that I was still expected to come up with something decent for a Friday blowout.

And just like that, I was back in.

FREELUNCH HAD COST ME pretty much all my savings, and I wasn't the only one. The decision not to take commercial sponsorship on the project was well intentioned, but it had meant that the whole thing had to be funded by jerks like me. Worse: Freelunch wasn't a registered 501(c)(3) charity, so it couldn't even attract any deep-pocketed jillionaires looking for a tax deduction.

Freebrunch had been rebooted by people without any such Burning Manian anticommodification scruples. Everything down to the circuit boards had someone's logo or name on it, and they'd added a EULA to the project that said that by contributing to Freebrunch, you signed over all your "intellectual property" rights to the foundation that ran it—a foundation without a fully appointed board and no transparency beyond what the law mandated.

That had sparked a predictable shitstorm that reached the global newspapers when someone spotted a patent application from the foundation's chairman, claiming to have invented some of the interlock techniques that had been invented by Pug himself, there on the playa. I'd seen it with my own eyes, and more important, I'd helped document it, with timestamped postings that invalidated every one of the patent's core claims.

Bad enough, but the foundation dug itself even deeper when it used the donations it had taken in to pay for lawyers to fight for the patent. The schism that ensued proved terminal, and a year later, the Freebrunch was dead.

OUT OF ITS ASHES rose the Freebeer, which tried to strike a happy medium between the Freelunch's idealism and the Freebrunch's venality. The people involved raised foundation money, agreed to print the names of project benefactors on the bricks they dropped onto the moon's surface, and benefited from the Indian Space Research Organisation's lunar-mapping initiative, which produced remarkably high-resolution survey maps of the entire bright side of the moon. On that basis, they found a spot in Mare Imbrium that was as smooth as a baby's ass and was only a few hundred K from the Freelunch's final resting place.

Of course, they failed. Everything went fine until LEO separation, whereupon something happened—there are nine documentaries (all crowd-funded) offering competing theories—and it ended up in a decaying orbit that broke up over Siberia and rained down shooting stars into the greedy lenses of thousands of dashcams.

FREEBIRD.

(Supported, of course, by a series of stadium shows and concert tours.) Freepress.

(This one printed out leaked WikiLeaks cables from early in the century and won a prize at the Venice Biennale, held in Padua now that the city was entirely underwater. It helped that they chose cables that dealt with the American government's climate change shenanigans. The exiled Venetians living in their stacked Paduan tenements thought that was a laugh-riot.)

That took seven years.

THE LOST COSMONAUT CONSPIRACY theory holds that a certain number—two? three?—of Russian cosmonauts were killed before Gagarin's successful flight. They say when Gagarin got into the Vostok in 1961, he fully expected to die, but he got in anyway, and not because of the crack of a commissar's pistol. He boarded his death trap because it was his ticket into space. He had gone to what could almost certainly have been his death because of his belief in a better future. A place for humanity in the stars.

When you think of a hero, think of Gagarin, strapped into that capsule, the rumble of the jets below him, the mutter of the control tower in his headset, the heavy hand of acceleration hard upon his chest, pushing with increasing, bone-crushing force, the roar of the engines blotting out all sound. Think of him going straight to his death with a smile on his face, and think of him breaking through the atmosphere, the sudden weightlessness, the realization that he had survived. That he was the first human being to go to space.

We kept on launching printers.

Blight and I threw a joint seventieth birthday party to coincide with the launch of the Freerunner. There were old friends. There was cake. There was ice cream, with chunks of honeycomb from our own hive. There were—I shit you not—seventy candles. We blew them out, all of them, though it took two tries, seventy-year-old lungs being what they were.

We toasted each other with long speeches that dripped with unselfconscious sentiment, and Maya brought her kids and they presented us with a little play they'd written, involving little printed 3D printers on the moon.

And then, as we tuned every screen in the house to the launch, I raised a glass and toasted Pug:

"Let us live as though it were the first days of a better nation."
The cheer was loud enough to drown out the launch

FREERUNNER LANDED AT 0413 Zulu on August 10, 2057. Eight minutes later, it completed its power-on self-test routine and snapped out its solar collectors. It established communications with nine different HAM-based ground stations and transmitted extensive telemetry. Its bearings moved smoothly, and it canted its lens into the sun's rays. The footage of its first sintering was low-res and jittery, but it was all saved for later transmission, and that's the clip you've seen, the white-hot tip of the focused energy of old Sol, melting regolith into a long, flat, thin line that was quickly joined by another, right alongside it. Back and forth the head moved, laying out the base, the honeycombing above it, the final surface. The print bed tilted with slow grace and the freshly printed brick slid free and fell to the dust below, rocking from side to side, featherlike as it fell.

One week later, Freerunner established contact with the Freelunch, using its phased-array antennas to get a narrow, high-powered signal to its slumbering firmware. Laboriously, it rebuilt the Freelunch's BIOS, directed it to use what little energy it had to release the springs that locked the solar array away in its body. It took thirty-seven hours and change. We were on the Playa when we got word that the solar array had deployed, the news spreading like wildfire from burner to burner, fireworks rocketing into the sky.

I smiled and rolled over in our yurt. Igloo. Yurtgloo. I was very happy, of course. But I was also seventy. I needed my rest. The next morning, a naked twenty-year-old with scales covering his body from the waist up cycled excitedly to our camp and pounded on the yurt's interlocking bricks until I thought he might punch right through them.

"What," I said. "The fuck."

"It's printed one!" he said. "The Freelunch shit a brick!" He looked at me, took in my tired eyes, my snowy hair. "Sorry to wake you, but I thought you'd want to know."

"Of course he wants to know!" Blight shouted from inside. "Christ, Greg, get the man a drink. We're celebrating!"

The playa dust whipped up my nose and made me reach for the kerchief around my neck, pull it up over my face. I turned to the kid, standing there awkwardly astride his bike. "Well?" I said. "Come on, we're celebrating!" I gave him a hug that was as hard as I could make it, and he squeezed me back with gentle care.

We cracked open some bourbon that a friend had dropped off the day before and pulled out the folding chairs. The crowd grew, and plenty of them brought bottles. There were old friends, even old enemies, people I should have recognized and didn't, and people I recognized but who didn't recognize me at first. I'd been away from the Playa for a good few years. The next thing I knew, the sun was setting, and there were thousands of us, and the music was playing, and my legs were sore from dancing, and Blight was holding me so tight I thought she'd crack a rib.

I thought of saying, *We did it*, or *You did it*, or *They did it*. None of those was right, though. "It's done" is what I said, and Blight knew exactly what I meant. Which is why I loved her so much, of course.

STORY NOTES—Cory Doctorow

Some of the early conversations around this story took place on the Project Hieroglyph website in the "Remote Stereolunagraphy" forum, and with Mark Ganter, co-director of the Open 3D Printing Lab at the University of Washington. Thank you to Jekan Thanga and Katie Levinson for technical feedback. Thank you to Bre Pettis for suggesting the idea in the first place! Thank you to Esther Dyson for getting me involved with *Hieroglyph*. Thank you to Liminal Labs, my Burning Man campmates.

FORUM DISCUSSION—REMOTE STEREOLUNAGRAPHY: Materials and Engineering

Cory Doctorow, Neal Stephenson, and other Hieroglyph community members tackle some of the engineering and storytelling challenges of lunar 3D printing at hieroglyph.asu.edu/the-gadget.

TECHNICAL PAPER—Lunar Regolith Sorting

Read a technical paper from NASA's Microgravity University on sifting lunar regolith at hieroglyph.asu.edu/the-gadget.

TECHNICAL PAPER—First Demonstration on Direct Laser Fabrication of Lunar Regolith Parts

Check out a 2013 article from the peer-reviewed *Rapid Prototyping Journal* evaluating the feasibility of fabricating buildings, tools, and parts from lunar and Martian regolith at hieroglyph.asu.edu/the-gadget.

JOHNNY APPLEDRONE VS. THE FAA
Lee Konstantinou

HE DIED UNDER A Wyoming summer sky, high and blue and marbled with clouds, his interns at his side, just like he would have wanted. Fire nibbled at his rehabbed Volkswagen Westfalia Camper and then swallowed it whole. Its propane gas tank farted, rhythmic, and a tree of black smoke grew with mean leisure into the afternoon. Cars and trucks self-drove down I-80, swerving to avoid the hard heat. Another day, another domestic drone strike. Charlotte took my hand.

"Is this really how it had to end?" I asked.

She said, "He always predicted it would."

"It's my fault."

"We're all partly to blame, Arun."

The other interns looked at us, not wanting to believe Charlotte, but it was true. Still, I had played a special part. My gullibility gave the fucking FAA the opening that it needed. Most likely, anyway. We're still not sure what happened that day. He never told us his real name, never told us anything straight. Everyone called him Johnny Appledrone. The man was a fanatic, possibly crazy, but he finally won me over. He helped me see the world with new eyes.

An orange Fire Drone flew in low, its bladder swollen with chemical retardant.

JOHNNY APPLEDRONE WASN'T INNOCENT. Like all good gurus, he roped you in when you were vulnerable. I wasn't at my best when I met him. I'd earned my worthless social media certification from WCC Facebook Extension and sat on my sad unemployed ass for six months after that. No one wanted to hire a twenty-four-year-old social media grad. I was the first in my family to get something more than a gen ed certification, so I was a little proud. I was reluctant to take work that I thought was beneath me. Jobber, my job-counseling app, kept telling me that we lived in a new economy.

"The newest economy ever!" is actually what he said, dealing poisonous megadoses of algorithmic cheer.

The app came so highly recommended that Maa bought me a year's subscription on her precarious credit line. Jobber was a cartoon beaver, someone's symbol of hard work. "You gotta brand yourself, Arun," he advised me daily, "become a self-starting freelancer." On his advice, I consulted for free a couple times, helping local bands with their social strategy, but creatives are jerks when filling out Reputation Reports. You spend three hours customizing a promotional font, and then they suddenly decide they dislike it or blame you for printing costs.

"It's a vicious cycle, Jobber." I'd gotten into the habit of talking with him late at night, using him off label as a therapist. "If I keep working for free, everyone'll expect me to keep working for free. If I don't, I'll still get nothing."

"I understand you're frustrated, Arun. I hear it in your voice. But in my heart I know you'll find a paying client. Would you like to hear positive testimonials from other social media consultants whose Jobber profiles resemble yours?"

"No, I'm fine."

"I believe in you, Arun. I see your tremendous potential. My advanced analytics tell me you're not the quitting type."

I put Jobber into sleep mode, tears of frustration—and, okay, maybe gratitude—in my eyes. After two years learning frameworks and platforms that were already obsolete, I felt cooked. Living with my parents and sisters in Casper, I slept in every day, drank too much, and smoked up more frequently than was advisable with friends from my old gen ed playgroup, who were, like me, "structurally unemployed." But then one day, I woke up. I felt a fire inside. It wasn't anything particular that lit me up. I just realized that Jobber was right. At bottom, I wasn't the quitting type. I'd take anything, I swore. No matter how low the work, or how little it paid. You have to start somewhere, right? That's what Jobber told me, anyway.

I WORKED EIGHT-HOUR NIGHT shifts, six days a week, making sure BigMachine worked right. It was two hours from home, and it paid shit, but it was a job. The rambling complex was off I-80, a rest stop and Amazon-UPS droneport franchise. You could sometimes catch sight of mechanics in silhouette, quadcopters, tiny zeppelins, and fixed-wing aircraft taking off, landing nonstop. On my side of BigMachine, rigs came in, gassed up, loaded and unloaded cargoes. Truckers, ranging from chunky to obese, drank, ransacked vending machines, in search of diverting calories. Everything at BigMachine was automatic. Well, almost everything. Occasionally, a hose tangled up, an unusually big rat would die in the bathroom, a trucker would collapse drunk on a snooker table with a mighty thud, or a stray drone jammed up with bird poop would drop from the sky. I did what little the robots couldn't, a poorly paid ghost in the machine.

The bosses knew me only as a data plot on their management dashboards. Never met or spoke to me. My time was mostly open, as long as hoses behaved, spindly Lucite robot bartenders got orders right, temperamental vending machines belched out their goods to hungry shoppers, and drunken truckers didn't get too violent. Dimethyl ether fueled trucks; alcohol, people. My consulting career was a nonstarter, so I paid a big chunk of my new income, and burned through my extra time, retraining. Took classes in Microsoft Ampersand and then Iterated C, both at home and during work hours. When classes depressed me too much, I sometimes watched serials, but I never had much love for entertainment media.

Mostly, I was an eyewitness to the end of the age of the truckers. They told me that their days were numbered now that their rigs were mostly automatic. In the beginning, because robot trucks increased total trucking volume, truckers actually got *more* work. More trucks meant more legally mandated drivers, manning machines in case of trouble. But robotrucks became more reliable, and corporate lobbyists gathered in Washington. The law couldn't last. Truckers would eventually have to be sacrificed on the economy's automating altar.

I sympathized with them, though my sympathy wasn't entirely pure-hearted. If the truckers *liked* me—not just BigMachine, but *me* as an individual cog of that machine—my performance scores went up, my evals would reflect those scores, and I'd make a bit more money. So though I saw myself in them, those doomed truckers, though they found me genial enough to tell me their troubles, though they liked me enough to *like* me, I was, basically, whoring myself out for tips. And good at it.

I was surrounded by friendly folk all night, every night, but Big-Machine was a lonely place. I stopped talking to Jobber, ignored his increasingly urgent messages as my one-year subscription expired. It felt awful, like abandoning a real friend, like Jobber *missed* me, but I just couldn't face him. He reminded me of the person I once said I wanted to be.

EVERY HEAD IN THE bar turned. The truckers were too confused to cat-call. Kneeling in a corner, rescuing a reckless cleanbot, I forgot to breathe. When you spend the better part of six months hanging out with cranky middle-aged men, when you haven't talked to a woman your own age for the better part of a year, that's how you might react, too. Charlotte Wong came into BigMachine in full intern regalia: blue pleated pants, crisp white shirt, shoes with gold buckles, leather satchel under her arm. Her black bob shone fluorescently. I knew who she had to be. I-80 often gossiped about Johnny Appledrone.

Johnny was a *dronepunk*. His custom Volkswagen Camper drove up and down the interstate. Its ruined chassis had been replaced with fabbed hard plas. It had a custom sensor and control pack, which did an okay job at driving the vehicle, though sometimes the system rebooted unexpectedly, and the Camper veered off the road. Johnny was too busy to drive it himself. Was always tinkering in his mobile workshop, tweaking custom code for CAD freeware, making local-brew fabricator feedstock, building and refining drone prototypes, adding to forums, thousands of words a night, they said, spinning drone philosophy with the world community of dronepunks. If you were lucky, you'd see one of his small batches, freshly fabbed, rising from his open moon roof. They looked like hummingbirds, like butterflies, like largish cockroaches, sometimes like flying Wiffle balls, but they were basically airborne router/servers, designed to form mesh networks with like-minded devices.

© 2013, Haylee Bolinger / ASU

He was an engineer and an artist, already a legend, to some a hero, to the FAA a menace to the national airspace, which had in the last year become the site of a low-grade war between the agency and those who refused to obey its mandates. No warrant had yet been issued for his arrest. He'd lawyered up pretty good, the ACLU at his back. But the consensus was he couldn't walk free for long. Johnny was a hippie loser, the truckers said, but *whoo-whee!* those girls of his? Johnny's lovely interns? They dressed all Wall Street, were routed to him through the ACLU's pipeline, were committed to *this that or the other thing,* but still, wow. Man had some kind of thing for left-wing yuppie ladies.

"The vending machine," Charlotte said, nervous, which made me nervous.

"What seems to be, you know, the trouble?"

"It . . . It's better if I show you."

I said, "My name's Arun, by the way."

"What?"

"My name . . ."

"Charlotte," she said. "It's a mess. The machine, I mean. It told me you could help."

I FRIENDED HER, DEAR no-nonsense Charlotte. She was a New York City charter-school girl who, by way of Yale and then an ACLU paralegal job, had found Johnny, deferring admission to Columbia Law's certification program to support his mission. Through her, I met the others. All told similar stories: bubbly Beatrice (Wesleyan), Sandy of the Perpetual Smirk

(Vassar), gentle Zara (Brown), and then, when Zara lost her faith, icy Petra (Oberlin). Whenever Johnny's entourage came through BigMachine, usually just the Camper and a support vehicle or two, Charlotte made a point to stop in, say hi, fab skim lattes for the crew. Johnny himself never left the purple Camper. I saw his browned hands once, carpal tunnel braced, reaching out from the side of the van to take his latte and a bag of Extra Calorie Yum-E Pretzel Chips. His dreaded beard was momentarily visible, as if floating free of his face, and in that moment I imagined him as the love child of a sadhu monk and a survivalist Santa Claus.

Charlotte mostly (well, okay, *only*) talked about Johnny's mission. I'd heard about the Drone Commons from the truckers, but she taught me how it worked. Ordinary computers, ordinary networks—that is, the mediasphere—they're filtered end to end. You run illegal encryption software, say, or watch a movie without paying, and your phone knows, and the network you're on knows, and the platform you're using knows, and the servers those platforms are running on know, and soon enough the U.S. Department of Intellectual Property Protection, the National Security Agency, and the Federal Bureau of Investigation know. So you just don't do it, run the software or steal the movie, I mean, however tempting. The system isn't 100 percent foolproof, but it works well enough as a deterrent to illegal activity. The feds can always shut down the physical network if there's real trouble, like they did during that anti-Marriott strike two years ago in Chicago, whose organizers were using illegal encryption to organize the picket line.

On the Drone Commons, by contrast, nothing's filtered. No one owns it exactly, or you could say everyone owns it. It's just out there. Anyone can add devices to it as long as they follow the *Staskowski burst transfer protocol*. You need a special device to use it, since hacking a locked phone is a Class E felony. But it isn't hard to find open devices, Charlotte said, showing me hers (it looked like an ordinary phone), as long as it's made from a legal fabricator. And though it was technically illegal for someone to sell open fabricators, there were hobbyist loopholes, which the dronepunk community exploited.

Frankly, I didn't see why you'd defer your life for Johnny, why building the Drone Commons should amount to a near-religious life project, especially when you could use the perfectly good, ordinary mediasphere, what government PSAs called *hygienic networks*. Yes, the Drone Commons originally grew out of efforts to bring Internet coverage to rural areas, but mediasphere satellites gave better coverage now. And yes, the Commons wasn't technically illegal, but unless you were up to no good, why would you bother to use it? I didn't ask.

I developed a silly crush on Charlotte for a while, but my one-sided ardor faded fast. I realized we'd only ever be friends. Maa had been searching for a nice Indian girl for me to marry, a condition of my living at home. I wouldn't be single much longer. Better to forget Charlotte and Johnny, the romance of their mobile crusade. It was time to refriend Jobber, to plot my final escape from BigMachine.

ON MEMORIAL DAY OF that year, Martin Gallagher did what he did. He hacked the computer of his Freightliner D9000, hooked it up to what looked like a standard fifty-three-foot intermodal container that authorities would later determine had been fabbed in an ad hoc compound near Salt Lake City. Filled the container with fertilizer explosive. Drove to downtown Cheyenne, his own hands at the wheel, in control for once. Parked in front of the tallest building in the city, the newly built regional headquarters of the Department of Transportation, which had recently passed Directive 3482, a trial program experimenting with a small fleet of totally driverless trucks. At nine A.M. of that day, after six minutes and thirty-two seconds, during which time security cameras show him sitting stock-still, staring out his windshield, face neutral, he detonated his truck and himself.

An explosion the equivalent of almost one kiloton near vaporized five city blocks, killing 3,032 souls, injuring ten times as many. It was a miracle more people weren't killed. At that moment, Charlotte and I were having coffee. I'd gotten off my shift at BigMachine, and she was showing me a new prototype drone Johnny had built. A life-real killdeer, down to the smallest particulars. She controlled it with hand gestures, making it fly around my head, laughing at my discomfort, my bashful refusal to try it for myself. Then came a pop, a rattle. Seconds later, chimes cascaded through every phone in the diner. Charlotte got a message from Johnny and left right then, her coffee unfinished, Johnny's life-real killdeer drone left for me to dispose of.

MAA ALWAYS INSISTS I'M a likable guy. You might say my troubles all followed from that fact. Because, you see, Martin Gallagher didn't like much in his miserable life, but he liked BigMachine, and he *liked me*. I didn't make the connection at first—didn't think to check—but the FBI did.

"Let me see if I understand you, Arun. You're saying you don't remember ever talking to Martin Gallagher?"

"No. I mean, I don't know."

The second suited man: "Ten minutes ago, you seemed sure you didn't remember him."

"But then you showed me that video of us talking, and I kind of . . . I'm just saying it's pretty clear I *did* talk to him. I don't deny it. But so many truckers come through BigMachine. It's like *my job* to talk to them."

"Your pay partly depends on them liking you," said the first agent. "Isn't that the case?"

"I never said otherwise."

"So, tell us, did you ever do anything special to make Martin Gallagher like you?"

"You saw the video. I unjammed a vending machine for him."

"We mean anything *else*," said the second. "Because if you can't remember now, now that we've jogged your memory, and we find *another* video . . ."

Two special agents sat at our kitchen table, Maa at their side, more afraid than I've ever seen her. When you're on a work visa, you never forget what the bastards can do to you, even if your children are natural-born. The Fourth Amendment cyborg sat very still on our couch in the living room, her eyes flat clouded lenses, tiny wires burrowing into her head sockets, an occasional glance left, right, her movements sudden and odd. Because she had upgraded senses—enhanced vision, superhearing— she bypassed any Reasonable Expectation of Privacy. What her senses recorded was considered admissible evidence. The case law was ambiguous, Charlotte told me later, and the ACLU had been fighting Fourth Amendment cyborgs for years, courts indecisive on the question, no final settlement in sight. But the fact that the cyborg was there at all was a sign that I was of little importance, part of a broad sweep of data collection, no probable cause for a real warrant. Good news, I guess. But the hunt was ruthless. The FBI, agents of the Department of Transportation, and local law enforcement interviewed me six times. Interviews could last all day. When flesh-and-blood agents got bored or tired, they had me talk with interrogation software that directly accessed my biometric feeds. Then I worked all night. I burned through sick days fast, took a day of unpaid leave, spent what little money I had on legal-defense software, used Red Bull Xtreme Dermal Patches to survive savage shifts. I got groggy and irritable, started fighting with my parents and sisters. My work metrics crashed. Just as my legal expenses mounted, my income shriveled up. I couldn't see the bottom, but I knew that it was coming fast, and that it would hurt like a motherfucker when I hit.

THE CHEYENNE MASSACRE CHANGED BigMachine. Gallagher had released a video manifesto, a seven-hour soliloquy, a darkly frenzied attack against the Department of Transportation, against automated trucking, suggesting all manner of wild conspiracy theory. When asked, I made a point to say I hadn't seen it, wasn't interested in seeing it, and never would be. It was true, too. The truckers weren't sure how to respond. Everyone hated Gallagher, yes. At the same time, he'd taken action, while they, for all their whining and complaining, sat on their hands, waiting for the end, the day they'd finally be fired. The sympathetic chatter—cloaked beneath tortured disclaimers (*"I don't like what he done, but . . ."*)—made me sick. So many died at that monster's hands. How could anyone say a kind word, offer a single qualification or explanation for his actions, include the word *but* in any sentence about him? The truckers knew my views, and though they professed to feel the same way, liked me less than they once had, which further savaged my pay. Gallagher's video was all anyone talked about at BigMachine till the Department of Justice put the kibosh on it. It was material evidence in an ongoing investigation, the press release said. Might contain codes meant for other homegrown terrorists. One day, it was made to vanish from the mediasphere. The truckers, usually an animated lot, even in the darkest times, grew silent, as though they'd gotten some collective memo: *Shut the fuck up about Martin Gallagher.* Loose chatter was no longer allowed.

And then one day the secretary of transportation issued a new directive, and the truckers were gone, literally overnight, as if they'd never existed in the first place. Dozens were arrested, up and down the interstate. The entire trucking fleet of the United States of America became fully automated by fiat. Gallagher sped up what he'd meant to stop. My zone of BigMachine was now almost human-free. I had almost no work. Trucks still fueled up every hour of every day, guzzling DME, but the vending machines stayed full, and the bar was empty, the Lucite robot bartenders museum-still. My dashboard sometimes stayed green all night. Those green lights no longer signaled my diligence, but prophesied my obsolescence. It was just a matter of time before they let me go.

The droneport on the other side of the complex, meanwhile, livened up. Gallagher had used the Commons to plan his attack. He had uploaded his manifesto there, and the authorities couldn't take it down without destroying the physical infrastructure of the mesh network. Newly empowered by Congress, emboldened, the FAA subjected Class G airspace to martial law and policed higher altitudes with a new ruthlessness. The starless sky exploded, night after night. The war was on.

"JOHNNY NEEDS HELP," CHARLOTTE said.

I was wedged between Zara and Sandy in the back of the car. Charlotte and Beatrice faced me from the front seats. We were near Laramie, heading to a diner for an early breakfast. I was starved after a lonely night's work. It was a bit of a shock when Charlotte, who'd asked to meet me, came with the entire retinue of interns. Four months had passed since the blast. I hadn't seen any of them. But I'd messaged Charlotte about my situation at BigMachine, told her my job wasn't likely to last much longer, so they must have known I was desperate.

Charlotte added, "He's been making choices that are . . ."

"They're less than wise," Sandy said. "You might say they're *unwise*."

"We're really worried," Zara said. "Things are superbad."

Most dronepunks were lying low after the Cheyenne Massacre, but not Johnny, never Johnny, Sandy said. The effort to suppress Gallagher's manifesto only confirmed the need for the Drone Commons. The stubborn jerk never used the regular mediasphere, had no idea how the massacre was being covered, how public anger was getting rerouted against dronepunks. Antidronepunk rage was building, but Johnny didn't care. It didn't matter how insane Gallagher's ideas were, didn't matter that he used the Commons to plan his attack. You don't stop bad ideas by hiding them from view. You don't prevent crime by keeping everyone under 24/7 surveillance. Why blame innocent dronepunks for the actions of a madman? Why not blame the fucking Federal Highway Administration? he'd shout. The interns understood his perspective, and as always admired his principles, but they were near rebellion, especially Zara. He ought to quiet down temporarily, she interrupted, angry, wait for the paranoia and sadness to relax, as it would in time. Zara—the only one of Johnny's interns with local roots, the only one who lived at home rather than the motel trailer with the rest—was close to breaking ranks. The whole state was still furious. Everyone knew someone killed or injured by the blast. Someone from Zara's gen ed playgroup had been hurt.

Charlotte: "You've got a social media degree, Arun. Johnny's doing important work, but he isn't one to, let's say, communicate his mission effectively. He assumes you either understand what he's doing or can't be saved. But we've been talking, and we think—"

Sandy: "Look, Johnny needs someone to do publicity."

"And no one respectable will get within ten miles of the guy," I said. "You'd do it yourself, but you've all got, like, actual real work to do, and don't know the first fucking thing about this state and its people, except maybe you, Zara."

Sandy, almost with sympathy: "Bull's-eye."

"Don't be a jerk," Beatrice said. "We're asking for his—for your—*help*."

"Not that you're not respectable," Sandy added.

"His first male intern," I said.

"What's that supposed to mean?" Zara said.

"I'm just . . . I mean, at BigMachine, they say . . ."

"Johnny's not—"

Charlotte interrupted: "People say the most awful things about Johnny. But if you work for him, you'll need to check your assumptions."

"Sorry," I said.

"No, I'm sorry for approaching you this way," Charlotte said.

"Well, how much does Johnny pay?"

The long silence, followed by general snickering, was my answer.

"Oh, Arun. I thought . . . You know what an *intern* is, right?"

FBI AGENTS CONTINUED HARASSING me, casual but persistent. One time—an FAA stormtrooper at their side—they even asked about Johnny. Did he have any connection with Gallagher? Did I approve of his mission? Why did I seem to know his interns so well? On the advice of my legal software, I answered honestly, not mentioning the internship offer, and my answers seemed to satisfy them. When I was served, notified that my networks—and metadata—were under surveillance, most of my so-called friends abandoned me fast. Johnny's interns didn't defriend me, but under pressure from my parents I dropped them. Stopped answering Charlotte's calls. Not that keeping my distance helped. Baba lost his job, officially because of the Bad Economy, but we knew: I was to blame. My sisters still had to pay for their certifications. Only Maa and I were earning money, though I was bringing in less and less every day. BigMachine dropped my shifts. Not much for me to do, they said. If the trend line continued, my hours would zero out in less than a month. Our bank account was in bad shape. We might have to tap our meager retirement investments. I renewed my subscription to Jobber, buying another grossly expensive year of fruitless advice.

"I'm glad you're back, Arun."

"Things aren't going so well, Jobber. Things are, in truth, terrible."

"You can talk to me. Tell me about your troubles."

We talked all night. I'm not proud to admit it, but having Jobber back in my life was such a relief. Sometimes, I'd go to BigMachine to drink, sit alone at the near-empty bar, watch the robot big rigs, and we'd discuss my problems. Jobber revamped my résumé, started sending out hundreds of applications on my behalf every day. I got no interviews, no rejections even. For every open position, hundreds applied, most more experienced than me.

"I know how frustrating this process can be, Arun. But I believe in you. Is there anything we're forgetting?"

"What do you mean?"

"Any opportunities you might, in a self-starting fashion, make for yourself?"

"Well . . . no, nothing."

"I heard you hesitate, Arun. What were you thinking just now, that you didn't say?"

"I guess I've been, well, offered an internship."

"Why didn't you say so?"

"It's a bad internship."

"There's no such thing, Arun. Internships can always lead somewhere."

"It's probably illegal."

"Illegal? Are you sure?"

I told him about Johnny.

"But that's wonderful, Arun. It's an opportunity to work as a social media consultant, which is just what you trained to be. And my legal analytics say that it's not at all against the law to work for him. You can take Jobber's word on that. Our guarantee is always to find you employment in compliance with federal and state law."

"It pays nothing. Literally zero."

"Don't think of it that way, Arun. Think of it in terms of developing your reputation. Just imagine how much attention your work will get if you took on such a high-profile client! Our analysis shows that Mr. Appledrone is at the center of some very influential networks. If you do good work, which I know you will, your future will be unlimited."

I wondered whether I was still employed at BigMachine. I didn't have a shift scheduled for the next two weeks. That was what finally convinced me. When the sun was high enough in the sky that I wouldn't feel embarrassed to admit I was awake, I called Charlotte.

I CROSSED THE LINE. Charlotte picked me up from BigMachine, and we headed to Utah. As the car self-drove, our destination marked by a colorful confluence of hovering objects, drones alighting and taking flight, I decided that Charlotte loved me. Her love was not sexual—it went beyond mere sex—but was instead a sort of bottomless comradeship, togetherness, friendship, whatever. I was drunk. I smiled at her, and she smiled back, tense. The Third Dronepunk Congress was being held in Rockport Exxon Park, on the shore of a dazzling lake, yellow canoes and white sailboats peppering the water's deep blue, new condos rising, being built by robots, on the far shore. Hailing from all over the world, dronepunks circled their wagons, created a temporary city, ostentatiously occupied the recently privatized land. The community was partial to autonomous vehicles of one type or another. The authorities showed restraint, but the ad hoc encampment was ringed by private security, slickly armored in the latest paramilitary gear, armored drones mixing with the civilian variety. Charlotte had a registered pass and gave me a guest pass, allowing me into the fortified encampment.

A circus wheeled in the sky. I gawked at it, the constellation of animals, insects, zeppelins, hot-air balloons, demoniacal parade floats, hovering dolls in various states of undress, a life-real animatronic Superman swooping here and there, banners advertising myriad political views, reflecting the vast ideological range of the dronepunk community. It was a gathering of anarchists, anticopyright libertarians, hard leftists, soft liberals, civil libertarians, militant hobbyists, Pirate Party Scandinavians, transhumanists, Singularitarians, batshit entrepreneurs. Though he fashioned himself as something like the prophet of the dronepunks, Johnny represented only a thin slice of the activist spectrum, albeit a very vocal slice. It instantly seemed less strange to me that his interns dressed like corporate lawyers rather than punk rockers. Maybe I felt the way I did because I was so blotto, but *man oh man,* I thought, *what beautiful sky pollution,* what a dizzying, spiritual poetry of drones.

"C'mon," Charlotte said. "He's waiting."

THE CAMPER WAS PARKED near the WikiLeaks Foundation's thirty-foot-tall life-real inflatable statue of Julian Assange. Johnny had torn out the Camper's sink and gas range, replaced them with a fancy workstation—hoses, test tubes, circuit boards, small vials of fabricator mix—on which dozens of half-finished drone prototypes were splayed, pinned like exotic insects to corkboard. Where the front passenger seat should have been, a fridge-sized fabricator wheezed away. The cabin smelled of hot thermoplastic and human stink. The Camper's owner didn't often shower. In the midst of the beeping, whirring, buzzing machines sat the king, the venerable, wizened Johnny Appledrone himself, bedecked with his dreaded beard, on his ergonomic throne, which made subtle movements in response to thought or gesture. The Camper was an extension of his nervous system. He was overweight, very overweight, dressed in strangely colored military fatigues. He wore open-fingered gloves over form-fitting carpal tunnel braces, held in each hand a multitool, a Leatherman hybridized with some brutal offshoot of Cthulhu. On his face he wore a shiny Byzantine rig. You could call them glasses. Numerous lenses of various strengths and functions, three affixed loupes, rotated into his field of vision at unexpected times. When we entered, he looked up, didn't stop working on his prototypes, typing on primitive keyboards, scanning multiple monitors, also ancient, lashed against the window port.

© 2013, Haylee Bolinger / ASU

"They goddamn just bent over and said to the federal government and to the corporations, go ahead please and fuck us all in the ass!" was the first thing he said to me. "Do you understand?"

"I'd like to, sir," I said.

"You're a polite boy."

"I . . . try."

In its morning session, Johnny explained, the congress had issued a tepid statement offering condolences to the victims of the Cheyenne Massacre, defending the continued need for the Commons, but promising to work with government and law enforcement to help prevent its abuse.

He smiled. "Charlotte didn't warn you. I chew people up if they get in my way."

"No, sir." I looked at Charlotte, who gave me no guidance. "She thought—"

"Thought you might help me. But I'll ask you now, what is it you think you can do for me?"

"I have a social media certification from WCC Fa—"

"WCC?"

"Wyoming Community College. Well, the—"

"Tell me this, Arun. How you gonna explain me to the mainstream world when even my own so-called allies, as I say, bend the fuck over at the slightest challenge?"

I DON'T REMEMBER WHAT I said in reply, but Johnny decided he liked me. My first test would be to write up a press release for the afternoon session. He was part of a panel discussion called "Right to the National Airspace? A Roundtable," featuring Johnny as well as an ACLU lawyer, a technology reporter from *Finn* magazine who'd written three books on national airspace regulations, a sociologist from the University of Texas at Austin, and a representative from the Federal Aviation Administration. It was a headliner event. Promised to be a bloodbath. The room—or rather, the tent—was packed full, hundreds and hundreds jammed together. They booed when the FAA guy, in his cheap suit, took the stage. I was in the front row with the interns and Petra, an intern-in-training, on loan today from the ACLU.

WHEN EXACTLY DID IT come to blows? It's hard to say, even when you review the video, which I have, carefully, many times now. The elegant UT-Austin sociologist, who had an Eastern European accent, gave a jargon-clotted talk, which took far longer than her allotted seven minutes. At one point, she proposed that "reifying the skies" was a response to "secular ouranophobia." Some found her talk rousing, but most of us were perplexed. I understood maybe every fifth word. Bringing us back to earth, the journalist, a middle-aged white guy, gave a shallow, anecdote-filled talk, showing lots of clever slides, concluding with a fatalist shrug that, in the final analysis, the FAA more or less knew what it was doing. The woman from the ACLU—tense, precise—rapidly outlined numerous legal questions related to the peaceful civilian use of drones, hoping that these questions might be addressed in the Q&A period. The FAA guy, nervous as hell, cleared his throat, loaded up his boring-ass presentation, and tried to make the case for the need to control U.S. airspace. It was a matter of national security and public safety, he argued. When he used the phrase "Cheyenne Massacre," the crowd immediately turned against him. Boos, hisses mounted. Some in the audience, die-hard supporters of the FAA, stood and started shouting, "He's right! *He is right!*" Johnny gave a louche grin, leaned back in his chair, laced his fingers behind his head, and let the "FAA neo-fascist" (a term he'd used earlier) stew.

"I can't believe it," Zara whispered.

"What?" I said.

"Johnny's acting like such a jerk. Goading the audience."

"Johnny hasn't said a word," Sandy said.

"But look at him. Smirking like he's enjoying the poor guy's . . . It *was* a massacre. It's, like, a betrayal of everything he supposedly stands for. Johnny could end the boos with a word. Everyone here respects him so much. I . . ."

"Johnny has no obligation to do what you want him to do, Zara."

"I just feel—"

"You know," Sandy said acidly, "Johnny isn't your *boyfriend.*"

Silence choked the intern corner. A formidable taboo had been despoiled.

"I never . . . I *never* . . ." Zara stood up, her eyes wide with shock at what Sandy had said, the gall of it, *how dare she,* and left the tent.

The remaining interns glared at Sandy. They were proud of their professionalism, and Johnny had never even made a slightly inappropriate gesture toward any of them. My attention divided, subdivided. Onstage, Johnny had stood up at some point, resting his weight on the folding table, and was speaking, waving his index finger in outrage. I was supposed to attend to what he said. I had to write a press release about this event. Eventually, I would start managing his status updates, social network communications. "*—know who to feel angrier at, the neo-fascist FAA, or the weak-willed, easily intimidated so-called dronepunks who pretend—*" ("Sit down, fat man!" someone shouted from the audience.) "*—in anything resembling resistance to the corporate state, or if you believe that by asking for power's permission to resist you will—*" ("You have the right to shut the fuck up, Johnny, you fucking cocksucker!") "*—have the right to call yourselves dronepunks, you vile, obsequious, docile, fair-weather—*" I'm still not sure who hit me, but the last thing I remember, before the whole tent fell down around us, was a folded metal chair making its way toward my face.

WHEN WE LEFT THE congress three days later, sans Zara, Petra newly hired, I rode with Johnny in the Camper, my head still aching, my arm burning, now part of his circle of trust. Over instant Ramen cups, as we traversed the interstate, we discussed his social strategy. Johnny showed me his rump me-diasphere sites, of which there weren't many. He didn't bother arguing his side of the drone debate to nonspecialists, thought engaging with mainstream me-dia was beneath him. He had elaborate visions of alternate communications networks, alternate economies, alternate models of human governance. He showed me some of the dronepunk forums he frequented. The rumors were true. He'd written hundreds of thousands of words, sprawling, densely hyper-linked rants. I felt the force of his passion, half-comprehended the allure of the dronepunk community's vision of a genuinely decentralized communications network, no mediasphere satellites, no state approval, no corporate masters. The vision was powerful enough, urgent enough to draw hundreds to the con-gress, to inspire thousands to attempt to build the Commons, to provoke pos-sibly millions to bypass the official mediasphere. It was a universe unto itself, the Commons, a tiny photonegative of daylight media. I imagined explaining Johnny to Maa or Baba. His mission would mean little to them. It made sense only to those who were already converted. That was his main problem. John-ny would have, I saw, only limited public appeal, unless he changed his style. When I tried explaining this to him, at a rest stop, he didn't want to hear it.

"I didn't let you in here for your social media certificate, Arun." We were sitting in lawn chairs he'd set up in front of the Camper. Thousands of drones, disguised as locusts, flew from his fabricator's chute, through the moon roof, in a gorgeous spiral pattern. They were almost silent as they flew away, making only slight chattering noises, seeking out weak patches of the Commons network to fill in.

"Then what have we been talking about?" The day had grown unusu-ally beautiful. "What did I get beat up at the congress for?"

"All that stuff about mainstream social media is interesting enough, which is to say not at all interesting. What I really want to know about is BigMachine."

"You working for the FBI, Mr. Appledrone?"

Johnny slapped his armrest, laughing. "That's right, Arun. I'm a traitor to the cause, just like those motherfucking jerkoff delegates at the congress."

What Johnny wanted was a list of names, the names of truckers who'd liked me, some hint as to their allegiances. The "mainstream dronepunk" community, he explained, was selling itself out. "Give them a year, year and a half tops, and they'll just be some fuckwit political action committee or lobbying group. Which means the end of the Drone Commons as we know it. What I need, Arun, is an army, an army of the newly unemployed, people who need a sense of mission, who're still angry and stung enough to remember what they're fighting for. What's at stake. If you want to help the cause of informational freedom, which is the only true religion, your talents as a social media consultant are irrelevant. We're not trying to persuade the soccer moms to love us. What we need is motivated networks, and a man who can move networks. You seem likable enough, Arun, which is why I let my interns bring you to me, why I let you see the Dronepunk Congress. You know the community of truckers better than you probably realize."

"I don't know if I believe in your cause yet, Mr. Appledrone. The congress was amazing and scary and confusing. What I'm saying is, I don't even know if I fully *understand* your cause. That's what I thought I was trying to do, what Charlotte was asking me to do for you, to translate what you're saying so people like my mom and dad can understand it. If you can't do that . . ."

"Why did you take the job, if you're not sure?"

"I don't know, Mr. Appledrone. I'm unemployed at the moment, and my job-counseling app, Jobber, thought I could use the experience. And I—"

"You're saying Jobber *recommended* you become my intern."

As I answered, I understood my mistake. "He thought . . ."

"And you call Jobber 'he.' Oh, you dumb little boy."

Johnny jumped up from his chair, faster than I would've expected possible, and started poking his Camper with a scanning wand, stopping finally, after ten minutes of searching, near his minifridge. "Look at *that*. Just go *look at that*." Between his fingers Johnny held a big dead cockroach. "Now, you can see it's not one of mine. Bad craftsmanship." Johnny turned it over. Picked at it with his multitool till its legs started running uselessly. Pulled up its wings and unfolded a tiny satellite dish. It unfolded and unfolded. "You brought a friend, Arun."

"What is it?"

Johnny popped off the carapace, looked at its innards with a tiny loupe. "Insect media. *Bioelectronic*. Not meant to kill." Poke, poke. "Maybe surveillance. Possibly meant to hack my physical systems."

"How can you be sure *I* brought it?"

"Maybe it's just a coincidence, Arun, but it's spoofing your DNA. It was invisible to my scanners because I trusted your genome. You need more than a hobbyist fabricator to make this."

"Mr. Appledrone, I'm sorry if I—"

"Don't be sorry." Johnny looked up at the skies, worried. "Be useful.

Help me unload my stuff. Gotta make sure my van is bug-free. Charlotte and the others will be here soon. Called them up, This is a bad sign. While we're at it, we should nuke your phone. Do not trust that job-search app. Trust nothing on the mediasphere, Arun, and maybe someday you'll be less stupid."

IT TOOK A COUPLE hours before Johnny was satisfied that his Camper was clean. Charlotte, Beatrice, Sandy, and Johnny's newly christened intern, Petra, waited for him to give the all clear.

"Why's he so paranoid?" I said.

"Sometimes, he has reason to be," Charlotte said.

"Other times?"

Sandy shook her head, managing to communicate sarcasm without words.

We were hungry, so we decided to drive to a nearby Denny's. Halfway there, Johnny pulled over.

"Something's wrong with the Camper," he said. "I know it. I might need your help, so stay close."

Everyone remained stony. Johnny tested even those closest to him.

"You know," I said to Charlotte. "Johnny didn't want me to do social strategy for him. He wanted the names of truckers to convert. Pick them off while they're desperate."

"I told you," Sandy said. "I *knew* he was bullshitting us."

"What did you tell him, Arun?"

As I considered my answer, I watched Johnny limping toward the Camper. Beneath the fancy dronepunk gear, he was basically an old man, tired, out of breath, but determined. He was of a different era, had grown up in an America that he was, I imagined, sad to see die. None of us knew that other world. It took effort to see with Johnny's eyes, every second requiring tremendous concentration, dedication, and imagination. But thinking of the truckers at BigMachine, remembering their agonized stories, knowing that no mediasphere news site ever seemed interested in telling those stories, thinking how very deranged with despair Martin Gallagher must have been to do what he did, helped me understand Johnny, at least temporarily. "I don't know what I told him," I said, a second or two before what happened happened.

PEOPLE ASK HOW I felt. I don't like talking about it. They say it must have been hard to watch. I usually stay silent at such provocations, but yeah, okay, it was hard. It's only out of a sense of duty that I formulate these sentences, that I say that an unmarked matte-black quadcopter descended lazily from the perfect sky, that it approached the Camper unhurriedly, that we were less scared than confused when we saw it, that the Camper door was wide open. So we could see Johnny sitting atop his ergonomic throne, looking through workstation drawers, convinced that *something* was the matter. What was the matter was that a quadcopter carrying a small bomb was entering the Camper, flying through its open door. What was the matter was that Johnny looked straight on at the copter, blinked once, twice, turned to us, and then calm as could be, reached for his multitool, as if it might save him. What was the matter was that the quadcopter exploded with such force that it knocked us back. Debris flew in all directions. I suffered only minor injuries.

I, TOO, WAS PART of what was the matter.

"I trusted Jobber," I said, confused, half-crazed.

"Calm down. Don't blame yourself, Arun. We came to you."

"You came to me because *you* trusted me. You shouldn't have."

"If we couldn't trust you," Sandy said, "our work would be worthless."

"How do you figure that?"

"Because there'd be no one left to trust, Arun."

JOHNNY SUSPECTED THAT HE might be murdered. He had prepared for the possibility, had backed up his entire archive, all his research, all his notes, set it up to release automatically upon his demise. The Appledrone Archive, as it came to be called, was immediately banned on the official mediasphere, but you couldn't take it down from the Commons. In death, Johnny gained a following he never could in life. The drone that killed him was unmarked, untraceable. It was never clear who'd assassinated him. Most dronepunks were convinced that the FAA did it. The government claimed it was a rival from *within* the dronepunk community, a brilliant piece of propaganda, whether true or not. Other propagandists hinted that Johnny arranged for his own death—the ultimate form of "social media outreach"—to turn himself into the hero he so longed to become. Others spun stories more nefarious, stories involving undergrounds whose exis tence stood somehow athwart even the official shadow life of the republic, whose true motives—whose interlocking design—might never be put wholly into words.

As for me, I'm with the dronepunks. In my heart, I blame the FAA. Whatever the truth, Johnny's death generated huge interest in his mission. Even though Johnny would've hated it, his interns created a nonprofit to spread his vision. The Dronepunk Congress, meeting for a special virtual session, issued a strongly worded statement against the FAA, the FBI, the DOJ, the DIPP. The Commons grew larger as individuals and activist groups created new nodes on the mesh network, designed better encryption, more advanced onion routing schemes. After a week of silence, unusual tolerance, the FAA struck back. It escalated its suppression of the Commons. Soon after, the president signed into law the Hygienic Network Act, in the name of something like the nation's online spiritual health. The HNA closed the hobbyist loopholes that had allowed the Drone Commons to survive as long as it had. It was war, mostly bloodless, not bloodless enough. Everyone had to choose a side.

I TRUST YOU KNOW which side I picked. The FAA continues dismantling the Commons, but not faster than it can rejuvenate itself. That's a kind of victory, albeit temporary, but unless others join the effort, unless our march on Washington next month "changes the conversation," as some dronepunks say, the Commons won't last long. Sustained, mobilized state power is hard to beat. You might think mine is a sad story—my parents and sisters sure do—but don't make that mistake. We're building something, literally building it together. I want my sisters to live in an open republic, an open world, the world Johnny remembered or envisioned. We have our share of problems, but I'm not a pessimist. Haven't despaired. It helps that I won the first Johnny Appledrone Memorial Fellowship. I was, I will admit, a bit of an inside candidate. The award was small but has helped me pay my bills while I've worked to organize this protest. We're commemorating the one year anniversary of Johnny's death. He gave me hope that people working together can change things. His interns labor still, fighting for that better future. I see them now and again, when they pass through Wyoming, all except Charlotte, who returned to New York to get her law certification. We plan to meet up at the protest, to catch up, reminisce.

On reflection, my big mistake is obvious. I thought what I most needed was a job, but Johnny showed me that I needed a vocation. My vocation is to pass his story on. To fight the lies you've heard. Some of the lies are official. Johnny was right: don't believe anything unless you hear it on the Commons, and even then be careful. Don't be a dupe of power. Think for yourself. Organize. But there's an equally troubling effort to turn Johnny into a martyr or holy man. He didn't strike me as anything like that, just someone who was obsessed with informational freedom, someone who seeded the sky with drone poetry. It wasn't a bad obsession, not a bad life. But Johnny Appledrone was just the tip of a big, global iceberg. If you're hearing this, or maybe reading it, you know that much. All I can do is pass him on to you, to show you a jagged sliver of that iceberg through my small, particular memory of him. If you detect some lesson in his story, some abiding truth, go ahead and pass it on. Make it permanent, why don't you.

STORY NOTES—Lee Konstantinou

Citing Jim Karkanias, a researcher at Microsoft, Neal Stephenson defines a hieroglyph as a "simple, recognizable [technological] symbol on whose significance everyone agrees." Examples include "Isaac Asimov's robots, Robert Heinlein's rocket ships, and William Gibson's cyberspace." I prefer the *OED*'s definition of a hieroglyph: "A figure, device, or sign having some hidden meaning; a secret or enigmatical symbol; an emblem." The Drone Commons is meant to be a hieroglyph in this sense. It bears some secret or enigmatical political meaning that I'm not sure I can decipher yet. It's an emblem on whose significance I suspect few will agree. A hieroglyph is therefore, for me, an enigmatic science fictional symbol

about which we find ourselves compelled to argue—in the hope of achieving agreement or at least mutual understanding, in the hope of envisioning
a future that's better than the present. I make my hieroglyph public hoping
some of you will help me make sense of it.

I'm grateful to Braden Allenby, Julian Bleecker, Brenda Cooper, Melodie Selby, Greg Staskowski, and Darusha Wehm for giving me technical
feedback on this idea. I would also like to thank Kathryn Cramer, Ed Finn,
Chin-Yu Hsu, Matt Kirschenbaum, Julie Prieto, and John Mullervy for
reading early drafts of this story. I was inspired by some of the following
texts and projects: Jonathan Zittrain's *The Future of the Internet—And How to
Stop It;* the Electronic Frontier Foundation, especially its Surveillance Self-
Defense site; the New America Foundation's fascinating one-day conference "The Drone Next Door"; Google's Project Loon; the One Laptop Per
Child project; the Tacocopter hoax; the 2011 BART cell-phone shutdown;
the 2011 Internet shutdown in Egypt; as well as a *New York Times* article by
James Glanz and John Markoff, "U.S. Underwrites Internet Detour Around
Censors," on the U.S. attempt to use mesh networks to help foreign activists evade central authorities (in other countries, of course). Though I
encountered them after I wrote the initial draft of this story, I learned
from the dialogue-based book by Julian Assange, Jacob Appelbaum, Andy
Müller-Maguhn, and Jérémie Zimmermann, *Cypherpunks: Freedom and the
Future of the Internet;* Jussi Parikka's *Insect Media: An Archaeology of Animals
and Technology;* as well as reports discussing Amazon Prime Air and Facebook's efforts to build a drone-based Internet.

FORUM DISCUSSION—The Drone Commons

See how Lee Konstantinou pitched his idea for "Johnny Appledrone
vs. the FAA" to the Hieroglyph community at hieroglyph.asu.edu/
appledrone.

Response to "Johnny Appledrone vs. the FAA"—Sri Saripalli

Sri Saripalli, a roboticist at Arizona State University's School of Earth
and Space Exploration, discusses the realism of "Johnny Appledrone vs.
the FAA" at hieroglyph.asu.edu/appledrone.

DEGREES OF FREEDOM
Karl Schroeder

ROBERT SKY GOT THE call while helping his son pick out a new home in West Vancouver. After so many years in Ottawa, on the far side of the continent, he thought maybe his memory was playing tricks on him. He remembered this neighborhood differently—as a place where lichen and moss grew on the curbs, rain-drenched hedges rose twenty feet high, and garden slugs were as long as his thumb. Instead he stepped onto a clean cement sidewalk under blue sky and a hot sun. There were no hedges in sight, and sprinklers were trying to paint over the yellow that had invaded the normally rich green of the lawns.

"What do you think?" Terry spread his arms dramatically.

Rob looked up at the house they'd seen in the listing and grunted. Coral-pink stucco. Not a promising start. "How'd you find it?"

"Nexcity." Terry tapped his glasses.

"Shit, son, that's a nudge."

"It can be." Terry shrugged.

At this point Rob would normally have made some sarcastic remark about using augmented reality to make your decisions for you, but the fact was he had Nexcity open in his own glasses. Instead of saying anything, he took a moment to scout out the neighborhood. "What're they asking?"

"One five."

"Seems low. I wonder . . ." He turned around and saw why houses on this street might be priced lower. Two blocks away, his glasses showed the virtual wire-frame shape of a condominium tower superimposed against the towers across English Bay. The Nexcity app took data from plans registered at the city planning office and made them into a virtual skyline. The historical city; buildings now being built or renovated; what would or could exist here—all were visible through the glasses. Rob's ant-hill plugin annotated the condo project with projected desire lines showing which routes foot traffic was likely to take from the project to the new skytrain line. Much of it went right by the house.

"There goes the neighborhood," he said as he shut the car door. "You don't want to buy here."

"But, Dad, that tower's the only development." Had there been anything else registered at the planning department, it would be visible in Nexcity.

"Condos are like cockroaches. Where there's one, there's bound to be more."

Terry's wife, Margaret, was already inside, but she'd heard this exchange. Her laugh floated out of the foyer. "Check out the staging, boys!"

Whatever the place had looked like before, the fluffers had clearly been at it: all the interior walls were immaculate white, any rugs had been removed to show the blond wood flooring, and the furniture was clearly from some stager's warehouse: it was all utterly generic, like an *Architectural Digest* spread. Margaret was talking to the real estate agent, who looked like the usual bored-housewife recruit. Rob took the information sheet from her, held it up so his glasses could scan it, and overlaid the agent with a liaison for her company.

This synthesized face summarized the ratings given the company by thousands of customers. Bad reviews made it uglier; good reviews, more attractive. The face he saw was bland and unassuming. Not a *bad* company, at least.

Margaret was polite to the agent, taking another information sheet and tapping phones with her. As soon as the woman was out of earshot, she said, "Let's mess the place up a bit and see how it looks."

"What's the overlay?" asked Terry.

"Renovator Two. You got it?"

"Just a minute." Terry and Rob both opened store apps and found the overlay she was using. While they downloaded, she changed the wall colors and countertops in her overlay, then passed them on. The new view included renders of their paintings from back home—Kent Monkman originals, of course. Rob rolled his eyes, but actually, eggplant and lime green went better together here than he would have imagined.

Being pleased with something made him instantly suspicious. "The real estate companies pay these app makers, you know," he said. "Illusion of control. And the colors aren't what you'd actually see. Virtual paint ain't paint."

"Oh, Dad." As they looked at the bedrooms, he could see that Terry was convinced. Rob thought they could do better, but he would have happily gone along with Terry's decision had his son not suddenly said, "How's your Dorian look, Maggie?"

Rob snorted. "Oh, you've joined that damned cult, have you?"

"Dad, it's just more decision-support software."

"And you need more help making decisions? Pah."

At that moment Rob got the call. He stood there for a minute with his hand to his ear—motionless, so that Terry and Margaret shrugged and went to look at the en suite.

"Jesus," said Rob.

Terry poked his head out of the little bathroom. "What is it?"

"Should I come back to Ottawa? No, here's better, right . . . three hours." He blinked and looked over at his son. "No matter how hard we try, we can't escape our roots," he said.

"What do you mean?"

"A goddamned tanker's run aground in the Inside Passage. It's the worst possible moment, 'cause we've almost sealed the negotiations to build the Northern Gateway Pipeline." That pipeline was the last chance for Alberta's oil sands, as all other transportation costs skyrocketed and pipelines through the United States and east into Ontario had been stymied. "The First Nations were the roadblock, and they were about to sign on. That goddamned tanker just handed them a big environmental stick to beat us with. They're insisting on final, binding renegotiations of their original treaties. Land for oil, it's that simple. And guess who's leading the charge?"

"Oh. Don't tell me, it's—"

"You're always so proud to call them *our* people," said Robert Skaay. "Well, *our* people want a lands-claim settlement—and they're gonna use this spill to get it."

"The Haida are blocking the pipeline?" Rob could see the hint of excitement in Terry's eyes.

He sighed. "Not the pipeline, but the tanker terminal, which is pretty much the same thing?

"And it looks like I'm going to be across the table from them."

"FORTY THOUSAND TONNES DRY weight," said Krishnamurti, director of the Canadian Security and Intelligence Service. "We're not sure how much oil it was carrying but it's enough to make a hell of a mess. We're pretty sure the Haida are behind it."

Robert had taken over a conference room in downtown Vancouver and dimmed the lights so his glasses could take over, projecting a virtual rendition of the Ottawa room where the rest of the cabinet ministers sat. Like Rob, Krishnamurti was attending the meeting remotely.

The prime minister leaned back in his chair, arms crossed and obviously angry. "The Haida would never *cause* an environmental catastrophe! They're all about preserving the land, aren't they?"

All eyes turned to Rob. He sighed. "How would I know?" He stared them all down. After all this time they should know he'd never lived in the Haida Gwaii.

They should also know that, behind anything the Haida did these days, there was a couple hundred years' worth of frustration with the Canadian government's bad faith and broken treaty promises.

Krishnamurti cleared his throat. "It's not *their* shoreline that's threatened. There's a mosaic of overlapping First Nations around the Passage, like the Oweekeno and the In-SHUCK-ch. The Haida may have risked screwing them over for the greater good."

"More likely they're all in on it," said the minister of foreign affairs. "The bands that are affected can sue us for compensation."

Rob shook his head. "But why do you think the Haida are behind it? Was there a bomb on the ship?"

"It's purely circumstantial," said the CSIS director. "It's about timing."

"Can you pass Rob that overlay?" said the prime minister to Krishnamurti.

"Right." A flag in the corner of Rob's vision told him he had new e-mail with an attachment. He blinked at the symbol for the attachment and something loaded into his interface. "What is it?"

"Have you got a window to look out? It works best that way."

Warily, Rob rose and shifted the heavy curtain. Outside sprawled the green glass towers of downtown Vancouver. He could see the ski runs on Grouse Mountain, a green crosshatch under the summer sky.

Standing up out of the city in a protusion as thick as the surrounding forests were thousands of virtual flags. He poked at one and expanded it so he could see the caption. It was a man's name, vaguely familiar; a spiderweb of faint lines radiated out from it. "What is this?"

"It's an augmented reality overlay that tells you who owns what," said Krishnamurti. "A Big Data aggregation of publicly available information on real estate, machinery, infrastructure, you name it—linked back to the shareholders, boards, and individuals who own it. A map of who owns what . . . and not just modern financial data. It's got all the First Nations land claims. It was uploaded to the Vancouver Urban Overlays site six hours ago, just before the tanker ran aground.

"Whoever uploaded it did so from Haida Gwaii."

WHEN ROB WAS GROWING up, they'd still been called the Queen Charlotte Islands. An hour north of Vancouver by plane, the Gwaii nestled just under the Alaskan Panhandle. An inverted triangle of coastal rain forest, the islands were known for their gigantic trees and for the art that those had inspired. As inhabitants of one of the last areas of North America to be touched by European conquest, the islanders had a more direct connection to their ancestry than any other Canadian First Nation; their strength hadn't faded until around 1900 when smallpox devastated the islands.

That the aboriginal side of Rob's family was from there had always meant, well, nothing, to him. Artistic though they might be, the Haida were a footnote in North American history. Yet they had never entirely gone away, and they had never thought of themselves as a conquered people.

Maybe it was that one simple fact about them that made them dangerous.

He looked behind him. The augmented reality interface gave Rob the illusion that he was not standing alone in a commandeered conference room high above the Vancouver skyline but was in fact closeted with the rest of the cabinet back in Ottawa. Turning back to the window, he stared out at the unsettling skyline, wondering how many other people were looking at the city—the country—through the same new lens. This app was a step beyond Nexcity, which merely showed you the future of local real estate. This . . . this was inequality made visible

It wasn't just the present-day ownership tags. The whole visible vista of mountains and coast was subdivided by faint curving virtual walls, like the sheets of the northern lights, except tagged with the relevant treaty claims. All the betrayals by the British and Canadian governments over the centuries were visible, shimmering in the sky. Even the currency that the money was counted in—it wasn't dollars, but Gwaiicoin. That variant of Bitcoin was quickly becoming the most popular currency on the West Coast, and not just among the First Nations.

There was more.

The interface included something called *Fountains View*. When he tried it, the skyscape shifted; instead of shimmering walls of light, he was looking at . . . well, fountains. Fountains of money, rising off Indian lands and falling on the city, into glass-walled towers that wore the logos of logging and mining companies like crowns. Fountains of money that you could follow as they left the lands of the Aishihik and Te'mexw, the Klahoose and Nazko, and vanished into the vaults of white men—an accusation as clear as a cry from God.

"This can't be legal," he said. "Where are they getting the data?"

"It's all from legal sources. Shareholders' reports, mostly," said Krishnamurti.

"We think the same people somehow grounded the tanker?"

"We don't know it for sure. We're assembling a liaison for them. Here, I'll bring it up."

Rob turned back to the conference room, repopulated with the transparent images of his colleagues and a newcomer. A new figure sat in one of the previously empty chairs: a young aboriginal man, well dressed and calm, who gazed back at Rob through intelligent, dark eyes.

Rob shuddered. "Is it live?"

"Not yet; we don't have enough behavior of the group it models to bring it to life. When it is, maybe we can learn more."

"Meanwhile," said the prime minister, "let's look at our policy options. Your people have run the padgets?" Krishnamurti nodded and called up SimCanada. Back in Ottawa, it would be appearing on the wall screen; for Robert, the data sprang to life as a series of virtual screens floating in and even beyond the boundaries of the room.

There were sixteen Canadas up there, blotched with color that showed relative levels of political support for the Party, as well as economic well-being across the country, industrial measures, and even those new intangibles, the "happiness quotients" that were in such vogue now. Each map showed a different possible future for the country. The damned program provided only multiple futures, never a single projection, which was one of the things Rob hated about it. It had to do with how morphological analysis worked, but it was annoying anyway. What good was a system that let you see the future if it couldn't tell you *which* future was going to come to pass?

The sixteen maps showed Canadas six months from now, based on different policy choices the government was working on. These options were flight-tested in an agent-based simulation of the entire country that included the behavior of individual virtual citizens. The simulations were fed by real-time polling and econometric data, and by data from the padgets—policy-development gadgets—employed by the country's political parties. Krishnamurti used a slider on the screen to move forward and backward in time and sideways through the different options. "So here are the results with and without the tanker spill, depending on which of the response packages we select. As you can see, there's broad support for a crackdown to start with, but the padgets show quick deterioration of public support if the perceived threat declines . . ."

Robert expanded several of the maps to look at them more closely. That land-claims overlay was a dirty trick, and some of the Canadas showed the effect it might have if this was just the opening salvo in a more sophisticated information war. The scariest one was where the electorate somehow woke up to the fact that only 16 percent of the eligible voters had cast their ballots for the sitting government. Robert's party had muzzled Elections Canada back in 2014 so the bureaucrats couldn't even study the actual numbers, much less tell the public that less than 50 percent of them had voted last time. Rob only knew because the Party could afford to pay for private studies.

The more he looked at the sims, though, the more puzzled he became. "The only scenarios where we can win the next election are ones where we finally negotiate binding land-claims settlements with the Haida and the other First Nations," he said. "How do they get to extort us and pull a propaganda stunt like that overlay, and still make us look like the bad guys if we don't come to the table?"

Krishnamurti exchanged a glance with the prime minister. "Demographics," said Bill Michener, who had been prime minister for four years and was comfortable in the job. "The aboriginal population's booming, while the rest of us are in decline; and lately, they're turning out to vote in record numbers."

"But there's more to it than that," added the CSIS director. "Five years ago only we could afford the processing power for something like this." He nodded at the SimCanada maps. "And only we had the data. Now . . . so much information is publicly available, and with block chains running on mobile phone meshnets . . . we think the Haida are running their own SimCanadas. They've been war-gaming this scenario, maybe for months. This isn't just a bunch of boys who got all fired up and decided to make a roadblock. It's a calculated power play directed against the federal government of Canada."

"It's not about either of these stunts on their own," said Bill. "It's the overall pattern. They want to do our jobs for us.

"They represent a clear and present danger to Canadian sovereignty. That is why we're having this meeting.

"If the Haida win, there's going to be a domino effect. The First Nations have land claims on *one-third* of Canada's landmass. They're experiencing a baby boom and are growing far faster than the rest of the population. We're aging, retiring, and hopelessly mired in debt while they're debt-free, young, and just entering the workforce.

"Put it all together; the math is easy.

"This is a power grab."

THEY'D BEEN FLIPPING THROUGH scenarios for an hour when Bill sent Rob a back-channel request. Rob accepted, giving himself and his old friend an encrypted private channel.

"Bill, what are we really going to do about this?" said Rob before the prime minister could speak. "This isn't Quebec and whoever they are, those hackers aren't the FLQ. They're not trying to separate; they want something else. But what?"

"Yeah, as to that . . ." Bill stared pensively off to his left, which for Rob was a blank wall but was probably the window on Bill's end of the connection. "You know I used to go to the Davos conferences. Couple years back, the president of Paraguay comes up to me and he says, 'Do you have any power?' I mean, I wasn't the PM yet, I had your job, but . . . At first I just stared at him. But he says he's been talking to prime ministers, presidents, CEOs, you name it, and they all say the same thing. Ten years ago, they could have done things. But now? There's international treaties and grass-roots watchdogs, NGOs, churches, even reality shows all tramping around in what used to be our space. Most of all, there's the block chain, this thing they say runs Bitcoin. If you're, I dunno, some kid living in Africa, and you've got a smartphone, you don't need to use your nation's currency, you can use Bitcoin. But that's just the tip of the iceberg. You can register anything with the block chain: property ownership, health status, laws, citizenship . . . That kid in Africa doesn't *need* his government—he's got the Internet.

"Miguel said that everybody's having the same experience. Either they've finally gotten to the place where they expected to have real power only to discover they don't have it, or they've been in power for twenty years and watched it drain away over that time."

"Yeah." Rob shrugged. "I thought that's why the NSA tried to take over the Net. 'Cause it was a threat."

"Sure." Bill had a rueful look on his face. "Problem is, the block chain and all that other stuff—like that ownership overlay—really has little to do with what's happening. It's more about economics, education, mobil-ity . . ."

Rob sat down so he could get a better look at Bill without the interface shaking. They'd talked about the need to clean up the Canadian political landscape before, but mostly back in university. The subject hadn't come up since they'd actually risen to become the country's leadership. Both of them had been laying the groundwork for a purge for years, secure in the knowledge that the other had his back. So what was this bullshit about the president of Paraguay?

"Look, there's nothing going on we can't manage," he said. "You know we have something on everyone. Journalists, activists, housewives—anybody who ever used the Internet. It's in the Criminal Leads database, and Krishnamurti has it. Everybody's accidentally stumbled into a kiddie porn website or pirated movies or exchanged dirty e-mails with a coworker. Everybody's done something we can hang over their head."

"I don't think that'll help," said Bill, but Rob smiled.

"What I'm saying is we don't need to impose the War Measures Act to deal with something like Haida secessionists. A while back I had the NSA/ CSEC database cross-linked with the enemies list in CIMS."

"You what?" Bill sat up straighter. "You combined the files?"

The Party's Constituent Information Management System was the confidential database where all its friends and enemies were listed: at its simplest, it noted who'd donated to the Party, and who had told the canvassers to go to hell. Previous governments had not had enough fore-sight to divide up a constituents list so neatly into friends and enemies— remarkably naive of them.

"The NSA was more than happy to give us the data and CSIS mined it for incriminating patterns. I covered our asses by using the Freedom of Information Act to do a ministerial request with another pretext. You could say the data fell off the back of a truck and into the Party database. All it takes now is a single query to produce a list of enemies plus the grounds for issuing warrants for them. They can all be rounded up by tomorrow, if you want."

The prime minister shook his head. "The NSA didn't dismantle American privacy because they thought the Net might *become* a threat. They felt the power slipping through their fingers for years by that point. They did it 'cause they were scared. And it would have worked during the dot-com boom—but by the time they did it, secrecy wasn't where power hid any longer.

"If the bastards we're dealing with can make an overlay like the one you just saw, they can also make one based on your list. They may not *have* the list, but they'll have a pretty good idea who we're likely to be watching. And you can bet there's buggers out there who data-mine arrest reports looking for patterns just like the one that'd show up if we did what you're suggest-ing. They'll stick the data in the block chain where we can't censor it, even with War Measures in place and your man in the RCMP on side. Once the dust settled there'd be a nonconfidence vote and we'd be out of power.

"The fact is we're going to negotiate." He laughed at the expression on Rob's face. "To start with, I mean. It'll go wrong, it always does. And when it escalates—and we both know it will—we'll have our pretext and the approval of the public when we come down on them like the proverbial ton of bricks. Your job is going to be to do the negotiation."

And keep the status quo, thought Rob. Well, of course; stalling on land-claims settlements was a great Canadian governmental tradition.

"We have to get a handle on these hackers first. That's . . . another reason I wanted to talk to you."

"Because of the CSEC data?"

"No. Listen, Rob, I don't think you have anything to do with what's going on here, but you know somebody who does—somebody, in fact, who's a silent partner bankrolling a goodly portion of the Haida Gwaii meshnet. The money's in Gwaiicoin, but we were able to follow it." Bill told him where the trail had ended. Rob leaped to his feet, swearing.

"You've got to be kidding me!"

"There's a traitor in your house, Rob. I'm going to trust you to take care of it."

Rob shook his head. He'd come to expect betrayals in his long career, but this one . . .

"I'll deal with it, Bill. Tonight."

"YOU REALLY DIDN'T HAVE to come, the tanker thing's all over the news," said Terry as he made to close the door; then he noticed the RCMP security squad on the steps and scattered down the walk. "Oh. I guess you're not staying for supper . . ."

"Hi, Dad!" Margaret emerged from the kitchen carrying a tray of deviled eggs. "You heard we bought the place?"

"That's not why I'm here. Listen, I need to talk to you," he said to Terry. "About the Haida negotiations."

Terry glanced at the security team. He went down the hall to his little home office and Rob followed. Once they were inside, Terry shut the door and leaned on the computer desk, crossing his arms.

"What can I do for you, Dad?"

Rob had thought about how he would handle this. Krishnamurti had some damning information—but not enough. His relationship with Terry hadn't exactly been . . . comfortable, the past few years. If Krishnamurti was wrong, and Rob blew his stack at Terry . . . he made sure he smiled as he said, "The Haida don't want to use the usual conference format. They're insisting the negotiations happen in public and on the Net. I spent the afternoon having website addresses and acronyms thrown at me until my head spun. I don't understand this stuff, and I need somebody who does."

"Oh." Terry smiled. He looked genuinely happy. "What tools are they using?"

Rob rummaged in his coat pocket for the paper he'd been writing on during this afternoon's briefing. Of course CSIS and CSEC had people who could explain this better than Terry. "They're picking delegates via sortition from a pool that's developed using something called"—he squinted—"dynamically distributed democracy. What the hell?"

"Ah." Terry waved a dismissive hand. "That's just where people delegate other people to represent them. Rather than voting for some candidate, you might delegate me because you don't have time to look at the issues but you trust me; other people might do the same, and then I might delegate my aggregate to somebody who I trust. It sounds cumbersome, but you can use a networking protocol called Promise Theory to implement it right down to the hardware level—"

"Whatever. And what about this website, Wegetit.com? They're insisting that I register. Something about using it during the negotiations. Is this something they're gonna use to manipulate the process?"

Terry shrugged. "No more than Robert's Rules manipulates a meeting. Less so, actually. I can help you set it up."

"I'm gonna end up with a *profile*," grumbled Rob, "and then they're gonna use it against me. This is like those damned Dorians you and Maggie were using this morning, isn't it?"

"Nobody's using the Dorians against us, Dad. Dorians are just little pictures of yourself, one for each major decision you're thinking of making. Let's say you're thinking about quitting smoking. Your Dorian takes the data you give it—your age, health, and if you use a sports tracker it'll take your fitness levels, if you buy through a grocery delivery site it'll know your diet—and compares it to known outcomes for that demographic. Those little pictures of you—the Dorians—look happier or sadder, richer or poorer or sicker depending on the outcome. The Dorian for you in ten years if you smoke like a chimney is going to look different from the one where you quit cold turkey right now. And your Dorians get combined, so if you quit smoking but take up, I dunno, marathon running, then the good might counterbalance the bad. The game is to get your Dorian looking better and better—healthier, richer, and happier. If I want to do something like, say, buy a house, I tell my Dorians, and they look at outcomes for people like me and draw me a spectrum of faces based on usual choices."

© 2013, Nina Miller / ASU

"That's ridiculous," said Rob. But Terry shook his head.

"People have a huge amount of neural wiring dedicated to reading faces, so if you want to map a complex set of data in such a way that people can recognize tiny but significant changes between versions, the best way is to chart it as two or more faces where the differences are in how close together your eyes are, or how many crow's-feet you've got. A difference that's so minuscule that you'd never see it on a chart will be instantly visible as a face.

"That's just cognitive science. The analysis of your buying habits, social attitudes, health, and so on is the Big Data crunching that makes the data. How's that a cult?"

Rob's heart sank. He could hear it in Terry's voice, see it in the enthusiasm in his face. Krishnamurti wasn't wrong. The only question now was what to do.

"They're holding the treaty negotiations on Haida Gwaii," he said. "I'm flying out there in three days.

"Do you want to come along?"

THE RUNWAY WEST OF Queen Charlotte was drenched with rain as Rob and Terry stepped out of the little prop-driven commuter plane. Knowing what they were in for, they'd dressed in raincoats and brought umbrellas.

Climate change hadn't yet had much impact on the Gwaii. South of the new airport lay Bearskin Bay, a stippled gray surface backed with fog.

To the west were jagged, snow-capped mountains fronted by rough shore line; north and east the land was carpeted with giant lodgepole pines, a rain forest unlike any other on Earth. The deep underbrush below the trees was lush, full of broad-leafed plants whose greens were not subdued by the gray skies. It smelled dizzyingly wet and cold and fresh.

Rob and Terry hadn't spoken much on the flight out. Rob's assistants had most of his attention as they briefed him on the whos and whats of the place. That was just an excuse, and Rob knew it; he was hiding behind his aides. But he just couldn't talk to Terry, especially not at a time like this.

Rob paused at their hired car to look around. Beyond the dismal rain, towering trees scraped the vague underside of the low gray sky. Set back from the runway, but just in front of the trees, was a row of totem poles. Not those Disney imitations you saw everywhere else in the world, he noted with a small, grim hint of satisfaction. These were real, the animal shapes in them softened and gray with age. Once, there had been men named Skaay who carved them.

"Impressive, eh?" Terry was standing next to him, grinning at the poles. Rob shook his head.

"Impressive for the Stone Age. But that's not where we are. And that's the whole problem."

As they reached the car the driver opened the door for Rob; no driverless cars on the Haida Gwaii, at least not yet. As he made to get in, the man said, "Oh, I'm sorry."

Rob blinked at him. "What?"

"You're angry. I'm sorry for whatever it is I did." The man's face was local; the rest of him was invisible under a yellow rain slicker and broadbrimmed hat. And, Rob noticed suddenly, he was wearing AR glasses.

"Why do you think I'm mad at you?"

The driver tapped his glasses. "I have Asperger's. My glasses can recognize emotions on people's faces and tell me what they are. They say you're angry right now."

"Not at you." As he did up his seat belt he thought, *And I'm not angry anyway, dammit!* He scowled out at the monotonous trees as they headed into town and answered the aides' questions and suggestions with terse yeses and nos.

Despite his attempts to focus on the business at hand, he couldn't help but notice how Terry was avidly staring out at the landscape. Rob found his own attention reluctantly following.

The road curved and lowered, meandering south toward the bay and Skidegate Inlet. They passed a road sign that said they were on Oceanview Drive. It led toward a narrow strip of houses—just three or four streets deep—that hugged a shoreline bristling with the masts of fishing trawlers.

North of here, Graham Island fanned out, an inverted triangle nestled into the Dixon Entrance, where the Alaskan Panhandle met British Columbia's shore. From the air he'd been able to see into Hecate Strait, which separated the Gwaii from B.C. If the pipeline negotiations worked out, soon a daisy chain of immense tankers from Kitimat would be heading up the strait—bound north and through the entrance, and then to Asia. They would be carrying ultraheavy crude from the oil sands in Alberta, and there was no way they would get through here without the cooperation of the local First Nations bands. The First Nations had fought for the power of that veto inch by inch, over several lifetimes. It wasn't official, treaty-sanctioned power. They'd had to acquire real power, and in so doing had tangled themselves deeper and deeper into the world. This might look like a little island, but there was nothing local about politics on the Gwaii.

At one point the driver suddenly braked, reducing them to a crawl. Because he was watching the forest, Rob knew there was nothing to see—and yet, after a minute or so, a pair of deer cautiously stepped onto the road ahead of them. "How did you know they were there?" he asked the driver.

The man grinned. As the deer fell behind and he sped up again, he said, "Happy to be back?"

Rob started to retort that he'd never been to the Gwaii before, but the driver was Haida . . . "Yeah," he answered.

This was the land of his ancestors, however much he might resent carrying that burden. He had to admit, the houses and stores they were passing looked . . . not exactly prosperous, maybe, but not as squalid as he'd expected. The Haida had been all but wiped out by disease at the start of the twentieth century. That was a story that repeated all across the Americas, but the apocalypse had taken four hundred years and had reached the Queen Charlottes last. Their culture was still intact when the smallpox hit; one result of this was that they didn't see technology as the weapon of a conquering power.

His father had once told him that in the old days they'd used slaves to erect the more important totem poles; when the eyes were finally carved so the spirits could look out of them, and they were raised upright, the slaves would be killed and buried at their bases. It was the same nowadays, his father had said, except that they used power tools to do the carving and it was these they buried.

"Hey," he said to the driver. "Are you on Wegetit.com?"

"Hate using the Internet. But they got a kiosk by the real estate place; when I'm going by, I answer a question or two sometimes. Why?"

"'Cause your side is demanding that I use it. Any idea why?"

"Oh, that's 'cause it's part of how we decide things now."

"Really."

When he got to the hotel and finally could put his feet up, Rob set aside his glasses, pulled out his tablet, and went to Wegetit.com. It wasn't his first time on the site, but this time he bit back his impatience and set up an account. Terry had funded this, after all, and he couldn't quite deny the curiosity of a father about what his son had been up to.

There was only one thing you could do on Wegetit.com: show that you understood someone's framing of an idea. There were two text fields, one for a word or concept (very short) and a longer one, for about a tweet's worth of definition. You could let fly your idea of what something meant and wait. After a while, people would respond with restatements of your definition. If you thought a restatement accurately represented your meaning, you could click the Wegetit button. There was no button for disagreement.

Ideas were usually presented in the context of some issue or problem area, such as, in this case, aboriginal land claims. That was the domain the Haida negotiators wanted him to stick to. He started with basic ideas like *government* and *agreement* and worked his way up to *emancipation* and *good faith*. He had no idea who the people he was agreeing with were—identities were anonymized—but somewhere out there were thousands of people who shared his understandings of many basic concepts, even if they might disagree with his politics. Wegetit was drawing lines connecting all those people, and every agreement strengthened the connections.

According to Terry, this made Wegetit.com the opposite of every other Internet site with a discussion forum, because however well intentioned they might be, by their very nature discussion forums manufactured mis-understanding. Divergence, not convergence, was the rule in a forum. But give a problem—especially a thorny political problem—to a constellation of connected people on Wegetit.com, and however diverse they might be in their perspectives and attitudes, they would at least understand one another when they talked about it.

It all seemed like bullshit to Rob; it became obvious the next morning that it was anything but bullshit to the Haida.

The negotiations would be taking place in the Haida Heritage Centre in Skidegate (or, as the locals called it, Sea Lion town). The place was along the shore, a collection of five large buildings reminiscent of lodges but built with modern materials. Six large totem poles stood at stately intervals fronting them. A bewildering amount of carving and block prints covered the walls of the meeting hall, all repeating the legends and tales of the culture. Tables had been set up in a giant U-shape, and there was the usual chaos of people running around making last-minute preparations.

The Haida insisted they needed a daylong scoping workshop to pre-pare for the real negotiations. Since they were the ones threatening to scuttle the pipeline project, Rob had decided to indulge them. He was as good at steering workshops in the direction he wanted as anybody in the country. He let his aides run interference on the preparations and run-ning around; he wanted to make sure he greeted the right people ahead of the formal ceremonies. Before he could do any of that, though, his senior administrative assistant, Jeffrey, hurried over. "There's a delay," he said.

"Of course there is." He would have been surprised if there wasn't. Rob had been counting heads and seats; there were a lot more of the latter than the former. "Where is everybody?"

"Some of the delegates have been dismissed," said Jeffrey. "They're telling me it's because of something you did last night."

"Last night? All I did was go to sleep. Well, I browsed that website for a while . . ." *Oh.* Jeffrey was nodding.

"I guess you did enough agreeing that they were able to tell who would know what you meant when you used the word 'the'—and who wouldn't. The delegates who didn't match up were either dismissed or they're being briefed on the differences; and they've called up a boatload of profession-ally qualified people—"

"A literal boatload, I suppose?"

"—from across the islands and the mainland too, who're within your agreements map. With an extra day or so of prep, they'll be able to make sure that everybody sitting around the table speaks the same language at the level of basic ideas."

"Fine. If they're going to play shenanigans, so will we." He brought out his glasses and put them on. Then he made a secure connection to Ottawa and spilled some copies of SimCanada into his sensorium. He wanted to see how the land-claims issue was tracking.

In between introductions to men and women with names like Ghaandl and Imkyanvaan and Gumssiwa—names and faces that triggered odd memories and recognitions in Rob—he was able to glance at the maps representing different policy outcomes. He could also see the status reports coming out of CSIS on the investigation, but he wasn't really able to read them with all the glad-handing he was doing. It looked like the tanker hadn't split yet, but it was on the rocks and they couldn't get near it. A spill was inevitable; the only question was, how bad would it be?

Yes, let's not forget this is a power play, he reminded himself as he pulled the glasses off for a photo op. Somehow the Haida had steered that ship onto the rocks. They were corrupting navigational data in the Inside Passage. If the damned spooks in CSEC could get their heads out of their asses and find out how, he wouldn't have to be here. As it was, the threat was clear: *negotiate now, or this happens again.*

Either the Haida were confident that they could repeat this stunt, or they were desperate. He'd have to find out which.

"Attention!" It was Todd Swanton, a conference organizer Rob had worked with before. Todd had been flown out here on a day's notice to facilitate. "Not all the delegates are physically here yet," he said, "but I'm told they're all connected and we can do a little teleconferencing while we get organized. I'm going to start by introducing the minister of aboriginal affairs, Robert Skaay . . ." He went on about Rob's pedigree, but the way he'd emphasized the name, giving the correct Haida pronunciation, galled Rob. If the press started playing up his connection with the island, they might start to question his objectivity, hence his ability to represent the government properly.

Todd called him up to give a speech, and he talked for fifteen minutes without notes or any plan; he was good at that sort of thing. He started to relax in the familiar conference setting.

After all the preliminaries, it seemed the locals wanted to air their grievances, and Todd didn't discourage them; he actually started inviting people up to the mic to talk about issues. This too was a familiar exercise to Rob, who was prepared to tune out and ignore the whole process. It would be the usual festival of misery as various elders and parents talked about underfunding, poor education, drug problems, lack of good employ-ment . . . He'd heard it all before. He would nod and look alert, but Bill had made Rob minister of aboriginal affairs because Rob knew the govern-ment couldn't help these people. A hundred years of trying had yielded nothing. If you were going to pull yourself out of poverty, you had to do it yourself. Rob knew that in his bones, because he had done it.

Except that it didn't quite play out that way. The people coming up to the podium weren't just random petitioners; they were people who'd used Wegetit.com to define an issue. Some of them had access to sophis-ticated interfaces such as augmented reality glasses; some were old folks who'd been polled by volunteers in the grocery store. What they shared in common was that they had either identified some key issue in lan-guage that everybody else here—including Rob—seemed to understand, or they'd proven they understood one on the site, and had been chosen to be here through the sortition process of dynamic distributed democracy.

Even Rob had to admit that the problems they described over the next hour were real. Their descriptions were sharply focused, comprehensive, and almost immediately understood by everyone. The summaries were so clear, in fact, that he found it a bit creepy. Usually when he encoun-tered such clarity, it was the result of a concerted propaganda effort. This, though—Wegetit didn't filter or distort ideas, it simply connected those people who were capable of understanding one another. The people in this room represented the network with the broadest, most complete common understanding of the issues surrounding aboriginal land claims. A net-work that he was apparently part of.

With the summaries out of the way, Todd turned the podium over to another consultant, some analyst from Toronto. "Now I'd like to do a little exercise," he was saying as Rob leaned over to Jeffrey.

"Who is this guy?"

"One of the founders of Wegetit," murmured Jeffrey. "Got his start in something called Structured Dialogic Design."

"Wonderful."

"What I'm going to do is ask a series of questions," the consultant was saying, "about the issues that've been identified on Wegetit.com over the past few days. I want you to put up your hands if you agree. Those of us who are still traveling can IM their answers. Let's start with this question: Do you think that cheap access to the mainland would help ease the problem of the 'barrier to employment' we talked about earlier?" Hands were raised. "Now, do you think that better access to employment opportunities would make access to the mainland easier?" Hands went up again.

This exercise went on for a while. Rob raised his hand with the others. Most of the answers to the questions were obvious to the point of inanity. He couldn't see how it helped to know that a lack of education hampered one's job prospects.

After half an hour, the consultant pushed his glasses back on his nose and said, "Right, we've got enough answers. Our software's been quietly working in the background, doing a root cause analysis on all the issues we've talked about. Here it is."

He brought up a diagram on the wall screen, and suddenly Rob snapped to attention. There, laid out in graphic boxes joined by lines—a kind of flowchart—were the problems the Haida and related stakeholders had identified, organized according to which problems caused which. The chart formed a tree, with issues like suicide rates and drug use and abuse clustered at the top. They connected down into poverty, schooling issues, cultural genocide, and so on. The tree continued through these too, down to the single root cause that the exercise had shown underlay almost everything else. That flowchart box contained the words *The Haida Do Not Control Their Land*.

Rob swore under his breath. He'd done scenario exercises many times, but never one that had so quickly, seamlessly, and completely nailed down an issue. The causal tree had emerged from a series of perfectly reasonable—even obvious—answers to questions about how social problems were connected. The problem was, the tree was upside down: all those obvious answers should have led to the obvious conclusion, namely that it didn't matter how the damned islands were governed, individual people had to take responsibility for their own lives. Instead it said the opposite.

Rob had agreed with every answer that had built this tree. How could he not agree with the result?

It had to be a trick; he wasn't sure how yet, but the game had been rigged.

It was break time, and Rob spent most of it being visible. He shook various newly arrived hands and congratulated the organizers on the amazing progress they'd made today. Eventually he was able to make it to the bathroom, where he rendezvoused with Jeffrey.

He leaned on a sink and glared at his aide. "Did we just get blindsided?"

Jeffrey looked uncomfortable. "They're following the program. It's just that . . . what's happening here is connecting into other systems, like Wegetit, in ways we hadn't anticipated. I mean, you saw . . . processes that normally take months are taking hours."

"Politics is slow for a reason. You don't steer a supertanker like you steer a canoe. Not without damage. Who are these people?"

"You mean the ones doing the systems stuff? Well, there's Wegetit, but it's just a front end. It's a filter that groups people according to how well they'll understand one another, but we've just learned that the data from it can be used by another set of tools in a system called 'Cybersyn 2.0.'"

"And what does *that* do?"

Jeffrey hesitated. "I think you'd better ask your son. He's the CEO."

The break over with, and all the attendees finally there, the conference went into full gear. Todd Swanton stood up and began to introduce the afternoon's agenda. "The technical term for what we have after two hundred years of tug-of-war between the Haida and the Crown," he said, "is a *wicked problem*. A wicked problem is not just a *problem*. You can solve an ordinary problem; at least, you can describe it. With a wicked problem— also called a *mess*—there's no definite formulation of the problem. There's no stopping rule for a mess—no way to prove you've fixed it. Solutions aren't either right or wrong, just different, and every solution is a 'one-shot' that can't be compared to any previous attempt at fixing it. You cannot fix a mess. The best you can do is improve it."

He smiled cheerfully. "We're here today to improve the mess we call Canada-Haida relations. We're going to start using one of those sophisticated techniques that used to be jealously guarded by small groups of highly paid consultants and doled out at great expense to rich clients. Like so many other things that computers have made cheaper and easier, they've made morphological analysis easy—so easy that we're going to turn it into a game. We're going to play the game for the rest of this afternoon. The name of the game is 'Addressing the Root Cause.'"

"What the hell," muttered Rob. It was too late to get out of it now—

he'd agreed to this scoping workshop—so all he could do was smile and look like he was enjoying himself, and think about firing Jeffrey. For the in it four hours Wegdit and the Haida pulled out all the stops, creating multidimensional matrices whose nodes were the various different aspects of the mess that was government–First Nation relations. Using projectors, glasses, tablets, and anything else they could get their hands on, the organizers spun around, expanded and focused in on, drilled down into, and exploded the dimensions, eliminating literally millions of potential configurations until they'd narrowed down the class of possible solutions. The name for this technique was morphological analysis, which was bad enough, but it wasn't just the name that was exhausting; the many solutions would have all blurred together in a migraine-inducing mass except for one thing:

Each solution was displayed on the screens as a face. They were goddamned Dorians, and Terry had been right—even the subtlest difference between two solutions was instantly visible as a slightly different expression, ethnicity, or emotion on the parade of faces. You could sort through twenty of them for the best in the time it took to scan your eyes across them. The best solutions were happy, healthy, youthful, and ethnically Haida. When the room unpacked the data on a solution, it always turned out that their instinctive assessment had been right, through a problem space containing millions of possible answers.

As they did this Rob found himself swinging between his own multidimensional matrix of reactions: annoyance, indulgence, euphoria, and shock. The problem—mess, rather—was too big for any one human being to understand all its parameters and possible solutions; but it wasn't too big for a group of stakeholders to understand, if they were guided properly through the process.

At the end he raised his hand and asked the consultant, "What do you call what we just did?"

The man smiled. "We call it 'rewilding politics.'"

They broke for the night. Swanton finished by recapping, then said, "I know we're all tired from today's mental workout, but luckily it's a different kind of work we're going to do in the next session. Today was all about finding the problems. The next session, in two days, will be about nailing down the shared understanding we developed today. It's been proven that the best way to share an understanding of complex issues is through storytelling, so that's exactly what we're going to do—and it's why we'll all need a day to prepare. We're going to share our stories, through speech, in writing, in song, and in dance. Everything that we've come to understand intellectually today, we're going to know in our bones by the end of that session."

As they filed out, everybody was exhausted but hyper, and conversations and arguments spilled out into the parking lot and beyond. Rob headed back to his hotel and called Krishnamurti. "I know my son's involved, but I want to know who else is. Who're they working for, who else is funding them—I want to know everything," he told the CSIS director.

It was a voice-only line, slightly delayed as satellite connections tended to be. It was also late in the evening, Ottawa time, but Rob didn't care. Krishnamurti should have been expecting this call.

"CSEC's been looking into Wegetit," said the director. "But also into the Internet in the Queen Charlottes. It turns out it's mostly a homegrown meshnet. The islanders aren't buying their Internet connectivity from Rogers, Bell, or any of the other regulated carriers. They're using solar-powered homemade antennas and store-bought routers. A lot of those are logging company data relays; they're piggybacking on commercial equipment. They either pay in Gwaiicoin, or in goodwill. They're a darknet, in fact—a whole Internet outside the official one. And there's hints they may be using autonets, too."

"What're those?"

"Body-to-body data relays using Bluetooth or near-field. Almost impossible to detect or counter."

"But who's behind it?"

Again the delay dragged out. "No one," said Krishnamurti at last. "At least, it may originally have been somebody in particular's *idea;* but now it's running itself."

He thanked Krishnamurti and hung up. Then he made another call.

"Hello?" said Terry.

"This is all your doing, isn't it?" said Rob.

There was that same brief silence he'd gotten from Krishnamurti—as clear as day a signal that the guy on the other end of the line was choosing his next words carefully.

"We've got a rest day before the next session, right?" said Terry. "Why don't you and me do something? I was thinking of visiting the old forest."

A father and son outing? That was just as clichéd and artificial as
house-hunting. Still . . .

Rob harrumphed. "You're on," he said.

THEY TOOK AN OLD dirt road with green shoulders through a cathedral
of inward-leaning trees. The brush was an impenetrable tangle, and Rob
pointed that out to Terry. "It grows so thick! Where are we going?"

"There's an outfitter on Yakoun Lake. He can give us a canoe."

"Canoe?" Rob laughed uneasily. "It's been years, you know."

"Oh, it's okay. They also sell aspirin."

The road curled its way to the edge of a spectacular lake backed by
white-capped mountains. On the shore a man in a red plaid shirt was
flipping over a canoe as if it weighed nothing. With so much water in
the air, the distant mountains were like silver cutouts, except for their
white tops. Rob was distracted by this sight as Terry negotiated with the
tour operator. When he looked back from the scenery, it was to see his
son had stripped off his shirt. He was putting on something that looked
like a sleek blue undershirt, and there was a second one draped on the
canoe beside him. Rob had seen a few of these peeking out from under
the clothes of islanders over the past couple of days. He'd assumed they
were insulated, like fleece, but the outfitter grinned and shook his head.
"You'll see," he said.

"I don't like wearing other people's old bowling shoes, why would I
wear this?"

"Disposable liner," said Terry.

Rob sighed. What with everything else that was weird about this, it
was just one more thing. "Whatever." He put it on.

They paddled slowly along the shoreline for an hour, then across to
the western side. When they beached the canoe and Terry brought out a
thermos of coffee, Rob looked back at the distance they'd come. The vista
was glorious.

Ahead of them lay something even more wonderful. The trees here
were ancient, but widely enough spaced that light penetrated to the forest
floor in hazy shafts. A covering of bright green moss, inches deep, draped
across the roots and boulders alike like crumpled velvet. More dripped in
long streamers from the branches, which started far enough up to offer

long sight lines through the boles. When Terry stepped into the green cathedral, Rob eagerly followed him.

He felt a kind of buzz on the left side of his torso; at that instant something bounded from behind a tree off to the left. He couldn't see it, but somehow the sound matched up to the buzzing sensation.

"Feel that?" Terry slapped at his chest. "A deer."

Rob stopped moving. He suddenly realized that this touch on his body wasn't the only one; he could feel other creatures nearby. He slowly turned to the right, then pointed. "What's that?"

"You got it! There's a bear about a kilometer that way. Feel how it has a different texture. And up there"—he pointed—"I can feel eagles. They're especially prickly, I don't know why."

Rob was amazed. "It's the shirt doing this?"

"It's called sensory substitution. You can replace one sense with another. These vests do something like that, but in this case they're using all the smart sensors scattered through the forest to identify the animals— what they are, and where they are. Then they paint a sensation across our skin. They're actually cheap to make; they use speakers and vibrators from discarded cell phones, weave 'em into the material. Gives you a new sense. It works best if you don't consciously think about it. Just let it wash over you. Come on, let's go this way."

They strode through the ancient forest, and as they did Rob felt his sense of where he was, and even who he was, grow out from his chest like an indrawn breath that never stopped expanding. He could *feel* the deer, the ravens and foxes and bears, even if he couldn't see them. His ancestors had lacked this sense, but maybe they'd made up for that with knowledge—reports from hunters and workers of what lived where and in what abundance.

He'd never felt any sense of connection with those people. They were like shadows, as dark and inaccessible as the inward darkness below the pine boughs.

Pensive, he followed his son, speaking less and less as the day went on.

Gradually he became aware that the life of the forest lay behind them. Something was up ahead, and he assumed it was the sea, until they came to the edge of the forest and he saw the churned landscape of stumps and bare earth that stretched away for kilometers. Clear-cutting: the whole forest had been logged here, and with his new sense he could feel how empty it was.

"Raven," said Terry, pointing. Rob looked, but all he saw was an old logging road, and a pickup truck. Terry was walking out to it, so he followed.

There was a man standing next to the truck. The raven sensation was coming from that spot; did he have a bird with him? No; as Rob came closer he couldn't see the animal, and yet the raven signal kept getting stronger. It was as if the man *were* a raven.

And yes—of course he was.

Robert remembered his grandfather telling him that their family was part of the Eagle clan. It had seemed silly and superstitious to him at the time, just one more piece of the past that he'd have to reject if he was to make some sort of life for himself in the modern world. He still felt that way. And yet . . .

They greeted the man, who was working with Parks Canada to do a census of the local bear population. As they walked back to the trees, Rob said, "He was wearing one of these sensory substi-whatits, wasn't he?" He'd seen a hint of blue under the red plaid lumberjack's shirt the guy had on.

When Terry shrugged, Rob said, "So was everybody at the workshop . . . they could all feel each other's clan, couldn't they? Including ours? Did that guy back there see two Eagles come out of the bush just now?" Terry didn't answer, which told Rob all he needed to know. He stopped, suddenly aware only of his son and not the moss-covered cathedral of trees where they stood. "I know everything, Terry. That you're the one who's backing this. You're a Haida separatist?"

He expected the kind of evasion or argument he used to get when Terry was a kid. Instead Terry laughed.

"Dad, this is the twenty-first century. We're way past separatism here."

His conversation with Bill echoed in his head. "What, is this some kind of takeover? The First Nations' revenge?" But Terry was still laughing.

"Dad, we can't separate because there's nowhere to separate to. The world's too small now. Nobody can do it. And take over what? Canada's not a well-defined thing anymore, any more than the States or anywhere else is. We're all crammed together. It's the global village, right?"

"So what is going on here?"

Terry crossed his arms, serious now. "The shirts, the Dorians, Wegetit . . . they're just people using cognitive science to improve their interactions. And their decision making. Hell, you use the stuff yourself!"

"I do not—"

"Oh, yeah? What about SimCanada? It's all through Parliament Hill."

"Those are just brainstorming tools."

"Tools to think with, right."

"You're saying the Dorians are just like SimCanada?"

"*Exactly* like SimCanada, Dad."

"I don't like it, Terry. You're letting a goddamned machine make your decisions for you."

"Your Dorians don't make your decisions. They're just making visible the invisible: the interplay of all the complicated factors at play in your life. Like which animals are around us, and where all our Eagle brothers and sisters are right now."

"As well as who owns what?"

Terry grinned. "Ah, you saw that overlay, eh? Wait'll you see the stranded assets overlay for the carbon bubble."

Rob carefully looked through the dripping green branches at the complex depths of the forest. "If I put on my glasses right now, what *would* I see?"

"Us," said Terry. "You'd see what you're dealing with."

Like mountains, the Haida and Tsimshian territorial claims would loom over the trees—not claims entirely of men and women anymore, but of Bear and Raven—and Eagle. And he was sure he would be able to see other things, too, like logging concessions, company names. Who owned what. How much the forest was worth in cold cash. In that moment he got it.

"You're not trying to build a new government. You've already done it."

Terry nodded slowly. "Not just out of augmented reality apps. We call those the prosthetic—the thing that lets you see power and ownership. Like I said, making the invisible visible. But it doesn't do the deciding."

"The deciding—that's Wegetit.com?"

"Wegetit and the system around it, which we call Cybersyn. It's built on the block chain, so it's totally decentralized, peer-to-peer. It provides trusted communications, fraud-proof voting, citizenship, and other services for a new governing structure. It's more fraud- and corruption-proof than the one we've got now. Except of course it's not just for Canada. It's worldwide."

Rob stared at his son. "It's a damned good thing I am who I am, Terry. You've just admitted to treason."

"Not at all. If I can *see* the carbon bubble and I say, 'I think the government should divest from fossil fuels,' and you don't, and it turns out that Canada gets burned as the bubble bursts, did I commit fraud? No. I *advised*, and you had the option of listening or not."

"But what you're doing with it here . . . that's not just advising. You're actually *running the island* with it, aren't you?" All these maps of power and wealth—they had visible concentrations, end points, and those corresponded to people. If you could see the whole network of power around yourself, you'd know who to talk to in order to get things done. Even if you were just some anonymous Indian on the street, you'd be able to see what needed to be done, even if you couldn't do it yourself. And using the block chain, it could all be implemented in a completely decentralized manner. No center of power to take down . . .

"We're running the island because nobody else is doing it. If the feds were doing any kind of a good job at it, we wouldn't have to." Terry said this without heat, but the words stung. Rob almost said, "We do what we can," but in the face of what he'd seen here, that was no answer at all.

He started walking again, no longer noticing the gorgeous scenery. Terry fell into step beside him. "We use Wegetit and the rest of it to develop public policy that's actually made *by* the public and tested alongside official policy in the national Dorian, which is just an open-source version of Sim-Canada. They're both Big Data apps. We see which policy works better in the simulations, and then we wait for reality to catch up and see what actually happened in the real world. And either we tweak the national model or we publish the winning policy choice as a *padget*—you know, a policy gadget like they've had in Europe since, oh, at least 2010. The local MLAs have been using the padgets to design policy for a year now; they love it because they actually get good advice for free.

"You see what we're doing here, Dad? We're offering you the chance to do the same thing, only on the national level."

The implication was clear. If the feds didn't play, the Haida could take it to the next level: they could start voting in the block chain and cut the government out of the loop entirely.

Rob crossed his arms. "I'm representing the whole country. *You're* representing a little group of hackers and malcontents."

Terry shook his head. "How many people voted in the last federal election?" There was an awkward silence. "We involve more people in decision making than you do," said Terry. "You do the math."

Rob thought about it for a while, then said, "Why?" He meant, *why you.*

Terry seemed to understand. "Because you raised me to want to make a difference. The Midwest United States is emptying of people 'cause the water table's gone and the president says he'll invade Canada if we don't agree to reverse the flow of the Hudson Bay watershed. It's the Garrison Diversion project on steroids—and that's in the supposedly most stable, richest, most democratic region in the world. There's water wars and mass migrations everywhere, disease, starvation, religious pogroms. Here's the thing: solving all these problems is easy, from a science and engineering standpoint. The science has been there for decades; so's the technology. We've got biotech, nanotech, access to space, robots, 50 percent efficient solar cells, nuclear fusion, for God's sake! We don't need to solve *those* problems. There's only one issue that's worthy of our time and effort right now, because if we overcome it, we'll solve all the others.

"The only problem worth solving is the problem of *how we govern ourselves.*"

Their feet made no noise as they sank into the moss. For a while father and son just walked together. Rob could feel the web of life radiating out from them, almost like invisible light. The animals, the epic trees, the moss and the inch-long slugs crawling on it; they were almost like a part of himself.

He knew perfectly well how this was supposed to make him feel. Oneness with nature, that was the game here. It made him mad, because it was all so obvious and naive—a tourist's version of the natural world. Try living out here without technology for a week. Try emptying Vancouver into the countryside to hunt the forests bare. The population being what it was, the only reason there were still places like this was because there were places like Vancouver. All this back-to-nature crap wasn't going to cease to be crap just because some new technology made a more compelling argument for it.

There was no point telling Terry this, of course; a sidelong glance showed Rob the quietly happy expression on his son's face. He thought that he and his dad were Having a Moment. It was one of those things he did; Rob could remember times when he'd used this tactic as a boy—used his happiness to try to change his father's mind about something important. Sometimes Rob had let him know he was being an asshole; sometimes, he just stood firm and ignored the ploy.

They'd come to a height that looked down on the shore. He could see their canoe waiting for them. Funny—he hadn't felt it, the way he felt the ravens roosting overhead, or the deer half a kilometer off to the right. The canoe was a hole in the landscape. Damned interface.

"Tomorrow, we can tell this story," said Terry, as he began picking his way down to the shore. Rob sighed, watching him for a few moments, then followed.

RESOLUTE HE MIGHT BE, but by noon the next day Rob was grateful for Krishnamurti's call—it saved his ass.

The whole morning had been given over to a festival—of art, song, traditional dances, and storytelling. Rob had known it was coming—he attended such events many times each year. So he'd set his glasses to overlay the briefs on the government's position, so he could be ready when the negotiations started. Except, he kept being distracted by the performances.

Each story, each song, and every work of art had been chosen to reflect the insights they'd collectively discovered on the first day. They'd been told this in the conference recap at breakfast, but what it really meant was only just dawning on Rob.

When Krishnamurti called, Rob had completely forgotten the briefs, was in fact staring through them at an old Tsimshian fisherman from Prince Rupert, who was telling his story. For every one of the government's positions, this man had a real anecdote that showed why it was awful, wrong, or would just be ineffective. The damnedest thing about it was that Rob was sure this wasn't a careful propaganda ploy. Taken by themselves the old geezer's experiences were as random as anybody else's. But hovering in the background, visible through the glasses that everybody was now wearing, was the causal root analysis diagram. Somebody had redrawn it as an actual tree, and as they were done, each story, song, and artwork was being pasted into it as a hotlink. Their argument was already won; that had happened when the people in this room, Rob included, had collectively built that tree the day before yesterday. This morning was all about absorbing the implications. Which weren't good for any of Rob's positions.

It didn't help that Rob had bought the sensory substitution shirt from the outfitter (paying with Gwaiicoin), and with Terry's help had connected to the conference feed he'd suspected was there. Now he could *feel* the complex web of kinship, shared history, and alliances that informed the identities of the people opposite him. Through the glasses, he could see the pyramids of power and money made visible by the rogue overlays. All the complexities of obligation, history, business, and government were there—you could almost reach out and pull the strings, twist them to and fro.

So when Krishnamurti called and told him the news, Rob actually grinned in relief. "Thanks," he said, moving his lips as little as possible. Then his eyes sought out Terry, who was sitting with the visitors near the door, and the smile vanished. This could get ugly.

There wasn't a dry eye in the place by lunchtime, except maybe for Rob's. He had to admit, the whole performance had been damned convincing. What he'd seen and heard here perfectly described everything that was wrong with the Indian Act and two hundred years of colonialism, and with the causal analysis in play, the reasons were obvious to all. "So," said Todd as he took the floor again, "we can now move on to our last two stages. First, commitment to change. And second, deciding the actual courses of action that we will all take to address the root cause. This will take up the rest of today, and all of tomorrow."

Except it won't, Rob thought grimly, *because I won't be here to rubber-stamp any of it.* As everyone rose for lunch he rose too, joints creaking from yesterday's canoe trip. He did the usual glad-handing but pressed inexorably toward the door. Out of the corner of his eye he could see some of the industry reps talking heatedly on their cell phones as they paced in the corners. Shit was happening, apparently.

He collared Terry in the parking lot and said, "Walk with me."

His son grinned and nodded in the direction of the bay. The water was gray today, reflecting the low tumbling clouds. "That was amazing, eh?" said Terry as they walked.

Rob shook his head and sighed. "I just got a call," he said. "We know the tanker running aground wasn't an accident."

Terry stopped walking, a shocked look on his face. "No shit?"

"'No shit' what? 'No shit' that it was deliberate, or 'no shit' that we found out? *You* knew all along."

"Dad, really." Terry looked hurt.

"Is that why you called me to come house-hunting with you? To get me to Vancouver in time for all this"—he waved at the center with its proud totem poles—"to go down?"

"You really think I'd do that?" Now Terry looked angry.

"Well, you are a Sky."

Terry glared at him. The moment dragged—and then his son laughed. "So what happens now?" he asked.

"This is serious, Terry. If the evidence trail gets back to you, you could be going to jail for a very long time."

"Except that it won't, we both know that. Besides . . ." Serious now, Terry gazed out at the ocean. "There's a Dorian for that."

"Terry, I'm done here. When this hits, I have to walk away. No more negotiations. The government's going to cry blackmail, and your little escapade here is going to fall apart."

Terry shrugged. "There's a Dorian for that, too. What's SimCanada got to say about it?"

"I . . ." He didn't know. "Dammit, who cares?"

"You're right, it doesn't matter." Terry crossed his arms, looking pensive. "If you pull out now, the conference will still go forward. Only you won't have any say in the results. You could pull some stunt right now, and split off some of the industry guys, the conservatives and government lapdogs. But even some of them are now convinced about what should be done. And everybody else . . . they'll still go on to make their commitments. You may preserve the Indian Act, but it won't be the reality on the ground after today."

"We'll see about that." Rob turned away. He'd only gone a few steps, though, when he stopped again.

"You know why I never came here?" he heard himself say. He hadn't meant to say this—he shouldn't have to defend himself. Terry waited patiently, so Rob grimaced and went on.

"It's not my roots," he said. "*I* get to decide what my roots are. And these ones, this stuff you're defending so cleverly . . . it's dead. There's no people in the world who can hold themselves together using band councils and elders and traditional dances. You can't go back. The world's moved on and sitting around a campfire *deciding* together just isn't going to cut it anymore. It's that simple."

Terry sent his dad a wry look. "You know, the first time I visited you on Parliament Hill, I was walking up the steps to the main doors, and all I could think was 'This place is handmade. Out of *stone.*'"

He sauntered off in the direction of the water.

Rob stalked across the parking lot, fuming. What the hell was that supposed to have meant? Of course Parliament was built of stone; it was old. Old . . .

He skidded to a stop. "Hey, wait a sec!" But Terry was already out of earshot. Rob sputtered, trying to say, "Yeah, it's old but not old like the band councils, not like that wisdom of the elders shit," but his son was too far away and besides, Rob could feel the world turning around him, the ancient and the new colliding in the goddamned sensory substitution shirt.

They could have sensory substitution banned; but there was still Wegetit.com. Maybe that could be shut down, but there were already imitators. The mesh networks, autonets, the block chain . . . they blurred into the legal in every direction. And the overlays, Structured Dialogic Design, Nexcity, and the Dorians—now that the genie was out of the bottle, there'd be so many improvements so fast, that soon every citizen on- and offline would have or have access to the kind of political second sight that previously, only rare people like Rob had possessed.

He didn't have his glasses on, but it blazed in his imagination: the Dorian of the only future that was going to work. The face of a new government was rising like a sun above the campfires and lodgepoles, above the halls of stone and oak—a government not dependent on any single technology, not even the Internet, but rather the accumulated crescendo of dozens of little nudges, techniques, and apps, and hundreds of new insights into cognitive and behavioral science.

It was obvious now: he'd only been invited out to Haida Gwaii as a courtesy, the way that he himself had invited elders to meetings so many times. To make them feel better while the real business went on invisibly around them.

He wasn't going to lose this negotiation, and he wasn't going to walk away from it either. He'd never really been a part of it.

Jeffrey was standing in front of the center, eyes darting around and a worried look on his face. When he spotted Rob, he rushed over. "I just heard. What are we going to do, sir?"

Rob let out a huff of breath—half sigh, half laugh. "We do what we always do, Jeff," he said.

"One way or another, we keep the conversation going. We can't give up now.

"Let's go back inside."

STORY NOTES—Karl Schroeder

Humanity's biggest problem isn't how to imagine or design solutions for our economic, environmental, and social woes; our problem is that we can't agree to implement them. By 2013, for instance, international agreement on curbing greenhouse gas emissions was further away than ever, despite years of conferences, meetings, expert panels, and millions of dollars spent on studies. This issue—of how we decide important things in groups—is the "meta-problem" that trumps all other issues. If we solve it, our other crises become manageable. If we don't solve it, it doesn't matter how many fixes we come up with. If we can't get them implemented, we might as well not have wasted our time.

Wicked Problems

Many of our most important problems are ill-defined. There's little agreement surrounding possible solutions to such problems, and there's no way to verify if a proposed fix will work or if one that's been tried has worked. These are called "wicked problems" because you cannot simply engineer a solution to them. Fortunately, methods do exist to manage them—if not to solve these messes, to at least *improve* them. One such approach is called Structured Dialogic Design, which was developed by the Institute for 21st Century Agoras, primarily by cyberneticist Alexander Christakis. SDD builds upon decades of research into small-group interactions to provide a process whereby people with radically different, even hostile agendas can sit down together and agree upon mutually beneficial plans of action. An introduction to the process can be found in the book *The Talking Point,* by Thomas R. Flanagan and Alexander N. Christakis.

Decision Architecture

There will be no "Facebook for politics," no single solution to the problem of human governance, because politics is a wicked problem. That doesn't mean we can't improve political processes at all levels, perhaps dramatically, by solving many smaller subissues using communications technologies, cognitive bias filtering software, decision-making strategies, and so on. SDD is

just one example of how to do this. The story "Degrees of Freedom" show-
cases a possible set of such improvements, just a tiny subset of the many possibilities. I've included more information about some of these below.

Dorians

Humans are hardwired to detect extremely subtle differences in facial
expression. In 1973, Herman Chernoff suggested using this capability to
make complex multivariant data more easily visible to analysts. Different
parameters of a complex data set are mapped to different features on these
"Chernoff faces," making it easy for viewers to perceive small differences
between sets.

Extending this idea, Dorians are pictures of yourself that are more or
less happy, healthy, or fit depending on how your current behaviors or habits
are trending. Basically, they show you your future self as you might look if
you keep doing what you're doing. Dorians are a natural and intuitive interface for "quantified Self" apps such as sports and fitness trackers, though in
this story they also interpret the results of more significant life choices.

You can think of the augmented reality app Nexcity mentioned in the
story as a form of urban Dorian (see SimCanada, opposite).

Liaisons

Liaisons are a concept I developed for a Canadian military foresight
project in 2009. A liaison is a Dorian that personifies a corporation, government, organization, or group. It can serve as your interface to that organization; for instance, when you do online banking you might choose to
do so by talking to the bank's liaison. The trick is that the bank doesn't
control how the liaison appears and behaves—instead, its personality is an
aggregate of the public's experience of the organization—its social media
"likes" and "dislikes," to put it crudely. A company that tries to paper over
bad practices, lies to its customers and the press, etc., will have a shifty-
looking liaison. One that promotes philanthropic causes will look saintly,
and so on.

Padgets

Padgets are a European Union experiment in democratic technology.
Padget stands for "policy gadget." You can find out how they work at the
project website, http://www.padgets.eu/.

SimCanada

The Intergovernmental Panel on Climate Change shows how large sets of diverse models can be ganged together to create robust quantitative simulations of the future. SimCanada and its imitators build on this technology by using climatic, economic, social, and cultural data to present constantly updated future versions of the country. Citizens can explore possible outcomes of economic and political policies, climate change, and wildcard events by running them through the model(s). With a gamified graphical interface, the system will even let you walk through your city or province as it might appear years from now—in effect, as a national or urban Dorian.

Gwaiicoin and the Block Chain

Gwaiicoin is an altcoin: a derivative of Bitcoin. Bitcoin itself, while interesting, is a sideshow to the more important technology underlying it. This technology is a cryptographic system known as the block chain. It can be used for far more than "just" creating a revolutionary new form of money. The block chain can support decentralized, fraud-proof implementations of nearly any kind of registry. Everything from voting systems, citizenship and ownership contracts, constitutions, corporate structures, and decision-making processes can all be done in the block chain. Faced with the question of "Who has ultimate authority?" on nearly any matter, the answer no longer needs to be some committee, statute, ministry, board, or person. The answer can be "the stakeholders, directly, using the block chain."

Project Cybersyn

Cyberneticist Stafford Beer partnered with the Chilean government of Salvador Allende from 1971 to 1973 to build a new form of government based on cybernetic principles. Project Cybersyn was a new model of socialism, a "third way" that was different from both capitalism and Soviet or Maoist communism. Cybersyn was based on advanced communications and feedback systems. The system was destroyed, and Allende killed, in the September 11, 1973, coup backed by the CIA and led by Augusto Pinochet.

FORUM DISCUSSION—The Future of Agriculture

Should we ban agriculture on Earth? Karl Schroeder, Bruce Sterling, and chemical engineering Ph.D. student Zach Berkson investigate at hieroglyph.asu.edu/degrees-of-freedom.

THE MATHEMATICS OF GAMIFICATION—Foursquare Data Scientist

Explore the mathematics of gamification with Foursquare data scientist Michael Li at hieroglyph.asu.edu/degrees-of-freedom.

RESPONSE TO "DEGREES OF FREEDOM"—David Guston

David Guston, the founding director of Arizona State University's Center for Nanotechnology in Society, responds to "Degrees of Freedom" at hieroglyph.asu.edu/degrees-of-freedom.

TWO SCENARIOS FOR THE FUTURE OF SOLAR ENERGY
Annalee Newitz

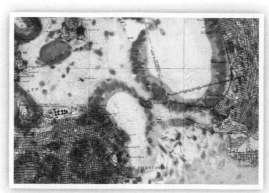

Biomimetic City

Driving in from the inland freeway, your car is a virus injecting itself into an enormous cell.

No, it's not your imagination—the layout of the City really was arranged to imitate the structure of a microorganism. In the mid-twenty-first century, they called it urban metabolic design.

When you see the glowing yellow sensor notices by the side of the road, you've reached the outer membrane. Privacy laws don't always work well with environmental ones, which is why we have to have big, ugly signs everywhere to warn people we are using surveillance to make sure the ecosystems aren't ruined. Most of our environment monitoring tech can't be used to track people or cars, but there you go.

We have tiny, networked sensors for tasting carbon and water levels in the air, camera-trapping the wildlife, and sniffing for chemicals. The sensors are too small to see, or they're camouflaged. But sometimes you'll catch a glimpse of the spider and dog robots patrolling up in the hills. They rescue animals who've done something ridiculous like eat a sensor, but mostly they repair the network and keep people from tromping around off the paths. If anything goes in the ecosystems out here, we'll know about it in just a few hours. We've got more than two centuries' worth of data on the kinds of fluctuations in life-forms you'd expect from wetlands and grasslands. If anything goes off the charts, we'll know.

It might get boring after a while, so I recommend tuning in to the camera trap live feeds. You can find them on the CityNet main page—they're some of the most popular channels. You can see everything from hawk nests and bear dens to foxes, fluffy little pikas, seals, and otters. Be careful, because the baby bear cam will suck you in for an entire day.

You'll also see metal spikes in the ground, which are part of the geo-grid that gives the City early warning on quakes and volcanoes. So far our record is a five-minute warning, but soon with better surveillance we'll be able to predict quakes *years* in advance.

Notice that the roads are made of fresh foam; your car will associate with the local network. That's where you'll see the solar and wind fields—these are the cell's chloroplasts (or mitochondria, if you prefer animal cells). We reuse nearly everything, so there are at least five generations of generator out there. Dishes, trays, planks, and slabs of blue-black light collectors slowly shift with the sun, some magnifying light with transparent lenses above their faces and some exposed directly. They're turning water and carbon into liquid fuel. The windmills have blades modeled on owls' wings, which is why they look like they're partially covered in spiny down. They're completely silent. They beat their wings over the fuel generators like weird birds from the Cretaceous.

Water for the fields comes from another part of the cell, a ring of recycling plants, factories, and farms that are a tangle of productivity. Call it the City's cytoplasm, full of proteins and organelles processing energy, waste, and everything else we need to survive. Factories are cooled by water reuse tanks clinging to the outside of their rough wood warehouse walls, and water vapor rises from their roofs. Water vapor is the only by-product allowed in chemical processing. Next door to a fab churning out glassware, you'll see a field of almond trees; and next to that, a tissue-growing operation where giant, rectangular mats of beef and chicken meat are grown on floor-to-ceiling tissue scaffolds the color of cream. Saucer-shaped robots hover at the edges of small farm plots, collecting run-off minerals to use in our matter printers.

These places are where all our food and water come from, as well as a lot of the primers we use for printing everything from computers and cameras to plates and toothpicks.

Most people treat their printers like magic—as if they just create rolls of toilet paper from random atoms floating around in the air. That's why I always tell visitors to drive through that cytoplasm, so they can see where all the matter actually comes from. We harvest it from the earth, and from recycled waste. No matter what the Singularitarians say, we don't live in a postscarcity era. We get all our atoms from the same places they've always come from—we're just better at manipulating them than people were a hundred years ago.

I think it was some old biologist who said that the nucleus is really just an unintended consequence of all the symbiotic relationships among different parts of the cell. If you think of the City proper as the nucleus, that's absolutely true. The closer you get to the places where people live, the more factory/recycling pods you'll see. Without them, the City would be unsustainable.

Crest the last hill and you will get an amazing view of all the towers and trains and rooftop gardens of downtown, darkly reflective against the clear waters of the Bay. Server towers dominate the skyline, the wastewater pipes crawling down their sides making them look like beautiful, veined bodies. The Market River cuts through downtown, its surface bobbing with boats and LEDs, and its banks lined with hundreds of stalls where you can buy everything from apples to circuit boards. Market's briny water flows south into the Mission Marsh, where the houses, hipster boutiques, and sidewalks are mounted on stilts above the muck. Silvery trains rattle over the streets, dipping underground to preserve as much space as possible. At night, the downtown dance clubs and crazy theme restaurants fluoresce in green and red.

This is where all the signals converge; it's the code that coordinates the entire cell. But it would be a mistake to say that the genome rules this synthetic body. Without communication between it and the rest of the cell, you'd have a broken metabolism.

A hundred years ago, this City was all nucleus and no cytoplasm. The cell's energy production, its food and fuel, came from all over the world, often traveling thousands of miles. People used energy just to ship more energy to the places that needed it. When you're high on fossil fuel fumes,

I guess almost anything can make sense. I love looking at photo galleries of what the City looked like back then, with giant trucks carrying things everywhere and all of nature totally unregulated.

What's weird is how similar things look, too. Especially in the nucleus. Buildings are taller and there are more wall farms. But a hundred years ago, you could easily see the same street scene I see outside right now. The only difference is that our walls are painted with sensors and everybody has spray-on windows now instead of glass. Also, the transit system is fantastic and robots keep things clean. The basic street grid is the same, the houses are still boxes made out of wood, and if you stumble out of a bar dead drunk at 2 A.M., there's a gutter to collapse in.

I forgot to mention that you'll have to park your car outside the City center and take the train in. There are usually some Cityshare electric bicycles if you want one and it's not too foggy to ride. Remember to stay on the foam. Riding off road messes up the diversity of the local ecosystem. You wouldn't want to get a ticket before you've even reached downtown!

Life in the Ruins

I'm sorry I'm late.

When it's my turn to feed the kitchen it takes me longer to get to work in the morning. The downstairs neighbors' air system has been dying in patches, and whatever is affecting their cyanobacteria is affecting ours now too. I'm starting to think we should call the gardener.

The blackened bits come off in flakes when I scrape the filter. I prep a new culture, spraying on a layer of nutrient and topping it with some fresh cyano from the small-batch brewer up the street. Once I've slid the whole thing back into its slot over the sink, I barely have time for a wash if I want to catch the train downtown. If all goes well, I'll come home to a thriving colony and we'll be breathing sweet, warm air. Plus we'll be bringing down carbon again, and that means fewer sad faces in April at tax time.

In the tub, I oil up and scrape off quickly, slapping a few tablespoons of dirty runoff into the bathroom bioreactor. It's never a good idea to waste skin microbes—you never know when they'll come in handy. Then I towel off, pull on yesterday's jeans, and bend the planks of the sidewalk as I race to the station.

Looking out the windows as the train crosses the river, I remember again why I moved here ten years ago. The place is gorgeous. In the distance, I can see the blocky, translucent warehouses that hold the cyano breweries, cooking up fuel. I like to imagine that I can see the columns of oxygen that the crops release into the air, invisible plumes of molecules that keep the planet cool.

Ahead are the rough, pockmarked Mounds of the business district, perfectly sculpted four-hundred-meter-high hills, their muddy slopes covered in a tangle of vines, grasses, antennas, and slow-moving escalators. I love a city with a long history, and this one goes back over a thousand years. Nobody knows much about the first people who settled the area, but you can still visit their eroded Mound ruins on the east side of the river. They didn't live inside their Mounds, though—instead, they built their villages and town squares in the shadow of those earthen behemoths, and rerouted the river to irrigate their farms.

You've probably heard that two hundred years ago, there would have been a stark contrast between the Mounds of the east and the buildings of the west side. In the industrial age, the whole city was running on fossil carbon—coal was a huge local industry—and everything was designed to accommodate that form of energy. So there were mines instead of cyano breweries.

Plus, the buildings were dumb. If the cement on the bridge cracked, it was finished. It didn't self-repair. You had to rip the thing apart, and maybe tear it down completely, wasting all those materials in the process. Roads were made of rust and tar, and houses were utterly dead inside. There were whole industries devoted to "pest control," which actually meant destroying all the bugs and molds and animals and microbes that I just devoted my morning to keeping healthy.

Picture a completely different world, where people built everything with their own hands and dumb machines. As my off-gridder uncle would no doubt remind me, everybody had a lot more freedom, too, because there were no carbon taxes and microbial regulation. But there was also really bad health care, disgusting food, and everybody lived in buildings that were constantly falling apart.

I get off the train downtown and grab some maté from a cart, weaving between the goats they've unleashed on the street to trim the grass. I must be hungry because I'm thinking, *Goat cheese, mmmmm goat cheese*. I skipped breakfast again. I crumple my cup and toss it on the grass, waiting briefly to see whether a goat will get to it before disintegration begins. The goats lose this time. The cup starts fraying into feathery strips of plant nutrients before I remember that I'm late.

The Mound where I work grew an unusual feature about thirty years ago during an especially bad storm season. It rained so much that the soil layers washed away and exposed its concrete to the sun. The concrete was a type of smart material that was designed to react with light, and something went wrong—the exposed areas just started to grow, kind of like a cancer. By the time repair crews had shut its metabolism down, there was this huge, irregular scab of concrete stretching from the roof to the ground in the exact shape of a water runoff stream.

The engineers who work here call it Scar Mound, which is our emo way of reminding ourselves not to ship twanged-out viral material. We build tiny environmental sensors out of modified virus shells, and that means you're depending on a little strand of occasionally unpredictable RNA to build the product. You don't want some sensor array to give the wrong readings because you forgot to block some basic pathway in its gene expression. I'm pondering that as I palm the reader next to a hatch about halfway up the scar. Its membrane thins and lets me through.

My office is lit by the redirected light from the vents. Luckily, my predecessor decided to decorate the roof with stars. She used different-colored algae to create a glowing field of yellow stars against a deep blue background. It looks like a kid's bedroom, but I love it. If you can't have a view of the river, at least the lights can be beautiful. And the carpet is a DIY grass mod that never gets too tall or scratchy. One day I'll figure out how to mod everything in here to reabsorb its own dying bits so that I don't have to dust plant crud off my projector every morning.

I get on the treadmill and start walking. The projector comes to life, filling the air with my unread messages, and I start swiping through them one by one.

Biomimetic City: What Would Make This Scenario Possible?

The biomimetic city is a purely technological and industrial creation that imitates biological processes in order to remain carbon neutral and sustainable. It isn't a city built from scratch—it is a retrofit of an existing city, San Francisco, and its metabolism was constructed over decades of incremental shifts in how citizens treated their environment.

This futuristic city might not look very different from cities today. The one noticeable change would be how energy and food are generated in nearby farms and factories. Though the actual buildings would be recognizable to anyone from the twenty-first century, they're made from very different kinds of materials. Roads, paints, windows, and even toilet paper are made using substances and processes that don't exist yet. Still, all these innovations could grow out of technologies we're developing today to create solar fuel generators.

The metabolic city is an unintended consequence of research into solar power technologies.

Today, researchers at the Joint Center for Artificial Photosynthesis (JCAP) at UC Berkeley and Caltech are working on solar fuel generators that will convert water, sunlight, and carbon into liquid fuel. To do it, they've had to invent a new, high-throughput method for testing possible materials that could be used to absorb light and create fuel.

Solar fuel generators have to act as light antennas, drawing in as many wavelengths as possible, but also as catalysts to split water and carbon into oxygen and hydrocarbon fuel. They have to be rugged and able to function in salt water, and they have to be cost-effective. We don't yet have materials that can be all these things—and work together.

Ian Sharp, a physicist who works with semiconductor materials at JCAP, is trying to figure out how to layer different materials on top of each other to create a device that can absorb light as well as transform water and carbon into fuel. Often, this means guiding electrons through ultrathin layers of material. "It's kind of like brewing coffee," Sharp says. "You want the coffee to make it into your cup, but you also want the grounds to stay where they're supposed to be. Except, with our device, the holes of the coffee filter are smaller than a few nanometers. And that means the system can become unstable, and you end up with a cup of coffee grounds."

In his analogy, the electrons are your coffee, and the water that contains those electrons are the grounds—you want to get your electrons to pass through into the semiconductor, but prevent water from coming in and corroding everything. The filter is designed to filter electrons out of water and keep the semiconductor nice and dry.

Ten years ago, scientists like Sharp would have had to mix and test new materials for their filters or light absorbers over months, exposing them to different levels of heat and corrosives to see how well they worked. JCAP scientists have retrofitted an ink jet printer to synthesize and print out tiny dots of metal mixed up from different amounts or types of elements. The result is a long, scrolling paper like what you'd get out of an old dot-matrix printer. Except each dot on it is a novel material that can be tested in parallel. Up to one million of these new materials can be produced in a single day.

Consider that this high-throughput synthesis of materials is being used in many other labs too. Though JCAP will eventually settle on a particular stack of materials for its light absorbers and catalysts, it will have created millions of other materials with novel properties in the process. It plans to make information about all those materials available for free online. Other scientists working on different problems in materials synthesis can consult JCAP's database.

This is a classic example of how taking on a big scientific project can lead to other forms of innovation on the way to a long-term goal. JCAP scientists want to generate solar fuel from carbon dioxide and water. Along the way, however, they'll make it possible for engineers in many other fields to discover new materials that could lead to what we saw in the biomimetic city: spray-on, high-performance windows, foam roads, sophisticated 3-D printers, superdurable environmental sensors, and extremely efficient water recycling systems.

It will also lead to actual solar fuel generators, another reason this futuristic city looks a lot like San Francisco today. Unlike current solar energy, which is intermittent and terrifically difficult to store, solar fuel can be packaged up in drums just like oil and gasoline.

We'd fill our gas tanks with solar fuel and use pipes to bring it into the city from the nearby generator fields. We'd retrofit a lot of our current infrastructure to work with this new, carbon-neutral fuel. The fact that we won't have to reinvent the way we deal with fuel could help us transform our cities sustainably, and slowly. Instead of tearing cities down, we'll recycle them and patch them up with new materials. Our cities will evolve to be more like biological organisms that are self-restoring.

On the road to developing efficient solar fuel generators, we could create cities whose technologies behave like components in an environmental system. As Sharp put it to me, "It's not a future that looks totally different, but the subtle differences are important. The result is very realistic."

Life in the Ruins: What Would Make This Scenario Possible?

Unlike the biomimetic city, the Mound city is actually biological. Everything from its water filtration systems to its solar energy production is done using biological organisms. Its structures aren't "smart" like iPhones—they are smart because they are teeming with bacterial colonies that respond dynamically to the environment. This city is the result of advances in synthetic biology that allowed engineers to use the photosynthetic process in cyanobacteria to convert water and light into hydrogen fuel.

Modeled on St. Louis, the Mound city looks dramatically different from cities of today—though, as our narrator explained, its architecture does resemble the styles favored by the Meso-American peoples who built Cahokia on the eastern side of the Mississippi River in the 600s CE. Historians believe that one reason Cahokia may have been abandoned in the 1200s is that the centuries-old city became polluted with waste and ruined by unsustainable agricultural practices. (There's evidence that the locals diverted rivers multiple times for irrigation.) Many of the problems that plagued people of that era are also issues for St. Louis's inhabitants today. The coal industry won't last forever, and droughts in the Midwest wreak havoc on the food supply.

That's why physicist Himadri Pakrasi has created an interdisciplinary initiative at Washington University in St. Louis called the International Center for Advanced Renewable Energy and Sustainability (I-CARES). The cornerstone of the initiative is a series of projects devoted to alternative energy, with Pakrasi focusing on genetically modified cyanobacteria.

A few years ago, Pakrasi made headlines when his lab created a strain of cyano that could produce far more hydrogen than average. If we could capture and use that hydrogen, he speculated, we'd have the beginnings of a new kind of sustainable fuel. Instead of drawing carbon from stores deep beneath the earth, this cyano would draw carbon that's already free-floating in the environment as part of its natural life cycle. This is the very definition of a carbon-neutral fuel.

When I visited Pakrasi in St. Louis to talk about how he imagined I-CARES would change the future, he suggested that one day his city would draw its energy from both algae and ultra-high-efficiency solar cells. His colleague Richard Axelbaum, an environmental engineer, gave me a tour of a model power plant facility at the university that the group thinks could represent a transitional phase between coal energy and algae energy. The plant is designed for "clean coal" burning, a process where the harmful by-products of coal burning are reduced and, in some cases, recycled. Carbon is siphoned off during combustion and fed to huge tanks of algae that will ultimately produce fuel. Tailings, instead of being stored in toxic ponds, are used in the production of asphalt.

This kind of energy plant, where coal burning feeds into the production of biofuel, is a reminder that we can't change over from one kind of energy production to another overnight. We have to move through transitional stages while corporations and the public adjust to the new carbon economy. To transition to the Mound city, however, we need more than hybrid fuel production facilities. The public must become accustomed to the idea that their city will run on genetically modified organisms.

Sustainable fuel from cyano could be the GMO that sets off a synthetic biology gold rush. After a generation grows up using GMOs for fuel, GMO panic might seem like an antiquated superstition. Today, we are already seeing the development of "smart" materials in labs—including bacteria-based, self-healing cement—but many people fear the idea of building with biology. It's possible that Pakrasi's strain of cyano, or something similar, could convert that fear into familiarity.

The result might be a place like the Mound city, where people use modified cyano for everything from air filtration to fuel. They also build with smart, self-healing materials, treating microorganisms the way we treat microprocessors today. Their Mounds are covered in vines and grasses that are an integral part of the city infrastructure.

However, Mound city isn't just the consequence of scientific advancement. If science were all that mattered for building a city, we could have a Mound city in fifty years. Cities are fundamentally social and economic structures. We'd need a social transformation that allowed for things like carbon taxes.

People living in the Mound city would also have dramatically different expectations about how they would live. Our narrator's home is in a densely populated building where her neighbors' cyano affects the functioning of hers—much the way a plumbing problem in one apartment can become a leak in another. She also doesn't own a car, nor does she expect to live in a place that is clean in the way most urbanites today would want. Dirt and plants are every where. And energy comes where you can get it. Most of the time, she powers up her computer by walking on a treadmill made with viruses that convert kinetic energy into electricity. For city dwellers of today, this might sound like a dirty, crowded, difficult existence.

To modern eyes, the Mound city would look like a ruin, with crumbling, scarred buildings that have been overrun with plants. But to people of the future, it would represent the apex of technology. Or rather, biology. Instead of building against the environment, Mound citizens would be building with the environment. They'd be using Earth's greatest source of energy: solar. It would be hard to know where the city stopped and the natural world began. It wouldn't be the sterile, orderly future of *Star Trek* that many of us were promised. It would just be Earth.

The biomimetic city and the Mound city are both imaginative products of a long-term scientific search for new kinds of solar energy. They remind us that every great innovation spawns more inventions than we intended.

As we move forward, new technologies and new social ideas may make the future as strange to us as a new city is to visitors from out of town. But if we choose our scientific projects wisely, we can harbor a rational hope that there will be friendly tour guides in centuries to come, willing to show our descendants around.

FORUM DISCUSSION—Urban Sustainability

Vandana Singh, James Cambias, and other Hieroglyph community members debate sustainable cities, community gardens, and the "zoopolis" at hieroglyph.asu.edu/solar-city.

A HOTEL IN ANTARCTICA
Geoffrey A. Landis

© 2013, Nina Miller / ASU

MAYBE IT STARTED THE day his laser company failed, the day his best friend, Saladin, drove off into the sunrise on his motor scooter, taking along the girl that Izak Cerny had always planned would be his girlfriend, and he stood on the curb waiting for lawyers and police cars to take everything he'd worked for, watching the sun rise, wondering what to do next.

Zak had stayed at a hotel that night. His credit cards were no good, but the banks hadn't yet flagged them for fraud. The hotel bill would just add a few more meaningless numbers to an epic bankruptcy. In a few days he would be thirty years old.

He'd never thought much about hotels before then. But—with his company imploded, and his thoughts circling in meaningless spirals—it was the only thing he could latch on to. He needed to think about something else or go crazy. And so he studied the hotel, Mistry Majestic Long Island, in obsessive detail. How would it be different if it were on the moon? On Mars? In orbit? He decided that yes, it might work. It just might work.

"I'm an entrepreneur," he said. "I can do it." It was midafternoon on a weekday. He was alone in a hotel room three grades fancier than anything he could have afforded, and he was talking to himself. He walked past the queen-sized bed, threw open the sliding glass doors, stepped through to the tiny balcony, and shouted to the ocean, "I can do this."

Or maybe it had all started long before that, the summer after his sophomore year at MIT. They had planted a seed, and Zak had carried it with him all those years.

That all-night session in the lounge outside their dorm rooms, they had been too young to legally drink, but with the help of some French grad students who didn't think much of American rules about alcohol, a small group of them were splitting a cooler full of Narragansett. Zak was expounding on how to colonize Mars, something he worked out in great detail, from the air-handling and regeneration system all the way to the sewage system. Saladin, always the voice of cynicism, pointed out at every opportunity "you don't know that," and "that's never been tested," and "what if it breaks down, and you need a spare part you don't have?" Eventually, Saladin made an argument. "Look, Zak. Seriously. Mars is way more hostile than you can imagine. It's colder than Antarctica, has less air than the top of Mount Everest, is drier than the Mojave, and is harder to get to than the bottom of the Marianas Trench. You say people are going to live there; it's our destiny? Fine. So we need room that bad, how come we don't have condos in Antarctica? Why no cities on the bottom of the Pacific? Why isn't the Gobi Desert populated? Those are vastly easier places to live than Mars. Yet nobody lives there."

"People live in the Gobi Desert."

"Maybe one person in a hundred square miles. You know how freaking big the Gobi is? It's empty."

"People live in Antarctica, too."

"Yeah, right—science stations. I mean, people who really *live* there, not just scientists on a glorified camping trip. You think humanity needs room? There's a whole continent we're not using.

"You think you can build a colony on Mars? Prove it. Build a hotel on Mount Everest. Or Antarctica; a hotel in Antarctica. That's a thousand times easier, but it's still damn hard. A hotel in Antarctica, that will show me you've got a clue, Zak. Call it an existence proof."

"Don't be silly. Who in the world would you get to stay in a hotel in Antarctica?"

He looked around the room for support, but to his surprise, a handful of the sophomores were nodding. One, a kid whose name Zak had long

ago forgotten, said, "Me. I'd go." Another kid said, "Sure. Awesome skiing. Make it a ski lodge." "Penguins," another kid said, at the same time a
fourth one said, "Set up tours to see the aurora."

"See," Saladin said. "There you go. Extreme tourism, that's the ticket.
You got a market. Make me a hotel."

"Drunken sophomores?" Zak said. "That's a market?"

"Build it and they will come."

Some twelve years later, Izak Cerny slid a sheet of hotel stationery
from the fake mahogany desk of a hotel room he couldn't afford. Underneath the letterhead "Hotel Mistry," he wrote: "A hotel in Antarctica 1.
Because it's really cool. 2. Because it's never been done. 3. Because it's
expanding humanity into a new frontier. 4. As a step toward Mars. 5. To
make money. 6. Because it's really cool, also penguins." Then he wrote
"people will want this." He circled that twice and wrote in the margin,
"!!emphasize this point!!"

The desk drawer held a privately printed autobiography of Gajadhar
Mistry, founder of the hotel chain. An identical volume was in every room
of the hotel: promotional reading for a million bored businesspeople who
had already finished the *Wall Street Journal*. The motto of the founder was in
boldface across the cover: "What others call obstacles, I call stepping-stones!"

Zak mined the book for relevant details, and then swiveled over to his
laptop. He already had eight windows open, with searches on the geography and ecology of Antarctica. He opened a new browser window and
typed in "Gajadhar Mistry." He would try Google first and then check
LinkedIn. He knew a lot of people. Somewhere in his network of friends
and connections and friends of friends, there was someone who could put
him in touch with Gajadhar Mistry.

GAJADHAR MISTRY HAD BLOW-DRIED silver-gray hair that made him
look like the uncle character in a Bollywood thriller. But other than that,
he still had the body of a much younger man, muscles showing that he regularly worked out with his personal fitness trainer. He wore a T-shirt and
jeans. When you're a billionaire who owns top-end hotels in twenty countries, apparently you don't care what anybody thinks of how you dress.

"My friends tell me that I should talk with you," Mistry said. "So, tell
me. *Why* should I talk with you?"

"I want to tell you about an idea—"

"Yes, yes." Mistry waved his hands. "You want to build a space colony I read the package you put together. It's crazy."

Zak interrupted. "It's not a crazy idea. The space colony is just an example. It's about a self-sustaining biosphere to live in a hostile environment. Antarctica—"

Mistry raised a hand. "I have no problem with crazy ideas. The fact that your ideas are crazy is not a downside for me, Mr. Cerny—" He broke off. "Mr. Cerny, that's formal, and I am not a formal kind of guy. May I call you Izak?"

"Just Zak."

"Zak. Excellent. Please call me Jerry. Now, Zak. Your ideas are crazy. Antarctica! Space hotels! Crazy indeed. But I like crazy ideas. I will let you convince me. And maybe your idea is not so completely crazy at all."

"It's not."

"Let me tell you," Mistry said. "I have made a small fortune building luxury hotels catering to the extreme tourism market. My first hotel was for the jungle-trekking tourists, in Chiang Mai. You already knew that? Ah, you've read my book. Excellent, I see you do your homework. Tourists love elephants." He waved his hand at the wall of the office. It was covered with photos taken at his various hotels, half of them featuring wild animals, with tourists on elephants in two of them. "The hotel in Chiang Mai was built on the backs of elephants—not literally, of course. Everybody loves elephants. Wonderful beasts. Penguins, now—I expect that some people would pay something to frolic with penguins, yes. And skiing, of course. Especially when it is summer in Japan and America.

"Now. Space colonies I have no interest in. But Antarctica? Crazy, but maybe crazy in a good way. Crazy the way I like."

Mistry leaned back in his chair and folded his hands together, fingertips to fingertips. "But my question is, why should I talk to *you*? You already gave me your idea."

Zak started to object, but Mistry raised his hand for silence again. "Yes, you gave it to me. Ideas can't be copyrighted. Once you sent me your package—thank you, and you have no ownership. I read your résumé. You have a physics degree from MIT, very impressive, you worked for several small technology businesses. Then you broke away to form your own company, which I see failed and went bankrupt in a most spectacular fashion. Now, maybe I like your idea. A hotel in Antarctica. I like the audacity. I'm *charmed* by your idea."

He leaned forward and placed his elbows on the desk. "But I don't see that you know anything about building hotels. Why do I want *you?*"

Zak looked him in the eye. Mistry held his gaze and waited. "You don't know me," Zak said. "You don't know this about me." He enunciated each word separately, as if it were its own sentence. "I. Will. Make. This. Happen."

Mistry rocked back in his chair and laughed. "Perfect! Really, that is most excellent. I admire your certainty. My first two companies failed, did you know that? I don't hold your failures against you, not as long as you learned what you needed to know. That is what I look for in a person. You're hired. Convinced me."

"I was thinking to work as a consultant," Zak said. "I can—"

"I'm sorry," Mistry cut him off. "If you work for me, you will work for me. I will assure you that, as long as I like your work, you will not be objecting to the salary I offer, but I have this thing, Zak, perhaps it is a flaw. Perhaps not. But I demand control. Nonnegotiable."

Mistry held his gaze, and for a moment neither one spoke. Finally Zak broke the silence. "Accepted."

Mistry smiled. "Excellent. Most excellent. Now, there are some people I need you to meet . . ."

IT TURNED OUT THAT "people that Mistry wanted him to meet" consisted of a woman in her sixties: Mrs. Jeanne Binder. She wore an enormous pair of round eyeglasses and, as far as he could see, a perpetual scowl. "I trust Mrs. Binder with everything," Mistry told Zak. "Whatever she tells you, please be assured that I say exactly the same thing."

Zak and Mistry were back in Mistry's office, in the penthouse suite of an art deco hotel in Miami Beach. As he talked, Mistry went through a large pile of paperwork methodically, signing things without, as far as Zak could see, looking at them.

"What does she do?" Zak asked. "What do I need her for?"

"Everything," Mistry said.

"She's an architect? Structural engineer? Hotel manager? What?"

"If that's what you need, yes."

"She can't have expertise in everything."

"She most certainly can. She *hires* expertise."

"But what does she do?"

"My friend Zak, your ideas may be crazy, and I told you I like that. But one thing cannot be crazy. It is Mrs. Binder's task to make sure that the thing that is not crazy is the money. Mrs. Binder is your accountant."

"Great," Zak said. "An accountant. And she's running the show?"

Mistry clapped him on the shoulder. "You'll be great friends."

BEFORE HE LEFT—MISTRY APPARENTLY never spent more than a few days anywhere—he had an entire floor of the hotel in Miami Beach cleared out, converting a large conference room into a war room for the minions whom Mrs. Binder was to hire, giving her an office with a large glass window looking out over the beach, and Zak one looking west toward the intercoastal waterway. The floor was still mostly empty. Zak was sitting at a huge, empty desk wondering what he was supposed to be doing when Mrs. Binder came to his office. He was doodling sketches of geodesic domes. She came in holding a stack of glossy color brochures. She placed them carefully on his desk before turning to talk.

"Mr. Mistry tells me that I'm to make sure that you don't spend your time exploring outer space," Mrs. Binder said. "He informs me that you are going to design a hotel in Antarctica. Quite a desolate place, I'm told. I'm not sure that it's much better than outer space. How many units are you projecting to build? What capacity fraction do you think you can fill? What are your estimates for projected profit margin per unit?"

"It'll fill up," Zak said confidently. "I don't have any details yet. I know it'll work."

She looked at him over the rim of her glasses. "Your business plan doesn't include a number of units?"

"I don't have a business plan. There are too many variables—"

She took her glasses off and polished them with a corner of her blouse. "No business plan."

"Sorry, no. I've never been much for business plans. I like real things—"

"No business plan. Hmm. Mr. Mistry tells me that your previous business venture failed. I believe I see why."

He hung his head down. "I—"

"A business plan is a real thing, Mr. Cerny. As real as rocks or rockets."

"So what?"

"What? What, I would say, is we make a business plan."

"I'm not good with that kind of stuff."

"Trust me, Mr. Cerny." She looked at her now well-polished glasses and then put them in a breast pocket. "It will be brilliant."

The brochures she had left on his desk were glossy flyers advertising a wide range of extreme tourism activities, from zip-lining in the rain-forest canopies of Honduras to BASE jumping from a skyscraper in Singapore. This was what she saw as his market.

Somewhat grudgingly, he admired her thoroughness. Her network of contacts seemed to include people from all around the world. She polled travel agents specializing in vacations into uncomfortable and dangerous areas of the world. She found a list of cruise ships offering tours to Antarctica and put together a spreadsheet analyzing which ships, how many sailings and what times they sailed each year, estimates of the fraction of cabins sold, length of the trip, and the price and profit margin per passenger.

"I do believe you may have found a viable market niche," she said. "I had no idea. Over eighty companies are offering cruises and tours to Antarctica. It's a short tourist season, though: starts in November and goes to April. Four or five months."

"Sunlight," Zak said. "After April the days get too short."

Mrs. Binder nodded. "That. And since it's a ship-based service, they have to wait for ice to clear. We'll need airline service."

"I was figuring that."

"We'll build an airstrip. Dock facilities too; we want those cruise ships."

"Of course," Zak said.

"Current market for Antarctic tourism is fifty thousand tourists a year. In the first year, we'll aim at capturing twenty percent of the market. Figuring for double occupancy, five-night stay, twenty-five thousand room-nights. At a thousand dollars a night, comes to an annual net of twenty-five million."

"Twenty-five million dollars a year?"

"Plus profit from selling tourist activities," she said. "At fifty percent occupancy, figuring a five-month tourist season, we need just over three hundred rooms. There's your baseline plan, Mr. Cerny."

Zak's head was spinning. "You sure?"

She looked at him. "Of course I'm not sure. If I had a crystal ball, I'd use it. Until then, I work with the numbers I have."

"Twenty-five million dollars," Zak repeated. "I should ask for a higher salary."

Mrs. Binder looked at him over the top of her glasses, a gesture that Zak was beginning to understand meant that he had just said something unbelievably stupid. "That's gross income, Mr. Cerny, not profit. That won't be paying very much of your salary, much less mine. There isn't any local minimum-wage labor to staff the hotel. This will be very expensive to run.

"No, that just buys us into the market. Once we get established, long term, we need to grow that market. And lengthen the tourist season. The profit comes when—and if—we grow to ten times that. We want every skier in Europe to take winters in Antarctica. We do that, and then we'll make some money."

"A hundred thousand tourists?" Zak said.

"And don't forget the housing for the employees as well." She looked at him. "You said you wanted a city. Here's your city, if you can build it."

"I can build it."

"That," Mrs. Binder said, "we shall see. There's a lot of work to do first."

"We should just build the thing," Zak said. "Doing something is always the best way to learn how to do it."

Mrs. Binder took off her glasses. "Just build it."

"Right. You learn from experience, not endless analysis."

She found a piece of napkin left over from lunch and started polishing her glasses. "You do not 'just build' a hotel."

"Yeah, yeah, I know. You analyze it to death first. Look, let's just do it. You're afraid we'll get things wrong? Fine, we'll probably get some things wrong. We'll fix them. We'll learn as we go."

"And where, exactly, should we 'just build it'?"

Zak shrugged. "Anywhere. Find a spot. As long as it's in Antarctica, wherever."

"Who owns that spot? Who do we buy the property rights from?"

"Nobody owns Antarctica. We build on it, we own it. Right of possession! You think somebody's going to take a bulldozer and knock us down? I don't think there even are any bulldozers in Antarctica."

"Mr. Cerny, your ignorance of international law is astounding. Saying 'I call dibs' does not serve as a legal claim in any international court in the world. Before Mr. Mistry puts a billion dollars into constructing a hotel, he will be certain that there is at least one nation in the world recognizing our right to build on that spot. Right now, I believe that Argentina is likely to be that nation; they have claimed a large portion of Antarctica. We will work with them."

"I haven't thought about that."

"I expected you hadn't," Mrs. Binder said. "That's why I hired a team."

"When it's your billion dollars at stake, Mr. Cerny, you are certainly free to 'just build it.' Meanwhile, I have a business to put together."

THE NEXT CRISIS HAD nothing to do with property rights. When Zak came to the hotel the next day, he saw the stucco facade of the building spray painted in bright red with graffiti: SAVE THE PENGUINS and DON'T LET CORPORATE AMERIKA RAPE ANTARTICA and KEEP ANTARTIKA WHITE.

"Mr. Mistry has been informed, and he is flying in from Martinique," Mrs. Binder told him. "He is not happy."

Mistry was indeed not happy. He entered the offices unaccompanied by the usual staff and slapped a thin magazine down on the conference table, scattering to the side a pile of drawings Zak had been working on with designs for snowmobiles looking like Easter eggs on wheels. "Who the hell leaked to these clowns?" he said.

Zak looked over at Mrs. Binder and then picked up the magazine. It was labeled *Rainbow Earth!* and had a full-color picture of fuzzy penguin chicks on the cover, looking disconcerted at finding themselves staring into a camera. A bright pink Post-it note marked a page in the middle, and Zak flipped to it. The headline, in huge type, was A HOTEL IN ANTARCTICA? and under that, in slightly smaller type, "If hotel billionaire Gajadhar Mistry gets his way, the last unspoiled continent on Earth is about to get trashed." The article was signed "Anjel Earth." The facing page juxtaposed another penguin with a photograph of a garbage dump with a hotel in the background. The logo on the hotel—MISTRY ACAPULCO—was prominently visible.

"Photoshop," Mistry snarled. "I don't build hotels next to garbage dumps. I'll sue those bastards for defamation."

"You will not," Mrs. Binder told him calmly. "You know that is exactly what they want." She picked up the magazine and examined it. "Pretty high production values. I'm impressed."

"To hell with their production values." He looked directly at Zak. "Who leaked our plans?"

Zak had just published a technical paper in *Acta Astronautica*, comparing the requirements for a moonbase with the requirements for a hotel in Antarctica, with a detailed analysis of wastewater recycling. He suddenly realized that publishing his plans might not have been a good idea. He stared at the floor and said, sheepishly, "I am afraid that maybe—"

Mrs. Binder cut him off. She tossed the magazine back on the table. "They don't have any details; it's all blue-sky speculation and inspired guesses. They're fishing. They heard rumors, and they're firing a shot across our bows to see if we react."

"*What* rumors?"

Mrs. Binder shrugged. "Could be anything. We're talking with the Cousteau Society for advice on the scuba diving in Antarctica; they doubtless have contacts with these Rainbow Earth people. Or the IAATO, the Association of Antarctica Tour Operators. Or half a dozen other people."

"You are telling me that everybody you meet knows that we're looking at Antarctica?"

Mrs. Binder looked at Mistry over the top of her glasses. "We are building you a hotel, Mr. Mistry. If you are under the impression that we are secret agents, I'm afraid you are misinformed."

"At least *try* to be discreet."

"Discretion is overrated," she said. "Right now, we could use a bit of publicity. In the right places. And this"—she tapped the magazine—"is exactly the right place."

"The hell it is," Mistry said. "They're saying I plan to strip-mine—hell, look at this. They imply I'm going to rape baby polar bears and skin the fur off the bloody carcasses to keep rich tourists warm." He paused. "Are there even polar bears *in* Antarctica?"

"I do believe that's a joke," Mrs. Binder said. "And I believe you're missing the point. This is the audience we want to hit, and they are doing our job for us, better than we could do it ourselves." She picked up the magazine again and flipped page after page, color spreads of snow-covered mountains and underwater photography of penguins flying gracefully beneath the surface. "This is gold. Who cares what the editorial says? This is a direct hit on our target audience. They're doing our publicity for us."

"You are crazy," Mistry said. He picked up the magazine and looked at it again. "Really?"

"The fact that they are protesting," Mrs. Binder said, "says that these people think we have an idea worth pursuing."

THEY WERE WORKING ON the third-floor patio of the hotel. Mrs. Binder had insisted that since they were in Miami they should work outside when it was nice. Her definition of "nice" could be debated, since the weather was hot, even in October. The tourists were mostly gone and the patio was empty. Papers, held down with conch shells, were spread out across a number of tables, each one with its own red-and-white umbrella.

The pool bar's specialty was margaritas—twenty different kinds. But Zak was drinking Pepsi, and Mrs. Binder tonic water. She wore a bright blue-and-yellow floral sundress and had traded her usual owl glasses for sunglasses with equally large round lenses. Zak wore a Hawaiian shirt of garish colors. He was beginning to like Florida. He was even beginning to think that Mrs. Binder was okay, for an accountant. He had never worked up the nerve to ask her about Mr. Binder. It was a subject that she never brought up on her own.

The negotiation for the nuclear reactor had been going poorly. Zak's plan had been built around NASA plans for a reactor called SP-100, designed to power a lunar base, which turned out to be just about the perfect size for the hotel. In the NASA version, waste heat from the reactor was radiated away in space, but in his design it would be circulated through hot-water pipes to keep the habitat warm. Unfortunately, he had run up against rules forbidding the export of nuclear technology. Since the plan was to put the hotel in the part of Antarctica claimed by Argentina, even though nothing in the design was actually classified, they hit a brick wall in trying to get an export permit from the State Department.

Mrs. Binder had put her contacts on the problem, though, and had found a workaround: the Ukrainian navy had an old, Soviet-era nuclear-powered corvette. It was heavy and slow by modern naval warfare standards, undergunned, and completely useless in any sort of battle. But it carried a nuclear reactor of Soviet military design: simple, rugged, and nearly maintenance-free. Most important was that, stripped of its weapons, the Ukrainians were happy to sell the ship for little more than the price of the scrap metal, as long as the buyer guaranteed that they would take it far away and never bring it back.

"Not very efficient, by American standards," Mrs. Binder summarized, "but it solves the problem of how we transport it to Antarctica."

"The inefficiency is a bonus," Zak said. "That means more of the energy dissipated as heat, and we can use all the heat it can generate."

"It's one of a kind, though," she said. "When we expand, we'll have to solve the problem all over."

"So, we'll have the same solution," Zak said. "The Ruskies must have tons of Cold War junk they can't get rid of. Submarines. Aircraft carriers. Who knows?"

"I'll make inquiries," Mrs. Binder said.

"LOCATION, LOCATION, LOCATION" WAS the catchphrase of real estate. "And double that for hotels," Mrs. Binder said.

Topping their list of required features were penguins—tours to a penguin colony would be one of their main attractions. That part of their search became easier when they found, in an obscure scientific journal, the penguin-poo map. The accumulated droppings from ten thousand penguins spending four months at a winter nesting site made a distinct spectral signature identifiable in satellite images. They made extensive maps showing Antarctica's penguin rookeries.

Additionally, they wanted a site with good skiing possibilities. That meant far enough south that the slopes would be snow-covered even at the peak of summer. The site also needed a good harbor, for both cargo and cruise ships, and for jet-skiing. And finally they needed a flat plain large enough for a nine-thousand-foot runway, so they could bring in jets full of tourists, although that would not happen for some years after the hotel was opened.

Mistry's contacts in Argentina were enthusiastic about sponsoring the hotel as an opportunity to emphasize Argentina's land claims. But, after poring over maps and satellite images, none of their candidate locations fell within the Argentinean claim.

The spot they finally rated number one was in an area claimed by New Zealand, on the Ross Sea south of the Adare Peninsula. Nestled up against the Trans-Antarctic Mountains on one side, it had a natural harbor on the other side.

"A claim staked under New Zealand law may be better for us in any case," Mrs. Binder said. "It's easier to negotiate when you're speaking the same language."

"If you call it the same language."

"We already have three hotels in New Zealand," she said. "We can navigate the required permits. All in all, I think I like it." She looked at him. "It's just about summer in Antarctica. You have plans for Christmas?"

In fact, Zak had gotten a letter from Kayla and Saladin. An actual letter! So quaint. But his old e-mail had gone belly-up along with his company and his finances, and they probably had no other way to reach him. They had invited him to visit for the holidays. But if they were happy together, it would only depress him to visit, and if they had broken up—being as Saladin was still, despite everything, his best friend—it would depress him even more. Besides, what would they do? Reminisce about the good old days, when they had maxed every credit card they could apply for and every loan they could scrounge in a doomed attempt to keep his business from going under before launch?

"No," Zak said. "I'm free."

PREPARING TO VISIT ANTARCTICA was, Zak discovered, much like preparing to visit the moon. They moved their base of operations to the Mistry Oreti in Invercargill, New Zealand, the southernmost hotel in Mistry's chain. This would be the hotel that Mistry would use to send tourists to Antarctica. So in a sense their expedition was a dry run for the tourist trade.

The flight from Miami took more than thirty hours on Virgin Australia. The final hop to reach Invercargill was on Air New Zealand, but Mistry had booked them business class, instead of crammed into tiny seats like cattle to slaughter. There were some advantages to working for a billionaire. Zak spent the flight thinking about transportation. Could they send tourists to Antarctica on zeppelins? Back in the day, the *Hindenburg* had flown passengers from Germany to Rio de Janeiro, so Miami to Antarctica should be doable. He made some calculations and sketched designs. Mrs. Binder also spent much of the flight on her laptop, working on what, Zak could not tell.

Once they arrived, the first order of business was acquiring supplies for the trip. There was a list of "suggested" gear supplied by Scott Base, the New Zealand scientific station that would be their first stop. The list of required clothing was twenty-eight items long, starting with long underwear and moving layer by layer to an outer shell. Each item had to be tried on, to verify that it fit over the layers underneath and was roomy enough to allow a full range of motion.

"This is like a space suit," Zak complained.

"That's what you asked for," Mrs. Binder said.

"I'm thinking microwave heating," he said. "We could have a phased-array microwave antenna, sending a low-power beam to keep the suits warm. No reason Antarctica clothing should be any heavier than it needs to be."

"Tourists might find that scary."

"Feedback circuitry to make sure it doesn't overheat. And microwave-absorbing sun-goggles, to make sure the beam doesn't get to the eyes. That's the only part of the body that's really affected by microwaves."

Mrs. Binder was checking out gloves. Oddly, although she didn't strike him as a skier, she already had most of the extreme-weather clothing on the list.

"You don't need to join this scouting trip, you know," Zak said.

"That's sweet. I do like to see property before we place money on it, though. It's surprising what you don't see until you actually *see* it."

"We'll be taking photos. Lots of photos. You won't need to be there in person."

"I'll be okay." Mrs. Binder shrugged. "I don't expect it could be any worse than the scouting trip for the Mount Everest hotel."

Zak was astonished. "You wanted to build a hotel on *Everest?*"

"We scouted a site. The numbers ended up looking marginal, and the politics even more marginal, so we didn't follow through."

"Shit," Zak said. "And I thought I was the crazy one." That did explain her cold-weather gear. "I picked Antarctica because I thought Everest was too hard."

Across the street from the hotel in Invercargill was an enormous billboard with pictures of penguins, and the huge slogan "Save Antarctica for the Animals." Zak gazed out the window. "That's the Rainbow Earth

Coalition. The people who ran that magazine objecting to the hotel. They know we're here?"

"Anjel Earth runs that organization," Mrs. Binder said. "If he knows that we're planning to build in Antarctica, he might guess we'd come here first."

"That can't be his real name," Zak said.

"I couldn't say. But it wouldn't take a genius to figure where we'd stay, and according to the newspapers, he's a pretty sharp guy. Or it may just be coincidence."

"Kind of creepy," Zak said. "Isn't he the guy who rammed that Japanese whaling ship?"

"I thought that was a different group," she said. "I think these guys just harass them—circle around the whaling ships with motorboats and shout at them through megaphones."

"Great."

THEIR TRIP SOUTH WAS on an Australian-flagged icebreaker, *Opal Star*. A Rainbow Earth ship shadowed them out of the harbor.

The crew Mrs. Binder had hired as assistants included a civil engineer from the hotel's staff, a polar geologist, a biologist, and a pilot. Their names, he had learned, were Ashanti, Anita, Alexander, and Steve, but he had already lost track of who did what. If he had a question, he would randomly ask one of them.

As they left the port of Bluff, the day was beautiful as a postcard for a New Zealand vacation. Zak watched from the rail at the stern of the icebreaker; the Rainbow Earth ship followed about a quarter mile behind. It was about a hundred feet in length, rugged but clearly powerful, and painted with orange and black leopard spots.

Steve—or was it Alexander?—was looking through a pair of binoculars borrowed from one of the crewmen. "Can you see what the banners say?" asked Zak.

Steve—if it was Steve—adjusted the focus. "The banner on this side says 'People Before Profits.'" He put the binoculars down and put his hand up to shade his eyes.

Zak borrowed the binoculars. He could now make out the ship's name, *Earth Avenger*, and could see a pair of bright yellow Zodiacs hanging on one side. He'd seen that ship on television. It was a decommissioned

Coast Guard cutter that the Rainbow Earth Coalition had repurposed for harassing oil tankers, whalers, and trawlers fishing in protected waters. The Rainbow Coalition were the good guys in all the news stories; it felt odd to have them on his tail.

"They're following us," he said. "I doubt that s coincidence."

"Yep," said Steve.

"Looks faster than our boat."

"Yep."

Zak focused the binoculars on the man standing at the prow. He was perhaps thirty, with a full beard and a long ponytail of chestnut-brown hair, wearing a tie-dye shirt in swirls of green and blue. Zak said, "He's staring at us."

"Who?"

"Anjel Earth."

Zak brought the fact that they were being followed to the attention of one of the icebreaker's crew. The only response was "We noticed." When he pressed further, the captain told him, "It's a free ocean. If they're still following us in another day, I may radio over and ask them what they're about."

Once they got out on the ocean, the voyage quickly turned boring. Zak went back to his cabin and took out his laptop to do some work. But with the rolling of the ship he found that if he focused on the screen, he felt queasy. It was going to be a long trip.

On the flight in, Zak had come up with another new idea: the hotel would be made from ice. Not the main structural element—that would be a trusswork of cold hard steel—but as a shell outside an air-gap insulating layer, the ice would serve as a second layer of insulation and stiffening at the same time. It would be translucent to allow natural light in. And it would make the building appear to be a natural part of the landscape. It would make a dazzling sight, glittering in the sun.

At night they could shine lasers on it—it would be magnificent.

Seasick or not, he needed to do some design work, get the idea fleshed out. He went back to his computer.

IN A FEW DAYS they started seeing ice. Zak had never realized that an iceberg would be such a startling crystalline blue. He stared, fascinated. Mrs. Binder came up beside him.

"Is this natural?" he said. "Are they always that color?"

"I believe so."

She pointed off to his left. "You're looking in the wrong direction, though. Look there."

He stared in the direction she was pointing. "Where?"

"To the left of that iceberg. See the spouts?"

"Yes?"

"Wait. Okay, now—there! See it? Whales."

"Oh my God."

Sometime after the first icebergs appeared, *Earth Avenger* stopped following, possibly because the captain wanted to avoid the potentially ship-killing bergs, or perhaps because Anjel Earth was more interested in following whales.

As the icebreaker approached the Ross Sea, the coast of Antarctica loomed up on the starboard side, rugged peaks like the gleaming white molars of ancient giants. They glided past mountains, each one more magnificent than the last. Zak, whose experience of mountains had been mostly limited to the foothills of the Appalachians, had never seen anything like it.

Despite predictions, they did not have to smash through floating ice to reach Scott Base. "It's been a warm spring," Ashanti (Was she the polar geologist? Zak wondered. Or the pilot?) said. The sea was covered by a jigsaw-puzzle pattern of ice, but the only ice they had to break shattered at the first touch of the ship's bow. "The ice isn't usually thin like this."

"All the better for us," Mrs. Binder said. She had spent most of the trip in her cabin, possibly suffering from seasickness. Or perhaps she was just catching up on an unending backlog of work. She had joined them on the deck as they cruised up to Scott.

After they left the ship, they were transported the last few miles to Scott Base by what was called a "taxi." This taxi turned out to be a Toyota troop-carrier, painted bright red, equipped with snow tracks instead of tires. Scott Base was a collection of lime-green buildings scattered higgledy-piggledy across the slope of a hill. "Why in the world did they choose that color?" Zak wondered aloud.

"Makes them visible," Mrs. Binder said. "Harder to get lost."

"How lost can people get? This is an island."

Mrs. Binder shrugged.

"You think this place is ugly, you should see McMurdo," Steve said.

"We made a wise aesthetic choice when we ruled this out as the hotel site," Mrs. Binder said.

They were welcomed to Scott Base by a burly man with a bushy beard nearly matching the orange of the down vest he wore. He called them all "cuz" and introduced himself as doctor something or other with such a strong accent that it sounded almost like a Scottish burr. They carried their luggage to their dorm. The small dorm rooms were equipped with bunk beds and tagged with old Christmas decorations.

They weren't going to stay long at the base, though. In the morning—to the extent that there was a morning, in a place where the sun barely broke the horizon—they were to undergo Antarctic Field Training, a mandatory class for people arriving at the base. Then they would board the Twin Otter for their scouting trip.

Training complete, the orange-bearded scientist saw them to the runway, a section of ice that had been flattened by tractors. He maintained a running commentary that, after Zak got used to the short vowels of his Kiwi accent, he almost understood. The gist was that he loved Antarctica, loved the idea of a hotel, thought that everybody on Earth should visit, and oh, wasn't the weather amazingly warm for the season. "So you're to go tramping for a squiz at the wop-wops, eh?" he said. "Beaut of a day, cuz. Beaut."

Zak wouldn't have called it "beaut," but he did think that the dire warnings that they needed layered parkas or they would die had been overkill, aimed at scaring people away from Antarctica rather than practical travel advice. Scott Base was no colder than a bad winter in Boston.

Their first trip was to be just a flyover, Zak and Mrs. Binder photographing the site from the air, with Steve as pilot and Ashanti as copilot. So it seemed Steve and Ashanti were *both* pilots.

The airplane was an old Twin Otter, equipped with skis instead of wheels and painted brilliant green like everything else in the camp. "Magnificent airplane," Steve said, and thumped the side of it with his fist. "Solid like a brick. They don't make them any more reliable than this." He looked up at the sky. "Wish I had a decent weather report, but it looks good to me. Let's go."

"What's wrong with the weather report?" Zak asked.

"Weather service won't give us more than a six-hour predict," Steve said. "Don't get me started."

"No. Really."

Ashanti answered. "Turns out that a weather satellite covering North America went out of service, and there wasn't a spare ready—budget cuts. So they shifted the satellite that's supposed to cover here to take over there until a new one is launched. So, end result, the meteorologist can't get a good squiz on what's over the horizon."

"Squiz?" Zak asked.

"Sorry," she said. "Been talking with too many Kiwis lately."

"So," Zak said. "That a problem?"

"Nah," Steve said. "We're not going to be gone that long."

They had filed a flight plan, but it had been deliberately vague, "aerial surveillance along the ice shelf and the coast toward Cape Adare." Mistry had given firm instructions to not reveal the exact location they had their eyes on. That was clearly paranoid—no other hotel chain was about to outbid them for the spot—but Mrs. Binder seemed to accept it as standard procedure.

Antarctica was even more impressive viewed from the air than from the ship. They followed the Trans-Antarctic mountain range, flying over glaciers and snowfields. Seen from the air, it was very different from how it had seemed on the maps and satellite views Zak had studied. He saw several possible sites he'd missed before. He kept the map and a GPS in his lap, making notes every time he saw a good place for a hotel, or a possible tour excursion.

After about two hours in the air, they reached the hotel site that they had identified. As Steve circled, they both photographed out the windows and exchanged comments. The steep northern face of the peak that they had tagged "ski mountain" on the maps was barren gray rock. But the south slope looked perfect, with a thick blanket of smooth snow. Below it, the slope leveled out to a patch of land with an ice-free harbor on the east, and a snow-covered glacier to the south.

"I can take us down, if you like," Steve said.

"Land?" Zak said.

"Sure, no problem. The plane's built for this. That glacier's as flat as an ironing board. That was where you were planning on putting the runway, right?"

"Yeah," Zak said, dubiously.

"That glacier is twelve thousand years old," Ashanti said. "It's a hundred meters thick, if that's what you're worried about. It will take the weight of the plane. A hundred planes."

"How do you know that for sure?" Zak asked.

Ashanti looked at him. "I'm a glacial geologist. That's what I do."

"I thought you were a pilot."

"Well, yeah," she said. "That too."

"Besides, oil pressure on the starboard engine has been running a bit low," Steve said. "I wouldn't mind looking at it."

The landing was so smooth that Zak wasn't quite sure when they touched down. The Twin Otter coasted on the skis for what seemed like a mile before it slowed to a stop and Steve finally turned off the engine.

The snow was about a foot deep, but beneath that, the ice was firm. It was no colder than the weather had been at Scott Base, but the wind across the glacier, unbroken by hills or trees, was biting. Now he had a better appreciation of the need for the cold-weather equipment. He pulled on the wool cap he'd been issued—up until then he had carried it but not worn it—and then pulled the parka's hood up over his head. With the goggles, only the tip of his nose was left exposed. He looked back toward Mrs. Binder, just coming down the folding stairs out of the airplane. "We should have brought snowshoes," he said.

Mrs. Binder held up her bag. "I did."

Meanwhile, Ashanti helped Steve carry out a folding ladder. They set it up next to the engine on the right side. "Better stick pretty close," he called out. "I'm not sure I like this weather blowing in; I'll take a look at this engine and then we'll get back up and out of here."

"Got it." Zak walked out onto the snow. The scene was a landscape in shades of white. "Antarctica," he said. "I love it!"

Mrs. Binder looked at Steve and Ashanti and then turned to Zak. "If he's so worried about getting back," she said, "why did he land in the first place?"

Abruptly, an enormous bang echoed across the landscape. He whipped his head around to look back at the airplane, but the sound hadn't seemed to come from there. Steve and Ashanti were also looking around, just as puzzled as he was. Across the landscape, nothing moved. "What the hell was that?" he said.

"I have no idea," Mrs. Binder said. "Sounded like a cannon."

Over at the airplane, Steve and Ashanti had turned back to the engine. They seemed to be removing parts from it.

"I don't think that looks good," Mrs. Binder said.

When they got back to the Twin Otter, Steve and Ashanti were inside, Steve talking earnestly on the radio. "No, it's not an emergency," he was saying. "We're secure. But we sure would appreciate the help when you can send it."

Ashanti turned to them. "Oil pump," she said.

"What does that mean?" Zak asked.

"Dead. Turns out we've been leaking oil for the last fifty miles or so. The engine's okay—other than that—but we can't fly."

"Great," Zak said. "You mean we're stuck here?"

"Not permanently." She inclined her head toward Steve. "Scott doesn't have the part, but they passed us along to McMurdo, and they have parts. They'll send a mechanic out by helicopter. It's an easy job—should be fixed in no time."

"So we have an unscheduled layover. We can scout the site, I guess. How long do we have?"

"They say they'll send him out as soon as the storm blows over."

"What storm?"

She gestured at the horizon. Dark clouds were moving in. "*That* storm."

They pulled in the folding stairs and shut themselves in the airplane. The storm rolled in with remarkable speed. One moment the sky was still, and then the sun vanished behind a wall of white.

With the storm came a loud series of booming crashes. "Sounds like we're being bombed," said Zak.

"That's unusual," Ashanti said. "Usually Antarctica is too cold to get much lightning."

The temperature in the cabin dropped to where they could see their breath. Steve started up the port engine, and Ashanti took her place in the copilot's seat.

"You're not planning on taking off in this, are you?" said Zak. He had to shout to make himself heard over the storm. The windshield of the airplane looked as if it had been painted white.

"One engine? Zero visibility?" Steve shook his head. "I'm not crazy. But we're not tied down. If I don't keep the nose pointed into the wind, the plane is likely to flip." He was steering the airplane mostly with his feet, making small adjustments as the wind shook the plane. "Now shut up and let me concentrate."

Another boom, and the whole airplane lurched. "What the hell was—"

With a noise like the eruption of Mount Doom, the ground tilted. The airplane slid backward, and then sideways. Steve fought to bring the nose around, but with no airspeed he had only limited control. The airplane rolled at a crazy angle. The left wing dipped, touched the ground, bent, and then crimped. Zak felt more than heard it when the propeller hit the ice, a series of staccato jolts shuddering across the plane.

The engine abruptly cut out, allowing them to hear the grinding and crashing all around them. They could see nothing outside except a pale cottony light filtering in through the windows. But they could feel the airplane sliding, one wing scraping as it skittered across the ice. Steve had not even the illusion of control anymore. But he still fought the controls, trying vainly to bring the nose around.

They slid backward until the airplane crunched to a stop, hard, against something behind them.

Whatever it had fetched up against apparently held it firm. Steve tried the radio, but it was dead, along with the rest of the plane's systems.

THE INTERIOR OF THE airplane had dropped to what seemed to be nearly cryogenic temperature. They were wearing all their extreme-weather gear and huddled in their down sleeping bags as well. Although the sun would not drop below the horizon for another month yet, the interior of the plane was dark. Nevertheless there was enough light for Zak to see that Steve and Ashanti shared the same bag.

When New Year's came, Zak proposed a cheer.

"I'm not sure your crew is in a proper holiday mood, dear," Mrs. Binder said. "Perhaps we should wait until we get back."

"If we get back," Steve muttered.

They tried to sleep. The storm increased in intensity, but they eventually learned to sleep through the irregular lurching of the airframe.

By the afternoon, the caterwaul of the wind started to subside. The windows were completely caked with ice, but when it was down to a mere whistle, Ashanti judged that it was time and opened the door.

The Twin Otter was rolled over at such an angle that the door opened down rather than out. Ashanti looked, and then cautiously backed away. "No exit that way," she said.

The right side of the plane had only a small emergency exit with a fire extinguisher mounted on it. Ashanti had to climb to get to it, and pulled herself out with her arms. Zak followed her lead, and then Mrs. Binder, with Steve only reluctantly abandoning his post at the now-useless controls.

A thin stream of icy snow sprayed down against their faces, but a brightness on the horizon—east? Zak had lost all sense of direction—suggested that the storm was abating.

The airplane was tilted and half buried in a hard-packed drift. It was perched precariously on a twenty-degree slope, with the right wing extended skyward, and only the shards of the left wing, wedged like pitons into the ice, preventing it from sliding down the remaining twenty feet to the restless water.

The flat plain of snow had vanished. In every direction, no more than a hundred feet away, they were surrounded by ocean.

"We're on an iceberg," Zak said.

The water was dark and choppy, undulating up until a spume of water broke against the ice, shooting white spray into the air, and then subsiding. Now that he was cued to it, Zak could feel the subtle rolling of the ice beneath him as the iceberg responded to the swells. All around them were dozens, no, hundreds of other icebergs, edges jagged as cut diamonds, some small as schoolbuses, others the size of mountains.

He found a level spot and sat down, looking across at the crumpled airplane. "What happened?"

Mrs. Binder said, "It would be prudent to get our equipment out of the airplane. As quickly as possible."

They all looked at the airplane. It had seemed to be firmly planted into the ice, but now they could see it flexing slightly as the iceberg rocked back and forth in the swell.

"I'm not sure that's wise," said Steve.

Mrs. Binder walked back to the airplane. "We'll need at least the tents," she said. "And emergency supplies." She climbed up onto the airplane and disappeared down into it.

"Does that woman have brass balls?" said Steve. "Or is she just clueless?"

"She's got more of a clue than we do," Zak said. "'Cause if that airplane slides into the water, we're dead without those tents." He stood up and headed after her.

It took a minute for his eyes to adjust to the dimness. Inside, the rocking of the airframe in response to the swells now seemed ominous. Mrs. Binder appeared out of the darkness and shoved a load in his arms. "Take this."

He levered himself up out the door and found Steve. He shoved the package at him. "Here!" He went back inside for another load.

With a shuddering crash, the ice beneath them suddenly tilted. Zak lost his footing and tumbled into the dark. Something snapped, and the aircraft slid a good five feet, then stopped. "What was that?" he shouted.

"Got hit by another iceberg," Steve shouted back. "Get out. Fast!"

With one hand Zak grabbed whatever was closest, and with the other he pulled himself toward the square of brighter light that marked the door. Before he reached it, the floor dipped under him. He could feel a nearly subsonic vibration as the two icebergs ground against each other, and then the floor jerked up again as the icebergs separated. The plane bounced.

The bouncing had jarred the door almost shut again. He squeezed through the opening and turned back for Mrs. Binder.

She had a flashlight in her teeth and both arms full of equipment. She gestured with her head, and it took him a moment to decode her meaning: *Get out of the way.* He scrambled up and out, shoved his bundle at Steve, and reached back to pull her out.

The package he had grabbed, he discovered, was a bag containing six inflatable life vests. Not much use. If any of them fell in the water they would die from exposure long before drowning. Mrs. Binder had salvaged the cold-weather tent, two down sleeping bags, and a case of emergency rations.

Ten minutes later, the airplane slid into the ocean. Another iceberg had drifted over and the Twin Otter slid into the wedge between them. For a minute the plane hung there, pinned between the two. Pushed by the ocean swells, the motion of the bergs twisted and crumpled the fuselage, until with a final wrench of metal, the plane disappeared beneath the dark water.

They found a nook behind a knob of ice, a reasonably flat spot to shelter. The wind had picked up again, and low clouds raced by overhead. The sound of the ubiquitous grinding of ice against ice was all around them.

Mrs. Binder turned to Steve. "Do they know where we are?"

Steve paused. "I'm not sure. We were supposed to call back with coordinates when they were ready to send the mechanic out."

Mrs. Binder inclined her head toward the water where the airplane had vanished.

"Yeah," Steve said. "Probably not broadcasting."

Zak turned to Ashanti. "Now, can you tell me just what the hell happened?"

Ashanti sighed. "The glacier fractured."

"What?"

Ashanti settled back into the nook. "A glacier is a river of ice. This one was blocked from flowing into the sea because of the ice shelf. Kind of a natural dam.

"With a long enough warming trend—a decade, maybe two; ice shelves don't melt fast—the ice shelf melts away underneath. Eventually it fractures.

"Ice shelves don't break up slowly. Once they start to break, each crack releases pressure that puts stress on another part of the sheet. The fracture propagates exponentially. When it fragments, it goes all at once."

"You said it was twelve thousand years old," Zak said.

She shrugged. "So, apparently, the climate's warmer now than it's been in twelve thousand years."

Zak thought about that. "So, what—the storm triggered it?"

"That was coincidence," Ashanti said. "Just bad luck. Or, wait, maybe not—the storm surge must have put extra strain on the shelf. That could have triggered the fracture, come to think of it.

"Once the ice shelf fragmented, it released pressure on the glacier. The seaward edge fractures. That's what we were hearing—the booms that sounded like explosions. It was ice fracturing, all around us."

"You said the ice was a hundred meters thick!" Zak said.

Ashanti shrugged again. "When it goes, it goes fast. It's happened before. A different glacier, a different ice shelf. Back in 1995. An Argentinean science team on the ice heard it. They said it sounded like a volcano erupting. It sounded like the end of the world."

"What happened to them?"

"They were rescued by helicopter before the ice sheet fragmented."

Zak looked up. The clouds were thick and opaque as a chocolate milkshake, so low that the peaks of icebergs in the distance cut swirls through them as they raced by.

"No helicopters for us," he said. "We're stranded."

Suddenly a thought came to him. He looked at Steve with suspicion. Hadn't it been just a little too unlikely? The problem with the engine that conveniently allowed them to land but not take off; the fact that they took off just before a storm that hadn't been forecast—

"You're with him," Zak said.

"What?"

"Anjel. The Rainbow Earth people. This was all a trap; you stranded us deliberately. To sabotage the hotel."

"Do I look suicidal?"

Zak stared at him. "That wasn't an answer."

"Okay," Steve said. "Here's an answer: no. No, I did not strand us deliberately. Am I an idiot? No, I absolutely did not strand us deliberately. I may be a member of Rainbow Earth, sure, but I didn't—"

"You're a member of Rainbow Earth?" Mrs. Binder said. "That explains how they were so good at figuring out what we were doing."

"Well, sure, I'm a member, yes, but hey, I didn't crash the airplane. And, anyway, Anjel Earth isn't a bad guy. Give him a chance."

"What do you mean, give him a chance?" Zak said, his tone bitter. "We're dead. We're not giving anybody a chance. It's over. He won."

"Listen," Steve said.

Even as Steve said that, another, fainter sound was beginning to penetrate Zak's awareness. He had been hearing it intermittently, when the wind abated, but not recognizing it, just another noise buried in the shriek of the wind and the rumble of grinding icebergs.

Zak turned around and grabbed one of the life vests from the package he'd salvaged, ripped open the plastic, and yanked hard on the lanyard. The orange vest inflated with a soft whomp, and the tiny strobe light on the collar pierced the dimness like a flash of lightning.

He waved it over his head. The wind slackened for a moment, and in the abrupt quiet, all of them heard it. In the distance, but steadily getting louder, the sound of motors.

Rounding an iceberg ahead of them, first one, and then the other, two bright yellow Zodiac boats skipped toward them over the swells.

WHEN THE ZODIACS HAD brought them to the cutter, Anjel Earth welcomed them on board. With his chestnut beard and piercing eyes, he seemed perfectly comfortable in the weather, as if he were born to live in Antarctica. He poured them each a large mug of hot tea from an enormous thermos, instructed them to call him "Anjel" and then corrected their pronunciation, and took them to a large cabin at the back of the ship to warm up.

The tea was sweet and seemed to be half milk, not the way Zak ever drank it. It was, he thought, the best tea he had ever tasted.

After they had shed their cold-weather gear and wrapped themselves in thick quilts that Anjel had provided for them, Steve looked at Zak. He looked over at Mrs. Binder, who nodded at him to start the conversation. He looked at the walls. They were covered with posters, some with phrases like "Act before it's too late" and "Save the planet," and others with photographs of rain forests and desert flowers.

"Well," he said, "we owe you a debt, Mr. Earth. Thank you for the rescue."

Anjel smiled. "Yes. Out here, we learn to look out for each other."

"I'm surprised, though," Zak said. "Why did you save us?"

"You must think we're barbarians," said Anjel with an exaggerated expression of shock. "We talk with McMurdo. They said they lost the signal from your plane's transponder, and they were snowed in but feared you were in trouble. I said we'd go take a look, render what assistance we could."

"Thank you for that."

"Well, you're welcome." He paused. "You work for Mr. Mistry, am I right?" Zak nodded, and he continued. "A hotel." He paused, apparently lost in thought. "A hotel in Antarctica. How about that."

"Yeah," Zak said. "It was a dumb idea. We all can see that now. This is no place for it. It's just too hostile."

Anjel Earth waved his hand. "Nonsense. Wait a few days, and the sky will be such a clear and crystalline blue it will dazzle your eyes. You won't believe it's the same continent. You'll change your mind."

Zak stared at him. "But I thought—"

"I saw the paper you had in *Acta Astronautica*," Anjel continued. "The one comparing a hotel in Antarctica to a moonbase." At Zak's blank look, he said, "What, do you think I only read nature magazines? You had some good ideas there. I like the way you think. The idea that we have to learn how to make an ecosystem work. Perhaps if we do, we can begin to understand just how wonderful our planet is, how everything works together."

Anjel Earth fixed Zak with his eyes. "When I first heard rumors of your hotel, I wasn't sure. I wrote the article in my magazine, trying to figure out what to think about it—that's what I do; I write to sort out how I think. What surprised me was the reactions I got. Some were against it. But almost half the letters asked when it was going to open, where to get reservations.

"My people wanted your hotel, Mr. Cerny. And I thought, what if they're right? Maybe it would be a good thing. Getting people to really experience Antarctica and the ecosystem and the ice and the interconnectedness of it all—isn't that just what we were working for? It's a mistake to lock Antarctica away, keep it as a preserve that nobody ever sees. If it were done right, like a moonbase, self-sufficient, and not trashing the land the way humans have done for thousands of years, it would be an example to the world.

"Make your hotel, Mr. Cerny." Anjel Earth's eyes bored into Zak's. "Give us that example. We need you."

Zak lowered his head. What was Mistry's motto? Obstacles. Steppingstones.

Through the window, the sky was still dark, but at the very horizon, a line of sky showed brilliant blue, above icebergs glistening white in the sunshine.

"We will try," he said. "We will try."

FORUM DISCUSSION—An Idea Is Born

Geoffrey Landis introduced the concept of a hotel in Antarctica to James Cambias, *Hieroglyph* coeditor Ed Finn, and other Hieroglyph community members in June 2013. Watch the idea gain momentum at hieroglyph.asu.edu/hotel-antarctica.

STORY NOTES—Geoffrey A. Landis

In my first-ever attempt at crowdsourcing a story, I wrote this story with assistance of the participants on Project Hieroglyph's web forum, http://hieroglyph.asu.edu/forums. Contributions to the discussion were made by Ed Finn, Aleks Antic, Larry Orr, James L. Cambias, Will Holz, John Fogarty, Brenda Cooper, and Bruce Sterling. Not all of your comments made it into the final story, but I would like to thank you all for helping me with your imagining.

Particular thanks to Will Holz for pointing me to the "penguin poo map," http://www.sciencedaily.com/releases/2009/06/090602122621.htm, a novel way of locating colonies of penguins.

FORUM DISCUSSION—Location, Location, Location

What's the best spot for a hotel in Antarctica? Observe Geoffrey Landis's brainstorm at hieroglyph.asu.edu/hotel-antarctica.

FORUM DISCUSSION—Ice as a Building Material

The idea of using ice as the primary building material for the hotel was proposed and developed by Hieroglyph community members. Read their conversation with Geoffrey Landis at hieroglyph.asu.edu/hotel-antarctica.

FORUM DISCUSSION—Through the Valley of Death

Geoffrey Landis discusses how to avoid the innovation "valley of death" at hieroglyph.asu.edu/hotel-antarctica.

RESPONSE TO "A HOTEL IN ANTARCTICA"—George Basile

George Basile, an expert on green business practices and biotechnology at Arizona State University, responds to "A Hotel in Antarctica" at hieroglyph.asu.edu/hotel-antarctica.

PERIAPSIS
James L. Cambias

I WENT UP TO Deimos for the contest two days after I turned seventeen. My father turned up at the Pavonis terminal to see me off. Good thing, too—just about every media feeder on the planet was there, hoping to get a word with me.

My baba drove a construction crawler and was built like a crawler himself. He lowered his head and stuck out his elbows and plowed through the crowd. I stuck close behind while people and flying eyes tried to get in my face.

Before I passed through the checkpoint, I turned to my father. "Thanks for coming. It was good to see you."

"People say you shouldn't go," he said, tipping his head back at the crowd behind him.

"I know." I'd heard more about brain drain that past month than I ever wanted to hear in my life. "There are things I want to do, and I can't do them on Mars."

He nodded. "You coming back?"

"I'll be back in a week if I don't get picked."

"Don't come back," he said. "Win it. Good luck, Ying." He took my hand in his for a moment, then turned and shoved through the mob. He didn't look back. I stepped through the checkpoint. An hour later I boarded the elevator to Deimos.

Deimos was the Big Time, like Jakarta or Mexico City. It was the gateway to Mars, the launch point for the outer system, and even supplied volatiles to Luna and the Lagranges. The Deimos Community had its fingers in everything that went on from Low Earth Orbit out to the Kuiper Belt.

Smart, ambitious, and attractive people flowed toward Deimos. Everybody wanted to be there. It wasn't just to get rich—it was to be part of the scene, to be where the cool stuff was happening. To be *there*.

The Deimos Community picked a population target of two million and enforced it. The only way new people joined was when there was a deficit between births and deaths. Hardly anyone ever left voluntarily.

Most years only a few places opened up. The Community filled them by inviting scientists, artists, or other talented people to join. Sometimes they'd auction off a couple of slots, which just made Deimos that much richer.

But every so often the Deimos Community kept a couple of places open for young people with potential instead of grown-ups who already had a reputation. You had to be between sixteen and twenty-five, willing to leave your family behind, and confident enough to enter a competition without knowing what you'd be doing. Kids from all over the system applied. The top eight came to Deimos to compete.

I was the only kid from Mars who made the cut. My academics were decent, not great—90th percentile ratings in physics and math, but only 75th percentile in language. I had a couple of wrestling trophies and you've heard me play keyboard. I knew I was a long shot when I applied.

But I had one advantage: I'd spent the previous year at Eos working on exotic propulsion systems with the Cavorite Club. They were a bunch of underfunded young genius lunatics led by an old genius lunatic named Chou Yu, trying to find ways to break the laws of nature. I slept four hours a day in a public hot-rack, mooched meals, and learned more about engineering and advanced physics than I could have in a decade at Harbin or Monterrey.

I wasn't sure if being part of the Cavorite Club would work for me or against me when I applied to join Deimos. The Pavonis Treaty gave Deimos a monopoly on moving stuff from Mars into space and the Community frowned on Martians building spaceships. I guess being a teenage rocket scientist was impressive enough to make up for it.

Once news got out I got a lot of crap for wanting to compete. Moving up the string was like treason—and the fact that Mars's best and brightest kept doing it just made it worse. I lost a lot of friends when I applied, and the rest when I got accepted.

The Deimos Community put all eight competitors in the Hotel El Dorado. I wound up across the hall from Sofia Komu. Yes, *that* Sofia Komu.

The first time I met her was when her suitcase banged into the door of my room. It sounded like some kind of horrible disaster, but there wasn't an alarm. I looked out and found a girl my age trying to manage two absolutely titanic bags. She was nearly my height and wearing a loose, warm-looking outfit that covered everything but her face.

I snagged one bag, and it almost pulled me out of my shoes. "What have you got in here?" I asked.

"The barest essentials," she said. "Books and clothing."

"You brought all this from *Earth*? I've only got twelve kilos and I rode the elevator!"

"These things are important, and they are mine," she said.

Neither of us said anything as we looked each other up. She was Sofia Komu, from Rhapta Special Economic Zone. Her résumé was scary: accredited by East Africa Open University with near-perfect scores in art history, biochemistry, ecosystems, memetics, and statistical analysis. Top-rated dancer, won the landscape design competition for Rhapta's mangrove park, two organism patents. Related to a dozen big names in the Africa Renaissance. A serious rival.

Worse yet, it looked like we were falling in love. According to my biomonitor, my heart rate and hormone levels shifted when I spoke with her—four standard deviations above my usual when talking to a girl my age. The hallway sensor net confirmed that she had a strong positive reaction to me. Her pupils dilated like the lights had gone out, and her respiration and skin temperature both increased.

Like any proper Martian I took steps to damp all that down. Too many people packed into fragile habitats made that a matter of survival for the early settlers, and the habit stuck. I hit hard on dopamine antagonists to keep me from getting infatuated. I was going to need my serotonin and testosterone to stay competitive. I figured she was doing the same.

"Well . . . see you at the opening, I guess," I said.

"Good luck," she said, and moved her bags one at a time into her room.

THE COMPETITION GOT UNDER way with a reception in Lupita Forest.

When they first settled Deimos, the Community blasted out a huge bubble a kilometer across under the east pole, filled it with air, piped in sunlight, and then turned some of the solar system's finest species designers loose to create a wonderland. The centerpiece of the park was a titanic bao-bab tree, with trunks leading off in all directions to the walls of the cavern. The branches and buttresses soared and coiled to form a green wood spiral galaxy half a kilometer wide. Grapevines, almost unmodified, stretched through the whole space like a demented spider's web. The thicker vines had footholds and guidelines to serve as bridges or ladders, depending on which way you were going relative to Deimos's ghostly gravity. Thornless roses, orchids, and bromeliads grew on the branches and vines. Most of the flowers were built with bioluminescent pigments, so when Deimos went into eclipse behind Mars at midnight, the cave turned into a spectacular swirl of glowing colors.

The reception was right in the center of the tree, where floors on several levels were anchored to the surrounding trunks and limbs. All of us contes-tants showed up exactly on time—except Sofia Komu. I didn't see her.

I called Micromegas, the main AI for Deimos. "Where is Sofia Komu?"

"Ms. Komu is currently in her room."

Sick? Bailing out of the competition before it began? The stress was pretty intense.

We milled about for half an hour. I tried not to look as nervous as I felt. Heavy use of adrenaline antagonists; my brain stem was trying to con-vince my body it was time for a mammoth hunt or something, churning out fight-or-flight chemicals that were no help at all.

"Good evening!" In the center of the lowest floor a spotlight circle picked out a tall, spindly man in a severe black outfit, with just a hint of gold at his neck and wrists. Text boxes in my vision identified him as Piers Tyana, one of the referees. "I'm so glad to see all of you here, and I'm sure everyone is very excited about the competition. There will be three con-tests; each of you will be scored individually by all the interested members of the Community. At the end, the person with the highest score will join Deimos as a full member."

Failed contestants from earlier youth competitions had a tendency to burn out, disappear into freaky subcultures, or apply their creativity to killing themselves.

While Tyana bragged about how great it was to be part of the Deimos Community, all us contestants were waiting for him to describe the tests. In the past they varied, with no predictable pattern. But as soon as he described what we'd be doing, eight very sharp brains would go into overdrive.

Everyone in that vine-walled room at the center of the baobab tree turned to watch Sofia Komu as she floated gracefully down to a prime seat just outside the spotlight. It was impossible not to notice her—she'd timed her entrance to coincide with Deimos entering eclipse. As the flowers around us began to glow, her outfit outshone them. She was wearing sensible tights, with some interesting transparent bits to show off her dancer's body, and luminous ribbons streamed from her arms and legs, swirling around her as she dropped, like the wings of some fantastic bird. When she landed neatly in her seat, the ribbons configured into a skirt and a wide collar.

This was going to be harder than I'd thought. I'd been approaching the competition as a project. Show what you know, solve the problems, work hard, produce good results. I could do that. Sofia understood the event was a *performance*.

Tyana resumed as if nothing had happened. "And now we come to the subject in which all of you are really interested: the nature of the contests. This year we have decided to choose competitors on the basis of creativity, imagination, and ability to solve problems."

Good: they were playing to my strengths.

"The first contest is free-form: create something. There will be another reception in this space in exactly one sol, and the contestants will show us what they have made. Impress us. Once that is done, you will learn the nature of the second contest. Good night; I'll see you in twenty-four hours and thirty-eight minutes." He finished up just as the clock hit 0001.

WE ALL HAD SEMI-UNLIMITED fabricator access, so actually making whatever we decided to create would be trivial. The real test was our ability to dream up something.

I'd like to say I developed my idea by some rigorous process of logic and research, but on my way down to the workspace it just popped into my head: the Most Beautiful Mask. The Deimos Community still makes a decent amount every year from licensing my Mask. (Yes, we had to sign away the rights to everything we created for the competition. Deimos didn't get incredibly rich by letting people keep valuable ideas.)

The concept was so simple that the first thing I did was a search to make sure nobody else had thought of it. It's still cool: a mask of smart plastic that changes its shape and color, with a simple brain linked to the local network. It uses the ambient sensors to watch whomever the wearer is interacting with, and it changes in response to that person's reactions. So while you're talking to someone, the Mask becomes more and more attractive to them. It works better with people who aren't regulating, but even with the most locked-down Martians it can pick up on eye-tracks and attention time.

They gave us a big unadorned section of ten-meter tunnel with a steel mesh floor to work in, with four big fabricators and eight workstations with smart-matter tools. Flimsy partitions gave us the illusion of privacy, but of course anyone in Deimos could look over our shoulders through the network.

While I got my station set up I was already roughing out the design. I could use freeware for most of the systems. I had the basic machinery done by 0400, napped for an hour before tackling the software, and sent my design to the fabricator at a minute before 1100.

I couldn't resist the urge to peek a little at what everyone else was doing. Sofia's workstation had a couple of big tanks on it, with something feathery-looking growing in the liquid. She was curled up in her chair having a nap. She'd changed out of her smart matter and looked comfortable in a loose coverall made entirely of unmodified plant fiber.

Haruko Sato, from Luna Farside, had the biggest project, a tall cylinder with massive power inputs, and four spider bots working on it. She gave me a haggard glance, and I waved, but she turned back to her bots without acknowledging me.

I kept the Mask wrapped until I got back to my workstation. The blank silver face was still for a moment, then it started to shift as it responded to me. At first it worked perfectly: the face narrowed, the eyes widened, the skin tone shifted from shiny silver to a more realistic tan color. And then . . . it got freaky. The eyes began a weird oscillation, one growing while the other narrowed, then switching. The rest of the features reacted to my consternation by squirming around like something out of a horror show.

Obviously a software issue. I could run tests to figure out which piece of kitbashed algorithm wasn't playing well with the others . . . or I could just rewrite the whole thing from scratch. Which I decided to do because I knew I'd wind up doing it anyway and it made more sense to start at 1130 rather than try to power through it at 2350.

After about six hours of writing code I needed a break. We had unlimited allowances at the El Dorado dining room, so I went up there and binged on protein—broiled chicken, steamed shrimp, fish balls, tamagoyaki, and some sausage-stuffed peppers for my vegetable.

"Mind if I join you?"

I looked up from my plate and saw another contestant—Reinette Luz, from Deimos itself. She was a *pathik,* one of the permanent guests who live in hotels and rental space but aren't part of the Community.

"Sure," I said.

While she took the chair opposite I checked her info. She was older than I'd thought—twenty standard years, though she looked about fifteen. Heavily modded: what I'd taken for an elaborate paint job was actually her skin, shifting colors in elaborate patterns that always drew your eyes back to her face.

My heart rate and hormones took a little jump despite the antagonists I'd hit myself with. I decided not to monkey with them. Hers were elevated, too.

"Are we feeding you enough?" she asked.

"It's better than anything downstairs," I said. Martians think of food (when they bother to think of it) as nutrition, not "cuisine."

While I spoke, she sent me a private message. "I've been watching the feeds," she sent. "There's a lot of chat about the eight of us." At the same time she said aloud, "The Community has some of the best chefs anywhere. How's your project coming?"

"Almost done," I said. "How about yours?"

"I already finished," she said. She added a silent message: "We need to fall in love."

"What?" I sent back, while I managed to stammer aloud, "You work fast."

"This isn't just an exam," she sent back. "It's entertainment. That African girl understands it—I loved her entrance last night. But we have to take it beyond just looking good. The audience wants drama."

"You want to fall in love in order to get eyeballs?" I sent.

"Yes. Just enough for people to notice. Work up some will-they-or-won't-they suspense. As we get closer to the final decision, we can play up the conflict: lovers and rivals. Maybe a fight. What do you think?"

Aloud she added, "People are going to love what I've made."

"That's a lot to think about," I sent her. "You must really want to win this thing," I said aloud.

"Absolutely," she said. "I've lived here since I was little, but I want to be inside. I *belong* here. What about you?" she asked after a moment. "Why is a Martian trying to join the Community? I thought you people hated Deimos."

Maybe her skin pattern had subliminals in it, or maybe I wanted to impress her. I don't know. "I've got this idea," I sent. "It's big. Really big. Too big to create on Mars. I need the Community's support to make it real." For the cameras I just shrugged.

"What is it?" she asked privately. Her eyes were bright.

I almost spilled it then, but I couldn't tell who she might talk to. Plenty of smart people there—one hint could let someone make the same jump I'd made back at Eos.

I said, "Got to get back to work."

She looked a little startled. Silently she sent, "What about falling in love with me?"

"I'll tell you tonight at the unveiling," I messaged. Aloud I said, "Nice meeting you," and got out of there.

It took me another three hours to get the Mask up and running, and by then it was time to go back to my room and clean up. With my door locked and all the privacy filters set to max, I opened the box and looked at the Mask once more. The smooth silver skin shifted to a flesh tone, the eyes widened, and the cheeks and jaw changed shape. After just a second, I could recognize the face. The features were a little exaggerated, the proportions a little neotenous, but the face was recognizably that of Sofia Komu.

I stuffed it back into the box and reset everything.

SOFIA AND I WERE the only ones in the center of Lupita Forest at the beginning of the second night's reception.

I showed up early because my Mask was as ready as it ever would be. Sofia was there because she had accurately predicted what all the others would do, copy her late arrival the night before, and wanted to monopolize the attention of the Deimos Community. A hundred people were physically present, and a big slice of the rest was watching. She looked fabulous in a loose tunic and pants made of silk, which turned out to be made by invertebrates.

Sofia set up her project, the Mycofilter, on a stand near the entrance. She'd brewed up an aerophyte mushroom, a cloud of feathery mycelia filtering moisture, dust, skin cells, mites, and other debris from the air. According to the pop up box she'd written, it would produce about a gram of protein per day and clean a million liters of air. She tried to make it pretty, with bioluminescence against a flat-black background, but under the spotlight it just looked like a mass of gray threads. Some of the more serious-looking people stopped to talk to her about it, but most just gave it a glance and passed by.

My Mask stayed in its box. When people stopped by my table, I just told them, "You'll find out at midnight," and smiled. When I checked the Deimos media feeds, I was gratified to see a minor buzz of anticipation.

Reinette Luz showed up about twenty minutes into the reception. She was wearing something medieval-looking in velvet and leather. Her skin was gold now, with faint cracks in it, so she looked like an old painting in a church.

"So what have you got?" I asked her.

"It's a business plan," she said. "I'm more of a strategy person than a techie."

She had a projector displaying a plan to set up a colony of robots on a sun-grazing metallic asteroid, smelt the thing using solar mirrors at perihelion, use the same mirrors to boost it into a Mars-grazing orbit, and finally park the mass of finished metal at one of the Trojan points along Mars's orbit.

"I can give the Community a century's supply of low-cost metal. That's our biggest import," she said, as much for the benefit of invisible viewers as for me. "My analysis shows a return on investment of 65 to 200 percent over ten years, *and* it will make Deimos independent of Mars and Luna for minerals."

Which would lock in their hegemony for good. It made sense, really, but I couldn't resist the urge to needle her a little. "You realize you've just given this plan of yours to the Community, right? Even if you don't win, they can still use it."

Her smile didn't shift a millimeter. "That's fine with me," she said. She added a silent personal message: "I've worked out a counterplan I can pitch to Luna investors if the Community wants to go ahead with this. Like I said, I'm a strategy person."

I poked around some of her pop-ups and supporting files and found out why she'd been able to finish so soon. She'd been working on this idea for a couple of years. The only thing she'd done that day was to jazz up the visuals and tailor the text to appeal to the Community. Clever. I hadn't even thought of repurposing one of my old ideas.

Over Reinette's shoulder I saw Sofia explaining her air-mushroom. She happened to look in my direction, and just for an instant her confident, engaged expression slipped.

By that point all the competitors were setting up, so it seemed like a good time to make my move. "Have you got a second?" I asked Reinette. "You can be the first to try out my project."

"I'd be delighted," she said, and followed me over to where the box holding the Mask sat in the spotlight. A small crowd gathered as we approached.

I cleared my throat and tapped into the sound system. "Members of the Community and guests, I present to you my entry for the first round of the competition: the Most Beautiful Mask." I opened the box with as much of a flourish as I could manage and took out the mask. Reinette looked a little confused at the blank silvery face, so I held it up to her own. "Put it on."

She did, and I could tell she was watching the local feed to see how it looked. I didn't want to make it turn into Sofia again, so I deliberately looked away while the Mask optimized itself for the journalist standing next to Reinette waiting to talk to me. For her it turned androgynous and pouty-lipped. For the older man who came up next, the Mask became an elfish-looking face with big eyes and a tiny mouth.

"Now let's see how it works for you," I said, and took the Mask from Reinette. I put it on my own face and watched the local feed. As she looked into my eyes, the Mask adjusted itself until . . . a duplicate Reinette looked back at her.

There was some polite laughter about that. I handed the Most Beautiful Mask off to the older man. He held my look long enough for me to see the Mask changing into a high-cheekboned face with dark skin and a narrow chin. Sofia again.

"I guess this means you didn't like my suggestion," said Reinette in a private message when she saw what the Mask looked like.

"I haven't made up my mind yet," I sent back.

"I think your mind has made itself up. I wonder what *she's* going to do with that information," she replied.

THE COMMUNITY VOTED ON our creations, but the results were secret. Of course people could speculate. There was a thriving prediction market, and plenty of outright betting. The line at Helium Colony on Mars had me in second place at even money based on my strong showing with the Mask. Even allowing for a little home-planet bias, I was definitely in the top half.

Right at 2438, Piers Tyana called for everyone's attention and took over the sound system. "And now for the second challenge. We all know the saying that you can't make an omelette without breaking some eggs. Well, that's what we'd like our competitors to do. By this time tomorrow we want you to bring us an omelette made without breaking any eggs. There will be four tasters for each omelette, and people will see and hear their reactions, so flavor and consistency do count. You will also be judged on how creative and interesting your solution to the problem is."

Great. A food challenge, and me a clueless Martian rube. No quick and easy win for me this time. I decided to play it straight. How to get the contents of an egg out of the shell without breaking it? Maybe they hoped one of us would invent teleportation or space-folding or something.

The first thing I needed was a couple of hours of sleep. Whether the tests were based on creativity, technical ability, or salesmanship, all of them required excellent sleep-regulation chemicals. I wondered if the Community created this whole competition as part of a plan to breed a subspecies that never slept.

I napped, adjusted my brain with a cup of tea, and went down to the workspace to get started. It took me four hours to come up with my basic approach, and another twelve to actually implement it. I figured out how to get into an egg without breaking the shell.

See, eggshells are porous, and even a brittle material like calcium carbonate has some elasticity. So I fabbed up a tiny multiaxis retractor with a pressure sensor and inserted it into one of the little micron pores, then started slowly ratcheting the pore open, stretching it nanometer by nanometer with pauses to let the material rest, until I could get a pipette inside and suck out the yolk and white. It sounds simple but I went through about fifty eggs before I got six where the calcium carbonate didn't actually fracture.

Then I had to make an omelette. Nowadays I can whip one up without even thinking. Back then I had never actually cooked much. When I was little, my family ate in the cafeteria in whatever habitat we were living in or traded washing up for cooking with our neighbors. As a little boy I learned to make tea, boil rice, and . . . well, that was it, really.

I needed to see someone make an omelette. I thought of calling someone back home, but even the best telepresence isn't the same as standing next to someone. Plus there was the gravity issue—making an omelette on Deimos wouldn't be the same as doing it on Mars. So I took my eggs in a sealed flask and went to the El Dorado kitchen.

Sofia was there ahead of me, with a bowl of something egglike. She was practicing her own omelette-making so I watched her. When she finished her final fold, she looked over her shoulder at me.

"You've come to do some cooking?"

"I've never made an omelette before. Mind if I watch you?"

"It's tricky in this low gravity. The egg spatters like crazy when you pour it. On the other hand it makes turning it very easy. You can flip it one-handed like a professional."

"So how'd you get the egg out without breaking it?" I asked her. "I promise I won't tell anyone."

"This egg never had a shell. I made it out of vegetable protein."

"Cool! I just found a way to get my egg open without breaking it."

"Oh?"

"Hyperspace," I said. "Rotate it through hyperspace so the shell's on the inside."

I think she believed me for about a second.

"You're terrible! Just for that I'm not going to show you how to make an omelette." She had a great smile.

"I think I've got the basics from watching. I'm going to practice with some hotel eggs before I use my hyperspace eggs."

It was then that I noticed her responses were going crazy. Interest and a hint of arousal, fatigue, and a hefty dose of fear.

"You're not regulating?" I asked her.

"I don't do that," she said.

"You don't have any implants?"

"Of course I have implants, silly. But they're to keep me healthy, not to change how I feel. If you don't feel temptation, you're not making moral choices. Now watch: you beat the eggs until they're just slightly bubbly, but you don't want them all frothy. See?"

I bookmarked the sensor images of what the eggs looked like. "So . . . you like me? You're not turning on the attraction on purpose?"

"Yes, I like you," she said patiently. "What do you think of me?"

"Well, I damped myself down pretty hard to stay focused. This isn't the time to start a relationship."

"Martians," she said with a shake of her head. "Anyway, once you've got your eggs properly mixed, you have to make sure the pan is properly hot."

"What temperature?"

"I don't know," she said, with a funny smile as though she was only just realizing it herself. "Just . . . when it looks right. When the butter is just about to brown."

"How do you know when it's about to do something?"

"Experience, practice—and smell! When it starts smoking like that, it's too hot!" She snatched the pan off the heat and put it in the wash pile, then started with another one.

I took note of the temperature. Just above 130.

"That looks right," she said, and scraped the egg mix into the pan. "It takes so long for things to pour here."

"You've never been off Earth before?"

"I took a ride up the Kenya Elevator once, but I didn't take the time to cook anything." For some reason her fear levels rose as she spoke.

"Didn't like it?" I asked.

"What? Oh, I loved the view, and the microgravity at the top was wonderful."

I sent her a private message. "What are you scared of?"

She looked at me, and then at the omelette. "Oh, dear. That's overcooked. See? It's too rubbery. We weren't paying attention," she said. While she scraped the floppy egg disk into the organics bin she sent me a private reply. "If you must know, I am afraid I won't win."

"Why do you care?" I sent back. "You can just fall back to Africa and run the place, right?"

"You don't know anything," she said aloud, and banged the pan. "Make your own!" She took her stuff and moved to the opposite side of the kitchen.

While I mixed up some practice eggs and got the pan ready again, I checked her history. Obviously I'd touched a live cable. Micromegas put it together. Sofia's family *had been* key figures in the Africa Renaissance before she was born, but they'd been losing out in the political realignments ever since. They had the bad luck to be part of a wealthy minority group, which is always dangerous. Her adult relatives outside the Rhapta SEZ were either imprisoned or suspiciously dead. The projections showed their faction was about to lose control in Rhapta as well. Having a family member in the Deimos Community would give the Komu side a friend with a big stick.

I tried another couple of practice omelettes, watching the temperature and time carefully. My failures got better, but they weren't anything I'd feed to a human.

After my third try, I took a break and went over to Sofia. "Listen," I began.

"I'm sorry I snapped at you," she said. "I'm nervous and spoke without thinking. Will you forgive me?"

"No—I mean, yes! I forgive you, but it's my fault, really. I'm sorry if I said something to upset you. I didn't know about your family."

"Please, just let it drop," she said. Everyone in Deimos was probably looking up Sofia's family now. I went back to my eggs.

The guy from Ceres won that round, hands down. He stretched the whole "without breaking an egg" definition to the limit by dissolving the shells in acid, but his finished product was really amazing. Turned out he was an expert at microgravity cooking and produced a Spanish omelette that looked like a cloud. The ecstatic expressions on the tasters made the rest of us grit our teeth in frustration.

Sofia did pretty well. Her eggless creation looked and apparently tasted just like a classic French omelette aux fines herbes. Reinette Luz took a more creative approach and made a candy omelette out of marzipan, which got a good response.

My own effort got some interested nods for how I got the egg open, but the reaction to my finished dish was perfunctory. Nobody spit it out—which actually happened to the poor girl from Luna, who also tried to make a substitute egg out of yeast and invented something absolutely inedible.

When I checked the odds out of Helium, I found that they had me rated at five to one. Sofia was holding at three to one, and Reinette was now tied with her.

THEY GAVE US ONE sol off before announcing the final challenge. We all slept a lot.

I did some sightseeing around Deimos: the Lagado Academy, the spacecraft yard, and the water sculpture park. I found a café on the Rue Candide and watched the crowds go by.

I'd been there an hour when Piers Tyana found me. He was dressed casually in a suit liner—though when I looked again I saw it was actually a woven silk bodysuit, tailored and dyed to look exactly like a beat-up old suit liner. "Are you waiting for anyone?"

"Just sightseeing."

"May I?" He took the seat across from me, and the crowd noise faded as he turned on the sound cloak.

"Is something wrong?" I asked him, suddenly afraid I had broken some unknown rule.

"Oh, no, no," he said, with a reassuring smile. "I'm not here as an official. This is entirely informal."

A bot arrived with a globe of white wine and a pair of samosas for him, and he took a bite and a sip before continuing.

"You're a very talented young man, Ying," he said. "The tasters weren't very impressed with your cooking, but our more thoughtful members still consider you a very strong candidate."

"Thank you," I said.

He took another bite of samosa. "What's your big idea?"

I just stared at him for a second. "How did you hear about that?"

He smiled and drank a little more wine. "Members of the Deimos Community enjoy absolute privacy in their communications and network activity. It's one of our fundamental rights. *Visitors,* however, may be monitored for the good of the Community. Even personal messages. Some of us in the loop are curious: What's your big idea?"

"When I was working at Eos, I started fooling around with some advanced propulsion concepts. I think I've found a way to—"

I stopped. I'd been messing with the old Alcubierre drive concept—squeezing space-time to move faster than light without breaking the rules—and I'd come up with a way to get around the problems that had scuttled the idea a century ago. Chou had looked over my notions and couldn't find anything wrong, but it would take a hell of a lot to develop.

"To . . . ?" he prompted.

"To change the way we move spacecraft around," I finished. I could feel myself getting sweaty and nervous, and I gave myself a big hit of adrenaline blocker. Not that it would help; Tyana could probably hear my pulse from where he sat.

He waited, then finished his first samosa. "You're listed as a team member on three projects of Dr. Chou's group—"

"It's not any of that," I said.

"As I said, I'm not here officially, and we've got full privacy. You don't have to worry about anyone stealing your idea."

That was all very well, but *he* was listening—and of course Micromegas was, too. And anyone with a "need to know." For the good of the Community. I was just a visitor, after all.

My idea was a game changer, no question about it. Spaceships with an Alcubierre drive wouldn't have to worry about minimum-energy orbits or available propellant. It would give us the stars! Deimos wouldn't be the hub of all space travel anymore—just one more rock in one more star system.

Unless, of course, the Community controlled the drive. Then they'd own the universe.

"It's still just conceptual," I said. "Not ready to publish yet."

He finished his samosa and looked at me, and I looked back. *You want what's in the shiny box? You have to let me in. Otherwise I'll show my shiny box to someone else.*

"Here in Deimos we really are a community," he said. "It's not just a name we call ourselves. All of us contribute."

I said, "I think I have a lot to offer."

Another long pause while he emptied the wine globe. "Well, thank you for this little talk," he told me. He got up and shot off into the traffic stream, and the silence faded away around me.

I WENT BACK TO my room and used my hotel credit to order a meal. But even after the bot set a table for me, I felt lonesome.

So I took my food across the hall and knocked on Sofia's door. "Would you like some dinner? I've got a big plate of fried fish and chips and it's too much for me," I said.

"I'd been thinking of something more like a salad," she said.

"Suit yourself." I started to turn away.

"—But maybe I'll have a little," she said, and stepped back to let me in. Her room was nicer than mine. They were identical, of course, but she had done some cool stuff with the settings. The walls showed a city of white and gold towers in a green river delta under blazing sunlight, and we sat on a colorful carpet. Not smart matter but an actual carpet made of animal hair, which she had actually hauled all the way out of Earth's gravity well and across half an AU just to sit on.

The fish was okay—that is, it tasted better than most things I'd eaten in my life before that, but Sofia got out a little jar of hot pepper paste to dip it in. I wished for something stronger than tea to soothe my throat.

We ate in silence, even though she had the room on full privacy. Ever since my conversation with Piers Tyana that afternoon I figured everything I said and all my network traffic would be watched by someone.

"Who do you think will win?" she asked me when there was nothing but fried potatoes left.

"I've got no idea. You, maybe? The prediction markets have you in the lead."

"The contest is still wide open," she said. "If I do badly on the last round, it could be you, or maybe Reinette Luz."

"Reinette? Not Rakesh?"

"Not him. All he does is food."

We finished the potatoes, then I decided to bring up the subject we'd been avoiding. "When I met you, I think we were falling in love."

"I noticed that too," she said. "But you've got meds for that."

I did something brave then. "When this is over, are you . . . ?"

"What?"

"Do you want to get together?"

"Will you allow yourself to love me?" she asked.

"Only one of us gets to join Deimos," I pointed out.

"You are cruel," she said. "Did you know that? Are you even capable of understanding? I love you already. I'm not all pumped full of chemicals to regulate me. I've been wrestling with this devil's choice since I saw you. If I win, I get to join Deimos, help my family back home—and lose you. If you win, I'll wind up in exile somewhere, or betray my family so I can stay in Africa, and I'll still lose you."

"What if neither of us wins?"

"Then we're two bright people who've already lost our fondest hopes. I suppose we could be unhappy together."

"Do you think they planned this?"

"Perhaps. I think the Community has goals of its own, which not even the members understand. A rock full of clever people who've cut themselves off from the rest of humanity may not be best for the members, but it's good for Deimos."

I hoped someone was listening when she said that. "I'll see you tonight," I told her, and went back to my own room.

THEY USED A MODEST meeting room in the hotel to announce the final competition. We had assigned seats in color-coded pairs—two red, two green, two blue, and two gold. I was in one of the green chairs, and Sofia sat to my left in the other. Piers Tyana was at the head of the table. Although the entire Community was watching, it felt more private.

Tyana started off with a speech about how wonderful we all were and how the experience of the competition would enrich us no matter who won. Finally he got to the important part.

"This final round will test your ability to work with other people. The Deimos Community values creativity and initiative, but it is very important that all our members are able to cooperate."

The eight of us were smart. The pairs in matching seats looked at each other.

"As you may have guessed, we have paired you up for this assignment. The pairing is not random—Micromegas has analyzed which pairs have the strongest emotional reactions to each other. We've chosen the most difficult people for you to work with."

The bastards, I thought. Match me up with a girl who is in love with me. Maximize the distraction for both of us.

"And now your task. Deimos is a wonderful place, the gem of the solar system, but no world is perfect. We want you to add something. Identify a need or a lack, and create something to fill it. You have one sol to complete it. Any questions before we start the clock?"

Sofia spoke up before anyone else. "Are there any restrictions on what we can do?"

He nodded, looking pleased. "Not many. You can't use any space or matter currently being used for some other purpose, and you can have a maximum of ten kilowatts sustained load. Otherwise, you have priority on fabricators, robots, and material processing for the next twenty-four hours. Be aware of the time limit: unfinished projects are failures."

Nobody had anything else to ask. I could see the other pairs already starting to brainstorm. I set up a private link to Sofia.

"You're the artist," I sent. "Pick something that will impress them."

Her eyes were flicking around like crazy as she interacted with Micromegas, so I waited until she sent me a reply. "I think I've got something. Let's go someplace we can speak privately."

We wound up back in the workspace area with full sound damping on. "I've been thinking about Deimos ever since I got off the Cycler," she said. "Have you looked at the people here?"

"What about them?"

She opened a window showing Rue Arouet. "If you look, you can tell the Community members apart from the visitors. Do you see it?"

"You mean their pop-ups?"

"No, I mean the way they look, physically. It's not phenotypes—they're strong on genetic diversity here—and it's not just the gravity. Contract workers and travelers get plenty of microgravity experience, but they don't look like members."

"The clothes," I guessed.

"No. *Look*. That man's wearing disposable coveralls, but I can tell he's a member. Those two women over there are in very stylish outfits, but they're not from here. Probably Earth."

"I see what you mean," I said after a moment. "But I can't put my finger on what I'm seeing."

"Confidence," she said. "They don't hurry, they don't flinch. Whatever they're doing is the most interesting and important thing going on anywhere. They're all perfectly self-assured."

I looked at the people and finally I saw what she meant. The members moved in straight lines at their own pace. Visitors and contractors flowed around the members, like wind around rocks.

"It's their moon—it's their whole solar system," she said. "The rest of us are just visitors and hired help." The idea seemed to bother her, much more than it bothered me.

"I still don't see how that gives us a project," I pointed out.

"They look inward. Except for the lounge at the elevator terminal and the viewing area at the spaceport, there aren't any windows on Deimos. I want to give them eyes on the universe."

"An observatory?"

"Exactly!"

"Well, that's . . . pretty easy," I said. "A mirror, some stabilizing gear, off-the-shelf software. They must have scopes already. IR to spot hostiles, targeting devices for the defense systems, probably some eyes on Mars and Luna."

"Yes, but that's all technical, inside-the-walls stuff. I mean a place where people can go to see the stars."

"I like it. We can split up the job. You design a viewing area and interface. I'll build us a telescope."

With twenty-two hours left, we got to work. She found a nonstructural volume of ice near the Rue Lagado and got permission from Micromegas to hollow it out. While she and some bots did that, I picked a ten-meter crater on the far side of Deimos and set to work transforming it.

It would have been simplest to just build a parabolic mirror and put it on a mounting, but I guess a little of Sofia's visual aesthetic had rubbed off on me, so I wanted something cooler. I graded the little crater as a simple spherical curve and lined it with vacuum-rated smart matter with an optical mirror surface. I put a high-quality camera on an arm and programmed the smart matter to form a parabolic mirror opposite the camera wherever it moved. The result was a silver pool that reshaped itself instead of moving around.

There were some trade-offs: it could only look at things within about sixty degrees of the zenith, but since Deimos circles Mars once a sol, you could look at most of the sky if you picked your time. The only blind spots were around Mars's celestial poles, and those aren't very interesting.

It sounds simple, but the actual work took a lot of time. I had to suit up and go supervise the bots because the job was so unlike their usual work. For instance: the first time they tried to grade the crater, they started on the outer edge and worked inward, which meant they screwed it all up as soon as they tried to crawl out again. I also had problems sticking the smart matter to the surface, until I finally just had them fuse the top ten centimeters into glass.

About sixteen hours into the project I was trying to write code for the mirror and supervise the bots building the camera arm at the same time, all in my sweaty suit with the capacity indicator blinking on the urine bag.

"How are you doing?" I asked Sofia.

"Have a look." She sent me an image of the viewing space she'd created. It was fairly intimate—a dozen seats under a dome-shaped screen. The overall aesthetic was based on Mughal architecture, as a nod to Jai Singh's observatory at Jaipur, but with what I now know are art deco elements echoing North American planetariums.

"Can you come up here? There's some stuff I need you to do," I told her.

About an hour later she came bounding across the surface toward me. She moved well in her suit, which was important.

"What do you need?" she asked as she made a soft landing a meter away from me.

"If you can take over the motion control coding, I can go fix that stupid actuator," I told her.

"Sure," she said, and then she looked up. "Ahh . . ."

"What?"

"The sky," she said. We were in Mars's shadow right then, so we stood on a black surface looking out at the universe. The band of the Milky Way stretched across our vision, and the stars looked close enough to reach out and touch. We watched in silence for a couple of minutes.

Eventually she gave a regretful sigh. "I guess we need to get back to work."

"Right, yeah." I dosed up on more stimulants and tackled the actuator.

What happened next looked just like one of those complicated failure chains you see in most space accidents. Sofia didn't know that the camera arm wasn't at its default position when she loaded her code. I had allowed my safety line to get looped over the arm. And my anchor piton was in a crumbly bit of regolith. I'd set it all up very carefully.

So when I replaced the faulty actuator and connected the power, the arm immediately swung itself to the neutral position, with the camera at ninety degrees above the mirror. It snatched me off my feet and ripped the piton out of the ground in one smooth motion.

I felt the twang as the line went taut as it slung me into space, then a couple of seconds of free fall. When I reached the end of the line, I felt a slight jerk as the piton snagged on the arm. For a moment I thought it would hold, but then it slipped away and I was off to outer space, no strings attached.

"Wu Ying! Are you okay?" Sofia called over the link.

"How fast am I going?"

Pause. "Six meters per second."

Escape velocity. I was now a moon of Mars. I'd have to call for rescue, unless someone helped me. "Sofia! I'll call this in myself! Finish the scope!" Then I waited.

Twenty seconds later something hit me. It was Sofia, of course. She'd used the arm to make a boosted leap after me, trailing her own safety line. She grabbed me around the knees, then pulled herself up until she could grab my safety harness.

"Clip on!" she said. I snapped onto her line and threw my arms around her for good measure. A second later we felt an almighty yank as the line hit maximum extension—and held. Both of us let out our breath.

I didn't let go of her. "We're on direct link. Nobody can hear. How much money do you have?"

"What? I don't know. It's all in buildings and infrastructure."

"Enough to fund a tech project? Ten, twenty megawatt-hours?"

"Why are you asking me now?"

The ground was rising up toward us. I'd never been so glad to fall. "My big idea. Starships! I can do it; I just need backing. Forget the competition, forget Deimos. Do you trust me?"

"Will you love me?" she asked.

"Yes!"

A second later we smacked down on the surface, bounced, and finally came to rest. I held on to her until we stopped tumbling. I could see the local network icon again at the corner of my vision. "Hello, Micromegas?" I said.

"Do you need help?" asked the AI.

"No, we're fine." I took a breath and looked at Sofia through two face-plates. "We quit."

REINETTE WON, BUT HARDLY anyone noticed. We sold the drama rights to pay our way to Earth—hibernating in a slow freight payload. Your grandparents were ready to kill us both when we came down the elevator, until Sofia and I showed them what we'd been working on.

That's the whole story, really. You should sleep now. We've all got a big day tomorrow.

STORY NOTES—James L. Cambias

I started thinking about the implications of rapid prototyping via things like 3-D printing and more advanced forms of "matter fabricators" combined with the continuing advance of expert systems. I think that pairing will be a huge boost to all forms of creativity. We're approaching the point where the barriers between the mind and physical reality are vanishing: we have only to imagine something and we can build it.

Regarding the setting: Physics suggests that if humans ever build a civilization encompassing the solar system, the Martian moon Deimos is the natural hub for traffic. Stake your claim now!

RESPONSE TO "PERIAPSIS"—Alex MacDonald

Alex MacDonald, an economist in the Civil and Commercial Space Division at NASA's Jet Propulsion Laboratory, responds to "Periapsis" at hieroglyph.asu.edu/deimos.

FORUM DISCUSSION—Longer-Than-Lifetime Projects

Stewart Brand, Joel Garreau, and other Hieroglyph community members join James L. Cambias in a conversation about ambitious projects that take longer than a human lifetime to complete at hieroglyph.asu.edu/deimos.

THE MAN WHO SOLD THE STARS
Gregory Benford

Vain is the word of that philosopher which does not heal any suffering of man.

—Epicurus

2016

Harold Mann idled at a corner and watched an enormous guy come out of one of the adult movie houses and stride over to his Harley.

Harold was on his second job—at fifteen, using a fake ID—driving a cab on South Jefferson Street of St. Louis. Business late on a sweltering night was slow. The big bearded guy's bike was under a light post next to a Honda Hawk. The man in black leather pants and a black T-shirt shouted at the whole street, "Who parked this turd next to my bike?"

He then grabbed the Honda Hawk, grunted as he lifted it, and threw it all the way across the street. It hit another Japanese bike, a yellow Kawasaki. The clanging smashup echoed in the moist night.

Some gasoline dripped from the Kawasaki and the man walked over, puffing on a brown Sherman's cigarette, and—dropped it. The gasoline *whomped*, sending flames licking across the sidewalk. The biker glared at Harold and walked up to the cab window. He pulled out a big Bowie knife, grinning. Harold looked straight ahead and heard the tapping on the window.

"What ya think a dat?" He slurred the words and spat on the blacktop.

Harold rolled down the window and looked into the scowling sweaty face. "I don't think you threw that rice burner hard enough."

Glowering: "Yeah?"

"Man's got to throw long in this life."

The biker walked away laughing. The bikes burned. Harold finished his duty time, drove to the cab station, and quit. *Maybe not my best line of work,* he thought.

Five months later he had turned sixteen and had another fake ID saying he was twenty-one. He pitched a smartware app to a start-up company in St. Louis, by walking in cold and asking to see the vice president. The app assisted robots with finding their footing and orientation while working in Low Earth Orbit. They could then assemble parts for the first orbital hotel.

The key to the app was using the new composite carbon girders with holes punched every half meter. Robots could count on having a dual-pivot purchase no more than fifty centimeters away, to torque or support a mechanical advantage. This increased their mobility and mass-carrying capacity.

The vice president was intrigued. While his engineers looked over the app he asked Harold for his credentials. He gave them a certificate saying he had graduated from MIT with a degree in astronautics, remarking that it was the same program in which Buzz Aldrin had gotten his Ph.D. The e-certificate was authentic, though he had artfully hacked it to omit the detail that he had done the classes entirely online in three years without ever being in Boston.

The start-up bought his app and he got a job. Within two years he was their CEO, and they issued an initial public offering. His share was nearly a million, since he had worked mostly for stock options.

Driving home that night, he saw the same biker guy coming out of a bar. Harold pulled over and bought the guy a drink, never saying why.

HE RECALLED HIS FIRST job as he watched the vids from the latest big satellite telescope. The deep resolution views were striking, and they brought back a moment when he was ten years old.

He had rented beach chairs to tourists down at Orange Beach, Alabama. All day long he let nobody get past him without a friendly, insistent, "A chair to make you more comfortable? The sand's hot. Just five bucks for the day."

The usual brush-off he eased by with, "Keeps you away from the sand flies, sir"—and that usually did the trick, especially if he had a woman with him. She would usually wrinkle her nose and badger the man into it.

Decent money, and he was only ten. His father thought it was good training and Harold did, too—the Great Recession was not yet in the rearview mirror. The tourists officially had the chairs till sundown, but many stayed with their beer and got fried oysters from the stand down the way. He stayed late, reading used paperback science fiction novels under the fluorescents of the greasy burger stand. He was an addict; science fiction sold the sizzle of the science steak. Even when he got tired he remembered to be polite, smiling and using the *yes sir* a lot—and so he discovered tipping.

Some just left the chairs strewn around, so he had to drag them back, two in each hand, to the shed. He had just finished stacking chairs and was turning to plod down to the bus stop to ride home when he turned toward the surf and saw them.

Saw them truly, for the first time. The whole grand sprawl of jewels across the blue-black carpet, hovering above the salty tang of gulf waters like a commandment. The Milky Way spanned the sky, vanishing into the horizon, glows shimmering of emerald, ruby, and hard diamond whites.

That's what we're part of, he thought. *The real, ultimate way the universe is, not just this moist curtain above a sandy stretch. Reality, big and strange and wonderful.*

2023

At twenty-two he decided to tint his black hair gray to appear on his first business panel, about resource extraction from asteroids. With dark glasses and long sideburns the tinting made him look older. The moderator was the famous Interplanetary Resources exec Peter Diamandis, who deftly kept the talk flowing without digressing.

A steely-looking woman in a stylish blue suit got into an argument with a panelist guy from NASA, saying, "Your main goal appears to be not to fail. In the bigger space companies and academia, the mission has to work. So you gold plate everything and your price soars."

"And you're about profit, period," the guy shot back.

"People give us money, their choice, we pay them with dividends. You take taxes with laws."

He said slowly, "Lockheed, Northrop Grumman, the rest—they have great track records."

"They're monuments, this is a movement."

The audience murmured and people started arguing with each other. Harold surveyed the discontent with a bemused smile.

He'd seen their likes before. Merit-driven products of the test-prep industry, capable cogs. And yet they did their jobs while thinking they were countercultural rebels. Their generation loved the Standard Story-line: insurgents fighting the true establishment, that distant dull group that was always somebody else. They were sharp and from Ivy Leagues, Stanford, Caltech. That unconscious attitude prevailed in corporate boardrooms, so they could rail against the establishment over cabernet in the evenings.

As he watched this woman he reflected that in a way he had accomplished the life goals his parents had taught him, mostly by example. He had found a good way to make a living, had started a business, and enjoyed it all. He got up each morning eager to get to the office. But this woman made him realize he had other goals left to achieve.

The focused woman said, "If you're young and lean, things can *fail*. For the big space companies the whole competition is just getting the government contract, then it's all risk aversion. It's not at all about doing something cool, first to market, then making money so you can do more. That's what I like: not playing it safe. To shift gears, to follow your nose."

She seemed startled when she got applause. Harold nodded and smiled at her. His talk was next. Fairly technical, about universal joints, AI linkages, and space applications—but she listened intently as he outlined a rock-prospector team of robots he had worked out and tried in the Arizona desert.

Moving on, Diamandis commented that for robots, deserts might be easier than space. Then on a concluding note, he asked where all this work would lead. "Prosperity!" the woman said. Someone in the large audience called, "To the stars!," and another voice shouted, "The stars? Impossible! Why do it anyway?"

She glanced at the moderator and said, "Why go to the stars? Because we are the descendants of those primates who chose to look over the next hill. Because we won't survive on this rock indefinitely. Because they're *there*."

The panel met in the bar with Diamandis for drinks after. He could not take his eyes off her, even when she was talking to Diamandis. He learned her name was Sara-no-h—Sara Ernsberg. As the group broke up he said impulsively, "Do you dance?"

They got back to the hotel at 3 A.M. He slept in her arms till noon, and they missed the entire morning session, including his own talk.

2029

"You're going off the deep end," Sara said. They were in his office with a big view of Pike's Peak. The slender mountain had snagged a looming purple thundercloud on its slopes. Lightning flashed in its belly. *Mine too,* Harold thought.

"I can make a billion in a year if we can repeat the old Air Force test trials, make 'em work," Harold said. "It's a calculated risk."

"Look, the public's against nuclear rocketry."

"Has anybody really asked? The nuke flies up cold as a salmon. SpaceX can deliver it. We turn it on after we've flown a tank of hydrogen up and mated it to the nuclear thermal unit. That assembly flies my robot team to the candidate asteroid and runs a nuke power source for their exploration."

She twisted her mouth in a skeptical red-lipsticked torque that he loved. "It never comes back into Low Earth Orbit?"

"Never. We use it for smelting in orbit beyond the moon."

Sara said, "I prefer more conservative invest—"

"In five years this *will be* conservative. It'll be raining soup and we'll have a bucket."

"So this is gambling on a certainty."

"Launching a nuke rocket core, piggybacking on a two-stage to orbit, it makes economic sense."

"Nukes. The UN can block you."

"Elon says he can launch us from mid-Pacific. His platform's not a UN member—or subject to nation-state controls." Elon Musk, Jeff Bezos, Richard Branson—they had been like the Carnegies and Rockefellers of high vacuum, just a generation before, and were still big players.

"Any skeptical legal advisor will say"—she frowned, did a bass growl—"'You could be sued for every double-yoked egg a hen lays after launch.'"

Harold flicked on a complex legal flowchart. "Ah, that old mink case as 'proximate cause'? Nope, we'd legally have to be sued on the moon. The parent company is Blue Sky Nuclear, incorporated as of today on Luna."

"Luna? There's no—"

"I and some investor friends sent a robot office clerk there. They'll have to argue for years over whether that's a legal registry. I'm happy to let them go trotting down that alley."

"Sorry. You've still got enough minimum contacts with the planet for them to get personal jurisdiction. It just might take a while—or you might end up losing that Laguna mansion."

Harold shrugged. "Keegan over at Consolidated will be after us for sure."

"Then there's the Outer Space Treaty—the United States is a signatory."

"Yeah, Consolidated will work that. That's how the Microsoft competitors shamelessly worked with the Clinton administration to take down Microsoft."

"You've got it all figured out."

"Nope, just the fun parts. The rest I leave to you."

"Me?!"

"I need a pretty face with a razor mind to present our target asteroids to the excited investing public."

"I haven't said I'll put anything into this swan dive off a skyscraper—"

"Take your pick." He flashed a list onto the wall using his thumb command.

Most Cost-Effective: 2000 BM19, a very small O-type asteroid (diameter less than 1 km). Makes several close approaches to Earth. Estimated value is $18.50 trillion and an estimated profit of $3.55 trillion (USD).

Most Accessible: 2009 WY7, small asteroid with regular close approaches of less than 1 AU. A silicaceous or "stony" object that has a high accessibility score on Asterank of 7.6577. Some hints of water content. $1.53 trillion.

Most Valuable + Most Profitable: 253 Mathilde, a 52.8-km-diameter carbonaceous asteroid. Estimated mineral/metal value of over $100 trillion. After robot mining and transport, estimated profit $9.53 trillion.

She shook her head. "Your audience is venture capital guys, not astronomers."

"I want to snag their economic ambition, not their intellect. You can charmingly smooth over the distinction. Now, come with me into the board meeting." He spread his arms wide, gave her a sunny smile.

"What?!" She looked terrified, which was actually rather attractive.

Five minutes later he was gesturing at a 3-D PowerPoint slide without looking at it. *Always face the audience.*

The nuke fission rocket idea he had prepared the board for, so it took only some cheerleading from Sara and a fast finish after the tech details: "Look, remember the 1990s and the 2000s? Computers toppled and then rebuilt industries. Retail sales—Walmart and Amazon. Banking—ATMs, online services. Finance—high-speed online investing down to milliseconds, global markets you needed a stopwatch to work in. Entertainment—web streaming, downloads, YouTube. Publishing—e-books took down old-style print media, aggregators did in paper news, so nobody goes to 'press' anymore. The march of time."

A well-known savvy techno-skeptic sniffed and gave them all a bemused scowl. Harold had invited him on the board, knowing the name alone would raise stock value. "Thanks for the history lesson. How's that tell us what comes next?"

"The big demand now is for raw material." Harold stood up and spread his hands expansively. "So we butt into the old mining company territories by bringing in new sources—the asteroids. Next we do communications—we provide cheap, easy repair to geosynchronous comsats that have gone dead. Energy—we go get the Helium-3 that's just sitting in the first few meters of the moon's surface, along with plenty of rare earths as a bonus."

This provoked a full hour of discussion, some heated. The skeptic stormed out, angry—only to return fifteen minutes later, red-faced, claiming he'd just gone to the bathroom. Sara got in some telling jabs, even some laughs. Finally the board turned to a plausible scenario for the mining operation. As usual, many trade-offs and unknowns, as always in blue sky investing—"or black sky," one board member joked. Harold grinned and decided to go radical on them.

"Friends, a chunk of high-quality metal twenty meters across generates an impact explosion on the scale of megatons, granted. But!—without radioactive fallout, and it doesn't spray much on impact, especially if it hits sand." He flicked a wrist and a satellite view of Earth rotated on the wall screen. The board leaned forward, studying sites picked out in livid color.

A graphic showed a fiery dot skating down through the atmosphere, diving in suddenly, and spiking into a bleak tan Mexican desert.

"There are plenty of remote deserts we can hit to make an impact safe. All the miners need do is to find a mostly metal asteroid on the appropriate orbit, give it a calculated nudge. Let our robots work metal and rare earths out of its crust. Save that, bundle the sludge with some orbital debris, and fuse it as a shell over the refined metal. Do your smelting where the robots can blow it off. The solar wind picks up the waste, takes it to interstellar space. Do this while the rock's in transit. Get the robots off with an unmanned shuttle. Pilot the metal into orbit so it can skim along the upper atmosphere, maybe skip it like a rock on a lake. Then bring it down, slam it in, mine it."

He finished with a 3-D budget, detailing axes: profit and loss and cost. "I'll take you the board to, let's say, Libya to watch the fireworks."

Mermin raised his big hand. "Reality check. You'll never get clearance."

"Your reality check will bounce. The UN Security Council is a debating society. Current ideas evaporate in societies struggling to feed their people. If a desert country can gain a new industry by letting rocks drop into their land, they will. Libya already says it will."

An investor said mildly, "Genuine realpolitik trumps wishful-thinking realpolitik these days."

Bo Duc Anton, CEO of Astroprospects, smoothed her classic Chinese cheongsam and said, "Start small."

"How?" Harold asked.

"My company has a Spacefarer contract to find and de-orbit debris. I can compact some of the space junk we collect with robots: booster rockets, lost gear, urine-icicles, dead satellites. We just grabbed Explorer I! Not typical—we'll bring it down to sell to collectors. Real junk we can bundle and drop back in as a trial, into a desert."

"Isn't all that supposed to go into the ocean?" someone shot back.

Bo Duc shrugged. "Sometimes we miss." Laughter. She blinked; it had just popped out, before she had a chance to really think it through. Harold knew how to get momentum going. Another objection about bad publicity made him shrug, saying, "Some days you're the pigeon, and some days you're the statue."

"Make it a small mass," Sara said. "You need to test targeting anyway."

Another woman said, "Better to start out clean, have a contract with Libya. They need the cash and the mining business."

The corporate lawyer began, "Risk is too high to allow—"

"Committees don't open frontiers—people do," Harold said. "We've got to look beyond the Official Future people learn in business school. It's risky to *not* do this."

2031

Their trial package came screaming down like an orange arrow. It hit within two hundred meters of their bull's-eye and Sara shouted as the shock wave hit them in a rolling roar, from two kilometers away. Sand rose in a tan wave above the Libyan desert and crashed in front of them like dirty foam.

She and Harold were the only ones who dared to stand this close. His simulation group was confident that with the cladding Sara's company provided, made from orbital junk, it would shed red-hot debris and follow a predictable path. Unlike the earlier satellites that had come flaming down, this was dense and hard and so kept to its programmed path.

The shock wave blew her hair straight back in the thunderclap roar and she laughed as he kissed her.

He realized then that others had sports like golf, or risky rich-guy hobbies like flying experimental aircraft, or just ran through a series of ever more expensive women . . . and he didn't. He liked to work, and Sara was just the right balanced love he needed, no more.

Whenever he needed to feel his inspiration, he could turn from his meetings and engineering details and deal-making . . . and simply look up into the night sky. The frosty splendor of stars glimmered there, eternally beckoning.

2032

His company had an executive retreat of a rather different sort in the high Sierras. They all went backpacking out from Mammoth Lakes and after some grunting and swearing got camped around Deer Lake at ten thousand feet. Harold liked to see how people did when not behind a desk. Some seemed to see the natural world as an exotic, hostile place. One groused about no cell-phone service.

Lying outside and staring lazily into the crisp, clear night sky, he recalled the same sensation of awe at the grand silvery sweep of the Milky

Way that he had felt as a boy. He couldn't see Alpha Centauri from here. Could a star be closer, yet undiscovered? Could he get there? The planets he would reach, sure, but *stars* . . .

As a boy in 2013 he had read a book about starships and how they might be built, following a century of burgeoning interplanetary commerce. After all, Columbus had found the New World in caravels designed for warm, tranquil Mediterranean waters, not the Atlantic. But within a generation the promise of gold and land spurred rugged craft that grew steadily larger.

Going to the stars would be harder than anything ever done, maybe more than life's laboring up out of an ocean and onto land. The true vast extent of the problem was the charm of it, too.

The next night around their snapping campfire along the John Muir Trail he talked about building capability to reach the stars. It would be a step-by-step process, a side effect of developing the solar system economy.

His execs rolled their eyes and looked at their CEO as if he was going loopy on them. *Well, maybe I am*, he thought. *For now.*

2033

One year later the Chinese tested a nuke rocket engine in the open air, just as the USA had in the 1960s and 1970s. There was little escaped radiation. They even blew up a nuke configuration with implanted explosives and found very low residual radiation—also as the Americans had. Intelligence found the Chinese had simply bought the entire program developed by the Soviets at Semipalatinsk; the Russian nation was having a fire sale. Now the Chinese were rapidly improving on the old designs.

This alerted the world and became the next "Sputnik moment." It was almost as if the new Chinese semidemocracy, struggling to pacify its nationalist faction, was trying to deflect internal stresses into an external competition. Soon enough, it quite obviously was.

Suddenly capital rained from the skies. Harold was ready with his bucket. He had made his deals to get a program under way for his company, FarVoyager, and their test bed results were good. They orbited the first test nuke half a year later.

The Chinese were still reorganizing after the overthrow of the old Red regime, their politics a factional scramble. They decided to not launch a nuke rocket from the ground, even though there was little escaped residual radiation. So they converged on the American design of assembly of the cold nuke rocket and command module with regularly supplied fuel tubes that inserted into the big liquid pods. This became the standard method for fission transport.

HAROLD WAS A PRIVATE sort of man who made a point of letting no one at all, even Sara, call him Harry. Still, at the celebration of the first nuke burn from Low Earth Orbit, he let himself go. It had gone perfectly, the hydrogen jetting out in luminous fury to boost a major tonnage of comsats and a few working zero-grav laboratories to high orbits. Proof of principle. Now the whole solar system seemed to yawn open at last.

COMMITTEES DON'T OPEN FRONTIERS—PEOPLE DO.

Somebody on his staff had put it up without asking. *Good,* he thought. Then he burst into a song he had written:

> *A fact without a theory is like a ship without a sail.*
> *Is like a boat without a rudder.*
> *Is like a kite without a tail.*
> *A fact without a theory is as sad as sad can be.*
> *But if there's one thing worse*
> *in this universe,*
> *A fact you just can't hack—*
> *it's a theory*
> *without a fact.*

Though he hit every note perfectly, he never sang in public again.

SOON SPACEX LOFTED ANOTHER long gray tube of liquid hydrogen to fly alongside the FarVoyager engine. Specially designed Astrominer bots mated fuel to engines. The craft ignited and left orbit, bound for a near Earth asteroid to carry out a prospector mission. It visited five water-rich asteroids that were energetically easier to reach than the surface of the moon. Orbital Sciences and Virgin Galactic, deeply into their orbital hotel businesses, offered their services for a second flight.

The Chinese had built an industrial empire with autocratic methods, but they had never opened a frontier before. They found it hard to let enterprises compete. The instincts of Late Marxism were hard to over-come. On the other hand, they were an eager market for products from space. Toward the end of the decade, Chinese billionaires competed to top the latest lavish champagne party in the Spherical Hilton.

2037

Harold and Sara took their first flight to the big new Spherical Hilton together. The two-stage to orbit shuttle was smooth, in a big rugged composite airframe. Out the porthole they could see Phoenix, now more like Jericho or Ur, with it shriveled relics of golf courses and the dusty hulls of swimming pools beside abandoned homes.

The Spherical was ornate in its lightweight way. They had a suite, which meant a big bubble window they could float within and see the universe passing in review. Hanging there in an ocean of night, they made love. Each time with her he felt a new depth, an unexpected flavoring. She was moist and cool as diamond-sharp stars drifted behind her. Energy rippled along their skins, somehow liberated by the weightlessness. Yes, here was their center. Bodies said what their words could not.

They had a preference for the spherical swimming drop. He plunged into the ten-meter-diameter shimmering cool ball and felt it coil around him in a way water on Earth did not. He hung suspended and kissed her foot, grinning madly. Kick, stroke, and he was back in air, barely in time, gasping.

The hotel furniture was as light as air. Carbon fibers with diamond struts, all puffed into a foamy shape. Their stick-to chairs faced the huge window where Earth slid by. The sights somehow loosened their tongues as they sipped from wine spheres. Lightly, Sara revealed that before him she had been the happy hypotenuse of a triangular domestic ménage.

"You gave that up for me?"

"No, for me. That way I got *you*."

Over dinner she finally got him to talk about his odd childhood. Maybe the altitude gave perspective? He grimaced. "Look, the information age rewards people who mature fast, are verbally and socially sophisticated, can control their impulses. Girls were way better at that. Schools praised diversity but were culturally the same. Different skin color, same opinions. The girls ran my senior class and I slept through classes."

"So you got out." They watched a gyrating hurricane, the fifteenth already this summer, churn across the Atlantic.

"They wanted to teach me how to share. I wanted a curriculum that taught how to win." He grinned. "And how to lose. I've done my share of that, too."

She turned to look at him. "Teachers wrote my parents that I was 'a fiercely rambunctious girl.' After a while they found out they couldn't tame me by assigning some of those exquisitely sensitive Newbery-award-winning novellas."

"Yeah. Social engineering ain't that easy. You're always going to get malcontents who like money and movement more than contentment."

"You're after the money?"

He noticed that she had deftly turned the talk back to him, but let it go. "Oh, you mean those investments in nanotech and 3-D printing? Sure, to get cash for the Botworks orbiter up here."

"What about all that opposition to nanotech? They teamed up with that failed campaign to stop your launches of cold nuke rockets."

"Marches don't stop markets. So maybe nanotech pushes noses out of joint. Big social impacts, sure. Life's like that. The world's getting stranger and I'm going to get stranger right along with it."

WHEN THEY TOOK THE trans-orbital shuttle to the Botworks in higher orbit, Australia was burning again. An angry black shroud north of Melbourne cloaked the already parched lands. Geoengineering with aerosols in the stratosphere was redistributing rainfall to counter this, but imperfectly. At least it was cooling the world and avoiding the terrible droughts of the early 2030s. Meanwhile chemical plants steadily worked to offset the rising alkalinity of the oceans.

Harold immediately used his phone to call through to his company office, Astromines AU, in Melbourne. "Give extra compensations to staff in the burn area," he said to his operations manager. "And make a corporate donation, say a hundred million, to the disaster zone."

He could tell from Sara's expression that she was surprised. "Y'know what I miss most in this warming-up world—the North Pole." He pointed to the south, where Antarctica was smaller but still brilliant white. To the north no sea ice remained.

She nodded. "Maybe we should spread more aerosols, bring the summer sea ice back?"

"The Russians want the sea lanes open wide. It's a trade-off." He sighed.

The Botworks were served by the big nuke complex and the attendant rocket, floating like a shark beside a clumpy whale. Astromines had snagged into high orbit a nominal working asteroid fifty meters across. Bots swarmed over it, directed by an octagonal manager craft secured to the dark rock by a carbon-fiber tower. Bots walked on this, their thick legs swinging from one toe-hold to the next with startling speed. They then spread over a mesh that grasped the asteroid, helping the smelting units grind and heat. The nuke power plant gave electricity and hot smelting fluids through a flexible, stark white piping array.

"Looks like a spiderweb around its prey," Sara said.

"Not far wrong," Harold said. "The Chinese have one like this, but many more people. See that hab on top of the command ship?" He pointed at the busy octagonal assembly. "Has three crew, all women. They work together better out here, seems like."

"The *Journal* says they're undercutting your price."

Harold shrugged. "They want to win not a space race, but a space marathon. They learned the big lesson from the 2020s. Manufacturing is all that matters in the long run. Service economies only shuttle money from person to person. Manufacturing creates wealth, services distribute it."

"The Euros want to keep space public—something that every citizen feels like they're involved in, a public utility rather than a private playground."

"Yeah," Harold said, "I saw that speech. 'Not just billionaires doing their bungee jumping in reverse.' Good line, bad logic."

The three women aboard were all agog that the CEO had come out to see them. Sara and Harold got into skinsuits and "the gals" tugged them around the asteroid, pointing out bots as they performed complex tasks. Bots all had AIs that knew kinetic tasks down to the millimeter, and bots never tired. "They don't get retirement plans," Harold remarked.

Their departing gift was a chunk of the ore. Sara sniffed it. "Smells like gunpowder."

"Smells like the future," Harold said.

After they left, Sara said, "My, they prettied themselves up for you. Skirts in space?"

He shrugged. "A nice gesture."

"They didn't know I was coming, did they?"

"I may have neglected to mention it."

"I almost laughed at how their faces fell. Didn't your staff send a manifest?"

"I don't use staff much. Like to work hands-on."

"Obsessive, the *Journal* said."

"People exaggerate."

That evening, their last in orbit, she said, "I'm not going to marry you."

He blinked just once. "How did you know?"

"Private pod dinner, stunning view, waiter who says nothing, gleam in eye—little clues."

"And—no?"

"I'm CEO of three companies, you of two. We have cross-lateral contracts with constraints under that damned ExoLegal legislation. Even a contract marriage—"

"I was going for the whole thing."

"Trad marriage? I'm not an antique."

He returned the already palmed ring back to his jacket pocket while she sipped from her wine bulb. "Okay, but a contract marriage of five years—"

She leaned over and kissed him slowly. "It's a wonderful thought, and we love each other, but—look at our lives. Always on the move. Eighteen-hour days. Legal thickets."

"At least we couldn't testify against each other."

"Now there's an incentive! Just what a girl wants to hear." She smiled into some distant future.

"So long as we don't commit any crimes, it'll keep the lawyers off us."

"No, I like it better this way. I'm here because I want to be. And you realize that Marquand fellow I also see isn't going to hedge you out, yes?"

He raised eyebrows, pursed his lips. "I was kinda hoping."

"I don't need a ring to stay with you. Or you me. We see others, we live intersecting lives. Great lives."

He nodded. Most of the way down from orbit they were relaxed, discussing how Harold could arrange to designate countries as "commission-aires" rather than wholesalers of raw metal in cylindrical ingots. Because commissionaires never took possession of ingots, which would mean paying taxes on them, an agent in France could sell them on behalf of a subsidiary in low-tax Singapore, people he had never even seen. The ingots themselves never saw Singapore, either. They came down in capsules that parachuted directly onto the grounds of assembly factories. Once in the landing yard, robots took ingots to processors.

From that commissionaires' maneuver he got money to pay for more astronomy studies, for finding new asteroids to visit, prospect, mine, for new engineering designs. Plus he could intervene where governments were slow to act, as with the Australian fires. Capital could move faster.

A few months later, exhausted with work, he needed some downtime. He spent a week on Maui having his longevity looked after, using a service LifeCode had just started.

Most of aging was failure to do maintenance. The latest innovation used genetic information to spot repair genes, then stimulate them into doing better. While a team poked and prodded him, fed him odd, thick, slurpy drinks, and got him into lab-rat-style exercises, he let his mind roam, thinking about his boyhood dreams.

It was time to fund them.

His excuse for spending the money was a celebration. Sara had finally agreed to a five-year contract marriage. The stock in his companies leaped over 10 percent.

2040

Dr. Katherine Amani looked up from her work. Harold said, "I made an appoint—"

"You actually *are* Harold Mann. I thought it might be a joke."

"Uh, that's what I said, ma'am—"

"I thought it was a . . . boast."

"More like a confession."

He knew her wry look. Didn't this man know that in the '30s no sophisticated person divulged wealth or talent or ability? It was unseemly, unsettling, and rude.

"Or a prank—that was my second guess."

"Your friends masquerading?"

"Last week my boyfriend . . . never mind. What do you want?"

"I want to know about the follow-on to the Wide-field Infrared Survey Explorer satellite."

"What? Oh . . . WISE."

"Oh, should've known. Nobody uses full names; I really am out of it."

"WISE, that's ancient . . . and there was no follow-on."

"My people tell me one was built, but not launched."

"Ah, that. Too expensive back in the Drawback era. Still is. It's probably sitting on a shelf in Maryland."

"You agreed with the conclusion—no brown dwarfs closer than five light-years?"

She got up and made a graphic display open on the well. "Here's the final 3-D plot. We surveyed the sky—well, nearly all—"

"How much did you miss?"

"About two percent, as I recall. Some cycling glitch with the 'scope."

"How sure are you of the five light-year number?"

She grinned. "You mean the contradiction with the average density of brown dwarfs? It was indeed a puzzle. There should've been several closer, but we didn't see them."

He decided to use a method that worked in business planning. "Suppose I told you there was one? What would explain why you missed it?"

"Um . . . I always wondered if our method was right. See, we surveyed in three spectral bands and used the ratio of luminosity between those bands to see if it was a dwarf."

"How did you know the ratio test?"

"Modeling of dwarf atmospheres. See, dark stars have methane clouds at the top of their cold atmospheres. We used metalicity plus methane and water absorption bands to select out the millions of faint dots we had."

"How about a pure hydrogen dwarf?"

She gave him the wry look again. "You've read up on this. A pure hydrogen star would be undetected in these kind of model-driven observations."

"Good answer. How much would it cost me to have all the data examined again, using a less narrow band model?"

She blinked. "Funding like that—maybe a million, even."

"You and a team could do it? I'll make it a gift to the university."

"Uh, yes, we could. And . . . wow. We never see such grants anymore."

"Hard times. Sad. And stupid." He leaned against a filing cabinet. "How does an infrared astronomer like you get new data?"

"Mostly we don't."

Harold allowed himself a smile. She was still trying to take in his offer. He liked keeping people off balance; they told you more that way. "How much would it cost to pull that old WISE satellite off that shelf, update all the electronics, launch?"

Another blink, eyes to the ceiling, lips moving. "Um . . . we haven't gone much further in e-development, and launch costs are down thanks to—" She stopped. "To you guys, I guess."

"And a hundred million others."

"With people living full-time offworld, too." He could see the question in her eyes. *A tycoon comes visiting an astronomer? What's up?*

"Estimate the cost of a new WISE with broader modeling in the analysis?"

"Maybe two hundred million."

"Okay, let's redo the old data first. And work up a sharper cost estimate for a relaunch."

She was still trying to take it all in when he left for a business appointment, feeling the old dazzle of opportunity lifting his eyebrows. The university got out the paperwork in three days; they were feeling the long-term research pinch. He delivered the check himself and then took her out to dinner with her postdocs. She got a bit tipsy.

2041

The several-year recession—even worse than the Great Recession—took its toll on his enterprises. Trimming programs and people was part of business, he knew, just like gardening. Indeed, he took up gardening to get his mind off the failures.

Chief of these was the inevitable collapse of the Muslim countries that had run for a century on oil revenues. Their reserves were depleting, green tech was lowering consumption, and their vast overpopulation was getting ugly in the streets. The Arab states began their collapse, plus Indonesia. Of course that didn't affect Pakistan and the other Stans, or the coming Muslim majority in Sweden. Older countries stiffened their immigration, letting few in but the very skilled. Financial markets turned turtle, heads in, going nowhere.

Plus he put some of his own money into a start-up study of building a space elevator. It seemed like a great idea, a crucial component to get into space cheaply and effectively. There were superstrong composites, part diamond, and his self-managing AI bots made it seem plausible.

His engineers used a junk debris mass left over from mining to build the first lengths, with multiple redundant cables with cross-strapping to distribute loads around a break. When a meteorite or dead satellite inevitably hits, you would only need to replace a small part.

But the first high launch tower went into rapid launch mode then, chopping lift costs considerably below even the traditional two-stage to orbit. Plus there were tech failures and the corporate treasurer turned out to have his hand in the till It was the big, final hit. Harold could not for the life of him hold together the investment coalition to build further.

He had to fold and take a considerable haircut. The unfinished cable became an embarrassment. He finally sold the useful parts for orbital scrap use, just to stop people taking pictures of it and laughing.

For three years he took a dollar-a-year salary and sent his stock option profits to the astronomers for their infrared work. Sara offered to help, but he thought it safer to keep their assets separate. She got miffed at that, and they didn't see each other for two months.

Then she appeared at his skyscraper office at quitting time, in a fine new red dress. Red was always a signal between them, better than roses any day.

"That damned treasurer," he said to Sara that evening. "Takes all kinds but—"

"It must." She smiled as she shed the red. "They're all here, like 'em or not."

2043

His first target back in the 2020s had been an asteroid rich in rare earths. That paid back all start-up costs in a single shipment.

Spin could throw the robots off, so he paid rockhounds, with their satellite telescopes and fast-flight sail craft, to find one with a tiny spin and good elements. The key innovation was a rock filter that worked best in microgravity, and not at all on Earth. It separated molecules by charge and mass, using tribocharging induced by simple friction, the same process that yielded sparks on doorknobs after walking across a rug. His first half-dozen asteroids made him rich, and then he got started on truly adventurous ideas.

As soon as he had robots that could manage well even on the surface of rocks that spun around several axes, he made spin an asset. There was board opposition, but he called in favors and won a straight up/down vote with the board.

A new class of robots spun out long, rigid armatures of carbon fiber, creating a throwing arm. Cargo got hoisted out on the arm, and then released. Careful calculation of spin phase and orientation made it possible to send packages on precise trajectories to High Earth Orbit. With a midcourse correction nudge, they nosed into nets waiting to receive them—free transport, paid for by a slight decrease in the asteroid spin. Fuel depots, orbital factories, and hab colonies got their goods delivered, for the minor trouble of snagging them as they passed by.

The "right to mine" industry took off then. Brokers traded those rights and gathered capital. Only when shipments started did he fully own the rock he had paid options on. There were plenty of tricky accounting riffs to play, especially since the rules kept changing. The U.S. Geological Survey, which originally had been formed in 1879 to discover ore and stimulate the mining industry, was still in the Department of the Interior. It soon became an interplanetary agency. Then under the North American Community rules, taxes and deductibles became even more fraught with peril.

Plus a new one: hijackers could grab the cargoes in flight. It did not take long for other companies operating in near Earth space to figure this out. Such pirates then inadvertently supplied a defense against the main danger— big masses missing their targets and slamming down through Earth's atmosphere. But with better beacons and tracking, piracy dropped off.

Three multiseason series about the exotic gangs of 'roid pirates had run on worldwide 3-D—all before Harold ordered arming of his robot 'roid escorts.

2045

He got to Katherine Amani's office within an hour. "Where is it?"

She grinned. "Less than a light-year away. Small, cold, but there."

"How?"

She blinked, used to his abrupt questioning style by now. "We had those suspicions, recall? Early estimates predicted as many brown dwarfs as typical stars, but the WISE survey showed just one brown dwarf for every six stars. So how could we have missed some? If they were close to us, they could move enough between our two surveys. Not showing up again eliminated them."

He nodded eagerly. "So you looked at them again."

She nodded and showed him a star map of many small blotches. One she circled. "It took a while. Atmosphere temperature is a tad above this room's."

He pursed his lips and leaned forward. "Wow, lower end of the Y dwarf range. And close!"

"As you wished." She smiled.

Harold got up, started pacing, then looked at her intently. "You saw last month's discovery—an Earthlike with an ozone line?"

"Yes, great, clearly a biosphere. Nearly a hundred light-years away. All attention's focused on it. Both the Chinese and USA/Euro want to put up new satellites to pick up as many pixels as they can, analyze the atmosphere, maybe get a picture."

He stopped pacing, sat down. "It'll get all the attention. Let's keep this quiet for now. How about putting WISE 2 up?"

Her eyes widened. "Withhold—? Ah, I see. Let them ignore infrared studies while we get more data."

"If you don't mind." *What's my action item here?* he always asked himself. "I like springing surprises, but they have to be substantiated."

"There's not much chance anyone's going to revisit this old data soon. If you have the money to put up another, better WISE . . . I suppose so . . ."

There. "Done, then." She blinked. Her mouth opened and nothing came out. *She's being handed a hundred million bucks, after all. I know CEOs who can keep their cool at moments like this, but they are few. So . . . keep it mellow . . .* "Let's keep all this quiet for now. Meanwhile, I want to put some money behind a way to get there."

"But our rockets would take—"

"Better than rockets. We can leave the engine on the ground."

2052

He discovered a useful rule: If you want to know what's going on, don't ask the person in charge. To get the truth, especially from the edgy government bodies that regulated space industries, you had to come in from the top management, and then drill down.

That was how he learned of a new profit angle—asking actual astronomers, not NASA managers. The craters near the moon's north and south poles were like the dusty attic of the solar system—an attic in a deep freeze. In a hundred-square-kilometer area there were a billion gallons of water in the top meter of dirt—and even better, the same load of mercury. Water made the place livable for the few shivering humans who had to run the robot teams mining the metals. Pure hydrogen poured out when

a reactor's waste heat warmed the soil, capturing the harvest in big balloons inflated by the gases. This rocket fuel spread throughout the swelling fleets of mining craft.

All this wealth squatted in the dark craters. After exhausting the several hundred asteroids that were energetically easier to reach than Luna,
the frozen poles were the latest economic hot spots.

2055

By now Harold Mann was one of the *ultras*, the chummy though distant club of the trillionaires. Some said there were mysterious others, the
transcendental rich, or "transrich," but Harold didn't think they existed.
If they did, they left no signs among the vast and fast trading markets.
The constrained AIs who governed those provinces would not say if any
transrich existed, but then, they were coy.

Definitions didn't interest him. He was of the *determined elderly* now,
rich and harboring the ambition of those who knew they had little time to
accomplish more . . . much more.

Sara said, "You're exercising those stock options close to the line, given
all this new legislation."

They were swimming off Maui, so the subject seemed odd. "I need
cash for R&D."

"I've picked up some legal sniffers around my operations," she said.
"The North American Community needs cash so—"

"They always do. Hey, see if we can bodysurf this wave!"

His advisors told him not to discuss his ambitions so much, and certainly not his intricate finances, what with all the suffering in the world.
The vast differences between economic levels had led to the fashionable view humans had messed up enough worlds already. So if life were
detected on a distant Earthlike world, humanity had best leave it alone.

The same argument had arisen over the subsurface life discovered
on Mars decades before. That life, organized through microbial plants,
was remarkably strange and showed clear signs of consciousness. It was
entirely anaerobic, oxygen-free, and of separate and earlier origin than
Earth's. Many scientists thought that the undeniable connections between
Martian and Earthly DNA, going back to the Archea ages, proved that we
were Martians. Thus we were not damaging an entirely separate phylum
of life. There was no damage anyway, since human Martian colonies had

no biological transactions with the true Martians at all, which were far below ground.

Still, Harold made no secret that he had plans for future exploration. He wouldn't say what they were, ever. He funded propulsion studies by exercising stock options in several minor companies, taking his profits, then plowing them into secretive companies pursuing low-probability/high-payoff technologies.

Secrets created their own fandoms, in the sprawling, intensively interacting solar economy. He was quite surprised when the mysterious aura around his name made the public like him more; people wanted intriguing puzzles now, a sense of things coming.

2059

Some asteroids were icy, with up to 20 percent water and frozen carbon dioxide; miners called them iceteroids. Melt the 'roid rock with circulating nuke heat fluids and the water comes off first. Condense and separate it out, squirt it into expando spheres for packaging and let it freeze in free space. Hang the spheres on frames holding a bare nuke engine, with no shielding needed. Then robo-ship the whole unlovely contraption to near Earth habitats for life support or, with the CO_2, for propellants.

The rocky, metal-rich asteroids got teams of mining craft that deployed smart minebots, which could siphon off metals by weight and fluidity. Platinum was the biggest prize, so prospector bots sought it first when they touched down on a new rock. "Fat plat" was pure strain metal that could go straight into Earthside catalytic converters. Auto-facs and 3-D printers made electronics or even jewelry. High-value ore shipped in low-energy orbits arrived at Working Earth Orbit space with its market value already set—never less than $50,000 New Bucks a kilogram—because it had been mass spectrum sorted by bots along the way. Those rugged devices could take all the time they needed to get the measures right. They were slaved to the MarketWatch integrators, beyond question more honest than a human could even pretend to be. The lesser stuff—iron, copper, aluminum—got fed into orbital factories to make spacecraft fittings and hulls in vacuum-dry foundries. Behind all this was the laser comm Net that kept bots coordinated and standards aligned.

Yields accelerated in what became known as the Astro Moore's law, though in fact the similarity was superficial. The true driver was the plentitude of free fresh mass, coasting out there among the planets.

His was not the first mining company to go out into the main asteroid belt. It wasn't even the tenth. But it lasted.

So did Harold's personal R&D budget. He was surprised one morning to find a news story calling him the biggest research funder except for China, the USA, and Europe, in that order.

2060

Dr. Katherine Amani handled the press well. Harold sat in the back and watched her proclaim discovery of not one but two dwarf stars nearer than Alpha Centauri. Yes, she said, she had taken the years of study essential to be quite sure these stars were truly there. *One of the virtues of not reporting to government panels,* he thought, but said nothing.

Press attention was still focused on the distant, Earthlike world called Glory by the public. Of course no expedition was feasible, but reporters immediately asked about this new star. Did Redstar, the nearest, have planets?

Dr. Amani demurred. It was too early to tell, but "anonymous donors" were readying a far more sensitive infrared study of the region close around Redstar.

The possibility of going there got little attention in the press. The current worldwide depression had bled most of the sense of opening possibilities from the general class who paid attention to more than just getting through their difficult days.

And who named this dull dwarf Redstar, anyway? Surely the International Astronomical Union had naming rights?

Dr. Amani opened her mouth and looked at the back of the room, but Harold was already gone. You get better coverage if the media uncover the story themselves, he had learned—then feed their eager faces.

2063

Harold sighed. "Did you ever think that we're just stuff, the odd sort of stuff that comes into consciousness, reproduces, swims through this universe, and dies, that's it?"

Sara frowned. "You don't believe that."

"No, I don't. But I could."

They were inside a tight capsule of Mooncrete, heavy shielding against a solar storm of great lancing ferocity. This first trip to the L1 resort was not turning out very well and Harold felt claustrophobic—the most common affliction among deep space travelers.

She kissed him. "Have another glass of wine."

2069

Often when he was in an immersion tank having his body scanned, inspected, and improved, he would reflect that the meeting about WISE 2 was where his life began to accelerate. The sensation of time collapsing along its own axis was common with aging, of course. It arose from the lack of novelty in later life. Travel, new friends, fresh hobbies—these helped. But he had been to every country he wondered about, eighty-seven of them when he stopped. Friends were fine, too, though he never had hobbies. Intense interests outside of work, yes—but they were always pointed at the sky, the solar system, the stars.

First came the sails. Entrepreneurs had already developed the fundamentals of solar sailing, a thrifty way to survey and prospect myriad asteroids. The sun's photons were free, but skimpy. Better to focus a microwave or laser beam on a sail and shoot it out of Low Earth Orbit, saving it years of climbing up Earth's gravity well. Better still, coat its inner face with a designer paint that, heated by the beam, would blow off—an induced rocket effect.

But the real kick came from diving deep. *Sundiver I* had already plunged to within a few radii of the sun, shed the asteroid that shielded it, and unfurled before the furnace star. Its gossamer disk carried an intricately designed burden that now warmed furiously. Painted on, this layer blew off under high temperatures, a momentary rocket exploiting a bit of Newtonian physics: change velocities when the craft has high speed, and the boost gets amplified. A blue-white jet arced for tens of minutes. Once gone, the painted fuel revealed a blazing white sail. That intense hour sent it shooting outward at speeds rocketeers only dreamed about.

Sundiver I had entered the far reaches of the Kuiper Belt by the time Harold assembled the Inner Network System of microwave and laser beams. This INS made considerable profit by lowering commcosts among mining communities, asteroid habitats, bases on Mars, and even the new exploration teams around Jupiter's moon Ganymede.

Sail development accelerated, making quick exploration of the outer solar system efficient. Harold bought into several small sail start-ups. By the time they had found some ripe iceteroids ready for steering into the inner worlds to be harvested, he exercised his options and extracted profits on the expectations bounce tech stocks often get—for a while.

By the time *Sundiver XI* came speeding out from its searing solar encounter, the INS system was ready to pour radiance on its kilometer-wide sail whenever it passed nearby. Timing was exquisite, intricate, a marvel equated in the media to ballet. THE INS GOES OUT one headline proclaimed. Headed for Redstar.

2073

Fusion nuke rockets had become the Conestoga wagons of the solar system, and the lunar poles were their frigid watering station. The reversed-magnetic-field configuration had finally made big-bore fusion rocket chambers practical, and they had higher thrust per kilogram than fission. Shipping got cheaper.

Harold had a piece of polar development, mostly because he wanted to drive toward ever-larger nukes. The Chinese and Arabs who threw in with them tried the same approach, but proved to be slower to respond to the myriad problems that arose. The poles were *cold* and gear refused to work unless warmed by the waste of big operating and distilling nuke plants. Harold had investments in breeder reactors and recycling reactor wastes, so he benefited from both ends of the enterprise.

Soon AI piloted nukes ran whole mining parties to asteroids. Complexes grew, which demanded humans to supervise the smart but limited AIs who had narrow intuition and common sense.

On carbon-restricted Earth, such work cut back on wasteful, inefficient, and polluting processes to mine and smelt. There was much less digging, grinding, and greenhouse gas emission. Social benefits rebounded, wealth spread through largesse, and the workweek fell. Workaholics immigrated into space, where opportunity and hundred-hour weeks abounded. All that fervor and wealth came from spinning habitats and solar mirrors melting rocks way out in space.

2074

Harold imposed strict rules on how supplies and parts for his asteroid habitats got delivered. The specs laid out exact sizes of the storage canisters, plus where the securing bolts went, how latches fitted, corner configurations, and thickness down to the millimeter. His suppliers grimaced but complied, wondering why he was so exact.

"Your competitors aren't so damn picky," one said.

"But I pay more for it," Harold said. "You want the contract?" He smiled at the grudging nod.

He told no one the reason. His work crews dutifully unloaded the supplies and parts in zero grav, handing them to the bots who did the assembly of borers and smelters. Only then did the next bot crew appear, taking the shipping canisters apart, clicking together the light carbon-fiber walls—and producing the actual outer walls of the habitats. Spun up, the tight joins held full atmospheric pressures. He had gotten them delivered at the suppliers' cost, not his.

2081

"We can hold them off for a while but not forever," Lin said.

"You've done that for decades now," Harold said, hands clasped in front of him at the conference table. Sara sat beside him, shaking her head.

"Decades?" Sara said. "I forget details . . . Writing all the development costs off—"

"As business investment, yes," Lin finished for her. A 3-D lattice condensed in the air over their table. It mapped in axes of time, dollars, and legal spending avenues. A spaghetti of multicolored strands connected big orange dots. *Like a nightmare medusa,* Harold thought.

"All this was legal, deductible back when—"

"You started, yes." Lin gave him a wan smile. "Not anymore."

Sara looked startled as she followed the info-dense tangles. "These topo maps in cash and progress indices—there's a whole development line just in ion engines!"

Lin grimaced. "That doesn't get us off the hook anymore."

Harold nodded. "Our poor old planet has seen a lot. Environ damage, the greenhouse not going away as fast as we thought, resource scarcity, big collective regimes. So they go after offworld cash."

"And change the rules in the middle of the game," Lin said. "You've been in the game a long time, so you have to change the most."

"So . . ." Sara was still entranced by the luminous spaghetti and its projected territories. " . . . you can pay some back taxes?"

"Sure, if I strip myself of most that I own," Harold said. "Or—"

"You can fight," Lin finished for him. She obviously knew her boss well, Harold saw, and was one jump ahead of him. "Legal dodges, evidence of sequestering funds offworld, not available for testimony—"

"The whole suite of dances every business learns the hard way," Sara finished. "Let me guess—back taxes doubling every three years, retroactive penalties, a post facto nightmare."

"Can I go back to Earth?" Harold asked, eyes veiled.

"I don't advise it."

Sara jerked as though she had just come awake. "What?!"

"They can arrest you." Lin gave them a *that's how it is* shrug. "Not likely maybe, but it depends on who's got the helm of the North American Community when you land. You have enemies in the Mexican faction."

Harold remembered the friction surrounding the adoption of the Community Constitution. Yes, the Mexicans wanted a Right of Confiscation and he spent a lot to block them. The Mexican Constitution from over a century ago stopped foreigners from owning land in Mexico. Now there was a French-style tax on net worth, too. He sighed. "It doesn't take a very big person to carry a grudge."

Lin said softly, "The sitting chairman called you out publicly for using corporate funds to further your 'hobbies' yesterday."

"I thought hobbies were supposed to broaden you," Harold said. "Mine is R&D."

Sara's mouth twisted into a cautious tilt. "Silence is sometimes the best answer."

Lin said, "I started the legal defenses running."

"How about my reserves—and Sara's—in Earthbound accounts?"

"I got them posted free to Lunar Holdings last night. It caused a drop in several markets this morning."

Sara said, "No hiding when you're this big, I guess."

Lin nodded. "I had to sacrifice some transactions in progress. Resource plays, a convertible debenture or two."

Harold got to his feet in the 0.4 grav. "I smell Keegan over at Consolidated."

Lin said, "I do too. Rumor says he hates you. He wants to weaken you, maybe create opposition on our board."

"I'll work the board some." Harold shrugged. "Sometimes you get, and sometimes you get got. Let's go for a swim."

Their new swim sphere was forty meters in diameter. For safety a black cable lanced through the middle, so swimmers too far from air could haul themselves out quickly. He made a point of never using it and lapped furiously around the perimeter, letting drops scatter everywhere. The blue-green water cohered, enhanced surface tensions gathering up the drops amid the air currents. Sara was not so proud; she swam subsurface most of the time, using an oxy enhancer. When she surfaced, he was there with a frown, and after her first gasp for air, she said, "Don't worry, you've faced troublemakers like this before."

One of his signs of anxiety was a slight lapsing back into his southern accent. "The biggest troublemaker you'll prob'ly ever have to deal with watches you from the mirror every mornin'."

2085

In principle it was simple: stay in orbit, use the centrifugal 0.4 grav advantage that the Mars Effect people had shown did indeed lessen damage to the general neuro and cardio systems. But some were shy of orbiting at all, so they lost old friends. Harold and Sara were too tired of orbital life, of running their far-flung businesses electronically—so they had battalions of lawyers fight the Community edicts. This allowed them some immunity to prosecution and seizure while on the ground. Still, they made visits short, mostly to see the latest work on robotics and catch up with the red dwarf star scientists. A hobby of sorts, he still maintained for the lawyers.

2093

A reporter accosted him and Sara in their home overlooking Kings Canyon. It was an "arranged surprise opportunity" as his media advisors called it, so he feigned being startled.

"You're certainly the man behind Dr. Amani's announcement of Redstar's discovery, Mr. Mann. Now you're launching a probe to look at it." The reporter feigned astonishment, as required. "So you knew about it for years!"

"Decades, actually." Deadpan. *Hold Sara close*, he thought. *And smile, dammit.* After all, it was their umpteenth five-year-contract anniversary. She smiled, also obligatory. He couldn't hold his smile for long. He focused on the view. The distant pines and elegant granite peaks weren't clear and sharp like the old days, since the warming gave a heat ripple everywhere.

"Why did you and your scientists not announce—"

"I wanted to get my ducks in a row. Now the whole world is training their 'scopes on Redstar, to tell us what they can. I'll give us all a close-up."

"That's arrogant!"

"I suppose so. This isn't a hobby, it's a lifelong obsession. I wanted to do it my way."

"The entire world scientific establishment—"

"Is just that, an establishment. Funded by governments—that is, by you citizens of so many nations. I wanted to move faster than that. And make a profit while I built the INS."

"What will *Sundiver XI* find?" The reporter seemed to be getting desperate.

"I don't know. That's the point, yes?"

As they walked on Sara said, "Y'know, people are saying that, after all this, we'd decide to retire. We've finally accomplished everything we set out to do, so . . ." She gave him a raised-eyebrow glance.

"I don't think we're safe, just retired."

"Oh—the Universal Rights rules?"

The inevitable collision between a stressed, overrun planet and lots of retired but vigorous well-to-do was looking like a train wreck. The central political message seemed to be, *You have that cash, see, and I have this gun . . . and these lawyers.*

"So they'll come after us for more taxes," Sara said. "We can live with that."

"It's getting harder to stay Earthbound. There's no government space program anymore; can't afford to get it out from under their bureaucracies. That Exceptional Needs Tax alone—"

She jostled him, kissed him. "Enough worries! Don't let tomorrow use up too much of today. Let's go for a hike on the John Muir Trail."

She was right. He went. They had friends to meet later, a good cabernet tasting—life was good. He should lap it up. Even so, in the back of his mind on the trail that afternoon he thought of *Sundiver XI* and mulled, *Even better to see it in person. No, that's silly. Not that I can. Too damn old.*

2100

He and Sara arrived at the robo-control station in a high arc ship. The zero grav was a blessing to his joints.

As he swam through the transfer bubble, looking out through UV fil
ter walls, he saw a waiting array of ceramic and carbon-fiber bots. The
gliding serenity of deep space made a slow, artful ballet of even routine
industrial processes.

He knew their designs well, had even worked on some of the coupling
joints. Stubby robots sat dutifully in a fiber rack array, drawing power from
the idling nuke a few meters away at their backs.

Zero-grav bots had no front/back bias. They could spin their heads to
bring digital eyes or metal sensors to bear, all housed in a rotating platform
that sported microwave antennas and a laser feed, too. Omni-able, the
industry pundits called it. He was proud to be one of the fifty-nine inven-
tors listed on the patent—he had given his fraction to Sara when they'd
celebrated one of their five-year-contract marriages.

Bot bodies were chunky mech pistons and grapplers, driven by fluid
hydraulics. No beauty, but they were yellow and red and blue as suited
their jobs, so the control bot could tell them apart. People in space made
their habitats and work areas gaudy, a reflex against the surrounding black.
The color splashes would have driven an Earthside decorator to violence.

And here came the orange transfer pressure gate at the end of the tube.
The door dilated.

"Officer aboard!" a young woman declared firmly as he popped through
the dilating lock. Her name badge woven into her flexsuit said NGUYEN and
she gave him a grin. "It's protocol, sir—I know you're not an officer."

"Daddy Spacebucks aboard would be better," he said.

The man next to her laughed, but it seemed unlikely anyone here knew
the reference. "Yessir." He wore a T-shirt that proclaimed SAME SHIRT DIF-
FERENT DAY. Harold sniffed and was thankful that habitat air cleanup was
well developed. "Sorry you're not an actual daddy?" Sara said beside him.

"Um, what? Oh . . . I never wanted to be. I'd have been terrible at it."

"I felt the same, for me. We're better at making things work."

"Too bad about the genes not getting passed on."

She chuckled. "What makes you think that?"

He couldn't suppress his grin. "Okay, we've all got stuff stored. We live
quantified lives with backed-up selves. Your eggs . . . ?"

"I might want to use them someday. Or another lady."

"Way things are going, could be another, well, guy."

"So be it." She shrugged.

"We're here as a luxury to the species. We expand horizons—most people live inside them. Hey!" Harold looked around, uncomfortable with abstractions, as usual. "I'm here to catch that new rock work."

Later they watched the magnetic catapult cast an entire iceball cylinder to high velocity. It picked up considerable speed in the magcat, a big lumbering beer can with a snow-white cargo. Then the catapult sleeve fell away as the cylinder's ion jets cut in. It shrank with bewildering speed, faster than any takeoff he had ever seen.

"It can rendezvous up to what speed?" Sara asked Nguyen.

"A hundred klicks a sec," Nguyen said. "Maybe better."

"Um, what's the commercial app?"

"Emergency supplies needed in a habitat," Harold said crisply. "Funded it myself."

She smiled. "You belong out here, you know."

"I've been here, one way or the other, since I was driving a cab."

Man's got to throw long in this life, he thought.

2102

At first he had noticed the years accelerating. Now it was the decades.

He and Sara did all the new techy health things plus taking a special LifeCode series of molecules targeted on their own genes. They upregulated their repairs and kept their bodies fixing the innumerable insults of advancing age. Tedious, sometimes, but it worked. They wanted to be around when *Sundiver XI* arrived. Harold didn't say so, not even to Sara, but he wanted even more.

He had to tell his advisors repeatedly: *Become a mere steward of your own assets? Boring!*

A rich bank account did not mean rich ideas; in fact, often the reverse. The bigger your ass, the more you want to cover it.

So the second step was the comet-grabbers.

Investors care a lot more about return on invested capital than about optimized hardware or new technology. But give them dividends and they will give you your technologies. Start with an easy consumer come-on first.

Luna was in many ways a pleasant place—right distance from the sun, quite nearby, light gravity. But it was bone dry; if ordinary Earthside sidewalks had been there, miners would have leaped at them to suck out moisture.

With air and water, people would visit the moon's striking plains and mountains. For now, bubbles blown in excavated cavities would suffice for flying, the best sport of all. The retaining bubble was actually the new flux-diamond, a carbon liquid that condensed into a rigorous firm seal. So he invested in the new Lunatic Hotels and luck intervened. Their first cavity struck a totally unexpected lode of ice, so they had no water problems— the enterprise went profitable. Contrary to the conventional wisdom, Luna was a soft, stony sponge.

He paid off the support loans at the earliest possible no-penalty date. When the comet nuclei he had ordered sent in from beyond Uranus by robot crews finally arrived, they weren't essential, thanks to the lake discovery—and he ordered a swimming sea made of them. They crashed onto the surface, but succulent machines captured a lot of their moisture.

Nobody knew it, but this was the beginning of the terraforming process that would take many decades before a filmy skin of moist air clung to the lunar craters. That shallow gravitational well could still hold for ten thousand years the atmosphere slammed into it by a cascade of comets. But a full atmosphere could wait. Soft winds would blow across those ancient lava fields, eventually, but the Loonie Hotel business made profits *now*.

So did throwing ice and hydrocarbons sunward, the real point. The robot teams that snagged floating mountains of iceteroids and steered them inward had their troubles, but bots worked 24/7 with little maintenance cost, with no vacation time or health care or retirement plan. They benefited humans who loved the interplanetary splendor they saw on their screens, then went to the sunny sandy beach after their twenty-hour workweeks.

Profit made his own research teams possible. They developed a way of shaping iceteroids and torpedoing them at very high speeds into the hoppers of passing nuke rockets. Vapor flared in the nuclear chambers and forked out at furious speeds. The magnetic catapult system led to efficiencies in nudging comet-candidates onward. In turn this increased the profitability of supplying light molecules in shimmering spheroids to the inner solar system colonies.

But such distant wonders were scarcely the whole point. The shareholders thought so, and Harold obligingly said so. He owned the largest share fraction but ruled through a coalition on the board. Still, he ran his latest corporation, Farscape, with bigger goals in mind.

"I sold my debris companies," Sara said with a sigh. "We've done most of the job. Mop-up is boring, casting big sheets to grab small stuff. Time to get out."

"Good. I have a trip planned, we'll be free to go."

He lounged back while a nurse did the daily IV. He did not allow her to joggle his hand holding a vintage red wine; it was part of the medication, too. Deductible, even, though they had stopped thinking about such accounting matters decades ago. Then a good swim in the spherical pool, yes. They were on the 0.4 g level of the Great Cylinder Hotel, which seemed to be the right gravitation for longevity. Turned out the studies using lab mice and pigs had been right. Sara especially was aging very slowly; he had to hustle to keep up with her.

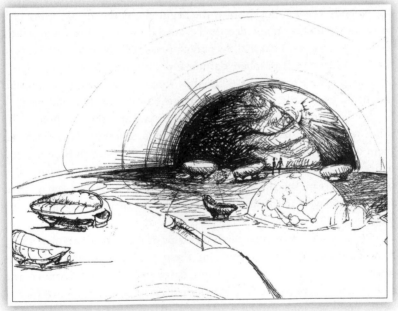

© 2013, Haylee Bolinger / ASU

She smiled. Time had been kind to her wrinkles; indeed, she had few. They had just recently finished a long celebration of their one hundredth birthdays, three months apart, and even a thousand kilometers from Earth the media hammered on the walls, metaphorically. It was hard to escape the grasping Earth.

"Where?" she asked.

"To the whatever end there is."

2103

Sundiver XI plunged by Redstar in less than a day. It ran on a high-efficiency, nuke-driven ion drive that gathered molecules from in front of the sailship. The combination shaved many centuries from the voyage. It also meant the big sail was a relativistic missile streaking through, swiveling its cameras and sensors to grab torrents of data.

Harold watched intently between Sara and Katherine Amani. The smart sail was tacking as well as it could, zooming by the star. All this had happened nearly a year ago, of course, delayed by the light travel time.

The team below them studied their screens and abruptly a startled shout came up from them. On the big screen appeared a reddish world with a shimmering ivory haze of atmosphere surrounding it. Harold saw an unmistakable glint of sunlight from the left edge. Polar caps were a dirty gray.

"An ocean," he said. "On a tide-locked planet."

Katherine Amani said, "We picked it up earlier but this is the freshest image. There are plenty of spectral signatures. There's an odd cutoff in the far infrared, something like the edge we see in light reflecting from Earth plants. This spectrum is really dark red, down to reddish brown to black."

The next image showed clear continents and somber seas, even big lakes and some white-capped mountains. Reams of data slid down screens around the room as the sail did its job.

Katherine said, "There's going to be so much to study—"

"I'm going," Harold said. "Now."

"No, no, no," Sara said. "*We* are."

2104

Lin was in a hurry. "You're not safe here anymore. The legal walls around you have come down."

Harold said, "It's that bad?"

"The North American Community reached a midnight agreement with the Euros. They got new laws passed, to let them seize assets and argue their case later. It applies to anyone offworld, too. No matter how big."

Lin had worked for Harold for decades, so he knew she was holding the worst back for last. "And . . . personally?"

"There are criminal charges available." She said it calmly but he could tell she wasn't.

"Could they come up here with warrants?"

"I'm afraid it's explicitly allowed for you two, plus about fifty others. The ones on Luna will get more warning—"

"But we're just an hour away," Sara said.

"Afraid so."

"Could this be just intimidation?" Sara asked.

"It doesn't smell that way," Lin said, presenting a projected summary of the legislation. Harold had read enough bad prose to know the bomb was buried in the footnotes, and with a tap Lin brought up their names.

Harold Mann, indicted.
Sara Ernsberg, indicted.
Subject to precautionary arrest.

Sara seemed undisturbed. "We're packed for a long boost. I've got our vital memorabilia in a carry case. Clothes, meds, the rest."

Harold watched the two women get the staff moving—hustle, bustle, rustle. He didn't regret growing older, it was a privilege denied to many. But he had trouble grasping the unspoken assumptions behind these new societies. Boundaries got redrawn at the point of a sword, and the legal frame followed. When he was growing up, the paradigm had been *with liberty and justice for all,* but now on a world stage jammed with swarming masses in desperate need, it seemed to be *three hots and a cot and whatever you got.*

"You were right, back decades ago," Lin said in passing, "going for high-efficiency boost. And building that development complex out in the asteroids, where bot teams could do the assembly."

"Bots don't blab," Sara said.

Harold smiled and nodded. "This is going to be more fun than retirement to a prison."

2105

Harold had started letting people call him Harry, now that he was over a hundred.

They pushed him into the ship on a zero-grav gurney. It was massive with med devices and monitors, all wrapped around a lean though not frail body.

Sara smiled beside him. "Are we going first class?"

"The only class. It's just us."

"Crew!"

"They bail out at Neptune. After that, bots."

"You planned it that way? From the first?"

"This was a worst-case option. The bots can do human coldsleep tending in flight. Our genomes and specs are already run in a lot of simulations and some lab trials." He shrugged. "Best I could do."

In the run-up preps he had rejected a mix of genes derived from naked moles and eagles to improve his hearing and vision. He also shook off, with an irritated snort, suggestions that for a trifling sum he could have his multiracial brown skin suffused with the fashionable golden scarlet. He had scrawled across the memo, *As is!*

"My, these look more like coffins than I'd like," was Sara's only remark when the immersion team helped them try on the big blue sleeves for the Sleep Crucibles. Harold's LongSleep company had tested for decades now the induced sleep pods he and Sara would use. With hydrogen sulfide bleed-ins and low temperatures, long cruise ships had been carrying slumbering passengers to the outer solar system for over a decade. This would be a logical but untried extension of those, by an order of magnitude.

The entire solar system media maze was now intent on Harold's "quixotic indulgence," but he had left all that behind. Some of it was amusing, though. Already crackpots were baying that Harold's fast probe would announce our presence to unknown alien bullies, who would come steaming in to trounce us. Their detailed explanations of why were useful diagnostics of the crackpots' problems, often amusing. The most common was that aliens with the right ontological bias would read out the state of our technology, our vulnerabilities, and deepest secrets. Then they would come for our riches.

"Maybe the Redstar carnivores will eat us," Harold mused.

"They'll have to catch us first," Sara said lightly. "If they exist."

They were lying in the crucibles while the team worked on their hookups.

It all seemed dreamy to Harold, yet he did not want to miss any of it. After all, he might not wake up. Still, when the team left and Katherine Amani leaned over them, he felt a longing for the world—no, worlds— they were leaving behind. "I will never forget you," Katherine said, and kissed each of them. Now she would go back Earthside to help his staff and companies face the consequences. For once he did not know what to say.

He fell asleep as the long burn began.

The automatic systems did revive them for system checks as they cleared Jupiter's orbit. When they passed Saturn, he insisted on getting up and looking at the big screen nearby. Saturn was just a dim glimmer, with the sun a glaring white coin. He held up his hand at arm's length and realized he was covering the entire orbit that Earth swung through. All the great acts of human history had played out on that scale.

Then their long sleep began, with the sour, stinky tinge of hydrogen sulfide cocktail swarming into their nostrils as the cold seeped in.

2192

© 2013, Jon Lomberg

He heard, "—hydrogen sulfide bind to cytochrome oxidase reversing complete. All blood oxygen returned to normal. Beginning neuro— alert!—is awake."

"You bet . . . I am," he croaked. "Sara . . . ?"

"Reviving." The voice was precise and melodious and of course a mech—an animated AI that seemed to swim in his blurred vision. It had eyes and a grille speaker mouth but those were the only concessions to humanlike appearance.

"We made it." He had harbored doubts, of course. Now a great feeling of triumph swelled in him.

"With conditioning, we will escort you to the world below," a mech said. "But you must undergo the restoration treatments."

"Anything the autodoc wants," Harold said. "Anything. Try to make it fun."

What had he used to say, back as a kid? *Committees don't open frontiers— people do. With smart machines.*

THE EXTRAVAGANT RUDDY SUN painted them pomegranate. Redstar had banded clouds of methane that echoed Jupiter, in a constant slow swirl.

"Let us see it better," he said to the mechs. "Tune helmet filters to our eyes." A strange new world, he thought.

"Full sensorium, please," added Sara.

Even though their helmets amped the visible spectrum, the effect was eerie. Stars shone in pale gray here against the inky black. The huge hull of Redstar hung as a burgundy disk cut off by the sea. Here and there across the long panorama of perpetual twilight, slanting rays of a deep Indian red showed floating plants, lapping on the waves in a somber sprawl. Everything glowed with infernal incandescence.

"Good to sit," Sara said. The mechs had brought them low sloping chairs from the descent vehicle. The 1.34 gravs here made walking odd and harder, although they had been reviving their muscles for five days aboard the main ship. He had learned to edit out the joint pain, too.

Down from the desolate slope to his left came an echoing cry, long and slow. In the thick air a thing like a huge orange gossamer butterfly fluttered on a thin wind. It swooped across a sky peppered with amber clouds and vanished with deliberate, long flaps of its enormous wings, behind a low eroded hill.

"Thick atmosphere, something that big can fly," Harold said, still trying to take it all in. This was far stranger than Mars, with an entire ecology on ready view. Most of the vegetation was low slimy growth, hugging the land.

"I wonder . . ." Sara said, and stopped. Something moved on the beach.

It looked like a reddish rock at first until he could see the legs articulating with a sluggish grace. A huge crablike creature with long antennae waving. Now that his eyes had adjusted to the odd light he could see other small forms. A big thing broke surface out on the oily swell, then slid away.

Slow-stirring life abounded on this stony beach. "Well-chosen landing site," Sara said to the mech crawler nearby. The machines kept their silence, as if understanding the importance of this moment.

He recalled that in the media storm before they departed, a faction had argued that some ethical imperative made ever visiting other living worlds morally reprehensible. Such people thought alien life should go undisturbed, never realizing that their notions would kill the very impulse behind astronomical curiosity. Why find it if you can't study it further?

They would never see such wonders as this. Still . . . something tickled at the back of his mind.

Then he felt it. They were sitting in seats that sloped back like loungers, and the old memory came fresh again. This subdued crimson landscape recalled Orange Beach, Alabama, where he had rented chairs to tourists. That night his boyish eyes had truly seen the stars for the first time and yes, the ideas had mingled. Learning to do a job, making money . . . and at work's end the sudden huge perspective of the galaxy itself, a sprawl of stars like jewels on velvet above the salty waters. He could see the design of his life in a single scene, leading to this alien beach.

"My life has come full circle," he said. Sara just grasped his hand through their suit gloves.

Her analytical gaze swept across the view. The crablike thing was still lumbering slowly down the shoreline, apparently looking for food in the slight surf. "I wonder how long we can live out here."

The nearby mech said crisply, "We will have to harvest supplies from this world, begin expansion of living quarters. I assume you wish to live on the ship, of course."

"For now," Harold said. "But to live down here, yes, that's my goal."

Sara studied him for a long time. "You know, we're nearing two hundred years old."

"Not done yet," he said.

HE AND SARA HAD decided to rest, just a quiet doze in their suits while sitting on the beach. Somehow the scene was restful.

So Harold was surprised when the mech called him up from a muzzy sleep.

"There is news," it said. "A signal."

"What? Um. Pop it through."

In oddly accented English a relayed voice said, "—hailing the Mann vehicle, we are approaching orbit. Harold Mann expedition there? In middle of doing a delta-V around the planet to lose last of our velocity."

"What?" Harold said, suddenly alert. "Who are you?"

"Translight expedition eleven, sir," the soft high woman's voice said. "Are you human or mech?"

"Human. Harold Mann."

"What? Then you survived! We did not expect—never mind, this is great news." The voice rose, elated.

Sara said, "How—?"

"We hoped to get here when your expedition was to arrive, but your transmissions were sometimes confusing. So you're there! Looks like—on the surface?"

Harold realized there must be video on this link too. "Yes, a relaxing day at the beach. Recliner chairs. Cocktail hour coming up."

"We're not equipped for landfall. This is just a compact carrier, experimental. We'll have to meet you—"

"Wait, how the hell did you get here so fast?"

"Translight, sir. It's a relativistic warp effect, been working on it for decades. Our teams have made some jaunts into the Oort, now this. I admit it was a long shot, trying to catch up to you. We're funded by one of your own companies, Galaxy Nautics."

"So . . ." Harold was having trouble following this woman's fast, odd accent. "Looks like I left the right people in charge."

"Some of them still are—we live much longer now. Mr. Mann, you're the first. You beat us here by maybe a few weeks. We're still getting the translight calibrated."

Sara broke in, her voice slow from just waking up. "So there's a . . . new method?"

"New physics, straight out of the new Insight. Is that—Mrs. Mann?"

Sara managed a dry laugh. "Ms. Ernsberg. Our five-year marriage contract ran out about a century ago."

"You both survived! Wonderful news. Estimated probabilities were less than ten percent, so—sorry, we came expecting to be talking to just the mechs. We'll have to rethink our procedures—"

Harold said firmly, "I believe you work for me, ma'am."

"I . . . suppose I do." The woman's voice hesitated and came back a bit subdued. "I can understand your Anglish! You're . . . the oldest people, ever. Not even our Optimals have gotten this many years logged. We didn't really think—well, anyway, we brought modern gear for your body upgrades. Our CEO insisted."

"Is that Mark Martin?"

"Well, no, he's chairman of the board now. But it may have been his idea, yes. We can do microrepairs, sort out your accumulated epigenetic effects from the long sleep—"

"Good, start getting your gear up to speed for us," Harold said. "My joints are aching and I need a high-mileage checkup."

The woman laughed. It felt good to be back in business.

Harold stretched against this planet's strong gravs. "Y'know, the formal name of this was the Forward Expedition. Let's call it that, okay?"

Sara glanced over at him and said to the general comm, "Pretty soon now, we'll have our mechs lift off this beach and get into orbit. Say, you don't have a warrant for us, eh?"

"What? I don't—oh, our AI shows the doc history . . ." They could hear the woman muttering to someone. "No, that regime killed a lot of people. No real records. No wonder you left in a hurry! They didn't last long."

Sara laughed and said, "When we left, Earthside had its same problem—too many humans on the planet using a destructive technology to live by. Has that changed?"

"Oh, plenty. Fewer of us now, getting the climate punched up, importing plenty from offworld."

Harold wanted to know everything that a century had unfolded, but restrained himself to: "Keegan over at Consolidated—what happened?"

A long pause. "Checked my infold mind. Both of them went under in some scandal."

"Ah." Perhaps it was small of him, but Harold grinned. "Good. Aim to rendezvous within two orbits."

"Uh, yes, sir. We're modifying our delta-V now. As soon—"

"Just get it done. I want to see your system specs as soon as we're aboard."

"Oh, yes, I think—my Lord, there are statues to you back home! I don't know how to—"

"Yeah, well, this statue talks. No pigeons around, either. Make it snappy. We've got work to do here."

ON BUILDING THE STORY—Gregory Benford

Some may recognize that "The Man Who Sold the Stars" is a direct echo and commentary on Robert A. Heinlein's classic tale from the 1940s, "The Man Who Sold the Moon." Both imagine a future, now soon to come, when space will be explored and developed by private companies. Heinlein was largely wrong—the U.S. government ran the first era. But of course nearly all the technology NASA used came from private companies, and in our second era now developing, companies also make the major decisions of what to do next.

Heinlein's Harriman sold the moon as a source of mining wealth, including gold. Arthur C. Clarke was closer to reality: he predicted geosynchronous satellites in 1945. I imagined repairing those geosats as a plausible industry, leading to asteroid mining—where, we now know, the true wealth awaits.

I suspect that space and science fiction tend to be cultural manifestations of rich, highly developed Western countries that can afford such pursuits. Now that other countries have come on board (China, India) as the global economy develops, people have enough free time to follow this dream. There will be global competition for the rewards of solar system industries, echoing the opening of North America centuries ago.

Companies are far better at this than governments. Russia has had Siberia for more than four centuries, yet still can't develop it well; there are about 30 million people in a land area comparable to the USA. (Historical analogy: California had 73,000 people in its first census, 1850, shortly after the USA took it from Mexico. Now it has more than 38 million and is a high-tech leader.) The principal directions for solar system development will entail technologies we can see now: 3-D printers in a variety of substances, for manufacture from materials found in space; advanced space-rated robotics, with artificial intelligences to control them; nuclear thermal rockets to carry large masses.

At first we'll see some space tourism (orbital hotels, etc.), then repair of high satellites, and on to asteroid mining. Beyond that, the frontier is open.

HERE ARE SNAPSHOTS OF ingredients that shaped the story, and vice versa:

• The symposium that kicked off the subject: http://www.centauri-dreams .org/?p=9979.

• This carries discussions and links to speeches that amplify the prospects for an industrial solar system economics: http://www.starshipcentury .com/.

• A central reference point, the Centauri Dreams website. For example: http://www.centauri-dreams.org/?p=18892; http://www.centauri-dreams .org/?p=13134.

• http://www.nasa.gov/wise.

• The second-nearest star to us is a brown dwarf double star system, which seems to have a planet as well: http://arxiv.org/pdf/1312.1303v2.pdf.

I didn't know this while writing the story, just imagined it plausible. We don't know if any brown dwarfs lurk closer still.

THE BASIC BOOK ABOUT asteroid mining is John Lewis, *Mining the Sky*. Robert Zubrin's *Entering Space* has many ideas. He shows how rocket planes, solar and magnetic sails, controlled fusion, and other technologies stand untapped as unique resources that will allow us to be more mobile and to reach farther. His bestseller *The Case for Mars* is still the best presentation of colonizing ideas.

From that and discussions many pathways emerge.

I DID A LOT of backgrounding for Harold Mann's business. Here are Notes in Summary of some key innovations needed for robot explorers and prospectors, which I never used:

1. Artificial intelligence for decades of operation without human intervention. Robotic governance of nonhuman exploration teams that can show originality, adapt to the unexpected, and bring forth new investigations. Space-ready robots will need autonomy for greater than one day on outer solar system missions in the next ten to twenty years.

2. General computational intelligence, with reactive decision making,

real-time choices from incomplete information, fault-detection and response, replanning capability. Miniaturization and cold-blooded avionics
and instruments are high priority for outer planets, icy moons, distant
small bodies.

3. Conventional propulsion: chemical, solar electric, radioisotope electric,
and nuclear thermal. All need propellants; the latter can use water. Need
long-life electric thrusters, lightweight radioisotope and nuclear generators.

4. Prospecting, mining, refining of consumables like chemical and inert
propellants. Radioisotopes more difficult to obtain in situ and may be
better to process in breeder reactor, or take along large quantities of Am-
241.

5. Solar and magnetic sails, to eliminate propellant near the star where
energy is available. Beamed energy and laser-driven sails, undeveloped
today. Beaming needs a free line of sight path and onboard batteries for
energy storage. These exist on most geosats now.

ENTANGLEMENT

Vandana Singh

. . . FLAPPING ITS WINGS . . .

. . . and flying straight at her. She ducked, averting her eyes. The whole world had come loose: debris flying everywhere; the roar of the wind. Something soft and sharp cannoned into her belly—she looked up to see the monster rising into the clouds, a genie of destruction, yelled—*Run! Run! Find lower ground! Lower ground!*

She woke up. The boat rocked gently; instrument panels in the small cabin painted thin blue and red lines. Outside, the pale Arctic dawn suffused the sky with orange light. Everything was normal.

"Except I hadn't been asleep, not really," she said aloud. Her morning coffee had grown cold. "What kind of dream was that?"

She rubbed the orange bracelet. One of the screens flickered. There was a fragmented image for a microsecond before the screen went blank: a gray sky, a spinning cloud, things falling. She sat up.

Her genie appeared in a corner of the screen.

"Irene, I just connected you to five people around the world," it said cheerfully. "Carefully selected, an experiment. We don't want you to get too lonely."

"Frigg," she said, "I wish you wouldn't do things like that."

There were two messages from Tom. She thought of him in the boat three hundred kilometers away, docked to the experimental iceberg, and hoped he and Mahmoud were getting along. Good, he had only routine stuff to report. She scrolled through messages from the Arctic Science Initiative, the Million Eyes project, and three of her colleagues working off the northern coast of Finland. Nothing from Lucie.

She let out a long, slow breath. Time to get up, make fresh coffee. Through the tiny window of the boat's kitchenette, the smooth expanse of ocean glittered in the morning light. The brolly floated above it like a conscientious ghost, not two hundred meters away. Its parachute-like top was bright in the low sun, its electronic eyes slowly swiveling as the intelligent unit in the box below drank in information from the world around it. Its community of intelligences roved the water below, making observations and sending them back to the unit, so that it could adjust its behavior accordingly. She felt a tiny thrill of pride. The brolly was her conception, a crazy biogeochemist's dream, brought to reality by engineers. The first prototype had been made by Tom himself, in his first year of graduate school. Thinking of his red thatch of hair framing a boyish face, she caught herself smiling. He was such a kid! The first time he'd seen a seal colony, he'd almost fallen off the boat in his enthusiasm. You'd think the kid had never even been to a zoo. He was so *Californian*, it was adorable. Her own upbringing in the frozen reaches of northern Canada meant she was a lot more cold-tolerant than him—he was always overdressed by her standards, buried under layers of thermal insulation and a parka on top of everything. Some of her colleagues had expressed doubts about taking an engineering graduate student to the Arctic, but she'd overruled them. The age of specialization was over; you had to mix disciplinary knowledge and skills if you wanted to deal intelligently with climate change, and who was better qualified to monitor the brollies deployed in the region? Plus Mahmoud would make a great babysitter for him. He was a sweet kid, Tom.

She pulled on her parka and went out on deck to have her coffee the way she liked it, scalding hot. Staring across the water, she thought of home. Baffin Island was not quite directly across the North Pole from her station in the East Siberian Sea, but this was the closest she had come to home in the last fifteen years. She shook her head. Home? What was she thinking? Home was a sunny apartment in a suburb of San Francisco, a few BART stops from the university, where she had spent ten years raising Lucie, now twenty-four, a screenwriter in Hollywood. It had been over a year since she and Lucie had had a real conversation. Her daughter's chatty e-mails and phone calls had given way to a near silence, a mysterious reserve. In her present solitude that other life, those years of closeness, seemed to have been no more than a dream.

Over the water the brolly moved. There was a disturbance not far from the brolly—an agitation in the water, then a tail. A whale maybe five meters in length swimming close to the surface popped its head out of the water—a beluga! Well, she probably wasn't far from their migration route. Irene imagined the scene from the whale's perspective: the brolly like an enormous, airborne jellyfish, the boat, the human-craft, a familiar sight.

The belugas were interested in the brolly. Irene wondered what they made of it. One worry the researchers had was that brollies and their roving family units would be attacked and eaten by marine creatures. The brolly could collapse itself into a compact unit and sink to the seabed or use solar power to rise a couple of meters above the ocean surface. At the moment it seemed only to be observing the whales as they cavorted around it. Probably someone, somewhere, was looking at the ocean through the brolly's electronic eyes and commenting on the Internet about a whale pod sighting. Million Eyes on the Arctic was the largest citizen science project in the world. Between the brollies, various observation stations, and satellite images, more than two million people could obtain and track information about sea ice melt, methane leaks, marine animal sightings, and ocean hot spots.

It occurred to Irene that these whales might know the seashore of her childhood, that they might even have come from the North Canadian archipelago. A sudden memory came to her: going out into the ocean north of Baffin Island with her grandfather in his boat. He was teaching her to use traditional tools to fish in an icy inlet. She must have been very small. She recalled the rose-colored Arctic dawn, her grandfather's weathered face. When they were on their way back with their catch, a pod of belugas had surfaced close enough to rock their boat. They clustered around the boat, popping their heads out of the water, looking at the humans with curious, intelligent eyes. One large female came close to the boat. *"Qilalugaq,"* her grandfather said gently, as though in greeting. The child Irene—no, she had been Enuusiq then—Enuusiq was entranced. The Inuit, her grandfather told her, wouldn't exist without the belugas, the caribou, and the seals. He had made sure she knew how to hunt seals and caribou before she was thirteen. Memories surfaced: the swish of the dog sled on the ice in the morning, the waiting at the breathing holes for the seals, the swift kill. The two of them saying words of apology over the carcass, their breath forming clouds in the frigid air.

Her grandfather died during her freshman year of high school. He was the one who had given her her Inuk name, Enuusiq, after his long-dead older brother, so that he would live again in her name. The name held her soul, her *atiq*. "Enuusiq," she whispered now, trying it on. How many

years since anyone had called her that? She remembered the gathering of
the community each time the hunters brought in a big catch, the taste
of raw meat with a dash of soy. How long had it been since those days? A
visit home fifteen years ago when her father died (her mother had died
when she was in college)—after that just a few telephone conversations
and Internet chats with her cousin Maggie in Iqaluit.

The belugas moved out of sight. Her coffee was cold again. She was
annoyed with herself. She had volunteered to come here partly because
she wanted to get away—she loved solitude—but in the midst of it, old
memories surfaced; long-dead voices spoke.

The rest of the morning she worked with a fierce concentration, sending data over to her collaborators on the Russian research ship *Kolmogorov*,
holding a conference call with three other scientists, politely declining two
conference invitations for keynote speaker. But in the afternoon her rest-
lessness returned. She decided she would dive down to the shallow ocean
bed and capture a clip for a video segment she had promised to the Million
Eyes project. It was against protocol to go down alone without anyone
on the boat to monitor her—but it was only twenty-two meters, and she
hadn't got this far by keeping to protocol.

Some time later she stood on the deck in her drysuit, pulled the cap
snugly over her head, checked the suit's computer, wiggled her shoulders
so the oxygen tank rested more comfortably on her back, and dove in.

This was why she was here. This falling through the water was like
falling in love, only better. In the cloudy blue depths she dove through
marine snow, glimpsing here and there the translucent fans of sea butterflies, a small swarm of krill, the occasional tiny jellyfish. A sea gooseberry
with a glasslike two-lobed soft body winged past her face. Some of these
creatures were so delicate a touch might kill them—no fisherman's net
could catch them undamaged. You had to be here, in their world, to know
they existed. Yet there was trouble in this marine paradise. Deeper and
deeper she went, her drysuit's wrist display clocking time, temperature,
pressure, oxygen. The sea was shallow enough at twenty-two meters that
she could spend some time at the bottom without worrying about decom-
pression on the way up. It was darker here on the seaweed-encrusted ocean
floor; she turned on her lamp and the camera. Swimming along the sea-
floor toward the array of instruments, she startled a mottled white crab.
It was sitting on top of one of the instrument panels, exploring the device

with its claws. Curiosity . . . well, that was something she could relate to. The crab retreated as she swam above it, then returned to its scrutiny. Well, if her work entertained the local wildlife, that was something.

A few meters away she saw the fine lines of the thermoelectric mesh on the seabed. There were fewer creatures in the methane-saturated water. Methane gas was coming up from the holes in the melting permafrost on the seabed—there were even places you could see bubbles. Before her a creature swam into focus: a human-built machine intelligence, one of the brolly's family unit. Its small, cylindrical body, with its flanges and long snout, looked like a fish on an alien planet. It was injecting a rich goo of nutrients (her very own recipe) for methane-eating bacteria. She was startled by how natural it looked in the deep water. "Eat well, my hearties," she told her favorite life-forms. Methanotrophs were incredibly efficient at metabolizing methane, using pathways that were only now being elucidated. Most of the processes could not be duplicated in labs. So much was still unknown—hell, they'd found *five* new species of the bacteria since the project had started. Methanotrophs, like most living beings, didn't exist in isolation, but in consortia. The complex web of interdependencies determined behavior and chemistry.

"If methane-eating bacteria sop up most of the methane, it will help slow global warming," she said into the recorder. "It will buy time until humanity cuts its carbon dioxide emissions. Methane is a much more potent greenhouse gas than CO_2. Although it doesn't stay in the atmosphere as long, too much methane in the atmosphere might excite a positive feedback loop—more methane, more warming, more thawing of permafrost, more methane . . . a vicious cycle that might tip the world toward catastrophic warming." Whether that could happen was still a point of argument among scientists, but the methane plumes now known to be coming off the seabed all over the shallow regions of the Arctic were enough to worry anyone whose head wasn't buried in the sand.

Maybe her bacteria could help save the world. With enough nutrients, they and their communities of cooperative organisms might take care of much of the methane; in the meantime the thermoelectric mesh was an experiment to see whether cooling down the hot spots might slow the outgassing. The energy generated by the mesh was captured in batteries, which had to be replaced when at capacity. The instrument array measured biogeochemical data and sent it back to the brolly.

Her drysuit computer beeped. It was time to return to the surface—or else she would run out of oxygen. She turned off the camera-recorder and swam slowly and carefully toward the light. "Message from Tom," her genie said. "Not urgent but interesting. Two messages from Million Eyes, one to you, asking about the video, the other a news item. A ballet dancer in Estonia saw an illegal oil and gas exploration vessel messing around the Laptev Sea. There's a furor. Message from your cousin Maggie in Iqaluit, marked Personal. She's in San Francisco, wondering where you are."

Damn. Hadn't she told Maggie she was going on an expedition? Maggie hardly ever left Canada so the trip to San Francisco must be something special.

"I'm coming up," she said, just as she felt a numbing pain sear into her left calf. The cold was coming in through a leak, a tear in the suit; her drysuit computer beeped a warning. Her leg cramped horribly. She looked up, willing herself not to panic—the surface seemed impossibly far away, and the cold was filling her body, making her chest contract with pain. She moved her arms as strongly as she could. She must get up to the surface before the cold spread—she had had a brush with hypothermia before. But as she went up with excruciating slowness she knew at once that she was going to die here, and a terror came upon her. *Lucie,* she said. *Lucie, forgive me, I love you, I love you.* Her arms were tired, her legs like jelly, and the cold was in her bones, and a part of her wanted simply to surrender to oblivion. Frigg was chirping frantically in her ear—calling for rescue, not that there was anyone in the area who could get to her in time—and then a voice cut in, and her grandmother said, *Bless you and be careful up there, I'm praying for you.* This was really odd because her grandmother was dead, and the accent was strange. But the voice spoke with such clarity and concern, and there was such an emphasis on *be careful*—and weren't there kitchen sounds in the background, a pan banging in the sink, so incongruously ordinary and familiar?—that she was jolted from the darkness of spirit that had descended on her. Her arms seemed to be the only part of her body still under her control, and although they felt like lead, she began to move them again.

Tom's voice cut in, frantic. "I'm coming, I'm coming as fast as I can, hold on," and Mahmoud, more calmly, "I've contacted the *Kolmogorov* for their helicopter—and the Coast Guard." But the helicopter had been sent over to a station in Norway that very afternoon. She saw her death before her with astonishing clarity. Then she felt something lift her bodily—how could Tom get here so soon?—an enormous white shadow loomed, a smile on the bulbous face—a whale. A *beluga?* She felt the solid body of the whale below her, tried to get a hold of the smooth flesh, but she needn't have worried, because it was pushing her up with both balance and strength, until she broke the water's surface near the boat. Hauling herself up the rungs of the ladder proved to be impossible: she was shaking violently, and her legs felt numb. The whale pushed her up until all she had to do was to tumble over the rail onto the deck. She collapsed on the deck, pulled off her mask, sobbing, breathing huge gulps of cold air. Her suit beeped shrilly.

"Get dry NOW," Frigg said in Mahmoud's voice, or maybe it was Mahmoud. She half crawled into the cabin, peeled everything off, and huddled under a warm shower until the shivering slowed. A searing pain in both legs told her that blood was circulating again. There was a frayed tear in the drysuit—had it caught on a nail as she was pulling it out of the cupboard? So much for damning protocol, something she never did if a colleague or student was involved. Her left calf still ached, and the tears wouldn't stop. At last she toweled off and got into warm clothes, with warm gelpacks under her armpits and on her stomach. The medbot checked her vital signs while hot cocoa bubbled.

"Frigg, tell Tom and Mahmoud not to come, my vitals are fine," she said, but her voice shook. "Tell them to call off the rescue." Her chest still ached, but as she sipped the cocoa she started to feel more normal. After a while she could stand without feeling she was going to fall over.

She stepped gingerly out on the deck. The sun, already low in the sky, was falling slowly into the ocean like a ripe peach. The first stars sequined the coming Arctic night. The belugas swam around the boat. She finished her cocoa in a few gulps and felt a shadow of strength return to her. A whale popped its head out of the water next to her boat and looked at her with friendly curiosity.

She put her arms between the railing bars and touched the whale's head. It was smooth as a hard-boiled egg. *"Qilalugaq,"* she whispered, and tears ran down her cheeks, and her shoulders shook. "Thank you, thank you for saving my life. Did *Ittuq* send you?" She realized she was speaking Inuktitut, the familiar syllables coming back as though she had never left home. *Ittuq,* she whispered. She had been too young when her grandfather died, too shocked to let herself mourn fully. Now, thirty-nine years later, the tears flowed.

At last she stood, leaning against the rail, spent, and waved to the pod as it departed.

Later that night, when she had eaten her fill of hot chicken soup, she talked to Tom on video. He was touchingly grateful that she was all right and excited about the whale rescue. Irene said, "Don't go around broadcasting it, will you?" She had no desire to see her foolishness go viral on the Internet. Fortunately Tom had something exciting of his own to share.

"Look! he said. "This is from this afternoon." A photo appeared on the side of the screen. There lay the enormous bulk of the artificial iceberg to which his boat was docked. An irregular heap lay atop it.

"Polar bear," he said, grinning. "Must have been swimming for a while, looking for a rest stop. Poor guy's sleeping off a late lunch. I tossed him my latest catch of fish."

"Stay away from him!" Irene said sharply. "Wild animals aren't cute house pets—remember your briefing!"

"You're a fine one to talk, Irene." He grinned again, and then, anticipating her protests, "Yes, yes, I know, don't worry. If I go aboard the berg with the bear on it, some kid somewhere is going to notice and send me a message. This morning I stepped out without my snow goggles and a twelve-year-old from Uzbekistan messaged my genie. Thanks to Million Eyes you can hardly take a shit in peace . . . er, sorry . . ."

"It's not *that* bad." She couldn't help smiling. Good for the kid in Uzbekistan. Tom could be absentminded. The screen image of the fake berg was impossibly white. It was coated with a high-albedo nanostructured radiative paint that sent infrared right back into the atmosphere, while leaving the surface cool to the touch.

"Another interesting thing happened today," he said, with the kind of casualness that betrayed suppressed excitement. "You know we have eight brollies on Big Lump?" Big Lump was the largest iceberg in a flotilla about fifty kilometers north of Tom's station. "They've been screening meltwater pools on the berg from the sun, refreezing them before they have a chance to melt deeply enough to make cracks. Well, three nomad brollies arrived from Lomonosov Station—just left their posts of their own accord and came over and joined them. Mahmoud just reported."

"*Very* interesting," she said.

It was not surprising that brollies were making their own decisions. It meant that as learning intelligences, intimately connected to their environment and to one another, they had gone on to the next stage of sophistication. Her own brolly continuously monitored the biogeochemical environment, knowing when to feed the methanotroph consortia their extra nutrients, and when to stop. Her original conception of linked artificial intelligences with information feedback loops was based on biomimicry, inspired by natural systems like ecosystems and endocrine systems. Her brolly was used to working as a community of minds, so she imagined that facility could be scaled up. Each brolly could communicate with its own kind and was connected to the climate databases around the world, giving as well as receiving information, and capable of learning from it. She had a sudden vision of a multilevel, complexly interconnected grid, a sentience spanning continents and species, a kind of Gaiaweb come alive.

"How much time before they become smarter than us?" she said, half-jokingly. "This is great news, Tom."

Afterward she watched the great curtains of the aurora paint the sky. She sat in her cabin, raising her eyes from the data scrolling down her screen. Temperature was dropping in the ocean seabed—the methane fizzler had perceptibly slowed since the project began. It was a minute accomplishment compared to the scale of the problem, but with two million pairs of eyes watching methane maps of the Arctic, maybe they could get funding to learn how to take care of the worst areas that were still manageable. Partly the methane outgassing was a natural part of a thousands-years process, but it was being exacerbated by warming seas. Didn't science ultimately teach what the world's indigenous peoples had known so well— that everything is connected? A man gets home from work in New York City and flips a switch, and a little more coal is burned, releasing more warming carbon dioxide into the atmosphere. Or an agribusiness burns a tract of Amazon rain forest, and a huge carbon sink is gone, just like that. Or a manufacturer in the United States buys palm oil to put in cookies, and rain forests vanish in Southeast Asia to make way for more plantations. People and their lives were so tightly connected across the world that it would take a million efforts around the globe to make a difference.

She touched the orange wristlet and the screen came on. "Frigg, call Maggie."

"Irene, Irene?" Maggie had more gray in her hair, but her voice was as loud as before. Demanding. "Where have you been? They told me at your campus you were in the Arctic, and I thought, dammit, she's come home at last, but I hear you're somewhere in Siberia?"

"Don't you keep up?" Irene said, growling, trying not to grin in delight, and failing. She blinked tears from her eyes. "Siberia is where it's at. I'm in

a boat, running an experiment on the seabed. Trying to stop methane out-gassing, you know, save the world, all in a day's work."

"Great, great, but I hate coming all the way here and finding you gone. I have to tell you, I saw Lucie. Yes, you heard me right. She's going into documentary filmmaking—expedition to Nepal—"

Nepal!

"Well, I am glad she's talking to you," Irene said, after a moment. "Is she . . . is she all right?"

"She's fine! Irene, she just needs to find her own way—you two have been by yourselves for so long . . ."

"By ourselves! In the middle of the empty streets of the Bay Area!"

"You know what I mean. Big cities can be terribly lonely. Why do you think I came back after college? Listen, Irene, nuclear families suck, and single-parent nuclear families suck even more. People need other people than just their parents. My kids have issues with being here in Iqaluit, but at least they are surrounded by uncles and aunts and cousins and grandparents—"

"How are your parents? How is everyone?"

"Waiting for you to come home. Come and visit, Irene. It's been too long. We all thought you were the one who was going to stay because of everything you learned about the old ways from Grandfather."

"The last time I came, when my father died . . . your mother threw a fish at me and told me to gut it."

Maggie laughed.

"Which I think you did pretty well. Surprised me. Now you have to come on up, Irene! Or down, I should say. Come talk to my boy. Peter's part of a collaboration between Inuit high schoolers and scientists. Hunters too. Going out with GPS units, recording information about ice melting and wildlife sightings."

Irene wanted to say, *Maggie, I almost died today, but* Qilalugaq *gave me the gift of life, and that means I have to change how I live. I need your help.* The words wouldn't come out. She said, instead:

"Maggie, I got to go. Let's talk tomorrow . . . we have to talk."

"Irene, are you all right? Irene?"

"Yes . . . No, I can't talk about it now. Tomorrow? If . . . if you see Lucie again, tell her—give her my love."

"I'm seeing her Friday for lunch before she leaves. I will, don't worry. Tomorrow, for sure then. Hang in there, girl!"

She waved good-bye and the screen went blank. The lights of the aurora reflected off the walls and desk in the darkened room. The boat swayed gently—out there, the pale top of the brolly floated. Something splashed out at sea, a smooth back. She remembered the small house in Iqaluit where she'd grown up with her parents and grandfather and two aunts and cousins. The great sky over the ice, sky reflecting ice reflecting sky in an endless loop. Her grandfather had been an immensely practical man, but he had also taught her to pay attention to intangible things, things you couldn't quantify, like the love you could feel for a person, or the land, or the whale. She had been rescued by a whale, a whale from home. What more of a sign did she need? She had stayed away first because it was inconvenient to go all the way, and then because she had been so busy, doing important work—and later because she was confused and ashamed. How to face them all, knowing that despite her successes she had lost her way, wandered off from her own self? How to return home without Lucie, knowing herself a failure in so many ways? Now she saw that the journey home was part of her redemption, and as the belugas migrated, traveling in great closed loops in the still-frigid waters of the Arctic, visiting and revisiting old ground, so must she. *Enuusiq,* she whispered, practicing. She thought of her daughter's eager, tender face in childhood as she listened to a story, and the bittersweet delight when Lucie went off to college, so young and beautiful, intelligence and awareness in her eyes, at the threshold of adulthood. She thought of herself as a small child, watching her mother weaving a pattern on the community loom: the sound, the rhythm, the colors, her mother's hands. The world she loved was woven into being every moment through complex, dynamic webs of interaction: the whales in their pods, the methanotrophs and their consortia, the brollys and their family units, the Million Eyes of eager young people trying to save the world.

"*Ittuq,*" she said aloud, "I'm coming home."

. . . IN THE AMAZON . . .

. . . there is a city in the middle of the rain forest: Manaus. This year there is a drought. The rains are scant. When they fall, they fall kilometers downwind of the city . . .

In the heat, outside the glitzy hotels and bars, there is the smell of rotting fruit, fish, garbage, flowers, exhaust. Rich and poor walk the streets with their cell phones or briefcases or Gucci handbags or baskets of jenipapo or camu-camu, and among them prowls the artist. He's looking for a blank wall, the side of a building. Any smooth, empty surface is a canvas to him.

His favorite time is the early morning. In that pale light when the bugio monkeys and the birds begin to call, he is there with black oil chalk, and a brush, drawing furiously in huge arm strokes, then filling in the fine-detail work. He never knows what animal will emerge from the wall—the first stroke tells him nothing, nor the next, or the next, but each stroke limits the possibilities until it is clear what spirit has possessed him, and then it emerges. When it is a jaguar, he, the artist, feels the bark of the tree limb; he flickers through the jungle on silent, padded feet. When a manatee emerges from the blank wall, the artist knows the watery depths of the river, the mysterious underwater geography. When it is a bird, he knows the secret pathways of the high jungle canopy.

Then he is done. He looks around, and there is nobody, and he breathes a sigh of relief. He slips away through the sleeping streets to another self, another life.

Fernanda stared out from the airplane window at the city that was her home. It was a bright splash of whiteness in the green of the Amazon rain forest. *Urban heat island indeed,* she thought. The city had grown enormously in the last decade, with the boom in natural gas and high-tech manufacturing—returning to it was always a surprise—a populous, economically vigorous human habitation in the middle of the largest forest in the world. Despite the urban forests that made green pools in the white sea of concrete, it lay before her like scar tissue in the body of the jungle. The Rio Negro was languid as an exhausted lover—the water was lower than she could remember since the last drought. She hadn't forgotten what it had been like, as a child, to stand on the dry bed of the river during the big drought, feeling like the world was about to end. Bright rooftops came up toward her as the plane dipped, and she tried to see if there were any green roofs—hard to tell from this height. Never mind, she would know soon enough, when she joined the new project.

"Been on holiday?" the man next to her said pleasantly.

Fernanda was caught off guard. She had spent three months in the coastal jungle studying the drought, counting dead trees, making measurements of humidity, temperature, and rainfall, and, on one occasion, fighting a forest fire started by an agricultural company to clear the forest. Her left forearm still hurt from a burn. The team had camped in the hot, barren expanse, and after two months she and Claudio had broken up, which is why she was coming back alone. They'd established beyond doubt that barren wasteland was hotter than healthy forest, and that less rain fell here, and that it was similar to an urban heat island. Far from being able to regrow the forest, they had to fight greedy marauders to prevent more of it from being destroyed. Claudio remained behind with the restoration team, and the rest of them had trekked through the deep coolness of the remaining healthy forest until they had got to civilization. She had grown silent as the forest muttered, called, clucked, and roared around her, had felt its rhythms in some buried ancestral part of her, and her pain had quieted to a kind of soft background noise. Now she looked at the man in his business suit and his clean-shaven, earnest face, the shy smile, the hint of a beer belly, and thought how alien her own species seemed whenever she returned from the forest.

"Business," she said coldly, hoping he wouldn't inquire any further. The plane began its descent.

The city was the same and not the same. She found out within the next few days that the cheerful family gatherings at Tia Ana's, which she'd always enjoyed, were a lot more difficult without Claudio, mostly because of the questions and commiserations. Tia Ana had that look in her eye that meant she was already making matchmaking plans. Her mother had tickets for two for a performance of *Aida* at the Teatro Amazonas, no less, which was something to look forward to. Inevitably she thought about that last fight with Claudio, when he accused her of being more sexual with her saxophone than with him. Not that she'd brought her sax into the rain forest—but she hadn't been able to take it out of its case as yet.

What was different was that there wasn't enough rain. When the clouds did gather, there might be a scant shower over the city, but most of the rain would fall about fifty kilometers downwind. Meanwhile the humans sweltered in their concrete and wooden coops—those who had air-conditioning cranked it up—the poor on the city's east side made do without, some falling victim to heat exhaustion. But for the most part the lives of the middle and upper classes went on much the same apart from the occasional grumbling. It seemed peculiar to Fernanda that even in this self-consciously eco-touristy city, people whom she knew and loved could live such oblivious lives, at such a remove from the great, dire warnings the biosphere was giving them.

The other thing that was different was the artist.

An anonymous graffiti artist had hit the streets of Manaus. Sides of buildings, or walls, were transformed by art so startling that it slowed traffic, stopped conversations. She heard about all this with half an ear and didn't pay attention until she went running the day before her new project began. White shorts and tank top, her black hair flying loose, along the harborway, through the crowded marketplaces with their bright awnings and clustering tourists, she ran through the world of her species, trying to know it again. She paused at a fruit stand, good-naturedly fending off the flirtations of two handsome youths while she drank deeply of buriti juice. There were ferries as usual on the Rio Negro, and the water was as she remembered it, dark and endless, on its way to its lover's tryst with the Solimões to form the Amazon, the Amazon she had known and loved all her life.

She turned onto a side street and there was a jaguar, about to leap at her from the windowless side of a building. She stopped and stared. It was abstract, rendered in fluid, economical brushstrokes, but the artist knew which details were essential; whoever it was had captured the spirit of the beast, the fire in its eyes, what Neruda had called its *phosphorescent absence*. For a moment she stood before it, enthralled, the jungle around her again.

After that she looked for more of the work, asking at street corners and market stalls. The drawings were everywhere—a flight of macaws, a sloth on a tree branch, or an anaconda about to slide off a wall onto the street. Wherever they were, there was a crowd. The three-dimensionality of the drawings was astounding. The ripple of muscle, the fine lines of feathers, the spirit come alive in the eye. She was contemplating a particularly stunning rendering of a sauim-de-coleira that a real monkey would be forgiven for mistaking for its relative, when a car full of university freshmen went by, loudly playing what passed for music among the young (she was getting old and jaded at twenty-seven!). The car stopped with a screech of brakes and the youngsters piled out, silenced, and Fernanda thought in triumph: *This is the answer to the oblivious life.* Art so incredible that it brings the jungle back into the city, forces people to remember the nations of animals around us.

But the next day, looking at the data from her rooftop lab, she was not encouraged. The city's pale roofs were glaring back at the sun. What impact did the city's heat island have on the local climate, compared to the drought-ridden sections of the forest? The drought was mostly due to large-scale effects connected with warming oceans and coastal deforestation, but she was interested in seeing whether smaller-scale effects were also significant, and by that logic, whether small-scale reparations at the right scale and distribution might make some difference. It was still a controversial area of research. She spent days poring over maps on her computer screen, maps generated by massive computer models of climate, local and regional. Could the proposed green-roofing experiment be significant enough to test the models? How to persuade enough people and institutions to install green roofs? Scientists were notoriously bad at public relations. Tia Ana would say they weren't good at other kinds of relationships either, although that wasn't strictly true. Her former advisor, Dr. Aguilar, had been happily married to his wife for half a century.

There was a private home in the Cidade Nova area that was already green-roofed according to the design—native plants, chosen for their high rates of evapotranspiration, mimicking the radiative properties of the rain-forest canopies. If they could get enough city officials, celebrities, and so on to see a green roof in action, maybe that would popularize the idea. The home was in a wealthy part of town, and the owner, one Victor Gomes, was connected to the university. She went to see it one hot afternoon.

It was quite wonderful to stand in a rooftop garden with small trees in pots, shrubs in raised beds arranged with a pleasing lack of respect for straight lines, and an exuberance of native creepers that cascaded lushly over the walls. There were fruits and vegetables growing between the shrubs. This was the same model that the restoration team was using in the drought-ridden portions of the Atlantica forest—organically grown native forest species with room for small vegetable gardens and cacao, rubber, and papaya trees, inspired by the *cabruca* movement: small-scale agriculture that fed families and preserved the rain forest. Fernanda looked over the railing and saw that the foliage covered almost the entire side wall of the house. A misting sprayer was at work, and a concealed array of instruments on poles recorded temperature, humidity, and radiative data. It felt much cooler here. Of course, water would be a problem, with the rationing that was being threatened. Damn the rains, why didn't they come?

But she was encouraged. On her way back, her smartphone beeped. There was a message from Claudio that the initial plantings had been completed in the experimental tract, in the drought-ridden forest, and that the local villagers were tending to the saplings. The grant would help pay for the care of the trees, and when the trees were older, they would bear fruit and leaves for the people. There were only a few cases worldwide where rain forests had been partially restored—all restoration was partial because you couldn't replicate the kind of biodiversity that happened over thousands of years—but it was astonishing how things would grow if you looked after them in the initial crucial period. Only local people's investment in the project would ensure its success.

Claudio sounded almost happy. Perhaps healing the forest would heal him too.

The heat wave continued without respite. Fernanda saw people out in the streets staring up at the sky, now, looking at the few clouds that formed above as though beseeching them to rain. The river was sullen and slow. Everyday life seemed off—the glitter of the nightlife was faded too, and the laughter of the people forced. She spent an evening with her cousins Lila and Natalia at the Bar do Armando, where the literati and glitterati seemed equally subdued. The heat seemed to have gotten to the mysterious artist too, since there had been no new work for several days.

Fernanda found herself making the rounds of the graffiti art in the evenings. There were tourist guides who would take visitors to the exhibits. Small businesses sprouted up near these, selling street food and souvenirs. There was outrage when one store painted out the drawing of macaws on its side walls. Each time Fernanda went to see the art-work there would be people standing and staring, and cameras clicking, and groups of friends chattering like monkeys in the jungle. Once she bumped into the man she had sat next to on the plane. He was stand-ing with his briefcase balanced against his legs while he tried to take a picture. She thought of saying hello, apologizing for her coldness on the plane, but he didn't look her way.

She noticed him on three other occasions at different parts of the city, clicking away at the graffiti with his camera. He was photographing the crowds as much as the graffiti. Just a businessman with a hobby, she told herself. But one day, he dropped his briefcase and papers flew open. There were sheets of accounts, tiny neat numbers in rows, a notepad, a note-book computer, a badly wrapped half-eaten sandwich, and a piece of black chalk. The chalk rolled near where Fernanda was standing. The people near the man were solicitously bending over and picking up his things, but he looked around at the ground wildly. Without thinking Fernanda put her foot over the piece of chalk. She dropped her bag, bent down to retrieve it, and got the chalk in her purse with a fluidity that surprised her. It was hard and oily, not at all like ordinary chalk. There was a loose sheet of paper not far from her that the crowd had missed—she picked it up, hurriedly scribbled an address on it, put her business card and the chalk behind the sheet, and gave the whole thing to the man, looking at him with what she hoped was the innocent gaze of a good citizen. She saw recognition leap into his eyes. *Obrigado*. He averted his gaze and hurried off.

She spent the rest of the day feeling restless. If only she could reassure him! She wasn't going to give him away. She'd seen the name of the company where he worked on top of the sheets. Now if only . . .

At home she touched her wristpad, turning on her computer. She scrolled through the news. The tornado in an eastern state of India. Arguments in the United States Senate about the new energy strategy. Floods here, droughts there, the fabric of the biosphere tearing. She thought of the Amazon rain forest, so often called the earth's green lung. Even some tourist guides in the city, taking their mostly North American charges into the jungle, used that term. Did anyone know what those words *meant*? She thought of the predictions of several models, that the great forest, currently a massive carbon dioxide sink, might turn into a *source* of CO_2 if it was stressed enough by drought and tree-cutting. What would happen then? *"Hell on earth,"* she said aloud. She wondered how many people looked up into the sky and imagined, as she did, the invisible river of moisture, the Rios Voadores, roaring in over the Amazon from the Atlantic coast. It thrilled her to think of it: flying river, the anaconda of the sky, carrying as much water as the Amazon, drawn in and strengthened by the pull of the forest so that it flowed across Brazil, hit the Andes, turned south, bringing rain like a benediction. What had human foolishness done to it that there was drought in the *Amazon*? The green lung had lung cancer. She remembered Claudio's face in the lamplight at camp, speaking passionately about the violated Atlantica forest, the mutilated Mato Grosso, the fact that nearly seven thousand acres of forest were cleared every year.

"What do *you* think—are we a stupid species, or what?" she asked the lizard on the wall. The lizard gave her an enigmatic look.

She rested her head on her arms, thinking of Claudio, his physical presence, his kindness. The work they had been doing had drawn them together—maybe the relationship had never been more than that. And yet . . . the work was important. To know whether such reparations would make a difference was crucial. She was usually so positive, so determined despite the immensity of the task. Perhaps it was the drought, the lack of rain when it should be raining buckets every day, that was making her feel like this. "What shall I do to bring the rain?" she asked aloud. The wristpad beeped, and then there was a kid's voice, distorted by electronic translation software. On the computer screen he was sitting in a hospital bed, his dark, thin face earnest. His ears stuck out.

Sing, he said. Behind the translation she could hear the kid's real voice speaking an unfamiliar language. He sounded tired. What had he said? *Sing,* he said again. *Sing for the clouds, for the rain.* He started to sing in an astonishingly musical voice. She could tell he was untrained, even though the musical style was unfamiliar. But it was strangely uplifting, this music that would bring the rain. She wanted his voice to go on and on, even though the translation software was off-key. Then abruptly the screen went dark.

Where had the kid come from? She had signed on to an experimental social network software device at a friend's urging, but the kid wasn't in her list of contacts. The connections were really bad most of the time. She hoped he was all right.

The next day the idea of music bringing the rain still haunted her. Of course such things didn't happen in the real world—as a scientist, she knew better. The vagaries of the climate were still beyond them, and the reparations, the stitches in the green fabric of the jungle, had just begun. The trouble with repairing the forest was that it would never be enough, without a million other things happening too, like the work at the polar icecaps, and social movements, ordinary people pledging to make lifestyle changes, and governments passing laws so that children and grandchildren could have a future. The crucial thing was to get net global carbon dioxide emissions down to zero, and that would take the participation of nearly everyone. The days of the lone ranger were gone; this was the age of the million heroes.

Still, she opened her saxophone case the next day and caressed the cool metal. It drew her, the music she had put away from her. She hadn't answered her bandmates' e-mails. Now she had to run to the lab—maybe this evening, she told her saxophone. We'll have a date, you and I.

But she never got to the lab, because her colleague Maria called her, excited. As a result she went straight to the home in Cidade Nova with the experimental green roof. She went around the house to the side wall, where a crowd had already gathered. People were getting out of cars, and there was even a TV truck. From behind the foliage cascading down the wall of the house peered a jaguar, a gentle jaguar, sleepy even, at peace with the world. Fernanda let out a long breath. The artist had understood her message. The owner of the house, elderly Victor Gomes, was standing with the crowd, his mouth agape.

Within a few hours, the news spread and the crowd swelled until the traffic became a problem. Sensing an opportunity, she talked briefly and urgently to Victor Gomes, and he gave an impromptu tour of the rooftop garden. Suddenly everyone was talking about green roofs. Imagine, if you went ahead and got one (and there was a grant to help you out with costs if you couldn't afford it), not only did your air-conditioning bills go down, but maybe, just maybe, the artist would come paint the side of your house.

© 2013, Nina Miller / ASU, adapting content from 2005,
Bibloq / Wikimedia Commons / Public Domain

Two days later there was a gala fund-raiser and awareness event at the Hotel Amazonas. Fernanda played with her old band. She put her lips to her saxophone and into each note she poured her yearning for the rain, for a world restored. The music spilled out, clear as light, smooth as flowing water, and she sensed the crowd shift and move with the sound, with her breath. During a break, when she leaned against the side wall of the stage, watching Santiago's fingers ripple over the piano keyboard, a waiter came up to her and handed her an envelope. Curious, she opened it, and inside was a paper napkin, and an Amazonian butterfly drawn on it, so vivid she half expected it to rise off the napkin. She searched for him in the crowd but there were too many people. Her wristpad beeped. *"A butterfly,"* she whispered, and she felt the wings of change beating in the light-filled air around her.

" . . . CAN CAUSE A TORNADO . . ."

" . . . but scientists now know more than they did only five years ago. We will now speak to an expert . . .

Can you please turn off the TV? I can't bear to see anything more about the storm . . . It was the same program this morning.

I am too sad to tell this story. You'll have to wait a moment.

I am sad because my grandfather the professor died. He was not really my grandfather, but he treated me like I was his own. I called him Dadaji. He let me sleep on the verandah of his bungalow, on a little cot. I felt safe there. I cleaned and cooked for him, and he would talk to me and tell me about all kinds of things. He taught me how to read and write. From the place where I slept I could look down a low incline to the village, my village.

Are you translating this into English? Does that mean I'll be famous all over India?

I want to help my village. I want people to know about it, even though it is only a Harijan basti sitting on stony ground. I want to make sure the world knows that we did something good.

Let me tell you about my village. The river is many hours' walk from us, but the floods are getting worse. Last year during the monsoons the water came into the huts and the fields and drowned everything except what we could carry. The ground where the village sits is very stony, and things don't grow well. We don't have fields of our own, not really. We are *doms*—most of us work in town, or for the big Rajput village—Songaon— two miles away. We do all the dirty work—sweeping and cleaning privies, that sort of thing. Me, I am lucky because the professor employs me and takes care of me and treats me as though I were not a *dom*. He doesn't observe caste even though he is a Rajput himself—he says it is already dying out in the towns and cities. He says the government laws protect people like us, but I don't know about those things because if the Rajputs are angry then they can do what they like to us and nobody can stop them. But the professor, he is a different kind of person—a *devata*. He even has me cook his food, and pats my head when I do my lessons well—and when there is a festival we share a plate of sweets together.

See this thing I am wearing around my wrist, like a watch? The professor gave it to me. He has been teaching me the computer and this thing makes it come on and we can see and talk to people from around the world. Once I spoke to a man all the way in Chennai—it was very exciting. It was really like magic, because the man didn't know Bhojpuri or Hindi and the computer translated his words and mine so we could both understand. The translator voices were funny. Mine didn't sound like me at all.

What I love most is music. In the early morning when the mist lies on the river, the first thing I hear is the birds in the bougainvillea bush. When I bring the tea out on the verandah and we have drunk the first cup, the professor gives me his tanpura to tune. Then he starts to sing *Bhairav*, which is a morning raga. Listening to him, I feel as though I am climbing up and down mountain ranges of mist and cloud. I feel I could fly. I sing with him, as though my voice is a shadow following his voice. He tells me I have a good ear. It isn't the same kind of singing as in the movies—it is something deeper that calls to your soul. When I told the professor that, he looked pleased and said that good music makes poets of us. I never thought that just anybody could be a poet.

From his house, I can see all the way to the river far beyond the village. In the last few years we have either had drought or flood. This year seems to be a dry year. Always there is some difficulty we have to deal with. But we have been changing too, ever since the professor came and began to live in his house. He has problems with his sons; they don't get along, so he lives alone except for me. He and some other people have been working with our basti. The other people are also dalits like us, but they can read and write, and they know how to make the government give them their rights. They have traveled all over the country telling villages like ours that the climate is changing, and we must change too, or we won't survive. So now we have a village panchayat, and there are three women and two men who speak for all of us. You see, new times are coming, difficult times, when Dharti Mai herself is against us because instead of treating her like a mother, human beings have treated her like a slave. Most of those people who did this are in America and places like that, but they are here too, in the big cities. It is strange because at first we used to think places like that were the best in the world, because of what we saw on TV, but the professor explained that living like that, with no regard for Dharti Mai, comes with costs. Why doesn't Dharti Mai punish *them*, then? I asked him that once. Why is she punishing us poor people, who have done nothing to cause the problem? The professor sighed and said that Dharti Mai was punishing everyone. So people ask him all the time, what can we do? This makes the professor happy because he says that earlier most people in our basti just accepted their lot—after all, for thousands of years it has been our lot to suffer. He is pleased because now we want to do something to save ourselves and make the world better. If all those rich, upper-caste people and all the *goras* have been wrong all this time about how they should live, maybe they're wrong about us too. Maybe our time has come.

But Bojhu kaku—he's the one who took me in when my parents died—he says what's the good in pointing fingers? Even the *goras* are changing how they live. The question is what can we do to heal Dharti Mai? How can we help each other survive the terrible times that are upon us? So in the village people take turns being lookouts when there is a bad weather forecast, and they help each other more, and they've got a teacher to come twice a week to teach them how to read and write. They sent Barki kaki off to the town to be trained by a doctor—she's the midwife—so that she can help us all be healthier. You should have seen her when she came back, she was so proud—she got to see how they work in the big hospital and she came back with pink soap for everyone. We now have our own hand pump and don't have to drink river water. All this is because of the professor, and because of people like Bojhu kaku, and Barki kaki—and Dulari mai, even though most people are scared of her temper. The professor and I are treated like royal guests whenever we go to visit. The professor studies people—anthro-pology—and even though he is retired, he hasn't stopped. He goes around all the local villages, tap-tapping with his cane—he's got a bad leg—and he tells people about the world.

Which is how we know about how the world is getting hotter, and even the *goras* are burning up in their big cities with all those cars and TVs. But that is not all. You know there is a big coal-mining company that wants to buy all the land around us? The professor gets angry whenever the coal company is mentioned, so angry he can hardly get a word out. It is burning coal and oil that is making the world hotter and Dharti Mai so angry with us. He says the government, instead of finding ways to use other things, is mining more coal and making more coal plants so that the people in the big cities can have electricity and cars and TVs, which warm the world even more. It sounds to me like when Dhakkan kaka gets drunk, he wants to keep on drinking. So maybe the way the rich people of the world live is like a sickness where they can't make themselves stop. Also most people in my village don't want to give up their ancestral land for the coal company, small and poor and stony though it might be, even though the government has promised compensation. That tiny piece of earth is all we have. But some of the young men think that the money would be good, and they can go to the big city and make it big. The professor told them that there are already too many people trying to make it in the city, but behind his back they grumble and talk about the good life they could have. It's mostly people like Jhingur kaka's older son, who is a malcontent. The Rajput village—Songaon—doesn't like the coal-mining idea either and the professor persuaded them to let us join a protest delegation in the town, although we had to keep our distance behind them. The professor sat with us and argued against the coal company from the back. You should have seen how furious the Rajputs were! They respect him for his education and his caste, even though he doesn't keep caste, but his ways upset them. Later, when we were walking back, one of them told him, "If you weren't an old man, and learned too, I would take my stick to you, for the example you are setting to our children." I know, because I heard him. It was Ranbir Singh. He is the one with the biggest mustache and the biggest, stoutest sticks, and the biggest temper. His mood changes so quickly, everyone is afraid of him. He even has guns. The professor just said quietly that if Ranbir Singh did that with every Rajput in the country who had broken caste, he would run out of sticks pretty quickly.

The day it all happened, in the morning we were listening to the classical program on the radio because the professor wanted to hear a new *bandish* that was playing. There were clouds in the sky but no sign of rain. Just then we heard a roaring sound. The radio crackled and the announcer said something about an unusual cloud formation. The sound of the wind became so strong that we couldn't hear the radio. The sky became dark, even though over the river it was still light. There was a tapping sound over our heads: hail! I was very excited. Hail has fallen only once in my village in my lifetime. I ran down the verandah steps to collect some, and then I saw the storm.

I had never seen anything like it. I saw a whirling monster towering in the fields behind the house, like a top spun out of clouds and wind. The professor looked alarmed. He said he had heard of things like this in other lands, and that it was called a *tur-nado*. He said we would be all right in a pukka house like his, but then he stared out into the distance toward my village. People were coming out of their homes and getting ready to walk to Songaon or the town for the long day of work.

"Bhola," he said to me, "I am going to check on the computer what we should do. Get ready to run down to the village and warn people."

Dadaji, will you be all right?" He's an old man, and lame, too. But he pushed me impatiently off, saying of course he would be fine. That's the last thing he said to me.

I ran down toward the village. The wind was strong, and I saw a crow in the sky struggling to keep its wings under control. It swooped down in a big arc and came right at me, flapping its wings, and hit me in the stomach. I grabbed it and held it to my chest—a full-grown crow. I thought it was dead, but I couldn't just throw it away. So I held it to my chest and I ran.

The sky darkened and the wind howled in my ears. I looked behind me at the house. The tur-nado was over it. The verandah was so dark I couldn't see the professor. I saw the lit screen of the computer disappearing as he went into the house. Above us the tur-nado looked like a monster. I have never been so scared. Then my wrist strap beeped. A woman's voice said out of nowhere, "Find low ground, low ground," and "Run! Run!" I wanted to see if the professor was all right, but he had told me to warn the village. So I ran.

There is a narrow ravine not far from the village. Old people say that it is a crack that opened in the earth during an earthquake. In the monsoons it fills with water, but right now it is dry, full of thorny bushes and rocks. The goats like it there. That was the only low place I could think of. I began to shout as I got closer, yelling to people to stop gawking and trying to lead them to the ravine. I couldn't hear my own voice because of the wind, but Dulari mai started to scream at people and gather them and point them to the ravine. Everyone worked quickly; they are afraid of her temper. There was even someone carrying Joti Ma, old Gobind-kaka's mother, on his back, the terrified children were all holding hands, some were carrying the babies. Behind me the tur-nado danced across the fields, ripping up everything in its path. It picked its way across the land. I saw people rushing toward the ravine, some carrying bundles with them. There was a lot of shouting but everyone was moving. I thought: *I'm not needed here, I could have stayed with the professor.* I thought I should see if I could go around the tur-nado and get to his house. I made my way back across the fields, keeping a careful eye on the storm.

When I was halfway there, I saw the children. It was Ranbir Singh's younger daughter and son, returning from school on the footpath through the fields. Usually someone takes them from Songaon to the town and back by bicycle, but they were walking home. She is older than me, maybe fourteen, and he is only about five years old. Her father once had Bojhu kaku's son beaten because he said he—Kankariya bhai—dared to raise his eyes and look at his daughter. Before I was born, there was trouble that nobody talks about and the Rajputs came and burned down some of our huts, and three people died. That's what I mean when I say they can do anything to us. I hesitated, because if I said anything to the children they didn't like, their father could have me thrashed and the village burned down.

The children looked scared. The girl was trying to use her mobile but she gave up and put it in her schoolbag, looking upset. They looked at me and looked away, and the older sister said to the boy, "Come," urgently, and pulled on his arm. He was tired and about to cry.

I thought: *Why should I try to help them?* But I pointed to the tur-nado raging behind us:

"Sister, that is a bad *toofan*. The professor told me we have to hide. We are all at the ravine near my basti. I can take you there."

I took extra care to be polite. I didn't want her to accuse us later on and get the whole village in trouble. She hesitated. The little boy said:

"Why are you holding a dead crow?"

The girl came to a decision. She said:

"Show me where this place is."

They followed me. There were leaves and branches flying around, and I saw the thatched roof lift off a hut and vanish. A brick came hurtling through the air and missed us by two spans of my hand. I didn't dare look back—we were racing over the fields. The little boy stumbled, and the girl picked him up. Panting, she followed me. It would have been faster if I'd carried the child, but she wasn't going to let a *dom* boy touch her brother. Then she half stumbled. She said: *"Wait!"* I almost didn't hear her but when I looked back she was crying. She thrust her brother at me. Her breath was coming in sobs. He was crying too.

"You want me to carry him? Your father will break my neck!"

She was wailing and shaking her head, and the tur-nado was very close, so I put the child on one hip and handed her the still-warm body of the crow.

"I'm not going to hold that," she said, scowling.

"Then take your brother back," I said, losing my temper. "This crow is a *vahan* of Shani Deva, and we must not disrespect it. Don't you keep pigeons!"

She wrinkled her nose but took the crow in her dupatta, and we ran the rest of the way until we were at the ravine.

It was dark inside, because the low, thorny bushes growing on the top edges of the ravine blocked the sky. Wind screamed over our heads and we heard the most terrible sounds, as though the world was being torn apart.

And then silence.

We all looked at each other. Bojhu kaku and the others saw that I was holding Ranbir Singh's son in my arms, and his daughter was standing next to me, holding the body of a crow in her dupatta, her eyes wide with fear.

"Bhola, what have you done?" someone said. Maybe it was Barki kaki. People gasped.

"I couldn't leave them to die," I said. The boy wriggled out of my grasp and went to his sister. She handed me the crow and held her brother close. Tears ran down her face.

Bojhu kaku said to the girl, "We will see you home. Come, there is nothing to be scared of."

So the children were escorted to Songaon by the crowd. If Bojhu kaku went by himself, he might have to bear the brunt of Ranbir Singh's mood. There was no telling whether he'd be grateful or angry. So Barki kaki said she would go, and then Dulari mai (and we had to tell her no because she would insult even the gods if she lost her temper, and where would we all be then?). So about fifteen people went.

We climbed out of the ravine. The village was smashed flat. There were pots and pans scattered about the fields, and bricks also. The bargad tree that has stood at the crossing on the way to Songaon for two hundred years was completely uprooted. The pathway was covered with big tree branches. Our homes were gone. You might say, *What's a mud-and-thatch house? It is nothing.* But to a poor person it is home. Our hands shape it, our hands weave the *bhusa*. It is where our hopes live. When you have very little, everything you have becomes more precious. We wept and in the same breath we thanked the gods for sparing our lives.

I didn't go with them. My duty was to my dadaji now, and I had a terrible fear growing inside me. I went to the house on the hill. Midway the crow stirred in my arms, and I saw that it was only stunned, not dead. I stopped in the field and found a pocket of moisture where some hailstones had fallen, and let a few drops trail from my fingers into its throat. Suddenly it struggled and flapped its wings. I opened my hands and it flew. It was unsteady at first, but it got stronger as it flew, making two big circles over my head before it went off. Then I went up to what was left of the house.

The windows and doors were gone, and I could see the sky through the roof. Two walls were down. I thought: *This is a* pukka *house, how could this have happened? How could brick and mortar come down like this?* There was dust in the air. It made me cough. There were pages and pages torn from his books, fallen everywhere like leaves. I saw that his computer had fallen under his desk and was all right. Bricks fell as I walked around. I fell too, and broke my arm, and hurt my leg. That's why I'm in hospital.

I was the one who found him. He was near the drawing room window, under a pile of bricks.

He was my grandfather, no matter what anyone says about caste and blood. He gave me everything I have—he was like a god to me. I would have given my life for him, but instead he is the one who is gone. He said I would grow up to be a learner and a singer—someone who could change the world. A *dom* boy like me—nobody has ever told me such things. I'm telling you, he was my dadaji; I don't care what anyone says.

His sons came for his body. I'm not allowed to be there for the last rites. But I know, and he knows, that I should be there. He used to tell me that if you look at things on the surface, you don't know their true nature. You also have to look with your inner eye. He looked at me with his inner eye. He was my dadaji and he's gone.

That's his computer on the table. His sons didn't ask about it.

Nobody has come to see me and I am scared.

What is that you say? Half of Songaon is destroyed? That is a terrible thing. Seven people dead!

I am glad Ranbir Singh's children gave a good account of us. It is strange for him to be in our debt.

Earlier today there was a TV program about the tur-nado. They interviewed an expert. He said that although a tur-nado is strong, it is also delicate. I think I know what he means. Before it is born, the tur-nado is a confusion of cloud and wind. It takes only a little touch here and there to turn the cloud and wind into a monster that can destroy houses. Even once it is made, you can't tell where it is going to go, because it is so delicate a thing that maybe one leaf on one tree might persuade it to go this way instead of that. Or one breath from one sleeping farmhand in the field.

When I leave the hospital, I'm going to help rebuild my village. And I'm going to collect all the pages of Dadaji's books that are scattered all over the fields. I imagine I will find the thoughts of a scientist or philosopher, or the speeches of a poet, stuck in a tree's branches, or blowing in the wind with the dust. I will pick up every page I find and put it together.

I have to find out how I can keep learning. Dadaji was going to teach me so that I could be a learned man like him when I grow up. How is it possible for a tur-nado to be so powerful and so delicate at the same time? How do we tell Dharti Mai we are sorry? How do we stop the mining company that wants to take our land? Please print that in your newspaper—we cannot let them mine and burn more coal, because that is destroying the world. Please tell the big people in the cities like Delhi and in faraway places like America. They won't care about someone like me, but ask them if they care about their own children. I saw just yesterday that it is not just the poor who will suffer in this new world they are making. Tell them to stop.

I have been seeing crows at the window all afternoon. They land on the sill and caw. The orderly says Shani Deva has shown me grace, because of the crow I saved. Everyone fears Shani Deva because he brings us difficult times. But crows remember, and they tell each other who is a friend, and maybe the crows will help us. It's their world too.

I'm very tired. In one day I lost my grandfather, hid my people from the tur-nado, saved two Rajput children, and became a friend of crows.

Something strange happened after dinner. I was half asleep. I heard a woman saying very sadly, "What shall I do to bring the rain?" Then I saw it wasn't a dream, because there was this young woman on the computer screen, a foreigner. I thought she must be one of the people who used to talk to the professor. She looked sad and tired. I told her, you have to sing to the clouds. You have to sing the rain down. Between the radio and my dadaji's lessons I have learned a little of the raga—*Malhaar,* the rain-calling raga. I sang a line or two for her before the connection broke.

Dadaji told me once that sound is just a tremble in the air. A song is a tremble that goes from the soul into the air, and thus to the eardrums of the world. The tur-nado is a disturbance of the air, but it is like an earthquake. Perhaps it is the song of the troubled earth, our mother Dharti Mai. One day I will compose a song to soothe her.

... IN TEXAS ...

   ... it was the kind of day Dorothy Cartwright's husband wouldn't have allowed. Wasn't it just a year and a half ago—he'd gotten so mad at the heat wave at Christmastime that he'd cranked up the air-conditioning until she had to go find a sweater? But they'd had the traditional Christmas evening fire in the fireplace, and weather be damned. It was nowhere near Christmas Day, being March, but it was hotter than it should be, the kind of day when Rob would have had the AC going and the windows closed. Closed houses always made her feel claustrophobic, no matter that her old home had been over four thousand square feet—just the two of them after their son, Matt, grew up and left home. But now Rob was dead of a heart attack more than a year ago, and Dorothy lived in a little two-room apartment in an assisted-living facility. She could open the windows if she felt like it. She did so, and turned on the fans, and checked the cupcakes baking in the oven. There was a cool breeze, no more than a breath. The big magnolia tree in the front lawn made a shade so deep you could be forgiven for thinking evening had come early. She arranged the chairs in the living room for the fifth time and glanced at the clock. Fifteen minutes and they would be here.

   As she was taking the cupcakes out, the phone rang. She nearly dropped the tray. Shaking, she set it on the counter and picked up the phone. It was Kevin.

   "Gramma! Guess where your favorite grandson's calling from?"

   He was cheerful in the faked way he had when he was upset. Which meant—

   "I'm in rehab and this time I'm going to quit for good."

   "Of course, hon," she said. Who could believe the kid when he'd been in and out of rehab six times in two years? She remembered Rob's cold fury the last time the boy had been over. Her grandson was adrift, and she was helpless and useless. The other day she'd watched a show on PBS about early humans and how the human race wouldn't have survived without old people, other people than the parents, to help raise the young and transmit the knowledge of earlier generations. Grandmothers in particular were important. That was all very well, but in this day of books and computers and all, who needed grandmothers? They lived in retirement homes, or in huge, echoing houses, at the periphery of society, distracting themselves, waiting for death. Times had changed. Kevin was beyond anyone's help. She gripped the edge of the counter with her free hand. An ache shot through her chest. She felt a momentary dizziness.

"I'll send you some cupcakes," she said. All she had been able to do for the people she loved was to offer them food, as though the trouble in the world could be taken away by sugar and butter and chocolate. She said good-bye, feeling hopeless.

He had sent her an orange wristlet, rather pretty. It had jewellike white buttons on it that allowed her to communicate with her new notebook computer (a gift from her son) with a touch. She looked at it and thought how nice Kevin was, to get her a present. She touched the button and her notebook computer lit up, and there was an image of a woman in a diving suit suspended in murky blue water, her arms working, and a reedy electronic voice like a cartoon character saying something about cold Arctic waters and repeating a name, Dr. Irene Ariak, Irene Ariak. Surely she had heard the name in some show or other. A scientist working in the Arctic. What a dangerous thing to do, to go up there in the cold and dark. "Bless you and be careful up there, I'm praying for you," she said. The cartoon voice said, *Mrs. Cartwright, thank you!* And the screen went blank. Dorothy wondered if she'd heard right. Well, this was a new world, to be sure.

The doorbell rang as she was setting the cupcakes on a plate. Patting her hair, glancing at the small oval mirror over by the little dining table (her lipstick was just right), she went to the door.

There they all were, smiling. Rita, with her defiantly undyed white hair in a braid tied with rainbow-colored ribbons (Rob would have thought them loud), said, "How nice of you to host the meeting, Dorothy!," and planted herself in the comfortable armchair. The others, Mary-Ann, Gerta, Lawrence, Brad, Eva, and three women she didn't know, crowded into the small living room. Dorothy handed around cupcakes and poured tea and coffee and felt as awkward as a new wife hosting her first dinner party. She scolded herself: *Now, then, you've known these people for eight months, and you've hosted more parties in your life than you can remember!* This was about reinventing herself. Stretching outside her comfort zone, learning new things. Rob would have never allowed these people in their house—there was something not *done* about their passionate intensity. "Aging hippies," Rob would have said. He would have told her what was wrong with each of them, and she would never have invited them again. Once she'd had a local mothers' group over for tea; Rob came home early. He'd been pleasant enough greeting them and had gone upstairs. The women were upset about the firing of the principal at the local elementary school, and one of them had raised her voice emphatically, making her point. Rob had banged the bedroom door so hard upstairs that the reverberation made the windows rattle. She'd never invited those women over again.

She sat down and let the conversation swirl around her, trying to ignore the tightness in her chest. Keeping up the smile was becoming difficult.

"Well," Rita said, "our energy-saving campaign has been successful beyond anything we expected. Management has stopped grumbling. We've saved them $14,504 in energy bills, annually!"

"New lightbulbs and more insulation, and cranking down the AC so it isn't freezing in the middle of summer, and one set of solar panels . . . who'da thought it?"

"Our see-oh-two emissions are down by . . . let's see . . . 18 percent . . ."

"Multiply individual actions by millions or billions, and you're looking at real global difference . . ."

It was one of the new women, a blonde with intense blue eyes. Not from the apartment complex. Dorothy had already forgotten her name. Now the woman was smiling at her a little uncertainly.

"Mrs. Cartwright, we need to recruit people for the protest. The pipeline is coming to us. Janna Helmholtz's land is being *violated*—they got a court order to cut a corridor through her woods to bring the oil pipes through, and we're going to protest. Can we count on you?"

"Yes, yes, of course," Dorothy said, feeling foolish. What had she agreed to?

" . . . they say fracking for shale oil and gas is going to reduce carbon dioxide emissions, but can you believe they base that on completely ignoring the methane emissions from the fracking?"

"Methane is twenty times worse than see-oh-two . . . cooking the planet . . ."

"My objection to fracking is entirely on another plane—see, less coal burned here means coal prices fall, and it gets exported elsewhere, so coal usage will go up somewhere else if fracking happens here in the United States—idiots don't understand the meaning of *global* . . ."

"Yes, but there's also the issue, I told him that, I told him just because you work for Texas O&G, try to have an open mind for fuck's sake—I told him, think about switching to green energy. Fracking for oil and gas just means putting off what we need to do. Like, you know, you need to fucking quit, not go from cocaine to . . . to meth!"

Rob wouldn't approve of the f-word either. Dorothy told herself to stop thinking about Rob. Rob used the f-word as much as he liked, but he couldn't stand women swearing. Generally, he said that meant that either they were common, or they needed a good lay. *Shut up about Rob,* she told herself.

"Well, Mrs. Cartwright?"

She cleared her throat. What had they been talking about?

"I don't know," she said. What could she do? Her life behind her . . . she felt a sudden wave of utter misery.

"What can I do? I'm not trained . . ."

"Dorothy, you don't need training for this," Rita said, in her proselytizing voice. Rita was a You-nitarian, You-niversalist, as Eva had once said in mincing tones—*Rita, there's so much You in UU, where's the room for God?* They'd had quite a spat about it, but they stayed friends. Rob had always said you could only be friends with people who thought like you.

"Honey, there are retired people all over the country like you and me who care about the world we are leaving our grandchildren—"

"—hell, everyone thinks we are old fogies, useless relics, and I say we are a totally untapped resource, a revolution waiting to happen . . ."

Lawrence ("not Larry") nodded. "We have experience, and knowledge of human nature—Dorothy, just by being who you are you can make a difference—"

She found herself signing up to recruit five people and be at the meeting place today in three hours. Janna Helmholtz had called to say the earthmovers were going to be on her property ripping up the trees her granddaddy had planted and she needed them to be there. Three hours! (*Well, the fracking company doesn't wait at our convenience, honey; besides imagine if you were in the middle of the workday, you wouldn't be able to make it. But we have the time and the determination! So be there or be a quadrilateral!* This from Eva, retired math teacher at Pine Tree Elementary.)

After they had all left, Dorothy found herself putting the dirty dishes by the sink in a mood of despair. How was she going to go to wing 5 and recruit five people? She couldn't imagine being able to convince anyone. Talking to people was difficult anyway, especially when they didn't wear their hearing aids or were taking a nap. She heard Rob's voice: *You're being a fool, Dottie. We Cartwrights don't get into other people's business. Do you really think you can make a difference?*

It was hard to remember that she had been second valedictorian at her school, and that she had got into a prestigious college and been on a debating team. After she met Rob—he'd chased and flattered her relentlessly—she had seen the possibility of another life, the kind that she'd only glimpsed through the iron lattice gates of rich acquaintances—a life of going to theater and art museums and raising children to send off to the best schools. Who in the world would love her like Rob? She remembered when they were both young, and he had lost his first job, how much he'd looked up to her, needed her. She began to scrub the baking tray, thinking of Rob's love for her cooking. He'd always praised her culinary skills to his business friends whenever there was a party. She sighed. He would not have been pleased about her involvement with this cause. But she'd given her word— what had made her agree to talk to five strangers? She wiped her sudsy hands absently on the towel, and her wristlet beeped. "I'm no use to anyone," she said aloud. "I don't know what to do." And she heard a voice from the little computer on the mantelpiece say, with the utmost conviction: "Something good will happen to you today." Very clear English, but a strange accent. She went and picked up the computer but the screen had gone dark.

She rearranged her hair and put on fresh lipstick and went determinedly down the hall to wing 5. There were several people in the lounge. She told herself *second valedictorian* and made herself smile and say hello. By the end of an hour she had recruited eight people. Would have been nine, if Molly hadn't had her annual physical that afternoon. *Damn, you're good*, Rita said, when she called and told her, and Dorothy thought, with pleased surprise, *Yes*.

In an hour they were loading into cars, driving over the long, empty roads soon to be filled with rush-hour traffic, over to Janna's place. Janna had a big house on a hundred acres, and there was already a crowd in the middle of a field, and at least half a dozen cars, and my goodness, was that a TV truck? There was Janna, with a new perm and her big smile, waving to the newcomers walking over to her. The sun was hot. Along one side of the field ran a dark line of woodlands, presumably the place where the pipeline was going through. Dorothy walked over determinedly, ignoring the odd breathlessness that caught her at moments, gritting her teeth, closing her ears against Rob's voice. *That woman should never wear shorts, her legs are too*

fat, and that one, dressed like a slut, tells you what she wants. These wannabe hip-
pies are a laugh. Can barely walk and they want to change the world! Well, that bit
was true of some of the protesters, old ladies with walkers and even a man in
a wheelchair. There was Rita, high-fiving him. Dorothy found herself standing at the edge of the crowd, grateful for her hat. There were the earthmovers roaring up in front of them. A young man at the helm of each, one of
them grinning, the other one nervous. The sun glinted off the windshields.

A black woman was making a speech. Eva nudged Dorothy and whispered, "Myra Jackson, professor over at the university."

"It's not just about land," the woman said. "Global warming is real,
and we have to do something about it now, not tomorrow. Shale gas only
puts off what we really need, which is green energy, and a new alternative-
energy-based economy. Germany's already ahead of us in solar energy. We
need a Marshall Plan for the ecological-economic crisis!"

There were cheers.

Now they could hear police sirens getting louder. The protesters began
to shout slogans. Dorothy's heart began to beat thunderously in her ears.
What had she gotten herself into?

There was Janna, yelling above the noise.

"Y'all pack up your equipment and get outta here, we're not gonna let
you clear my family's woods! No more fracking!"

There were signs now going up, and cameras flashing, and people
yelling "Don't frack Texas!," and the big yellow machines kept coming,
although slowly. The professor woman jumped off the table—she was too
young and fit to be one of the oldies—and someone moved the table away.
The cops arrived, waving the protesters to the side so that the machinery could get to the trees. The crowd shifted and surged, without backing
away. The man in the wheelchair waved his stick at a policeman and yelled
something. Handcuffs clicked, cameras rolled. The giant machines kept
inching forward. Dorothy found herself ignored by everyone, even the
cops. She felt the cool air of the woods at her back, through her thin cotton
dress. She was just in front of one of the machines. She stared at the young
man in the driver's seat. He looked like Kevin. She wondered why his face
was set—goodness, the boy was nervous! She thought of him suddenly
as a sacrifice, like all the young men in her life, her son gone to the army,
returned a silent shadow of his former self, her grandson beset by demons,
all that youth and strength turned wrong. She thought of the poor woman

out in the bottom of the ocean in the Arctic trying to save the world so
that her grandchild, Dorothy's grandchild, and all, everyone's grandchild
could live in the world. And she thought how cruel the world that makes
young men hold the guns against their own temples, the knives at their
own throats, so that their own hands poison the earth and its creatures
that the good Lord made—and Rob said in her mind, *Dottie, you're talking
like a fool*—and something broke inside her.

She was standing with a Tupperware box of cupcakes—stupidly, she
waved it in front of the boy like an offering. She walked toward him, her
own face set, as though she could save him, as though she, Dorothy Cartwright, B.A., M.R.S., could do anything. The kid's eyes went wide, and he
waved frantically at her, and she turned around and saw the great yellow
arm of the other machine swing, and the horrified face of the other man,
who saw her only at the last minute—then it hit her shoulder, and the side
of her head, and then she was falling, and cupcakes falling everywhere.

She awoke in the hospital. The light was too bright. Someone drew the
curtains across the window. She could hear some kind of hubbub outside
her door. She slept.

Hours later she woke feeling better. A lantern-jawed doctor who
looked like a very tired Clint Eastwood told her she had a mild concussion,
and a cracked bone in her shoulder. The man at the bulldozer had turned
the thing off just in time; it was the momentum that had gotten her. Otherwise she might be dead. She was really lucky. All the scans were clear,
but they were going to keep her overnight for observation. After that, six
weeks of rest for her shoulder.

"I can see you're a wild young rebel, Mrs. Cartwright, but promise me
you won't be up to those shenanigans for a while," he said, smiling.

She told him, smiling back, surprising herself, "You do your job, I'll
do mine."

Her son called. Matt was driving over the next day. He sounded more
bemused than anything. She thought with satisfaction that she had finally
managed to surprise someone.

And then Molly was there, praising her like she had done something
heroic.

"Wish I could have been there," she said wistfully. "Rita and Eva are in
jail, and that black professor too, and about ten other people. They're probably going to charge you as soon as you are well."

Dorothy couldn't imagine going to jail--but Molly made it sound like it was the thing to do. Well, it had been some day. She decided not to worry. Over the doctor's objections she let two journalists interview her and take pictures. Her mother used to call her a chatterbox, a trait that had disappeared with time and Rob, and now she couldn't stop talking.

'When my husband was still alive," she said, "he used to tell me how impractical it was to worry about the environment. Practical people run the economy, make sure things work. That attitude, combined with greed, has ruined the earth to a degree that threatens our grandchildren. I'm only a housewife, but I know that we need good, fresh air to breathe, and trees to grow, and we need the wild things around us. As a grandmother, I can't think of one single grandparent who wouldn't want to do the best for their grandchildren. That's why I believe we need to protect what the good Lord gave us, this blessed Earth, else how can we live? And what's more practical than that?"

After they had all gone, in the silence of the room, she lay back against the pillows, spent. An incredulity rose in her. What had she done? The whole day she had been putting herself forward, Rob would say. The elation subsided. She hid her face in the pillows.

Then the phone rang. This time it was Kevin.

"Gramma! I saw you on TV! You kicked ass!"

She laughed. It was so very nice of him to call. They talked for half an hour, until the nurse came and frowned at her.

"Gramma, I'm going to get clean this time," Kevin said. Dorothy took a deep breath.

"Kev, soon as they let me out of here I'm going to come see you. This time you *will* get clean, love. You've got a life to live."

And so do I, she thought after she hung up.

Lying back in the darkened room, she saw from the digital clock on the side table that it was nearly midnight on March 16. Heavens, no wonder Rob had been haunting her all day—it was his birthday! And she had forgotten. Well, at least she had baked his favorite cupcakes. She thought about how her life had changed in one day, and the work left to be done. It wasn't going to be easy, and she had no illusions that she was any kind of heroine, or that her few minutes of fame were going to lead to any major changes. But Molly had told her that the phone lines of No Fracking Texas were swamped with calls from other assisted-living facilities and retired people's associations. It seemed the old ones, the forgotten ones, were coming out of the woodwork. In times gone by, the old were the ones to whom the young turned for advice. Now the old had to bear responsibility for ruining the earth, but they also, by the same logic, bore the responsibility for setting things right. The press was calling it the Suspender Revolution. The Retirees Spring. Kind of disrespectful, but they'd show them. And she, Dorothy Cartwright, had helped it come about. *Viva la revolución,* and poor Rob, rest in peace, and Happy Birthday.

The End.
    The Story Begins
    Or does it end here?
    It ends, the young man thinks, as he climbs the last mountain, emerging into the last alpine valley. It ends with his own life winding down as he climbs to the roof of the world. The strength that has allowed him to leave the busy streets of Shanghai and journey to this remote place in the Himalayas is like the sudden flaring of the moth caught in the flame. Lately he's had a vision of simply lying down in the tall green meadow grass, and falling asleep, and feeling the grass stalks growing through his body, a thousand tiny piercings, until he is nothing but a husk.
    He pauses to catch breath against the rocky wall of the cliff. His breath forms clouds of condensation in the cold air. His rucksack feels heavier now. He can't remember when he last ate. Probably at the village he left in the morning. He takes out a flask of water, drinks, and finds a small bag with trail mix and walks again.
    When he emerges from the narrow pass, he finds himself at a vertiginous height. Below him, lost in mist and distance, is a rocky, arid valley through which a silver river winds. On the other side the mountains are gaunt and bare, the white tongues of melting glaciers high on the slopes. But the place he seeks is immediately to his right, where the path leads. The stone facade of the monastery comes into view, a rocky aerie impossible to conceive of—how could anyone build here, halfway up to the sky?—but it is solid, it is there. So he walks on, up the narrow path, to the great flight of steps. The tiers of windows above him are empty, and there is an enormous hole in the roof of the entrance hall, through which he can see a lammergeier circling high in the blue sky. Could it be that the last refuge is destroyed after all? He had dreamed of a great university hidden deep in

the Himalayas, a place where people like him could gather to weave the web that would save the dying world. He had dreamed of its destruction too, at the hands of greed and power. Can it have happened already?

Wearily he sinks down on the dusty floor at the top of the steps. In the silence he hears his own breath coming fast, and the faint trickle of water in the distance. He is conscious of being watched.

A man is standing on a fallen column. He is tall, dressed in rough black robes. There is some kind of small animal on his shoulder, brown, with a long, bushy tail—a squirrel, perhaps, or a mongoose?

Yuan bows, clears his throat.

"I dreamed of this place," he says in English, hoping the monk can understand him. "I came here to try to do something before I die. But it's too late, I see."

The monk gestures to him, and Yuan stumbles over broken pieces of stone, follows him around a corner into a small, high courtyard open to sun and sky.

"Sit," the monk says, indicating a low wooden seat. There is tea in a black kettle, steaming over a small fire. "Tell me about your dream of this place." There is white stubble on his shaven chin, and deep lines are etched on the brown face. His English is fluent, with an accent that is vaguely familiar. Yuan clears his throat, speaks.

"It was a monastery first, then a university. It was a place for those who sought to understand the world in a new way, and to bring about its resurrection. I saw the humblest people come here to share what they knew, and the learned ones listened. It didn't have the quietude of the monastery it had once been—at every corner, in every gathering, I heard arguments and disagreements, but true peace is dynamic, not static, and rests on a thousand quarrels.

"It wasn't a secret, although not many people knew about it. It was rumor and it was real, because at the university where I studied in Shanghai, there was a woman—a scientist from Nigeria—who spoke of this place. She came and taught for five days and nights. After that we were all changed. I got a new idea, and even though I was dying, I made sure it came to light. Then I thought I needed to find her, my teacher, and this place. Here and there I heard rumors that it had been destroyed—because there are people who will try to hasten the end of the world so they can make a profit. And this place stood in their way.

"It was the hope of the world. I heard that there were branches in a few other places. There was an idea about connecting it through small world architecture to webs of information, webs of knowledge and people, to generate new ideas and, through redundancy, ensure their survival. If it hadn't been destroyed before that hope was made real, its disappearance may not have mattered so much."

His voice fades, as he slumps to the ground. The monk gathers him up and carries him effortlessly through long corridors into a room of stone, where there is a rough bed. He wakes from his faint to see the wild creature sitting on a wooden stool by the bed, staring at him with dark, round eyes. The monk helps him up so he can sip hot yak butter tea, rich and aromatic. Then Yuan sleeps.

Over five days and nights they talk, the monk and Yuan, sometimes in this room with its narrow windows, sometimes in the high, sunny courtyard.

"This place was destroyed in an avalanche," the monk tells him, pointing to the mountain behind them, from the high spur on which the monastery perches. "The glacier melted and brought down half the mountain with it. It rained boulders. Many were killed, and the place abandoned. I live here alone, except for the odd scientific team that comes to study the glacier."

Yuan is silent. *So much for the university that would save the world.* But how could his dreams be so vivid, if they weren't true?

When he feels a little better, Yuan goes with the monk to a high terrace from which he has the best view of the glacier. The terrace is broken in places—holes have been torn out of it, and the room below is littered with massive stones. The still-intact portions of the floor make a zigzag safe pathway across the terrace.

The terrace is open to wind and sun, and the immensity of the mountain overwhelms him for a moment. Squinting, he looks up at it and nearly loses his balance. The monk steadies him.

Far above them, what remains of the glacier is a bowl of snow above sheer rocky walls. A great, round boulder bigger than a house stands guard at the edge of the bowl, rimmed with white.

"Don't worry," the monk says. "If that falls, it will fall right here and finish off this terrace, and what's left of the western wing. The part of the monastery where we sleep is not going to be affected—see that ridge?"

Yuan sees a ridge of rock high above and to his right, rising out of the steep incline of the mountain. A fusillade of snow, ice, and boulders falling down the slope would be deflected by it just enough to avoid the eastern edge of the monastery, which is why it is still intact.

Yuan begins to shake. The monk guides him silently across the broken floor, and they return to the room. He sinks onto the bed.

"Why do you remain in this terrible place?" he cries.

The monk brings him tea.

"Thirty-three died in the avalanche," he says, "my teacher among them. So I stay here. The others left to join another monastery."

Yuan is thinking how this does not answer his question. He is beginning to wonder about this monk and his excellent English. After a pause the monk says:

"Tell me about yourself. You said you came up with an idea."

Yuan rummages in his rucksack, which is at the foot of the bed. He draws out a handful of orange wristlets. Each has a tiny screen on it, and some are encrusted with cheap gems.

"I am a student of computer engineering," he says. "In my university in Shanghai I was working toward some interesting ideas in network communications. Then she came—Dr. Amina Ismail, my teacher—and changed everything I knew about the world.

"Most of us think there is nothing we can do about climate disruption. So we live an elaborate game of denial and pretend—as though nothing was about to happen, even though every day there are more reports of impending disaster, and more species extinctions, and more and more climate refugees. But what I learned from my teacher was that the world is an interconnected web of relationships—between human and human, and human and beast and plant, and all that's living and nonliving. I used to feel alone in the world after my parents died, even when I was with friends or with my girlfriend, but my teacher said that aloneness is an illusion created by modern urban culture. She said that even knowledge had been carved up and divided into territorial niches with walls separating them, strengthening the illusion, giving rise to overspecialized experts who can't understand each other. It is time for the walls to come down and for us to learn how to study the complexity of the world in a new way. She had been a computer scientist, but she taught herself biology and sociology so she could understand the great generalities that underlie the different systems of the world."

"She sounds like a philosopher," the monk says.

"They used to call scientists natural philosophers once," Yuan says. "But anyway, I learned from her that whether we know it or not, the world and we are interconnected. As a result, human social systems have chaotic features, rather like weather. You know Lorenz's metaphor—the butterfly effect?"

"I've heard of it," says the monk.

Yuan pauses.

"She said—Dr. Ismail—that we may not be able to prevent climate change because we've not acted in time—but perhaps we can prevent *catastrophic* climate change, so that in our grandchildren's future—my teacher has two grandchildren—in that future maybe things will start turning around. Maybe the human species won't go extinct.

"So one day I was walking through the streets, very upset because my girlfriend and I had just broken up, and I didn't look where I was going. I got hit by a motor scooter. The man who was driving it yelled at me. I wasn't seriously hurt—mostly bruises and a few cuts—but he didn't even stop to ask and went on his way. I dragged myself to the curb. People kept walking around me as though I was nothing but an obstacle. I thought— why should I go on with my life? Then a man came out of a shop. He bent over me, helped me to my feet. In his shop he attended to my cuts, and he gave me hot noodle soup and wouldn't let me pay. I stayed there until I was well enough to go home.

"That incident turned me away from my dark thoughts. I realized that although friends and family are crucial, sometimes the kindness of a stranger can change our lives.

"So I came up with this device that you wear around your wrist, and it can gauge your emotional level and your mood through your skin. It can also connect you, via your genie, to your computer or mobile device, specifically through software I designed."

He sighed.

"I designed it at first as a cure for loneliness. I had to invent a theory of loneliness, with measures and quantifiers. I had to invent a theory of empathy. The software enables your genie to search the Internet for people who have similar values of certain parameters . . . and it gauges security and safety as well. When you most need it, based on your emotional profile at the time, the software will link you at random to someone in your circle."

"Does it work?" said the monk.

"It's very buggy," Yuan says. "There are people working on it to make it better. The optimal network architecture isn't in place yet. My dream is that one day it can help us raise our consciousness beyond family and friend, neighborhood and religion, city and country. Throughout my journey I've been giving it away to people. In every town and village."

He taps the plain orange wristlet on his left arm.

"I'm connected right now to seven other people, seven strangers. The connection is poor, but sometimes I hear their voices or see them on my notebook screen. On the way here I stopped at a grassy meadow crisscrossed by streams, a very beautiful place. The reception must have been good because all at once I saw an old woman on my computer screen. She was standing at a kitchen counter feeling like she had nothing to give to the world. Helpless, useless, because she was old. So I told her—I didn't know what to tell her because I felt her pain—but finally I told her something clichéd, like a fortune from a fortune cookie. I said, 'Something good will happen to you today.' I don't know if that turned out to be true. I don't even know who she is, only that she's from another country and culture and religion, and I felt her pain like it was my own."

The monk listens very carefully, leaning forward. The little creature has gone to sleep on his lap.

"Perhaps you suffer from an excess of empathy," he says.

"Is that a bad thing? I suppose it must be, because of how I've ended up. As you grow up you are supposed to get stronger and harder, and wiser too. But I seem to be less and less able to bear suffering—especially the suffering of innocents. I saw a photo of a dead child in a trash heap, I don't know where. The family was part of a wave of refugees, and the locals didn't want them there. There was violence. But what could these people do? Their homeland had been flooded by the sea. They were poor.

"I once saw a picture of a dead polar bear in the Arctic. It had died of starvation. It was just skin and bone, and quite young. The seals on which it depended for food had left because the ice was gone.

"There are people who don't care about dead polar bears, or even dead children in trash heaps. They don't see how our fates are linked. Everything is connected. To know that truth, however, is to suffer. Each time there is the death of innocents, I die a little myself."

"Is that why you are so sick?" the monk says harshly. "What good will it do you to take upon yourself the misery of the world? Do you fancy yourself a Buddha, or a Jesus?"

Yuan is startled. He shakes his head.

"I've no such fancies. I'm not even religious. I'm only trying to learn what my teacher called the true knowledge that teaches us how things are linked. My sickness has nothing to do with all this. The doctors can't diagnose it—low-grade fever, systemic inflammation, weight loss—all I know is that no treatment has worked. I am dying."

The monk walks out of the room.

Yuan sits up weakly, finds the cooling yak butter tea by the bedside, and takes a sip. He is bewildered. Why is the monk so upset?

Later the monk returns.

"Since the third day you came here," he says, "you haven't had a fever. Once your strength returns, you should go back, down into the world. You have things to do there."

Yuan is incredulous.

"Even if what you say is true," he says after a while, with some bitterness, "how can I trust myself? My vision of this place—remember? The university I dreamed of—the hope of the world. My reason to keep going. It was all false."

"Maybe it was a vision of the future," the monk says gently. "After all, your teacher was real. If she mentioned this place to you, then that must mean that others are dreaming the same dream. Go back down. Do your work. This malady, I think it is nothing but what everyone down there has. Most of the time they don't even know it."

He gestures savagely toward the world below and falls silent.

Yuan has not allowed himself to feel hope for so long that at first he doesn't recognize the feeling. But it rises within him, an effervescence. He looks at the monk's averted face, the way the animal on his shoulder nestles down.

"If I am cured, then you have saved my life. You took me in and nursed me back to health. The kindness of strangers. I am twice blessed."

The monk shakes his head. He goes out of the room to attend to their next meal.

As Yuan's condition improves, he begins to explore the ruined monastery. There are rooms and rooms in the east wing that are still intact. The meltwater from the avalanche has filled the lower chambers of the west wing. In that dark lake there are splashes of sunlight under the holes in the roof.

"We got all the bodies out," the monk says.

Then one afternoon, when he is exhausted from exploring and has taken to his bed, Yuan is woken by the monk's little pet. The animal is scrabbling frantically at Yuan's shoulder, whimpering. Sitting up, Yuan looks around for the monk, but there is no sign of him. There is a great, deep rumble that appears to come from the earth itself.

At first Yuan thinks there is an earthquake, because the mountain is shaking. Then he realizes what it is. He rushes out of the room, conscious of the little creature's scampering feet on the stone floor behind him. He runs up the stone stairway to the broken terrace that lies directly in the glacier's path.

The monk is standing on the terrace, gazing upward, his black robes billowing behind him. The enormous boulder that was poised at the lip of the glacier has loosened and is thundering down the mountainside, gathering snow and rocks with it.

"What are you doing?" Yuan yells, grabbing the man. "Get away from here—you'll be killed!"

He grabs the man's robe near the throat, shakes him. The monk's eyes are wild. With great difficulty Yuan pulls him across the shaking, broken terrace floor, toward the stairs.

"You die here, I die here too!" he yells.

At last they are half falling down the steps, running down the broken corridors, over to the east wing. When they get to the terrace, there is a sound like an explosion, and the ground shakes. It seems to Yuan that the whole monastery is going to go down, but after what seems like a long, endless moment, the shaking stops. They look around and see that the east wing is still standing. The small creature leaps up the monk's robe and trembles on his shoulder. The monk caresses it.

There are tears in his eyes, making tracks down the lined face. Yuan sits him down on the low wooden seat. The kettle has fallen over. He brings water from the great stone jar, pours some into the kettle, gets the fire going.

When the first cup of tea has been made and drunk, when the monk has stopped shaking, he starts to speak:

"I'm not a monk. I'm only the caretaker. They took me in when I came in as sick as you, but where the world made you feel like you would die of grief, it made me burn with anger. I was a city man, living what I thought was the only way to live, the good life. Then some things happened and my life unraveled. I lost everything, everyone. I ran away up here so that I wouldn't hear the voices in my head. I was full of anger and pain. My sickness would have killed me if the monks hadn't calmed it, slowed me down. Instead thirty-three of them died when the avalanche came—my teacher among them. And I lived."

"So you were waiting for that last rock to come down," Yuan says slowly, "so you'd have your death."

The man starts to say something, but his eyes fill with tears, and he wipes them with the back of his hand. The creature on his shoulder chitters in agitation.

"Your little animal needs you to live," Yuan says. "He came and called me. That is why you are alive."

The man is holding the animal against his cheek as the tears flow.

"Life is a gift," Yuan says. "You gave me mine, I gave you yours. That means we are bound by a mutual debt, the kind you can't cancel out. Come back with me when I return."

Several days later, much recovered, Yuan made his way back the way he had come. His companion had decided to stay in the village nearest the monastery. Here, under a sky studded with stars, Yuan heard the man's story. Yuan left with him an orange wristlet, even though the satellite connection was intermittent here. When they parted, it was with the expectation of meeting again.

"In the future that you dreamed of," said his friend. "Don't be too long!"

"I'll be back before you know it," Yuan said.

After he had passed through the high mountain desert, Yuan descended into the broad alpine meadow. He lay down in the deep, rich grass and felt his weight, the gentle tug of gravity tethering him to the earth. Around him the streams sang in their watery dialect. Sleep came to him then, and dreams, but they weren't about death. His wristlet pinged, and he woke up. He must be back in satellite range. He heard, faintly, music, and the sound of a celebration. A woman's voice spoke to him, a young voice, excited. Two words.

"**. . . A BUTTERFLY . . .**"

STORY NOTES—Vandana Singh

I am indebted to the following researchers for their willingness to spare a considerable amount of time to share their expertise: At Arizona State University: Dr. Hilairy Hartnett, ecosystems biogeochemist, for fascinating conversations on remote diving in polar seas, methane outgassing and methanotrophs; Dr. Ariel Anbar, geochemist and astrobiologist, for discussions on geo-tweaking versus geo-engineering and the possibility of trips to Enceladus; Netra Chhetri, geographer, for insights on local community action in Nepal with regard to climate change; Zhihua Wang, engineer, for invaluable information on the Urban Heat Island effect and multiple resources; and Michael Barton, anthropologist, for useful conversations on how social change occurs.

I'm also immensely grateful to these researchers outside ASU: Dr. Shari Gearheard, research scientist at the National Snow and Ice Data Center, for crucial information on Baffin Island and Inuit culture; and Dr. Henry Huntington, anthropologist with the Pew Charitable Trust, for discussions on the impact of climate change on indigenous people in Alaska as well as local action and participation in scientific data collection. I also thank scientists from Los Alamos, the Carnegie Institution for Science, Woods Hole Oceanographic Institution, and Stanford University for sharing their expertise on climate change, deep sea diving, and high-albedo materials.

FORUM DISCUSSION—Biomimicry and Eco-Friendly 3-D Printing

Read Vandana Singh's post about biomimicry and eco-friendly 3-D printing at hieroglyph.asu.edu/entanglement.

FORUM DISCUSSION—Methane Burps in the Arctic and Climate Change

Vandana Singh, Gregory Benford, and other Hieroglyph community members consider the risk of "methane burps" caused by warming oceans at hieroglyph.asu.edu/entanglement.

RESPONSE TO "ENTANGLEMENT"—Christian Etter

Designer Christian Etter responds to "Entanglement" and discusses how technology can help make people aware of the global consequences of their actions at hieroglyph.asu.edu/entanglement.

ELEPHANT ANGELS
Brenda Cooper

© 2013, Haylee Bolinger / ASU

FRANCINE CRACKED OPEN HER window, filling her tiny apartment with damp cold that slapped her cheeks and helped her blink awake. She smelled coffee from the breakfast food-truck below and breathed in the slightest hint of Puget Sound salt. People scurried through the bare gray of early morning, fleece coats pulled tight around them, gloved hands clutching purses and briefcases.

She watched until she spotted her granddaughter's face, brown and round, with dark eyes and a long fall of black hair that ended just above bright yellow sweats.

A few minutes later, Araceli herself burst through the door wearing her smile of hiding. She produced a small cloth bag from behind her back. "I brought you something."

"And how are you?" Francine took the bag and fumbled it open. She pulled out a sky-blue shirt with a photo of an elephant on it. She stared, awed. It signified an approval she hadn't expected.

"You're one of us, now. They took your application." Araceli practically jumped up and down with excitement, a bounciness reserved for excited nineteen-year-old girls. She had helped Francine fill out forms online and spent hours teaching her how to be elsewhere, had run her through all the training simulations and tests before Francine took the real test.

The elephant on the shirt was a savanna matriarch, which Francine wouldn't have known a month earlier. The words ELEPHANT ANGEL had been hand-embroidered along the hem of the right sleeve.

"Try it on."

Francine went into her bedroom and pulled on the shirt, which fit her far better than she deserved. It looked good.

She found Araceli in the kitchen, stirring the special tea into a hotcup. She looked up and smiled. "Now. Your first shift is now."

"Really?" Francine's mouth dried and she felt dizzy.

"Drink your tea."

Francine took the cup to her easy chair and sat down. Araceli had mounted tiny speakers around the headrest, since earbuds tickled Francine's hearing aids. A small table held her teacup, her VR glasses, a pad of paper, and a blue pen.

Araceli perched on an old love seat across the room, her long legs draped over the arms and her flimsy open and glowing on her lap as the screen powered up. Araceli would see what Francine saw and hear what she heard, but would have no control. It would be in 2-D, like a movie. Part of the training had put Francine in that position, the watcher of the watcher, and it reminded her of the days when movies were flat.

After the first few sips, the bitter tea began to brighten Francine's senses, accentuating the tickle of the slender wires that rode her jaw and hooked behind her ears.

The last step was to drop her glasses down in front of her face and sip the dregs of the tea.

"Hello," a human voice whispered. "All clear."

"Thank you." The other pilot winked away as soon as the exchange ended, the transition instant so that the two pilots wouldn't crash in moments of confusion. As she'd been taught, she left well enough alone for a breath, trusting the expertise of the person she replaced to have left the craft on a stable trajectory.

The hot summer sun beat down, as if Africa kissed the Northwest.

Cicadas. Always the first thing she noticed, the sound so foreign to Seattle and so embedded in Africa. Wind sighed through trees, barely louder than the swish of the elephant's feet through grass. She had entered close-in, her view almost that of the mahout. She snapped her fingers wide and flat and drove her hands up, telling the tiny machine half a world away to rise.

Flying delighted Francine. It was as simple as the video games she'd grown up with, where her movements told cartoon characters on the screen what to do.

The tiny drone gained height.

The matriarch marched in front of a family group of six—four females and two calves, one about two years old and the other one younger. Only the matriarch hosted a rider, long limbed and dark skinned and almost naked, swaying with the elephant's steps. The girl had a slender waist, long legs, and barely formed round breasts. She wore long feathered earrings and looked as relaxed as if she sat in a beach chair instead of on an animal big enough to crush her with a single step.

Francine did her job and spun the drone 360 degrees. This gave her a slightly jerky view in all directions. Far off, a herd of giraffe walked with awkward grace. A kite wheeled through a dusty blue and cloudless sky. Nothing else obvious moved except for the elephants, although there were enough trees to hide all manner of birds, buzzing insects, and sleeping prey.

© 2013, Haylee Bolinger / ASU

Other Angels watched the satsites and evaluated data flowing from swarms of sensors as thick as the cicadas. Francine watched for the glint of sun on metal and listened for conversation or the interrupted call of any wild thing.

The elephants meandered. Twice they worked together to push over acacia trees and nibble at the tender, sweet tops. The rider stayed on the matriarch easily even as the big beast bent into the trees and strained. Even though Francine could hear and see the savanna, the only feeling she had was the sense of movement that came from the drone's feed, sort of a vague up and down and sideways that felt like an echo in her bones, and a very slight sickness in her middle.

These were her elephants. Would be her elephants. This was so frightening that Francine shivered briefly. She had not been responsible for anything outside of herself for at least twenty years. Or jointly responsible, she reminded herself. Each herd had help on the ground, in the air, and remotely. A universe of Elephant Angels.

She hovered above the girl's right shoulder, just behind the dangling feathers that touched her deep brown shoulders. Francine remembered the feel of skin that supple, remembered having joints that flexed and moved easily.

The matriarch watched the next biggest elephant lean forward and push against a tree almost as wide across as her wide, wide leg.

It exploded.

Not the tree itself, she realized. The ground around it.

It took a moment to recognize an attack. A rare thing, but the reason she flew a drone in Africa.

The drone sped away, up and back, a reaction to Francine's unintended jerks of surprise. The elephants' images grew small as the drone receded. Smoke from the explosion created a thin smudged line of white and black that rode the wind. Francine twisted her right hand and lifted her left, overcorrecting so that her cameras pointed at the sky and the ground and the far horizon in the wrong direction. She took a deep breath, and then tried again twice before the drone cameras yielded her the elephants.

The matriarch's head swung back and forth, her wide ears flapping. She held her tail out away from her body. Her shoulders twitched.

Her rider clung to the neck strap.

The wounded elephant lay on her side, trunk writhing, the skin on her chest and front legs peeled away as if she has been flayed with giant knives. Pink flesh glistened in the cuts.

Francine realized she had been hearing squeals and trumpets, had failed to pay attention to sounds with the sight below her so awful and the drone barely under control.

She flew close to the fallen elephant, who struggled to stand, failing.

Messages blossomed across Francine's glasses, and voices chattered with one another in her ears.

The elephants trumpeted again, the matriarch the loudest.

Pain. It was a sound of pain.

Or anger.

Francine felt what she heard in the animals' voices, anger and dismay and the sharp shock of going from a placid afternoon to death.

Thinking was hard. This was nothing like the simulated attack from training, which had been a man with a gun and a jeep she had been able to see coming. She tried to ignore the chaos for a moment, to let her brain breathe and review.

Poachers would know their trap had sprung.

The elephants were in mortal danger. She had been taught they would want to stay with the injured.

One of the babies approached the elephant on the ground, touched her with its trunk. Probably *her* baby. It made Francine want to cry or scream or both.

She sent her drone up high, spotted the dust blossoms of at least three vehicles.

The mahout struggled atop the matriarch, holding on to an ear with one hand and twisting to stay in the saddle as the elephant screamed a complexity of emotions.

Francine took the drone as close as she dared, using the smallest of movements so as not to startle anything or anyone. It took three tries before she got close enough to whisper, "Wasps," into the girl's right ear.

The girl turned and nodded, dark eyes wide. Francine flew higher and watched the rider touch a button on her belt. A swarm of autonomous drones the size of fingernails spread out behind the girl. The drones created sounds too low for humans to hear and harried the elephant.

Her rider hunkered down.

The matriarch trumpeted, stamped her feet, swayed, and stamped again.

Francine fretted.

The elephant began to lope. When the others—even the calves—caught up, she sped up.

Francine remembered her training and began to rotate the drone in all directions, watching the plumes of dust resolve into dusty jeeps. She recorded who came, and watched, still and horrified, as five men in shimmering active camouflage severed the elephant's wide trunk near her eyes and used carbon saws and chains to force the long, curved tusks free of the flesh.

She witnessed the moment the life left the elephant's eyes and was skewered by it.

Three more plumes of smoke appeared. A fourth. Angels, the drone indicated. They would already have her recordings.

She could go.

Francine hovered for a moment, torn. She wanted to know what happened next, but every delay opened more distance between her and her herd. Still, she hesitated. Would the poachers get away? Would there be a fight?

The world exploded.

A lens of one camera remained intact and fed her glasses, tumbling fast through blue on blue sky to green grass and resting near the bloody gray body. Francine had barely registered the new point of view, barely comprehended that she had been shot from the sky, when the last of whatever powered the camera flashed away.

Araceli lifted the glasses from Francine's head and turned them off.

Francine blinked away the silent dark of the drone's death and stared at her granddaughter. Tears fell down her cheeks. Araceli had seen what she saw. Francine's hand shook as she extended it and took her granddaughter's more slender hand in hers. "I lost my herd."

Araceli nodded. "Fucking poachers," she said.

"Don't use that word with me."

"Even now?" Araceli grimaced and wiped Francine's cheeks dry. "Let's get you some food."

Francine had been immersed in late afternoon, in summer. It shocked her to return to a winter morning. She shivered and pulled her blanket closer. She had failed her herd, failed in her new job.

Lost a drone.

Francine's body demanded attention, shaking softly with sorrow and postadrenaline crash.

Her granddaughter brought her oatmeal and half a slice of toast. The warmth infused Francine so she felt strong enough to ask, "What happens now?"

Araceli glanced at the lights on the body monitor Francine wore on her wrist. She was more adept at reading them instantly than Francine, and she said, "You rest. I'll stay with you today. You have another shift tomorrow."

"I need to know about the poachers. Did they catch them? What about the little mahout?"

Araceli nodded. "I'll find out while you rest."

"I want to know now."

Araceli obliged her by looking through the Elephant Angels webmesh until she found information. "The other elephants are safe. There is a fresh observation drone flying in now. They caught one poacher but not the others. There's a watch for the ivory through all local ports."

MAKENA TURNED ONTO HER belly and slithered down behind Delba's ear, clutching the neck rope until she could push off and scissor out away from her charge's huge side. She landed lightly on the calloused balls of her feet and regarded the herd. Delba seemed undecided. The matriarch stared back the way they had come. If a look could undo the past, hers would. Then she turned toward the calves, let out a long, low rumble, and trundled into the watering hole Makena had led them to. The other two adults waited for the calves and then followed.

Makena turned into the grasslands to find a place to pee while there was no drone to record it. There would still be watchers via satellite, but she would be small to them. She had insisted on seeing what the Elephant Angel watchers saw after she took the job and passed her six months' probation. Mostly they saw things in big pictures, on maps with moving dots that identified various individual animals. They saw weather and monitored the location of safari tourists from a distance. The drone was the only constant nag on her own privacy. She hated it even though it had saved her and the elephants at least three times.

A new person flew the drone today. She had been told that at the start of her shift. The pilot hadn't been clever enough to give a warning, although she *had* reminded Makena to loose the wasps.

She shouldn't have panicked. She stepped over the bones of a rhinoceros, long since picked clean, and looked back at the herd. The adults' trunks roamed the calves' sides.

Makena did not remember explosives ever being buried so close to trees. The area had looked normal and smelled good to Flower, which didn't seem right. Elephants could smell storms a day ahead.

The poachers had been clever.

She returned to the water and washed her body and her face carefully and slowly in the watering hole. The water barely felt cleansing.

Luis's voice in her ear. "Makena?"

"Catch them."

"I will. Are you okay?"

"After you catch these people, I will be fine," she told him.

"I'm sorry this happened."

"Stop talking to me and catch the poachers."

He broke off. Good. She didn't want to talk to anybody, not even handsome Angels from foreign lands. Not even sexy Angels, maybe especially not those.

Usually the watering hole was a happy place where the herd played and relaxed. Not this afternoon. They had run far, and their movements were as slow and unhappy as Makena's own.

They mourned.

Flower was dead. Makena had hated the name, bestowed by some fat American a decade ago. Donors bid big money to name African elephants, and in her few bitter moments, Makena supposed she was lucky none of them had paid to name *her*.

She had not hated Flower herself. Only her name. Flower had been strong and willing, and good at looking out for the babies.

Makena walked out into the water and stroked Bee's back. Flower's small son had nearly stopped nursing. He might live even after losing his dam. If he didn't die of a broken heart. She slopped water over his leathery skin and found herself crying. She had not cried since her mother died of AIDS a year ago, and the tears surprised her and then overtook her, so that she leaned on Bee with half of her weight and spilled her tears over his back.

He curled his trunk and touched her shoulder softly with the tip.

Before they came out of the water, Makena climbed back onto Delba's back and shimmied to her spot on the elephant's neck, her legs spread wide behind Delba's huge ears. She signaled the matriarch forward. Delba led the little band out of water and toward the closest stand of acacias.

Cicadas hummed and birds called back and forth to each other in the not-yet-cooling afternoon.

Makena used her wrist-phone to call Saad. "Be careful," she told him. "'The elephants are restless and there is one less. Flower was killed." She told him the rest of it, and he asked her if she had a video and she told him no, even though she was sure she could find one if he wanted it. She did not want to see it again. "You are bloodthirsty," she said.

"No," he said. "But I am sorry."

Mollified, she settled into worrying about whether or not it would be safe for him to come.

The slanted early-evening sun had started to edge the savanna's grasses and trees with gold. Flower would not see another sunset, and so Makena found it hard to drink in the normal peace of this last moment before the evening hunting started.

The sun hung just barely above the horizon when Makena's little brother sent her a message. "I am near."

She chewed her lower lip, watching the way the elephants walked and held their ears and trunks and how close they were to one another. She had no wasps left, but Delba was under as much control as the matriarch ever granted her. Generally, Delba did Makena's bidding, but she never gave up veto power. She seemed docile enough now. "Okay," she said. "Come out."

Saad stood where the herd could see him and where the wind would bring his scent to them.

Makena stopped Delba and waited until she was sure the elephant saw her little brother, now only a head shorter than her, but still clothed in the slenderness of boyhood. She helped him climb up onto Delba's back and seat himself right behind her. He handed her a bag of antelope jerky. "Poaching?" she asked him.

"Harry Paulson is."

She grunted but took the meat, which was tough and salty and tasted like heaven.

"I am an Angel," he teased her.

"Not yet."

"I will be."

"Maybe." Saad had been accepted as a courier for the Angels, allowed to bring Makena parts or supplies from time to time. He wasn't supposed to ride, or even touch, the elephants, but they took advantage of any times the drone wasn't around. "If you are taking jerky from poachers, how do I know you won't succumb to bribes for ivory?"

"I will not."

"You should stop talking to any poachers about anything."

"You are eating the jerky."

She wished she hadn't taken it, but it tasted fabulous.

"I will ride elephants when you go to the city."

"Maybe."

He stuck his lower lip out and she laughed softly at him. "I love you, little brother. When I have earned enough to go to Pretoria, I will tell them you should take my place. But that will not be until you are older. I'll have to wait."

"You can do that for me. Then you can be my Angel, too."

"I am already your Angel," she said.

"Truth, that."

Much later, Makena and her grandfather sat on their wooden veran-dah. The dusky time of hunting animals had passed, and the evening quiet had settled around their small house. Her grandfather had raised her and had taught her of elephants and zebras and lions and hyenas and white rhi-noceros. He had been a ranger at Dzanga-Ndoki before he retired, and she hoped he would understand more than Saad had. "They took an elephant from me today," she told him. "I have never lost one."

The faint and flickering light of a low lantern illuminated deep wrin-kles around his dark eyes. "Tell me."

She did.

"You are lucky *Delba* did not step on the IED. You might have lost the most important elephant."

His way of saying she could have been hurt herself. "I failed. It's unthinkable to lose even one."

"I lost a whole herd once. We let a monster storm drive us all inside, and the poachers were not so afraid of floods as we were. Rain and wind kept us inside for a day and a half. The tractor flooded and wouldn't start. We had to patrol on foot the next day. I found seven dead elephants. Two of their babies died over the next two weeks. We were only able to save the oldest." He sighed and stared off into space for a moment, as if he could still see the dead elephants. "All that because we did not want to be wet."

She spoke softly. "How were they killed?"

"Elephant guns. In my day we fought poachers with guns, not eyes and websites and satellites. They don't even give you a gun."

"I know." He had encouraged her to take his, but she had told him no. She would be fired if she were caught with a personal weapon.

He sipped his nightcap, a mix of tea and brandy that smelled so sour it made Makena's stomach light. "There are twice as many elephants now. Maybe more." He smiled at her. "There is more land for them, and more of them. There is progress."

"I know." She drank her water. "I still feel sad."

"Look up," he told her.

"Why?" But she did, and drank in the deepness of stars overhead, like a carpet of pinpricks in the nearly moonless night.

"My grandmother lived in the first bush, the wild bush. She told me that when an elephant dies, a star falls. Perhaps if we watch, we will see Flower's star."

Makena wrapped her arms around her knees and kept staring upward. The sky looked close enough to touch even through the mosquito nets. "What would your grandmother say if she knew the wildest elephants were ridden every day?"

"As long as she knew you were doing it she would be pleased."

"You're lying," Makena said.

He stood up and kissed her forehead with his cool, thin lips. "She would be proud that you are caring for the family. Are you coming to bed?"

"Not until I see Flower's star."

SAAD SMELLED OF ELEPHANTS. He lay on his bed and watched a Chinese professor with passable English stalk the stage, back and forth, using expressive hands to illustrate the economy of the commons. The class itself was *in* the commons and he could pay a little bit and take a test if he wanted the credit. An Oxford class. He expected to get an A even though he was only thirteen and living in resettled Africa. The commons was easier for him to understand than international trade or the physics of space elevators.

His sister, Makena, made a living sufficient for all three of them, riding a beast that had become the apex herbivore of the most famous commons of all: the wilds. The same commons had been stolen from his people long ago, and now it was a different place. Still, he almost expected Makena to show up in Professor Jiang's presentation.

Maybe he should send the man a picture of his sister.

He didn't. He took careful notes in longhand. When the class ended, he placed the paper in his lockable drawer and put the key on a string around his neck.

He'd learned to do classes with paper notes, to stay away from his gaming devices and just focus. For some classes, he locked his bedroom door and locked all of his extra machines on the far side of the door. That way, he'd have to take an extra step and that would make him stop and remember how much the classes mattered.

He wasn't allowed to ask the professor questions since he wasn't formally enrolled, but he wrote down the questions he wanted answered.

He retrieved his phone and opened a chat window. He called up an Angel Makena had connected him up with as a tutor, Luis Castanova. Luis had led him to these classes.

Luis lived and breathed international data and data synthesis, and Saad had never failed to find him online. "Luis," he typed. "Ask why the commons was so hard to sell into the middle of America."

Luis typed back. "Because commons had no value in a greedy, capitalistic society. How about if I ask why they're gaining in value?"

"Okay." Saad stared out the window, and then typed, "If the commons are gaining value, does that mean Makena gets a raise?"

"It means more people get hired."

"We lost Flower today."

"We all know," Luis responded. "I'm chasing her ivories."

"What?"

"I'll show you. We'll go together and you can be my witness."

Saad pushed the right buttons to slave part of his computer to Luis's and open a verbal window as well. Luis's image showed up on his screen. He looked as Hispanic as his name suggested, with wide lips, an easy smile, and long dark hair. Slight. Saad was pretty sure Makena had a crush on him, but his sister was too imperious to say anything when Saad asked.

Luis stared at something so intently it looked like he might fall into his screen, but then he noticed the completed connection and smiled.

"Take me away," Saad said.

"Okay. We're going to Cotonou. I'm looking for a ship there."

Saad pursed his lips. "Twelve hours since Flower died. Would the ivory have gotten there so fast?"

A map flashed up on the screen. A red X showed the place Flower had died, maybe twenty miles from Saad and Makena's grandfather's house. Luis's thick Spanish accent forced Saad to turn up the volume and stay as still as possible. "The drone pilot got footage of the three jeeps, but they shot the drone down before we could tell which one they put the ivory in. We caught one, and it didn't have the ivory. The other two went in almost opposite directions, one south and one west."

"Did they split the ivory up?" Saad asked.

"The jeeps were stealthed moments after Flower died. We could see where they went as long as they made dust, but no details. They disappeared completely once they hit pavement. We couldn't even tell how many people were in them.

"So both jeeps ended up in towns. They stopped in a few places and could have transferred the cargo almost anywhere out of sight. Or maybe they wrapped it up in invisible cloth . . . I don't know. No one reported any ivory and none of our Angels actually saw any." Luis raised an eyebrow. "But we did get a clue."

Luis was playing with him, stringing him along, having fun. But Saad was okay with that. He learned every time Luis talked with him. He played his part of the game and asked, "What's the clue?"

"We know who is planning to buy the ivory."

"Who?"

"A madame in Charleston caters to Chinese clients. They will pay well. She also has a deal to sell some ivory to a priest in Chicago."

"How did you find that out?"

"The priest's secretary likes elephants more than ivory rosaries."

"We are lucky."

Luis laughed. "Yes, Saad, we are very lucky. She told us about this six months ago, and about where the money is. She said to watch the money. It moved fifteen minutes after Flower died."

Wow. "Okay, so her tusks are being shipped to the United States. But there are a lot of ports in the United States," Saad said. Even a kid from Africa knew that.

"So how do you think I figured it out?" Luis asked.

"I don't know."

"Think about it. You tell me that, and I'll tell you the rest of the story."

Saad pursed his lips. Luis had never done this before, tested him this way. Maybe if he succeeded, he could get a job as an Angel investigator like

Luis. If he worked for Luis, he would miss the elephants. Still, this might be a chance. A good chance. "Let me work it out for a minute,"

"Okay, I'll go check on our question." His screen darkened.

Surely there wouldn't be an answer that fast. Maybe Luis would stop and call a girl. The thought of that made Saad shiver, but then he forced his mind away from girls and back to the problem at hand.

Twenty minutes later, he sent a text giving fair warning and reconnected to Luis. "I think I have the answer."

"Tell me."

"I used globenet to track every ship going to America from Africa by port. I used a time window that allowed the ivory to be driven to possible ports. That narrowed it down to thirty-seven ships."

Luis was smiling.

Feeling more confident, Saad continued. "Twenty are the wrong kind of ships—cruise ships or tankers. The tusks are probably in a container. So that left five ships. One of those was from South Africa. It goes to Miami. I think it's the best bet."

Luis was grinning from ear to ear and laughing. "Not right. But you are thinking really well. What if I told you ivory can be detected in containers now?"

"Then I would say it must be on one of the tankers." He imagined Flower's tusks tied down to the flat top of a supertanker and covered with blue tarps that blew in the wind.

Luis still shook his head. "Most regulated ships in the world."

"Then what?"

"What's left?"

"A cruise ship? Isn't that really busy?"

Luis had stopped laughing. "Did you notice the *Ruby Sea*?"

Saad drew his brows together. "No. I just set all the cruise ships aside."

"You were right to set aside commercial cruise ships. It's possible, but it would take more than one crewman acting together to hide something so big. I think the ivory is on the *Ruby*. She's private—only a few hundred cabins, and all of them bigger than your house. The cost of ten days on her would buy your house. There's stealthed stuff everywhere aboard her, from money to the daughters of sheiks."

"Where does she get in?"

"It doesn't matter. We're going to get the ivory before it leaves Africa."

"You'll come here?"

"No. But we have rangers we trust. I'll tell you about it after it happens."

"I hope you find the ivory."

"We will."

"Someone from here is going to be your mule?"

"You need to be older."

"That's not fair! You're barely older than Makena, and Makena is barely older than me."

Luis laughed. "There's two times two years in there."

"I can do math." But then he didn't want Luis to think he whined. "Did you get an answer?"

"The commons are getting more expensive because they are getting more beautiful as they become more protected. Even strips in cities."

"I want to do what you do," Saad reminded Luis.

"Graduate."

"One more year."

"Well, you have to be at least sixteen, too."

"Maybe I'll have my master's degree by then."

"Maybe you will."

"You said I could follow you to the port."

Luis grinned and then shut off his camera. "I'll slave the right window."

This wasn't as good as going with Luis in a drone. He'd have no view he could control.

"Watch," Luis said.

They were on a small dock. The *Ruby Sea* filled a berth. Brightly painted gangplanks spilled out over the sides. Music played from a band on the deck.

Swarthy men and veiled and covered women boarded, and occasionally he spotted a more Nordic face on a man or woman or a couple.

Security guards waited at the foot of every entrance, checking IDs casually, chatting, and here and there holding the hands of people boarding or kissing them on the cheek.

Saad loved the clothes. Men and women both wore flowing robes and colorful belts and scarves.

His and Luis's twinned point of view wandered through three different people. Saad kept trying to guess who they were, but they were professionals, and whenever he looked at where he thought he had just been standing virtually, the place was empty. He didn't dare talk since he had no idea if the sound would come out on the scene.

He could hear the band and the conversations, mostly in languages he didn't speak. His guess was that the people were Arab and Egyptian and perhaps American.

After an hour, everyone had boarded the ship.

"Did you learn anything?" Saad asked.

"I think it's there," Luis said. "I'm almost a hundred percent sure. But there was no sign."

"So now what?"

"I watch it sail, I watch it while it sails, and I watch it land."

"Thanks for taking me along."

"Anytime."

Saad dropped his connection and wandered out to see his sister. "How was class?" she asked.

"Great. We studied African literature." He struggled to remember that class, which he had actually passed months ago. "We studied Chinua Achebe."

"I didn't like his work."

"I like it that he was smart." *Like me,* he thought. *You don't see it yet, but my light will be very bright one day.* He never said this out loud, but it was his way of reminding himself he would surpass Makena in many things when he grew up. He had to bide his time, but someday he would please her by becoming greater than she could imagine, just like he was helping her to buy him an education far greater than any of them had imagined. "I talked to Luis. He may know where the ivory is."

"I heard." A slight blush touched her cheeks. She had showered. Even though she smelled more of slick shampoo now than of beast, he could feel Delba looking over her shoulder at him.

LUIS SAT ON A bench and sipped black coffee as the *Ruby Sea* approached Charleston Harbor. The open water between him and the dock she'd pull alongside reflected a nearly cloudless dawn sky and the wheeling forms of seabirds.

He'd been in Charleston for three days reporting what he knew to every agency that might care.

He wore dockhand work blues: jeans and a short-sleeved shirt with a light coat he'd buttoned against the cool and then unbuttoned over and over. Even this early in the winter, the air felt sticky. Thankfully, it wasn't hot—just thick and damp and full of the promise of heat.

Whatever he saw streamed back through his glasses to his watchers in five points of the world. "The boat's here," he told them.

He picked out Saad's voice. "Lucky day."

Makena chimed in from the top of Delba. "Get them. Delba knows something's happening. She's got her trunk up in the air and she's waving at you."

Luis fed a sat shot of the beautiful and brilliant Makena into the left window of his glasses and left it there so he could watch her. Delba's trunk was in fact up, and she trotted slowly around, the closest thing an elephant could manage to prancing. "For you," he whispered, talking to the elephant and her rider.

Makena sat like a queen of the savanna upon her massive gray throne. Her beauty always made his throat swell up and his groin tighten. He had never met her in person, and probably never would. But still, she had become his icon for the whole project. She and her brother, who was perhaps even more brilliant than Makena.

"I want these men," a new voice piped up. "For my grandmother."

"Hi, Araceli." Luis checked on the *Ruby Sea*'s progress. She hadn't touched the dock yet, but now she loomed close. "How's your grandmother doing?"

"She still has nightmares. She saw them cut out the tusks. She's taken two more shifts, and nothing happened on those. They haven't cleared her yet, though. The dumb Angel monitors think she might not hold together under stress, and they want me to babysit her through two more trips."

"That's two more times you both get paid," he reminded her.

"Just get these guys."

"I either did or I didn't," he said. "The work's already done." Still, he fingered a handgun in his pocket. He did know how to use it—he'd spent a few years on the drug-soaked and bloody border between the United States and Mexico when he was in his early teens. A friend here had loaned it to him.

Hopefully he wouldn't need it.

He had a knife with him, too. In his boot, the hilt scratched at his calf. Both seemed like bad ideas.

"Quiet now," he said to all of his lurkers. In addition to the three, he was being ridden by two senior Elephant Angels and a lawyer, It made him feel heavy for no logical reason.

As the *Ruby Sea* turned to present her broad side to the dock, her engines turned deep and throaty. Dockhands caught silver snakes of ropes and started the dance of tying her up, calling to each other.

Seabirds dipped above the *Ruby's* decks, calling mournfully and looking for scraps of food.

The cruise ship dock was a city-block-sized square of walkways. He stood onshore. Two sides of the dock went straight out to meet a thick white immensity of concrete with cleats as big as Luis's arms. The *Ruby Sea* had tied up just in front of an even bigger boat. Temporary fences served as security, each manned by armed, uniformed men in formal poses.

A few passengers and crew stared out over the rails on the second and third decks. This would be a port of call only, but it was also the first few hours the passengers had onshore since the *Ruby* left Africa.

Doors opened and bright orange gangways started to roll out.

"Can you get closer?" Saad asked.

"I'll kick you out if you're not quiet."

"Beast," Makena teased in a hushed whisper. She had the last word—his watchers all shut up and watched like they were supposed to.

A group of ten mixed Coast Guard and uniformed Port Authority police marched out onto the dock. Luis recognized some of the faces from agencies he'd been asking for help. He smiled.

They left a human barrier five people wide on the far side of the fence. The other five walked through the gate and past the watcher and up to one of the pursers. A policeman showed the purser a set of papers.

The purser shook his head.

Words were exchanged. Luis couldn't make them out, but they sounded determined.

The purser called two others over. Apparently he wanted them to watch the police, since the purser then disappeared into the bowels of the *Ruby Sea*.

The scene looked tense.

The gangways were all out now, bobbing from almost flat to slightly canted as the *Ruby Sea* reacted to slight and periodic jerks of her engines.

People started down the closest gangway. The guards by the fence let them through with no questions, but the five on the dock stopped them. Hushed but heated voices talked over one another in multiple languages.

Newsbots started arriving, many no bigger than his hand, a few even smaller. A mix of drones and UAVs jostled for position. One knocked another out of the air and it fell into the sea and floated.

The standoff continued for ten tense minutes.

Four huge men in suits came out of the *Ruby Sea*. Two stopped to talk to the authorities right outside and the other two moved toward the blocking police, talking the crowds out of the way.

Luis narrated as best he could. "These will be bodyguards, and maybe also lawyers." To his surprise, they only said about three sentences to the officers, and then the officers turned and left the dock, followed by a string of passengers.

"Anyone know what happened?" Luis whispered to his watchers.

The lawyer spoke. "Diplomatic immunity."

"Damn." Luis gave out a slow whistle. "On what grounds?"

The lawyer again, bitterly. "One of the women on the dock is the new ambassador from Benin."

"But we can still search the cargo areas, right?" Luis asked.

"If they've pasted a diplomatic seal on them, then, no. Otherwise, maybe. Watch."

The rest of the passengers disembarked. Some looked sleepy, some excited. Only a few had young children with them. Women carried purses and men and children backpacks, but none wheeled luggage.

The tusks weren't escaping this way.

He was even more certain they were here. Diplomatic immunity might succeed, too, darn it all. There had been nothing about it on globenet, but names and nationalities and bank accounts of passengers could be hidden by international law.

A bus and two cabs pulled up and collected the passengers. The newsbots floated slowly away. Nothing to see here.

He would wait until the ship left if he needed to. It was only here until nine in the evening. He had brought an apple and cheese in his bag, and although he was hungry, he decided he might be hungrier later. He thought of talking to Makena, but she liked her privacy. So he settled for waiting, staying as meditative as possible while watching statistics for the other Angel programs. Tigers and rhinos were doing well, but the world had lost four whales to three separate incidents—two to the Japanese whaling fleet, one that beached itself off Baja California, and a legal traditional hunt by Native Americans off the Washington coast.

He had applied for whales, but there were no openings there yet. He might not go now, even if they offered him a job. The elephants needed him.

On the dock, all but one of the gangways pulled back in.

THE EARLY MORNING WASN'T yet spilling light into Francine's window. Almost. While she watched her flimsy screen at the kitchen table, Araceli glanced at her grandmother from time to time. Francine flew the drone smoothly now, with a sense of grace in the flutter of her hands. She knew the elephants by name, too.

Araceli watched Makena through the drone's cameras. Spears of sunset bathed the elephants in hot orange light while Araceli shivered in a navy-blue hoodie and fuzzy slippers.

The animal tracking maps showed impala near the herd, and a family grouping of wildebeest, but no lion or tiger or human to threaten the scene.

Araceli noticed movement in her window to Luis. It was already midmorning in Charleston, and the shift in point of view as Luis stood up clued her that something had changed. A boat slid through the water from behind the *Ruby Sea*.

"MAKENA," SHE WHISPERED. "WATCH Luis."

"Yes," Makena said softly. "I already am. Two more boats are coming."

It was hard to see—her point of view was slaved to Luis, who appeared to be running; the scene in front of her jerked up and down. Then she heard a loudspeaker proclaim, "Stop! Coast Guard."

Two larger boats chased the medium-sized boat that had come from behind the cruise ship.

They weren't far from the dock. Too far to jump, but close enough to swim.

"Shit."

She had never heard Luis curse.

Men in black uniforms boiled up out of the center of the boat, shooting. At least six of them.

Shots came back from the Coast Guard boats.

Figures and guns fell into the water.

Newsbots zoomed over Luis's head.

Araceli's heart pounded in her chest as if she were there. She wanted Luis to back away so he couldn't be hurt, but she had no control of him.

The muzzle of a gun showed up in her viewpoint, looking like she was aiming. "Don't!" Araceli yelled. Luis could end up getting caught up in jail, or in trouble. Besides, how would he know who to shoot?

Makena's voice joined hers.

Luis's hand shook and then he breathed out. "You're right."

The gun disappeared.

There was no more gunfire anyway. Police and Coast Guard called back and forth to each other, coordinating. One of the two Coast Guard boats drifted away from them, but the other came up beside the smuggler and nudged it toward the dock. Luis's hand took a line and pulled, but then someone else took it from him. He let it happen and walked away. Araceli's view changed to the sidewalk in front of him. After a long time, he turned back so they could all watch from a distance.

"Luis," she said. "They got them."

"Thank God and Mary," he whispered back.

Someone dragged a body onto the dock, wet and dripping sea and blood. Another. The way they were treating the bodies suggested they were the smugglers.

Police cars rolled up one after another with lights and sirens, and then two ambulances and a fire truck.

The newsbot swarm grew again.

Araceli flipped to a news channel, which might actually be able to see more than Luis could. Her instincts paid off: they already had pictures of the bottom of the boat lined with ivory. "They got them!" she shouted out loud. She checked on Francine, who wore a wide smile on her face. Makena stood on Delba's neck with an arm touching the sky, like a triumphant ancient warrior. But then, Araceli was grinning, too. It felt like their shared happiness had jumped distance and time and infected them all with lightness.

Francine blinked at her and then returned to her watch, tears filling her eyes, looking incongruous above her smile. Araceli felt as if she had expanded. "They did it," she repeated to Makena. "They got them!"

"It is a lucky day," Saad said to them all.

Araceli flipped to Makena, sitting again now, and to the elephants. The two babies pushed at each other and touched trunks, flaring their ears and making short mock charges. Makena sat on Delba and watched the play with a great wide smile on her face.

The very last bits of summer sun from Africa kissed the cold Northwest.

STORY NOTES—Brenda Cooper

First, the idea of paying people to solve ecological problems (partially as a way to offset a probable future that will have chronic high employment) started with a short article I did for the *Futurist* magazine. Here's a link to that article: http://www.wfs.org/futurist/september-october-2012-vol-46-no-5/22nd-century-first-light/forecasts/where-wild-things-are-not.

So then the World Future Society asked me to speak at their conference, and I started doing research. That research morphed into my Backing into Eden blog series at http://www.backingintoeden.com, which then got picked up at a few other places. One of my posts for Backing into Eden is about elephants—which gave me the idea of writing a story about elephants. I was working on that blog post as I was working on this story. Here's a direct link: http://www.brenda-cooper.com/2013/06/25/backing-into-eden-chapter-10-the-elephant-angels/. The emotional drive for this story came from my elephant research . . . the things humans do to these beautiful beasts make me very angry.

The post from Project Hieroglyph that was most related to ideas in this story was Karl Schroeder's talk about vertical farming, and the idea that if we start to do a lot more vertical farming we might be able to rewild some spaces, which sent me off to work on reading about the commons, which is also a theme in this story.

Of course, other bits of background in the story, like its global and multinational set of characters, came out of some of the general reading I do as a futurist.

FORUM DISCUSSION—Protecting Protected Land

Brenda Cooper introduced her solution to guarding protected and preserved land to Vandana Singh and other Hieroglyph community members in June 2013. See the conversation unfold at hieroglyph.asu .edu/elephant-angels.

COVENANT
Elizabeth Bear

THIS COLD COULD KILL me, but it's no worse than the memories. Endurable as long as I keep moving.

My feet drum the snow-scraped roadbed as I swing past the police station at the top of the hill. Each exhale plumes through my mask, but insulating synthetics warm my inhalations enough so they do not sting and seize my lungs. I'm running too hard to breathe through my nose— running as hard and fast as I can, sprinting for the next hydrant-marking reflector protruding above a dirty bank of ice. The wind pushes into my back, cutting through the wet merino of my baselayer and the wet MaxReg over it, but even with its icy assistance I can't come close to running the way I used to run. Once I turn the corner into the graveyard, I'll be taking that wind in the face.

I miss my old body's speed. I ran faster before. My muscles were stronger then. Memories weigh something. They drag you down. Every step I take, I'm carrying thirteen dead. My other self runs a step or two behind me. I feel the drag of his invisible, immaterial presence.

As long as you keep moving, it's not so bad. But sometimes everything in the world conspires to keep you from moving fast enough.

© 2013, Haylee Bolinger / ASU

I thump through the old stone arch into the graveyard, under the trees glittering with ice, past the iron gate pinned open by drifts. The wind's as sharp as I expected—sharper—and I kick my jacket over to warming mode. That'll run the battery down, but I've only got another five kilometers to go and I need heat. It's getting colder as the sun rises, and clouds slide up the western horizon: cold front moving in. I flip the sleeve light off with my next gesture, though that won't make much difference. The sky's given light enough to run by for a good half hour, and the sleeve light is on its own battery. A single LED doesn't use much.

I imagine the flexible circuits embedded inside my brain falling into quiescence at the same time. Even smaller LEDs with even more advanced power cells go dark. The optogenetic adds shut themselves off when my brain is functioning *healthily*. Normally, microprocessors keep me sane and safe, monitor my brain activity, stimulate portions of the neocortex devoted to ethics, empathy, compassion. When I run, though, my brain—my dysfunctional, murderous, *cured* brain—does it for itself as neural pathways are stimulated by my own native neurochemicals.

Only my upper body gets cold: though that wind chills the skin of my thighs and calves like an ice bath, the muscles beneath keep hot with exertion. And the jacket takes the edge off the wind that strikes my chest.

My shoes blur pink and yellow along the narrow path up the hill. Gravestones like smoker's teeth protrude through swept drifts. They're moldy black all over as if spray-painted, and glittering powdery whiteness heaps against their backs. Some of the stones date to the eighteenth century, but I run there only in the summertime or when it hasn't snowed. Maintenance doesn't plow that part of the churchyard. Nobody comes to pay their respects to *those* dead anymore.

Sort of like the man I used to be.

The ones I killed, however—some of them still get their memorials every year. I know better than to attend, even though my old self would have loved to gloat, to relive the thrill of their deaths. The new me . . . feels a sense of . . . obligation. But their loved ones don't know my new identity. And nobody owes *me* closure.

I'll have to take what I can find for myself. I've sunk into that beautiful quiet place where there's just the movement, the sky that true, irreproducible blue, the brilliant flicker of a cardinal. Where I die as a noun and only the verb survives.

I run. I am running.

WHEN HE MET HER eyes, he imagined her throat against his hands. Skin like calves' leather; the heat and the crack of her hyoid bone as he dug his thumbs deep into her pulse. The way she'd writhe, thrash, struggle.

His waist chain rattled as his hands twitched, jerking the cuffs taut on his wrists.

She glanced up from her notes. Her eyes were a changeable hazel: blue in this light, gray green in others. Reflections across her glasses concealed the corner where text scrolled. It would have been too small to read, anyway—backward, with the table he was chained to creating distance between them.

She waited politely, seeming unaware that he was imagining those hazel eyes dotted with petechiae, that fair skin slowly mottling purple. He let the silence sway between them until it developed gravity.

"Did you wish to say something?" she asked, with mild but clinical encouragement.

Point to me, he thought.

He shook his head. "I'm listening."

She gazed upon him benevolently for a moment. His fingers itched. He scrubbed the tips against the rough orange jumpsuit but stopped. In her silence, the whisking sound was too audible.

She continued. "The court is aware that your crimes are the result of neural damage including an improperly functioning amygdala. Technology exists that can repair this damage. It is not experimental; it has been used successfully in tens of thousands of cases to treat neurological disorders as divergent as depression, anxiety, bipolar disorder, borderline personality, and the complex of disorders commonly referred to as schizo-phrenic syndrome."

The delicate structure of her collarbones fascinated him. It took four-teen pounds of pressure, properly applied, to snap a human clavicle—rendering the arm useless for a time. He thought about the proper application of that pressure. He said, "Tell me more."

"They take your own neurons—grown from your own stem cells under sterile conditions in a lab, modified with microbial opsin genes. This opsin is a light-reactive pigment similar to that found in the human retina. The neurons are then reintroduced to key areas of your brain. This is a keyhole procedure. Once the neurons are established, and have been encouraged to develop the appropriate synaptic connections, there's a second surgery, to implant a medical device: a series of miniaturized flexible microproces-sors, sensors, and light-emitting diodes. This device monitors your neuro-chemistry and the electrical activity in your brain and adjusts it to mimic healthy activity." She paused again and steepled her fingers on the table.

" 'Healthy,' " he mocked.

She did not move.

"That's discrimination against the neuro-atypical."

"Probably," she said. Her fingernails were appliquéd with circuit dia-grams. "But you did kill thirteen people. And get caught. Your civil rights are bound to be forfeit after something like that."

He stayed silent. Impulse control had never been his problem.

"It's not psychopathy you're remanded for," she said. "It's murder."

"Mind control," he said.

"Mind *repair*," she said. "You can't be *sentenced* to the medical proce-dure. But you can volunteer. It's usually interpreted as evidence of remorse and desire to be rehabilitated. Your sentencing judge will probably take that into account."

"God," he said. "I'd rather have a bullet in the head than a fucking computer."

"They haven't used bullets in a long time," she said. She shrugged, as if it were nothing to her either way. "It was lethal injection or the gas cham-ber. Now it's rightminding. Or it's the rest of your life in an eight-by-twelve cell. You decide."

"I can beat it."

"Beat rightminding?"

Point to me.

"What if I can beat it?"

"The success rate is a hundred percent. Barring a few who never woke up from anaesthesia." She treated herself to a slow smile. "If there's anybody whose illness is too intractable for this particular treatment, they must be smart enough to keep it to themselves. And smart enough not to get caught a second time."

You're being played, he told himself. *You are smarter than her. Way too smart for this to work on you.*

She's appealing to your vanity. Don't let her yank your chain. She thinks she's so fucking smart. She's prey. You're the hunter. More evolved. Don't be manipulated—

His lips said, "Lady, sign me up."

THE SNOW CREAKS UNDER my steps. Trees might crack tonight. I compose a poem in my head.

The fashion in poetry is confessional. It wasn't always so—but now we judge value by our own voyeurism. By the perceived rawness of what we think we are being invited to spy upon. But it's all art: veils and lies.

If I wrote a confessional poem, it would begin: *Her dress was the color of mermaids, and I killed her anyway.*

A confessional poem need not be true. Not true in the way the bite of the air in my lungs in spite of the mask is true. Not true in the way the graveyard and the cardinal and the ragged stones are true.

It wasn't just her. It was her, and a dozen others like her. Exactly like her in that they were none of them the right one, and so another one always had to die.

That I can still see them as fungible is a victory for my old self—his only victory, maybe, though he was arrogant enough to expect many more. He thought he could beat the rightminding.

That's the only reason he agreed to it.

If I wrote it, people would want to read *that* poem. It would sell a million—it would garner far more attention than what I *do* write.

I won't write it. I don't even want to *remember* it. Memory excision was declared by the Supreme Court to be a form of the death penalty, and therefore unconstitutional since 2043.

They couldn't take my memories in retribution. Instead they took away my pleasure in them.

Not that they'd admit it was retribution. *They* call it *repair.* "Right-minding." Fixing the problem. Psychopathy is a curable disease.

They gave me a new face, a new brain, a new name. The chromosome reassignment, I chose for myself, to put as much distance between my old self and my new as possible.

The old me also thought it might prove goodwill: reduced testosterone, reduced aggression, reduced physical strength. Few women become serial killers.

To my old self, it seemed a convincing lie.

He—no, I: alienating the uncomfortable actions of the self is something that psychopaths do—I thought I was stronger than biology and stronger than rightminding. I thought I could take anabolic steroids to get my muscle and anger back where they should be. I honestly thought I'd get away with it.

I honestly thought I would still want to.

I could write that poem. But that's not the poem I'm writing. The poem I'm writing begins: *Gravestones like smoker's teeth* . . . except I don't know what happens in the second clause, so I'm worrying at it as I run.

I do my lap and throw in a second lap because the wind's died down and my heater is working and I feel light, sharp, full of energy and desire. When I come down the hill, I'm running on springs. I take the long arc, back over the bridge toward the edge of town, sparing a quick glance down at the frozen water. The air is warming up a little as the sun rises. My fingers aren't numb in my gloves anymore.

When the unmarked white delivery van pulls past me and rolls to a stop, it takes me a moment to realize the driver wants my attention. He taps the horn, and I jog to a stop, hit pause on my run tracker, tug a headphone from my ear. I stand a few steps back from the window. He looks at me, then winces in embarrassment, and points at his navigation system. "Can you help me find Green Street? The autodrive is no use."

"Sure," I say. I point. "Third left, up that way. It's an unimproved road; that might be why it's not on your map."

"Thanks," he says. He opens his mouth as if to say something else, some form of apology, but I say, "Good luck, man!," and wave him cheerily on.

The vehicle isn't the anomaly here in the country that it would be on a city street, even if half the cities have been retrofitted for urban farming to the point where they barely have streets anymore. But I'm flummoxed by the irony of the encounter, so it's not until he pulls away that I realize I should have been more wary. And that *his* reaction was not the embarrassment of having to ask for directions, but the embarrassment of a decent, normal person who realizes he's put another human being in a position where she may feel unsafe. He's vanishing around the curve before I sort that out—something I suppose most people would understand instinctually.

I wish I could run after the van and tell him that I was never worried. That it never occurred to me to be worried. Demographically speaking, the driver is very unlikely to be hunting me. He was black. And I am white.

And my early fear socialization ran in different directions, anyway.

My attention is still fixed on the disappearing van when something dark and clinging and sweetly rank drops over my head.

I gasp in surprise and my filter mask briefly saves me. I get the sick chartreuse scent of ether and the world spins, but the mask buys me a moment to realize what's happening—a blitz attack. Someone is kidnapping me. He's grabbed my arms, pulling my elbows back to keep me from pushing the mask off.

I twist and kick, but he's so strong.

Was I this strong? It seems like he's not even working to hold on to me, and though my heel connects solidly with his shin as he picks me up, he doesn't grunt. The mask won't help forever—

—it doesn't even help for long enough.

Ether dreams are just as vivid as they say.

HIS FIRST WAS THE girl in the mermaid-colored dress. I think her name was Amelie. Or Jessica. Or something. She picked him up in a bar. Private cars were rare enough to have become a novelty, even then, but he had my father's Mission for the evening. She came for a ride, even though—or perhaps because—it was a little naughty, as if they had been smoking cigarettes a generation before. They watched the sun rise from a curve over a cornfield. He strangled her in the backseat a few minutes later.

She heaved and struggled and vomited. He realized only later how stupid he'd been. He had to hide the body, because too many people had seen us leave the bar together.

He never did get the smell out of the car. My father beat the shit out of him and never let him use it again.

We all make mistakes when we're young.

I AWAKEN IN THE dying warmth of my sweat-soaked jacket, to the smell of my vomit drying between my cheek and the cement floor. At least it's only oatmeal. You don't eat a lot before a long run. I ache in every particular, but especially where my shoulder and hip rest on concrete. I should be grateful; he left me in the recovery position so I didn't choke.

It's so dark I can't tell if my eyelids are open or closed, but the hood is gone and only traces of the stink of the ether remain. I lie still, listening and hoping my brain will stop trying to split my skull.

I'm still dressed as I was, including the shoes. He's tied my hands behind my back, but he didn't tape my thumbs together. He's an amateur. I conclude that he's not in the room with me. And probably not anywhere nearby. I think I'm in a cellar. I can't hear anybody walking around on the floor overhead.

I'm not gagged, which tells me he's confident that I can't be heard even if I scream. So maybe I wouldn't hear him up there, either?

My aloneness suggests that I was probably a target of opportunity. That he has somewhere else he absolutely has to be. Parole review? Dinner with the mother who supports him financially? Stockbroker meeting? He seems organized; it could be anything. But whatever it is, it's incredibly important that he show up for it, or he wouldn't have left.

When *you* have a new toy, can you resist playing with it?

I start working my hands around. It's not hard if you're fit and flexible, which I am, though I haven't kept in practice. I'm not scared, though I should be. I know better than most what happens next. But I'm calmer than I have been since I was somebody else. The adrenaline still settles me, just like it used to. Only this time—well, I already mentioned the irony.

It's probably not even the lights in my brain taking the edge off my arousal.

The history of technology is all about unexpected consequences. Who would have guessed that peak oil would be linked so clearly to peak psychopathy? Most folks don't think about it much, but people just aren't as mobile as they—as we—used to be. *We* live in populations of greater density, too, and travel less. And all of that leads to knowing each other more.

People like the nameless him who drugged me—people like me— require a certain anonymity, either in ourselves or in our victims.

The floor is cold against my rear end. My gloves are gone. My wrists scrape against the soles of my shoes as I work the rope past them. They're only a little damp, and the water isn't frozen or any colder than the floor.

I've been down here awhile, then—still assuming I *am* down. Cellars usually have windows, but guys like me—guys like I used to be—spend a lot
of time planning in advance. Rehearsing. Spinning their webs and digging
their holes like trapdoor spiders.

I'm shivering, and my body wants to cramp around the chill. I keep
pulling. One more wiggle and tug, and I have my arms in front of me.
I sit up and stretch, hoping my kidnapper has made just one more mistake. It's so dark I can't see my fluorescent yellow-and-green running
jacket, but proprioception lets me find my wrist with my nose. And there,
clipped into its little pocket, is the microflash sleeve light that comes
with the jacket.

He got the mask—or maybe the mask just came off with the bag. And
he got my phone, which has my tracker in it, and a GPS. He didn't make
the mistake I would have chosen for him to make.

I push the button on the sleeve light with my nose.

It comes on shockingly bright and I stretch my fingers around to shield
it as best I can. Flesh glows red between the bones.

Yep. It's a basement.

EIGHT YEARS AFTER MY first time, the new improved me showed the IBI
the site of the grave he'd dug for the girl in the mermaid-colored dress. I'd
never forgotten it—not the gracious tree that bent over the little boulder he'd
skidded on top of her to keep the animals out, not the tangle of vines he'd
dragged over that, giving himself a hell of a case of poison ivy in the process.

This time, I was the one who vomited.

How does one even begin to own having done something like that?
How do *I*?

AH, THERE'S THE FEAR. Or not fear, exactly, because the optogenetic and
chemical controls on my endocrine system keep my arousal pretty low. It's
anxiety. But anxiety's an old friend.

It's something to think about while I work on the ropes and tape with
my teeth. The sleeve light shines up my nose while I gnaw, revealing veins
through the cartilage and flesh. I'm cautious, nipping and tearing rather than
pulling. I can't afford to break my teeth: they're the best weapon and the best

tool I have. So I'm meticulous and careful, despite the nauseous thumping of my heart and the voice in my head that says, *Hurry, hurry, he's coming.*

He's not coming—at least, I haven't heard him coming. Ripping the bonds apart seems to take forever. I wish I had wolf teeth, teeth for slicing and cutting. Teeth that could scissor through this stuff as if it were a cheese sandwich. I imagine my other self's delight in my discomfort, my worry. I wonder if he'll enjoy it when my captor returns, even though he's trapped in this body with me.

Does he really exist, my other self? Neurologically speaking, we all have a lot of people in our heads all the time, and we can't hear most of them. Maybe they really did change him, unmake him. Transform him into me. Or maybe he's back there somewhere, gagged and chained up, but watching.

Whichever it is, I know what he would think of this. He killed thirteen people. He'd like to kill me, too.

I'm shivering.

The jacket's gone cold, and it—and I—am soaked. The wool still insulates while wet, but not enough. The jacket and my compression tights don't do a damned thing.

I wonder if my captor realized this. Maybe *this* is his game.

Considering all the possibilities, freezing to death is actually not so bad.

Maybe he just doesn't realize the danger? Not everybody knows about cold.

The last wrap of tape parts, sticking to my chapped lower lip and pulling a few scraps of skin loose when I tug it free. I'm leaving my DNA all over this basement. I spit in a corner, too, just for good measure. Leave traces: even when you're sure you're going to die. Especially then. Do anything you can to leave clues.

It was my skin under a fingernail that finally got me.

THE PERIOD WHEN HE was undergoing the physical and mental adaptations that turned him into me gave me a certain . . . not sympathy, because they did the body before they did the rightminding, and sympathy's an emotion he never felt before I was thirty-three years old . . . but it gave him and therefore me a certain *perspective* he hadn't had before.

It itched like hell. Like puberty.

There's an old movie, one he caught in the guu this one time. Some people from the future go back in time and visit a hospital. One of them is a doctor. He saves a woman who's waiting for dialysis or a transplant by giving her a pill that makes her grow a kidney.

That's pretty much how I got my ovaries, though it involved stem cells and needles in addition to pills.

I was still *him,* because they hadn't repaired the damage to my brain yet. They had to keep him under control while the physical adaptations were happening. He was on chemical house arrest. Induced anxiety disorder. Induced agoraphobia.

It doesn't sound so bad until you realize that the neurological shackles are strong enough that even stepping outside your front door can put you on the ground. There are supposed to be safeguards in place. But everybody's heard the stories of criminals on chemarrest who burned to death because they couldn't make themselves walk out of a burning building.

He thought he could beat the rightminding, beat the chemarrest. Beat everything.

Damn, I was arrogant.

MY FORMER SELF HAD more grounds for his arrogance than this guy. *This is pathetic,* I think. And then I have to snort laughter, because it's not my former self who's got me tied up in this basement.

I could just let this happen. It'd be fair. Ironic. *Justice.*

And my dying here would mean more women follow me into this basement. One by one by one.

I unbind my ankles more quickly than I did the wrists. Then I stand and start pacing, do jumping jacks, jog in place while I shine my light around. The activity eases the shivering. Now it's just a tremble, not a teeth-rattling shudder. My muscles are stiff; my bones ache. There's a cramp in my left calf.

There's a door locked with a deadbolt. The windows have been bricked over with new bricks that don't match the foundation. They're my best option—if I could find something to strike with, something to pry with, I might break the mortar and pull them free.

I've got my hands. My teeth. My tiny light, which I turn off now so as not to warn my captor.

And a core temperature that I'm barely managing to keep out of the danger zone.

WHEN I WALKED INTO my court-mandated therapist's office for the last time—before my relocation—I looked at her creamy complexion, the way the light caught on her eyes behind the glasses. I remembered what *he'd* thought.

If a swell of revulsion could split your own skin off and leave it curled on the ground like something spoiled and disgusting, that would have happened to me then. But of course it wasn't my shell that was ruined and rotten; it was something in the depths of my brain.

"How does it feel to have a functional amygdala?" she asked.

"Lousy," I said.

She smiled absently and stood up to shake my hand—for the first time. To offer me closure. It's something they're supposed to do.

"Thank you for all the lives you've saved," I told her.

"But not for yours?" she said.

I gave her fingers a gentle squeeze and shook my head.

MY OTHER SELF WAITS in the dark with me. I wish I had his physical strength, his invulnerability. His conviction that everybody else in the world is slower, stupider, weaker.

In the courtroom, while I was still my other self, he looked out from the stand into the faces of the living mothers and fathers of the girls he killed. I remember the eleven women and seven men, how they focused on him. How they sat, their stillness, their attention.

He thought about the girls while he gave his testimony. The only individuality they had for him was what was necessary to sort out which parents went with which corpse, important, because it told him who to watch for the best response.

I wish I didn't know what it feels like to be prey. I tell myself it's just the cold that makes my teeth chatter. Just the cold that's killing me.

Prey can fight back, though. People have gotten killed by something as timid and inoffensive as a white-tailed deer.

I wish I had a weapon. Even a cracked piece of brick. But the cellar is clean.

I do jumping jacks, landing on my toes for silence. I swing my arms. I think about doing burpees, but I'm worried that I might scrape my hands on the floor. I think about taking my shoes off. Running shoes are soft for kicking with, but if I get outside, my feet will freeze without them

When, When I got outside.

My hands and teeth are the only weapons I have.

An interminable time later, I hear a creak through the ceiling. A footstep, muffled, and then the thud of something dropped. More footsteps, louder, approaching the top of a stair beyond the door.

I crouch beside the door, on the hinge side, far enough away that it won't quite strike me if he swings it violently. I wish for a weapon—*I am a weapon*—and I wait.

A metallic tang in my mouth now. *Now* I am really, truly scared.

His feet thump on the stairs. He's not little. There's no light beneath the door—it must be weather-stripped for soundproofing. The lock thuds. A bar scrapes. The knob rattles, and then there's a bar of light as it swings open. He turns the flashlight to the right, where he left me lying. It picks out the puddle of vomit. I hear his intake of breath.

I think about the mothers of the girls I killed. I think, *Would they want me to die like this?*

My old self would relish it. It'd be his revenge for what I did to him.

My goal is just to get past him—my captor, my old self; they blur together—to get away, run. Get outside. Hope for a road, neighbors, bright daylight.

My captor's silhouette is dim, scatter-lit. He doesn't look armed, except for the flashlight, one of those archaic long heavy metal ones that doubles as a club. I can't be sure that's all he has. He wavers. He might slam the door and leave me down here to starve—

I lunge.

I grab for the wrist holding the light, and I half catch it, but he's stronger. I knew he would be. He rips the wrist out of my grip, swings the flashlight. Shouts. I lurch back, and it catches me on the shoulder instead of across the throat. My arm sparks pain and numbs. I don't hear my collarbone snap. Would I, if it has?

I try to knee him in the crotch and hit his thigh instead. I mostly elude his grip. He grabs my jacket; cloth stretches and rips. He swings the light once more. It thuds into the stair wall and punches through drywall. I'm half past him and I use his own grip as an anchor as I lean back and kick him right in the center of the nose. Soft shoes or no soft shoes.

He lets go, then. Falls back. I go up the stairs on all fours, scrambling, sure he's right behind me. Waiting for the grab at my ankle. Halfway up I realize I should have locked him in. Hit the door at the top of the stairs and find myself in a perfectly ordinary hallway, in need of a good sweep. The door ahead is closed. I fumble the lock, yank it open, tumble down steps into the snow as something fouls my ankles.

It's twilight. I get my feet under me and stagger back to the path. The shovel I fell over is tangled with my feet. I grab it, use it as a crutch, lever myself up and stagger-run-limp down the walk to a long driveway.

I glance over my shoulder, sure I hear breathing.

Nobody. The door swings open in the wind.

Oh. The road. No traffic. I know where I am. Out past the graveyard and the bridge. I run through here every couple of days, but the house is set far enough back that it was never more than a dim white outline behind trees. It's a Craftsman bungalow, surrounded by winter-sere oaks.

Maybe it wasn't an attack of opportunity, then. Maybe he saw me and decided to lie in wait.

I pelt toward town—pelt, limping, the air so cold in my lungs that they cramp and wheeze. I'm cold, so cold. The wind is a knife. I yank my sleeves down over my hands. My body tries to draw itself into a huddled comma even as I run. The sun's at the horizon.

I think, *I should just let the winter have me.*

Justice for those eleven mothers and seven fathers. Justice for those thirteen women who still seem too alike. It's only that their interchange-ability *bothers* me now.

At the bridge, I stumble to a dragging walk, then turn into the wind off the river, clutch the rail, and stop. I turn right and don't see him coming. My wet fingers freeze to the railing.

The state police are a half mile on, right around the curve at the top of the hill. If I run, I won't freeze before I get there. If I run.

My fingers stung when I touched the rail. Now they're numb, my ears past hurting. If I stand here, I'll lose the feeling in my feet.

The sunset glazes the ice below with crimson. I turn and glance the other way; in a pewter sky, the rising moon bleaches the clouds to moth-wing iridescence.

I'm wet to the skin. Even if I start running now, I might not make it to the station house. Even if I started running now, the man in the bungalow might be right behind me. I don't think I hit him hard enough to knock him out. Just knock him down.

If I stay, it won't take long at all until the cold stops hurting.

If I stay here, I wouldn't have to remember being my other self again. I could put him down. At last, at last, I could put those women down. Amelie, unless her name was Jessica. The others.

It seems easy. Sweet.

But if I stay here, I won't be the last person to wake up in the bricked-up basement of that little white bungalow.

The wind is rising. Every breath I take is a wheeze. A crow blows across the road like a tattered shirt, vanishing into the twilight cemetery.

I can carry this a little further. It's not so heavy. Thirteen corpses, plus one. After all, I carried every one of them before.

I leave skin behind on the railing when I peel my fingers free. Staggering at first, then stronger, I sprint back into town.

RESPONSE TO "COVENANT"—Joel Garreau

Joel Garreau, Lincoln Professor of Law, Culture and Values at Arizona State University, responds to "Covenant" at hieroglyph.asu.edu/covenant.

FORUM DISCUSSION—Hacking the Human Mind

Elizabeth Bear discusses the ethical and practical aspects of hacking the human mind, and the difference between our minds and our brains, with James Cambias and other Hieroglyph community members at hieroglyph.asu.edu/covenant.

FORUM DISCUSSION—Neuroplasticity, Neurobiology, and the Brain

Check out a discussion of neuroplasticity and neurobiology with Elizabeth Bear, Lee Konstantinou, and other Hieroglyph community members at hieroglyph.asu.edu/covenant.

QUANTUM TELEPATHY
Rudy Rucker

"**WHAT DO YOU THINK** of this guy?" asked my old pal Carlo. It was a fall day in Louisville. I was slouched in my soft chair at the back of my nurb store. Carlo was holding something he called a qwet rat, pretty much shoving the thing into my face. Patchy gray fur, yellow teeth, and a naked pink tail.

"He's skungy," I said, laughing a little. "Who'd ever buy that?"

"Skungy!" echoed Carlo, flashing his version of a sales-conference grin. "The perfect name." He raised the rat high into the air, as if displaying a precious vase. The rat's black-bead eyes twinkled with intelligence. His pink-lined ears made small movements, picking up our voices, the rustling leaves of the branches on the roof of my store, and the all-but-imperceptible buzz of the gnat cameras that had followed Carlo in.

"This rat's really your prototype?" I asked.

Flaky Carlo had managed to get a job in business, working at a start-up company run by one of our high school friends, Gaven Graber. In his new persona as a marketeer, Carlo was wearing a jacket patterned in scrolls and cut from the latest termite-cloth. He'd been getting gene-cleaning treatments, and he had a youthful air.

"First thought, best thought," said Carlo, lowering the rat back to the level of my face. "Especially from a qrude dude like you. Hell, we ought to use 'Skungy' as the name for our whole qwet product line."

"What's qwet supposed to mean anyway?"

"Quantum wetware. Nice buzz phrase, huh?"

"You guys are crazy," I said, addressing the gnat cameras as well as Carlo. I figured Gaven Graber was watching us via the swarm.

I sold odd-looking nurbs in Live Art—my store. My products had all been designed—or at least enhanced—by independent artists like me. We took pains to make our quirky nurbs seem friendly and cute. The dog-sized house-cleaner slugs were hot pink, for instance, and they giggled. The wrist-band tentacles on our portable squidskin screens were small, demure, pastel. Our bourbon-dripping magic pumpkins had a jolly, drunken air—drifting in the air like heavy party balloons. Our web-spine chairs were tweaked to take on elegant, sculptural shapes. But this rat—

"It's all about product placement," said Carlo. "Gaven wants to go for that outrider chic. He's itching to show the world that Louisville can mud-wrestle with the wild hogs. Letting a qrude like you launch the product is a good step." Carlo gave the rat a sharp tap on the crown of his head. "Bring us luck, Skungy! Drag home big cheese."

The rat glared up at Carlo and emitted a series of rapid, reproving squeaks that were—I gradually realized—actual words. I could even hear some insults in there. Asshole, maybe. And stupid turd. He had a bit of a Kentucky accent.

"And Gaven's quantum wetware tech is so special because—?" I began, only to be interrupted by a yelp from Carlo. Skungy had bitten the tip of his finger.

"Oh no!" screamed Carlo. Nurb bites could have horrible side effects.

A bright drop of blood welled out, very red. Wriggling free, the nurb rat leaped onto my sales counter, which grew out of my store's floor like a tall toadstool.

© 2013, Haylee Bolinger / ASU

"I've got my rights!" shrilled the excited rat, rising onto his rear legs. "I'm every bit as smart as you. I shouldn't oughta be for sale!"

If I mentally dialed up my listening speed of my ear, Skungy wasn't that hard to understand. Uneasily I wondered if he might be segueing into a lethal rampage. These things happened more often than nurb dealers liked to admit—especially with wetware tech's rapid rate of change. None of our products were sufficiently pretested.

"Calm down," I told the rat. I rose from my chair and drew my denurbalizer stick from beneath the counter. The stick was the size of a billy club. I brandished it. "I'll melt you if you keep it up, Skungy. Act right. Aren't you supposed to be, like, Carlo's helper?"

The gnat cameras circled us, taking in the scene from every side. Combining a swarm of gnat-cams' viewpoints gave the user an interactive 3-D image.

Carlo found a Voodoo brand healer leech on a shelf and put it on the spot where Skungy had bitten him.

"Oh please God don't let me be infected," muttered Carlo. "Goddamn this rat. He's two days old and he's running amok. But don't denurbalize him quite yet, Zad. Gaven's got a couple of million bucks in this prototype. You know what denurbalizing means, Skungy? Your DNA and protein molecules uncoil and you shlup down into a puddle of slime. We'd hate to decohere your sparkly quantum wetware. Be grateful, you piece of crap. You should think of Gaven as God. And I'm God's promo man." The tiny flying cameras rocked their wings in agreement.

"Eat shit!" said the rat. His tensely twitching whiskers were like insect antennae—constantly in motion, alert for the slightest incursion into his space.

I had to laugh. I liked the nurb's bad attitude. He was wilder than any I'd seen since my very first roadspider—the short-lived Zix.

"You wave on the rat, huh?" said Carlo with a tense smile. "You're a troublemaker too. An artist. That's one reason why we fingered you as our go-to guy. Not to mention that you're one of the only registered art-nurb stores in Louisville. And thanks to our crazy Kentucky laws, you're allowed to sell art nurbs without federal Department of Genomics approval. We'll give Live Art an exclusive on our Skungy line for a month. You'll have a buttalicious high-end market to yourself."

"I'm not sure I'd want to stock this rat, Carlo. What kind of discount would you give me?"

Carlo was ready for this. "Gaven says you could have your first two dozen Skungies for free. A test run. You charge what you like, you keep the money. As the inevitable glitches and nurb attitude problems arise, we'll pump out the upgrade patches. Meanwhile the chain stores are hanging back, watching for lawsuits, waiting for the Department of Genomics to certify the quantum wetware rats for the wider market."

Skungy was pacing around my counter, surveying my shop, and sniffing at the faint scents of food that wafted from my living quarters out back. My wife, Jane, had thrown me out of our fancy housetree condo, see, so I'd grown a bachelor pad onto the back of my shop. I had my bed in there, and a stash of my remaining *Cold Day in Hell* slime-mold paintings.

There were some of my *Cold Day in Hell* pictures on the walls of my store too. But they weren't selling at all anymore. For that matter, the Idi Did gallery on Bardstown Road had dropped me from its roster. I'd had about seven good years as an artist, and I'd managed to marry wealthy, chic Jane, heiress to the Roller nurb chow fortune. But now the thrill was gone. As of this spring, Jane was tired of me. She had her own life, energetically running her Jane Says public relations agency. And me—according to Jane, I was dead and hollow.

I snapped back into the present. This nurb rat, this Skungy, he didn't seem particularly task-oriented. He was more like a pool-hall idler, drifting on the tides of his random thoughts. Noticing me watching him, the rat laid a fecal pellet on my counter.

"I don't know," I told Carlo, weighing his offer. "What if the rats kill a cat or gnaw a baby?"

"Naturally Gaven covers any legal problems you have," said Carlo. He handed me a crisp, folded paper from his silky termite-woven jacket's pocket. "Legal waiver for you, qrude. Gaven really likes the idea of us three launching his product. Like he's nostalgic for the old times. Back in Louisville after his big score with the Gaven Graber housetrees."

Carlo mimed a salute in the direction of the gnat cameras. Right now the iridescent green dots were grouped into a shifting blob near the ceiling.

"I don't think Gaven was all that fond of me in high school," I said, setting down the waiver. As far as I was concerned the paper could have held hieroglyphs written with smears of shit. I was an artist all the way.

Not like Gaven. Remembering the numerous times we'd disrespected him back in the day, I directed a grimace toward his swarm of spy-gnats. I was making one of the faces I used to aim at him—drawing back my chin, putting my tongue between my teeth and puffing out my cheeks. Gaven's gnats zoomed at my head, perhaps meaning this in a jolly way.

"Have you physically seen Gaven since he moved back to town?" asked Carlo, not smiling.

"Just the once," I said. "That big welcome dinner at the Pendennis Club in March. Louisville's favorite son. I hardly got to talk to him. You were there too, Carlo. You were drunk. From those whiskey pumpkins bobbing around the room."

"Don't remember," said Carlo.

"The rest of us do," I said, a sharp note in my voice. "Jane especially. I was still living with her then, right?"

"Too bad about you two breaking up," said Carlo quickly. "Sweet Jane. Why are you looking at me that way? Did I say something bad to Jane at Gaven's party?"

"You asked her how it felt to be married to a washed-up loser," I said. "It was the last straw. The tipping point. The next day Jane threw me out. You're a jerk."

Even though I meant these words, I didn't put all that much heat in them. Carlo and I had been sniping at each other for thirty years. We were comfortable together because we could be as insulting as we liked. He was that kind of friend.

The rat was still twitching his nose toward my apartment in the back. "Your nest smells nice," he told me.

"Think of it as a kitchen midden," I said, lightening up. "A future archaeological dig."

"What all's ripe today?" asked Skungy, swinging his tail to bat tiny turds off my counter.

"We have our local specialty," I said, pointing to a greasy crust of what they called Derby pizza. The cheese on these things was made from the bourbon-scented milk from merry mares. "Jolly pizza," I told the rat. "Nummy num."

Amusing himself with some some quantum wetware-brained routine of being world-weary, Skungy flopped onto his belly and dragged himself across the counter, moving like a parched traveler in a desert. When he came to the edge, he leaped off it, doing a midair flip, and hitting the floor running. Moments later he was back on the counter with his prize, his tail writhing as he devoured a pizza scrap the size of his body. The merrymilk seemed to be relaxing him. A little pool of urine spread beneath his feet, dampening his fur.

"So anyway, no hard feelings about Jane," said Carlo with a vague wave of his hand. "At that party—I'm sure I was trying to help. You don't do me justice. My point is that you need to change your presentation. The upgrade package you bring to the table. Otherwise—"

"Don't you go bird-dogging Jane!" I cried, suddenly imagining I saw the old hustle in his eyes.

"Au contraire," drawled Carlo. "I myself would like to see you and Jane back together."

"Why?"

"Jane Roller is rich. I like having her in my circle of friends. And I care about you, qrude. I'm sad to see you going under. But keep in mind that Gaven Graber's feelings about Jane may be more conflicted."

"In other words I'm screwed."

"Zad, the reason you're having problems is that you're logging way too much time in your dreamchair. Webzombia, qrude. Each era gets its own madness. Melancholia, neurasthenia, schizophrenia, bipolar disorder—webzombia. Let me ask you this, Zad: When you sleep, do you dream you're on the web? Key, key danger sign."

I didn't like being called out on my use of my special chair. Webzombia? I'd never heard the word. Clearly a bullshit concept. I liked my busy, convivial hours on the web. Now and then I sold some nurbs or some art that way, or even cajoled a virtual customer into physically visiting my shop. The web was where I lived these days, and I didn't want people trying to root me out.

"You're the zombie, not me," I snapped. "You and those fountain of youth treatments you're getting all of a sudden. You look like you're fucking eighteen."

Carlo cocked his head, giving me a silent, sympathetic smile. And now Skungy glanced up from his pizza—as if finding me pathetic as well. A nurb was sorry for me?

"I should shove that filthy quantum wetware rat down your throat!" I yelled at Carlo, fully losing it.

"Our rat's seeming filth is a marketing move," said Carlo calmly. He enjoyed seeing me crack. He'd scored a point in our never-ending game.

"When people see a scuzzy rat they think New York City. And that's a plus."

"Skungy sounds more like he's from Kentucky."

"Well, that has to do with how we programmed him. We had to take a shortcut. But later on we hope to have our qwet rats sounding totally NYC. Manhattan is so luxor just now. The theme park thing."

"Luxor," I echoed, catching my breath. "Yeah. I'd like to go to Manhattan again myself. It's been two years. I've been watching the retrofits from my chair. The honking nurb cars, the flydinos gliding among the classic skyscrapers—yeah. An old-school city of the future. When I watch, it's like I'm there."

"I bet it is. You sitting in your dreamchair." The pitying look again.

Something within me gave way. "Okay, yes, I admit it! I'm sick of my life. I'm going nowhere. I need a change."

"He felt a wistful yen for a life that was real," intoned Carlo. "And the answer was—a Skungy! A quantum wetware rat even smarter than his friends!"

"Smarter than you and Reba Ranchtree," I muttered. "That's for true."

"Why are we even arguing, Zad? It's all coming together. Win-win. Did I mention that we're calling our company Slygro? Louisville's moving up the food chain. Enough with the bourbon and the tobacco and the horses and the Roller nurb chow. With Gaven in town, Louisville can productize some radical nurbs. A whole line of Slygro qwet rats. Spies, messengers, thieves—"

"What about Skungy being a biter?" I interrupted.

Carlo looked down at his finger. "I am a little worried about that," he admitted. "Gaven's not totally sure about what this quantum wetware shit can do. But never mind, we're working all that out."

I got into waving my denurbalizer stick at little Skungy. "Nobody wants a nurb that bites," I scolded him. "And if the biter is smart, that makes it worse."

"I'm not a biter," piped the rat, his mouth full of Derby pizza. "Not ordinarily. Your pal smacked me on the head. He was asking for it. Once we grow out a nice big pack of qwet rats, we'll get respect."

Carlo glared at Skungy. "Keep it up with the loose-cannon bullshit, and you'll be the very last qwet rat that Slygro ever makes. Gaven and I need to see some willingness to please. Right now, Skungy. Start kissing my butt."

"That's a metaphor?" said Skungy, laying a fresh turd on my counter. Incongruously he began rocking his pelvis and singing, his little voice raspy and sweet. "I want to liiiive," twanged the rat, for all the world like a Grand Ole Opry performer. "I want to raise up a famileeee!"

A faint odor of qwet rat had permeated the store by now. And Skungy's plangent melody caught the attention of the other nurbs—the bin of floor lickers, the web-cruising chairs, the wristwatch squidskins, the buoyant magic pumpkins, and even the stack of flat, leathery house seeds—all of them were nodding and twitching in sympathy—and Gaven's gnat swarm was folding upon itself like ghostly dough.

The scene reminded me of those primordial black-and-white cartoons where all the objects on a farm start jiving to a tune. Even I was falling under the music's spell. Skungy had an ability to get all of us into his channel. Was this part of the quantum wetware thing? The rat seemed taller than before, his fur lustrous and beautifully groomed, his motions eloquent and filled with worldly-wise tenderness and wit.

Relishing his power over us, Skungy rasped a final chorus, then took a deep bow with his paws outstretched. An appreciative murmur passed around the room. We loved him.

Well, maybe not Carlo. "That part about raising a family?" Carlo said, his voice cold. "That's out of the question, Skungy. You're sterile. Like all the other nurbs."

"Man, that's harsh!" said Skungy, feigning exaggerated surprise.

"Think about it," I put in, thinking I needed to comfort the rat. "If you nurbs were to start hatching out litters, what would retailers like me even sell? How would producers like Slygro pay their development expenses?"

"Oh, Skungy knows damn well he's sterile," said Carlo. "He's just jerking your chain."

"I'm gonna make babies," said Skungy. "I'm not a simple tool like those other nurbs you got. They're soft machines. Me, I've got free will and I'm sneaky, see?"

Carlo sighed and peeled the Voodoo healer leech off his finger. The wound was gone, with skin grown back into place. "I keep telling Gaven he should reprogram the Skungy personality," said Carlo, studying his finger. "But he won't. He's so impatient about impressing us local yokels. In a rush to buy our respect."

"Buying is fine with me. I'm close to tapped out."

"Oh, did I mention your bonus?" Carlo dug into his jacket and hauled out a serious wad of hundred-dollar bills. "To help you with any transitional issues. While you're distributing and patching the rats."

An odd thought struck me. "You think Gaven could make a quantum wetware patch for me? If I had an aftermarket personality upgrade—"

"Love makes the world go square," said Carlo with a simpering smile. "That's from an old Broadway musical. Square like fuddydud?"

"Broadway musical, qrude?"

"I'm seeing a woman who likes musicals. Kind of a geek. Went to Stanford in California? She's the head wetware engineer at Slygro. Rikki Shimano. Slygro's a tiny company, you understand. We're working out of a barn on Gaven's horse farm. I met Rikki the first day that I signed on as the marketeer. That night Rikki and I were in bed. Seems like just my type. Reckless, self-confident, completely innocent. Me, I'm all jaded and courtly. We're talking volcanic geek-girl sex. I might have some video I could—"

The gnats appeared upset—to the extent that tweaked insects can show emotion.

"What now?" said Carlo, noticing the swarm's chaotic tremors. "You're jealous, Gaven? Them that asks, gits. Learn from the rockabilly qrudes. Stop being a code monkey."

"I'm in a dry spell myself." I sighed. "I need a blinding light. A big aha. Before I wither and drop like an autumn leaf."

"Everyone's getting so sad and serious!" said Carlo, shaking his head. "Just because we're thirty? We'll be giving you ten qwet rats on Monday, Zad. Keep Skungy for your helper. I'm sensing a mutual resonance between you two."

I looked down at the qwet rat. As if overwhelmed by the Derby pizza and his performance routine, he was lying limp on my sales counter. Asleep? He didn't look so nasty to me anymore. He looked like he belonged. He wouldn't bite me. I wasn't a jerk like Carlo.

"Deal," I said. "I'll keep Skungy. But I'm warning you that business isn't good. I know you're giving me that incentive fee, but it'll only cover the hassle of housing your qwet rats for—let's say a month. If they're not selling by the end of October, I get more money or Gaven takes them back."

"Incentive fee," echoed Carlo, savoring the tasty phrase. "Let me tell you this. If you don't bungle the qwet rat test run, Gaven might let you do trial marketing for more new nurbs. Even better, he might let you market this special treatment he'd like to start selling people. He has a whole bunch of loofy things to spring. Lucky little Louisville. Gaven says we'll be, like, the epicenter of the qwet wave."

"Let me ask you this," I said, uneasy with any grandiose plans. "Do you remember my first roadspider? Zix? Untested nurbs can get into these dark and surreal fail-modes. Tragically inept. Endangering lives. People know this. A barn-brewed uncertified trial-market nurb is a very tough sell."

"Your art shop sells to the fringe," said Carlo. "The eccentrics, the loofy debs, the qrudes among the horsey set. You'll be selling them forbidden fruit. But they feel safe getting it from you. You're a society artist. One of them. Your shop is in the eleganto old-town district, down here on Main Street, surrounded by redbrick buildings and the up-to-the-minute Gaven Graber high-rise housetrees by the river. I can hear the tintinnabulation of the ice cubes in the merrymilk highballs on those balconies. You're at the core, qrude. Totally luxor." Carlo's eyes were liquid, sincere. He had a way of getting deeply into whatever line he was feeding you.

"I'm living in the back of a store," I said flatly. "And the best thing that's happened to me today is that I'm feeling this weirdly organic bond of sympathy with a weird nurb rat."

Despite my doubts, I really was getting a strong gut feeling that Skungy would be of great value to me. A rapport was forming between us two. At this point I realized that Skungy wasn't actually asleep.

"He's using a cosmic mind state to merge his quantum waves with yours," explained Carlo, giving me a perspicacious look. "A qwet rat does that with his new owner. They're kind of telepathic. You're feeling his glow, qrude."

I myself was no mind reader, but with the qwet rat focusing on me, I imagined I could feel his little breaths, the rapid patter of his tiny heart. I even glimpsed the dancing triangles of his ratty thoughts. Cat noses, rat vulvas, corners of cheese.

"I do wave on this rat," I murmured.

"Here's his special food," said Carlo, handing me a sack of golden-brown cubes—addictive Roller nurb chow for Skungy. The chow smelled like tobacco—which was indeed one of its ingredients. As long as I controlled Skungy's chow, I was at the center of his life.

Carlo was ready to move on to other topics. "So—with Jane temporarily out of the picture, what are you doing for sex? Fucking sex nurbs?"

Carlo swiveled his head, keenly scanning my store. "You still stock them, don't you? Slit spheres, magic staffs, like that?"

"No, you moron. Sex nurbs are over. The Live Art shop is about quality and grace. And when I get antsy, I go out behind the shop and work on my new car. Sublimating randiness into craft. Thereby enhancing my he-man charm."

"Car?" said Carlo blankly.

"I've got an antique show car," I said. "It's the same model as the black convertible where JFK got shot a hundred years ago. That president? Wife wore a pillbox hat? My car's a Lincoln Continental stretch limo from a bankrupt car museum out on Shelbyville Road. Sizzler Jones bought out the place—you remember him from school? Sizzler's a land developer now. I traded him one of my living-slime-mold installations for this particular vehicle. I let him have *Cold Day in Hell: Why You Believe in God.*"

"Always with that same title, Zad?"

"My brand. It still works a little bit. Sometimes. Rack up a fat sale by Louisville's beloved rebel qrude artist, Zad Plant!"

"You said it was a trade to Sizzler Jones," corrected Carlo. "Not a sale."

"It's the same," I said impatiently. "Anyway, Sizzler Jones is razing the museum and planting a grove of Gaven Graber housetrees. There's rolling fields and a lake, see, and Sizzler put a few thoroughbreds in the pasture. Nurb merry mares, actually, but whatev."

"Look, I gotta get going," said Carlo, losing interest.

"Let me finish! You're gonna do business with me, we gotta chat, right? Whittle and spit and talk about cars! Like our grandfathers used to do." I was oddly excited, and talking fast, running my hand across the damp fur of the sleeping rat all the while. Petting him. Picking up traces of his dreams. Strange about this rat. I kept on talking. "My Lincoln Continental even has a working internal combustion engine. Not that I have gas, but the engine is there under the hood—Detroit pig iron. Heavy metal."

Carlo was at the front door, ready to make his exit. "Roadspiders and flydinos are what matter," he said, pointing at the sky. "There's Reba Ranchtree on her flydino right now. Slygro's biggest investor. Yeah."

For a while after high school Reba had been my girlfriend. She'd been very bitter when I dropped her for Jane. And then she'd dated Carlo. Always the same little circle of people in my life, nothing ever forgotten, all of us endlessly mind-gaming each other. Louisville's like that.

Following Carlo out to the grassy street, I peered up into the swaying housetrees by the river. It was getting on toward the evening of a late September day, a Thursday, the sun low and brassy, the temperature bearable, an evening breeze beginning to stir.

Reba's condo was in the same tree where I'd been living with Jane. I could indeed see Reba lying on her stomach on the back of the oversized leather-winged nurb dino that she rode. Tiny and far as Reba was, she somehow managed to see Carlo and me, and she gave us a wave. Maybe the wave was cheerful, but I took it to be lofty. Like a queen acknowledging ants.

"Reba and her rhamphorhynchus," I said with unexpected bitterness. "The savage, toothy beak. The walnut-sized brain." Loser that I'd become, I hated anyone who was doing well.

"And Reba's snobby about—what?" said Carlo, getting into my trip. "That's what I always wonder when I see her these days. Why does she think she's better than me? Because her parents died and left her a fortune? I mean, both of us were her lovers ten years ago. That should make for happy memories, right?"

"Actually she treats me okay," I had to admit. "But it's like she's sorry for me. Little does Reba realize how nice my shop's spare room is. Little does she grasp that I've attached a giant nurb garden slug to the underside of my obsolete metal car. I drove the thing around the block last week. Did you hear about that?"

"Maybe, yeah." Carlo was mildly interested again, and he let me draw him back into my store.

"My big ride, she slime around so nasty," I said, my spirits rising. "Low and slow, qrude. A luxor assassination limo with a slugfoot. I might relaunch myself selling retrofitted cars."

"Fuck retro. But a giant slugfoot—that's good. I want to ride in that car. When I have more time."

Skungy was snuggling against my hand. Brother Rat. He rolled onto his back to expose his white underbelly. I caressed him with my fingertips.

"Before you go, Carlo, give me some background. For pitching our qwet rats to the slobbering marks. Like what the fuck is quantum wetware?"

"Well—wetware is, like, your body's chemistry. The genes and the hormones and the brain cell goo. Like you're a wet computer? And your brain has this switch that Gaven calls a gee-haw-whimmy-diddle."

"Huh?"

"The name is a hillbilly thing. It's a wooden toy that, like, your country cousin Dick Cheeks whittles to sell to the slickers at the Shelby County Fair? You've seen them. It's a thin bumpy stick with a propeller on one end? You rub another stick along the bumps, and you holler 'gee' or 'haw' like you're talking to a mule, and the propeller spins the one way or t'other. Fun for the young, fun for the old."

"And Gaven's using this phrase to acknowledge his glorious Kentucky heritage. Fine. And your brain's wetware gee-haw-whimmy-diddle switch does—what?"

"The ultranerds say that a quantum system can be smooth and cosmic—or jerky and robotic. Gaven's quantum wetware lets you wedge your brain's gee-haw-whimmy-diddle switch wide open. You can stay in the cosmic mode. And if your buddy does that too—why then the two of y'all get into a kind of telepathy. What we call qwet teep."

"You've got telepathy? You're saying that Skungy can read minds?"

"In a weak way, yeah. But he only does the full mind merge with someone else who's got the quantum wetware. What we'd call another qwettie."

"I've always wanted to have telepathy."

"We'll probably be marketing it pretty soon. But it's not like you think it is. The teepers don't exactly remember it afterward. That's a problem. Gaven had drummed up some secret military funding, and now he's had to tell the war-pigs that qwet teep's no use for their messages. So they cut him off. And our man's on the edge of a financial cliff. I'm telling Gaven he should go ahead and start selling people the qwet teep treatments, but he's being all cautious and holding back."

"Let's back up for a second. Can Skungy read my mind or not?"

"Let's just say he's good at picking up people's vibes. Thing is, as long as you're physically near a qwet person or a qwet nurb, you'll get these little brief touches of qwet teep with them. On account of the qwettie's smell. Each scent molecule does a mini-zap on you."

"And when two full-on qwetties get together?"

"You can get a full-on merge. Qwet teep's gonna be a superbig product. But for now, just to warm up, Gaven used qwet teep to copy a qwet guy's whole personality over to the qwet rat."

"So Skungy's a person?" I echoed, more bewildered all the time.

"Yeah, baby," said Carlo. "And we're rats." He put his hands up under his chin with his wrists limp. He cheesed his teeth at me, nibbling the air. A comedy routine.

I held my hands like rat paws too. Skungy, Carlo, and I looked at one another, our six eyes glittering with glee. A multilevel goof was filling the room, fueled by Skungy's rank qwet scent. I could feel his individual odor molecules impacting my smell receptors. Pow, pow, pow.

"Where did Gaven get Skungy's particular human personality?" I asked, wrestling myself out of my trance.

"Joey Moon," squeaked Skungy. His rough little voice was warm. "I am Joey Moon."

"Moon works on Gaven's farm these days," said Carlo. "Kind of a caretaker. He's twenty-five, has a wife and three kids, always broke. A pale guy with big dark eyes. Kind of rowdy. Drinks, gets into speed. I think he calls himself a painter—like you? They say he's rough on his poor wife."

"Yeah, I know him," I said shortly. "Not exactly the ideal personality you'd want to implant inside a consumer product."

I'd seen Joey around town over the years, riding a scorpion or drunk in a bar. He was nearly ten years younger than me, and several notches wilder than my crowd had ever been. He said he was an artist too, and he'd come to my gallery once or twice, trying to set up a show of some paintings that he was unwilling or unable to show me in advance. They were supposed to be portraits of some type, but he didn't want to let anyone see them until they went on sale. He was afraid that some "art star" might "steal his big idea." From the few hints that Joey dropped, I was guessing that the so-called pictures might be empty frames or glass mirrors. His stories were always changing. It was like he wanted your approval, but he wanted to completely mock you and prank you—all at the same time.

"I didn't like using Joey either," said Carlo. "I wanted someone from New York. But Joey was handy. And, hell, we're only in prototype mode. Gaven paid Joey for a legal waiver and full mental access. Gave him a nice block of founder's stock as well. And then he made Joey qwet. So he could teep the rat."

"I still don't get it."

"The point of a qwet teep merge is that you don't write or evolve the target nurb's personality—you just copy it from a living template. Only takes an hour or so. But the qwetting process had some effects on Joey. He's not coping. We're still waiting to see how all that pans out. Before we start selling qwet teep treatments all over the place."

"Joey Moon sold his soul for his litter of pink baby ratties," put in Skungy, loading the pathos into his grainy voice.

"And the other Skungies?" I asked. "The qwet rats to come? Will they be copies of Joey too?"

At this, the gnats began buzzing in Carlo's face, and the squidskin on his wrist went wild with messages.

"That's enough whittlin' and spittin' on the courthouse steps, old son," said Carlo. "More details later. Gaven's throwing a prelaunch picnic on his farm starting about now. You and Jane are both invited—Gaven already messaged her. He messaged Reba too. That's where she was headed on her flydino, no doubt. Come on over soon as you can. Maybe you'll get laid! You're gonna like it on the Slygro team, Zad. We keep our big ole balls in the air."

And then Carlo was out in the street, jouncing off on his roadspider.

I closed up my shop, got into my slugfoot Lincoln, and headed for Gaven Graber's farm as well. I had the car's roof down and my qwet rat Skungy was perched on the dash, enjoying himself, now and then dispensing some bullshit Joey Moon advice. Route directions from a southern hipster rat.

The Lincoln was a dream to drive. With her slimy foot, she rocked and rolled like a luxor boat. I followed the old river road along the Ohio, heading toward the horsey end of town. Most of the asphalt and concrete was gone from the roads, replaced by tight, impermeable nurb grass. This might have been a problem for a car with wheels, but not for my slugfoot.

A few people waved to me along the way—the guy running the BBQ stand near the waterworks, an art collector tooling past on her roadspider, a realtor friend of Dad's on a zigzag-backed flydino. The news about my slugfoot Lincoln was out. Chatty little Louisville. Even if I hadn't sold jack shit for a couple of years, I still had my glamour. That qrude and loofy artist, Zad Plant.

It wasn't until Skungy was guiding me up the long green driveway to Todd Trask's old place that I grasped that this was where Gaven Graber lived. Todd himself had died of a nasty flesh-eating disease a few years back. The word was he'd caught it at a debutante sex nurb party in New York. Trying too hard to be a jaded roué.

The nurbs had brought along some new health risks all right. Sometimes a nurb would incubate a human disease, and the bugs would leak back out a thousand times as strong. At first people hadn't realized that could happen. But by now most of us knew better than to fuck nurbs.

Poor Todd. I'd given me my start. Naturally we'd made friends again a few weeks after the roadspider fiasco. And—just as Jane had predicted— the gory incident had helped launch my career. Todd managed to buy himself two new thoroughbred colts by flipping one of my *Cold Day in Hell* pieces. But my glory days were gone. At least for now.

Halfway up the driveway, I spotted the party group by the old pond where we'd picnicked when I was a boy. A rangy security guard waved me to a stop.

"I'm Zad," I told him. "Zad Plant."

"Right," said the guard. "I'm Artie. Hell of a car you got. Just drive on down across the pasture."

I swung down the gentle slope to join the gang. They were lounging on nurb chairs beneath a big oak tree, with Reba's flydino wallowing in the pond. The flydino was pale purple, with bat wings and a pelican beak. The September sunset was coloring the sky. Very idyllic.

Even though it was not all that hot of a day, Gaven had three jumbo AC bullfrogs croaking cool, dry air—they had icicles in their mouths like white teeth. Iridescent skeeter-eater moths were fluttering around. Bluegill fish with little pink legs were walking around the edges of the pond and its cattails, rooting up worms. Gaven was making some amazing shit.

He was standing next to my wife, Jane, intently chatting her up. A mental warning bell pinged. Meanwhile Reba Ranchtree was talking with Carlo and with a pleasant-faced woman I hadn't seen before—I figured was the Rikki Shimano whom Carlo had been talking about. *Volcanic geek-girl sex,* he'd said, building himself up.

Off to the side, a pale, twitchy guy was tending a fire and arranging some food at the mouth of a nurb horn of plenty. Joey Moon. I hadn't seen him for a while, and I was a little sorry to see him sunk so low. Working on Gaven Graber's farm. Not that I much wanted to talk to him. He'd just start running one of his wheedling cons on me.

I noticed hot dogs on the table. Cool. A nostalgic Trask farms weenie roast coming up. A full-lipped woman stood behind a table laden with drinks. She had oily skin and what I thought of as a gypsy look. Joey Moon's wife. Now she was someone I did want to talk to. I'd seen her around, but I'd never actually met her before.

"Hi," said Jane, walking over to me just then, graceful and composed. "Your weird car's finally working. Very luxor."

"The farthest I've driven it so far," I said. "You look wonderful, Jane. I miss you."

"Oh, Zad. You look nice too. And right at this minute I don't feel like shaking you and screaming in your face until I'm so hoarse that I can't talk."

"We've done enough of that," I said. "Both of us. I keep wondering if—"

"At least we never had children," interrupted Jane, staving me off. "Makes things easier. But I do wish you'd get the vat of nurb paint off my balcony. I keep asking you to do this, and nothing happens. I'm ready to have someone denurbalize the slime and cart the vat to the dump. I want to put a little garden on my balcony."

"My balcony, my balcony," I parroted.

"Zad, let's not keep going back to square one. The Live Art shop is yours. The apartment is mine. A clean break. Now about that vat—are you ever planning to make a slime-mold painting again?"

"I want the vat, yes. Even if I don't paint with the mold, it's my friend. You know how I can coax the stuff into sticking up dozens of little heads and they all jabber at one another?"

"I do like that trick," said Jane. "But your nurb paint won't do anything for me. I think it's sulking. Look—let's get someone to cart the vat over to your shop and you can keep it out back. The rain won't hurt it. You can throw trash in it, and it'll grow."

"Fine. And when it gets deep enough, I'll drown myself in it."

"A perfect exit," said Jane. "Your slime-mold paintings will get a nice bump in the market."

It was nice to be talking to Jane; our conversations were like a graceful dance. "Speaking of slime—here comes the big guy."

The creature that had carried my car was wriggling out from beneath it. A twenty-foot yellow mollusk with globular eyes on stalks.

"Eew!" exclaimed Reba, wandering over to join us. "Is that thing safe? You ride the scariest things, Zad Plant." She mimed a comic expression of awe.

"Sluggo needs his supper," I said, popping open my old car's bank vault of a trunk and dumping a bushel of nurb chow onto the ground. The big yellow slugfoot was on the stuff in seconds, but not before Skungy had scampered over and claimed a nugget for his own. The slug begrudged this, and actually went for the rat, but Skungy skittered out of reach and clawed his way up my pants and shirt to find a perch on my shoulder. Finishing off the chow, the slug humped across the grass to join Reba's flydino in the pond.

"Zad's a pirate!" cooed Reba, not snobby at all. I had a feeling she was expecting to hook up with me tonight. Reba and Jane were good friends. Maybe they'd made a deal to hand me off.

"So you like your qwet rat?" said Gaven. He was six inches shorter than me, but bigger around. And he wore a geeky black holster with some kind of nerdy instrument in it. Not that any of this made him less confident. "Carlo tells me you're going to be repping us in your gallery. On the winning team at last!"

"Me on your team?" I said. "Or you on my team?"

"Rude and qrude," said Gaven, with a tight laugh. "Same old Zad. Do you know I own one of your paintings? *A Cold Day in Hell: Louisville Flood.*"

"That's a good one," I said. "I like when the Ohio overflows in the spring. The mental liberation around a natural disaster. Everything flat and shiny along River Road. Weird shit floating around. Like the inside of my head. People go down to the floodwaters and party. Atavistic."

"I never went to many parties," said Gaven. "You know how it was. But Jane's helping me find my way into the qrude Louisville scene at last. The Jane Says agency."

"You're working for Gaven?" I asked Jane, surprised. "I hadn't heard."

"Working like a Trojan," said Jane, kind of proud. "What does that expression actually mean? It's disgusting. Anyway, yes, Gaven wants to launch a whole raft of high-profile products in Louisville. And I'll be zinging my connections. It was my idea to let you handle the prototype qwet rats, Zad."

"Carlo said I might be test-marketing a whole series of things," I said, wanting to get this clear. "Like maybe qwet teep? Right, Gaven?"

"One step at a time," said Gaven. "The qwet rats are just a start. In a month or two—well, I don't want to rush into things. Nondisclosure!"

Jane laughed, clearly in the know. It bugged me to think of her and Gaven having secret plans. It would be just like that grotty little geek to try to get something going with my wife. His day in the sun at last.

"I do like the little ratty on your shoulder," Jane told me. She could tell I was tense, and she wanted to cool me down. "You named him Skungy? I hear he's practically human."

"I contain multitudes," said Skungy in a genial tone. "I aim to pee."

"That rat bit me today," put in Carlo.

"I saw when that happened," said Gaven. "Show me the spot."

"This finger," said Carlo, sticking out his right index. "At first I thought it was healed, but, look, it's swelling up."

"Are you feeling any, ah, personality inflation?" asked Gaven. "Any expansion of your psychic boundaries?"

"Maybe," said Carlo. "I'm keeping all that down with the bourbon."

"Soldier on," said Gaven, not seeming very worried.

"I could treat the bite with something," said the woman whom Carlo had been talking to before. "But if it's what Gaven and I think it is, it's too late. I say we let it run its course. And learn from the process."

"Agreed," said Gaven.

"Is this whole routine some giant revenge trip?" I asked Gaven, starting to lose it. "You've come to Louisville to destroy your high school tormentors? Steal my wife and kill Carlo? You're really that lame?"

"Cool it," snapped Carlo, shoving his hand into his pocket. "Don't blow our deal, Zad. I can take care of myself."

"I do admire you two guys," said Gaven, rocking back on his heels and grinning at us. Like he was watching a video. "You gotta know that. You're the qrudes. Have you met Zad, Rikki?"

"Hi there," she said, stepping forward. She had an odd coiffure, with her dark hair up in two flat buns—a little like lacquered mouse ears. "Rikki Shimano. I'm a fan of your paintings. All the Wet E majors at Stanford admire you. Like, yes! He knows that nurbs are beautiful!"

"Thanks," I told Rikki, shaking her cool, dry hand. "Carlo was praising you to me, too."

"We all need flattery," said Rikki. "Pile it on. I'm very insecure. The bright girl with no social skills. Carlo's latest victim." She looked at him and giggled. "He thinks. It's so strange coming to Kentucky from California. Like I'm visiting another country. Your secret histories. Social taboos. Folk garb."

"Folk garb!" cackled Reba. "Are you talking about my patchwork-plaid suit with the wiggle beads?"

"I would like to know where you found that thing," said Rikki. "I'd like to go home with one of those."

"I'll give you mine," said Reba. "We're about the same size. And it's not an outfit I'd wear over and over."

"I wouldn't wear it once," said Jane.

"Those beads," asked Rikki. "Are they nurbs?"

"How's Joey Moon holding up?" I asked Gaven, lowering my tone.

"He's stuck in that qwet teep state," said Gaven, glancing over at Joey, who wasn't doing much of anything right now. "But Rikki and I feel that people ought to be able to adjust to it. There should be a market for it. It's not what you expect, but even so—"

"Joey Moon!" exclaimed Skungy on my shoulder. The rat himself was kind of out of it himself, but he was half listening to some of the things we said. He raised his little voice and chirped louder. "Joey Moon!"

Joey didn't seem to hear the rat. He was staring up into the oak tree as if lost in thought. Seized by a sudden enthusiasm, Skungy leaped to the ground and scampered over to confront his template. The qwet rat squeaked shrilly at the distracted hipster, who shook his head and kicked savagely at the quantum amplified animal, even trying to stomp on him. Abashed, the rat retreated to the dashboard of my car. The woman at the bar—Joey Moon's wife—remonstrated gently with her husband.

Wanting to learn more, I went over and asked her for a bourbon and water. "I'm going to be marketing those rats," I announced. "I'm Zad Plant?"

"I'm Loulou Sabado," said the woman. I hadn't known her name. She had a low, purring voice. "And that's Joey Moon." She frowned at me. "And you know all about us. Thanks to that rat."

"I only just now got the rat," I said, wanting to placate her. "And certainly I don't plan to—"

"You know a good lawyer, Zad?" put in Joey Moon, a little unsteady on his feet. As usual, he seemed resentful and pissed off. And he stank like a goat. "Your friend Mr. Graber, his experiments messed me up. I'm hearing voices in my head, and it's getting worse. Even this tree is talking. Not voices, exactly. Nudges and winks. And I know what you're thinking about my wife, you poncey son of a bitch. I ought to—"

"Oh, stop it, Joey," said Loulou, shaking her head. "Christ!" She set my drink on the table with a clack. "Here you are, sir."

"I need a drink, too," said Joey. His goat smell was invading my nose, sensitizing me to his tangled thoughts.

"No, you don't," said Loulou, fed up. "Sit down and stop bothering people."

Before slinking off, Joey addressed me again. "Don't forget that I'm an artist too, Zad. Even though you won't show me in your gallery. I'm not a hotshot who gets everything handed to him on a silver platter. But I'm just as good as you."

"Sure, man. You've had it hard." Anything to calm him down.

Joey went and sat down at the base of the tree, glaring at us and making odd little gestures meant to show that he knew our inner thoughts. It seemed that, as long as I could smell him, I was in some weird, partial teep connection with him. For sure he was accurate in what he was reading from me—my fear, repulsion, and guilt toward him—and my lust for his wife. It was a drag.

Be that as it may, we had a party to do. I knocked back another bourbon and smoked a cornsilk bomber with Carlo. He seemed to be turning into another Joey Moon.

"I sense your essential mockery of me," he said. "And I'm picking up on Rikki's low opinion of my intellect. Her attraction to me is merely physical. Nobody really likes me. I'm a court jester, a hired fool."

"Oh come on, Carlo? Is Gaven spreading this teep shit like a plague?" I paused, studying the cornsilk's clearly etched tendrils of smoke. I picked up an odd odor in the air. Something from Carlo. "Are you wearing cologne, qrude? That's how far into the dark side you are?"

"It's a probiotic skin culture transferred from kangaroos. It's called Tailthumper. Women like it."

"Sure they do. But anyway, if you've got some teep, can you, uh, tell me about Loulou Sabado?"

"She's dangerous," said Carlo. "She's five years younger than us. Five years older than Joey. Worldly. I think she might be a teeper. If I even look at her, I feel like I'm going to explode. Like going into a carnival funhouse." Carlo stared down at his hand, trying to control his careening thoughts. "This rat-bit finger, man, I can't understand why nobody wants to help me. Rikki's over there talking to Joey Moon. She's got this weird, sick attraction to him. There's something physically twitching inside my finger, Zad. A horrible parasite alive inside me."

"You're wasted, man. You're on a head trip."

"Hey, you two!" said Reba, grown very jolly. "My old beaux. I don't usually have this much fun on a Thursday night. Eeny meeny miney moe, catch a qrudie by the toe." She was moving her finger back and forth with the words, and she ended up pointing at me. "Aren't you lonely sleeping in your store like a janitor, Zad?"

And now here came Gaven, walking with his arm around Jane's waist.

"How can she stand letting him physically touch her?" said Carlo, blurting out exactly what was in my mind.

"Shall we dine *en plein air*?" said Gaven, coming on all smooth and baronial.

"You sound like Todd Trask," I told him. "Guy who used to live here. Piss-elegant."

"A good role model for me, no?" said Gaven. "Landed gentry. I'm upgrading my image. But do let's eat." Gaven turned loose of Jane and gestured toward the horn of plenty. "Sausages, shrimp, burgers, quail— whatever you feel like grilling. Do it yourself. Or ask Loulou."

"But don't ask Joey," hollered Joey Moon, fifty feet away by the base of the tree with Rikki Shimano fluttering around him. Joey was overly tuned in.

"If all of our qwet rat template providers experience psychiatric dislocations of this nature, it could pose a workflow problem," said Gaven in a bloodless monotone. "Not to mention the public relations fallout regarding the market for qwet teep."

"For the rats, we just use Joey's personality over and over," said Carlo, wrenching himself back into business mode. I could almost see the smoke coming out of his ears. "Use Joey's personality for every single rat. By copying it across from Skungy. No need to deal with Joey or with any other human template again."

"No more Joey," echoed Gaven. "Put him into treatment, in a place where he's safe."

"And that way Zad gets a clear shot at Loulou," said Carlo, beginning to enjoy himself again.

"Is that really what you're thinking?" Jane asked me. "You'd go for a slutty woman like that?"

"That's not your business anymore, is it?" I said. "Especially if you're dating Gaven. And Loulou's not slutty."

"That's what you think," said Jane. "You're so unaware, Zad. It's pitiful." She put on a blank, simpering expression. "La, la, la, I'm the unworldly artist."

"Let's scroll back," interrupted Carlo. "Back to Skungy being, like, the standard meter for the qwet rat personalities. My bright idea."

"I've got your platinum diamond meter stick right here!" screamed Joey. "Me!" He was pulling down his pants.

Smoothly Rikki backpedaled away from him.

Gaven was murmuring into his cupped hand. "Code red, Artie. Calm Joey down."

Artie was as smooth as silk. He loped down from the driveway to spray some nod into Joey's contorted face. Joey took a halting step, then collapsed to the ground, his body limp, his pants around his knees. Loulou said something sharp to Artie, pointing her finger. The guard shrugged, then fastened up the inert Joey's trousers. Loulou looked deeply unhappy.

"Time for grub," said Gaven. "I think we're all a little on edge. You can go back up to the driveway, Artie."

"Is Joey going to be all right?" I asked.

"Artie only gave him a light dose," said Rikki, rejoining us. "He'll bounce back in fifteen minutes or half an hour. We've had to do this before. Sadly. Joey's really such an interesting character. Do you know him at all, Zad? He says he's an artist, too."

"Yeah," I said. "Being an artist is hard. Making the stuff and selling it. Both are impossible. I don't see Joey as doing too well at either of those ends. Though God knows he's colorful, with his teep issues. The public likes an eccentric artist."

"We'll get the teep snags ironed out," said Rikki. "Once this line of qwet rats is established, we want to sell qwet treatments to people. We see a big market for teep, right, Gaven?"

"But if teep hits everyone the way it hit Joey—" I began.

"It won't," said Rikki. "We've tested other people. Should I tell Zad, Gaven?"

"I really don't want to be talking business," said Gaven. "And what you're telling Zad is supposed to be a secret. You signed a nondisclosure agreement, you know."

"So what," said Rikki. "Slygro is moving too slow. If we creep along, United Mutations is going to ace us. And our founder's stock won't be worth a cent. I'm telling Zad right now." She stared at me, and I seemed to feel a tingle from the touch of her clear eyes. "I'm qwet already," she said, nodding her head. "And so is Gaven. We made the change a week ago. It feels good. And I think we should start selling it as soon as possible. Like tomorrow."

"I think I'm turning qwet too," said Carlo, shaking his head. "Thanks to that screwed-up rat biting me. I have this, like, creepy free-floating feeling of empathy? It's like I'm a social worker. Is it teep, Rikki?"

"Palace revolution," said Gaven, increasingly annoyed. "Am I the only one who's hungry? Come over here and check the food. Open up some of that German white wine for us, Loulou."

Wordlessly she nodded and took a deep breath. My heart went out to her.

"I remember my family coming to a cookout, exactly here," I told Loulou, wanting to lighten the mood. "Thirty years ago. One of my first memories. Thanks for all the help today."

She mimed an expression of extravagant gratitude and interest. Probably sarcastic. I wasn't getting over at all at this party.

I skewered a hot dog with one of the supple green branches that Loulou had prepared. I held the thing out over the fire, enjoying the gentle bobbing of the weighted branch. The stumpy AC frogs made the heat of the fire bearable.

"I see this man knows the drill," said Gaven.

"Be a dear, Zad, and roast some of those divine little sausages for Jane and me." This from Reba, in a faux high-society voice. She and Jane burst into laughter.

"And I'll sizzle up a couple for Rikki and me," said Carlo, pulling himself together. "Gaven here can handle his own weenie. As per usual." The drinks were making us silly. The horizon was a dappled maze of gray and gold. Reba's flydino and my slugfoot were peaceful in the pond. Joey was still flat on his back.

"Something I just remembered," I said. "Those cattails—they look like hot dogs on sticks, right? And when we came here when I was five, I was sure that if I could manage to yank one of those things out of the pond, it would roast up just as good."

"I can make that happen for you," said Gaven, feeling at the gizmo he wore dangling from his belt. "With my qwetter and a little teep."

"You can turn a cattail into a hot dog right now?"

"You have no idea how easily I can do real-time wetware engineering now. Thanks to the qwet teep techniques. I invented this qwetter gizmo last month, by the way. It sends a thicket of branching quantum vortex fields into the target organism's cells. Makes it qwet. I used it on Joey and, yes, on Rikki and me. We'll be running it on walk-in customers before too long."

"What does this have to do with the cattails?"

"Okay, I'm qwet already. I have teep. And if the cattails are qwet, I can wreak my will on them. I can look at them and tweak their internal biocomputations. Change the genes, the enzymes, the works. And their tissues reorganize immediately."

The qwetter device had the rough outline of a pistol—but cobbled together from a hundred little parts. Fins, tubes, chips, condensers, magnets, mirrors, a tiny helium tank—like that. Gaven held out his arm and aimed. Unnerved by his gesture, the flydino and my giant slug splashed to the other end of the pond.

The qwetter hissed, and the air around the cattails got wiggly. And then Gaven stared at the cattails for a very long time. His lips were slowly moving. He made some mystic passes with his hands. It was like he was hypnotizing the cattails. And then he snapped out of it.

"I rule!" he crowed. "I'm the ascended master of qwet teep tweaks. Harvest time, Zad."

"Here, Reba," I said. "Hold my hot dog sticks for a sec."

"I think not. Let Loulou do it. Could you, dear?"

Wordlessly, moving in slow motion, Loulou took over my sticks. Her hand brushed against mine, and I felt a slight thrill—followed by guilt at thinking about her that way with her poor husband all screwed up and lying on the ground conked out by the bodyguard's nod mist—followed by a weird sense that Loulou knew everything I was thinking.

Oh well. By now I was pretty drunk. Drunk enough to wade into the pond with my shoes on, and to yank up three of the transformed cattails by their roots. And, sure enough the cattail bulges at the tips had turned to meat. Or something resembling meat. Pale, a bit like veal or chicken.

"No way am I eating that crap," said Carlo. "I know better than to sample every single batch of the Slygro moonshine. Bad enough that I'm infected by that fucking rat."

"Feed Joey Moon a cattail!" whooped Reba. She'd always had a bit of a mean streak.

As if roused by the sound of his name, Joey jumped to his feet and, moving unbelievably fast, pinwheeled over and snatched the qwetter from Gaven's hand.

"No!" roared Gaven. "Don't start spraying everyone! Guard! Artie! Stop him!"

"I'm already qwet!" cried Joey, brandishing the qwetter. "I'll show you how it feels!" He was teeping into his own body, doing something to his wetware, warping his body's configuration.

Slowly, and then faster, Joey took on the look of a child's awkward drawing. He had conical legs, an oval body, and a dome of a head with thick bristly lines for his hair. His mouth was a crooked slash, his eyes were wobbly, scribbled dots. His sausage arms waved frenetically, with the qwetter still clenched in one of his three-fingered hands.

Artie the security guard was almost upon Joey.

"Wheenk," whooped Joey, whirling around just in time to spray the agent with the qwetter. Narrowing his eyes, Joey fixed the guard with the full force of his will.

Artie dropped to all fours—and became a crude cartoon of a pig—round, bulky, wobbly, pale pink with dark spots. The sketchy pig rubbed his snout across the ground, as if sniffing for acorns. He was crapping from his other end. My rat Skungy, frightened by the chaos, clambered onto my shoulder.

Moving slowly, regally, as if fascinated by his wobbly magnificence, Joey tumbled the contents of the horn-of-plenty nurb into his gaping maw of a mouth. As the food sank in, Joey grew in size—he was a saggy blob of perhaps three hundred pounds. He scowled at us, a sour meat mountain with waving spikes of hair, preparing to—

Cuing on some unseen signal of Gaven's, one of the big cooling frogs flipped his thirty-foot tongue and glommed the qwetter tool from Joey Moon's great paw of a hand. And then, in a flash, Gaven had retrieved the qwetter from the frog's mouth. Rushing forward, he fixed his eyes on Joey and the rooting pig, thinking at them, teeping into their bodies to restore the former states of their genetic codes.

"Undo, undo, undo," cried Gaven, his voice shrill with the joy of winning. I remembered that tone of his from our schooldays—when he'd gloat about his perfect grades.

Moments later, Joey and Artie looked like their old selves. Joey collapsed to the ground, shuddering, with a mound of sloughed-off meat lying shapeless beside him. Despair radiated from him like a physical force. Artie the guard took on human form and rose to his feet.

"Put Joey under physical restraints," Gaven instructed Artie. "And call in that psych clinic we were talking about. Have them send an ambulance. Why are you staring at me so hard, Artie? Are you okay?"

Artie ran a trembling hand across his features, checking that everything was in place. He had mud on his nose, and a bit of acorn in the corner of his mouth. "I—I can see into Joey's mind. And into yours, Gaven, and into Rikki's and—"

But now Artie was interrupted by Carlo screaming bloody murder. Right in my ear.

"What is your problem?" I snapped.

"My finger! It's splitting open. Oh my God, a tiny rat is crawling out. Shit, shit, shit!" The newborn rat dropped wriggling to the ground.

Skungy snickered. He was still on my shoulder. "Carlo said I couldn't make babies. He was wrong. That's my daughter. Call her Sissa. I grew her from a bud inside Carlo. And now I'm sending my personality into her. I'm making her just like me."

"Oh hell," moaned Carlo, holding his head, with blood dribbling from his split finger. "It keeps getting worse. The cattails are singing, but I can't hear the words. And Joey and Gaven and Rikki and Loulou—they're like cyclones of colored fog. I've been this way for an hour, but I thought I could—oh, shit. Help me, Rikki."

Rikki Shimano wrapped a Voodoo healer leech around Carlo's finger. Carlo goggled at her, increasingly disturbed by his teep impressions of her thoughts. He cursed again and stumped across the grass to get himself another glass of bourbon.

"He's messed up like Joey Moon," said Rikki. "I have the worst taste in men. But Joey's more artistic, don't you think? Those qwet tweaks he did on his body were stark. He'll be a grand master if can learn to enjoy his teep. And he does have some shares of Slygro founder's stock."

"Thank God this is a private party," said Jane. "I've never seen such a fiasco."

"But you like the excitement I bring," said Gaven. "Right?"

Jane studied the man. She seemed midway between attraction and disgust. I caught her eye just then, picking up her vibes. Married-people telepathy. I could tell Jane wanted to get what she could from Gaven. A strategic decision. It disgusted me and made me jealous, but for now I had to let it go.

Down at my feet, the new little rat Sissa was shaking her body—letting the Skunginess stink in. And now the wised-up baby rat made as if to climb my leg like her father had done. Skungy scampered down my leg and bared his teeth at her.

"Zad's mine," squealed the older rat. "You be Loulou's helper. That woman right here."

Loulou was at my side, as if magnetically drawn by my attraction to her. "Get me out of here, Zad," she said in a low, vibrant tone. "It's too crazy."

All right! I led the mysterious woman to my car, followed by our two qwet rats. The Lincoln's slugfoot was back in place beneath the chassis.

"We're outta here!" I whooped, mania in my voice. "Thanks for everything!"

And now I was speeding away from the Trask farm with a woman again—just like with Jane, ten years ago. Ah, Jane. The voices behind us rose in remonstrance and complaint. And then Loulou and I were out the driveway and heading for River Road.

WE RODE IN SILENCE for about ten minutes, letting the night air beat against our faces, each of us gathering our thoughts. It was a moonless September evening—the air hot, moist, luscious. A night of mystery and promise. I was picking up a lovely musky scent from Loulou, and with it came little pings from her personality. Carlo had said that Loulou had qwet teep too.

"Pull into the next road on the left," she said in her husky voice. "That clearing behind the old Ballard school? Nobody will bother us." She nodded, emphasizing her plan.

Synch beyond synch. The Ballard bower was exactly where I'd gone with Jane on that night I'd just been thinking about. The first place where Jane and I'd had sex.

As soon as we stopped, Loulou started kissing and rubbing on me. Five minutes later we were naked and fucking in the backseat of my car. It was romantic to be doing it outdoors, behind the Ballard school, a return to the glories of youth.

On the hood of my car our two qwet rat helpers danced in celebratory glee, savoring our rich sensations.

After sex, Loulou and I lay on the smooth old leather of my car seat, looking up at the sky, with Loulou nestled naked on my chest. I felt very close to her and to the world around us. Closer than close. Close like never before.

It was more than Loulou pinging me now—I was blending with her thoughts, right inside her skin. I was feeling the minds of our qwet rats, and, in some undefinable way, the shapes of the gently swaying trees and the scuttling of the insects in the rotting leaves on the ground. Nothing specific, everything loose and impressionistic. Like the hues in nurb paint before you tightened them up. All the walls were down.

"I see the I's—" I stammered, having trouble with my words. "I see you."

"Please don't freak," whispered Loulou, her lips against my cheek. "Please get used to it."

"You're teeping too? You've been that way all along."

"I caught it from Joey. They switched Joey over to quantum wetware last week, right? So he could merge his mind with your rat's."

"And you made me qwet just now? By having sex?"

"It's contagious if you're intimate. You might say that—telepathy is a sexually transmitted disease?" She let out a warm, two-note giggle, higher on the second note. "Teep can be good, Zad. You heard what Rikki said. You don't have to go nuts like my husband."

"Are you sorry for him?"

"Sure I am. But Joey and I were done, even before this happened. And now he hasn't washed for a week, yuck. You're my knight. Maybe we'll be right. Relax into it, baby. Qwet is like a magic power."

Easy to relax, but a little scary. I didn't want to drown, didn't want to be a piece of dust in the cyclone of the minds. But like it or not, I was merged with Loulou, and with our two qwet rats, and now, like sensing lights in the distance, I was feeling the minds of Carlo, Joey, Rikki, Gaven, and Artie the guard as well. Gaven was drooling over Jane. Carlo was putting the move on Reba Ranchtree, and Joey—he was in a straitjacket inside the shell of a road-turtle about to take him to a clinic downtown. Rikki Shimano was riding in there with him. Artie was staring up at the sky. All their little voices were in my head, blurred and unclear.

I let myself wave with it. Loulou was right. I didn't have to fall apart. I could still be me. I was reaching into the other mind flows, tasting them, not knowing what I was doing, but somehow changing my vibe.

Trying to integrate what was happening, I fell back on the image of cruising the web. As if the other minds were websites I was browsing on multiple screens. But the screens were weirdly invisible, as if out in the flickering zone of my peripheral vision.

Maybe I hadn't been wasting time cruising the web half asleep in my dreamchair. I'd been getting ready. Ready for qwet teep.

FORUM DISCUSSION—Quantum Telepathy

Rudy Rucker unpacks the concept of quantum telepathy on the Hieroglyph forums at hieroglyph.asu.edu/quantum-telepathy.

Excerpt from *The Lifebox, the Seashell, and the Soul*

Read an excerpt from Rudy Rucker's book *The Lifebox, the Seashell, and the Soul* about language, telepathy, and the dynamics of human cognition at hieroglyph.asu.edu/quantum-telepathy.

TRANSITION GENERATION
David Brin

"I SWEAR, I'M THIS close to throwing myself out that window! I don't know how much more I can take."

Carmody yanked his thumb toward the opening, twenty-three stories above a noisy downtown intersection. Flecks of rubber insulation still clung in places, from when old Joe Levy pried it open, during the market crash of '65. Fifteen years later, the heavy glass pane still beckoned, now gaping open about a handbreadth, letting in a faintly traffic-sweetened breeze. A favorite spot for jumpers, offering a harried, unhappy man like Carmody the tempting, easy way out.

They should have sealed it, ages ago.

Though really, would that make a difference?

"Tell somebody who cares," snarked Bessie Smith, who managed the Food & Agriculture accounts via a wire jacked into her right temple. She allocated investments in giant vats of sun-fed meat from Kansas to Luna, grunting and gesturing while a throng of little robots swarmed across her head, probe-palpating chin, cheeks, and brow, crafting her third new face of the day. Carmody found the sight indecent. A person's face ought to be good for months. And the transforming process really should be private.

"Yeah, well, *you* don't have to handle the transportation witches," he retorted. "They've stuck me with a doomed portfolio that . . . aw hell!"

Symbols crowded into Carmody's perceptual periphery, real-time charts reporting yet another drop in Airline futures. His morning put-and-call orders had wagered that the industry's long slide was about to stop, but *there it goes again!* Sinking faster than a plummeting plane. He could forget about a performance bonus for the sixth week in a row. Gaia would sigh and cancel her latest art purchase, then wistfully mention some past boyfriend.

And she could be right, fella. Maybe your wife and kid would be better off . . .

As if summoned by his glowering thought, Gaia's image sprang into being before his tired gaze. Her dazzling aivatar shoved aside dozens of graphs and investment profiles that, in turn, overlay the mundane suite of office cubicles where Carmody worked. At least, he assumed that the ersatz goddess manifesting in augmented reality was Gaia; her face looked like the woman who sat across from him at breakfast, bleary eyed from all-night meetings with fellow agitators on twelve continents, fighting to extend the Higher Animal Citizenship Laws one more level, this time to include seals and prairie dogs.

What next? Voting privileges for crows and cows and canids? How was that going to work?

Back in fine fettle, Gaia shone at him with active hair follicles framing her head like seaweed, rippling from blond to brunette and rainbow shades between. A blast of enhanced charisma-from-a-bottle made Carmody curse and shut off the smell-o-vision feature of his goggles.

She knows I hate that.

Gaia's aivatar made a pointed gesture with one, upraised finger, waving the finger like a wand, casting forth a series of reminder blips:

STOP AT AUTODOC TO ADJUST YOUR IMPLANTS. FIX THAT DAMN MALFUNCTIONING MOOD FILTER!

ELDER-CARE SAYS PICK UP YOUR DAD, OR WE'LL PAY STORAGE OVERCHARGES.

GET EGGS.

Carmody winced, hating whoever invented aivatar-mail, endowing the voluptuously realistic duplicates with artificial intelligence. Of course, he *could* spend time mastering the latest tricks . . . like assigning an aivatar of his own to reply automatically, fending off work interruptions . . .

He tried to will her image to a far-back corner of the percept. *Mr. Patel will have my hide if I don't file my report on transportation trends. I still think they indicate a turnaround in air freight that—*

Gaia's aivatar clung to one of his maglev-zep performance charts, resisting his efforts to dismiss her, continuing the series of chiding reminders while his impatient, leave-me-alone wind pushed her backward. The chart collapsed and surrounding data got caught up in the meme-storm as she blew backward in a blur of data-splattered robes.

Carmody's percept reached some kind of overload. One corner contorted as graphs and prospectus appraisals whirled around each other, crumpling into a funnel-cyclone, like dirty water circling a drain, sucking his entire week's labor—and his wife's protesting analog—toward some infosphere singularity.

"Cancel!" Carmody shouted. "Restore backup five minutes ago!"

He kept issuing frantic commands but nothing worked. Reaching and grabbing after the maelstrom, he did something wrong, triggering a cyber lash-back! Searing bolts of *lightning* seemed to lance between his eyes.

Shouting in pain, Carmody tore off the immersion goggles, clutching them in both hands. Laying his face on the cool surface of the desk, he suppressed a sob.

I used to think I was so hip and skilled with specs and goggs. Now, kids are replacing them with contact lenses and even eyeball implants that juggle ten times as much input.

Can I really be so obsolete?

"Bob?" A real voice, grating in his real ears. "Bob!"

It was Kevin's voice. Standing next to the desk. Carmody didn't move.

"Are you okay, Bob? Is there a problem, man?"

Glancing up, eyes still smarting and misty, Carmody shook his head.

"Just resting a sec." He put up a brave face, knowing better than to show any weakness to this young jerk, his assistant, clearly angling for Carmody's job.

"Well, I'm glad of that," the younger man said. But a smug expression told Carmody everything. The breakdown of his percept and loss of all that work . . . he knew it was Kevin's doing! Some trick, some hackworthy sabotage that Carmody would never be able to prove.

Does he have to gloat so openly?

"I thought I better let you know, Mr. Patel is on his way down. He wants a word with both of us." Kevin's look of anticipation was so blatant, Carmody had to quash a troglodytic urge to erase it with his fist. *Kevin might have learned some surface tact if he had gone to university or worked at a regular people job. But no. His generation absorbs technical skills directly, like suckling from a—*

The right metaphor wouldn't come. Strangely, that was the last straw for Carmody.

Enough is enough.

"You look terrible," the younger man added. "Maybe you better visit the loo and clean up, before . . . Where are you going? Mr. Patel wants . . ."

Carmody had one hand on the windowpane and the other on its frame. Staring through the gap and down twenty-three stories, he inhaled, feeling resolution build, overcoming panic, layering upon the panic, *amplifying* his panic into something that felt more manly.

Determination.

Time to end this.

Carmody felt eyes turn his way, staring as the window swung wide. His left foot planted on the sill, pushing till he stood, teetering along emptiness.

"Bob. What're you doing?"

Carmody smiled over his shoulder at his coworkers, none of whom rose to stop him.

"I'm taking the easy way out."

And—he jumped.

© 2013, Haylee Bolinger / ASU

CARMODY'S GUT ROILED WITH caveman terror as the first few floors swept by. At least his life didn't pass before him.

He knew he should compose himself, but as wind stung his eyes and tugged his hair, a shadow loomed from an unexpected direction—another figure hurtling Earthward. Business suit flapping, clenched fists outstretched as if racing Carmody to the pavement. Dickerson of accounting.

That sonofagun always seemed much too tightly wound.

Oh? an honest part of himself replied. *And what are you? Taking the coward's way out.*

Carmody tried to focus on what mattered, with little time left. *Is anything important, at this point?*

Abruptly, he heard someone speak. A shout, over the throbbing wind, but conversational, nonetheless.

"Dickerson is such a maroon! I was at the same meeting when Mr. Saung told us all to jump. But you don't see me showing off like that!"

Glancing left, he saw a woman dressed in the slick, pinstripe uniform of a company attorney. He'd seen her around. Instead of plunging superhero style, she had arms spread like Carmody, delaying the inevitable. A rightward eyeflick detected no sign of Dickerson. So now it was the two of them.

Told you to jump? Boy, that Saung is a hard case. Much worse than Patel. In fact, maybe I should have stayed and fought it out . . .

Carmody almost replied to the woman—dark humor about falling *with* her, not *for* her. But she frowned in concentration, preparing for the fast-looming street.

That's what I should do.

Grimly, Carmody, strapped the goggles back on to his head. Bearing down and gritting his teeth, he mentally recited a personal chant.

I am a son of light. I am a son of light. I am a son of light . . .

Nothing. Opening his eyes briefly, he saw that he was halfway to the ground, with much *less* than half the time left before . . . going splat upon the broad apron that now surrounded every downtown building, protecting pedestrians and vehicles from plummeting jumpers.

Splat. Me? Come on, focus!

I am a son of light. I am a son of light. I am a son of light . . .

He tensed muscles in his arms, back, and thighs—and felt electric tension course along his spine, at last. A crackling that was molten, electric, and fey, all at the same time, seemed to fizz from every pore. It hurt like hell! But he kept up the mantra, frowning hard and willing power into his fists. His feet.

I am a son of light. I am a son of light. I am a son of light . . .

From his scalp implants to the tips of Carmody's toes, power erupted, along with pain.

I am a son of light . . . and I can fly!

Bottoming out a couple of stories above the splat barrier, he made second-floor windows shake with the roar of his passage.

Carmody flew . . .

. . . **AND ALMOST COLLIDED** with half a dozen others, amid a throng zooming above Broadway. Carmody's percept throbbed with warning shouts and small fines applied against his commuter account. But he managed to maintain concentration, leveling off and settling into an uptown flight path without injuring anyone.

Damn, no wonder they say you should always use a standard launching catapult. Skyscraper-jumping is for idiots! Or, at least, folks who aren't out of practice like you, fool.

He turned onto Seventh Avenue, banking in a wide swoop that gained altitude as well. It almost felt . . . *fun,* for just a bit, though the tight maneuver made his stomach churn.

Okay. What had Gaia reminded him to do? Assuming he was about to be fired and become a house-husband, he might as well cover the checklist.

Oh yeah. Pick up Dad.

Carmody turned on the goggles' aroma detectors and followed a scent of liquid nitrogen. He descended to a low-slow lane, barely dodging a skylarking vette, and did a body tuck to land squarely in the catcher's mitt at Seventh and Fifty-Eighth Street.

With ringing ears and scraped palms, Carmody dusted himself off, wincing as body-repair implants dealt with the usual bruises and a fractured finger.

"Watch out!" came a cry from above. He stepped aside to make way for the next flying person, coming in for a semi-crash landing.

"There's got to be a better way," Carmody muttered. "Sometimes I wish we still had subways."

Ten minutes later he had signed at the desk for his father. The old man was tucked into a carrier pouch, strapped to Carmody's chest. Awkward and heavy, but with room left to stuff in that carton of eggs.

If I took the car, I'd have to pay ecobal fees and parking . . . but I'd also have a spare seat to strap him into. Or the trunk. Oh, well, being unemployed will have compensations.

He took an elevator to the fifth-floor catapult room, paid his dime, and stood in line till it was his turn. Enviously, he watched as some teenagers hustled past the people-launcher to an open-air platform, where each one took a running start and then *sprang* into the sky. Well, of course anyone could do that, if you had plenty of free time to practice . . . and the agility of youth. Why, twenty years ago Carmody had been quite a big deal at his local hoverboard park. And he wondered if anyone still used them anymore, so graceful, silent-smooth. And it didn't *hurt* when you rode a board! Only when you fell off.

"I am a son of light," he murmured, preparing his mind for the coming jolt-and-fling, always disagreeably jaw-jarring. "I am a son of light."

"*You're MY son,*" groused a voice within the carrier pouch. "*And need I remind you that it's dark in here?*"

Carmody rolled his eyes.

"Hush, Dad. I gotta concentrate."

But he unzipped the pouch to a safety stop, so his father's gel-frozen head could see out. Carmody focused on the mantra, controlling his implants much better this time, with less emotion and a bit less pain, as the robot attendant held a taut saddle for him.

"I am a child of light . . ."

This catapult needed tuning. It flung him with a nauseating initial spin. Fighting to correct, Carmody gritted his teeth so hard he wondered if he chipped one. This time, at least, he managed to enter traffic without too many micro-fines.

"I can fly . . . I can fly . . ." he convinced himself, while roaring ahead, weaving two hundred meters above the street, tired but homeward bound.

"I . . . can . . . fly . . ."

DAD JUST HAD TO keep kvetching.

"You call this traffic?" he demanded, as they cruised over the southwest corner of Central Park. "When we first moved to this city, during the Big Reconstruction, only taxis and buses could fly! And just in narrow lanes! At least once a month, some fool would do a forced landing onto the groundstreet, clogging things, like the traffic jams you see in old movies. Just look at you punks, complaining about getting to flit about like gods!"

Carmody glanced toward the free zone above the lake, where no rules held—where fliers darted about with abandon, doing spirals, spins, and loops. Sure, that looked kind of godlike, if you thought about it. Maybe Dad had a point.

But miracles don't seem that way when they become real-life chores.

"Like my own pa used to bitch and moan about his airplane flights." Dad's voice—querulous and chiding—emerged from the encapsulating globe. Now transformed from expensive cryo-cooled to economical plasticized-state, he wasn't legally a person. The comments were produced by an inboard AI whose algorithms query-checked their estimated reactions against the billions of neurons in Dad's gel-stabilized brain, staying relatively true to what he *might* have said.

"My pa would fly from Raleigh to Phoenix on business and then back in two days, eating peanuts and watching movies while crisscrossing a continent that *his* great-grampa took a year to cross by mule, and almost died! But all he could talk about were narrow seats and luggage fees. And went on and on about having to take his shoes off."

Yep, this sure sounds like my old man—the same lectury finger-waggings, without fingers. If I hadn't promised to keep him on the mantel for at least ten years, I'd dump his nagging skull in that lake over there.

But Carmody knew he wouldn't. Within a decade the emulation would be much better, perhaps simulating the old guy's better, deeper side, maybe even some wisdom, too. And perhaps, someday, the glimmering, ever-alluring promise of "uploading" to wondrous realms of virtual reality. *If I want my own kids to take care of my head, I suppose I should set an example.*

Anyway, wasn't this just another example of what Gaia had been nagging him about? A crappy attitude, taking everything too hard. Oversensitivity to life's harsh edges. An imbalance of grouchy sourness over joy. Okay, things weren't going too well, right now. But something was definitely wrong *inside*, Carmody had to admit.

He'd been resisting adjustment, and no one on Earth could force him. *I can straighten out all by myself,* he grumbled, knowing how puritan and old-fashioned it sounded.

They used to prescribe drugs. He shuddered to imagine what an unsubtle bludgeon that must have been. Nowadays—

I suppose it wouldn't hurt to adjust my implants, to let me see a picture wider than just downsides. So I can choose to cheer up easier. Especially if I'm going to be looking for another job. Be a better husband and father. Maybe go back to my music. Or at least concentrate better when I have to fly!

On impulse, Carmody swung left at Eighty-Third and cruised between condominium towers with their own landing ledges on every floor. Wary for incautious launchers, he slowed to a near hover at the end of the block, exertion stinging his eyes as he looked down and west at P.S. 43, where little Annie attended second grade.

The school's protective force field shimmered like reflections off the Hudson, a kilometer farther west. A brilliant safety feature, invented to give parents some peace of mind that their children were safe—the dome sparkled every time an object crashed into it, erupting with half-blinding brightness. In just the few seconds he had been watching, dozens of flashes forced Carmody to damp down the filters of his goggles.

Thank heavens for the dome.

WHAM! Another collision, as a student slammed against the inner surface, caroming amid a cascade of electric sparkles before zooming off again, to swoop and cavort amid some incomprehensibly complex playground game. Giving chase, a girl sporting red boots, garish epaulets, and a ponytail struck the force field with her feet, amid a shower of sparks. Crouched legs helped her spring off again, in hot pursuit.

Carmody had no such endurance. Concentrating, biting his lip, he managed touchdown on the condominium building's roof. Then he stepped to the edge, muscles and nerves twitching.

Kids. Their generation takes it all for granted. They're the ones who'll roam the sky with real freedom, painless and comfortable—all of them—with the powers of superheroes. He sighed. *I just hope some of them appreciate it, now and then.*

He looked for Annie . . . and the goggles picked her out from the recess throng. A small figure, dark hair kept deliberately natural, though with a tidy ribbon, she flew amid a formation of friends, in a calmer, less frenetic game. Annie's own specs must have alerted her to the parental presence, because she split off from her pals, doing a lazy dolphin glide just inside the closest part of the barrier, back-stroking, giving Carmody a wave, a smile. It filled his heart, in such a heady rush, that he swayed.

Then a bell sounded. Recess ended. Juvenile implants tapered down, damped by teacher control, forcing them to land. He stood there, intending to watch till Annie filed back inside the school . . . only then Carmody's phone rang. A curt, businesslike summons, impending at the left edge of his percept.

The boss. Crap. And just when I was remembering how good life is. Well, let's get this over with. I was a company hotshot till last year, so there ought to be a decent severance.

Mr. Patel's image wasn't aivatar but true-view, beamed from his office. Carmody grimaced, knowing that his own glowering expression would be conveyed to the manager. Resigned, he felt determined to face what was coming, with dignity.

Look, I know this wasn't a great day . . . he was about to start. But Patel spoke first.

"Bob, I wish you had stayed, but I understand your reasons. Look, I know things haven't been great, lately . . . I didn't pay close enough attention to personnel dynamics and thought you were exaggerating your concerns about Kevin. But his stunt today proves you were downplaying, instead—"

Carmody interrupted.

"Then you know it was his doing—?"

Patel shrugged. "Sure. Oh, he used a new grilf trick that's hot on the streets, right now. But come on! Like we don't have people out there, hovering over the new? Arrogant putz, his worst sin was having such a low opinion of our skills!"

"Huh . . . then my work . . ."

"I've got the report. It needs several polishes before I take it upstairs, but I think your trend analyses are unassailable. You just underestimated market obstinacy. It needs a phase factor of at least two weeks to take into account how everyone holds on to their biases and assumptions. But we can pounce on the transport upswing in ten days. Good work! You'll have my notes for those polishes by the time you get home."

Carmody reversed his own assumptions. Instead of asking about his severance package, he decided to switch tracks.

"Not tonight. It's been a rough week and I'm decompressing. Taking the family out for a sunset picnic and a fly-stroll. Tomorrow can wait."

"Well, okay. Tomorrow then. Only fly carefully, will you? I just replayed your jump today . . . *everybody* has. They're calling you Mr. Almost-Splat!"

Carmody couldn't stave off a wry smile. That sort of nickname could do a fellow good, in his line of work.

"Tomorrow, then." He clicked off.

He glanced again at P.S. 43, now quiet under its almost-invisible protective dome. It was still another hour and a half till school would let out. Annie was in a carpool, anyway, so no need to wait around. In that case— maybe he could make it home in time to surprise Gaia. That is, if anything ever surprised his wife.

Carmody looked across the expanse of roof and pondered. The nearest public catapult was a block away . . . and Mr. Almost-Splat was feeling pretty daring.

"Son, are you sure you want to . . ." asked the gel-stabilized head of his father. Then the old man's gelvatar wisely shut up, letting Carmody concentrate as he sped along the rooftop toward the farthest edge.

We'll have our revenge, he thought, while his legs pumped hard, picking up speed. *The best kind of revenge, for having to watch our kids surpass us in every way. The satisfaction of watching THEIR children surpass them!*

Heck, I'll bet Annie's son or daughter will come equipped with warp drive!

They'll bitch and complain about it, though. It's just the way we are.

Suddenly filled with fire and pain and a volcanic sense of utter thrill, a child of light launched himself over the parapet edge, toward the great, orange ball of a setting sun.

Oh yes, he added. *Eggs.*

Mustn't forget eggs.

"SHARING THE FIRE"—Ed Finn

Read "Sharing the Fire," an essay on thoughtful optimism and collective agency by Ed Finn, *Hieroglyph* coeditor and founding director of the Center for Science and the Imagination at Arizona State University, at hieroglyph.asu.edu/transition-generation.

INTERVIEW EXCERPTS—David Brin

David Brin explains how science fiction can help us prepare for the future, what science fiction writers can learn from history, and more in an interview at hieroglyph.asu.edu/transition-generation.

RESPONSE TO "TRANSITION GENERATION"—Jim Bell

Jim Bell, a planetary scientist at Arizona State University's School of Earth and Space Exploration, discusses how science fiction inspires scientists at hieroglyph.asu.edu/transition-generation.

THE DAY IT ALL ENDED

Charlie Jane Anders

BRUCE GRINNORD PARKED ASLANT in his usual spot and ran inside the DiZi Corp. headquarters. Bruce didn't check in with his team or even pause to glare at the beautiful young people having their toes stretched by robots while they sipped macrobiotic goji-berry shakes and tried to imagine ways to make the next generation of gadgets cooler-looking and less useful. Instead, he sprinted for the executive suite. He took the stairs two or three at a time, until he was so breathless he feared he'd have a heart attack before he even finished throwing his career away.

DiZi's founder, Jethro Gruber—Barrons' Young Visionary of the Year five years running—had his office atop the central spire of the funhouse castle of DiZi's offices, in a round glass turret. Looking down on the employee oxygen bar and the dozen gourmet cafeterias. If you didn't have the key to the private elevator, the only way up was this spiral staircase, which climbed past a dozen Executive Playspaces, and any one of those people could cockblock you before you got to Jethro's pad. But nobody seemed to notice Bruce charging up the stairs, fury twisting his round face, even when he nearly put his foot between the steps and fell into the Moroccan Spice Café.

Bruce wanted to storm into Jethro's office and shout his resignation in Jethro's trendy schoolmaster glasses. He wanted to enter the room already denouncing the waste, the stupidity of it all—but when he reached the top of the staircase, he was so out of breath, he could only wheeze, his guts wrung and cramped. He'd only been in Jethro's office once before: an elegant goldfish bowl with one desk that changed shape (thanks to modular pieces that came out of the floor), a few chairs, and one dot of maroon rug at its center. Bruce stood there, massaging his dumb stomach and taking in the oppressive simplicity.

So Jethro spoke first, the creamy purr Bruce knew from a million company videos. "Hi, Bruce. You're late."

"I'm . . . I'm what?"

"You're late," Jethro said. "You were supposed to have your crisis of conscience three months ago." He pulled out his Robo-Bop and displayed a personal calendar, which included one entry: "Bruce Has a Crisis of Conscience." It was dated a few months earlier. "What kept you, man?"

IT STARTED WHEN BRUCE took a wrong turn on the way to work. Actually, he drove to the wrong office—the driving equivalent of a Freudian slip.

He was on the interstate at seven thirty, listening to a banjo solo that he hadn't yet learned to play. Out his right window, every suburban courtyard had its own giant ThunderNet tower, just like the silver statue in Bruce's own cul-de-sac—the sleek concave lines and jetstreamed base like a 1950s Googie space fantasy. To his left, almost every passing car had a Car-Dingo bolted to its hood, with its trademark sloping fins and whirling lights. And half the drivers were listening to music, or making Intimate Confessions on their Robo-Bops. Once on the freeway, Bruce could see much larger versions of the ThunderNet tower dotting the landscape, from shopping-mall roofs to empty fields. Plus everywhere he saw giant billboards for DiZi's newest product, the Crado—empty-faced, multicultural babies splayed out in a milk-white, egg-shaped chair that monitored the baby's air supply and temperature in some way that Bruce still couldn't explain.

Bruce was a VP of marketing at DiZi—shouldn't he be able to find something good to say about even one of the company's products?

So this one morning, Bruce got off the freeway a few exits too soon. Instead of driving to the DiZi offices, he went down a feeder road to a dingy strip mall that had offices instead of dry cleaners. This was the route Bruce had taken for years before he joined DiZi, and he felt as though he'd taken the wrong commute by mistake.

Bruce's old parking spot was open, and he could almost pretend time had rolled back, except that he'd lost some hair and gained some weight. He found himself pushing past the white balsawood-and-metal door with

the cheap sign saying ECO GNOMIC and into the offices, and then he stoppe.
A roomful of total strangers perched on beanbags and folding chairs
turned and stared, and Bruce had no explanation for who he was or why
he was there. "Uh," Bruce said.

The Eco Gnomic offices looked like crap compared to DiZi's majesty,
but also compared to the last time he'd seen them. Take the giant Intervention Board that covered the main wall: when Bruce had worked there,
it'd been covered with millions of multicolored tacks, attached to scraps
of incidents. This company is planning a major polluting project, so we
mobilize culture-jammer flashmobs here and organize protesters at the
public hearing there. Like a giant multidimensional chess game covering
one wall, deploying patience and playfulness against the massive corporate engine. Now, though, the Intervention Board contained nothing but
bad news, without much in the way of strategies. Arctic Shelf disintegrating, floods, superstorms, droughts, the Gulf Stream stuttering, extinctions
like dominoes falling. The office furniture teetered on broken legs, and the
same computers from five years ago whined and stammered. The young
woman nearest Bruce couldn't even afford a proper Mohawk—her hair
grew back in patches on the sides of her head, and the stripe on top was
wilting. None of these people seemed energized about saving the planet.

Bruce was about to flee when his old boss, Gerry Donkins, showed
up and said, "Bruce! Welcome back to the nonprofit sector, man." Bruce
and Gerry wound up spending an hour sitting on crates, drinking expired
YooHoo. "Yeah, Eco Gnomic is dying," said Gerry, giant mustache twirl-
ing, "but so is the planet."

"I feel like I made a terrible mistake," Bruce said. He looked at the
board and couldn't see any pattern to the arrangement of ill omens.

"You did," Gerry replied. "But it doesn't make any difference, and
you've been happy. You've been happy, right? We all thought you were
happy. How is Marie, by the way?"

"Marie left me two years ago," Bruce said.

"Oh," Gerry said.

"But on the plus side, I've been taking up the banjo."

"Anyway, no offense, but you wouldn't have made a difference if you'd
stayed with us. We probably passed the point of no return a while back."

Point of no return. It sounded sexual, or like letting go of a trapeze at
the apex of its arc.

"You did the smart thing," said Gerry, "going to work for the flashiest consumer products company and enjoying the last little bit of the ride."

Bruce got back in his Prius and drove the rest of the way to work, past the rows of ThunderNet towers and the smoke from far-off forest fires. This felt like the last day of the human race, even though it was just another day on the steep slope. As Bruce reached the lavender glass citadel of DiZi's offices, he started to go numb inside, like always. But instead, this time, a fury took him, and that's when he charged inside and up the stairs to Jethro's office, ready to shove his resignation down the CEO's throat.

"WHAT DO YOU MEAN?" Bruce said to Jethro, as his breath came back. "You were *expecting* me to come in here and resign?"

"Something like that." Jethro gestured for Bruce to sit in one of the plain white, absurdly comfortable teacup-chairs. He sat cross-legged in the other one, like a yogi in his wide-sleeved linen shirt and camper pants. In person, he looked slightly chubbier and less classically handsome than all his iconic images, but the perfect hipster bowl haircut and sideburns, and those famous glasses, were instantly recognizable. "But like I said: late. The point is, you got here in the end."

"You didn't *engineer* this. I'm not one of your gadgets. This is real. I really am fed up with making pointless toys when the world is about to choke on our filth. I'm done."

"It wouldn't be worth anything if it wasn't real, bro." Jethro gave Bruce one of his conspiratorial/mischievous smiles that made Bruce want to smile back in spite of his soul-deep anger. "That's why we hired you in the first place. You're the canary in the coal mine. Here, look at the org chart."

Jethro made some hand motions, and one glass surface became a screen, which projected an org chart with a thousand names and job descriptions. And there, halfway down on the left, was Bruce's name, with "CANARY IN THE COAL MINE." And a picture of Bruce's head on a cartoon bird's body.

"I thought my job title was junior executive VP for product management," Bruce said, staring at his openmouthed face and those unfurled wings.

Jethro shrugged. "Well, you just resigned, right? So you don't have a title anymore." He made another gesture, and a bright-eyed young thing wheeled a minibar out of the elevator and offered Bruce beer, whiskey, hot sake, coffee, and Mexican Coke. Bruce felt rebellious, choosing a single-malt whiskey, until he realized he was doing what Jethro wanted. He took a swig that burned his throat and eyes.

"So you're quitting; you should go ahead and tell me what you think of my company." Jethro spread his hands and smiled.

"Well." Bruce drank more whiskey and then sputtered. "If you really want to know . . . Your products are pure evil. You build these sleek little pieces of shit that are designed with all this excess capacity and redundant systems. Have you ever looked at the schematics of the ThunderNet towers? It's like you were *trying* to build something overly complex. And it's the ultimate glorification of form over function—you've been able to convince everybody with disposable income to buy your crap, because people love anything that's ostentatiously pointless. I've had a Robo-Bop for years, and I still don't understand what half the widgets and menu options are for. I don't think anybody does. You use glamour and marketing to convince people they need to fill their lives with empty crap instead of paying attention to the world and realizing how fragile and beautiful it really is. You're the devil."

The drinks fairy had started gawking halfway through this rant, then she seemed to decide it was against her pay grade to hear this. She retreated into the elevator and vanished around the time Bruce said he didn't understand half the stuff his Robo-Bop did.

Bruce had fantasized about telling Jethro off for years, and he enjoyed it so much he had tears in his eyes by the end. Even knowing that Jethro had put this moment on his Robo-Bop calendar couldn't spoil it.

Jethro was nodding, as if Bruce had just about covered the bases. Then he made another esoteric gesture, and the glass wall became a screen again. It displayed a PowerPoint slide:

DIZI CORP. PRODUCT STRATEGY
+ Beautiful Objects That Are Functionally Useless
+ Spare Capacity
+ Redundant Systems
+ Overproliferation of Identical but Superficially Different Products
+ Form Over Function
+ Mystifying Options and Confusing User Interface

"You missed one, I think," Jethro said. "The one about overprolifera-tion. That's where we convince people to buy three different products that are almost exactly the same, but not quite."

"Wow." Bruce looked at the slide, which had gold stars on it. "You really are completely evil."

"That's what it looks like, huh?" Jethro actually laughed, as he tapped on his Robo-Bop. "Tell you what. We're having a strategy meeting at three, and we need our canary there. Come and tell the whole team what you told me."

"What's the point?" Bruce felt whatever the next level below despair was. Everything was a joke, *and* he'd been deprived of the satisfaction of being the one to unveil the truth.

"Just show up, man. I promise it'll be entertaining, if nothing else. What else are you going to do with the rest of your day, drive out to the beach and watch the seagulls dying?"

That was exactly what Bruce had planned to do after leaving DiZi. He shrugged. "Sure. I guess I'll go get my toes stretched for a while."

"You do that, Bruce. See you at three."

THE DRINKS FAIRY MUST have gossiped about Bruce, because people were looking at him when he walked down to the main promenade. If there'd been a food court in *2001: A Space Odyssey*, it would have looked like DiZi's employee promenade. Bruce didn't have his toes stretched. In-stead, he ate two organic calzones to settle his stomach after the morning whiskey. The calzones made Bruce more nauseated. The people on Bruce's marketing team waved at him in the cafeteria but didn't approach the ra-dioactive man.

Bruce was five minutes early for the strategy meeting, but he was still the last one to arrive, and everyone was staring at him. Bruce had never visited the Executive Meditation Hole, which also doubled as Jethro's pri-vate movie theater. It was a big bunker under the DiZi main building with wall carpets and aromatherapy.

"Hey, Bruce." Jethro was lotus-positioning on the dais at the front, where the movie screen would be. "Everybody, Bruce had a Crisis of Con-science today. Big props for Bruce, everybody."

Everyone clapped. Bruce's stomach started turning again, so he put his face in front of one of the aromatherapy nozzles and huffed calming scents. "So Bruce has convinced me that it's time for us to change our product strategy to focus on saving the planet."

"You what?" Bruce pulled away from the soothing jasmine puff. "Are you completely delusional? Have you been surrounded by yes-men and media sycophants for so long that you've lost all sense of reality? It's way, way too late to save the planet, man." Everybody stared at Bruce, until Jethro clapped again. Then everyone else clapped too.

"Bruce brings up a good point," Jethro said. "The timetable is daunting, and we're late. Partly because your Crisis of Conscience was months behind schedule, I feel constrained to point out. In any case, how would we go about meeting this audacious goal? 'Enterprise audacity' being one of our corporate buzzsaws, of course. And for that, I'm going to turn it over to Zoe. Zoe?"

Jethro went and sat in the front row, and a big screen appeared up front. A skinny woman in a charcoal-gray suit got up and used her Robo-Bop to control a presentation.

"Thanks, Jethro," the stick-figure woman, Zoe, said. She had perfect Amanda Seyfried hair. "It really comes down to what we call product versatility." She clicked onto a picture of a nice midrange car with a swooshy device bolted to its roof. "Take the Car-Dingo, for example. What does it do?"

Various people raised their hands and offered slogans like, "It makes a Prius feel like a muscle car," or "It awesomeizes your ride."

"Exactly!" Zoe smiled. She clicked the next slide over, and proprietary specs for the Car-Dingo came up. They were so proprietary, Bruce had never seen them. Bruce struggled to make sense of all those extra connections and loops, going right into the engine. She pulled up similar specs for the ThunderNet tower, full of secret logic. Another screen showed all those nonsensical Robo-Bop menus, suddenly unlocking and making sense.

"Wait a minute." Bruce was the only one standing up, besides Zoe. "So you're saying all these devices were dual-function all this time? And in all the hundreds of hellish product meetings I've sat through, you never once mentioned this fact?"

"Bruce," Jethro said from the front row, "we've got a little thing at DiZi called the Culture of Listening. That means no interrupting the presentation until it's finished, or no artisanal cookies for you."

Bruce sighed and climbed over someone to find a seat and listened to another hour of corporate "buzzsaws." At one point, he could have sworn Zoe said something about "end-user velocitization." One thing Bruce did understand, in the gathering haze: even though DiZi officially frowned on the cheap knockoffs of its products littering the third world, the company had gone to great lengths to make sure those illicit copies used the exact same specs as the real items.

Just as Bruce was passing out from boredom, Jethro thanked Zoe and said, "Now let's give Bruce the floor. Bruce, come on down." Bruce had to thump his own legs to wake them up, and when he reached the front, he'd forgotten all the things he was dying to say an hour earlier. The top echelons of DiZi management stared, waiting for him to say something.

"Uh." Bruce's head hurt. "What do you want me to say?"

Jethro stood up next to Bruce and put an arm around him. "This is where your Crisis of Conscience comes in, Bruce dude. Let's just say, as a thought embellishment, that we could fix it." ("Thought embellishment" was one of Jethro's buzzsaws.)

"Fix . . . it?"

Jethro handed Bruce a Robo-Bop with a pulsing Yes/No screen. "It's all on you, buddy. You push Yes, we can make a difference here. There'll be some disruptions, people might be a mite inconvenienced, but we can ameliorate some of the problems. Push No, and things go on as they are. But bear in mind—if you push Yes, you're the one who has to explain to the people."

Bruce still didn't understand what he was saying yes to, but he hardly cared. He jabbed the Yes button with his right thumb. Jethro whooped and led him to the executive elevator, so they could watch the fun from the roof.

"It should be almost instantaneous," Jethro said over his shoulder as he hustled into the lift. "Thanks to our patented 'snaggletooth' technology that makes all our products talk to each other. It'll travel around the world like a wave. It's part of our enterprise philosophy of Why-Not-Now."

The elevator lurched upward, and in moments they had reached the roof. "It's starting," Jethro said. He pointed to the nearest ThunderNet tower. The sleek lid was opening up like petals, until the top resembled a solar dish. And a strange haze was gathering over the top of it.

"This technology has been around for years, but everybody said it was too expensive to deploy on a widespread basis," Jethro said with a wink. "In a nutshell, the tops of the towers contain a photocatalyst material, which turns the CO_2 and water in the atmosphere into methane and oxygen. The methane gets stored and used as an extra power source. The tower is also spraying an amine solution into the air that captures more CO_2 via a proprietary chemical reaction. That's why the ThunderNets had to be so pricey."

© 2013, Lauren Pedersen / ASU

Just then, Bruce felt a vibration from his own Robo-Bop. He looked down and was startled to see a detailed audit of Bruce's personal carbon footprint—including everything he'd done to waste energy in the past five years.

"And hey, look at the parking lot," Jethro said. All the Car-Dingos were reconfiguring themselves, snaking new connections into the car engines. "We're getting most of those vehicles as close to zero emissions as possible, using amines that capture the cars' CO_2. You can use the waste heat from the engine to regenerate the amines." But the real gain would come from the car's GPS, which would start nudging people to carpool whenever another Car-Dingo user was going to the same destination, using a "packet-switching" model to optimize everyone's commute for greenness. Refuse to carpool, and your car might start developing engine trouble—and the Car-Dingos, Bruce knew, were almost impossible to remove.

As for the Crados? Jethro explained how they were already hacking into every appliance in people's homes, to make them energy-efficient whether people wanted them to be or not.

Zoe was standing at Bruce's elbow. "It's too late to stop the trend, or even reverse all the effects," she said over the din of the ThunderNet towers. "But we can slow it drastically, and our most optimistic projections show major improvements in the medium term."

"So all this time—all this hellish time—you had the means to make a difference, and you just . . . sat on it?" Bruce said. "What the fuck were you thinking?"

"We wanted to wait until we had full product penetration." Jethro had to raise his voice now; the ThunderNet towers were actually thundering for the first time ever. "And we needed people to be ready. If we had just come out and told the truth about what our products actually did, people would rather die than buy them. Even after Manhattan and Florida. We couldn't give them away. But if we claimed to be making overpriced, wasteful pieces of crap that destroy the environment? Then everybody would need to own two of them."

"So my Crisis of Conscience—" Bruce could only finish that sentence by wheeling his arms.

"We figured the day when you no longer gave a shit about your own future would be the day when people might accept this," Jethro said, patting Bruce on the back like a father, even though he was younger.

"Well, thanks for the mind games." Bruce had to shout now. "I'm going to go explore something I call my culture of drunkenness."

"You can't leave, Bruce," Jethro yelled in his ear. "This is going to be a major disruption, everyone's gadgets going nuts at once. There will be violence and wholesale destruction of public property. There will be chain saw rampages. There may even be Twitter snark. We need you to be out in front on this, explaining it to the people."

Bruce looked out at the dusk, red-and-black clouds churning as millions of ThunderNet towers blasted them with scrubber beams. Even over that racket, the chorus of car horns and shouts as people's Car-Dingos suddenly had minds of their own started to ring from the highway. Bruce turned and looked into the gleam of his boss's schoolmaster specs. "Fuck you, man," he said. Followed a moment later by, "I'll do it."

"We knew we could count on you." Jethro turned to the half-dozen or so executives cluttering the roof deck behind him. "Big hand for Bruce, everybody." Bruce waited until they were done clapping, then leaned over the railing and puked his guts out.

STORY NOTES—Charlie Jane Anders

Until recently, I was always intimidated to approach real scientists and experts to check the science in my stories. I figured they're busy people and don't have time to worry about my weird flights of fancy.

But I've found lately that scientists really like getting the chance to have input into science fiction, and working on my story in *Hieroglyph* really helped me get over my fear of being an annoying author.

For my story in *Hieroglyph*, I was hoping to pull off a fake-out—you think the story is going in one, fairly depressing, direction, and then it suddenly turns out to be something quite different. And for that to work, I needed there to be some technologies for mitigating environmental damage embedded in these apparently useless gadgets that everybody is carrying around.

So the great part about writing, and especially revising, this story was getting to have a crash course in different technologies that could absorb carbon. I exchanged tons of e-mails with two people at Arizona State University: Braden Allenby, Lincoln Professor of Engineering and Ethics, and Jean Andino, Senior Sustainability Scholar with the Global Institute of Sustainability. And I also e-mailed a lot with Jez Weston, a policy analyst with the Royal Society in New Zealand who had given a talk about geoengineering at Nerd Nite Wellington.

The thing I learned from all three of these experts was that doing things like reducing a car's emissions below a certain point, and capturing carbon from the air, are difficult and expensive to do—but there are things that could be coming along, even if they would be expensive to implement. (Perfect for the overpriced gadgets in my story.) Braden Allenby suggested you could spray sodium hydroxide into the air and capture carbon for storage underground. And then Jean Andino came up with an even better solution—you could use liquid amines to capture the carbon, with solar power used to regenerate them. Dr. Andino, who had done a lot of vork for Ford Motor Corporation, also suggested a technology that uses a photocatalyst to convert CO_2 emissions and water into methane, which could be used as a fuel source. You could even capture the CO_2 within the car's cabin.

This was a really fun research gig, and a chance to learn something about the cutting-edge technologies that could help save the planet someday.

"THE DAY IT ALL ENDED": THOUGHTS OF A TECHNOLOGIST—Brad Allenby

Brad Allenby, an engineer and ethicist at Arizona State University, discusses the radical worldview of "The Day It All Ended" at hieroglyph .asu.edu/DiZi.

TECHNICAL PAPER—Carbon Capture

Read an article from the peer-reviewed *Journal of Materials Chemistry A* about the production of solar fuels, coauthored by "The Day It All Ended" collaborator Jean Andino of Arizona State University, at hieroglyph.asu.edu/ DiZi.

TALL TOWER

Bruce Sterling

MY WIFE WENT TO the Tall Tower. She left for orbit, never to return to Earth. Gretchen so wanted to go on up there.

I got pretty lonesome. The Tall Tower commenced to weigh heavy on my troubled mind.

To dream big and to build big, that was the big idea of the Tall Tower. To build a tower that touched the cosmos. In weightlessness they build bigger than the green Earth can allow.

Big dreams do come true sometimes, but time goes on, despite the size of dreams. I'd fulfilled some dreams. A loving bride, two fine sons. I'd gotten in my full share of trout fishing and campfire songs with the guitar.

I had built a home, and I'd run a good business, too. I was a historical tour guide by trade. My horse, Levi, and I led a mule train of tourists together, down into an old-time copper mine.

That hole in Arizona was one of the biggest structures humankind had ever created—and in my own day, it was a mighty ghost mine, a feral wilderness of landslides, rattlesnakes, and cactus.

Levi and I made that Arizona copper mine into an exotic tour business. We kitted out for every season in our heritage cowboy gear: me with my white hat and blue jeans, plus a six-shooter and a lariat. Levi sported his shiny silver saddle and his blue-and-white-striped horse blanket.

The tourists were generous to me, while the tourist kids always loved Levi. In the off-season, Levi and I ventured far over the horizon, sometimes as far as the tumbledown ruins of El Paso and Tucumcari. The two of us were restless souls by our natures as man and beast.

Time had made me an older man. Being a horse, Levi was downright elderly.

That being said, the time had come for me to venture to the Tall Tower. Plenty of room up in orbit for a man's soul to grow to vast dimensions. Living in outer space, I would have a superhuman life span and wield superhuman powers. I'd be up among the stars, with the highest of the high technologies.

But one simple matter bothered me. What about my horse? To become "superhuman" is a great thing, obviously. But what about the "superequine"?

It was the wife who had first put that problem into my head. "It just don't seem fair," Gretchen told me one summer evening, as we sat on our back porch together at the rancho, drinking homemade beer. "Our animal friends will never share our bliss, when we're Ascended Masters up in Outer Space!"

My wife, Gretchen, enjoyed an intense spiritual life. Gretchen had always lived within sight of the Tall Tower. The Tall Tower cast its morning shadow from Arizona clear to Los Angeles.

Nothing mankind had built could match the steely splendor of that six-legged derrick soaring toward the stars. Big lights glared upon it, and small lights twinkled brightly, up and down the curves of its almighty slopes. Pretty swarms of drone-planes flew among its cross-braced beams.

Flower gardens hung off it. Trailing clouds rippled from the Tall Tower like pennants, because it pretty much made its own weather.

Since its completion, no earthly structure had ever matched the Tall Tower. Why build two of them? And why build such things on Earth? You had to build off the earth to outbuild the Tall Tower. The Tall Tower was the tallest, grandest possible structure that the earth could support.

The tower sang to us as it stood there. Every night there were launches, the passenger ships firing off. Those space-trains carried crowds of eager human beings, shedding all earthly limits, abjuring all worldly ties.

As mankind departed from Earth to build grander things in outer space, the healing Earth grew green and wild again. A man on a good horse could follow the empty highways from the Yukon to Honduras, and never set an eye on a fellow human being.

With technology lofted to the starry realm, the bears, wolves, and bald eagles returned to rule Earth's rivers, plains, and peaks. Longhorn cattle abounded. So did rugged mustangs, like my Levi. The earth abided under a night sky swarming with satellites.

Gretchen respected the Ascended Masters, putting faith in them for her salvation. Each and every night, cartridges of human astronauts were loaded into the Tall Tower's base. A narrow launch tube ran up the tower, a rifle barrel to the stars.

These spacecraft capsules, nestled within, would get quantumly transposed, through the astral technology of the Ascended Masters. The capsules existed down at the tower's base, and yet also existed far up at the tower's remote summit, both at the same cosmic instant.

When that wave-form probability collapsed, the quantum spacecraft would fling themselves from the tower straight to the heavens, squirting off slick as watermelon seeds.

When Gretchen betook herself upward, we didn't fight about that matter. The Ascended Masters had astral capacities. They lived in stellar paradises forged from the iron of asteroids, great space cities so colossal that I saw them in the daylight with my naked eye.

We human beings knew as much about their cosmic science as my horse, Levi, knew about saddle-stitching. The Ascended Masters were nano, and robo, and bio. We human beings were their larvae. The Ascended Masters never reproduced—for they left that vital task to us, humanity.

Through their own wise choice, the Ascended Masters were celibate. The greatest of them were astral, boneless entities, all telescope eyes, nerves, and megatons of living brain, floating through the cosmos in shining steel shells.

Earth was their cradle. The Ascended Masters called us from that cradle, to become their recruits. We ventured up there to join them in the heavens, once we felt good and ready for it, and until then, they kept their starry distance from us. That was a sensible arrangement.

Now, to tell the truth, some people had some problems with this state of affairs. Human nature is crooked, and sometimes we balk at salvation like a horse will shy at a shadow. So I will confess that I, too, had a problem. What about my horse?

That arrangement excluded my horse. A man is a being. And a horse is also a being. But humans are aspirational beings, who imagine, and speculate, and plan, and build.

No horse does all that. Yet Levi also had his dignity and worth. Because Levi wore the saddle and was dutiful. Levi had met his bargain with me. Now I found myself alone with him. My boys had grown, my wife had gone her own way. It was just him and me, under those bright stars and satellites.

Call me stubborn, or call me a sentimental fool, but I owed something to my sturdy beast.

So I settled my affairs. I sold off the spread, and I gave away my earthly possessions. I took a last farewell look around, and I saddled him up. The two of us headed for the Tall Tower to meet our destiny.

NEVER ONCE HAD I ventured to the remote and icy peak of the Tall Tower—I had only seen it, stenciled on the skyline like a promise of redemption. But I had been to the wicked city that grew within the spread legs of the tower's mighty base.

This thriving, noisy desert metropolis, crowded with space-bound pilgrims of every size, shape, and creed, bore the name of "Desconocido."

Because it had a giant tower standing on it, Desconocido was a mighty easy town to find. Finding trouble in that town was even easier. Those who dwell in the shadow of the gods will always make fun of the divine. The townsfolk of Desconocido were sharp-witted and crooked people, always full of their own schemes, with the much-mixed pigments of a whole lot of local color.

Desconocido was an oasis by its nature. The Tall Tower collected ice on its slanting, cloudy spars. Meltwater trickled down through a host of pipes. Giant steel shadows crawled across the city every day, sundial style. Every neighborhood had its own climate.

So as to get shot off up into orbit, pilgrims came to Desconocido from every corner of the world. Commonly, these sacred pilgrims would have some final fit of the nerves before they left Earth forever. They naturally desired some farewell glutting of the fleshpots. The locals were more than ready to oblige.

So Desconocido was a fine place to wake up next to a stranger. A place to discover new tastes for ancient human vices. A place to get robbed, or to get killed, maybe. Maybe all of that would happen to you in one single day.

My own needs were simple and my aims were clear. My horse, Levi, and I had long been partners. I refused to become superhuman until Levi was superequine. I had made up my mind that Levi would transcend the innate limits of the horsely.

Somebody in Desconocido would help me with my ambition. Obviously this notion of mine could not be entirely new. Nothing was entirely new to Desconocido.

I therefore commenced to look around the town, with the caution of my worldly wisdom, being a man of mature years.

My first concern was proper shelter for my horse. I found that stable above the city.

The Tall Tower had vertical farms. Vast expanses of steel real estate sloped upward. Crops could grow within chosen spaces that were cooler, wetter, drier, or brighter, all according to taste.

So I found a perpendicular hacienda run by some kindly Jewish folk. These religious sectarians had strict dietary requirements. Their ancient scriptures didn't allow them to eat modern foodstuffs.

Modern dining was based on microbes, algae, and insects, as one might well expect from agricultural science. The Jews found that prospect bothersome. Nobody else did, but the chosen folk had never been just anybody.

My new hosts were hard to beat for industriousness. They had staked up a regular Hanging Babylon for themselves, with steel gardens of baths and troughs and tubes and pumps and shelves, for nigh on a vertical kilometer.

My hosts had practical use for a horse on the Sabbath, when they forbade themselves electricity. So these farmers and I came to a cordial arrangement. They sheltered my horse, fed him his grain, and me my spinach, and also, they loaned me a cot. In return, I sought out new markets for their vegetable produce, among the other folks downtown.

I made it my business to inquire among all the numerous cults, breeds, and creeds of tower dwellers. The Tall Tower had attracted every breed of mystic to itself, from the Amish to the Zoroastrian. Those of a spiritual bent clung to the tower like iron dust to a steel magnet.

I made it my business to inquire among these believers. Mankind had always been perplexed about God, and life's meaning, and the soul, and immortality, and human purpose in the world. Most of us had it figured that the Tall Tower had resolved these issues through sheer mechanical engineering.

However, I soon learned of other ways of thought. These mystical creeds had many good answers ready for my heartfelt spiritual questions. They all had different answers to offer me, though.

After we'd discussed spiritual matters for a few hours, I might change the subject and offer them some kosher vegetables. Commonly they would buy.

My questions about superanimals were already known to these wise folk. I learned about supercanines and superfelines. Many tenderhearted pet owners had desired to share their spiritual aspirations with their family companions. Attempts were made, and some results were found.

That news encouraged me. I followed up on every lead. My ambitions were rewarded.

I learned about superbirds from the Parsees. The Parsees, too, were Tall Tower folk. For centuries on end, these Parsees had been the smallest of mankind's great old-time religions.

It had long been the sacred practice of the Parsees to expose their dead to vultures atop a great "Tower of Silence." Thus the affinity, for such was the ancient Parsee ritual.

Most everyone in the tower felt a deep respect for the Parsees. For the tower people, the presence of the Parsees among them was a touching validation of their chosen way of life.

Unfortunately, the sacred vultures of the Parsees had all died out from

Earth's climate change. As the earth's stricken skies cleared up somewhat, the Parsees had struggled to revive—or rather to reinvent—their extinct, sacred, corpse-eating birds.

With much cleverness and effort, the Parsees had bred themselves a superbuzzard. These superbirds nested within the Tall Tower.

These artificial Parsee supercondors were the size of small aircraft. The ultrabuzzards had become a common sight, drifting over the American Southwest, where they followed the bison herds for the sake of the carrion. Splendid creatures. A poetic sight, and truly a gift to the world.

But to tell the truth, their Parsee hearts just weren't in this achievement. The superbird project didn't satisfy their deeper aims. So these genteel, noble people, who had an unbroken spiritual tradition of four millennia, had reached the end of their trail. The only direction left for the Parsees was up. One by one, they were all becoming superhuman spacefolk. Soon the earth would know their faith no more.

That tale well nigh broke my heart. I might have joined the Parsees, if they accepted converts. But these vanishing folk were a proud and dignified people, and just weren't having any of that. So, instead, I just sold them some aquaponic rice and some saffron.

Next, I tried out my vegetable wares with the tower's big-time grocers. Businessmen are a practical people, so they sold modern scientific foods made from bugs and algae. I convinced the grocers to stock old-fashioned vegetables as window dressings. I threw in some pretty flowers to settle that deal.

These antique displays made the shoppers stop and gawk. I would drop by the stores in my fancy cowboy gear and publicly devour some vegetables, for the sake of the show. That was a pretty good business.

In return for this service of mine, a grateful grocer informed me about superhorse feed: a high-performance fuel, purpose-brewed for racehorses.

This sticky, salty goop had every nutrient that the peak-performing athlete horse could require. Levi commenced to dine on that substance and began to perk up right away. I also arranged some regular blood filtering and growth-hormone management. Results were gratifying. Old Levi's mortal horseliness began to visibly slough right off him.

The dingy hair of his dappled palomino hide fell out in clumps. A spry new superhorse fur grew in, thick and shiny. His gnarled yellow teeth turned white at the roots. His cracked hooves grew in hard and smooth.

The Jewish folk grew somewhat afraid of Levi. So I had to rent Levi a fresh stall in an old metal foundry, where he could buck, kick, and crash into things without hurting anybody.

Through these incidents, I came to know the men of steel who repaired and maintained the Tall Tower. These high-steel roughnecks faced a tough situation. I understood and I sympathized.

Back when the tower was first built, it had been a prestigious undertaking to acquire millions of tons of high-performance construction steel. But in our own more modern day, we had so many abandoned cities that steel was a pestilence to us. We had to pay people to haul steel away.

These roughnecks and I enjoyed a few drinking sessions at their favorite cantina. I convinced them that they should rethink their public image and take due pride in their historic steel.

The best way to do that, said I, was to throw some big heritage banquets, where the people ate old-fashioned vegetables. These civic festivals would restore public appreciation of old-fashioned materials like steel. The steel men could ensure that their Tall Tower was maintained only with authentic metal.

It took some doing to bring my idea to fruition. Nobody changes Rome in a day. Bit by bit, though, Tall Tower sentiment turned against newfangled rubbish like silicon nitride and foamed carbon nanotubes, and back to the real deal of steel.

Every city is an open conspiracy between the politicians who run it and the technicians who build it and maintain it. A million tons of steel is a whole lot of city business. Once a city has a good steady business, the city's people want to buy into that. Our cities shape us, and then we shape our cities. The people of Desconocido had hearts of steel. As a stranger, I always knew that about them, and after a while, they agreed with me.

The locals took a shine to me after that episode, and I found myself mixing with the Tall Tower's higher circles.

The Tall Tower's jet set traveled by private plane. The finer folk had always lived it up in the heights.

Rich folks have all the human troubles, just richer ones. The Tall Tower itself had been built by some hugely rich guy—a computer lunatic, or so the story went.

The original builder of the Tall Tower wasn't much remembered in my own day—I'd never even heard his last name. But he'd been a typical

old-timer, because he'd built himself a Vegas-style gambling casino way
up the top of the tower. He had also built an air-conditioned toy train that
could spiral up the tower's sides, to reach this neon utopia at the peak.

That brash casino was sorely doomed. Every day it suffered harsh
blasts of raw, paint-peeling Arizona sunshine, unfiltered by the earth's
atmosphere. That ordeal commenced long before the local dawn at ground
level, and it lasted till way after sunset.

The casino had fried and gone bust, and the toy train followed suit.
That little train had to run through killer jet-stream winds at nine kilome-
ters. Up around twelve kilometers was a lightning-blasted "death zone."
Above that menace, the Tall Tower narrowed down into "the Neck."
Nobody lived "above the Neck" except surveillance spies and the military:
grumpy, secretive folk.

The tower folk had adapted to reality in their always colorful fashion. They tore down their broken old train. They found new means of
traveling their tower. Drone taxis and helicopters were the commonest.
A spiderweb of cable cars was popular for a while. Pneumatic tubes like
big blowpipes worked for some folks. Magnetic limousines ran silently up
the steel girders. Big catapults were built, and by "big" I mean levers big
enough to throw vacation houses due upward.

On ceremonious occasions, the tower people visited their tower's peak.
Important tower rituals occurred up there—some public, some secret.

To reach the peak, the pilgrims flew halfway to the summit, then took
airtight pods through a creaky series of derricks, cable cars, and elevators,
all owned by a variety of greedy interests, all of them with their hands out.

This cumbersome arrangement struck me as decadent, frankly.

Why not ride a horse to the top of the Tall Tower? It seemed to me that
a horse and rider should be able to venture, from the ground level, all the
way to the tower's summit, through the main strength of man and beast.

I believed that feat could be achieved. Of course it would be difficult.
The brave horse would require an airtight space suit of some kind, with an
oxygen helmet and an intravenous feed. The rider would have to guide his
beast through the killer jet-stream winds at nine kilometers.

Past twelve kilometers was the Neck, where the Tall Tower narrowed
down in a near vacuum, with deadly cold and blinding solar radiation. The
Neck was the tower's dangerous choke point, full of defunct giant turbofans,
lidar surveillance devices from forgotten national spy agencies, weather

modification efforts that had never worked out—a historical junkyard.

The final stage, beneath the tower's peak, was rumored to be especially dreadful. Strange breeds of lightning chewed at that dry, icy steel: sprites, blue-devils, black ball-lightning clusters, and space-weather things with no human names.

The worst obstacles the horse and I would confront would be human beings. Desperados lurked up in the stratospheric badlands. I'd heard thrilling tales of vacuum robberies and ambushes, with airless arrows flying hither and yon, and tomahawks, and Bowie knives. Nobody dared to venture to the tower's summit without native escorts and uniformed guards.

I knew that these Wild West tall tales must outpace the reality. But those who meet reality may not live to tell the truth.

I decided to go through with this adventure because I thought it was best for my horse. In climbing to the peak of the Tall Tower, my horse would perform a superequine feat. Levi would become a famous horse, with a name that would live to posterity.

That prospect made every kind of sense to me—and I even had a vision that stretched a ways beyond that.

If the two of us survived the trip, maybe we could make a regular tour business out of a Tall Tower climb. We had once led tourist mule trains deep into a giant copper pit. Why not climb steel ledges to the roof of the world?

This adventure was a spiritual quest. To carry it through, Levi and I needed a generous and sympathetic patron. Someone with deep pockets, who understood the idealistic nature of our mission.

Since Fortune favors the bold, Lady Luck smiled on me and my horse. It turned out that I already knew my patroness. Louisa was from the Dakotas, just like me. We'd known each other as kids.

The last time I'd seen my childhood friend Louisa, she'd been the prettiest girl in the wreck of a Dakota shale-oil boomtown. Even at age six, Louisa been a girl to sit on the swing with a simper, so some big boy would come along and push her higher. She always had her eye fixed toward the top.

Nowadays, my childhood friend Louisa had become a rich widow. Louisa had done hair, scarlet lipstick, smoldering eyes, clattering heaps of turquoise jewelry, and a tailored jacket of the finest buckskin. The pretty girl was a pretty fine lady now, and she owned a big airtight spread six kilometers up.

Inside, Louisa's palace was full of aerospace curios—racing trophies, parasails, quadcopters, ornithopters, and suchlike. The rich businessman who'd made Louisa a lucky widow was one of those hard-driving, over-achiever types. When his heart blew out, he left Louisa as a Tall Tower dame in fine standing, a famous patroness of local culture and the arts.

I explained to her my aspirations for the horse.

Well, no ten-year-old girl could have been more eager to see Levi. In short order, Louisa swanned into the derelict foundry where I'd hidden old Levi away. Levi had grown mighty restless. His superequine qualities were itching at the palomino. Levi was bigger and more muscular in every horsely dimension. He was glowing like a stove.

I feared that Levi might take a big bloody nip out of Louisa, but Louisa had never lacked for dainty charm over man and beast. In short order that horse was eating right out of her hand.

"I know just the artistic craftsman to design a space suit for this noble animal," Louisa declared, tipping up the brim of her velvet sombrero. "For his great adventure, he'll wear steel plate armor, airtight, like a deep-sea diver! Then he'll charge right up my tower like a battle horse for knights and ladies, in the days of goddamned yore!"

I allowed that it might be hard to fit a growing horse into airtight steel plates.

"You can let me take care of the costuming," said Louisa, having at my horse's spiky hide with a steel-toothed currycomb. "Veterinary medicine is one of the fine arts! Let's get this beast out of this rusty place and into a proper spa!"

The kindly friendship of this tower lady made my special mission so easy—but then things got personal.

"So when are you ascending into outer space?" she asked me, fitting the bridle bit between Levi's big new tusky teeth.

"I hadn't thought that out yet," I told her.

"Well, you must be flying into outer space! That's what people do, who come to the Tall Tower. Don't you have your launch date set yet? I could help out with the waiting list."

"I hadn't made up my mind about it."

"You are a mortal human being, Cody Jennings! You could slip on the soap in the shower! Then you'll never turn extraterrestrial!"

"Well, you see, ma'am, my special mission here is all about my horse."

"You are a hick," Louisa decided, knitting her pretty eyebrows. "You're a long, tall drink of water straight off the range. Life sure hasn't changed you much, Cody. You've got a whole lot to learn about civilization."

All that might be true, but I didn't much care for the lesson. "Well," I countered, "why haven't you gone off into outer space your own self, then, Louisa?"

"I'm waiting here on Earth to find my one true love," said Louisa. She commenced to lament about that subject, all through the length of the day and well into the scarlet evening.

Louisa confessed that her search for true love was the meaning of her womanly existence. So she couldn't possibly ascend up to outer space, and go all floaty and brainy and stellar and celibate, without first finding and uniting with her true earthly soul mate.

Fine ladies do like the cowboys. It had been quite a while for me. So we had at it.

At first, it was lovely. We had some nice fun, and we saw eye to eye about the horse business. We made good progress arranging the mission to the top of the Tall Tower.

Slowly, it dawned on me that I wouldn't be numero uno on Louisa's checklist. A beauty queen already has a steady guy: the mirror.

Levi and I found ourselves caught in Louisa's stable. Levi was all cyborged up with his new monitoring systems, implants and sensors and drip feeds. I was like some bronze statue of a cowpoke, kept inside a glass jar.

We had company, too. Louisa was a kindly soul, even after she got bored in the bedroom. The grand dame had a regular mule train of the beautiful people, traipsing in and out of her palace.

I had to share the far end of the mahogany dining table with a character named Renato. Renato and I were manly rivals for our lady's charms, so likely we should have knifed each other. However, we got to sharing the crystal wine decanter. We both saw the humor in our situation.

I took a good liking to him, for Renato was a lively, talented, clever character with a sideways eye. This artist could see certain things that I couldn't see and do things that I couldn't do. A man like that has a value.

"We live in a unique period of art history," Renato confided one day, as we killed some time drinking vintage whiskey in Louisa's airtight study. This handsome trophy room was chock-full of fine leather-bound art books. Nobody had opened them in four hundred years.

"Even in artistic prehistory," said Renato, "prehuman beings made petroglyphs. Nowadays, we human beings remain on this planet as a thin and temporary remnant. Few in number, we dwindle away toward the stars. We humans persist between our remote past as primates and some unknowable state of transcendent being."

"So, Renato, what's that all mean?" I said.

He sipped his whiskey. "In terms of art practice, it's not much different. Just cut out some studio space and get the work done. Ship it while you can still feel it. And never trust a critic."

I asked Renato what he'd been working on lately. I had learned that this was always a good question for artists.

Renato needed to show me that personally. So we made a break for it, left Louisa's fine mansion, and ran along, breathless and freezing, up a long, crooked set of corrugated metal stairs.

We broke through the creaky airlock of his artist's studio. Renato's atelier was a rust-stained garage pod, where everything stank of paint, solder, plastic, and Renato's unwashed clothes. Still, his studio had excellent lighting and a mighty fine view.

"I have found a way to make an authentic human gesture, even in the present day," said Renato. He sat on a stool and plugged in his work lamp and teakettle. "I do this by re-creating ancient works of performance art. These performances date to an era when every human was mortal, and there were no superhumans."

"Okay," I said, coughing into my fist. That thin, cold air had brought up the dirt from the bottom of my lungs.

"Reviving a work of performance is like thawing a frog out of ice," Renato told me. "If it jumps, then it's still alive."

"I get it," I told him. "That's just like playing an old campfire song." Some songs were mighty old, yet still mighty sad.

Renato opened a paper volume and showed me the archival description of his work of performance art. This was written in some lost European language that wasn't even English.

"What is a 'Polaroid camera'?" I asked.

"That was my own question, too," said Renato, closing the book. "Those devices were extinct machines from a long-lost media technology. As part of my art practice, I re-created a working replica of a Polaroid camera." Renato opened a cabinet with a key from his work pants.

Renato pointed his strange device at me. He pressed its trigger. A whirring noise came, and a thin slice of plastic slid out. It was white and blank. Renato shook it around and slapped it.

Then a picture blossomed out of it, like a colorful bruise under unbroken skin. This was a "photo-graph" of me. In the picture, I looked appropriately surprised.

"Can I keep this?" I said.

"Everybody asks that!" Renato smiled. "Of course you can keep it, my friend! I am an artist, and such is my gift!" He handed me the machine. "Here, try it yourself."

I pressed the red tab with my finger. The camera jumped. The blank slab of photo-graph came out.

My photo-graph was crooked and cluttered, but it was a living piece of reality. I looked at the picture, and looked at the scene I had photo-graphed, and then I looked at the picture again.

Who could ever think up such an amazing achievement? Humanity was the damnedest thing ever. "Your picture art is tremendous, Renato! I stand in awe."

"The camera is merely a technical instrument," said Renato. "Performance art is of a different order of experience."

"It is?"

Renato handed me a packet made of paper. The packet had a small poster stuck on it, with some old-time political leader, and a slogan in a dead language.

I was bewildered by this time, there being so many fine things in the art world that I knew nothing about.

"This was once called a 'mailing envelope,'" said Renato. "People wrote their news on sheets of paper, with ink. Then they put their paper messages in these envelopes and sealed them. They wrote an address on the envelope and bought this special little emblem from a government. With this stamp attached, these mailing envelopes would be physically carried, by uniformed officials, anywhere on this planet!"

I had never imagined such a thing. It was even more amazing than the photo-graph.

"Think of those vast networks of moving paper!" Renato preached. "Billions of sealed letters carried from sender to receiver! The postal systems lasted for centuries, crossing huge expanses of space and time. That is history, and it's all entirely true."

"I am a lucky man to see this," I said. I had always thought that the Tall Tower was the grandest thing mankind had ever built—but now I realized that we were capable of other great things.

Renato nodded at my compliment. "The art performance is as follows. Find a woman you might love, but never will love. Take her picture with the Polaroid camera. Before the image can develop, put the picture inside the envelope. Then seal the letter. Never send the letter to anyone."

For some dark time, I thought hard about this strange ritual. There was something deep, and holy, and even frightening about this ancient thing Renato had revealed to me. This performance art was more disturbing, in its own way, than the Parsees and their flesh-eating condors.

There was something entirely Tall Tower about the situation in which I had found myself. This ritual was trying to speak to me. I stood upon the brink of understanding.

Testing myself, I took up my photo-graph, and I slid it inside the mailing envelope. These two objects fit together perfectly. The two long-lost things, these two long-dead technologies, had been built for each other. They would never again be united.

I looked at what I had done, held it in my own hand, and I understood performance art. I felt it in the sudden, painful, wordless way that a horse might feel a stick.

Renato handed me the camera. "My friend, I have performed this work of art. You should perform it, too."

So, through this help from a generous colleague, I became a performance artist. The performance worked, too. It worked just as well as it had ever worked for any human being.

MY TRIP TO THE peak with Levi became our act of performance art.

After declaring myself to be an artist, I was able to advance toward my goal. Step by step, I was able to map a route, and gather supplies, and create equipment. Those were engineering problems—but if I'd called myself an engineer, the tower people would have forbidden me to try my feat, and maybe even jailed me. Their politics required me to be artful. Art was good for people problems.

The people of the Tall Tower were a subtle, complex, and long-established people. They were the citizens of a great monument, and the occupants of a great religious center. Therefore, they were a perverse people.

They never told me everything they knew. They never meant everything that they said. They played fast and loose with things that shouldn't be mocked. They made me promises that they never meant to keep.

Some of them despised me. They wanted me to fail. They meant me harm. My worst enemies within the Tall Tower were people like myself.

The worst people were interlopers like me, invaders like me, outsider people and wilderness people. These were people in the tower, but not of the tower.

Up above the Neck, where the Tall Tower grew slender, but somewhat below the top, where the tower spread out in its crown—the tower had a wilderness.

This distant zone of the tower was so icy and airless and hateful to human flesh that it had never pleased anybody. Those steely badlands had every disadvantage that the tower offered, and none of its joy or its glamour.

It was deathly cold up there, airless, heavily radiated, and poorly maintained. It was always in motion, too. Up above the Neck, the tower swayed.

Bad men fled up there, because they could hide and not be apprehended. Hidden, yet at a great height, they could see things they were not meant to see—they were eagle-eyed, these predatory men, the mountain bandits.

Other men went up there because they were ordered to restore control. Rugged men, tough men, the alpine soldiers.

Time passed, as is its habit. The men of the Tall Tower's heights, those bandits and soldiers, they could not remain adversaries. The bandit who turns his coat becomes a thief-catcher. The soldier who disgraces his uniform becomes a warlord. Once they learn that they are feared by other men, they soon find their kinship and commonality.

Women of bad intent went up there to seek evil men. Evil children were born.

Those natives of the great heights cared nothing for what seemed good or bad by the standards of those below. They were a naked, rude, and simple people. Their bare steel homeland was poor and miserable, deprived of even the earth's most basic riches, of water, air, and topsoil.

Somebody had made them suffer. So somebody had to pay.

The more subtle and courtly and complex people of the Tall Tower—they were afraid of those few wolfish predators who dwelled in the steel hinterlands high above their heads. But time passed, and they found themselves forced to pay the ones they feared. Mostly, the peaceful people paid to be left alone. This is the worst sort of payment, because it guarantees outlaws paid to stay outlaws.

As more time passed, the tower people created social customs from their social problems. They paid these wicked people to do certain awful things that they themselves secretly wanted done. Most of those human crimes had very old human names.

But some crimes were new crimes. The biggest had to do with a great device built within the structure of the tower. This was a working space-launch machine, but of an old-fashioned, merely human sort. People called this tower machine "the Whip."

The Whip was a large and powerful contraption, installed into the tower well above the Neck. The Whip was like the free-spinning reel in a tall fishing rod.

This Whip had a strong fishline, plus geared wheels and counterweights. The Whip was a human aerospace technology, built at great expense.

The Whip was designed to claw up a small burden from the surface of the earth. Any modest object with the heft and the shape of a barrel, or a packing crate, or maybe an atomic bomb.

Then it would reel that burden up at sudden crazy speed and "crack the Whip," just toss its payload into the very heavens, at a lashing, supersonic speed.

If this flung device was a rocket, it would ignite and fly into orbit. If that rocket carried steel nails aboard, that rocket could burst.

A rocket full of orbiting nails was a cruel and deadly thing. A bucket full of steel nails, spreading out as stinging space junk, was a long-lived, ever-spreading nuisance that even the Ascended Masters would fear.

What man can't fear a man who doesn't fear to make the gods afraid?

The people of the Tall Tower direly feared the Whip. They were also immensely proud about it. They respected and adored anyone who dared to possess it. Their oppressor was always one of themselves—the underworld tyrant of their steely overworld.

There had been many of these tyrants in the Tall Tower. These bold desperados wore a crown of blood. Every gangster king had a fancy name and an epithet, the Tall Tower's heartfelt folk poetry. The Head of All Heads, the Flying Ace, the Signor of the Skies, the Man of Steel, the Chief Engineer, maybe you catch my drift.

Nobody bluntly admitted that this dark business was the state of affairs within the Tall Tower. This was no simple matter of bad engineering. This was a darkly human, civilized complication. Everybody was implicated. Nobody had clean hands.

Rather than decry the situation, the victims wrote ironic, knowing songs about their plight. Every clean and simple solution to this grave problem had already been tried, and had failed. Repeatedly.

Once every other generation, some stout-hearted group of younger folk would rebel, and unify, and march to the heights, and depose the bloody tyrant at some cost in their own blood.

Once these adventurers were up there themselves, though, and in command of the heights, they would realize that they themselves now held the Whip over other people. The Whip was the Tall Tower's noblest human achievement. Nobody ever dismantled the Whip.

To reach the Tall Tower's summit, and to complete our quest, Levi and I had to gallop through these adversaries. They were many, while Levi and I were just a man and a horse.

I tried to beg an audience with the famous bandit chief who held the Whip. This brigand was called "the Astronaut." To grant this wicked man his due, the Astronaut was a man of supreme physical courage.

The Astronaut had climbed into a crude rocket attached to the Whip. The Whip had flung the Astronaut into orbit around Earth. So the Astronaut had seen outer space personally. He had even survived the descent back to earthly soil. The Astronaut had ventured into outer space and yet remained a human being.

This stunning feat sure made my sideshow with my horse look pretty small. The Astronaut had ridden a rocket into orbit, while I was trying to climb the Tall Tower by riding a horse. My request was modest—but the Astronaut was jealous about his prestige. He refused to hear from me. I was beneath his notice.

Mankind can build a Great Thing. Sometimes we do it. But then we have to live with the consequences of greatness. What does a Great Thing tell us about ourselves? Not that we are great, but that our Great Things are so rare, and so much abused. So many in our dreams, so few to loom like towers in the light of day.

After learning of this dark and decadent business, in its many secret scraps and sinful hints, and in taking that bad news to heart, I realized I was becoming a Tall Tower man. Through my intimacy with them, I was joining their civilization. I had come to think, feel, and live just as they did. Since I saw so much of this darkness within myself, I even came to love them for it.

Yet I persisted in my desire to ride to the top of the Tall Tower. This quest was about the union of me and my horse—and Levi was rarin' to go.

Ever the good listener to my troubles, the superequine horse had become all a horse could be, and more. Levi had become a living force of supernature. If I had my human doubts and fears, Levi had none of those.

To see Levi in his present state was to realize the potential of warm blood and a beating heart. Levi was noble. He was magnificent.

Having failed at my all-too-human problems, I let Levi take the lead for both of us. Levi was ready for adventure. He was eager. He was a great beast rearing and tramping in a suit of shining steel.

When we embarked for the top of the Tall Tower, Levi and I, we had a pretty good crowd to cheer us onward and upward.

Levi made no fine departing speech to the people, so neither did I. Anyway, I was all sealed up, just like him, in a homemade space suit. Levi, in his overlapping steel plates sealed with rubber rings, was every bit as big as a steel rhinoceros.

We cantered upward that glorious first day, with gangs of happy kids jumping and yelling at us, and my dear local friends placing some wily bets against my survival.

We left the lower city streets and commenced to climb.

There were lots of streets, then fewer streets, then more and more vacant air.

By sunset, we were up into a neighborhood of great refinement. In this cooler, cleaner air, the tower was graced with many fine villas and chalets. Every national tradition of architecture had conjoined up here and reached some final and humane agreement. These were the places of refined dwelling within mankind's last great human monument. They possessed taste and elegance.

I reached my chosen base camp at the estate of an obliging lady friend. I spent a day repairing leaks and tending to a blistered sore on Levi's fetlock. This was a marathon, and the hardest part was ahead of us.

On the third day, we climbed relentlessly, and the human habitations dwindled away beneath us. We found ourselves in an area of bared machinery, strangely overgrown with thriving alpine weeds. These hardy plants of the Rocky Mountains had been brought to the tower by the dung of migrating birds.

By the evening of day four, we had climbed well above the tower's snowline. Air was gently hissing through a dozen holes in our suits.

I made lavish use of an epoxy I'd brought. It cured without air, but it cured up mighty stiff. With every kilometer of height that we gained, Levi and I lost flexibility. His noble shining armor looked as patched as his palomino hide.

In these sparser surroundings, we still saw rich folks living in their pressure pods, waving a greeting from behind their exclusive plate glass.

For a few kilometers, some roughneck steel men kept us company in their sealed tractor. Sometimes a drone airplane would putter by with a pennant for us, some wisecrack from a skeptic, or a mash note from a lady fan.

After that, our climb got hard and lonely. Most people just plain gave up at these heights. Living without air is far worse than living without water, while the lack of water will destroy all living things.

As my horse and I gallantly ventured on, I could see all kinds of strange, haphazard methods and inventions. Big rubber bubbles. Hairy garages like soda-straw haystacks. Wheeled caravans that retreated downward to suck up fresh air and then returned to the heights. Cryogenic air conditioners that froze oxygen in steel pails of air, then reeled that air up all spiderlike, so that folks could somehow breathe.

There were lichen shelters, and barnacle shelters, that sucked in traces of air through a foamy lacquer and wouldn't let the air back out. These dogged human settlers of vacuum weren't beaten yet. After two hundred years of the tower's existence, the great steel aerial desert still had its diehards. Every once in a great distance, tucked into some steel niche, I would see a pale, sunless, bearded, crazy face at a porthole . . .

I, too, found myself engaged in fateful struggle with my own overlarge ambitions.

My horse and I, intimately joined at the saddle, had become two bloated bubbles of imperiled air. A swift death by freezing suffocation surrounded our every step. Our glassy helmets steamed up with our labored breathing.

With an effort, I could pull my bare hand out of my space-suit sleeve, squinch it down, and scratch the dew off my faceplate. So I could see to guide the horse—but then, frost formed all over my helmet. This was my human warmth and moisture, adhering to me.

Frosted up as we were, we were hard put to see the obstacles—even those directly in front of Levi's big airtight rubber horseshoes.

I had made a paper map to the heights, based on the best advice from past explorers. At kilometer six, a cruel gust of wind caught my map and bore it off like a tumbleweed.

Then I had to depend on Levi's instincts. To give him his due praise, the superequine horse was bold and tireless. Fed intravenously while huffing pure oxygen, Levi climbed as deftly as a mountain goat.

I could tell from the airtight reek of his heavy sweat that the beast was suffering, yet Levi understood our goal. If I died in his saddle, he would carry my corpse to the heights.

The broken guardrails, the half-collapsing ramps, the piles of defunct machinery, the dizzying aerial vistas of desert—they didn't daunt my horse. Iron stairs, he took two at a time. Burdened though he was by his steel armor, he didn't hesitate to jump.

Sometimes, when rounding some desolate iron corner, we would catch a vista from the awesome height we had achieved. We saw the curvature of the earth, and layers of haze in the atmosphere. We saw aircraft flying below us, small and bright as fireflies, and we saw the Tall Tower's long gray pennant clouds, wreathing and writhing in the tower's mighty slipstream.

The homely features of the planet's surface had gone all abstract with our distance. Homes were mere dots, roads were sore red scratches, gullies were crooked little veins, everything gone remote in the blended shades of planetary hues, olive, rust, dusty hazes.

At night, quantum launches rushed up the core of the Tall Tower. As we slept uneasily, stinking in our airtight suits, there would come a gutwrenching sense of unnatural motion, of a space-time twisting speed that was so much more than any earthly speed—these awesome sensations rippled through my puckered skin and Levi's horsehide, and I heard the horse bellow in the tainted, private atmosphere we shared.

Sometimes, I would dismount. The suit seals worked, but we lost some good air by doing it. Still, I had to move to ease my body's pain and stiffness, and also to set loose the emptied cylinders of oxygen, and lighten Levi's load.

We were lucky with the legendary winds of the heights. Those winds existed, and they direly wanted to blow us to hell, but we made haste, and the winds got weak on us faster than they could get vicious on us.

After our windy ordeal, we plodded up into a strange, glaring, silent place, where the sun was round like a golden coin, and shone crazy bright, and the bare, scorched surfaces did odd tricks. Rust patinas that looked steel-solid popped off and chipped like fingernail polish. Electrostatic dust clung to us, then crept around on us in little waves of living grime, and leaped off us in eerie haste.

Slow tremors ran through the great metal Tall Tower. Some of the shadowed cracks had dry ice in them, or some dirty, furry, frozen substance that wasn't honest water. Things decayed up here—but they decayed through methods unknown to living organisms. An airless, spacey, mummified degeneration.

There were metallic vibrations, and sometimes awful swaying rumbles, but no air to carry any audible noise. Every hut and pressured arch and citadel looked sun-scorched, gray, and entirely old.

There were no warning signs above the Neck, where the hostiles dwelled. No sign of any life that a native of Earth's surface would understand. But there were huge, archaic machineries, and there were death traps. At this height, even simple barbed wire could kill a man, for the barbs could rip his suit. There was barbed wire aplenty, in snaky tangles and coils.

Once Levi snagged a thin tripwire, where a big tumbledown trap of concrete blocks was poised to crush us like bugs. But that trap had been set decades ago, and a grit of static dust had glued the deadly blocks together.

There were mazes of fat white pipe, wrapped in shiny airtight tape. Slanted solar panels sat in tight nests of colored electrical wire. Sometimes I would see a gently steaming rivulet of icy sewage, in areas that should have no water at all. Machines were running up here, for I felt a rhythmic banging. Some of those bangs felt sinister and deliberate, like a drum-code conveyed by human hands.

I would like to claim that it was bravery and skill that got us to the tower's summit, but it was luck plus grim persistence. When we finally reached the peak, I was so weary, so chafed and stale in my own skin, that I had given up counting the oxygen bottles for our likely fatal trip down.

Levi and I plodded up one last interior ramp to the tower's flat summit. The Tall Tower was so huge that its great flat head was a desert plaza—an abandoned, airless ghost town.

We knew we had reached the top through the simple fact that there was nothing left to climb. Just the blackened sky overhead, stars visible in daylight, and glowing satellites, chasing one another through the heavens, in their stately and abstract fashion.

For a hard-breathing hour, Levi and I clomped around the airless streets of the long-dead casino, in a thin gritty film that seemed to be meteor dust. I was vaguely looking for some souvenir that I might loot, to prove to folks that I had really been up there.

Then I noticed footprints. Naked, savage footprints, in that gritty dust, at the very summit of the Tall Tower.

The horse and I followed that trail. I soon found many marks of toes and heels, even finger smears, of agile men running and falling, trampling one another in hasty steps.

Then we came upon the savage ceremony. They were naked and ferocious, these young men covered head to foot in warpaint grease. In their sacred ceremony, their secret ritual performance, they were flinging their bare human bodies from the peak of the Tall Tower toward the distant earth so far below.

These initiates of a mystical fraternity were casting themselves, headlong and gasping, into free fall toward our mother planet. They had built a BASE-jumping ramp, a skeletal tangle of cordage and lumber. They were scampering straight off that, naked but for odd little parachutes.

These fierce, savage teens, in order to attain the awesome privilege of jumping into emptiness, had to run through a gauntlet of their fellows.

These older, wiser brutes wore diving suits and homemade tanks like aqualungs. They also carried long canes, which they cheerfully deployed to beat the daylights out of the naked kids, whose bare ribs heaved convulsively at empty vacuum, before they flung themselves off in their frantic pursuit of the living sea of air far below.

These barbarians of the airless heights, born and raised within sealed chambers and as pale as ghosts, were performing this strange feat, not because it was easy, but because it was hard.

This soulful agony was a noble performance, and I had spoiled the art of it, for the medicine men saw my intrusion, and they were furious.

Instant confusion reigned. The remaining naked daredevils convulsed and fainted beneath their warpaint. The older warriors, those who wore the breathing masks, didn't know whether to kill me right away, or to rescue their smothering fellows.

It was Levi who proved my salvation. We had committed a grave offense, but not even the most reckless brave wanted to face this beast of mine, this uncanny rhinoceros clad all in steel.

To these natives of the heights, a creature like Levi was a wonderment.

The natives and I couldn't speak to each other—for there was no air for us to speak with—but I made it clear to the savages by hand signs that, whatever fate we met, my horse and I would meet that fate together.

Levi and I deserved punishment for the insult we had delivered—but to the eyes of these savages, our misdeed, so strange and unexpected to them, bore a mystical significance. Our intrusion was a sign.

We had to leave the sacred ground of the tower in one of two directions: down or up. As our savage judges saw the situation, up would be all right, and down would be all right, too. As long as we left, and we never returned.

The horse and I didn't care to leap to our deaths by walking that BASE-jumping plank. I allowed that we would prefer to be flung together upward into outer space.

It took some negotiations with the Astronaut—and his chief lieutenants Robur, Wernher, and Yuri—to settle this tangled situation.

But, through the passage of time, I'd become accustomed to the ways of the tower people. I had found the knack to befriend them. Sometimes, I could make these people see certain things that they could not see about themselves.

Levi and I chose to be thrown together into orbit. Let the Whip do its worst to us both, man and beast, I declared. Unlike most tower people, I was unafraid of the Whip. Because I knew that the Whip, this wicked device they all cherished so much, was really just some rickety contraption. They adored it, but it had weaknesses they never perceived.

The Whip might well throw me into orbit. Or it might throw Levi, if Levi was cut into separate horsemeat chunks and thrown repeatedly. But the Whip had never been designed or built to launch a man riding a horse. No matter how fearsome they are, machines can only do what is physically possible.

Superstition can decree whatever it wants: but physics is a science. An artwork can symbolize most anything—but engineering meets hard constraints.

BEING WHO THEY WERE, the tower people set to work to build a Whip big enough for both man and horse. Taxes were raised, and everybody cheerfully collaborated. A construction program arose within the Tall Tower. Everyone got busy and was forward-looking again.

I was solemnly sworn to become the sacrificial victim in the embrace of this spacey device. But I thought: Let them try. Let them build this instrument of my doom, if they think they can doom me. Me, and my horse.

To tell the truth, I was willing enough to die for the Tall Tower. Many have died for otherworldly aspirations. To perish as an old man, who has known his own worldly experience, that is not such a big, dreadful thing. Billions of us men have done it, cheerful and unflinching. The fear of dying is way overblown.

The people of the Tall Tower still work at that space program today. Like most great public works of mankind, it never seems to conclude. However, most everybody inside the tower has some cut of that action. The new prosperity has been spun off and spread around, with all the cunning of the locals.

While they plot and scheme and build their bigger, grander Whip, their older Whip, the original one, no longer works at all. They had to dismantle it to prepare for something grander, and I can't say it's much missed. The human race commonly substitutes big dreams for actual, existent engineering. Luckily, the tower people are long accustomed to overlooking the obvious.

I am pretty well known in the Tall Tower nowadays, although I am merely a white-haired old figurehead. It's my famous horse who is truly adored by the tower's people. Everyone is engrossed by this mighty, public task of lofting Levi into orbit—the first horse ever launched to outer space.

Being a mute beast of the earth, Levi doesn't make a fuss about it. This ageless beast has sired colts, the spindly-legged creatures of futurity, who are stabled far aloft in their vacuum stables. If my horse could write as I do, I think he would announce his satisfaction.

Clearly, this situation can't last forever. I know that, and you know that. But let's face it: nothing lasts forever, no matter how big it is. A man and a horse have to act within their own span of days. If not us, whom? If not now, when?

SADDLING THE FUTURE—Ron Broglio

Ron Broglio, a scholar of literature and sustainability at Arizona State University, responds to "Tall Tower" in the context of spirituality and human-animal relationships at hieroglyph.asu.edu/cowboy-tower.

FORUM DISCUSSION—Contemporary Skyscraper Construction

Bruce Sterling, Neal Stephenson, and other Hieroglyph community members search for the ideal location for the Tall Tower at hieroglyph.asu.edu/cowboy-tower.

SCIENCE AND SCIENCE FICTION: AN INTERVIEW WITH PAUL DAVIES

Ed Finn sat down to discuss Project Hieroglyph with physicist and cosmologist Paul Davies, director of the Beyond Center for Fundamental Concepts in Science at Arizona State University.

EF: I'm going to start with a very simple question: why do you write books?

PD: As a much younger man I came in for a lot of criticism from my peers. The feeling was that if you were writing what we might today call a popular book as opposed to a textbook, that this somehow meant that you couldn't be taken seriously as a scientist. Indeed, one colleague of mine said for every book you write, you should subtract ten from your journal publication list. That was the feeling in those days.

Why did I do it? I think partly because I discovered quite unexpectedly that I had a talent for communicating in plain language, using analogies, mathematics, and so on, quite advanced and subtle concepts in physics in particular. People seemed to like it when I did it, and there's nothing like having an appreciative audience out there to make you carry on.

I'm such a passionate scientist. I find science so deeply exciting and important and significant that I want to tell people the good news. When I talk to nonscientists, then I realize that they have no idea about things like quantum reality or the Higgs boson or what happened before the big bang or any of these sorts of really important things or even stuff about the nature of time that we've known for a hundred years.

They're missing out on this vast universe of excitement. I just want to share this, my own sense of excitement, and not just excitement of science, but its significance for what it means to be human and what it means to be living in this universe. A bit of a sort of missionary zeal. Then it all changed in the 1980s, partly because physics, which is really my discipline, was beginning to wither.

Students found it hard. They found it too abstract. Girls seemed to hate it. The whole subject was really in decline. Universities began to wake up to the fact that if they had someone writing really good, exciting popular physics books that that might improve student recruitment. Then Stephen Hawking wrote his famous book, *A Brief History of Time,* reaching parts of the reading public that the rest of us had been unable to reach.

Suddenly it was okay to write popular books. Then all my colleagues began doing it. Now I think it's almost part of the job description. It's obviously not obligatory, and not everybody can do it or do it well. The days when it was frowned upon are long gone, and I'm thankful for that. Although I think there are probably rather too many popular science books on the market at the moment.

EF: Would you say that's true primarily in physics or do you also see that happening in other scientific disciplines? Is there now a broader expectation of this kind of public communication?

PD: Biology has really stolen a march on physics. When I was first embarking on this, there weren't very many people doing popular science. Most of those were from physics or cosmology backgrounds. It's easy to talk about astronomy and cosmology because you can discuss objects that are out there like stars and black holes. Biology was rather the poor relation. That changed, perhaps because of Richard Dawkins's books. He writes very well. He really did popularize biology.

My first thought when I began to read Richard's books—which I think he just writes beautifully and I enjoy them immensely—my feeling was well, what's new? This is about Darwin's theory of evolution, it's 150 years old. *[Laughing]* Why is he writing about this stuff? It's old hat isn't it? But of course I guess it's anything but old hat. Now when you look at lists of popular science books, they tend to be dominated by biology.

Biologists have an advantage and a disadvantage. The advantage is that we can all imagine certain animals and plants. The concept isn't very abstract. The disadvantage is that at the molecular level it's so incredibly complex, and everything you want to talk about has some horrible unpronounceable name. *[Laughing]* It's only in recent years that they're coming around to doing what the physicists have long done [with naming]. For example, black holes. That's a pretty pithy explanation. In the beginning they used to be called totally gravitationally imploded stars or something.

Biologists now talk about things like junk DNA or they give genes funny names like hedgehog and NANOG. I think they've learned that if you're trying to communicate something, it really does pay to have some pithy acronym or description.

EF: Names have a lot of power, of course. So many names also come prepackaged with these metaphors—the black hole is a great example. It conveys very powerfully this particular image of what the thing is. There are so many popular science books out on the market now. What do you see as your responsibilities as a public communicator of science? How does one do it well?

PD: Don't pretend that doing science is ultimately for making money. There is this horrible trend among people who are trying to popularize science: *Why are we looking for the Higgs boson? Well, maybe in a hundred years somebody will make a buck out of this.* That's not why we're doing it. The reason that we do basic science is to understand how the universe works, and what our place is within the universe. It's a noble quest.

Not something you're going to devote 50 percent of the GDP to, but some small fraction of the GDP is spent basically exploring how the universe is put together, what the underlying laws are, and how it began, and how it's going to end. All these things are just as important as—well, for previous generations were the great religious questions. People built the medieval cathedrals in Europe. I suppose there were a few people who said, "Well, what is this doing for the GDP? Where is the productivity in this, all these resources?"

EF: Those people probably got their heads cut off.

PD: That's right. They were doing it because this was a great, collective human venture for trying to understand our place in nature. It was uplifting. It was giving people a sense of belonging and purpose. Science is exactly the same. It doesn't cost as much as the medieval cathedrals to do our type of science. I think science isn't just entertaining; it is part of what it means to be human.

If science leads to some practical application, that's a bonus. The prime reason that we're doing basic science—not *applied* science but *basic* science—is to probe the secrets of nature, to figure it all out. And I think that's a wonderful thing to do. I think authors who communicate that sense of wonder—that we're doing it, not because we're trying to invent a better type of can opener, or something—that this really *is* part of the human adventure! That's what goes over well.

What doesn't go over so well, and my literary agent cautioned me against it right at the outset, is to take a subject and just give a sort of rundown of it, a survey of the latest thinking about data mining or something. That isn't going to do too well. If it's something like *chaos theory completely transforms the way that we understand the relationship between cause and effect,* that's pretty deep. Quantum reality shows there may be parallel worlds. *That* is attention grabbing.

There's got to be something in it that—and this touches on science fiction—takes us outside of our daily world into another realm; some people might say an Alice in Wonderland realm of weird and wonderful concepts. Things that are counterintuitive, defy common sense, really lie outside the scope of everyday experience. Yet we can still understand them. That's the magic of the human mind. We can go into territory where our imagination and our common sense completely desert us. And yet we can still make sense of it. Science has the power to reveal how the world works, even in areas where we could never guess it just by looking.

EF: I want to draw out two things that you just mentioned. First, the cathedral metaphor, which I think is very apt. Second, the sense of wonder. What I love about the idea of cathedrals is that they were literally building an architecture of the universe. It was a way to make sense of the world by putting a frame around it.

I think that is very much what the scientific endeavor is, more abstract at times, but in an equally sweeping and ambitious way. Science fiction becomes a kind of cathedral of the imagination. It's a space to do that playfully, to do it in an exploratory way.

Tell me how you try to capture and convey that sense of wonder as a writer and then let's use that as our bridge into science fiction, which is of course for many people a core engine for that experience of wonder in the world.

PD: The great advantage science fiction writers have over people like me is that they can bend the rules, sometimes quite a lot. They can make up different laws of physics or pretend that some of the things that we now cherish will be overthrown.

When I'm writing speculative science, I really try to be very careful about, first of all, being honest. Second, differentiating between speculations, which are firmly rooted in accepted understanding of science, and those that might require some future change or ideas that are being kicked around in academia, which are sort of taken semiseriously by the scientist concerned, but may never work out. Often people will say, "All this stuff about string theory and so on. We can't take it seriously, can we?"

Well, the answer is maybe, to a certain extent. I always think it's really important if you're doing responsible science popularization to say, "This is a popular idea. It's a coherent idea. It's been worked on in a lot of detail. We know there's a lot of mathematical modeling of it, but there's not a shred of evidence at this stage that it's correct. It may turn out to be useful or may fade away." That's really important.

You can certainly push the boundaries. You don't have to remain exactly at a current state of knowledge. You can talk about ideas that challenge that. You can't just wave a magic wand and travel faster than light. If you're going to talk about faster-than-light travel, it's got to be done in this very cautious way.

EF: Much to the disappointment of many Hollywood screenwriters.

PD: Yes, if ever there is a spoiler for science fiction, it is the finite speed of light. It's a pretty big speed, but in astronomical terms it's very slow of course. It takes light one hundred thousand years to cross the galaxy. If you really believe nothing can go faster than light and you can't even send information faster than light, then that dissuades one from a lot of very popular science fiction scenarios. Now maybe one day we find out that this speed of light restriction is wrong, that there are ways of circumventing it. I personally don't think so, I think it's here to stay.

As a scientist I must always be prepared to be open-minded. The whole point is that nobody has the last word. All I can do is report to the best of my ability what is the current understanding of this or that subject area whilst being open to the fact that that may change in the future. If you take a sort of "anything goes" attitude—so I wrote a book recently called *The Eerie Silence* about the search for extraterrestrial intelligence. Well, a wonderland there of speculation. You could imagine all sorts of civilizations out there, all sorts of things going on and so on.

I am careful in the book to say, "Well, you know, if we can imagine super-civilizations as a possibility, why not invent civilizations that can travel faster than light? What effect would that have on looking for aliens?" What I point out is that really to do responsible speculative science you have to take the best understanding that we've got at this time in the knowledge that we may be proved wrong in the future.

If you take the attitude that we can make up anything, any laws, any old ideas that we want, then it becomes rather valueless: your speculation is as good as my speculation. It's got to be informed speculation, informed by the very best understanding we have of science in the full knowledge that we don't have the last word. There's more to come.

EF: How in your life have you seen the intersection of science fiction and science? Do you see that as a positive feedback loop? Were there science fiction stories that were particularly inspirational to you when you were younger?

PD: I don't think there's any doubt that not only myself, but many of my colleagues, particularly those who went into the physical sciences, were deeply inspired by reading science fiction, probably in their teens. I certainly did. For me, part of the love of physics and astronomy was reading those early books. I particularly liked reading Fred Hoyle, who was a practicing cosmologist. In fact, he gave me my first job. It was long before I had a professional relationship with him that I was reading his books, which I thought were very good because they were rooted, again, in the very best science.

Because I read Asimov, H. G. Wells, I've always been a little bit choosey in the science fiction that I liked to read, inasmuch as for me it's better if it's hard science fiction, close to what I feel I can believe. In some ways I think I enjoy rather more reading the biological stories than the physics-type stories because it's easier for me to suspend my disbelief in a field I don't understand so well.

Of course as a teenager, I wasn't so able to spot the flaws. I don't think there are any flaws in Fred Hoyle's stories actually. *[Laughing]*

This is a two-way street of course. Scientists are influenced by science fiction most often, but not always, when they're young. Then there's a question of how much science fiction writers are keeping up with and are influenced by new ideas and science. That's more of a mixed bag: some are, some aren't. Some people who write science *fantasy,* they might be aware of weird things like quantum locality or something like that, but they're not going to make a huge effort to get it right.

Some do. Stephen Baxter for example. I'm very impressed with the way he's able to follow and write about really pretty advanced stuff in quantum field theory, quantum gravity and so on, and weave a story around that. I think that's very skillful. David Brin as well is able to do this, to pull these things together. Frankly, I'm lost in admiration as to how they're able to do that because, even for a professional scientist, trying to keep abreast of those things can be difficult. To be a fiction writer as well is tremendously impressive.

I also, as you probably know, very much enjoy the books of Ian McEwan, though they're not science fiction. He often writes fiction about scientists. Again, I'm astonished at how well he seems to grasp even stuff at the very forefront of modern physics.

EF: When Ian McEwan was here visiting ASU, it was quite interesting to hear him talking about the choice that he made at a certain point in his career to pursue writing instead of a career in science, which was I think the alternative for him. He echoed your pleasure in seeing that there is more and more popular science writing. It has allowed him to remain involved in that discourse even though he can't do it professionally because he's too busy writing all those wonderful novels of his own.

PD: I think that is the point—that science fiction writers are not just there to entertain, not just there to write books for scientists to read in their downtime. *[Laughing]* They really do have an important social role, first of all as part of communicating the science process. A lot of people, particularly young people, first get their glimpse of difficult ideas at the forefront of science from reading science fiction.

In science fiction you're creating a sort of imaginary but plausible world. That can be used as a setting to develop all sorts of social or even political messages. H. G. Wells's *The Time Machine* was really not a book about *time travel*. It was a book about what would happen if society continued to develop its rampant capitalism, and to develop in the far future the division into the haves and have-nots.

It does provide that vehicle for social and political commentary. I guess that science fiction is as varied as any other genre. It'll be everything from an entertaining romp to something with much more serious sociological input.

EF: I think that's right. The mission of Project Hieroglyph is really to find that sweet spot of science fiction right at the intersection of science, trying in this very deliberate way to put writers directly into contact with scientists and engineers and get them to engage with the latest cutting-edge ideas, the newest research. And still give them the freedom to write stories that explore social, ethical, and cultural questions.

I think that's what science fiction can do in a way that nonfiction science writing often can't: create that imagined world and work out human conflicts in a future landscape where some new discovery or new technology exists. That can be quite powerful. That's how the rest of us can follow along in a sense and start to play out these issues.

I like to think of science fiction as this sort of imagination lab where you can play out scenarios and work through all the different possible consequences in a way that is probably quite difficult when you are focusing on technical problems.

The premise of Project Hieroglyph, the initial call from Neal Stephenson to come up with more optimistic science fiction: I'm curious to hear whether you agree with that and how you see the state of our cultural relationship to the future?

PD: Almost all futuristic fiction is dystopian. Maybe it always has been. I'm thinking back to H. G. Wells and George Orwell—I don't recall that as science fiction, but I mean it's worse now than he predicted for 1984. That's all coming true. *[Laughing]*

Do we see any utopian science fiction? Well, not a great deal. I mean, I think Arthur C. Clarke probably is a counterexample. It's not all utopian, but it's by no means doom and gloom. Science fiction can involve futuristic science, but also our same science but futuristic technology. Just taking what we see coming over the horizon and then imagining, taking it to some extreme in twenty years, fifty years, one hundred years—what would it be like?

Anything that involves truly dramatic transformation of society could be viewed as dystopian, even if it's not. Imagine a future world, as we so often do—*Brave New World,* in which the human reproductive process is managed very differently, and we're creating designer babies, transhumans, posthumans with carefully chosen attributes, controlled systematically by some sort of authority. It seems ghastly to us now.

If it were to *happen,* I could well imagine that in another hundred years, people would say that *our* age was the awful one: rampant overpopulation and plundering of resources and people behaving in a ghastly manner. How much better to have engineered genomes and controlled population, where people are better adapted to their society and to what they can contribute and to what they need from it; and the whole thing is planned and organized.

They might regard that as the Utopia. What is good and bad? It very much depends on the age. There are things that we are doing now in our society that people are comfortable with that would have been regarded as horrific fifty years ago. It's too simple I think to just say that the future is, as told by science fiction, always bleak.

EF: One of the best things that science fiction can do actually is complicate things a little bit or point out when we're leaning too heavily on certain assumptions. I think it's true in many ways that science fiction is a philosophical literature. The most outlandish, the most dangerous ideas that science fiction proposes often are really moral and philosophical questions rather than some radical new technological invention. It's ultimately about how we as humans use these things.

PD: You think ahead fifty years and probably the most profound changes will come from aspects of science and technology that we don't even know about yet. Or we might know about them, but we don't appreciate their significance. Time and again when I'm discussing these things about my own youth and reading books about the future, I think of the comics that I used to read and their images of cities in the year 2000 with people with jetpacks on our backs.

They completely missed out on the information revolution, which was there, but it was just out of sight. People didn't understand the significance. That's the fun, isn't it, of trying to pick what's next?

EF: That's a very interesting question. We are moving so quickly now in so many different arenas of discovery that we have a huge number of new ideas, tools, and systems that we have created, and we haven't realized what a tremendous impact they could have. That's one of the things that excites me the most about the premise of Project Hieroglyph: it's really almost science fiction of the present. What could we do *now* if we simply set our minds to it? Not relying on undiscovered technologies but simply reconfiguring or shifting the cultural frame to say, "This is important and here are these tools. Nobody's put them together yet, but you could really do this if you wanted to."

PD: I like to speculate about what we could achieve with current science and technology and the commitment and resources. One that I've been banging on about for years is a one-way mission to Mars. We could set up a Mars colony now with current technology. We don't need some really futuristic thing. We could go to Mars. We have the ability to get there. We could send people there. They may not live as long as they would if they stay behind on Earth, but it's not a suicide mission. We could build Mars colonies starting now.

Is that science fiction? I don't know. I suppose it's conceivable, but at the moment it's fiction. I think what's standing in our way is simply having a good reason to do it, or for nations having the ability to pull together their resources. Most of my career was dominated by the Cold War and the arms race, particularly in physics. To a certain extent, biology. But big science was driven by the military.

Things like particle accelerators, which are very expensive, big projects, or the space program—these things were riding on the coattails of the military budget. They were regarded as, if not directly military, at least sort of part of a national virility contest: your technological prowess to intimidate the opposition. A lot of people spoke in the early days about the peace dividend.

The plan was when we stop spending this obscene amount of money on armaments, you could always spend on really useful stuff like health-care programs, and the nonmilitary science would absolutely flourish. The exact opposite occurred. The peace dividend turned out to be negative once the arms race faded away. Big science became very difficult to fund. It's a bit of a tragedy that humanity can't pool resources in the spirit of cooperation rather than competition.

The truth is you get more out of people by having a race or a competition than you do asking them to cooperate. It says something about human nature, and it's true of individuals and it's true of nations. It's well known that if you want to achieve something, a million-dollar budget, and it's not enough, it's a ten-million-dollar project, you create a million-dollar prize—now I'm thinking the X Prize. It's a great way to get people to go to Mars: give them a prize.

EF: It's a powerful motivator and it reminds me of the cathedrals. The Cold War provided this frame that made a rational story out of the universe. It wasn't a terribly happy story. It was a story of these two competing superpowers with nuclear missiles poised at each other's cities. But it was a story that made sense, that allowed everybody to pull together and focus on these things. It had those elements of competition and ideology and self-interest.

The Apollo missions were part of the Cold War. The space race was part of this broader military struggle. Of course we had Wernher von Braun and we had our rockets. We weren't just using them to study moon rocks. Yet there was also a beauty and a selfless sort of majesty to the space missions as well, in taking that step for mankind.

I think you're quite right, those framing stories are so important. We seem to be struggling for a new one.

PD: It's a much more confused picture now. In our present society I think we can recognize something—there's a deep malaise running through our own liberal democracy, Western society, and around the world. Ideological conflicts now are really between the world of traditional Islam and Western democracy, whereas previously it was communism versus capitalism.

For a while people were talking about the New World Order with the end of the Cold War, that maybe it was now possible to have everybody integrated into some sort of common market, and everyone get wealthy together. Things are a lot better than they were, I have to say. People who tend to be gloomy about our present circumstances have forgotten what it was like, say, in the '70s or '80s. I think the world is better. Relatively speaking there is less poverty; it doesn't mean there isn't some. Relatively speaking there's less.

What I see is really the fragmentation of society; it's no longer the case that we can get behind these simple narratives, where it seems like there is an obvious trajectory that we want to follow. And then, if we try hard enough and are not derailed by the opposition or the alternative ideology, we'll get there.

When I talk to young people, they don't seem to have a real grasp of who they are, or what sort of community they're in, or where it's going. There's a terrible sense of living for the moment, of just instant gratification and no real commitment to a well-charted future. Maybe this is where science fiction really can help by giving some sort of structure to the way forward, and getting away from this notion of living in the here and the now and not bothering to plan further down the track.

I'm talking primarily of course about liberal Western democracies. It may be totally different in China.

EF: China is just beginning to develop a new wave of science fiction. As a cultural concept, it's of course very different. Soviet science fiction was fascinating if you look at something like Tarkovsky's *Solaris*. The way that you imagine the future is always a reflection of the present. We need to build this pathway forward, and not to the distant future, which is still the same as it was fifty years ago.

What's a goal that we could accomplish in the next ten years or twenty years? That was something that we had in previous generations. That was something that the cathedral builders had because they knew that ultimately they were going to finish building the cathedral, and it was going to be better than the cathedral in the city down the road.

PD: The spirit of the Apollo program was that it was deliverable within a human lifetime, and a big commitment, and everybody got behind it. It's easy to imagine doing things like that now. I mean, I've mentioned there's one way to Mars, but that's maybe a bit harebrained. We could imagine great projects here on Earth that we could do—if there was the commitment, we could do it. What these projects need to do is, in my view, to be unifying and not part of a national competition. What we need is great projects that can bring people together.

ABOUT THE EDITORS

Ed Finn is the founding director of the Center for Science and the Imagination at Arizona State University, where he is an assistant professor with a joint appointment in the School of Arts, Media and Engineering and the Department of English. His research and teaching explore the ways ideas circulate through contemporary culture, especially in digital form, and he is currently working on a book about the changing nature of reading in the age of algorithms. He completed his Ph.D. in English and American literature at Stanford University. Before graduate school Ed worked as a journalist at *Time*, *Slate*, and *Popular Science*. He earned his bachelor's degree at Princeton University with a comparative literature major and certificates in applications of computing, creative writing, and European cultural studies.

Kathryn Cramer is a writer, critic, and anthologist and was coeditor of the *Year's Best Fantasy* and *Year's Best SF* series. She has coedited approximately thirty anthologies. She was a founding editor of the *New York Review of Science Fiction* and has a large number of Hugo nominations in the Semiprozine category to show for it. She won a World Fantasy Award for her anthology *The Architecture of Fear* (1987). Her fiction has been published by *Asimov's* and *Nature* and in anthologies. Her story "Am I Free to Go?" was recently published on Tor.com. Kathryn holds a B.A. in mathematics and a master's degree in American Studies, both from Columbia University in New York. For five years, she taught writing at Harvard Summer School. More recently she has been a consultant for Wolfram Research, L. W. Currey, an antiquarian bookseller, and for ASU's Center for Science and the Imagination. She is a consulting editor for Tor Books. She lives in Westport, New York, in the Adirondack Park.

ABOUT THE CONTRIBUTORS

Charlie Jane Anders won a Hugo for her novelette *Six Months, Three Days.* Her writing has appeared in *Asimov's Science Fiction, The Magazine of Science Fiction and Fantasy,* Tor.com, *Tin House, Lightspeed Magazine, Strange Horizons, Mother Jones,* and elsewhere. Her novel *All the Birds in the Sky* is forthcoming in 2016 from Tor Books. She also blogs about science fiction and futurism at io9.com.

Madeline Ashby is a science fiction writer and strategic foresight consultant based in Toronto. She is the author of *vN* (2012) and *iD* (2013), the first two novels in her Machine Dynasty series. Her fiction has appeared in *Nature, FLURB, Tesseracts, Imaginarium,* and *Escape Pod.* Her essays and criticism have appeared at *Boing Boing, io9, WorldChanging, Creators Project, Arcfinity,* and Tor.com.

Elizabeth Bear is a science fiction and fantasy author based in Massachusetts. In 2005 she won the John W. Campbell Award for Best New Writer, and she has also won two Hugo Awards, for Best Short Story and Best Novelette. Elizabeth is an instructor at the Viable Paradise science fiction and fantasy writers' workshop and also teaches at Clarion, Clarion West, the WisCon Writer's Respite, and Odyssey.

Gregory Benford is a science fiction author, educator, and astrophysicist. In addition to authoring more than twenty novels, Gregory is a professor of physics at the University of California, Irvine, where he has been a faculty member since 1971. He has served as a scientific consultant for *Star Trek: The Next Generation,* is a Woodrow Wilson Fellow, and is a contributing editor for *Reason* magazine.

David Brin is a scientist, bestselling author, and tech-futurist. His novels include *Earth* (1990), *The Postman* (1985, filmed in 1997), and Hugo Award winners *Startide Rising* (1983) and *The Uplift War* (1987). A leading commentator and speaker on modern trends, his nonfiction book *The Transparent Society* (1998) won the Freedom of Speech Award of the American Library Association.

James L. Cambias is a science fiction author and game designer. His short stories have been featured in the *Magazine of Fantasy and Science Fiction, Nature,* and the *Journal of Pulse-Pounding Narratives*. He is a cofounder of Zygote Games, codesigned *Bone Wars: The Game of Ruthless Paleontology,* and has written or contributed to books for a number of tabletop role-playing games.

Brenda Cooper is a science fiction author, futurist, and technology professional. She is the chief information officer for the city of Kirkland, Washington, and a member of the Futurist Board for the Lifeboat Foundation. Brenda is the author of seven novels, including *The Silver Ship and the Sea,* which won the Endeavor Award in 2008.

Paul Davies is a theoretical physicist, cosmologist, astrobiologist, and bestselling author. He is a regents' professor, director of the Beyond Center for Fundamental Concepts in Science, and co-director of the Cosmology Initiative at Arizona State University. His award-winning books include *The Eerie Silence* (2010), *The Goldilocks Enigma* (2007), *How to Build a Time Machine* (2007), and *The Mind of God* (1992).

Cory Doctorow is a science fiction author, activist, journalist, and blogger. He is the coeditor of *Boing Boing* and the author of young adult novels like *Homeland* (2013), *Pirate Cinema* (2012), and *Little Brother* (2008) and novels for adults like *Rapture of the Nerds* (2012) and *Makers* (2009). Cory is the former European director of the Electronic Frontier Foundation and cofounded the UK Open Rights Group. Born in Toronto, Canada, he now lives in London.

Kathleen Ann Goonan is a science fiction author, educator, and critic. Her debut novel, *Queen City Jazz* (1994), was a *New York Times* Notable Book of the Year, and her novel *In War Times* (2007) won the John W. Campbell Award for Best Science Fiction Novel. She is a visiting professor at the Georgia Institute of Technology.

Lee Konstantinou is a novelist and scholar of post-World War II U.S. fiction. He serves as associate editor for fiction and criticism at the *Los Angeles Review of Books* and is an assistant professor in the department of English at the University of Maryland, College Park. Lee is the author of the novel *Pop Apocalypse* (2009) and coeditor of *The Legacy of David Foster Wallace* (2012).

Lawrence M. Krauss is a theoretical physicist, cosmologist, author, and science popularizer. He is the founding director of the Origins Project at Arizona State University and the foundation professor at ASU's School of Earth and Space Exploration and Department of Physics. His most recent books include *A Universe from Nothing: Why There Is Something Rather Than Nothing* (2012), *Quantum Man: Richard Feynman's Life in Science* (2010), and *Hiding in the Mirror* (2005).

Geoffrey A. Landis is a scientist and a science fiction writer. As a scientist, he is a researcher at the NASA John Glenn Research Center. He works on projects related to advanced power and propulsion systems for space and planetary exploration and is currently a member of the science team for the Mars Exploration Rover Mission. As a science fiction writer, he has won a Nebula Award, two Hugo Awards, and a Locus Award, as well as two Rhysling Awards for his poetry.

Annalee Newitz writes about science, pop culture, and the future. She is the editor in chief of *io9*, a publication that covers science and science fiction. She is the author of the books *Scatter, Adapt, and Remember: How Humans Will Survive a Mass Extinction* (2013) and *Pretend We're Dead: Capitalist Monsters in American Pop Culture* (2006) and the coeditor of *She's Such a Geek* (2006). Formerly, she was a policy analyst at the Electronic Frontier Foundation and a lecturer at the University of California, Berkeley, where she received a Ph.D. in English and American Studies.

Rudy Rucker is a science fiction author, philosopher, mathematician, and one of the founders of the cyberpunk movement. He worked for twenty years as a computer science professor at San Jose State University and has published a number of software packages. Rucker is best-known for The Ware Tetralogy (1982-2000), a four-novel cyperpunk series that won two Philip K. Dick awards. Other novels include *Turing & Burroughs* (2012), *Mathematicians in Love* (2nd ed. 2014), and *The Big Aha* (2014)—which grew out of "Quantum Telepathy."

Karl Schroeder divides his time between writing fiction and analyzing the future impact of science and technology on society. He is the author of nine novels and has pioneered a new mode of writing that blends fiction and rigorous futures research: *Crisis in Zefra* (2005) and *Crisis in Urlia* (2011) were commissioned by the Canadian army as research tools. Karl holds a master's degree in strategic foresight and innovation from OCAD University in Toronto.

Vandana Singh is a science fiction author and associate professor of physics at Framingham State University. Her short stories, which most recently include "Peripateia" (2013), "Cry of the Kharchal" (2013), "With Fate Conspire" (2013), and "A Handful of Rice" (2012), frequently appear in *Year's Best* and other anthologies. She also writes poetry as well as novels and short stories for children.

Neal Stephenson is an author of historical and science fiction, a technology consultant, and the principal provocateur behind Project Hieroglyph. He is the author of the three-volume historical epic the Baroque Cycle (2003–2004) and the novels *REAMDE* (2012), *Anathem* (2008), *Cryptonomicon* (1999), *The Diamond Age* (1995), *Snow Crash* (1992), and *Zodiac* (1988). He lives in Seattle, Washington.

Bruce Sterling is an author, journalist, editor, and critic. Best known for his ten science fiction novels, he also writes short stories, book reviews, design criticism, and introductions for books ranging from Ernst Juenger to Jules Verne. He is a contributing editor at *Wired* magazine, and in 2013 he was the Visionary in Residence at the Center for Science and the Imagination at Arizona State University.

COPYRIGHT NOTICES